HET

Jess of Roos Hall

Janet T. Sawyer

HALSGROVE

First published in Great Britain by Halsgrove, 2007

Copyright © 2007 Janet T. Sawyer

British Library Cataloguing-in-Publication Data
A CIP record for this title is available from the British Library

ISBN 978 1 84114 594 5

HALSGROVE
Halsgrove House
Ryelands Farm Industrial Estate
Bagley Green, Wellington
Somerset TA21 9PZ
T: 01823 653777
F: 01823 665294
email: sales@halsgrove.com
website: www.halsgrove.com

Printed in Great Britain by The Cromwell Press, Trowbridge

AUTHOR'S PREFACE

The principal characters in this book are fictitious: the rest is mostly History. Scenes of rural, social, naval and colonial life in the late 18th and early 19th centuries are combined with the story of the Jarvis family of Beccles, Suffolk, and the lives of two orphans, showing how the gentry dealt with their illegitimate offspring, and how their outlook and achievements were affected by ignorance of their true birth.

Roos Hall is reputed to be haunted by several ghosts, among them the pale face of a small girl peering out from the topmost gable window, and the lane which passes it by a black carriage and horses driven by a headless coachman and by Black Shuck, the fearsome dog of the marshes. My grandparents farmed at one of the Ringsfield properties and later ran a dairy farm in Beccles town. My parents were married at Beccles Church, where the parents of Admiral, Lord Nelson, were wed. All the manifestations of Black Shuck in this tale were witnessed by members of my family or their friends.

Janet T. Sawyer
Exmouth
Devon 2007

JESS OF ROOS HALL

CONTENTS

JESS OF ROOS HALL

CHAPTER I
The Witness

"The wind was torrent of darkness among the gusty trees,
The moon was ghostly galleon tossed upon cloudy seas ..."
From "The Highwayman" by Alfred Noyes

Indeed it was such a night as Betty Jarvis walked home from her employment as Housekeeper at that gloomy brick pile known as Roos Hall. It was late October and the leafless branches of the tall ancient beeches gleamed briefly in the intermittent moonlight as they clashed together far above her head. The fitful moon sent shapeless shadows leaping across her path as she hurried along close to the grass verge which bordered the roadside ditch. Gravel crunched beneath the heels of her stout leather boots, though as she carried no lantern she often had to splash through an unseen puddle or stumbled over a rut left by the many carriers' carts and occasional carriages which used this lane winding between the Suffolk border towns of Beccles and Bungay.

Of course there was no traffic to be expected at this hour of a dark winter evening, and the use of a lantern would only have attracted the attention of any cutpurse who happened to be passing. Besides, she knew her way so well - had she not tramped there and back daily these past thirty and some years, ever since she had entered service at the Hall as a girl of nineteen? She had wed a fellow-servant, the Butler of the establishment, a fact which had caused much friction and jealousy among other members of the household below stairs. However this situation did not last long as Betty's husband, a man of mature years, had died suddenly leaving Betty pregnant with child. She bore a daughter, whom she named Alicia after her own mother, as fair and pretty a child as anyone could dream of. Betty's employers, Sir Robert and Lady Mary Rich, informed her that she might return to her situation at the Hall, but only on condition that she had her child fostered out or adopted by a local citizen. Fostering charges would take up almost the whole of Betty's wages and she was desperate for a solution to her dilemma when a friend introduced her to Bob Jarvis, the son of the licensee of the Bear & Bells Inn to be found alongside the Old Market in the Town of Beccles. They took a liking to each other at once and married within a month. Bob then succeeded his father as landlord and this was the home to which Betty now hastened.

They had not had further children of their own, but Alicia had grown into a lively young woman. She had been educated at a local scholastic establishment and, it seemed, good fortune had endowed her with looks and ideas beyond her station. There were few opportunities for employment in the district; boys became farm labourers, fishermen or shipping clerks if they could take to book-keeping and a situation free of domesticity in Lowestoft or Yarmouth. For girls, even those who applied themselves diligently to their studies, of which Alicia sadly was not one, the most intelligent might become a governess or school-teacher, the rest went into service. Thus, when Alicia reached the age of fifteen and her education had come to an end, Betty sought and obtained for her a place as a chambermaid at Roos Hall where Betty herself had recently been elevated to the post of Housekeeper.

Betty had done her best to inculcate into Alicia the precepts and morality of her own strong Christian faith. She had always attended regularly services at the large church-on-the-hill in Beccles, that noble building of grey stone with its landmark bell tower which crowns the scarp of a curve in the course of the River Waveney, going twice on Sundays and never missing feast days and festivals. Alicia, sitting beside her mother in the wooden pew with her eyes supposedly demurely cast down, was actually furtively glancing sideways, firstly to ensure that she was better-dressed than her rivals, and secondly to spy out any good-looking youth who might merit further investigation. For Alicia was a flirt, but like many flirts she paraded her charms rather for her own benefit than that of anyone else. Betty suffered terribly at the onset of each new relationship in which her daughter indulged. Anxiously she watched for any tell-tale early signs of preg-nancy, but five years had passed and nothing untoward had occurred. Nay, Alicia had even declined several offers for her hand, two of them from the sons of Beccles tradesmen who had prospects, one might have supposed, of following in their father's line of business. Then, just as Betty had despaired of ever having her daughter "settled" and off her hands, she suddenly noticed one day that Alicia was suffering from morning sickness. But who was the father of her child?

* * *

The name Roos is a Dutch word, meaning red or rose-coloured. It might have been assumed that the term referred to the dark red, locally-made, bricks of which Roos Hall had been built, but in fact the first owner of the estate had been one William de Roos. Around the year 1300 King Edward I granted him the Lordship of the Manor, together with the farms of Ringsfield and Redisham, in return for the military assistance which William provided in Edward's wars against Scotland. Almost three centuries later the Hall had passed into other hands; its owner, a Mr Thomas Colby, married a local heiress named Ursula Rede, and in 1583 they had the half-ruined medieval manor house substantially rebuilt. Thus there are Tudor-style mullioned windows and the roof is crowned with several fine Tudor chimneys. The Colbys were also responsible for adding a separate side-wing containing a large kitchen and pantry, a feature of many noble houses at the time, and designed to keep kitchen fumes and the risk of fire well away from the fine fabrics and furniture in the residential apartments. Moreover, rumour had it in succeeding centuries that certain secret historical features, such as a priest hole, hidden stairways, and a tunnel leading into the woods, were all still to be discovered at Roos Hall, concealed behind its linenfold oak panelling, and that ghostly apparitions were occasionally to be observed in particular parts of the grounds.

Mr Colby did not retain the Hall for long - maybe its ghosts troubled him - for he sold it in 1610 to John Suckling, a distinguished Norfolk yeoman, who was elected Member of Parliament for the Borough of Dunwich in 1601 and for Reigate in 1614. John Suckling served as Secretary of State to James I under his Lord Treasurer, Sir Robert Cecil, and was knighted in 1616. When Sir John died in 1627 his widow took as her third husband Sir Edwyn Rich of Mulbarton in Norfolk, and Roos Hall and its farms then remained in the ownership of the Rich family, a family with noble connections for three hundred years past. In the later decades of the eighteenth century the fifth baronet, Sir Robert Rich, was the last of his line. When he died in 1785 it was found that he had willed all his property, several farms in Norfolk, Roos Hall and its farms in Suffolk, and Waverley Abbey House in Surrey where the family normally resided, to his only daughter Mary Frances, known in Polite Society as the Lady Marietta. This young woman had been presented at Court and had become one of the many ladies-in-waiting to Queen Charlotte, the popular consort of King George III. As a female member of a large and diverse family, Lady Marietta had scarcely expected to become an heiress and two years previously had accepted a proposal of marriage from a humble but aspiring clergyman, the Reverend Charles Bostock. Upon obtaining his wife's inheritance the Revd Charles did not hesitate to promote his own status. He assumed the surname and coat of arms of the Rich family and King George was persuaded, a few years later in 1791, to revive the baronetcy which had expired with Sir Robert and to grant it to his son-in-law, Charles.

In the summer of 1782, shortly before his marriage to Lady Marietta, Charles Bostock, or as we shall call him for now Mr Charles, had paid discreet visits to all his future father-in-law's rural properties, to the Mulbarton estate near Norwich and to the farms belonging to Roos Hall. When he called at the Hall he had introduced himself to Betty Jarvis who conducted him around the property. However he had asked Betty not to disclose his identity to the rest of the staff, and no, thank you, he would not accept accommodation at the Hall, for that was not quite proper when he was not yet officially affianced, but would seek a bed in Beccles town instead. What more natural than that Betty should refer Mr Charles to her husband Bob at the Bear & Bells, where he was immediately shown into a very comfortable, if simply-furnished, upstairs room which just happened to be vacant that night.

Now Miss Alicia Jarvis was possessed of insatiable curiosity. She had noted the good-looking stranger her mother was showing around the Hall and had taken every opportunity to browbeat Betty, unsuccessfully, for the rest of the day and during their walk home that evening - for they only lived in at the Hall on those infrequent occasions when the family and their guests came to visit - as to who the stranger was. Imagine Alicia's surprise and delight when on reaching the Inn she found the eminent gentleman cosily installed at her father's bar enjoying some convivial hospitality. Alicia immediately volunteered to take her mother's place behind the bar, for which both parents at the time were grateful, Betty because she could take an all-too-rare rest, and Bob because he could give attention to his many other customers, since it was Market Day in Beccles and keeping apace with the livestock auctioneer's rapid patter had always been thirsty work for farmers. Thus, save for a few brief interruptions, Alicia had the aspiring Mr Charles all to herself.

Mr Charles, finding he had such a ready and attentive audience, waxed forth about the pleasures of life at Court. He described Their Majesties, so devoted to each other and to their children, the Prince of Wales, a tall, affable and sociable young man a few years older than Alicia herself, the Duke of York who had chosen a career in the Army, and Prince William Henry* already serving as a young midshipman at sea. Alicia nodded encouragingly. Mr Charles went on to mention some of the duties of a lady-in-waiting, as performed by his future bride - he had proposed to the lady, he confessed, but her father's formal consent was still awaited. Alicia listened with wrapt attention. Oh to be part of such a world, she sighed in a whisper. Mr Charles mentioned Lady Jersey and Georgiana, the Duchess of Devonshire, as the current leaders of fashionable Society. They always appeared in the most elegant outfits which immediately sent every other self-respecting courtier to consult their dressmakers and the less well-off to visit the new emporia which had begun to grace London's Oxford Road. As for their hair-styles - and Alicia's eyes widened as she listened - there was nothing so elevated as the extravagant creations devised by the Duchess and copied by her rivals. With further encouragement from Alicia, Mr Charles went on to provide a thumbnail portrait of the balls and card parties given at Devonshire House and at other town houses of the Ton, as the upper echelons of Society were known, and were so labelled by an eager Press that reported in detail every scandal or piece of gossip whispered on the air.

Mr Charles now grew weary of his conversation - after all, he was chatting to a mere barmaid, or so he supposed for, although he had noted Alicia's presence at the Hall where she had been cleaning one of the rooms he had inspected, he was unaware of her blood connection with Mrs Jarvis, the Housekeeper. Poor people often did two or three jobs in order to make ends meet, so it was no surprise to him to find Alicia also serving behind the bar. He finished his drink and proposed to retire for the night.

Alicia, whose calculations of a brighter future for herself in the wider world well away from Beccles had been working overtime, looked up at Mr Charles with a flash of her large blue eyes and asked, "Would you care for a hot posset to send you to sleep, sir? I would be happy to prepare one for you, as I often do for myself."

"Thank you, young lady, indeed I would. I did not catch your name, by the by?"

"'Tis Alicia, sir, and I'll bring the posset up to you in about ten minutes, if that's convenient?"

"Thank you, Alicia, that sounds excellent,"

As Mr Charles turned to depart upstairs Alicia busied herself serving other customers. Some of the farmers had departed to their homes or their lodgings and she observed that her father's attention was fully occupied in chatting with those that remained. She tiptoed up to her father and took his arm. "Father, do you mind if I go up now? I'm feeling quite tired. Are you sure you can manage without me?"

"Of course, my dear," her father replied, "you go and take some rest. You have to be up in the morning earlier than I, and these are all regular customers who will be leaving soon. I've only to shut and bar the door after them. I trust you enjoyed your long conversation with Mr Charles? As your mother must have told you, he's likely to become Sir Robert's son-in-law." Alicia struggled to hide her blushes as she murmured a suitable reply.

Alicia slipped into the kitchen and prepared the promised hot posset. She placed the tankard on a tray and took it upstairs. There she paused in the corridor to lock her bedroom door from the outside and slip the key into her pocket, just in case either parent should think to look in upon her room during her absence. Then, with her heart pounding loudly with excitement, she walked rapidly back along the corridor to the room which Mr Charles had rented. She knocked on the door quietly, unsure whether her mother was still lying awake in the nearby bedroom. A voice within called, "Come in, please," so that she did not need to speak.

From the depths of a comfortable bed Mr Charles looked up with a smile. The girl was indeed devilish pretty and he was tempted. The clerical attire which Mr Charles was obliged to adopt from time to time had never sat easily upon his shoulders. Indeed he had often berated himself as something of an hypocrite for assuming it before a dissipated Court, as if to indicate a standard of morals superior to their own. Besides, this girl was a mere chambermaid and looked old enough to know her mind. From the manner of her glances at him all evening he deemed her well-accustomed to male company and much doubted that she was a virgin. If she were, however, there was always that old wives' adage that one couldn't get a virgin with child upon her first deflowering. And if Alicia did conceive, Mr Charles had such hopes of preferment at Court, once married to Lady Marietta, that he felt sure that a few guineas and a word here and there would settle the situation to the satisfaction of all concerned.

"Shall I wait while you drink it, sir?" Alicia asked with a blush.

"Yes, do," Mr Charles replied and made a flat space in the counterpane. "Why don't you sit here with me, Alicia?" he said. Alicia suffered easily from boredom; her life at work and at home in Beccles she viewed as provincial and useless. She had often contemplated escaping to the brighter lights of Norwich or London, but without funds she knew she would be obliged to take to the streets as a 'woman of pleasure', so that seemed not such a good idea. The arrival of Mr Charles fresh from the upper echelons of Society with connections to people of every rank suddenly presented her with a vision of a more promising future, especially now that her father had revealed that Mr Charles was likely to become their new landlord. It seemed obvious that an affair with the future owner was likely to bring forth an additional source of income. What did she, Alicia, care for the uncouth sons of civic merchants when a relationship with a member of Society offered to lead her into dazzling adventure?

So she sat on the bed, half demurely, half glancing at Mr Charles with her shining blue eyes under their dark lashes. Mr Charles put forth one hand, nicely warmed from holding the hot tankard, and raised her fingers to his lips, watching her all the while. Alicia smiled back at him. "What are you seeking from life, then, Alicia?" he asked. "A pretty girl like you should have no difficulty in finding herself a good husband."

"Oh no, sir, I want my independence," Alicia replied pertly, "at least for a while."

"Do you indeed," Mr Charles said with an answering smile, "and does that independence include granting this gentleman a favour?" He put down the tankard at his bedside, his left hand moving to her waist and the other smoothing her young breasts that peeped half over the neckline of her gown. She was not wearing any stays and warm panting flesh yielded to his touch. Nor was she wearing any drawers, as his right hand presently discovered. Alicia meanwhile unbuttoned her gown and let it fall from her shoulders. Then she stood up and allowed her gown to slide to the floor. The flickering candlelight revealed the shape of her young body beneath her thin shift. Mr Charles slid rapidly out of bed and turned the doorkey in the lock. Then he took Alicia into his arms.

But Alicia did conceive, to the fury of her parents when they eventually persuaded her to confess what had occurred. After much discussion with her husband, Betty Jarvis decided to put pen to paper: she could write a good letter when required, for her own education had not been neglected nor forgotten. This letter, though, touched upon a most delicate subject and several drafts were essayed - too bold, and Betty would risk her own continued employment at the Hall; too indirect, and the recipient would have every chance of denying or slipping away from his obligations. In the end Betty decided that a degree of firmness was indispensable and she wrote as follows:

Sir,
On the occasion of your residence with my husband, Mr Robert Jarvis, licensee,
and myself at the Bear & Bells Inn at Beccles in the County of Suffolk on the night

of 27th August last, our daughter Alicia has confessed to us that you took her into your bed, as a result of which she is four months with child.

Not wishing to state more than might be necessary concerning such an abuse of our hospitality, we are nevertheless constrained by circumstances to give careful consideration to the future wellbeing or our daughter and her child. We await anxiously your instructions, sir, as to the furtherance of this matter, until receipt of which we remain

Your obedient and obliging servants,
Robert and Elizabeth Jarvis

Mr Charles had left with Betty an address as 'poste restante at White's Club' in London, so that she rather doubted that she would receive a prompt reply. Nevertheless little more than a fortnight later a package arrived at the Bear & Bells by special messenger, thus giving rise to much speculation among the publican's customers as to its contents. Bob Jarvis waited until his wife returned from the Hall that evening before he opened it. He ordered Alicia to serve behind the bar whilst he and Betty studied Mr Charles' reply in an adjoining room.

My dear Mr and Mrs Jarvis, Mr Charles had written on 3rd January, 1783.
May I first offer both of you my most humble apologies for what has occurred. The contents of your letter furnished me with a rather severe shock: I had entertained no idea that Miss Alicia might be your daughter, but had assumed that she was merely an employee. The coincidence of observing her presence at Roos Hall earlier in the day should have warned me to enquire into her relationship with you, if any, but I confess that my mind being preoccupied with other matters I failed to do so. Moreover from Miss Alicia's manner towards me I took it that she had some experience of the World and was accustomed to distribute her favours, tho' I must admit that later I was inclined to revise that opinion. Have you every certainty that the child is mine?

By misfortune your letter has caught me upon the eve of my wedding to the distinguished lady of which we spoke during my visit, and we are then to depart to the Continent for a protracted honeymoon lasting several months. Accordingly I enclose herewith an Order for 200 guineas drawn on my Bank at Norwich which should defray at least the services of a competent midwife and any physician who may prove necessary. Please write to me again at this same address as soon as the child is born.

Once again, may I offer my most sincere apologies for what has occurred, and please extend my kind wishes to Miss Alicia for an agreeable confinement about which I would wish her to exercise the utmost discretion. Yours, etc.

Charles Bostock

"The devil, he raped my daughter! Now he thinks he can buy us off with a Banker's Order!" Bob Jarvis shouted.

"Hush, my dear," Betty urged, "or your customers will hear us in the tap room."

"Just dare he show his face here again and I'll throttle him, so I will!" Bob Jarvis raved with frustration, becoming quite purple in the face.

"Indeed you will not, dear husband, for then we would all be sent packing from our employment, Alicia and the babe included. I think that Mr Charles has been quite generous and indeed very practical. He has admitted his fault, has met our likely early expenses, and has asked to be informed at the child's birth, thus waiting to see whether Alicia goes full term with her firstborn and whether the child is born alive. Besides, it would seem from his letter that Alicia may have given him some encouragement. That's not what I have taught the hussy. She's developed ideas above her station, that one. No doubt Mr Charles entertained her with tales of his life at Court..."

"Yes, Betty, I did remark that they seemed to chat together rather amicably. It never occurred to me that Alicia might do such a thing. I suppose it is too late to marry her to one of her suitors from the town, and to tell him or persuade him that the child is his? Yes, of course it is. Why did Alicia not confide in us sooner, the deceitful little vixen? She deserves to have us turn her out of doors to avoid an unwelcome scandal for us, never mind what harm it causes Mr Charles, and he having just married Sir Robert's daughter too!"

"Husband, I have a suggestion to make," Betty continued. "Your nephew Alfred has a growing family at the Ringsfield Farm. We can send Alicia there to be confined. His wife Martha has all the necessary skills and experience, and Alicia can lend a hand with the household tasks since Martha's health is often fragile. I shall be obliged to hire another chambermaid at the Hall and to forego Alicia's wages, and you will need some assistance here at the Inn. Alicia's condition is beginning to show and I'll not have her serving behind the bar for your farmers to gawp at. Besides, Mr Charles would not wish it either."

"Excellent, wife, I agree to your plan. When I close for the night we shall confront Alicia and make everything plain. Nor shall she blame us; we may say we are following Mr Charles' instructions."

Needless to relate that Alicia was not at all enchanted to find herself excluded from the social delights of serving behind the bar. Her parents gave her the choice of sleeping in at Roos Hall or of transferring her person and labours to the Ringsfield Farm straight away. She chose the latter with reluctance, threatening dire revenge on every side, exclaiming that the mud would soil her clothes, that the farm stank and her little second cousins smelt unwashed, and that Martha was always complaining that she was too weak to keep them in order and to help her husband as she should. "That's precisely why we are sending you there," her mother replied tartly, "so that you can help Martha. The only labour you should eschew is the lifting of anything heavy. Always call one of the men if there's lifting or pushing to be done." Bob Jarvis delivered Alicia to the farm, taking her ignominiously in his waggon along with several empty barrels which he was returning to the brewery in Bungay. She could not have felt more angry or humiliated.

Yet within a few weeks Alicia was a changed young woman. She had hitched up the skirts of her plainest attire and had happily adapted to feeding the hens and collecting their eggs, with a little aid from Martha's children, Carrie and Hugo, who would always hunt out the extra one hidden away in a corner. She had learnt not to fear the geese - or rather those wise birds had learnt to accept her - and she could feed the calves and let them suck her fingers as she passed. When it came to milking a cow, that required a little more courage and patience, but she would master it. Meanwhile Martha was teaching her how to make butter, and to let the whey ferment with yeast to form a soft and creamy cheese, and how to bake bread in the capacious farmhouse oven. Time passed quickly, and it was there at the farm, amid the clank of milk pails, the lowing of the cows and the crow of the cockerel, that Alicia was safely delivered of a daughter in the late Spring.

A few weeks later Betty took pen to paper to write to Mr Charles from whom, indeed, nothing had been heard in the meantime.

Your Honour,

In your letter of 3rd January last you kindly requested that I write to you again once our daughter Alicia had been delivered of her child. On 15th May just past Alicia gave birth to a daughter who is of fair appearance and good health. Her mother has named her Jessica, which name we trust will meet with your Honour's approval. Unfortunately Alicia did not benefit so well from that event. She soon developed a fever from which she was unable to recover, despite the attentions of a trusted physician. Mr Jarvis and I have but now returned from attendance at her funeral.

Thus, not only have we lost our only child and with her our expectations for the future, but we have incurred the unlooked-for expenses of her funeral (and of a suitable memorial in due course), and of hiring a wet-nurse as well as additional help at the Inn to replace Alicia's duties.

Mr Jarvis and I have maintained complete discretion and confidentiality throughout this time, and we would inform you that, following your earlier correspondence, we sent our daughter to the Ringsfield Farm where she completed her confinement away from the public gaze. Even the wet-nurse believes that the child is that of the wife of Alfred Jarvis, the farmer, who has been too poorly to fulfill her maternal duties.

Your Honour, my husband and I await your further instructions in this matter as to how we are to proceed. We read with pleasure in the Norwich papers news of your Honour's recent marriage and send you and your lady wife our most humble felicitations. No doubt you will soon be beginning a new family of your own and so will be sensible of our anxiety for the future welfare of our granddaughter.

Awaiting your early response we remain your Honour's humble and obedient servants,

Robert and Elizabeth Jarvis.

As before, little more than a fortnight had passed when a special messenger knocked at the door of the Bear & Bells, again giving rise to much speculation among the farming fraternity of Beccles. They knew very well that Bob Jarvis had just buried his daughter who had been 'helping out' at the Ringsfield Farm, and that a young babe had been put out to nurse with Bob Jarvis bearing the expense. Now neither he nor Alf Jarvis, his nephew, was saying a word to anyone, and as for Alf's wife Martha, well she had not been seen in public for months and who knew what had happened to her? Be sure something scandalous was going on, but no-one would oblige them with even a hint of what it might be. The new package when opened disclosed a Banker's Order for 300 guineas and a letter which read as follows:

Dear Mr and Mrs Jarvis,
I thank you for your recent letter and regret most sincerely the very sad news it con-
tained. Indeed I am all too conscious of the pain you must feel at the loss of your
dear daughter. In my recollection she was such an amiable young lady that I too
have grieved for her, even tho' you may not consider such grief on my part accept-
able.

I enclose a draft for a sum which I believe will defray your present expenses
until such time as I can make my escape from onerous duties at Court and can
visit Beccles again. Until then, please leave the child with the wet-nurse whilst she
is weaned. Thereafter she may be removed to Roos Hall, there to abide at my
expense. The name Jessica appears perfectly acceptable to me and I will arrange
for the child to be christened in due course when I have made further decisions
about her future. In the meantime, please do not hesitate to apply to me again,
care of White's Club, should your circumstances so require.

And now there is a personal service in which I would be much gratified to have
your assistance, dear Mr and Mrs Jarvis. In a week or two I shall send to Roos Hall
by private carriage a young man, fourteen years of age, whom Sir Robert wishes
to spend his school vacation months of July and August in the pleasant surround-
ings of Beccles. His name is Ainsworth Rich and is an orphan whom Sir Robert
has taken into his care. We should be much obliged if both Mr Robert Jarvis and
his nephew Mr Alfred Jarvis might contrive to keep the boy well-occupied in their
respective businesses for the duration of his stay, so that he will lack opportuni-
ties to make mischief. I shall send further funds for this purpose care of Sir
Robert's agent, Mr Anthony Russell, who is to accompany Mr Ainsworth to Roos
Hall before proceeding to his home near Norwich.

I should be most obliged if you, Mrs Jarvis, would kindly make all arrange-

ments necessary for Mr Ainsworth's reception, and please inform the staff that he is a distant member of Sir Robert's family. Sir Robert himself does not enjoy good health these days and is unlikely to be able to visit Roos Hall or any of his other East Anglian properties for some considerable time. I would be most grateful it you would kindly report to me, dear Mrs Jarvis, upon Mr Ainsworth's safe arrival, and later upon his demeanour during his stay.

With my sincerest condolences for your personal loss and my grateful respects,

> *I remain*
> *Yours,*
> *Charles (Bostock) Rich*

"What do you make of that, husband?" Betty Jarvis asked as soon as she had finished reading the letter aloud.

"I think he's sending us another of his bastards, that's what I make of it," Bob Jarvis exclaimed emphatically. "You can see the convenience if he's married a wife and wants to sever his complications from the past."

"And Ainsworth, hardly a Christian name, is it?" Betty remarked. "'Tis a surname, surely?"

"It sounds like the surname of another chambermaid he's seduced, and probably without enquiring into her circumstances either. We're being made a convenience, Betty, and I won't allow that."

"But I do not think we may object to it, husband. If I were to leave my situation at Roos Hall we would have no command of the care of little Jessica. We wouldn't wish to contest her paternity with someone as wealthy and well-connected as Sir Robert or his son-in-law."

"Yes, Betty, you're right, wife, as you usually are," Bob Jarvis replied. "Can you pen him a reply acknowledging his letter and confirming our compliance with his instructions?"

"Indeed I will, husband, and you must proceed with finding extra help here at the inn, before your own health catches up with you. I've seen how tired you've been of late."

* * *

Mr Ainsworth duly arrived at Roos Hall, a tall, callow-looking youth with a crop of dark curls and a sullen glance. Nothing was good enough for him, though the cook prepared the most wholesome dishes and she, Betty, made sure the chambermaid had changed his sheets, warmed his bed and had set a fire in the hearth of an evening. Not though her husband. Bob took the lad about with him when he collected fresh supplies from the Brewery or returned the empty barrels, though he showed him how to pour ale and stout so as to give the drink a good head, and how to reckon up his business accounts, which he did at the end of every month and early on quarter days. The only time young Ainsworth had paid him any attention, Bob complained to his wife, was when he instructed him in the various types of wines available at his establishment, and even then his interest had depended upon whether he might taste a sample! Alf Jarvis had much the same experience at the farm. Feeding and caring for cows, sheep and pigs provoked no cooperation at all from the youngster, and when it came to harvest his sole enthusiasm lay in harnessing up the horses that drew the waggon. Every other task he performed perfunctorily, if at all. He was rude to the children and scarcely civil to Martha who was always ready to spoil a stranger. Moreover the farm dog, Horace, a cross between a collie and a lurcher, did not care for Ainsworth either, and, as Alf remarked to his uncle, "That dog is highly intelligent."

* * *

Seven years had passed since then. As Betty walked home on this windy October night she reviewed anxiously the changes which had taken place. Her granddaughter Jessica was now a child of seven, slight and fair-haired like her mother, but with dark eyes which must have belonged elsewhere in her ancestry. She lived now at Roos Hall where the cook, Mrs. Baines, saw to her meals as she did those of the rest of the household, and where the elderly footman-cum-handyman Briggs picked her up and rubbed her knees if she fell over. However the child was not receiving any education, save from Betty herself who had taught her to read and write in moments when she could be spared from her household duties. During the one visit he had made to Roos Hall not long after Jessica's birth, Mr. Charles had decreed that Betty should not disclose to the child her blood relationship with her granddaughter. Mr. Charles arranged and attended a private christening at which she was named Jessica Alicia Rich and during which he styled himself as both her godfather and her guardian. He then instructed Mrs. Jarvis that whilst Jessica might eventually learn the identity of her benefactor, she was not to be told her mother's name or circumstances. This to Betty was the most frustrating instruction of all, not to be able to reassure her own flesh and blood of a grandmother's tender care, having to leave the little one alone there in her room in that dark old house with only the cook and the footman sleeping upstairs in the attics after the other servants had departed to their homes.

And now Mr. Ainsworth was expected again; the young man himself had sent a message from London ordering what preparations he would have made for his coming. Ainsworth had not visited the Hall since his schooldays. Jessica was still being cared for by her wet-nurse then and had not impinged upon the surroundings of that rather nonchalant young man. What would happen now, Betty wondered?

* * *

The wind clashed on in the branches and a sharp shower of rain stung Betty's face. She shivered and pulled her cloak more tightly about her. She recalled that it had been a similar night to this, chilly and windswept even in May, the last time she had witnessed IT, that terrible apparition, the night before Alicia had died. Something was going to happen again tonight, she could feel it on the air. With one chilled hand she sought for the crucifix that hung about her neck and clutched it hard. Suddenly she felt a sensation of steamy warmth and turned to look behind her. Even though the lane was pitch dark her eyes could distinguish the movement. Someone or something was coming rapidly towards her, tumbling over and over and changing its shape like a breaking wave on the shore, a black wave of darkness. Then it was upon her, all around her, tearing at her cloak, her hat, her hair. Betty shut her eyes and prayed and prayed again. Then it was gone, vanished, leaving only a rank, rancid smell like that of a wet dog. Black Shuck, the ghostly dog of the marshes. How many times she had seen it on her lonely journeys home. Her husband had often lent her the Inn's dog, Horace, that had been retired from service at Alf's farm due to old age, but he liked to keep the dog with him on Market Days in case there should be any trouble among the merry and quarrelsome farmers.

"Thank God it was not the other one," Betty muttered as she resumed her journey. For 'the other one' was an apparition also known to haunt this road, a black carriage drawn by four black horses and driven by a coachman who was headless. That apparition was a portent of certain death, and it was that she had witnessed on the eve of Alicia's death.

With an overwhelming sense of relief Betty pushed in through the low doorway into the warmth and shelter of the Inn. Her husband Bob looked up and nodded. His young assistant Peter smiled cheerily. Now Peter Jones was a real orphan, a lad from Lowestoft whose mother had died of the smallpox and whose father had then committed suicide by leaping off the jetty into a stormy sea. Peter had lived with them, working hard and eager to learn the trade, for upwards of half a dozen years. It gave Betty much peace of mind to know that the only labours which awaited her attention at home were likely to be merely domestic.

As Betty stood removing her hat and cloak to hang them on the peg in the corridor beyond the bar, one of a group of four farmers sitting chatting earnestly in a window embrasure called for another flagon of malmsey wine. "In the cellar, I have sold all the stock I brought up this morning," Bob shouted over his shoulder as he served another customer.

"Don't you fret, Mrs. Jarvis, I'll go down and fetch some," Peter said. Taking a lantern from an empty table he climbed down the stairs into the cellar. There was a noise of a struggle and confusion and then Peter reappeared at the head of the cellar steps, his face white as a sheet and neither wine nor lantern in his hand. "I'm not going down there again after dark" he exclaimed.

"I'll go, Peter, I know what it was." As she stood at the top of the cellar stairs Betty could smell it, the rank, dank, stink of wet dog. It was not Horace, for he was resting peacefully, stretched out before the fire. It was Black Shuck! Betty took another lantern and descended to the cellar. Beside the fire, Horace clambered to his feet, crossed the floor and stood whining at the top of the cellar steps. Betty found the wine, extinguished the lantern which Peter had upset in his fright, and turned to climb the steps again. When she reappeared with the wine and the lighted lantern, she too had blanched but her crucifix was clenched firmly between her teeth. "That's the second time I've seen him tonight!" she whispered to her husband. "Something evil must be coming upon us."

CHAPTER II
The Victim

My name is Jessica. I am seven years old and I live at Roos Hall in the County of Suffolk. Indeed, I am nearly eight because my birthday falls on 15th May, only three weeks to wait now. I hope that our cook, Mrs Baines, will bake me a cake as she did last year, but I am not sure that will happen now that Mr Ainsworth is here. He doesn't like me, you see.

"I am a norfan," (sic). Our Housekeeper, Mrs Jarvis - she's an elderly lady who dresses in black and always smells of lavender, but she is very kind - she explained to me that a norfan is someone who does not have parents or even kith and kin any more. Either they are dead or they have gone away. Of course I did have parents originally, everyone does. Mrs Jarvis tells me that my mother was a very pretty lady. She had fair hair, though not as light as mine, but she had nice curls and I wish I had those. My mother had blue eyes, tho' mine are dark, and Mrs Jarvis says that probably I in-her-i-ted those from my father's family. He is a gentleman, Mrs Jarvis says, but he went away and left me and she will not tell me any more about him. My mother, of course, is dead. She died when I was just a few days old, so I do not remember her. All that I remember is being brought to live here in this big dark house where it is often so very damp and cold.

"It was my Nanny who brought me here. We came in a carriage and that was the first time I had ridden in one. Nanny had been looking after me because my mother was not able to do so. Nanny was a warm and cuddlesome person and I miss her very much. When we first came here she slept in my bedroom, so that if I woke during the night I would hear her breathing and would feel warm and safe again. However when she had been here a little while they sent Nanny away and said I was old enough to look after myself. Mrs Jarvis told me this was on my father's instructions and that he had sent a letter saying so, but if he cared for me at all he would know how lonely and frightened I felt to be left on my own. Mrs Jarvis said that Nanny was obliged to return home to look after other children. I think that is a much better reason, don't you?

"So then I had the big bedroom all to myself. I could spread out my toys all over the floor and I laid out my clothes on what had been Nanny's bed so that I could decide what to wear. Mrs Jarvis used to help me choose. On cold evenings Briggs, the handyman, would light a fire in the grate and put a metal guard around it so that I could not fall in, and Mrs Baines always looked in last thing at night to make sure I was asleep, and to put out my candle, since I was afraid to go to sleep in the dark. I still am really. All that changed when Mr Ainsworth arrived and I am not nearly so comfortable now.

"Mrs Jarvis explained that Mr Ainsworth is to look after the Hall on behalf of the owner. Well, I do not think he is making a good job of it. He is very strict and is rude to all the servants and often upsets Mrs Baines, Briggs, the chamber-maids and the groundsmen too. Nobody likes him and Mrs Jarvis is the only one who stands up to him, and he is often rude to her as well. He mopes around the house all day when it is bad weather, shouting orders at everyone and never say-ing 'thank you'. When it is fine he takes his gun and his dog, that is a black short-haired retriever named Arthur, and goes shooting pheasants in the park. Sometimes he brings back a deer. I do not wish to see animals killed, but we have to eat something and Mrs Baines always prepares such good dishes. Oh and Arthur, I like dogs and wanted to make friends with him when he arrived here with his master, but Mr Ainsworth forbade me to touch him. He says Arthur is a trained gun dog and must not be petted.

"It is just the same with Mr Ainsworth's horse - 'tis a beautiful bay-coloured hunter named P-H-A-R-A-O-H. I think that is how it is spelt; 'tis the name of the kings of ancient Egypt, so Mrs Jarvis tells me. But the housemaids swear it is spelt F-A-R-O after the card game that all the smart people play. The maids say that Mr Ainsworth chose that name because he gambles with money, but Mrs Jarvis insists that I must pay no heed to the gossip below stairs, as 'tis likely to be wrong any-way. As I was telling you, I went up to Pharaoh in the stable to give him a pat, as I've seen the stable-boy Ted do, and Mr Ainsworth came in just at that moment and smacked my hand away. He told me that his horse is a highspirited thorough-bred which he did not wish upset by a little ig-nor-a-mus like me.

"I wish I could have a pony of my own. There is plenty of room in the stables and I am sure it would not cost so much to keep. I did mention it to Mrs Jarvis but she replied she would need to seek her employer's permission and someone would have to be assigned to teach me to ride. It did not sound as if it would be very possible. But then if, as I suspect, her employer, our landlord, is also my father, I think it ought not to be too much to ask of him. If only he would call upon us I would ask him myself. I believe he may be Mr Ainsworth's father also, and *he* seems to obtain everything he sets his mind to.

"One day Mr Ainsworth called all the staff together in the dining-room after breakfast and told everyone he had invited guests to a house-party for the fol-lowing weekend. He made Mrs Baines take down a list of all the dishes he wished prepared, and so flummoxed her with the speed of his requests that the poor lady's hand was shaking as she tried to make a note of them. The stables had to be cleaned and tidied, he said, so that there would be room for more horses and their carriages. And then he came to the part that affected me - I was to leave my comfortable large bedroom and move up to one of the attics, so that the whole of the first and second floors would be available for use by Mr Ainsworth and his guests.

"At that Mrs Jarvis, who had quite incorrectly not been consulted about any of this, protested on my behalf and remonstrated with Mr Ainsworth that the attics were damp and had only tiny fireplaces not suitable for 'a child of my tender years', that is what she said. Mr Ainsworth replied tartly that since he was in charge of the Hall she should mind her duty and supervise Briggs and the maids in the making up of the beds and the lighting of warm fires to welcome his guests. Mrs Jarvis then, very boldly I thought and so did the other staff for they hushed with white faces, demanded of Mr Ainsworth how this event was to be paid for, since the expense could not be found from the housekeeping allowance made over to her by our landlord to cover all our domestic needs.

"I am Charles Rich's son," Mr Ainsworth replied angrily, "and he'll just have to stump up whatever is necessary to meet the tradesmen's bills. You can put everything on account, Mrs Jarvis, as most people do, and there's no need to pay them a shilling till they have begged for it on several occasions."

"That's not the way we do business here, Mr Ainsworth," Mrs Jarvis replied, rather tight-lipped, "and I doubt that Mr Charles behaves in that way either!" At that Mr Ainsworth, feeling somewhat worsted perhaps, tapped his riding crop hard against his boot and strode to the door. "See to it, all of you!" he shouted as he turned at the doorway.

"So now I sit shivering in my little attic room, the one with the high window overlooking the drive. At least I had the diversion of watching all the fine carriages turn into the drive for the house-party, and if I slipped into Mrs Baines' room I could put my head out of the window there and watch the visitors stepping out. However, as it was such cold weather, they were all wrapped in heavy coats and cloaks and wore hats and bonnets, so that there was not much to be seen. One evening, when there was dancing in the hall below, I crept down to the gallery to watch. But Mr Ainsworth glanced up and saw me, and he looked so cross that I ran right back to my room. Next morning at breakfast he started berating me for it, but then some guests came into the dining-room and he was obliged to desist. Later that day he forbade me the dining-room altogether and ordered me henceforth to take my meals with the servants in the kitchen wing.

"My bedroom is at the gable end of the house, so is exposed to the wind and the rain on three sides. Also the leads do not fit well into the window-frames and the curtains are too flimsy to keep out the draughts. So when I get up or go to bed I hurry into my clothes as fast as I can. Fortunately I can fasten most of my hooks and ties by myself now and do not need to ask for help. The covers on my bed are rather thin, just one blanket and a light counterpane, and those are not sufficient when the weather is cold. You see, this room was intended for use by a housemaid when guests were entertained, so Mrs Jarvis says, and she has promised to bring me an extra quilt from her home. She had better not let Mr Ainsworth know, for he will surely be disagreeable about it.

JESS OF ROOS HALL

"When the weather is bad I sit on the mat before the fireplace, tho' Briggs has orders not to light a fire for me between April and October, and I play with the few toys I have been given over the years, or else I read the books which Mrs Jarvis has given to me. I used to go downstairs to the Library and look at some of the big books on the shelves there - some of them have engravings and even painted pictures which are interesting to look at, but recently Mr Ainsworth entered when I was there and he sent me to my room. He says the books in the Library are too valuable to be touched by a child's sticky fingers. But I am always most careful with them and usually my hands are quite clean. I always wash them in the morning in the basin in my room when one of the maids brings me a jug of warm water.

"I wish I might go to school as other children do. I have asked Mrs Jarvis about it and she said she would obtain instructions from her employer, meaning Mr Charles again I suppose. From my window I can see the lane at the end of the drive and I watch the farm children going past each day on their way to and from school. The town is only half a mile away and I would be able to walk there with them, so would not need to be taken. I have tried waving to the children as they pass, but so far they do not seem to have noticed me.

"When the weather is fine I can take a walk in the park and watch the deer feeding. The fawns are so pretty beside their mothers, but they are all shy of me and move away when I call. Then I climb down the steep bank to the stream and sit where the sunlight dapples the shadows. There are trout in the stream, big brown ones, and Briggs says that when I am a little older he will teach me to fish, tho' I daresay that now Mr. Ainsworth is here that will be forbidden too. Sometimes when it is really hot and sunny I lie on the stream bank and make up stories, like the ones I have read about in the books Mrs Jarvis gives me. I am always the heroine, of course, and fight off dragons and monsters, until some brave and gallant knight comes to rescue me.

"However on other days I decide I should do something more worthwhile and go into the kitchen garden to help the gardener Easton and the other grounds-men. The kitchen garden is walled all round to keep it sheltered from the winds. On the walls where the sun strikes most in summer there are fruit trees which have been trained to grow sideways along strands of twine. These grow pears and in a good year some grapes. There are also some apple trees - which I can climb when no one is looking, tho' Mrs Jarvis will scold me if I dirty my clothes. There is a hothouse which is steamy and smells of manure but enables exotic fruit from foreign lands to be grown here, such as peaches and pineapples. And there is an ice-house outside the north wall of the garden which does the opposite, keeps food cool and allows Mrs Baines to make the most delicious cold and creamy desserts when the weather is hot.

"The rest of the garden is divided into plots for berry bushes and for vegeta-bles, and there is also a large bed of herbs. I am permitted to pull carrots and onions for the kitchen and lately I have been allowed to dig potatoes too, though one has to be careful not to put the tines of the fork too close to the plant or one spears the potatoes and they are not fit for use. They let me carry all the baskets of produce needed for the day to the kitchen where Mrs Baines will allow me to shell the peas or shred the beans. I enjoy watching her prepare our dishes and mean to learn more about cooking as I am sure 'tis a useful art. Moreover, as the kitchen is in a side-wing separated by a corridor from the main house, Mr Ainsworth is less likely to visit it, which means I can linger there all day without his finding a reason to send me to my room.

"Now I must tell you the really awful news: Mr Ainsworth has begun to use violence towards me. It began one day when he came indoors after riding. He walked through the hall just as my spillikins were spread all over the floor. The room being dimly lit through the latticed windows, Mr Ainsworth failed to see the sticks, fell down and slid right across the polished floor to the fireplace, sending the andirons crashing and clanging into one another. I ran over to him and started to apologise, for he was quite crimson in the face with anger. But he jumped to his feet, snatched up his crop, seized my arm and began to beat me hard with it across the back of my bare legs. I screamed and cried, but nobody heard. When eventually he threw me to the ground I ran up to my room, even tho' my legs hurt so badly that I could scarcely climb the stairs. An hour or two later, after my tears had diminished somewhat, I found that my legs had swollen and that there were horrible weals where the crop had struck. I was ashamed of them and dare not leave my room. When I did not come down for supper, Mrs Baines sent Briggs upstairs to see what had become of me.

"Briggs reported the matter to Mrs Baines who, she later told me, was heard to exclaim in horror, 'Oh, the poor little mite. You take that tray up to her, Briggs, whilst I serve 'is Lordship's dinner. Tell her I'll be up later with some ointment to put on those poor limbs'.

"I kept well out of Mr Ainsworth's way for several days after that, but whenever he has chanced upon me since he always raises his crop or his hand as if he would strike me,and I have no recourse but to run away and hide. This reminds me to tell you that I have discovered a new hiding place behind some panelling in the corner of the stairs. I call it my own secret place since nobody else seems to know of it. Mrs Jarvis has been working at the Hall for years and years and when she passed by the other day - I could see her through the crack of the panelling door - I stepped up behind her and she exclaimed: 'How you startled me, child. I did not know you were there.' When I first discovered the secret door, which opens from a catch carved in a wooden flower, the hinges creaked horribly. So I borrowed an oil can from the potting-shed and dosed my door when no one was looking. Now it opens quite silently and provides me with a niche into which I can slip very rapidly, and I do not have to clatter all the way upstairs to my room.

"There is just one problem though, I do not know how to open the door from within. I cannot see any catch, and indeed there may not be one for perhaps that recess was meant only to be used from the outside. This obliges me to leave the door open just a little bit and I keep a small twig inside the cupboard for use as a wedge, However I am always afraid that if Mr Ainsworth should chance upon my hideaway he might shut me into it and not let me out again. That is the reason why I have begun to write this Journal, which I hide in my bedroom, so that if I am missed for long enough they will make a thorough search and come upon it, and then will know where to find me. Of course I might have died of hunger by then if they do not search sufficiently. My other reason for writing this is that should Mr Charles pay us a visit I can show him my Journal and he may read for himself of all the matters that require his attention, and more particularly of the bad behaviour of Mr Ainsworth.

"Recently there have been other occasions upon which Mr Ainsworth has beaten me, several of them trivial and of little account, but some beatings have been severe and have arisen out of the most dramatic circumstances. Nearly two months ago, when it was no longer winter but not yet spring, and when the leaves had not quite burst from their swelling buds, as I walked in the park I took a fancy to sit by the stream and wait for the water rat or some other of the river creatures to appear. I had sat on the top of the bank to obtain the best view and was enjoying some breezy sunshine when I saw a mouse emerge from a hole in the bank. It sat up on its tail and looked right at me, twitching its whiskers and wiggling its large round ears. I leaned forward to take a closer look and, before I knew what was happening, my foot had slipped on a patch of mud and I tumbled down the bank, feet first, into the water!

"I knew the water to be quite shallow there, only ankle-deep in summer, though after the wet weather of winter it was a good deal deeper than that. However I thought I might easily stand up and scramble up the bank. Instead I found myself drifting slowly downstream. The water did not feel very cold because the sun had warmed it that morning, and anyway I was lying on my back, quite comfortable in fact, with my petticoats keeping me afloat. Then the pace of the water quickened, a cold chill began to penetrate the cloth, and I was conscious of sinking deeper and deeper into the flood. It was then that I remembered the weir where our stream enters a dyke that crosses the meadows to the River Waveney. There is a deep pool below the weir where the water scours around after flowing down the slope. I had better try to stand up right now, I thought, and did so, try, I mean, but could not! Suddenly there was water all around me, clutching at me with cold hands, whilst my soaking petticoats clung to my limbs and dragged me down, down, down. I rose to the surface and started to shout. I could see a distant figure in the park but there was so much water in my eyes that I could not make out who it was. Then there came a great splashing in the stream behind me and a large black shape seemed to tower above me. This force grasped the clothing behind my head and I felt my body being towed along till it reached the bank where a strong hand leant down and hoisted me upwards.

"Unfortunately the strong hand belonged to Mr Ainsworth who immediately began to belabour me with his walking cane. It was his dog Arthur which had plunged into the stream and seizing my floating collar in his mouth had ferried me to the bank. Mr Ainsworth beat my shivering limbs with his stick without even waiting to see whether I was still alive. Fortunately the wet clothes prevented his hurting me much and when he realised this he turned his attention to my bare arms and head which did hurt and I was afraid that the weals would show on my face so that everyone would know how naughty I had been. At that moment Arthur flushed a fox and Mr Ainsworth paused to recall the dog from his vain pursuit. I slid from his grasp and raced for the safety of the kitchen.

"There I ran straight into Mrs Jarvis who took one look at me and asked what had occurred. She was not best pleased with me either, for it seems I had ruined my clothes and Mrs Jarvis told me there was no money in the allowance from Mr Charles to replace them. I did not dare to point out that half the damage to my outer garments had been caused by Mr Ainsworth flailing at me with his stick. Instead I listened meekly to a lecture on my unseemly behaviour, that I should walk in the park like a young lady rather than scrambling about on the river bank, and that a means must be found for keeping me out of mischief.

"The other incident I must mention is the one which has led to my present humiliation and despair. It happened only a week ago and I have been blamed unjustly for what occurred. The stables here at the Hall consist of two buildings, one of brick with a thatched roof which has stalls for several horses and a tack room, and the other an old wooden thatched barn used to store the carriage at one end and bales of straw and hay at the other. Now during the winter the rain had got into the stack of straw through holes in the roof and it had started to rot; the smell was awful. Had the bad straw been laid down for Pharaoh it would have made him very sick, so Mr Ainsworth ordered that the carriage be taken out and thoroughly cleaned and polished while the remaining old straw was to be raked into the middle of the floor and taken away by one of the tenant farmers, a Mr Alfred Jarvis, who I think is related to Mrs Jarvis but I am not entirely sure. New straw and hay would be delivered by Mr Jarvis when he collected the old.

"Naturally I was interested in observing all this unusual activity which made a welcome change from hiding in my room. Also Easton and the groundsmen,who would normally have been at work in the kitchen garden, had been assigned to cleaning the carriage instead, so that I could not help them in the garden as usual. After watching the goings on out of Mrs Baines' bedroom window for a while, which afforded only an incomplete view of the proceedings, I went downstairs to the yard and asked Easton if I might help with cleaning the carriage. He gave me a couple of brass lamps to polish along with a rag and a bottle containing brass-cleaning fluid. I was very careful and achieved an excellent shine on the lanterns while spilling only a drop or two of the cleaning fluid on my pinafore. So I was feeling quite virtuous when Easton asked me to go into the barn to see what had become of Ted who had been sent in there to gather up the old straw.

"The barn door was heavy and took much effort to open further so that I could slip inside. It was very dark within after the bright sunshine out in the yard. At first I could see nothing at all, but then I realised that I was standing in front of a huge pile of straw; the rest was complete silence. So where was Ted? Then I heard a loud snore coming from the pile of straw. I ran around to the other side of the mound and there was Ted lying in the straw fast asleep. I also smelt smoke. Ted had been secretly smoking his clay pipe - in the barn! a thing totally forbidden to all the staff. It had fallen from his lips as he slept and the straw was beginning to smoulder! I tried stamping on the glowing straw but my slippers were too flimsy to have any effect. Then in the corner of the barn I espied the bucket used to catch rain leaking through the roof. I ran over to it, found it half full of dirty water and directed this at the flickering flames. Unfortunately my aim was poor. I had doused Ted who woke and sprang up with an oath. The flames began to burn all the more. Ted seized the bucket from me and started beating at the flames. At that moment Easton opened the barn door to find out what was afoot and the whole straw stack went up in a sheet of flame.

"Ted staggered out of the building coughing and spluttering from the smoke, but I was too frightened to move. I just stood there, paralysed, while the flames grew hot and frightful and the fire leapt out at me. I stared and stared back at it. Then I felt a funny tickling sensation at the back of my neck. It was a moment or two before I realised that my hair was on fire! I could hear Mrs Jarvis calling my name but still I could not move. Then a wet sack was thrown over my head and heavy hands beat out the flames and a heavy stick beat about the rest of me, and I knew who had come to my rescue - Mr Ainsworth!

"I was dragged out of the barn and thrown to the ground while Mr Ainsworth went to his horse, Pharaoh, and put a cloth over his head to lead him from the stable. There was every danger, you see, that the thatched roof would catch light from the sparks coming from the barn. Briggs was pumping water as hard as he could at the pump in the yard, and Easton and his men were running up with ladders and throwing buckets of water over the stable roof, for by then it was too late to save the barn. For the joists had caught light and the flames soon made their way to the roof and the walls. The heat was so violent that it cracked the glass of the tack room window. When the barn had been reduced to tumbled rafters and ashes, Easton and the others set about dousing the flames and Pharaoh was returned unharmed to his stable. At that moment Alfred Jarvis arrived with his waggon of fresh straw and hay and there was nowhere to store it. So the hay went into the tack room and some straw into a disused outhouse and the rest had to be piled inside the carriage which had just been so laboriously cleaned.

"All these details I had later from Mrs Baines, for I was still lying on the ground insensible at this stage, with the wet sack over my head and my clothes half-destroyed by the fire. It was many, many long minutes before Mrs Jarvis could call Briggs from the pump to carry me indoors to the kitchen settle so that my injuries could be examined. I have numerous burns on my legs and arms, all of which have been smothered with ointment and bandaged. These were then encased in thick knitted woollen stockings and knitted mittens with long cuffs to keep all the bandages in place. Mrs Jarvis thinks they are mostly scorch marks which will heal in time. However there is a serious burn on the back of my neck where my hair caught fire. This has been heavily poulticed and my head feels odd, as if it does not quite belong to me. At the moment I am easily confused and have no inclination to run around as I used. Probably that will keep me out of mischief for a while, Mrs Jarvis says.

"However, the very worst of my injuries is the loss of my hair. When they removed the wet sacking from my head, they found beneath it just a few singed spikes, much resembling the mouldy straw which had burned in the barn. The singed ends were cut off and all the wounds were rubbed gently with ointment. Now I must wear a cap, a horrid linen one borrowed from one of the maids It feels prickly where it touches my skin and adds to my discomforts. I look such sight that I dare not face anyone, not even the servants. But will my hair ever grow back again, or will it just grow in the undamaged patches so I shall appear half-bald? No one will wish to speak to me if I am to look like this for the rest of my life.

"Worse still at this time is the fact that I am being blamed for the disaster. I described what had happened to Mrs Jarvis and Mrs Baines while they were treating my injuries. Alas, Ted has refused to confess to smoking in the barn for fear of losing his position, and Easton, who is his superior, backs him up. Easton says that I must have lit one of the carriage lamps which I had been cleaning and have carried it into the barn with me, oversetting it on my way. Mr Ainsworth chooses to believe Easton, of course, especially as one of the carriage lanterns mysteriously reappeared from among the ashes of the barn, covered in dust. If anyone ever found Ted's clay pipe it was never mentioned.

"Mr Ainsworth called me into his study and when he shut the door behind me I was never more frightened in my life. I thought he was about to beat me again and that no one would come to stop him. But all that happened was that he was very rude. He informed me there was no money available to rebuild the barn and that he would have to apply to Mr Charles for extra funds. Then he laughed, a funny sort of hollow laugh with a twist of his lip. 'Ha!' he said, 'at least now no one will seek to marry you and you will remain a nobody for the rest of your days!'

"At that moment Mrs Jarvis opened the door of the study and informed Mr Ainsworth that Mr Alfred Jarvis had called for payment for the new straw and hay and for certain other monies owed him. Mr Ainsworth laughed even more loudly and said, 'Tell him he'll get paid when I have built a new barn. And take this piece of peasant rubbish with you!' he concluded, indicating me.

"So now I am sitting in my cupboard in the wall with my Journal on my knee. There is just enough light at present for me to see what I write. However it will soon be dark and I shall continue to stay here, let them look for me as they will, for this is the only place where I feel safe. All my wounds are hurting and my neck gives me especial pain. Some of the burns on my arms and legs are itching, but Mrs Jarvis says I must not scratch them or I will be scarred for life. I hardly care any more. If I am rubbish then it does not matter what becomes of me and I may just as well shut the door and entomb myself in this place."

(The Journal ends here ...)

CHAPTER III
The Prodigal

My dear Richard   July, 1791

"I am setting this down in the form of a letter addressed to you, the close companion of our schooldays, whether you ever read it eventually or no, both by way of a confession and an explanation of the abrupt manner in which we were parted. I have forgotten what details I furnished of my childhood, but let me start again at the beginning, insofar as the facts are known to me.

"I was born in February 1769 in a workhouse at Lewes, Sussex, where my mother had been granted refuge on dismissal from her employment when her condition had become known. I vaguely remember those earlier years, sleeping in my mother's bed, the cold, the damp, the poor food, and the old and the ugly who congregated there with their sores and infections. When I was about three years of age my mother obtained outside employment again but could not take me with her, so that I was left to fend for myself at an orphanage at Brighthelmstone. All I had to remember my mother by was a silver locket containing her likeness - I wear it still, as you have often remarked - and the name Ainsworth by which I was known henceforth. I suppose that to have been my mother's name or some name with which she had connections, for I do not believe it was ever other than a surname.

"I remained in that orphanage until the age of seven, fighting and stumbling with the other children, bullied by those who were older, and soundly chastised by the Warden, Mr Bulstrode. He never stopped to inquire the source of our misery, but administered equally all round thwacks from the heavy cane he always carried. We were supposed to be taught some rudiments of education, but I barely learnt to spell and write my name, and to count the number of pence in a pound. Then a most astonishing event happened. I recall that the year was 1776 in the month of July, when the weather had just turned hot and dusty and I had been rolling over and over in the yard engaged in bloodying the nose of my deadliest enemy, one Marcus Todd. It is curious how one can remember names and the merest trivia from the events of one's youth, and how they may return to haunt one still as adult life goes on.

"A carriage bearing a crest and coat of arms upon its doors turned into the yard through the open gates and pulled up before the Warden's lodgings. Mrs Bulstrode, who was plump and portly, and whom we hated as cordially as we did her spouse for the vicious slaps she distributed with generous liberality, stood on her threshhold with her jaw dropping wide open as she observed the elegant gentleman who descended to her door. Mrs Bulstrode attempted a curtsy and fell flat upon her face in front of the visitor. That brought all our games and squabbles to an instant halt as we gathered round, speculating avidly about what might be afoot.

"That visitor was the Reverend Charles Bostock, now ennobled as Sir Charles Rich. He waited patiently while Mrs Bulstrode struggled to her feet, not offering to assist her, he being of a superior class of person. We children enjoyed the scene hugely. Mrs Bulstrode was quite scarlet of countenance with embarrassment but nevertheless asked of the stranger what he required. The gentleman identified himself by reference to a letter he had evidently written to the Warden and confirmed that he had now come to collect the said boy and take him away. 'Oh yes, your Honour, you mean Mr Ainsworth,' Mrs Bulstrode replied. 'I'll call my husband if you would care to wait within.' With that the gentleman stepped over the threshhold.

"As soon as I heard my own name mentioned I wished I had not so dirtied myself or my clothes rolling over in the yard and began to dust myself down, running a grubby hand through my disordered hair. Unseen by me, Mr Bulstrode had come up behind me, and unseen by the gentleman, administered a kick upon my backside as he grabbed my arm and propelled me towards the doorway. 'Here he is, your Honour, a little dusty from his play, but he's a good child really, and a clever one,' he uttered with a fawning accent which was a delight to my ears, having received nothing but chastisements from him in the past.

"Here are his personal effects, your Honour,' said Mrs. Bulstrode, bustling forward. 'P'raps you'll just inspect them before I put them in this nice canvas bag.' I had a glimpse of a pile of neatly folded clean clothes which I had never seen before and certainly had never had the pleasure of wearing. They must have been hand-me-downs from some previous inhabitant who had ceased to require them, for at the orphanage if we were given a change of smallclothes after our Saturday evening bath in order that we might not offend the nostrils of the congregation as we filed into the neighbouring church the next morning, it was a miracle indeed.

"The Revd Bostock looked down at the pile of garments and turned to Mrs Bulstrode. 'Was there not some token of his identity, Madam, left with him when the boy was placed here?' Mrs. Bulstrode glanced swiftly at her husband.

"He coughed and replied, 'I will search our records, your Honour. We keep very careful accounts of personal trinkets, very careful indeed.' Mr Bulstrode turned and hurried into his office. Taking a large bunch of keys from a drawer in his desk he proceeded to insert one of them into the lock of a cupboard on the wall. He removed a large wooden box which he again opened with a key, and from the mysterious interior brought out the locket that I now wear. 'Is this the one your Honour had in mind?' he asked, half hoping that the gentleman might deny it so that it need not be relinquished. The Revd Bostock held out his hand, took the locket and opened it, spending a very long while, as it seemed to me, studying the portrait within, which I now know to be a likeness of my mother.

"'Yes, this is the one,' the clergyman replied, slipping the jewel into his breast pocket. The pile of clean clothes was inserted into the canvas bag and with the buckle fastened it was handed to the Revd. Bostock. He turned towards me. By this time my knees were shaking. Was this my father? Had he come to collect me at last? Was I being taken home to a loving family with my mother safely installed at its heart? But all he said was 'Ainsworth?' I nodded, dumbfounded by the sudden turn of events. He continued, 'Boy, you're to come with me.' He helped me into the carriage ahead of him, then climbed up after me and sat down. The coachman put up the step and closed the door. Then he mounted up, clicked to his horses, and we clattered out of the yard.

"I had never travelled in a conveyance of such elegance before and spent several minutes studying my surroundings, for I believe my mother must have used the stage waggon to transport me from Lewes to Brighthelstone. Then it occurred to me that I had scarcely seen anything of that town beyond the streets in the vicinity of the orphanage. Looking out of the window, which was halfway open, I could see the Channel, and then the Downs rising behind the town. You may imagine my excitement as the vehicle turned towards them and took the road north.

"However I soon turned my attention to the study of my travelling companion. In fact he had reclined in the corner of the seat opposite, had stretched out his legs diagonally and was engaged in reading a book, tho' from my distance I could not tell whether he read a romance or some improving homily. He was dressed as a man of the cloth, albeit rather elegantly. His shoes with their silver buckles were made of the finest leather. His hose was without wrinkles, his breeches well-cut and fitting smoothly to the knee. His waistcoat was of handsomely broidered brocade rather than being of plain clerical serge, and his topcoat bore a velvet collar. It was only his white stock and his black hat which truly identified his profession, since the hat was similar to that worn by the vicar at the church we orphans had attended, walking thither in procession, two by two, with Mr Bulstrode at the head well-armed with his cane, and his wife walking behind us to report any ill behaviour. The stranger had a pleasant expression, amiable rather than charitable, and his profusion of curly hair, which he wore unpowdered, marked him out to be a youngish man, I judged perhaps in his early thirties, and much younger than old Bulstrode in any event.

"You will imagine, dear friend, that I was all agog to enquire what relationship existed between us, and all afraid to address any incoherence of mine to such a fine gentleman. I found it hard to believe that I could be the offspring of a man of the Church without his having fulfilled towards me the duties of fatherhood, such familial obligations forming, as they do, a fundamental tenet of the Christian faith. Instead I managed to blurt out,'Sir, where are you taking me?'

"'We are travelling to Waverley Abbey at Farnham in Surrey,' the stranger replied. 'That is the country estate of Sir Robert Rich. You will be taken into his guardianship and will assume the surname Rich.'

"'Is that gentleman my father, then?' I enquired timidly.

"'No, he is not, but he has kindly agreed to bear the cost of your welfare and the expense of your education.'

"'I see, then, sir, are you perhaps my father instead?'

"'I regret, child, that I have been constrained not to disclose your parentage, and with that you must be content. It is enough that Sir Robert has taken you into his care in order to oblige a dear friend. You will be christened in the Abbey's private chapel within a few days, since I ascertained from Mr Bulstrode that you had not yet been formally blessed by the Holy Church, and we shall agree upon a suitable second name for you which may be preferred to the rather peculiar choice of Ainsworth.'

"Thus, a short while after my arrival at Waverley, the promised ceremony took place, it being conducted by the Revd Bostock himself, with Sir Robert and his Steward standing in as my sponsors. As my second name Sir Robert had hit upon the classical nomen Ignatius, after some ancient Bishop of Antioch who had the misfortune to be martyred by the Romans. Whether Sir Robert by his choice meant to signify that I was intended for the Church, or whether he was inspired by such thoughts as '*ignited* through passion', as one might refer to an ill-starred affair to be hidden in a choice of name, or whether he had determined that my origin was to remain unknown and *ignored*, I cannot say. Nor can I enquire of that gentleman, for he died some six years ago, at which point the Revd Bostock became his heir, being married to his only surviving child Mary Frances, or the Lady Marietta as she is presently distinguished.

"Needless to reiterate, I was not much impressed by my Guardian's choice of name, as I felt it unlikely to be popular among my peers. Moreover it provided me with the initials A.I.R. which furnished the subject of much mirth among our schoolfellows, as you are already aware. Thus I have adhered to the name Ainsworth, hoping that it might yet supply some link with my true past. Dear Friend, how I envy you your solid parentage, your participation in a regular family with brothers and sisters and both parents still living. For I fear that my own loss of identity has cast a blight over my philosophy and achievements which may haunt me for the rest of my life.

"In the meantime the carriage had reached Waverley. I obtained an impression of long boundary walls, high ornamental gates, parkland extending farther than I could see and, in the distance, the most enticing-looking ecclesiastical ruins which were swathed in ivy or peered out between clumps of trees. In short, to a boy who had seen no more of life than the grubby yard of an orphanage, with church parade on Sundays, it seemed to me that I had entered the Garden

of Eden. We reached the house and I became aware of a structure of noble proportions, then an interior graced with delicate plastered ceilings, and chinoiserie
wallpaper which now has fallen out of fashion but was much in vogue when it
was installed thirty years ago. There were many crystal chandeliers which tinkled
in the breeze by day and sparkled with candles at night, as well as much elegant
furniture, and busts and statuettes standing on pillars which I was ever afraid of
running into and toppling over. No call for further descriptions, I think, since
you will recall it well from your several visits, but I mention it only that you may
appreciate the awesome effect the experience had upon my humble person.

"Then there was the unexpected joy of having my own bedroom, after sharing a dormitory with thirty-something boys at the orphanage, all the length of
the attics, two to a bed and one blanket between us to quarrel over in our sleep.
There was even a fire lit in my new room of an evening which emitted a cheerful glow by the time I retired there. However all those around me were complete
strangers, for even the Revd Bostock left for his own home a few days later. I was
dumbfounded when the servants addressed me as 'Master Ignatius' and bowed
their heads to me within doors, or touched their forelocks in the grounds if they
were outdoor staff. I felt bewildered at my fate and began to wonder whether I
was not some very important person being kept incognito, perhaps a royal bastard. But any such dreams were dispelled immediately when the Butler caught
me stealing from his pantry and gave me the kind of thrashing that would have
made old Bulstrode proud. The Butler would never have dared to thrash me so
had I been a royal child.

"Who is or was my father, then, and where is my mother, if indeed either is
still alive? I confess I yet have no idea. No further information has been vouch-
safed to me, but from the manner in which he has always dealt with me, supervised my education, paid my debts and generally disciplined me, I would hazard
that Charles Rich knows a good deal more about my ancestry than he dares to
say. I remember how he spent some minutes studying the portrait in my mother's locket, and so I decided to adopt him as my progenitor, unless and until
some other should appear with a better claim to my respect.

"I had spent but a few months at Waverley, passed but one rapturous summer
exploring the Abbey ruins, creating my own fortresses and encampments among
the undergrowth, watching with round eyes the activity of birds, squirrels, deer,
rabbits and all the other natural creatures in which such a park abounds, even
being permitted by the Gamekeeper to help him train a gun dog to retrieve, and
also being taught to swim in the Lake by the Head Gardener's son, when I was
sent away again to school, our school, St Peter's-atte-Aldersgate in the City of
London. You will recall that I had endured the place for four whole years by the
time you joined us. When I arrived, being then small of stature, I became an
immediate target for the bullies, who lay in wait for me around every corner.
They christened me 'Airy Fairy' after my initials, and kicked and bruised me such
that all too often I went to bed in tears, and climbed out again with the greatest

reluctance next morning, dreading another day of pain. No more vivid contrast could be had than with Beauchamp Minor who, tho' a year or two older yet small for his age, because his father was a Duke could hold all the bullies in awe by his threats of dire retribution by his father's henchmen the next time they called to escort him home.

"I spent many a wakeful hour wondering what might be done to improve my condition. One morning I sought out Beeston, Johnny 'Basher' Beeston, the biggest and worst of the bullies. My conversation with him went much as follows: 'Sir?' I addressed him most politely, 'would you be agreeable to my becoming your fag?' (Strictly speaking he was not yet sufficiently senior as to be entitled to have one.)

"Basher's glance was all astonishment. He looked me up and down in a speechless sort of way 'Very well, Airy,' he replied, quite forgetting the 'Fairy' tag on my name, 'you do that. You look after me proper, clean my boots, have my linen laundered, come when I call and fetch what I require, then maybe, just maybe, we'll get along together.' Later that day I saw him lounging with his cronies on the bank beneath the oak trees. 'Airy, come here,' he called. 'Now you cut and run to Old Minto's on the corner of the Market and bring me two penn'orth of almonds, the big ones mind, not the tiddlers,' he ordered. Not only was I obliged to find the two pence up front, out of my meagre allowance (if any remained) or else by borrowing from a friend (Beauchamp Minor could often be relied upon in such matters), but I also had to break the school rules applicable to junior boys, climb a tree to get over the boundary wall, leap down the other side at risk of life and limb, and then thread my way through the hurly-burly of Smithfield Market, the trampling animals, the vulgar drovers, the muck-slippery ground or the swoosh of a cleansing bucket of water into the filthy runnels, to the far side of the square where a diminutive corner shop sold peppermint almonds and all sorts of other delightful confections beloved of schoolboys. You will remember that shop well, Richard, for the many occasions when we dodged classes to visit it.

"Then I had to return to the school surreptitiously, without being observed either by the porter at the gate or by any of the Staff, since only officially-appointed fags were permitted to leave the school grounds. As you know, there are many market stalls set up around Smithfield and its neighbouring alleyways. Some stalls sell freshly-made meat pies or plucked capons in association with the meat trade; others purvey quite different goods. One such, a draper, had his stall surrounded by a series of upright posts, joined at their branched tops by a rope over which it was his custom to hang his choicest linen, for the better attraction of the customer's eye. Stuffing the precious minted almonds into the pocket of my jacket, I uprooted two of these poles, which I observed not to have been securely anchored, slipped off the rope and let the linen fall to the ground, set the poles at an angle against the school wall and ran up them like a monkey. With the angry stallholder clutching at my ankles, I clasped the bricks topping the wall and using my elbows kicked up one leg after the other. On the farther side I dropped down into some bushes, quite unobserved by those within.

"I presented Basher with his treasured almonds with a polite bow. 'Well done, Airy,' was all he said, and of course he never offered to defray my expenditure. School life thereafter became a little more tolerable within the aura of his protection, tho' every day Johnny Beeston would select some task for me to perform, often unpleasant, sometimes dangerous, sometimes almost adventurous. Then, some two or three months later, on going out into the yard after lessons one day, I received a severe shock. Just entering through the school gateway, with the porter carrying his bags, was none other than my hated enemy from my days at the orphanage, Marcus Todd!

"At first he looked upon me with great astonishment. 'Whatever're you doing here, Ainsworth?' he demanded as he followed the porter into the main school building. The gentleman who accompanied the party was, as I later discovered, merely a family servant. It seemed only a few days had passed before my erstwhile rival began to taunt me, as he had during my years at the orphanage. 'Who's your family now, Airy?' he asked, having replaced 'Ainsworth' with the hated nickname adopted by other pupils at the school. When I explained that Sir Robert Rich had taken me into his household and was paying for my education, Todd exclaimed, 'Oh, you're a charity boy, then. I thought you might have been taken up by one of your parents. My mother, you see, tho' she fell into unfortunate circumstances before I was born, subsequently made a good marriage, and her husband - he mentioned a person of the landed gentry - proved agreeable to adopting me into his family. So, you see, I'm not an orphan any more.'

"This was the very scenario I had imagined for myself when the Revd Bostock had collected me from Brighthelmstone, that I might be travelling to some warm hearth presided over by my mother, or even by my real father with a kind-hearted wife. I could not help but be envious. Later Todd began to taunt me publicly in the schoolyard with 'Born in a work'us and brought up in an orphanage, so Airy Fairy he hasn't a family tree to stand on, not even the meanest branch of one. He's a charity boy. Pay no heed to him.' So I fought with Marcus Todd: I stated for all to hear that I had endured sufficient of his insults and every time he repeated them he could count on my animosity.

"A crowd of boys gathered around us, partly out of curiosity and partly to prevent the staff observing us, since both of us would get a thrashing if we were found out. It so happened that the skill of fisticuffs was imparted to pupils at St Peter's in an unofficial sort of way. During the daily hour allotted for relaxation, we would gather in an old shed if it was wet weather. There the school Usher of those days, who happened to have been a prize-fighter in his youth before taking up a military career, till he was wounded and invalided-out, taught us the principles of human conflict. He showed us how to stand easy on our feet, ready to deliver or to dodge a blow, how to fold our fists for the maximum effect, and the different sorts of punch we might employ, as well as the basic rules of the sport. So my battle with Marcus Todd was not fought rolling over on the ground as it had been at the orphanage, nothing so demeaning, but in our shirtsleeves, face to face, with fists raised and half the circle at least, those who knew me, egging me on. 'Go it, Airy,' I heard the cry through the fire of my indignation, 'give him a facer! Knock 'is teeth in!' So, whilst defending myself with my left arm, I let fly with my right fist and caught Todd once on the jaw and again in the solar plexus. At the same moment the cheat had been trying to trip me up with one foot behind my ankle. My second blow was delivered with such force that Todd lost his balance and fell over backwards. In a trice I was on top of him, ready to deliver the coup de grace. Todd clung to my shirt as he struggled to rise and ripped it from my shoulders.

"'Well done, Airy, that's enough. Save some for another day.' It was Johnny Beeston's languid tones from the sidelines. I clambered reluctantly to my feet, leaving Todd wiping his bleeding nose with fragments of my shirt. 'Here, have an almond, Airy,' and Johnny Beeston proffered to me the same paper bag of confectionery that I had purchased for him that morning from Mr Minto's shop. Nevertheless, to share the feast of the great before the gaze of one's peers, was an honour indeed.

"I retired to the 'dorm' to change my shirt, then realised that its alternative was yet in the laundry in the capacious fists of Mrs Sudworthy, ('Soapy Suds' to us, if you recall).

"'You looking for a clean shirt, Airy?' Beauchamp Minor had been passing the doorway and called to me.

"'Yes, my other one's in the laundry,' I replied, closing the door of my bedside locker.

"'Come to my room,' he said, 'I think I have one would fit you.' I entered his bedroom, a luxury he shared with just one other pupil due to their paters paying top fees for the privilege. It was situated above the kitchens, warm in winter and in summer had windows on both sides which opened to the city air - and to the stink of Smithfield Market when the wind was in the right direction! There were two beds with bedside cabinets, and a sitting space with two chairs and a table, supplemented by each boy's travelling chest. It was this he opened and pulled out a neatly folded shirt from the top of a pile. He held it up against me. 'Yes, it will do,' he said. 'Here, I have some marking ink so we can alter the label so that Soapy Suds will return it to you.' He took out of the drawer beneath the table a small bottle of very black ink, and seizing a well-worn quill he scratched out his own initials and placed A.I.R. beside them. I thanked him profusely; I was not often shown such kindness and generosity.

"'Don't fret at what Todd says about you,' Beauchamp Minor said, handing me the shirt. 'Let me have a close look at that locket you wear.' In courtesy I could not refuse his request, so removed the chain from my neck and handed it to him. He opened it and took it to the window, the better to study the portrait within. 'Who is this?' he asked. 'Do you believe it to be your mother, Ainsworth?' He had used my proper name without realising it. I confirmed that I did believe it to be my mother and that it closely resembled the vague memories I had before I was parted from her at the age of three.

"'She does not appear to belong to the labouring classes, quite the contrary,' Beauchamp Minor said. 'This is an expensive miniature, and the locket is made of silver. It would not surprise me to discover that your mother was well-born and fell upon hard times, just as happened to Todd. You study at your lessons here, Ainsworth, learn all you can, and you'll be as good as any of us, maybe even go up to Oxford as a scholar, just as my older brother has done.' How I wish I had been more diligent and had taken his sensible advice.

"You will certainly recall, Richard, that our school stood athwart a large court-yard bounded by a high wall. At one end of the yard lay a lawn with some oak and lime trees and the shrubbery we used for our play. A drive through the centre led to the gatehouse. Behind the building lay the kitchen garden, full of herbs and vegetables, some chickens whose eggs and carcasses made their way to the table on rare occasions, and an orchard whose trees we were supposed not to climb, but what hungry lad would forbear to scrump for apples? The entrance hall led through to the Chapel where we were herded for morning and evening prayers through the chill of winter as well as the heat of summer. In the right wing, facing south, was the High School where the High Master taught us the Classical texts, with the Master's house at the end of the building. On the left stood the Usher's lodging and the Lower School, where the Usher taught us French, Geography, History, and Accounts or whatever other modern subject might be among the talents of that particular incumbent. Overhead were the dormitories, each housing some twenty boys, and joined by the Minstrel Gallery running through the Chapel. At either end of the upper floor stood those scanty ablution stations which we loathed so heartily.

"The kitchen and laundry block stood in the grounds at the back of the main building, beside the Refectory. Above these were the half-dozen lodgings assigned either to Senior Monitors, as Johnny Beeston had eventually become by the time you arrived, or to the privileged wealthy few such as Beauchamp Minor and yourself. In that structure too lurked the large communal bath into which we plunged or were pushed, ten or a dozen at a time, shedding our dirty linen as we stripped and receiving clean as we emerged from the no-nonsense grasp of Soapy Suds. In the summer, and whenever the weather was fine, even though frosty and chill, we processed in groups through the streets east of Smithfield to the meadows and open-air bathing pools of the New River. New boys were always forcibly stripped and thrown in, whether they could swim or no, but I had learnt not to fear water at Waverley in the River Wey and I was soon splashing happily. Johnny Beeston nodded his approval when I emerged and proffered me another of his mint almonds.

"Use of the New River pools and meadows for our play was a facility we shared with other City Schools. You must remember how we used to long to encounter our deadly rivals, the Blue Coat boys, and if coming from Smithfield with its muddy lanes and refuse-blocked runnels, would endeavour to kick them about the shins in order to dirty their yellow stockings, and we would pull off their caps or tug at their loose blue tunics to do them as much damage as we might. Perhaps this was jealousy at their uniforms, for we had nothing so smart at St Peter's, just dark trousers, white shirts, a loose black cravat and a jacket and top-coat of any description. Some had caps and the monitors wore tall black hats, but in a congregation where some were surprisingly rich and others, such as some of the day-scholars from the metropolis, unremittingly poor, it would not have been economical to demand conformity.

"Into the midst of this roughcast atmosphere you arrived one autumn morn-ing when the sky was blue and the leaves on the limes were just turning to gold. I saw your cheery face framed in the gateway as you walked towards me, with your manservant and the porter carrying between them your heavy school trunk. I was impatient to know your name and to make your acquaintance, never happier than that I was to sit next to you in class, whilst that swot Beamish was placed upon the other side,so that he might prompt you in lessons if you were not as forward with your knowledge as we were professed to be. But you outshone us from the beginning, whether it was Tacitus, Virgil, Horace and Julius Caesar, or Homer, Xenophon and Sophocles, you were acquainted with them all. Our High Master at the time was Dr Payne, who lived up to his name by making us write lines in Latin for the most minor infringements. Just as willingly would he send us in a long queue to Captain Tanner, the Usher of your days who, as a retired officer from His Majesty's Navy, understood in precise detail the science of flogging. The grimace of displeasure or of exquisite discomfort that crossed Dr Payne's features as we recited the chosen poetic passage or parsed some Classic phrase, changed to a fleeting smile as you rose to your feet and held forth. And when it came to study in the Lower School, or the Lower Deck as Captain Tanner would have us describe it, how were we to know that since your mother was French you had been bilingual from earliest childhood, and that having been raised on the Continent your knowledge of Geography and History both was far superior to our insular-minded cognisance?

"The school vacation arrived - we had a fortnight's leave at Christmas, a week at Easter and at Whitsun, and two whole months in the summer. However I was only permitted to return to Waverley for the summer holiday. For the shorter breaks I was boarded out in lodgings in London, near Bloomsbury Square, with a widow called Mrs Bostock whom I understood to be Revd. Bostock's sister-in-law. She had two children of her own, both much younger than I, and several other lodgers from whom she derived her living. At first Mrs Bostock attempted to keep me indoors, except when she was accompanied by her offspring when she was glad enough for me to hold one of them by the hand so that he might not run out into the road and under the wheels of some passing carriage.

However, when she discovered that if restrained I had merely to open the window of my room and to slide down the guttering to the ground, I was able to come and go much as I pleased. Thus I explored many of the western districts of London as far as Tyburn where the gibbet still stood, tho' but a stone's throw from the new emporia along the Oxford Road. I roamed through the dark lanes and cheerful markets of Soho (whence I am ashamed to say that I acquired the sleight of hand necessary to remove desirable edible merchandise from some of the stalls), to the wide avenues around Whitehall and Westminster and the open spaces of St James's Park. Sometimes I would turn towards the river and either stroll westwards to the Pleasure Gardens at Vauxhall, or eastwards through the quays and docks to Blackfriars, the Fleet River, and St Pauls. I was lonely during those vacations and could not understand why my Guardian did not welcome me to Waverley with Christmas gifts and pleasant treats. Instead it was Mrs. Bostock who repaired my linen and supplied any replacements needed, who folded Beauchamp Minor's shirt into a clean neat package with a fresh tape label and made me write a note of thanks to accompany it.

"At school again, when other boys were instructed to write home to their parents, I tried to pen a letter to my guardian, Sir Robert Rich, but scarcely knew how to address him. However, when it came to the forthcoming summer vacation I knew what I wanted and wrote fluently to the old gentleman begging that you might accompany me to Waverley. By then I knew already that you were agreeable and had sought your father's permission. I was overjoyed to receive a response in the affirmative, even though the letter had been penned by Sir Robert's steward, for you will recall that my Guardian had lost his left hand at the Battle of Culloden back in 1746, and that his right hand and arm had stiffened, as if in sympathy with its fellow.

"How we enjoyed that first sweet vacation! Do you remember the watch tower we constructed in the Great Yew Tree that rears upon its roots among the Abbey ruins? The fish that we caught in the lake and that huge pike that the gamekeeper took from the river? We watched him skin and limb a deer, shoot pheasants for the table, and wring the neck of a cockerel that was taking too many liberties with the hens. Three blissful summers we passed in the same delights, and we had just schemed that I should be invited to share the Christmas celebrations of your large family, when disaster fell upon us.

"One sunlit morn, after you and I had filched a decanter of brandy from the dining-room as we retired to bed and had sat up late around the fire in my room, discussing the world and his wife as young people do, we had then fallen asleep together in bed, as we had often done at St Peter's where you had a private room which I was often invited to share. One bright dawn, I repeat, Sir Robert happened to enter my room just as the manservant had thrown the curtain wide, and he encountered the two of us in bed together, stark naked and with our arms and our bodies intimately entwined. As we sat up rubbing our eyes, Sir Robert instructed us gruffly to wash and dress and to report to his study before breakfast. We were, in our innocence, or at least innocence then on my part, all bewildered at what might have occurred, and indeed you were afeared that some mischance might have overtaken your family which Sir Robert was about to disclose.

"We tiptoed into my Guardian's study together, after a timid knock on the door and a gruff 'come in'. 'Stand there, both of you,' Sir Robert ordered, pointing to the space in front of his desk. 'When I entered your room this morning, Ignatius,' - he persisted in using the name he had chosen for me - 'I was astounded, simply astounded, and yes, horrified. I will not tolerate boys having carnal knowledge of each other in my house'. What is this 'carnal knowledge' I wondered in my innocence, for I had been so used to sleeping two to a bed at the orphanage, and also at the school when there were often insufficient beds to go round? 'Such intimacy is not only an offence against my hospitality,' Sir Robert thundered, 'but it is an offence against the Criminal Law of England!' I dared not look at you to observe your reaction.

"That being so, you will be separated immediately and forever,' Sir Robert continued. 'My housekeeper is packing your things as we speak, Richard, and you will travel home shortly in my carriage, accompanied by my steward. He will deliver a letter to your father which will explain the situation in which I came upon you, and which will request him to agree with me a future course of conduct. Only one of you will return to St Peter's and as yet I cannot say which one of you it will be. You will leave the room now, Richard, whilst I continue to reprove Ignatius. You may shake hands before you go.'

"And we did, with tears in our eyes. Scarcely had the door shut behind you, my dear friend, than Sir Robert continued his severe homily. He reminded me that I had been born in poverty and had been rescued from an orphanage at the behest of a friend and sent to a fee-paying school. 'I do not disburse good coin and expect to receive dross in return,' Sir Robert declared with evident indignation. 'Your High Master, Dr Payne, has written to me that your attitude in the schoolroom is inattentive and indolent. He also describes you as being much under the influence of one of the Senior Monitors, John Beeston, whom you apparently serve as 'fag'. Whilst it will certainly do you no harm to prepare the gentleman's tea or to clean his boots, I must now ask you to tell me the truth - and please think carefully before you reply. Does John Beeston take you into his bed?'

"'No, sir,... er, that is, yes,' I stammered,

"'What?!!'

"'I get into his bed and warm it for him on cold nights, sir, but I leave it again when he comes to bed and return to my own bed in the dorm. 'Tis a part of my duties as a fag, sir.'

"'And the two of you do not lie abed together?'

"'No, sir,' I assured him.

"'Very well. I will speak to you again later, once I have a response from Richard's parent. You may go now and consume whatever breakfast has been left for you in the dining room,' my guardian concluded. I swallowed the food as if it were cardboard, finding no taste whatever in it, but fearful that if I failed to obey the instruction I would only bring down upon myself further reprimands. Then I went out into Waverley Park and across the stone bridge into the ruins of the Abbey which were knee-high with summer grass. I threw myself down among the bees and the flowers and I wept.

"Dear Friend, I write at such length because I hope to evoke the happy memories of our friendship, and that these may persuade you to renew our acquaintance. I learnt at St Peter's upon my return there that your father had purchased you a Cornet of Horse, and somewhat later that your Regiment was even now serving abroad, probably in India. I propose to seek your address from the War Office and trust that this long missive will reach you, wherever you may be upon this Earth.

"For myself, I have had a very thin time of it since you departed. I returned to St Peter's but found that Beeston had also left the school. There was a rumour that he had chosen a military career, and another that he had gone to Oxford along with Beauchamp Minor. So I felt most isolated, but persisted with my studies in the hope of pleasing my Guardian sufficiently that he would either send me to university or place me on the first rung of some other ladder to professional success. I spent my short vacations with Mrs Bostock as usual, but when it came to the next long vacation I was forbidden to return to Waverley. Instead Sir Robert's Bailiff of his Norfolk estates, Anthony Russell, collected me from St Peter's by the carriage and we drove to a place in East Anglia, spending a night at an inn at Ipswich on the way. My destination, for Mr. Russell himself went straight on to his home near Norwich once he had delivered me, was a rather gloomy old Manor House named Roos Hall, at Beccles on the border of Suffolk. This is another of my Guardian's properties, but it is older and in a more parlous state than his elegant establishment at Waverley. I was met by the housekeeper, Mrs Jarvis, a stern and rather forbidding person, who divided my time between working as a labourer either for her husband who is the licensee of an inn in the town, or for his nephew who manages one of the farms on my Guardian's estate. Neither situation afforded me much pleasure and for once I was glad to return to school. Life then proceeded much as normal for a further two years, except that when it came to the last long vacation I was able to return to Waverley once more since my Guardian had died. I found the Revd Bostock in charge of affairs there. Apparently no arrangements had been made for my future in my Guardian's will and it was just as though I had never existed.

"The Revd. Bostock appeared briefly at Waverley but spent most of his days at Court along with his wife Lady Marietta in attendance upon Their Majesties. During one of his visits he informed me that he had taken over from Sir Robert financial responsibility for completing my education, and also that he was about to assume the surname Rich, apparently with the express blessing of Sir Robert. The following year I sat the customary examination at St Peter's for entrance to

Oxford, but being neither as diligent in my studies nor, frankly, as academically suited as my provider might have wished, I failed to win a scholarship. This obliged my new Guardian to pay my tuition as well as my keep and I was sent instead to Cambridge, as far away as possible from my former acquaintances at Oxford.

"At College I joined a new set of young Radicals and became closely involved in the political aspirations of the Whig Party. I think much of this was prompted by the fact that Revd Bostock, in his proximity to the Crown, belonged to the Tory philosophy, which we students scorned. I had wished to study Law at Cambridge, but was obliged by the College to persist with the Classics, at which I knew I would never succeed. So I conspired with my fellows to lead a student riot - you may have read about it in the Press, or perhaps not if you are indeed in India. This was the summer of 1789, two years ago. Some of us, lacking sympathetic domestic retreats, had stayed up all vacation. In France, exponents of similar Radicalism had just stormed the Bastille, freed its prisoners, assassinated the Governor and had caused mayhem in the streets. Our fellow-students were returning from the Continent with tales of fiery oratory, bread riots, lootings, burnings and feastings. In Paris there was an orator in every square, a lively discussion upon every street corner and the atmosphere was like wine. The People had come alive, had risen up against Oppression, and who knew what the future might hold!

"I should explain, in case you are perchance unaware, that the diet available in lodgings at University is remarkably similar to that we endured at St Peter's, namely porridge or roll and butter for breakfast with coffee or tea, soup with bread for luncheon, with the main meal of the day being reserved for the early evening after the close of formal studies. Only the wealthy can afford good food, and my modest allowance from Revd Bostock did not often stretch that far. Thus we Radicals felt some kindred spirit with the starving Revolutionaries in France. Moreover, some who had first hand experience of the events in France and had suffered disruption of their journeys or adventurous hazards along their way, arrived back in Cambridge at the very moment when our discontent was reaching its climax.

"There was a Lodgings Master named Sharp who aroused our particular ire since he was notoriously mean and we believed that he was retaining for his own use a substantial percentage of our costs. In addition he served as a professor of Greek, though was not a leading academic, and in any event I had grown to hate that subject. Ergo, we conspired to besiege his own lodging when he was within, with the aim of obliging him to confess his sins. First we nailed planks across the doorways. Then we closed the shutters over the windows and nailed them shut, even as he opened each one of them in turn and looked out at us, shouting and gesticulating with rage. From downstairs he was forced to go upstairs in order to continue the dialogue, which he did from quite an inconvenient height above the ground. When the evening came we lit braziers which we had borrowed from some artisans, and set up a rota of watchers who were well-primed with beer so that they might keep up a raucous performance all night and prevent Sharp from obtaining any sleep. We had detained his manservant, whom we had bribed to divert himself at the Newmarket Races. This enabled us to imprison Sharp without provisions, since his only source of water was the pump in the yard. By the third day he had run out of drink and begged us for water. We rigged up a pulley in an overhanging tree and sent up a bucket - which was full of our piss! However we relented a few hours later and hoisted up some supplies by the same means, water, bread, a little cheese and butter and some cold tea. Each day till the end of the week we followed the same procedure. Then we removed the planks from the doors. At first the victim did not understand that he was free to escape from his involuntary imprisonment. When he did, he came out in his smallclothes and an overcoat, tumbled down the steps in his haste and ran screaming through the campus and out of sight.

"Now it happened that the lodging in question was in a remote part of the College grounds and everyone passing at night had assumed that our watch-fires were manned by the artisans who were so busy there by day, trimming trees, building fences and carrying out repairs with the timber that we were gaily burning by night. Thus no one became aware of Professor Sharp's plight until he presented himself so curiously undressed and disshevelled at the door of the Principal's office. In the meantime we had taken advantage of his absence to invade his abode and had, after much searching of cupboards and loose floorboards, discovered a strong-box. The key thereof took somewhat longer to locate and we removed the box and ourselves to another part of the grounds in order to examine its contents. As we had suspected, it was stuffed full of money, both in coin and in banknotes. Whilst the core of our group yet sat around the coffer, starting to count the money and discussing what to do with it - some were for sharing it among the poorer students, others for taking it to the Principal and explaining our case, we were ignorant of the fact that the latter gentleman had already sent a message to the Sheriff, and that a detachment of City Watchmen was even now searching the College grounds for sight of the miscreants! They came upon us, *in flagrante delicto*, with the strong-box open before us and banknotes piled upon the ground.

"We were hauled before the Principal, accused of theft rather than riot, and in vain did we endeavour to explain our objective. Everyone apprehended by the Officers of the Watch was sent down with immediate effect, though any supporters who were not present received no punishment at all. We were informed that a circular letter was being despatched to all parents and guardians of students stating that anyone participating in a similar 'disturbance' would be summarily dismissed. Our only consolation was that Professor Sharp also lost his post, though what happened to the strong-box and its contents I was never able to ascertain.

JESS OF ROOS HALL

"I returned to my lodgings to be informed by my landlady that I must leave at the end of the week. Bad news always seems to travel fast! Little remained of my weekly allowance from a Cambridge bank, so I sought out an address I knew and placed bets on a couple of runners for the next day's races at Newmarket. The sons of their owners were college friends: I knew the reputation of their horses and it was by no means the first occasion upon which I had recouped unwise expenditure in that way. I had good fortune and won just enough to pay for a seat on a post-chaise to London and a couple of nights' decent lodging when I arrived.

"Now you should be advised that the most important skills that a fellow acquires at College are those connected with the understanding of Loo, Faro, Whist, Backgammon and a host of other card games and gambling tricks, and at these I had become one of the most proficient. I dared not travel to Waverley after the disgrace which had occurred, and nor could I trouble Mrs Bostock, so I called upon one of my school companions, a former day-boy whose address I knew, and he obliged by introducing me at hostelries and other venues of a modest nature where I might play a hand. By this means I soon earned enough to keep a roof over my head, and through the good offices of yet another former schoolfellow I moved into a superior social set within a few months of starting out. Presently I was playing among the gentry and aristocracy and was invited to become a member of a Gentlemen's Club, Brooks's of St James's. I thought myself fine and secure there, being aware that Revd Bostock's club was White's and that due to their disparate political affiliations 'never the twain shall meet'. But they did, for one day as I was pondering over what for once was a devilish bad hand, a weight fell upon my shoulder. It was Revd Bostock.

"I backed out of the game immediately – that was one means of avoiding the consequences of miserable cards – and my Father (for I am still sure that he is, even if he gives me no overt sign of it) took me to a private alcove where, over a glass of port and one of his cigars, he pleaded with me to return to Waverley and he would assist me to find some suitable position where I might exercise some of the education I had received. He mentioned the occupations of schoolmaster, that of copyist in a legal office where I might take Articles if I were so bent upon the Law, or of assistant to a publisher if I wished to enter into the literary world. None, it seemed, offered a salary above twelve pounds a year, and I had already been winning heavily at cards at a hundred guineas or more a time. I thanked my Father for his kindness but refused his assistance, stating boldly that if ever I returned to Waverley it would be only as his heir! Then I put down my glass and walked out into the night.

"Of course I was back at Brooks's again next evening and many a night after that. My Whig connections acquired at Cambridge now became of use as I smartened my appearance, took lodgings in St James's and began to meet some of the leading figures of the day, especially those who had gathered around the Prince of Wales. Then my luck turned; just as if Fortune had suddenly spun a

46

wheel backwards, I started to lose heavily and began hastily scribbling IOU's for hundreds and even thousands of guineas. One elderly man, whom I had thought a genial and harmless old gentleman, abruptly called in the sum I owed and gave me no leeway to recoup my losses. He had been introduced to me as Sir Everard Wilmington. The name sounded familiar but I was unable to place it at the time. On receipt of his card demanding settlement I remembered exactly who he was, the stepfather of Marcus Todd! I was too proud to plead for mercy with such a person and he had recourse to Law. Presently I found myself in the Fleet Prison with all my goods and chattels taken by the Bailiffs in lieu of rent. I had just sufficient small change in my pocket to purchase paper and pen from the Turnkey and to write a letter to my Father informing him of my fate.

"Whether the letter took its time to find Revd Bostock – I had addressed it to Waverley but probably it had to be forwarded to Windsor or to Kensington Palace – or whether my Father intended that I should stew in my misfortune, I know not, but some twenty days elapsed before I was removed from jail, my debt paid and my other affairs inquired into. I was taken to Waverley, but only briefly while the inquiries were made. My Father was not there but at Windsor where his wife, Lady Marietta, was expecting her second or third child, so that I knew then that I was unlikely to become my Father's heir. Instead it was Anthony Russell, the Norfolk Bailiff, who had the task of escorting me once more to my present abode, Roos Hall, near Beccles in the County of Suffolk. Here I am to act as sub-agent, learn about management of the estate, and to keep careful account of the revenues against Mr Russell's next visit.

"Roos Hall is built of dark red brick, faced around the windows and elsewhere with pale sandstone. Constructed two centuries ago, it has seen but little improvement since, especially in its sanitary arrangements. Whilst running water is now supplied from a storage tank to the kitchen, which is found in a separate wing to one side of the main building, the same privilege does not extend to the house itself and we still rely on maids running upstairs with jugs and buckets of water to fill basin and bath. There is a water closet on the first floor, just one, the limitations of which became evident when I held a house-party here a few weeks after my arrival. For all other uses we rely on a pump in the yard which, from the colour of the water it delivers, I take it that it is piped direct from the stream which flows through the grounds. There is a Park of adequate acreage, stocked with deer and game, and a garden growing fruit and vegetables for the house, but nothing like the exotic fare which is produced so expertly at Waverley.

"There are several farms nearby forming part of the estate, and more in Norfolk, though those are managed directly by Mr Russell from his home near Norwich. All the farms here have leasehold tenancies, long-established ones, which makes it very difficult for me to impose any fresh direction upon them, even when I have received good advice from Mr Russell or from other landowners in the vicinity. Moreover the allowances which I am permitted to deduct from the farm revenues are insufficient to support the expenditure incurred at Roos Hall, let alone any monies necessitated by accidental contingencies, so that I have constantly to apply to my Father for additional funds. The Housekeeper, Mrs Jarvis, still the same forbidding figure who presided over my previous visit, receives a separate allowance to cover the household expenditure and the remuneration of the staff. Thus, my scope for making much of myself here is severely limited and I long to return to the lights of London and the lively company I kept there. Sometimes I ride to Yarmouth or Lowestoft in search of diversion, but the hostelries there are dens of low vice with the comings and goings of bibulous sailors on shore leave, and the importunate port doxies whose charms are not of the slightest attraction to me. You observe that I do so lack your excellent companionship, my dearest Friend.

"Moreover, there is another matter here which I have yet to disclose to you, and that is the presence of a young girl named Jessica who is around eight years of age. Though to all appearances she is an orphan child, I have discovered from the Estate Accounts that Mrs Jarvis receives a separate allowance from my Father for her upkeep. This would seem to relate to his person alone and to have had no connection with Sir Robert who had been my Guardian. As the child's mother is dead or departed and the child's birth occurred at about the same time as my Father's marriage to the Lady Marietta, who by all accounts has not visited Roos Hall since her own childhood, I am beginning to suspect a scandal. In short, I fear that Miss Jessica may have a better claim to my Father's affections and to his estate than do I. This I deprecate since it would please me to be Lord of the Manor here, as Waverley is already spoken for, I presume, for the heirs of my Father's marriage.

"The child Jessica is an unattractive waif with an unfortunate propensity for causing calamity. Even when I beat her for it, that does not seem to bring about any improvement in her conduct. Last winter she fell into the river in the park. I had a mind to leave her there as an obvious accidental death. Alas, my dog Arthur, who is a capital retriever, plunged in and dragged the girl to the bank, where, for the sake of loyalty to my dog's achievement, I had perforce to scramble down to the water and pull the girl out. More recently the barn was set on fire and burned to the ground. Jessica had been sent in to find the stable lad Ted who had been clearing out some old straw. It was thought at the time that she had taken with her one of the carriage lanterns which might have been lit. Only much later did Ted confess to smoking a pipe in the barn and letting it fall from his lips. He should have been dismissed instantly, but the head groundsman stood up for him and threatened to quit if Ted was sacked. Thus I lack that control of my staff which is appropriate to a head of a household. I was obliged to report the accident to Mr Russell, who rode over to inspect the damage, and then applied to his employer for funds to rebuild the structure. Fortunately the neighbouring stable housing my fine bay hunter named Pharaoh was undamaged.

"I did not trouble to exculpate Jessica, who had been singed by the fire and lost all her hair, as I thought the lesson would do her good. Moreover, by the time I learnt the truth Jessica had disappeared and a search of the house and grounds by the staff failed to find her. My dog Arthur then started whining and pawing at the wainscoting of the staircase. Mrs Jarvis called Jessica's name but received no reply. I was surprised to observe that rather stiff and dignified lady upon her knees on the stairway and pressing various items of carving which decorate the panelling. Suddenly there was a loud click and a panel swung open, revealing an alcove which had perhaps once been used to hide a recusant priest. The girl was within, slumped against the wall unconscious. The servants lifted her out and put her to bed, and with the application of smelling salts, a glass of my brandy and a visit from the physician, she is likely to make a recovery.

"Now my Father, newly ennobled as Sir Charles Rich, writes me that Jessica is to attend school, the same one as that attended by the girls from one of our farms. He mentions no allowance for the matter so I suppose that too is to be deducted from the revenues of the estate.

"Time presses, dear Friend, for I spent most of yesterday writing you this long screed. I am in London with Mr Russell to meet with Sir Charles concerning building plans for the new barn, and will take my chance to apply at the War Office for your address. I beg of you, Richard, if you still bear me any friendship at all, to respond with news of all your accomplishments since we parted.

Yours, most affectionately,
Ainsworth Rich."

Note : This letter was found many years later among Mr Ainsworth's papers. It was marked 'Return to Sender' from an address in India.

CHAPTER IV
The Farmer

A pony-trap was bowling along the Halesworth road to the south of Beccles. It carried Bob and Betty Jarvis, stiffly starched in their Sunday best, on their way to visit their nephew Alfred at the Ringsfield Farm. Bob Jarvis had hired the vehicle from Wilson's Livery Stables just behind the Bear & Bells, something he often did when the brewery waggon he kept under shelter in the inn yard would not have been appropriate to his needs. A well-chosen bottle of wine had paid the charge and there was no cause to trouble the coinage of the Realm. Jack Wilson also stabled the dray-horse that drew the brewery waggon, and the cost of that useful service was carefully recorded in the Inn's accounts, which Bob cast up regularly at the end of each month, and early on Quarter Days. Time was when the Inn had kept its own horses and had supplied the coaching trade, but now that the Old Market had closed and a new square had developed in the Town Centre, the large and stately King's Head Hotel had taken over that function. The Inn's stables and the remaining horses had been leased to Jack Wilson, and turnover at the Bear & Bells had diminished. That was one reason why Betty's position and wages made such an important contribution to their income and why Bob discussed with Betty as they travelled whether they could afford to keep Peter Jones working at the bar now that his age and experience entitled him to a raise in a few months' time at the year end.

This was by no means the only problem which faced their family, for Betty had come to discuss with Alf and his wife Martha how their children were to meet with Jessica and then in the autumn to escort her to and from their schools in the Town. More important still, how this was to be accomplished without anyone getting wind of the fact that Jessica was Betty's illegitimate granddaughter, so breaking Sir Charles' instructions.

Betty's attention was thus distracted from her husband's concerns and, quite uncharacteristically, she replied to him in monosyllables, until he turned to her in exasperation and asked, "What's keeping you, woman? You haven't listened to a word I've said!"

"Sorry, husband, I was thinking of little Jessica and the need to keep her origin secret," Betty replied

50

"I know, my dear, but Alf and Martha are sensible people and will soon devise what to tell their children when they ask."

Bob Jarvis flicked the whip and adjusted the reins so that the pony turned right into the lane which led to the farm. It was always known in the family as the Ringsfield Farm, even though it had its own individual name. This was because it was the largest tenanted farm of the Ringsfield Estate. It was a fine warm summer afternoon and the rose-coloured bricks of the farmhouse were bathed in a golden glow as the pony-trap turned in through the gateway, past the beech trees which lined the lane, and drew up before the front door which was recessed, painted white and boasted a fan-light shaped like a scallop-shell. For this was quite a prosperous and generously proportioned building with five sash windows in the upper storey and two each side of the doorway below. The steep roof had stepped gables and tall Tudor chimneys like those at Roos Hall, and perhaps had been built by the same architect as that employed by Thomas Colby. Behind the main building a row of lower, two-storey cottages, tiled, plastered and whitewashed, housed the Head Stockman, Jim Caldicott, and his family, the farm's communal kitchen, and the dairy for cooling the milk and preparing the whey, buttermilk, cheese and butter that were the by-products of a substantial dairy herd.

The remaining farm buildings formed three sides of a yard to the right of the farmhouse, a large barn, and an open-fronted shelter for the larger agricultural equipment, two ploughs, a harrow, the hay-wain and a pony-cart, long-disused for lack of a pony. There was a shed containing the smaller items, scythes and their blades and sharpeners, mallets, hammers, and fencing and hedge-laying tools. Next to that stood stabling for the farm's horses, a pair of Fenland Blacks* who did the heavy ploughing, sowing and harrowing, and a pair of Sorrel horses[†] kept for lighter duties, for pulling the hay-wain, especially when that vehicle went off to market at a spanking trot overflowing with Alfred Jarvis, Martha and their four children.

The third side of the yard was occupied by the cow-byre with comfortable space for the thirty Suffolk Dun cows that were the pride and joy of Alf Jarvis's ambitions. Outside the barn on the southern side of the buildings stood a number of tree-shaded wooden pens, variously occupied by Alf's dozen Suffolk White pigs and by his four score of black-faced Norfolk Horned sheep when they were brought in for shearing and dipping, but presently sheltering the farm's hens and geese during daylight hours. Nearby a new pen had been constructed, quite small and with high wooden fencing all around it. This held the farm's latest arrival, Tommy, the Norfolk Shorthorn bull, for Alf Jarvis was a forward-looking stockman, always seeking to improve his bloodlines.

To the east of the farmhouse, facing the morning sun, lay the kitchen garden and an orchard, as well as a bower of climbing roses against the end wall of the house. This was much beloved of Martha who would sit there with her sewing on quiet days after the cows had been milked and their creamy produce was

---

*Now known as the Shire Horse
[†]Now known as the Suffolk Punch

cooling slowly in the dairy. Twin thatched cottages half a mile along the lane housed the two milkmaids, the ploughboy who cared for the horses, and the shepherd who looked after the sheep and the pigs. Counting the Head Stockman's wife, Jeannie Caldicott, who helped Martha in both house and dairy, there was a staff of eight running this modest farm of some 200 acres.

As the pony-cart drew to a halt before the farmhouse door, it opened and Martha emerged with a warm smile. "Welcome, Aunt Jarvis, and Uncle Bob," she said as she greeted them. It was the custom to use first names only with blood relatives and Betty was therefore known to them all by her surname. Martha was slight of stature, with dark hair and a pale skin, not Suffolk-bred with red hair or Scandinavian fairness but of Devon ancestry, for Alfred had met his wife at the Smithfield Market where she had accompanied her father who had driven his stock all the way to London from the West Country. "I've sent the children into Beccles with Jeannie and her two. They have gone to the Fair on the Common, so we shall not be disturbed for a change," Martha explained as she helped Betty down from the pony-cart and ushered her indoors, while Bob tied the reins to the hitching rail and gave the pony a bag of hay.

"Come in, Aunt Jarvis," Alf greeted her at the doorway. "Afternoon, Uncle. Good to see you. I've been awaiting your visit as there are some ideas and other matters I would wish to talk over with you, a second opinion, so to speak."

"I'm not sure there is much qualified advice I can give you, nephew, but I'll be happy to assist in any way I can," Bob Jarvis replied.

"Then I suggest we leave the ladies to discuss their side of the family over a dish of tea whilst we stop by my office for something a little stronger before we go out in the yard." Alf led the way, past the parlour whither Martha and Betty had retreated, and past the central hall where a finely-carved wooden staircase led up to the gallery and several bedrooms, to the north-west corner of the house which had been walled off to make a snug office. There was a small fireplace with a window either side looking out into the yard, and a window in the southern wall overlooked the entrance to the dairy. Beneath this stood Alf's large bureau with its tambour roll-top permanently pushed back to betray ranks of wooden cubby-holes stuffed with all manner of bills and papers. Despite the existence of three windows, the daylight they afforded was severely obstructed by the piles of almanacs and books laid upon each sill. Rolled-up plans and charts festooned the top of the bureau and ledgers were scattered across its table-slide, so that there was scarcely room in between for a stand of quills, a penknife, cut plain paper, a bottle of ink and a box of sand for drying the script. A hook protruded from the ceiling; in the past it had probably served for the hanging of game or bacon, but now it carried a lantern which Alf was accustomed to light whenever he worked on his farm accounts after dusk.

Alf opened one of the small cupboards at the back of the bureau and produced a bottle of brandy. Then he stepped quickly through to the dining-room on the other side of the corridor and retrieved a couple of glasses from the dresser. "Sit you down, Uncle," he said, indicating one of the two chairs in his office. Bob Jarvis sat obligingly and received a glass containing a generous tot of brandy. "My chief problem is this, Uncle," Alfred Jarvis began. "I have a mind to make a number of improvements to my stock and to the way we do business here. When I meet with my fellow farmers at the stock market in Norwich, or even here in Beccles, I hear about the many changes they are making; more modern machinery, different cropping systems, better feed for the animals, and above all more productive breeds of cattle, and sheep, and pigs too for that matter. I wish to introduce some of those changes here – I'll describe them in detail as we go about the yard – but that will require the application of capital which I just do not have.

"In the past I have been able to write to Sir Robert Rich direct," Alf continued, "and he has either questioned me as necessary in writing, or has used one of his visits to the Hall to walk over the farm with me and to authorise such improvements on the spot, always leaving me a Banker's draft for the sum required prior to his departure. Now that that young bounder Ainsworth Rich is in charge at the Hall I have no chance of making progress. He knows nothing about farming, any more than when he visited here as a boy, you will recall, and he will not even pay the relatively minor sums he owes me for the loads of hay and straw I have taken over the Hall ever since that barn burned down. I have tried writing to Sir Charles, but he responded only after a long delay, saying that he knows little of farming practices and he referred me to his Bailiff, Mr Russell, who runs the Rich family's farms in Norfolk. I then applied to Mr Russell, who replied that he had instructions to leave such matters to Mr Ainsworth, who must learn the business by experience! Unfortunately it is my livelihood and the security of my family which are at stake here, not the whim of a dilettante youth!

"Common gossip has it that Mr Ainsworth has been rusticated here from London upon gambling away a fortune that Sir Robert would have ill afforded after losing his post with the Government. Poor man, he was a good employer and 'tis no wonder that the anxiety sent him to an early grave. Now we have Sir Charles who has honoured us with his presence on only a couple of occasions, he and his lady being so preoccupied with attendance at the Court. The absence of good direction means that my land's productivity will fall behind that of our neighbours, reducing our revenues and tempting Sir Charles, or most likely the heartless and heedless Mr Ainsworth, to foreclose my tenancy and assign it to another. The safety of my family is at stake, dear Uncle, and I need some way of turning the situation in my favour. Does Aunt Jarvis have any influence with Mr Ainsworth at the Hall?"

"No, Alf, she certainly does not, I regret to say," his uncle replied. "Mr Ainsworth is scarcely civil to her and is most uncivil to the other staff. The only exception is young Ted who takes care of Mr Ainsworth's hunter and whom he looks upon with some favour. Betty tells me that Mr Ainsworth is always ordering various extravagances from the tradesmen and leaving Betty to settle the bills, the which she is hard put to do out of the allowance she receives from Sir Charles. The only suggestion I may make is that you seek the assistance of one of the other landlords in this neighbourhood who is also distinguished at Court, and ask him to intervene with Sir Charles. Rather a ticklish thing to do, though, if Mr Ainsworth really is Sir Charles' bastard son, as Betty has heard him lay claim."

"Thank you, Uncle, I will see about it when next I visit the Norwich market, for that is where the most progressive-minded stock-breeders are to be found. Now, if you have taken enough of the brandy, let us go into the yard." They stepped down through the back door of the house into the dairy and thence into the yard. Alf took his uncle straight to the cow-byre which was empty, since the cattle had returned to pasture after milking. "The cows are over the hill by the Barsham lane now, as the grass there is still moist and sweet at the end of summer," Alf explained. "I think you have not seen the new flooring I have put down. I have covered that earthen floor with hard-standing and have sloped it to a drainage channel at the rear end of the beasts, so that their muck can be flushed more easily to the heap out there by the field. As you see, there is no straw to be mucked out, though that may change when I bring them in for the worst of the winter. The beasts seem to stand and lie just as comfortably as they did before, and probably with less disease too. My herd is purebred Suffolk Dun, as you know, which are lean to look at but let down a lot of milk into their big bags. I would wish to cross them with another strain to produce heifers which could be sold in the market for breeding beef calves, since the Dun calves are not much valued. That requires permission from Sir Charles or his deputy. You see my difficulty. In anticipation I have leased a Norfolk Shorthorn bull from Fred Coombes over at Ilketshall St Margaret, have paid for a year's servicing and now have the expense of his keep. I'm beginning to wonder whether I should have done so."

Their stroll led them next to the stables whose occupants' inquisitive noses were leaning over the doors of each stall. "Do you need all four horses for the farm?" Bob Jarvis asked his nephew as he patted one of the Fen Blacks.

"Well, I could manage for most of the time with just the two Blacks, but the Sorrels also have their uses, especially on social occasions when I take the family in the hay waggon, and of course the children have learnt to ride on them as they're shorter in the leg and narrower across the withers. Why do you ask?"

"I was thinking that you might offer them out for hire, say through Jack Wilson's livery stables whence I borrowed the pony and cart. You could ensure that they are available when you need them and that might help pay for their keep."

"Thank you, Uncle, that's a useful idea," Alf commented. They passed on to the farm equipment and Alf pointed to a shiny new ploughshare on one of his sets. "That one's made of steel," he said, "and replaces the old Norfolk cast iron one. 'Tis stronger, stays sharper, cuts better and allows the mold-board to turn the earth over more completely. I paid for it myself, not daring to bother Mr Ainsworth with it. I just expect to obtain a better return from the Big Field when we harvest it shortly. The turnips seem to like it too, leastways I have a heavier growth of tops this time for the livestock, and will be able to sell the surplus roots rather than keeping all of them to feed the cattle this winter." As they strolled on Alf said, "There's another thing, I would wish to purchase my own seed drill, one of the new improved ones, but I lack the capital to do so. At the present I'm obliged to hire one from a farm near Norwich. I lose a day's labour each way sending Frank Briggs there to fetch it with the hay waggon and the Blacks. If I had my own I might hire it out in the neighbourhood and obtain a return on the investment."

Tommy the bull looked up and snorted softly as Alf and his guest appeared around the end of the barn. Alf had tucked a bunch of fresh hay under his arm and the animal had already smelt its sweetness. Alf fed him slowly and ran his hand through the curly red and white hair on the animal's forehead. "See how short his horns are. My Duns have no horn at all. I always think horns are a waste of growth on cattle. Tommy watches the cows every day as they come and go. I trust this pen will hold him when one comes into season. I have not yet haltered him because I believe in giving the beast as much freedom to move as he can, to keep his legs strong for the task ahead."

"Indeed, he does look a handsome beast," Bob Jarvis remarked as they left Tommy behind and passed on to the pigs who looked up from their foraging, grunted, and returned with renewed concentration to the consumption of their feed.

"They will be put in the Big Field after harvest," Alf told his uncle while scratching the back of a large porker who had come up to investigate the presence of a stranger. "I shall fence off one side for them and the other for the sheep. They're in the far meadow over there at the moment. They're Norfolk Horn sheep and that is another bloodline I would wish to amend," Alf continued. "That's the ram there with the curved horns; the ewes have straighter ones. Their meat is sweet and lean, so they sell easily and they're prolific; they have twins as often as not and their wool is short but plentiful. But they do suffer so from the scrapie, and there's no solution to that but to slaughter every one of them that is affected. Now people at Norwich stock market tell me that if I were to cross these sheep with Lincoln or Leicestershire breeds, the new stock, that is, not only would I be rid of the scrapie but I would also obtain a heavier crop of wool and that without putting on too much fat, I reckon, if I follow the proper feeding plan.

"Come, Uncle, that's enough of my problems when you have plenty of your own," Alf concluded. "'Tis time we rejoined the ladies. If we walk through the garden they will see us approaching and finish off their chat. A good crop of apples this year, you'll note. They say much fruit is the sign of a cold winter to come, but I reckon it was just the dry spell we had late in the spring, plenty of bees at the blossoms and not much rain to make new leaves. Martha will lay those down in the attic and we'll have apple pie till we look like it all through the winter," Alf grinned as he led the way indoors.

"I've put the kettle on for a fresh pot, husband," Martha greeted Alf as they entered the parlour. "You'll wish to chat with Aunt Jarvis, no doubt, whilst I see to the tea. What did you think of the bull, Uncle Bob? Ain't he a fine fellow?"

"Yes, indeed he is. Alf has been explaining his proposals to me – most modern and progressive, I must say."

Once Martha had returned with a fresh pot of tea and it had brewed and been poured to their taste, along with the milk and sugar, not to forget the shortbread which Martha always baked whenever there was space to spare in the large bread oven, the conversation turned to the outcome of the ladies' discussion of that other family problem, the bringing up of Miss Jessica under the restrictions imposed by Sir Charles.

"Husband, I've been telling Aunt Jarvis about the schools our children attend. I thought you might wish to apprise her of our future plans," Martha prodded her spouse with wifely tact.

Alf Jarvis took a sip of tea from his dish, decided it was cool enough to drink, consumed the remainder of that which he had poured into the saucer and replaced it and the cup on the small table beside his chair. "My son Hughie, he's ten this December and attends the Sir John Leman School in Ballygate," Alf began. "'Tis a scholarly establishment with high standards, and its students have often gone into the Law or to business, have become physicians or have even taught at the Cambridge colleges. So you will understand that I wish to keep Hugo there as long as I possibly can. However, there is a snare. The school's charter allows for the education of 48 pupils, all boys, two being invited from Gillingham, two from Ringsfield parish, and the rest from Beccles. 'Tis a charitable foundation so there is nought to pay save incidental expenses, and there's no comparable school nearer than the boarding schools at Norwich, Ipswich, Bury or King's Lynn. My son is one of the two boys permitted from this parish, the other being Jake Martin's son Benjamin from Ilketshall St Andrew. Benjamin has just left the school and has gone up to London to complete his business studies. His younger brother Luke is to take his place, but Luke has had to wait until the age of nine to do so. I reckon we shall have a similar delay with our youngest, Peter, who is presently just six. I would wish him to start his schooling as soon as he can, but for that I shall need to withdraw Hughie and either put him to work on the farm, which the boy is not that anxious to do, or pay for him to attend another school as a boarder, something I cannot afford, especially as we do not know where we are for the future of this farm with our current landlord.

"The girls are rather better served, in a way, even though we must pay for their education," Alf Jarvis continued. "They cross Ballygate to the Angel Inn where they sit in an upstairs room over the carriage house." Alf chuckled, "Carrie says the girls are freezing cold in winter since their teacher, Miss Hayle, is rather plump and insists on placing her own chair right in front of the coals in the fireplace! Miss Hayle teaches reading, writing, drawing, sewing and poetry – Martha will correct me if I have omitted anything. However when the Usher of the John Leman School takes the boys to the Common for cricket or football twice a week, or to the Swimming Place in summer, the Headmaster, Dr Davey, crosses the street to the Angel and teaches the older girls English Grammar and Mathematics, while Miss Hayle takes the younger girls to the John Leman schoolyard for their play. Thus Carrie, who is thirteen now and in her last year of schooling, is as adept at those higher subjects as Hughie who is conning them every day. I have set the two of them the task of teaching young Peter to read and sign, so that he will not lag far behind if he has to wait to attend school. Lucy, the middle one, I regret does not apply herself to her lessons at all, is that no so wife? She persists in believing herself the baby of the family."

"If I remember well," Betty Jarvis broke in, "young Lucy is almost the same age as Miss Jessica. It will be interesting to watch the effect upon them both of the new situation. Jessica does not meet any children of her own age, indeed none at all other than Ted, the stable lad, and he is no example to a sensitive child."

"Aunt Jarvis and I," Martha interposed in a break in conversation while they sipped their tea and nibbled the sweet shortbread (Bob Jarvis sneaking yet another piece of it when he was sure Betty wasn't looking), "we have been racking our minds in vain to think how we may conceal Jessica's parentage from her and from all our children. It appears that Jessica is half-convinced that Sir Charles is her father, so Aunt Jarvis tells me, but she has no idea of the identity of her mother. On the other hand, Carrie and Hughie will remember Alicia's visit and the fact that she gave birth in this house. They know that she died and was buried in the Beccles graveyard. They saw the headstone there and have often asked me what became of the child, was it a boy or a girl, and had it been fostered out somewhere in Beccles, so that they might one day expect to make its acquaintance. I cannot now recall whether I ever mentioned that the baby was a girl, nor the reasons I gave at the time for not keeping the child with us at the farm. They will remember, though, children always do, and they'll put me to the lie in whatever information I've disclosed."

"I think Jessica herself will ask questions too," Betty Jarvis broke in. "I found a journal she had started to write, prompted I believe by the discomforts caused her by Mr Ainsworth's arrival. In it she repeated the little I had told her about her mother, that she was a pretty lady with fair curly hair and blue eyes. Blessed with that description and Jessica's birth-date it will not take long for your older children, Martha, to put two and two together and make a tidy sum."

"The most important consideration we should remember," Bob Jarvis intervened, having demolished the one remaining piece of shortbread, "is that news of the relationship must not go outside the family, and therefore the children must be taught the responses they should give at their schools. I am sure Sir

Charles would be most inconvenienced if his secret were to come out, and we must protect our own position as his employees and dependants."

"But everyone knows already that Mr Ainsworth is his bastard son, that young man is always proclaiming it," Alf Jarvis protested.

"Indeed he does say so, nephew," Bob Jarvis replied, "but your Aunt has always been in doubt about that. Mr Ainsworth was originally a ward of court of Sir Robert Rich, and Sir Charles may merely have inherited him along with the family estates."

"Such a charming inheritance, from all I observe!" Alf remarked sarcastically.

"So we are agreed, are we not," Bob Jarvis renewed his leadership of the conversation, "that the children shall be instructed what they are to reply, both to Jessica herself and to the other children?"

"Yes, husband," Betty added, "and I suggest that we instruct just the two older ones and advise them how to fend off questions from Lucy and Peter. I think we ought also to arrange for Jessica to come here and meet the children. I believe she would enjoy meeting the farm animals too, as she has made the acquaintance of Mr Ainsworth's horse and his dog, despite all his efforts to stop her."

"Oh, yes, that would be very right indeed," Martha echoed, "for them all to meet up beforehand. Then the children will not feel so reserved at dealing with a stranger."

Just then there came a scrunch of footsteps on the gravel drive and the front door burst open to admit a mob of tousled and breathless children. They paused at the parlour doorway, struck silent on observing the solemn-faced adults sitting within, while Jeannie Caldicott coming up behind said, "Oh dear, I think I've brought them back rather earlier than expected and you haven't finished your discussion."

"No matter, thank you Jeannie," Alf replied. "Hugo, Catherine, we have something to say to you." Alf Jarvis only called his children by their given names when there were serious matters afoot. The two older children glanced at each other.

"I'm starving," Hugo announced, "is there any milk? I suppose you have eaten all the shortbread?"

"In the kitchen, Hughie, under the cloth on the tray beside the stove. I saved some for you specially. The family milk is in the churn nearest the kitchen door. There's a clean dip beside it. Use it, please," Martha called to her son who was already scampering halfway along the corridor. "Jeannie," Martha continued, "could you please take Lucy and Peter and give them their supper along with your two?"

"Will do, Mrs Jarvis."

"But I wish to show Mama my new doll," Lucy protested.

"And my puzzle horse," Peter squeaked at her side.

"After supper, children," Alf decreed, "before you to go to bed." They turned away disappointed and accompanied Jeannie and her toddler twins, who were too tired to say anything, even though she and Carrie had shouldered one apiece on the long walk to and from the Fair.

Hugo and Carrie returned to the parlour with mugs of milk in one hand and chunks of shortbread in the other. "Hello Aunt Jarvis, Uncle Bob," they both uttered dutifully between crumbs as they sat down on chairs which their father had drawn up. Alf allowed them to finish their refreshment before he began.

"We have some news for you," he said. "Aunt Jarvis has come to ask for your assistance." Both children brightened considerably at this announcement. Hugo was a tall, wiry, intelligent-looking boy for his age, and Carrie was just as pretty, without being beautiful, and as resolute a young person as any farmer's wife could wish. "There is a young girl living at the Hall," Alf continued. "She is a distant relative of Sir Charles Rich, our landlord, and she is to be sent to school. Describe her, Aunt Jarvis, if you please," Alf had reached the limits of his male discretion.

"Yes, indeed. Her name is Jessica Rich and she is eight years old, in fact just two months older than Lucy. But she is an orphan," Betty drew a long breath until she had mastered herself again, "and does not know who were her parents. She is not fortunate as you are, living here on the farm with your own mother and father. Moreover a sad accident occurred to her a few months ago which has much affected her appearance. Your father will have told you that the barn at Roos Hall burned down. Well, Jessica was involved in that fire."

"Did she set the barn on fire, then?" Hugo asked breathlessly, his eyes wide with anticipation.

"No, it was thought so at first," Hugo's father broke in. "You will remember me telling your mother about it when I came home after delivering the new straw, but it eventually came out that Ted, the stable lad, had been smoking in the barn. You will also remember that I gave you a stern warning about that at the time."

"So Jessica was blamed unjustly," Betty Jarvis resumed. "The poor child was injured by the flames, and though most of her wounds have healed, her hair, which was burned right off, has yet to grow again, so that she has to wear a cap, not just over the top of her head, as you do Carrie, or should do when you go to Church or to school, but over the whole of her head which makes her look rather peculiar. That is why, when she starts her schooling, we thought it would assist if the two of you and Lucy would escort her, collect her from the Hall and bring her back, and protect her from teasing by the other children."

"Is she very ill?" Carrie, who had not yet spoken, asked very quietly.

"No, child," her great-aunt replied, "but she is lonely and feeling rather sad, so going to school with other children will provide some much needed diversion."

"Can we meet her beforehand, Papa?" Hugo asked. "After all, she is a complete stranger and I think we should see what sort of a person she is if we are to be asked to stand up for her."

"That is just what we were discussing, Hughie, as you arrived," his mother replied. "Aunt Jarvis and I will agree on a day when she will be brought to meet you, probably one afternoon next week, before we start to harvest the Big Field. You and the others will be able to show Jessica around the farm and introduce her to the animals."

"Son," Alf interjected with a hand on his son's shoulder, "because Miss Jessica is an orphan, there may be some unpleasantness about her living at Roos Hall, some jealousy from the other children, perhaps even from Lucy. That is why your Mother and I have called on you specially this afternoon to take charge of Miss Jessica and see that she comes to no harm."

"Yes, Papa, we will, won't we Carrie?" Hugo replied.

"Of course," Carrie responded. "Now can I show Mama the new bonnet I bought at the Fair?" she asked, slowly turning her back around to face her parent.

"Carrie! You're surely not intending to wear ribbons of that colour?" her mother asked, horrified.

"I am indeed, Mama," Carrie replied, "but not perhaps when we go to church," she added with a laugh and rose to leave the room.

When both children were out of earshot Betty Jarvis murmured, "Youth! That so reminded me of my dear Alicia."

CHAPTER V
The Children

The bees buzzed drowsily among the soft white and pink petals of the arbour's roses when Carrie and Hugo took refuge there the following morning as soon as their tasks had been completed. Carrie had been helping her mother pour the morning's milk through the cooler and into the churns which Hugo had been set to flush out under the pump in the yard. In summer every extra pair of hands around the farm was a welcome addition to the work force, freeing Jim Caldicott to check over the stock and Alf to catch up with his paperwork. Later in the morning the local milkman, Ben Ollenshaw, would clip-clop into the yard with his cob-drawn waggon to collect the milk for sale. This he would distribute around Beccles and the neighbouring villages, Ringsfield, Barsham, Shipmeadow, Ilketshall St Andrew, St John and St Margaret, wherever the cottagers did not keep a cow of their own. Any milk left over at the end of the day would be taken to the dairy shop in Ballygate, though that had other suppliers, or to the Angel Inn where the landlord's wife, Mrs Porter, made it into bread puddings for her guests' supper.

"What do you think, then, Sis? Who do you reckon this girl is, the girl from Roos Hall?" Hugo asked.

Carrie, posed along the length of the seat in her flower-printed gown and summer slippers, adjusted a tortoiseshell comb in her heavy brown locks and a smile crossed her fresh complexion as she replied, "I think we have not been given the whole story. There's much that our parents are not telling us, Hughie; otherwise they would not have needed to discuss it with us conveniently out of the way for the afternoon at the Fair. You heard what Mrs Caldicott said upon our return. She feared she had brought us home too soon. I suspect there may be some scandal attached to Miss Jessica, and the grown-ups don't wish questions asked.""

"That's what I think, too," Hugo responded as he sat on the end of the seat with one leg hooked up under his chin and the other kicking a hole in the grass beneath. "After all, you heard what Papa has to say about that Mr Ainsworth who supposedly is our landlord but does not know a thing about farming. Why is he living at Roos Hall when Sir Charles should be living there instead, or at least should be visiting us to see how his estates are faring?"

"They seem like forgotten people, don't they, Mr Ainsworth and Miss Jessica," Carrie mused, "like characters among a crowd that no-one pays any heed to. I wonder what Jessica is like? Will she be priggish and too fine to play with us, or maybe as she hasn't had any schooling so far she will be really dull and stupid."

"I should hate that," Hugo said forcefully, "because we would be paying attention to someone who would provide less company than a sheep!"

Carrie laughed and added with a little feminine spite, "Well, if she has lost all her hair already, at least she will not need to be shorn!"

"Yes, that must make her look quite pathetic," Hugo replied. "I wonder what my school-fellows will say if they see me escorting someone looking like that? I'm sure they will call me a sissy and tease me rotten. There'll be bullying from the older boys, like Mather and Weedon, to cope with all over again. I thought I had outgrown all that."

"I doubt whether Lucy will favour it at all, " Carrie continued. "I have difficulty enough managing her behaviour through school hours as it is, without having another person to overlook as well."

"Is it as bad as that, Sis? I had no idea. I know she is behind in her lessons and cannot even read properly yet," Hugo commented.

"You don't see her as I do," Carrie replied. "Lucy behaves much better when you are there: she looks upon you as her model. But when we leave you and walk into the yard at The Angel, she begins to behave like a vulgar hoyden, shouting at the top of her voice, picking on the younger girls, making faces in Class, and mimicking Miss Hayle as soon as our teacher turns her back to write upon the blackboard or to stoke the fire."

"Have you told Papa?" Hugo asked.

"I haven't dared, Mama knows though."

"What does Mama know?" Lucy suddenly appeared around the rim of the arbour, leaving the older children wondering how much of their unfavourable remarks she had heard. Fair curly hair, blue eyes, chubby cheeks and a lively look gave Lucy the appearance of an angel, though her nature immediately belied it. "I know what you're talking about," the cherub intoned. "I heard Mama telling Mrs C that we have to collect a girl named Jessica from Roos Hall on our way to school and take her home there afterwards. I also heard them say she's been burnt in a fire. Does that mean she'll look all black and charred, like wood in the grate?"

"No, silly," Carrie replied, "but she has to wear a cap right over her head because all her hair has been burned off."

"Oh, she must look awful," said Lucy, tossing her own fine head of curls. "I also heard Mrs C ask ...." and at this juncture Lucy dropped her voice to a whisper, "whether Jessica is il-le-git-i-mate. What does that mean?"

"Huh!" Hugo exclaimed with a glance at Carrie, "you explain, Sis."

Just at that moment there was an eager shout from Peter who came running up bursting with news. "Mama's just made buns, right out of the oven this minute, and there's sour cream to go with them from the dairy!" All four children rushed indoors without another thought.

A few days later Jessica paid her first visit to the Ringsfield Farm. Betty Jarvis had hired the pony-trap from Wilson's again and drove it herself with Jessica sitting on the bench beside her. The girl was dressed in a gown of white muslin embroidered with green leaves and pink flowers. Over it Betty had made her wear a green cloak which she hoped would protect the muslin from undue contact with muddy earth or inquisitive animals. On her wounded head Jessica wore not only a muslin cap but also a Dutch hood made of starched cotton, with long ribbons that tied beneath her chin. The outfit made her look old for her years, but the child was excited by the outing. She had never left Roos Hall and its park and gardens ever since Nanny had brought her there, and she looked about her with her large dark eyes. However her expression was wistful and sad. These people she was to visit were not hers, not her family. She was not really welcome here, not one of their own: they were merely people who had received their landlord's instructions to escort her to and from school.

Betty Jarvis halted the pony-trap beside the hitching-rail and climbed down slowly; she was getting a little stiff these days. She tied the reins firmly and gave the pony its hay-bag. All this while Jessica had sat frozen with fear, watching her. "Come along, Miss Jessica," Betty helped her to alight. By the time they reached the front door Martha stood there ready to greet them, with the children crowding behind her.

"Martha Jarvis, this is Miss Jessica," Betty said.

"How do you do, Mrs Jarvis?" Jessica uttered in a quiet apprehensive tone, holding out her small gloved hand.

"Come in both of you and meet the children," Martha ushered them indoors.

The children stood and stared at Jessica for what seemed an interminable pause. Then one of them moved. "How do you do, Jessica? I'm Hugo," he crossed the room and shook her hand.

"And I'm Carrie," said the eldest, giving Jessica's hand a little squeeze. "And that's Peter," she added, pointing to her younger brother who was already back on the parlour floor, trying to put together the puzzle horse he had brought home from the Fair. It was made up of intricately carved wooden pieces, which he had taken apart easily enough, but now was at much pains to put together again. "Lucy?" Carrie turned round to look for her sister.

Lucy had taken refuge behind her mother's skirts. "I don't wish to speak to her, whoever she is," Lucy stamped her foot, her face flushed with rage at finding someone else the centre of attention.

"Lucy Jarvis, come out here this minute and greet Miss Jessica properly," her mother grasped her arm and pulled her forth.

"Shan't," said Lucy, hanging her head and stamping her foot again. Martha propelled her forward until she was within arm's reach of where Jessica stood, small, still and pale, and with tears beginning to well into her large dark eyes.

"Don't wish to know you," Lucy blurted out suddenly, "you're il-le-git-i-mate!"

There was an astonished gasp from the adults, and the older children looked aghast. "Goodness Lucy! Wherever did she learn that word?" Martha demanded.

"Lucy heard Mrs C asking you, I fear," Carrie replied.

"Miss Jessica is an orphan," Betty Jarvis broke in firmly, "she merely doesn't know who were her parents. That does not mean necessarily that she was ill-born, but she should not be teased about it. That is why we wanted her to meet you all before she walks to school with you."

"Huh! I'm not going to school with her! I won't have her anywhere near me!" Lucy shouted and burst into tears.

"Lucy, go to your room this instant," Martha ordered, and Lucy ran out of the parlour and upstairs, her howls of anguish echoing behind her as she went.

"Oh dear, poor Lucy's put out, I see." It was Mrs Caldicott bringing in a tray of tea, well primed with a plate of currant cookies and mugs of milk for the children.

Jessica was introduced to Mrs C as Martha Jarvis's chief assistant around house and dairy, and sipped her milk. "It tastes different," she remarked.

"It should do," Martha replied, "that was fresh from the cows this morning."

"May I see the animals?" Jessica asked wistfully.

"Of course you can, my dear," Martha replied, "though you'd be better to do so in one of Lucy's pinafores than in that cloak, if you don't mind my saying so, Aunt Jarvis. Slip upstairs and fetch one, will you Carrie, and if Lucy is feeling more amenable she may come down for her cookie and join you later." Jessica was duly enveloped in one of Lucy's pinafores, whose ties, since Lucy was taller and chubbier, more than met behind her tiny waist. Accompanied by Hugo and Carrie, they ran out into the yard.

"Make sure she minds the pancakes," was Martha's last admonition as they went.

"Which pancakes?" Jessica asked.

"These," said Hugo, indicating a large moist deposit in front of the cow-byre.

"Oh," said Jessica, "horses are much tidier, I think."

Carrie collapsed in giggles and then said, "Look, the cows are still being milked. Would you like to watch, Jessica?"

"Please," Jessica murmured shyly. They peeped in through the doorway, and then Hugo took Jessica by the hand and led her inside. The air was hot and steamy, there was a munching of hay, a soft lowing from time to time as each animal started or finished yielding its burden of milk, and a hissing sound as the streams of milk from the teats hit the sides of the wooden pails and cascaded down into the creamy froth below. Jim Caldicott and the two milkmaids, Bessie and Anna, were busy at work with their backs to the children, but Jim's two collie sheepdogs, Pip and Shep, rose from their resting place beside their master and came to greet the newcomers. They sniffed over the stranger very cautiously, and Jessica smiled and stood still while they did so. Then they wagged their tails and put up their heads to be petted.

"Those two obviously approve of you," Hugo commented as he led Jessica forward to meet Jim and introduced her.

"Pleased to meet you, Miss Jessica," Jim said, rising from his three-legged stool. "Would you care to have a try?"

"Me?" asked Jessica, amazed.

"Go on," urged Hugo, "we have all learnt how to milk in case one of the maids falls sick." Jessica sat down carefully on the wooden stool, pushing her skirts out of the way behind and beneath her. Jim showed her how to gently pull and squeeze the teats until a stream of creamy liquid emerged. Jessica took two teats in her hands and tried to copy Jim's movements. He guided her to start with, then left her alone as she succeeded by herself.

"Bravo!" Hugo said as Jessica stood up, "now come and meet the cow." The pale yellow creature had turned its head, watching with liquid eyes the unusual proceedings at its tail end. "This is Lucille," Hugo said, "one of our favourites. Lucille, meet Jessica. I expect you will see more of her from now on." The cow allowed herself to be petted, then returned her attention to the manger in front of her and its protruding bunches of hay. Carrie introduced Jessica to the two milkmaids and then the children left the byre, crossing the yard to visit the horses in their paddock beyond the toolshed.

"She's not what I expected," Bessie remarked to Anna. "I thought she'd look grand, all dressed up and speaking proper, but she isn't. She's no different from the other children, except for her head, the poor little thing."

"Yes, neither of us would wish to lose our crowning glory," Anna replied as she continued milking.

The four horses came ambling across to the fence as soon as they noticed the children's approach. Carrie and Hugo had both paused to pull handfuls of long sweet grass from the sward growing in the shadow of the farm buildings and Hugo gave some to Jessica. He watched with approval as she placed it on her open palm and stretched out her hand. The older of the Fenland horses, named General, paused as he towered above the small, slight child, then blew softly on her hand as his flexible lips with their moustache of long white whiskers nimbly picked up the grass. His companion, Major, came shouldering his way to the fence alongside his colleague, and Hugo offered him a handful of the sweet greenery. Both animals spent a minute or two studying the newcomer and sniffing at her hood. "They seem to like you, Jessica," Hugo remarked. "You're not afraid of them, I see."

"No, I'm accustomed to petting Pharaoh, Mr Ainsworth's hunter. He does not wish me to, really, but since he discovered that I was not to blame for the fire in the barn at the Hall, I do not think even he has the spite to stop me."

"Is he very beastly to you?" Hugo could not help asking, even though his mother had told him not to pry.

"Yes, sometimes, but sometimes I expect I deserve it."

"Does your head still hurt from the burns?" Hugo, asked, full of curiosity.

"Yes, there is a bad burn on my neck which has yet to heal over, and Mrs Jarvis has to dress it every other day. My scalp is healing slowly but Dr Crowfoot, our physician, says it may be year or two before my hair begins to grow again."

Carrie came up just then, having dispensed her long grass to the two Sorrel horses, Captain and Corporal. They walked beside her along the fencing and investigated the newcomer for themselves. They sniffed at her hood and Jessica tickled their noses. "You seem to be at ease with the animals," Carrie remarked. "Come and meet Tommy, our new bull. He is another one who enjoys being fed," she added as she replenished her supply of sweet grass. Jessica and Hugo did the same.

After they had fed Tommy, had inspected the hens and the geese and the pigs in their sty, and Carrie had duly warned Jessica not to stand too close to those, and never to enter their pen, as Hugo had apparently done once and received a good bruising form the porkers and an even bigger thrashing from his father for his disobedience, they wandered over to the sheep pasture and began counting the flock. Everyone made it a different total and they all laughed, but Carrie and Hugo were gratified that Jessica could count as well as they did. Just at that moment Lucy joined them. She did not utter a word, but with one thumb in her mouth and a glare at Jessica from her brilliant blue eyes, she clutched Carrie's hand and accompanied them across the width of the farm, along the edge of the Big Field with its crop of harvest-ripe wheat, and thence to the turnip field with its second growth of green leaves. Hugo explained to Jessica that the turnips were used as winter-feed for the stock, particularly the cows and the sheep, whilst the pigs survived on household slops, and whey and buttermilk from the dairy. Sometimes Uncle Bob Jarvis would bring the pigs a few barrels of malt waste from the brewery at Bungay whence he collected his stock of beer and ale, and this was mixed with the pig feed. If one added too much at a time, Hugo said, the pigs would fall over themselves to consume it and become riotously drunk. He had received another thrashing from his father, he admitted, after experimenting with that very process, from a mischievous delight of watching a pigpen in mayhem!

The next field contained oilseed, which Carrie explained was made into a kind of cake which added goodness to the cattle's winter diet. Hugo reminded her that it was sometimes spread on the crop fields to fertilize the soil, although they normally used marl when they could afford it, or red clay if they could not. Next they passed fields of oats and barley, grains with which Jessica was familiar since they formed a part of Pharaoh's feed. There were also smaller plots for growing peas, potatoes and cabbages. Finally the skirted the long swathes of green pasture which bordered the Beccles to Bungay road. Carrie pointed to a double row of hedges that formed the farm's eastern boundary. "The lane between those bushes is the one we take to school. It joins the Bungay road very near Roos Hall, so it will be the easiest thing for us to call for you each morning."

"I know of the lane," Jessica told them shyly, "I have watched you come and go each day. My bedroom window is the one at the top of the gable and I have often waved to you, but you did not notice."

"Oh, I'm sorry, we shall not fail to look for you in future, even when there is no school. By the by, Jessica, Aunt Jarvis told us you had not attended school before. Are you able to read and write, or will you need tuition? Hugo and I are presently teaching Peter to read and to con the alphabet. We may help you too, should you wish. It would save you from extra lessons with Miss Hayle."

"I have already learnt to read and to write, thank you," Jessica replied. Mrs Jarvis taught me some time ago and she keeps bringing me books to read. I suppose she borrows them from the circulating library, since she seems to have a regular supply." Carrie and Hugo looked at her in amazement. Far from accompanying a dunce to school, they realised that Jessica was probably as nimble-minded as themselves and far more erudite than Lucy, who scowled hideously at this revelation, her thumb dropping right out of her mouth.

They turned back toward the farmhouse, passed the paddock again, petted the pony that had brought Jessica and Aunt Jarvis as it waited patiently at the front of the house and went indoors. Alf Jarvis had arrived in the meantime and greeted Jessica whom he had often seen when delivering farm produce at Roos Hall. "How did Miss Jessica seem to you?" he asked Hugo whilst the others were busy chatting.

"Oh, Papa, Jessica can read and write already," relief was evident in Hugo's voice, "and she cares for the animals too."

"I hear she sat down and milked old Lucille, is that so, Miss Jessica?" Alf called her over. "Don't you fret about Lucy's behaviour. I shall promise her a special treat if she will learn her lessons as well as you," he said. "I hope you enjoy your schooling, Jessica. Would you care to join us for harvest, that is if Mr Ainsworth will permit it? Every pair of hands is welcome and all the children take part?"

"Thank you, Mr Jarvis. I will ask Mr Ainsworth if I may do so and see what he says."

When Betty Jarvis and Jessica arrived back at Roos Hall later that afternoon, it was to find Mrs Baines wringing her hands and Briggs and the maids all of a tizzy. It seems that Mr Ainsworth, who had been in a foul temper all morning and nobody knew why, ordered Ted to saddle Pharaoh as he wished to take a ride. Now there was nothing unusual about that, but then Mr Ainsworth packed a couple of bags and slung them over his saddle, pronouncing that he was off to Yarmouth for a few days and would return when it pleased him.

"Well, that's a fine thing," Betty Jarvis exclaimed, "just when Mr Russell is due to ride over tomorrow to meet with the builders about starting on the new barn. That leaves us nicely in the lurch. At least we will not have to seek Mr Ainsworth's permission for you to go to the farm again tomorrow, Miss Jessica. If he is not here we cannot ask him, can we?"

The following morning Mrs Jarvis asked one of the chambermaids to escort Jessica along the track to the farm and to return once the buildings were in sight. She knew that either the children or one of the farm hands would bring Jessica back again at sunset. That left Betty free to make sure that the house, gardens and yard were ready for Mr Russell's inspection, so that he might find no cause of complaint other than Mr Ainsworth's inexplicable absence. She ordered Mrs Baines to prepare one of Mr Russell's favourite dishes for his dinner, with some of her creamy desserts cooled in the ice-house to follow on this hot, dry day of late summer, and she herself made a careful selection of delectable wines. If the builder had met with Mr Russell's approval, Betty imagined that he too might be invited to partake. Once that business had been concluded Betty had it in mind to tackle Mr Russell about Alf Jarvis's plans for the farm, on which her husband Bob had briefed her in detail. She hoped that Mr Russell would be so put out by Mr Ainsworth's absence that he would agree to take up those matters direct with Sir Charles.

Meanwhile Jessica, dressed in an old gown, pinafore, boots and the starched Dutch hood, was running along the grassy track towards the farmhouse. It was quite a deep lane with tall bushes on one side and a wood on the eastern side for most of the way. Had she been walking there alone, Jessica thought she would have found it rather intimidating, a place for encountering ghosts and spirits. However the knowledge that the grass had been well worn by the passage of the children comforted her. She knocked on the front door of the farmhouse, but no-one answered, so she ran around to the yard and in the dairy found Mrs Caldicott cooling the morning's milk whilst her two toddlers played on the floor beside her. "Morning, Miss Jessica," Mrs C said, "Mrs Jarvis is in the kitchen there, but everyone else is down in the Big Field. Would you like some fresh milk?"

Jessica walked through to the kitchen where Martha greeted her, putting a hot buttered crust in one hand and a mug for the milk in the other. Jessica's face was quite radiant: she did not often meet with such kindness. When she reached the field she found the harvesters working their scythes in a line, starting at the top of the slope where the crop was driest and moving gradually downhill. Alf Jarvis, Jim Caldicott, Ben Ollenshaw, the shepherd Bill Foster and the plough-hand Frank Briggs, the grandson of the handyman at Roos Hall, were all scything away. Pip and Shep ran in beside them, together with Ben's terrier Buster, all barking madly and chasing after any rat, mouse or shrew, as well as the occasional partridge that emerged from the corn.

The younger children, Hugo, Lucy and even little Peter, trotted along behind the scythes, gathering up the fallen stems into bundles and making sure that the heads of corn all pointed the same way. They deposited their bundles at the feet of Bessie, Anna and Carrie, who twisted straw in a wreath around each sheaf, tied it tightly and stacked every half-dozen or so sheaves into 'shocks' or stooks. Jessica noted the pretty red poppies, blue chicory and purple corn-cockles which the cutting of the corn had exposed to the light, as well as the clover and vetch-es upon which the pigs and sheep would soon be feeding.

"Hello, Jessica, I'm glad you could come," Carrie called to her. "Would you help Hughie, Lucy and Peter in gathering up the corn, if you please." Jessica received welcoming smiles from all except Lucy as she joined the team. She soon found she was quite adept at handling the long straw stems, and could help Peter too when his bundles were not quite large enough to make a full-sized sheaf. Around midday everyone paused and sought shelter form the sun under the hedge, where Martha and Mrs C replenished their strength with ale for the men, milk for the children, and a selection of pies, cheeses, crusts and cookies, all piled into overflowing baskets. Ben Ollenshaw left them to make his daily milk round, but Buster stayed behind as his services were considered indispensable.

They finished their labours as the sun was setting and Alf Jarvis spoke to Jessica for the first time that day, thanking her for her help and enquiring how she had enjoyed the task. Alf said that he was glad that Mr Ainsworth had given her permission to join them. "Oh, but he was not at home today, Mr Jarvis," Jessica replied. "When Mrs Jarvis and I returned to the Hall yesterday we found him gone to Yarmouth on Pharaoh, and with no promise of when he will be back."

"Did he now?" Alf responded, "and wasn't it today that Mr Russell was to come from Norwich to meet Josiah Mason that's to build the new barn?"

"Yes, Mr Jarvis, and Mrs Jarvis was most put out to be left alone when Mr Ainsworth is supposed to be in charge of the Hall."

"Why, so he is. Do you think, Jessica, that Mr Russell is still there at the Hall, or will he have ridden back to Norwich already?"

"I'm not sure, sir, but I heard Mrs Jarvis order Mrs Baines to prepare something special for his dinner."

"Is that so? Miss Jessica, would you have any objection if I was to escort you personally along the path to Roos Hall?"

"Not at all, Mr Jarvis, I should be most obliged," Jessica replied with great dig-nity.

Dusk was falling in the lane as they set out. The shadows were deep. A light breeze whispered among the trees and there were rustles in the woods where a deer or a fox had quietly crept away. At one point, Alf took Jessica's hand and showed her a barn owl that fluttered silently along the hedge like a large white moth. They reached the Bungay road in twenty minutes and were soon walking up the darkened drive to Roos Hall. Mrs Jarvis stood on the doorstep looking about her rather anxiously until she saw them arrive.

"Here she is, Aunt Jarvis, home safely and in one piece," Alf Jarvis said.

"Did you enjoy yourself, Miss Jessica?" Betty Jarvis enquired, and being reas-sured in the affirmative went on, "You're covered with dust, child. Ask Lizzie to help you to a hot bath before you go to bed. Your supper's ready in the kitchen." Jessica smiled and vanished.

"She seems a bright little thing," Alf commented and then asked, "Is Mr Russell still with you, or has he returned to Norwich?"

"No, he's just had his supper and I've made him up a bed for the night. The discussions with the builder took longer than expected since the price was raised above the estimate and Mr Russell had to beat him down again," Mrs Jarvis replied.

"Would he be agreeable to my having a word with him?" Alf enquired.

"I'll just go and ask him, Alf. You come and wait in the hall," Betty said. Presently she returned and ushered Alf into the wood-panelled dining room of the Hall. Mr Anthony Russell, tall, dark-haired and athletic-looking since he rode to hounds regularly, rose from his seat at the candlelit table and shook Alf Jarvis by the hand. He offered Alf a cigar and a glass of port. Alf declined the former but accepted the latter as the evening chill had begun to penetrate after the heated labours of the day, and he had escorted Jessica in such haste that he had left his jacket behind. He excused his disshevelled appearance as having some straight from the harvest and without more ado spoke his mind.

"Mr Russell, I have been cogitating over a number of improvements to my stock at the farm, the which I have brought up with Mr Ainsworth, but as soon as I gave him to understand that the schemes involved a certain expenditure of capital he refused to discuss them with me. I am anxious to avoid any loss of productivity from my land, or any reduction in its revenues, and I believe that my plans represent a positive increment of its value."

"Mr Jarvis," Anthony Russell interrupted him, "Mrs Jarvis has already apprised me on your behalf. So far as I can tell, what you propose is much in line with the improvements I am carrying out at Sir Charles's Norfolk properties. Now that I have been obliged to spend the night here and plan to return to Norwich tomorrow, may I suggest that I call upon you in the morning, shall we say around eight of the clock, and you shall explain everything to me at first hand."

"That will do splendidly, sir. I thank you most kindly." Alf downed the remainder of his glass of port and took his leave. He found Betty hovering in the hallway. "Thank you, Aunt Jarvis, for speaking up for me. Mr Russell comes to see me in the morning. By the by, if Miss Jessica wishes to do some more harvesting, we'll be cutting the oats this Friday and shearing the sheep next week. The shearer is promised for Wednesday. She did well today, bless her, joined in with the others and soon had the hang of things."

"If Mr Ainsworth is still absent she'll come, I'm sure, and if he returns – I'll think of some way of persuading him," Mrs Jarvis replied.

Alf left the lantern-lit doorway and trudged down the drive to the Bungay road. Apart from night-time excursions with Jim Caldicott to shoot foxes that had plagued his hens and geese, Alf seldom had reason to be out alone in the dark and far from his familiar farm buildings. He shivered as the chill dank air struck through his cotton shirt and was glad that he had accepted the glass of port. He thought of his Aunt Jarvis walking back to Beccles along this road every night after her duties were done, and gave credit to her courage and determination. After all, this lane had a certain reputation for manifestations of the supernatural. Was it not here that Betty Jarvis had encountered Black Shuck on more than one occasion? And she never did reveal exactly what it was that had frightened her so on the night before Alicia had died. Alf felt a creeping sensation run down his spine, and the hairs on his neck and arms stood erect and goose-pimply. There was definitely a presence here that was alien to human kind. He reached the wicket gate that marked the end of the path to his farm and turned aside gratefully. The path was in complete darkness as he stumbled along over the rough grass-tussocked ground. Thankfully, school classes ended early in winter, he thought, as he would not wish his children to be wending their way homeward in such blackness. Some invisible creature crossed the path in front of him and went crashing away through the undergrowth. Alf guessed it was a deer, but he was never more glad to reach his own front door.

Mr Russell rode over to the Ringsfield Farm the following morning and did not return to Roos Hall until well past noon. He paused to refresh himself and his mount and to thank Mrs Jarvis for her services. Then, as there was still no sign of the errant Mr Ainsworth, he wrote that gentleman a note deprecating his absence and indicating that he had been obliged instead to instruct Mr Alfred Jarvis to supervise the building of the new barn at Roos Hall. He had also discussed with Mr Jarvis certain improvements he wished to make to his stock and would be taking up those matters with Sir Charles. Mr Russell would be sure to notify Mr Ainsworth of the outcome, he wrote, and signed his name with a flourish.

It was fully a fortnight later that Mr Ainsworth returned to Roos Hall. Indeed the staff scarcely recognised the scarecrow figure atop his elegant horse. He was dirty, drunk and feverish, and his saddlebags were empty, the contents having been sold to pay for his lodging. Even Pharaoh's fortunes had fluctuated during his excursion, for it later transpired that Mr Ainsworth had gambled away his hunter and then had continued to play until he was able to buy it back again. And any promissory notes given upon the last throw of the dice or the last bad hand at cards? For the moment no one suspected their existence.

In the meantime, Jessica had paid almost daily visits to the Ringsfield Farm. She helped in the harvesting of the remaining grain crops and the loading of the wheat sheaves on to the hay waggon. Then she watched as Jim and Frank tossed the sheaves expertly atop the growing ricks with their pitchforks, where Alf pushed and prodded them into position. Their grain would not be threshed until later in the year, when the price was right and when their cattle had consumed sufficient hay so as to leave bare that portion of the barn floor where they would wield their flails. These ricks were circular and traditionally were topped with an individual message or motto created from twisted straw. The Jarvis dictum was "Time & Harvest" on one rick and "Wait for no Man" on the other.

Jessica had also observed the shearing of the Norfolk flock, all 79, or 80, or 81 of them, in one afternoon. The shearer with his boy had made his way from farm to farm hiring out his services. A month before he had attended the Holkham estate of Sir Thomas Coke (pronounced Cook), a famous gentleman farmer whose agricultural improvements were the talk of the Norwich and Beccles stock markets. Alf Jarvis always quizzed the man eagerly for any tips or news of fresh developments that he might be persuaded to divulge. As the fleeces fell to the ground the children rolled them up, dirty side out, and placed them in a heap in the barn. Presently Bessie and Anna would sort and clean them, wash them in a tub of unslaked lime and warm soapy water, rinse them under the pump and set them to dry on a wooden rack. Then they were packed into large hessian sacks and sold as ready for combing and spinning by the cottagers of the neighbourhood. The naked sheep would be dipped to cleanse them and rid them of remaining ticks and fleas, any wounds would be medicated with ointment or hot pitch, and then they were released into the empty Big Field to nibble the clover.

Summer and the harvest had come to an end. It was time to think about pulling the turnips and for the children to return to school. The first morning of a new term is always a solemn occasion. There are new faces to meet, perhaps a new schoolmaster to respect, and a changing structure of lessons as one progresses through the school. So Hugo felt extra apprehensive that morning when he left his sisters waiting at the gates of Roos Hall whilst he ran along the drive and stretched up to reach the bell-pull at the front door. It was opened by Briggs, and not by Mr Ainsworth as Hugo had feared. "The lass is ready, Master Hugo," Briggs said and called back into the hallway, "Miss Jessica!" Jessica came flying down the stairs, her cloak billowing behind her, and a radiant smile shining from underneath her hood.

From the Hall it was a matter of some ten minutes' walk to the boys' school where Hugo would leave them. His school had been founded in 1631 by Sir John Leman, a distinguished local magnate who had served as Lord Mayor of London in 1616-17, for which service he had been knighted. In his old age Sir John had determined to establish a school as a charitable foundation based on his own house in Ballygate and on associated farmland whose revenues would meet all running expenses, including the salaries of the Head Master and the Usher, his assistant. Education would thereby be provided free of charge for forty-eight boys. They were to learn reading, ciphering (the old name for writing) and casting accounts (which meant basic arithmetic); in addition they were to be governed by "the religion now established in this realm", which meant the Anglican practices of the current reign of Charles I, in contrast to the Protestantism of his predecessors and the Puritanism of the Commonwealth which followed the Civil War in the middle of the Seventeenth Century. Sir John was evidently a particularly discerning gentleman of his day.

By the time that a century or more had passed since Sir John's death his house, which was formerly thatched, had fallen into disrepair, and a substantial renovation was carried out in the middle of the Eighteenth Century. Thus the building which Hugo entered on the north side of Ballygate had a fine tiled roof, and a neatly trimmed flint frontage pierced by windows in the Tudor style. Through a side gate where the school motto read "Disce aut discede", which may be translated as "Learn or Leave", he entered the gravelled schoolyard. A porch topped by a bell tower housed the entrance to the schoolrooms, while the Headmaster's house with its accompanying outbuildings stood at the far end of the yard.

Beyond the schoolyard wall, which was inevitably climbed over daily during the noon break in lessons, wooded slopes led down to the River Waveney. The more serious-minded scholars sought refuge there among the trees and away from the rough and tumble of the playground. Hugo was a sociable child; as a member of a large family he was well accustomed to the company of other children. Fit and wiry by constitution, he enjoyed playing football or cricket in the yard when his elders had a mind to organise a game, but leapfrog and other minor pastimes he felt were beneath him now that he had moved up to the Head Master's class. Instead he had developed a friendship with a studious boy slightly younger than himself named Joseph Arnold. Being one of the peace-loving scholars, Joseph was often teased and bullied by the more boisterous pupils, and Hugo was then obliged to defend his friend as well as himself from the physical damage that their elders sought to inflict.

Thus the pair frequently sought refuge in the woods beneath the wall, where Joseph would fossick among the leaves for beetles and woodlice, or turn over a rotting log to count the snails and slugs concealed on its underside. They watched the fluttering passage of butterflies and moths, followed the spotted woodpecker to its nest in a tree-trunk, or parted the foliage around a dunnock's nest in the bushes. Red squirrels with their flicking tails and tufted ears would chatter at them from the trees and the occasional weasel or stoat would vanish among the bushes at their approach. Joseph carried a magnifying lens in one jacket pocket and in the other a small wooden box, which when opened disclosed his sadly-departed pet, an enormous black horned stag beetle!

This particular morning, however, the greeting which his fellow scholars gave Hugo was far from peaceful. Several of them had observed him walking along Ballygate beside his sisters and an apparition concealed in a long cloak and a large white hood. "Who's the fright that was with you?" the bullies Mather and Weedon demanded, crossing the yard and landing Hugo a punch on the shoulder, one from each of them.

"Her name is Jessica Rich," Hugo replied in accordance with his father's instructions, "and she lives at Roos Hall."

"And is she, rich I mean?" Mather enquired, landing a second punch on Hugo's sternum.

"I don't know," Hugo replied.

"Then what are you doing walking with her?" Weedon emphasised his question with a cuff at Hugo's head, and which the boy saw coming in time to duck most of its force.

"We are required to escort her to and from school by our landlord, Sir Charles Rich."

"Is he her father?" Mather asked, accompanying that with a blow at Hugo's ribs which half-winded him.

"No, she's an orphan," Hugo struggled dutifully to reply.

"Unlikely to be rich, then," Weedon concluded, then went on, "By the by, Jarvis, you'll be joining us in the senior class this year. Just remember that we're the top scholars, so don't you show yourself to be too bright, or we'll have to teach you a lesson or two of our own!" Fortunately for Hugo the school bell rang just then and all the pupils filed indoors in alphabetical order whilst Mr Barker, the Usher, ticked off their names in a ledger.

Meanwhile, Carrie, and a scowling Lucy who had not addressed a word to Jessica during their walk to Ballygate, reached the archway leading into the yard of the Angel Inn. Like the Bear & Bells, the Angel had once been a coaching inn and the yard would have been full of vehicles, stamping horses, and ostlers running hither and thither with feed and buckets of water. However, since the development of the New Market and the building of the King's Head Hotel, it too had declined. Coaches still halted there indeed, but only infrequently to put down passengers of the less wealthy sort, together with their meagre luggage. The Angel was therefore keen to welcome other business to boost its income; Mr Barker, the Usher from the boy's school, had his lodgings there during term-time, and Miss Hayle had set up a genteel academy for the young ladies of Beccles in the attic above the half-empty carriage-house. She taught girls of all ages, setting the older ones some written task or to drawing a still life study of objects grouped upon her desk, while she gave her attention to teaching the six to ten-year olds to read and write. Those who became adept rose to inclusion among the senior girls, whilst those who still needed individual discipline and encouragement lingered behind for further tuition. There were twenty pupils altogether and Carrie was among the half-dozen oldest, whilst Lucy still struggled with her lessons among the juniors.

Once the girls were fluent at reading and could copy in a neat hand, or even compose a short letter of condolences or acceptance of an invitation, most people would have considered them sufficiently prepared for the humble rôles awaiting women in Beccles. However Miss Hayle added to this some arithmetic, addition, subtraction and multiplication of numerals and pounds, shillings and pence, before handing over responsibility twice a week to Dr Davey who provided some further training in mathematics and also taught them English grammar. It goes without saying that a knowledge of foreign languages and the Classics were viewed as quite unnecessary accomplishments for country girls who were most likely to marry and die here in the provinces.

Dr Davey's arrival was a signal to Miss Hayle that the boys from the John Leman School had marched down the road two-by-two, accompanied by Mr Barker and his heavy wooden cane, to play sports on the Common according to the weather and the season. Thereupon Miss Hayle would take the junior girls across the street to the John Leman schoolyard where they might play organised team games, thus leaving Dr Davey's pupils to study in peace. It was a system which worked extremely well.

Jessica's advent into this somewhat cloistered world caused quite a stir. She had walked there beside the others, but it had been Lucy and not Jessica who had clutched Carrie's hand, and she had put her thumb into her mouth again. This came out immediately Lucy observed some of her school cronies and she ran forward to greet them. Carrie took Jessica by the hand and began introducing her to the more senior girls. There was a hush in the Inn yard as all the juniors turned round to stare at the newcomer. At that moment Miss Hayle arrived from her cottage further along Ballygate. Now it happened that Betty Jarvis had called upon Miss Hayle and had prudently apprised her of Jessica's unusual appearance. The plump lady therefore bustled up with a kindly expression, holding out her hand to be shaken and exclaiming for all to hear, "You must be Miss Jessica. So pleased you are to join my classes. Ladies," she turned to address the junior girls with a particularly firm glance, "this is Miss Jessica Rich who lives at Roos Hall on the Bungay road. Please welcome her to our midst." There was a scattering of applause from the senior girls who knew what was expected of them, and a continuation of hostile stares from the juniors, especially when Miss Hayle continued, "Jessica will join the preparatory class for the time being, until I am able to assess her abilities. She will sit beside Marion Mather, who will guide her until she becomes familiar with our customs. Marion?"

"Yes, Miss Hayle," Marion looked rather pleased to have been selected as she accepted the instruction.

"Now, indoors everyone," Miss Hayle said as she unlocked the door that led to the attic. "Hang up your cloaks and bonnets, and take your places. Good morning, Miss Carrie, I'm glad to see you are still with us this year. It is so important for young ladies to continue their education if they can."

Young Lucy was absolutely furious that she had not been given charge of Jessica's introduction to school life but that Miss Hayle, prompted no doubt by Betty Jarvis who had observed the child's hostility, had chosen Marion Mather, a nine-year old who was a quiet and careful pupil. Marion's older brother, Benedict, was one of the notorious bullies at the boys' school, and all who knew the family, prosperous Beccles attorneys, were amazed at the contrast between the siblings. There were gasps or surprise and further stares as Jessica removed her Dutch hood and hung it on a vacant peg at the end of the row behind the door. When she sat down in class, those sitting around her immediately noticed a lack of curls peeping from under her muslin cap, as well as the high neck of her gown which bulged at the back, whereas the other children mostly wore round-necked gowns with simple flat collars leaving their necks bare. Their pinafores followed the same neckline, and here Jessica's garments corresponded with theirs, as did her footwear. What was the reason for the particular style she wore? A whispering and murmuring began among the ranks.

"Silence!" Miss Hayle addressed them. "Catherine will read us the Morning Prayer," she said, indicating Carrie, "for which we shall all stand, and when we sit down afterwards I shall expect complete quiet unless asked to speak, is that clear?"

"Yes, Miss Hayle," everyone murmured, and Jessica's school life had begun.

CHAPTER VI
A Family Conference

Two years have passed. Jessica has done well in her lessons and has already joined the class of senior girls. Lucy has also made good progress, partly through rivalry with Jessica and partly because Alfred Jarvis has spoiled her with many a treat. Hugo is still struggling with Latin declensions and translations of the Classics at the John Leman School, while little Peter, now eight but never likely to prove a scholar, still waits for his formal education to begin. Carrie has left school and is at home helping her mother, which is just as well as Mrs C has been delivered of another pair of twins, girls this time, while her former toddlers are now active four-year olds and making just as much mischief as a pair of fox cubs.

At the Bear & Bells, Peter Jones has been given a partnership and therefore expects to take over the licence upon Bob Jarvis's retirement. Peter now carries out all the hardest tasks, such as handling the barrels and driving to and from the brewery, leaving Bob to lean over the bar to chat with his farmer friends. Betty Jarvis still walks daily to Roos Hall, though increasing stiffness in her limbs makes active labour more painful. Briggs is a little more frail, but the remaining staff are unchanged. There is a fine new barn, brick-built and tiled so that it cannot easily be burned down again. There is more room inside it, so that a pony-cart has been acquired which Mrs Jarvis may use for errands required by her position. In the stable next to the noble Pharaoh is a skewbald pony called James which, when not required by Mrs Jarvis, Jessica is permitted to ride about the estate. Ted, the stable lad, now somewhat wiser for his years and full of contrition every time he sees Jessica's head still wrapped in its muslin cap, and with only the slenderest stray blonde hair escaping from beneath its pleated rim, has given of his own time to teach Jessica how to ride and how to groom and feed the pony. Of a Saturday afternoon, and in secret defiance of Mr Ainsworth's instructions, Jessica has ridden James to the Ringsfield Farm and has helped Peter and Mrs Caldicott's older twins, Jonathan and Christopher, to learn to ride on a mount more suited to their size than the Sorrel horses. Indeed the latter have been hired out to Wilson's Livery Stables where they spend most of their days, but Alfred Jarvis has realised that this still does not cover the entire cost of their keep. He has it in mind to sell them and leave the Black heavy horses to take on all the work of the farm.

JESS OF ROOS HALL

And what of Mr Ainsworth? When that gentleman returned, much the worse for wear, from his excursion to Yarmouth, he was furious to learn that his tenant, Alfred Jarvis, had been left in charge of the building of the new barn, and that work upon the project had actually commenced. Mr Ainsworth had assumed that his own absence would ensure the postponement of the project. This would enable him, he thought, to take for his own use the funds supplied by Sir Charles for the building work. He would then rely upon subsequent income from the estate to pay the builder in due course, and a very distant course at that. In order to make good the shortfall, Mr Ainsworth raised the Ringsfield rent by as much as one third, and he took every opportunity to slight Alf Jarvis, both in conversation and in denying him access to the grounds of Roos Hall, or in sending him upon some other errand, anything which would prevent him from working closely with Mr Josiah Mason. Fortunately that craftsman had sufficient respect for Mr Jarvis, with whom he had family connections anyway, to make an honest job of his task.

However, before Mr Mason was able to present the account for his labours, Mr Ainsworth betook himself to Yarmouth again, and inquiries made there on Mr Mason's behalf failed to locate him. This time Pharaoh had been left safely at home in his stable, and Mr Ainsworth had ordered Ted to drive him into Beccles in the pony-cart so that he might take the public conveyance from the King's Head. Mr Mason's emissary troubled to inquire for Mr Ainsworth at all the most respectable lodging houses and hostelries in Yarmouth, but drew a complete blank. To all intents and purposes that gentleman had vanished. There was much anxiety among the staff at Roos Hall at this news, and Mrs Jarvis was debating whether she should inform Mr Russell, or even Sir Charles Rich, when Mr Ainsworth returned, scruffy and drunk as before, and riding upon the back of a waggon heading for the brewery at Bungay. Mrs Jarvis was even obliged to pay off the carter for his kindness.

One grey autumn afternoon some months later, two very strange gentlemen called at Roos Hall. They arrived in a curricle of a rather careworn appearance and drawn by a carriage horse that had evidently known better days. Briggs, looking out from the window beside the front door, saw them descend from the vehicle and observed that one of the gentlemen was very tall and bulky, whilst the other was much shorter and quite thin. Both men wore tall black beaver hats, the fat man's being wider in circumference and with a curlier brim that that of his companion. Both wore black frock coats and black cravats over their white stocks. The gentleman of more ample proportions sported a florid embroidered waistcoat and russet coloured breeches above his pale hose, while the thinner fellow was garbed all in grey down to his black shiny boots. Ted, whom Mrs Baines had roused from an hour of pleasant post-prandial somnolence in the warmth of the kitchen, had stepped to their horse's head, allowing the two gentlemen to advance side by side to the front door. Now Briggs had taken an instinctive dislike to the cut of these two visitors and had asked one of the maids to alert Mrs

Jarvis. Thus, when the front door was opened in response to an imperious pull at the bell, it was the indomitable Housekeeper whom the callers faced.

Both gentlemen lifted their hats and bowed their heads in unison and as if with supreme condescension. The thin one spoke, whilst the larger man merely observed the scene with a somewhat fatuous grin spreading from side to side of his chubby countenance. "Good afternoon, Madam. We have reason to believe that Mr Ainsworth Rich lives here. Is he at home?"

"I regret not," Mrs Jarvis replied with all the firmness she could muster, and thinking what very poor company Mr Ainsworth must keep if these fellows were two of his friends. "I am Mr Ainsworth's Housekeeper," she said, "may I assist you?"

"Let us introduce ourselves, then," the thin one continued. "I am Mr Doom and this is my colleague Mr Junkett." Mr Doom kept a very doleful expression as he spoke. "We are debt collectors, Madam, 'Junkett and Doom'. We have come from Yarmouth, but it may be that our renown has preceded us here at Beccles."

"Fortunately, gentlemen, I have never had the necessity to make your acquaintance," Mrs Jarvis replied tersely, guessing intuitively what was coming next.

"We represent a number of persons residing in Yarmouth and nearby with whom Mr Ainsworth Rich is accustomed to play cards; also some Captains and other officers serving with His Majesty's Navy upon ships which have called at Yarmouth or Lowestoft in recent months. You will appreciate, Madam, that for various reasons these gentlemen are unable to present themselves in person and have commissioned ourselves to pursue these matters on their behalf. Here is a list of the sums involved, Madam, if you would care to peruse it," and Mr Doom handed to Mrs Jarvis a page of foolscap paper bearing a long list of items.

Mrs Jarvis studied the list for some minutes. Here indeed were substantial amounts, sums which exceeded the monthly allowance she received from Sir Charles for the maintenance of the whole household. Were she to hand the list to Mr Ainsworth – and he had only gone riding into Bungay and might return thence at any instant – he would be bound to refuse payment entirely, giving rise probably to legal action; or he would deduct such debts as he deigned to pay from the revenues of the Estate and they would all suffer as a consequence. Why, he had already increased Alf Jarvis's rent out of sheer spite, and who knows what further threat Mr Ainsworth's actions might involve to the safety and livelihood of those living and working at Roos Hall, and particularly to little Jessica.

Mr Doom felt it was a propitious moment for some additional prompting as he enquired, "We are unsure, Madam, whether Mr Ainsworth Rich is a gentleman of independent means, or whether there is anyone else to whom we should apply for the satisfaction of these debts?"

This furnished Betty with the same conclusion as that she had reached already. "Quite right, Mr Doom," she replied, "if you wish to obtain a rapid outcome, I would advise you to apply to Mr Rich's Guardian, that is to Sir Charles Rich at Waverley Abbey House at Farnham in the County of Surrey."

"Is there no-one else nearby, Madam?" Mr Doom enquired. "Only we shall be obliged to incur additional charges if we have to refer this matter to one of our London correspondents instead."

Betty Jarvis hesitated for a moment, wondering whether Mr Russell might make a suitable intermediary, but she concluded that the matter was too private for that. Then she considered whether she should forward the list to Sir Charles herself, but again reached the same conclusion. To despatch these gentlemen to seek out Sir Charles would allow more time to elapse for the debts to be paid, and would give her an interval in which to report to her employer the visit received from these unpleasant characters. "No, I regret there is no-one else, gentlemen," she said, praying that there would not be a clip-clop of Pharaoh's hooves in the lane before they had departed.

"As you wish, Madam. We bid you good-day." Messrs Junkett & Doom bowed as one, turned on their heels and strode towards their vehicle. They observed as they went that Ted was no longer standing alone by their horse's head, but that Easton and the two groundsmen had silently arrived and had placed themselves alongside him, whilst in the kitchen doorway stood Mrs Baines with a huge iron ladle in her upraised hand. "Just in case they proposed any fisticuffs, Mrs Jarvis," as she explained later, "just in case it had come to that."

As the curricle left the driveway and turned back towards Beccles, Betty Jarvis felt a tremor run through her limbs and gladly accepted a dish of tea brewed by Mrs Baines while she recovered her composure. Confidentiality prevented her from revealing any details of the matter to the other staff, but they had all realised that the advent of Messrs Junkett & Doom represented a threat to their security, and were reassured to learn that Mrs Jarvis intended to report the visitation to Sir Charles.

Betty was glad of the interval before Mr Ainsworth returned from his ride, as this enabled her to put her thoughts in order and to consider how she would place them on paper to Sir Charles. She would feel most embarrassed at having to go behind Mr Ainsworth's back, but for all their sakes she felt obliged to do so. Presently there came the sound of hoof beats along the lane and Pharaoh galloped into the drive, but he was riderless! The reins swung wildly about his forelegs and were in great danger of bringing the animal down. Ted ran out into the yard and caught the uncontrollable creature, whose coat was all of a lather and whose eyes rolled white-rimmed with fear. While Mrs Jarvis hurried to join Ted, Mrs Baines hastened to call Easton and the groundsmen from the kitchen garden. They came running up as Ted shouted, "Mr Ainsworth must have had a fall somewhere!" They looked up and down the lane but heard and saw no one.

"We must go and search for him," Easton said. "Tom, do you bring sacks and two long poles from the outhouse, in case we need to make a stretcher."

They had gone quite a distance along the lane, past the woods and hedges that bordered the Ringsfield Farm, and were descending Barsham Hill within sight of the Church and just where the bridleway branches off to the right towards it, when they heard a dog barking. It was Arthur who came dashing out of the bushes, his teeth bared and his hackles raised. On seeing Ted, Easton and the other men, he quietened a little and led them through the willow brush and reeds to the edge of the flooded marshes. There Mr Ainsworth lay on the ground covered in mud, groaning but unconscious. He had obviously tried to keep hold of the reins after Pharaoh had unseated him, for there was a wide swathe cut through the brushwood to the spot where he lay. Mr Ainsworth must have hit his head on a willow stump or something hard, for blood was pouring from a wound in his temple. Ted took off his kerchief and made a pad of it which he pressed against the wound, whilst the others set about making a stretcher by cutting holes with a pocket knife in the closed ends of two large sacks and threading them on to the poles. Then they lifted Mr Ainsworth by his clothes as gently as they could on to the stretcher, in case he had any broken bones, and bound Ted's kerchief to the victim's wound with a second neckcloth. The return journey to Roos Hall seemed long and tedious.

Mrs Jarvis was at the gates as the stretcher party arrived. She made them lay the stretcher on the large oak table in the hallway, so that he could be attended to more easily when Dr Crowfoot had been called. Ted was sent to fetch him with James and the pony-trap, whilst Easton went to sponge down and quieten Pharaoh who was stamping and kicking in his stall, threatening to injure himself or to break out completely. They all realised that something unusual must have terrified the poor animal. Arthur too seemed unhappy, howling quietly to himself while he padded from stable to hallway, until he eventually resigned himself to lying down beneath the long table on which his master lay.

On arrival Dr Crowfoot called for some vinegar, hot water and plenty of clean bandages. He sent all the staff away except Mrs Jarvis. She helped him strip Mr Ainsworth to his underclothes as the doctor felt each limb one by one. Dr Crowfoot had received training as a naval surgeon by the East India Company, so he was well accustomed to diagnosing serious injuries. It seemed that Mr Ainsworth's legs were sound, though much scratched by their transit through the bushes. His ribs seemed to be in place and there was no sign of blood on his breath, so no puncture to his lungs fortunately, as Dr Crowfoot remarked. As the physician slipped Mr Ainsworth's coat from his right arm Mrs Jarvis heard him utter an oath. "He has fractured a bone in his lower arm," he said, "and I suspect that the shoulder is also affected. Yes, I thought so, a broken collarbone too. No puncturing of the skin, though, so I shall bandage the arm to his chest and he must stay like that for several weeks until it heals. I'll cup the head wound to draw out the bad blood, then we'll swab his injuries with vinegar. His skull feels intact, Mrs Jarvis, so he should recover from his concussion quite soon."

Mr Ainsworth, transferred to his bed with his right arm tightly bound to his chest and his head wound similarly swathed, did not recover consciousness before the doctor left. "If he does not wake by midnight, call me again," Dr Crowfoot said. "If he wakes of his own accord but cannot see, or his vision is impaired, call me also as the wound will have to be reopened and cupped once more. I will not cup him elsewhere as your stable lad told me he had already lost a deal of blood. Needless to tell you, Mrs Jarvis, that good broth and a rest in bed will heal him faster than you'd expect."

Fortunately Mr Ainsworth did recover consciousness that evening and the first words he said were "Hello, Arthur," to his dog, who had risen from the floor and had come to his bedside, on the left side where lay the uninjured hand. Mrs Jarvis, who had been dozing whilst keeping vigil in an armchair, rose and came across to the patient to enquire after his health. Of course, as soon as he was conscious, Mr Ainsworth started to swear, but then calmed a little as he took the glass of water Mrs Jarvis proffered him and considered his various injuries. His arm and shoulder and his head, he told her, hurt like the devil, and why was he all trussed up like a goose for the oven? This being explained, he pronounced that he ached all over but supposed these were bruises since he had no other sharp pains. Betty Jarvis then enquired what had occurred to cause the accident.

"I was riding along the bridleway past Barsham Church," Mr Ainsworth began, "and had come down the incline to the point where the path meets the marshes, which are naturally flooded at this time of year. I was paying attention to my horse and not looking about me, but Pharaoh must have noticed something strange for he began to fidget. Then I suddenly became aware of a dark shadow out on the marshes, changing its shape like smoke rising from a bonfire. Arthur started to growl and bark as I observed that the black shape was bowling towards us, tumbling over as it came. Pharaoh started to buck wildly and Arthur simply ran off howling down the track with his tail between his legs. Then the black creature was upon us. I cannot think of it in any terms other than some malignant being, for it enveloped me in its darkness and I smelt the foul stink of its breath."

"Like a wet dog?" Mrs Jarvis asked quietly.

"Yes, like a dog that's been rolling those marshes. Pharaoh kept bucking so wildly, and while I could see nothing for the darkness I fell out the saddle. Pharaoh set off at a gallop; I still had hold of the reins but he dragged me along through the bushes till I came to the water at the edge of the marshes. I thought that if I held on further I might drown. I believe that the cut on my forehead came from one of Pharaoh's hooves as he galloped away.

"What was it I saw, Mrs Jarvis?" Mr Ainsworth demanded. "Was it Black Shuck, that evil creature they talk of in the taverns, the one which attacked people praying in the Bungay and Blythburgh churches during the Great Storm two hundred and more years ago? They say 'tis a harbinger of death, Mrs Jarvis. I suppose that means I am likely to die of my injuries?"

"Oh, we hope not, Mr Ainsworth, not if you rest and eat well as Dr Crowfoot has instructed. As for Black Shuck," she continued, "I have seen him several times in the lane between here and Beccles, and I'm still alive to tell the tale. I've even felt the creature's presence in the cellar of our own tavern. Whenever I encounter it, I merely hold tight my crucifix and pray hard, and that seems to send it away."

"But some people in those two churches were burned to death, were they not? I felt no burning sensation at all, just slimy warmth and a choking of my breath," Mr Ainsworth continued.

"Yes, but there was a storm raging all those years ago," Mrs Jarvis explained, "and lightning struck both churches repeatedly, whatever the parishioners said they saw looking like a savage black hound breathing fire racing up the nave to cause death and destruction before the alter. There wasn't any lightning about yesterday, just a damp and chill gloom."

"I seem to have had a fortunate escape," Mr Ainsworth sighed and fell into a natural sleep, and Arthur lay down again on the rug at the foot of his bed.

Betty Jarvis had already decided she should spend the night at Roos Hall while Mr Ainsworth's condition was in doubt. One of the housemaids, who normally left the Hall at dusk, took a message to Bob Jarvis at the Bear & Bells. Then Betty sat down at Mr Ainsworth's escritoire to write to Sir Charles. Now that she needed to report the accident to Mr Ainsworth's Guardian it would be much easier, she thought, to mention the advent of the debt collectors at the same time, almost by way of a postscript to her main theme. After giving a full account of Mr Ainsworth's injuries and indicating that his horse had thrown him after being frightened - she was careful to avoid indicating the presence of any supernatural manifestation – Betty added the following paragraph:

"This same afternoon we received a visit from two gentlemen from Yarmouth who professed themselves to be debt collectors and asked to see Mr Ainsworth. They pressed for settlement of some expenses, which have apparently been incurred in that town. Taking into consideration Mr Ainsworth's incapacity, I took the liberty of referring these two gentlemen, named Mr Junkett and Mr Doom, to yourself care of Waverley Abbey House. I trust that I have acted correctly and in accordance with your wishes. I also intend to advise Mr Russell of Mr Ainsworth's condition, in case there may be matters regarding the direction of the Estate which need attention prior to Mr Ainsworth's recovery."

Mrs Jarvis addressed the letter to Sir Charles care of White's Club, believing that it would reach him there in advance of any action taken by Messrs Junkett & Doom.

It was the following evening, when Mr Ainsworth was seemingly on the mend, but sore and in pain (and calling loudly for supplies of alcohol which Mrs Jarvis dispensed only sparingly), but without any apparent ill effects from his concussion, that Betty Jarvis allowed herself to walk home to the Bear & Bells, rather later than usual. She wondered, as she walked along the pitch black lane this dark moonless night, guided merely by a candle twinkling in the window of a distant cottage that marked the junction of the road with Ballygate, whether she might expect to experience Black Shuck tonight, since he had seized upon Mr Ainsworth so recently. Yes, the dog or evil spirit, or whatever it was, was certainly the harbinger of ill fortune, for a Mr Doom had called at the door and now Mr Ainsworth's sins at the gaming table, and his irresponsible use of his Guardian's funds, were about to catch up with him.

Bob Jarvis and Peter greeted her warmly when she reached home. "Sit you down by the fire Mrs Jarvis," Peter said, "and I'll bring you a tot of brandy. You must have had a trying time and it will do you good." Presently the last customer left the tavern, Bob Jarvis bolted the door for the night and he and Peter joined Betty at the fireside. "How is Mr Ainsworth?" he asked.

"He seems to be recovering successfully," Betty replied. "There have been no further effects from his concussion. Dr Crowfoot called again today and says that the breakages are simple fractures which should mend easily in time. Briggs is staying up to watch over him tonight. My chief concern was to keep Mr Ainsworth from drinking large quantities of wine or spirits. That would only make his blood flow again, and with a head wound Dr Crowfoot advised against it."

"What happened to cause the accident?" Bob Jarvis enquired. "The girl you sent with a message told me Mr Ainsworth had fallen from his horse, but she gave no further details."

"It would seem that Mr Ainsworth had an encounter with Black Shuck," Betty replied. The two men looked shocked as she repeated the facts which the victim had given her, concluding with the thought that it was only Arthur's loyalty which had shown the men where to find him.

There was a pause and then Peter said, "Now I may tell you something which I have not dared to mention before. I have seen Black Shuck myself along that same stretch of road. I was driving the waggon with a load of empties and Jack Wilson had given me Beavis, that bay gelding that's the steadiest of his horses. The thing, and even by daylight I could not make out more than just a black shape, changing its form as it approached, rather like a large hairy dog when it runs, as I say, it came out of the bushes beside the road, crossed it and vanished up the slope on the other side. Beavis was entirely terrified and leapt forward at such a pace that half the empty barrels bounced over the tailboard. It took me ages to stop him and return to retrieve the barrels, and even then I was shaking too lest I came upon that thing again. That's the second time I have met with the creature, the first being down in the cellar here, as you will recall."

"'Tis supposed to bring bad luck, even death," Bob Jarvis commented, "but Mrs Jarvis has met with it several times and she's still with us, are you not, my dear, and in reasonable health for her age. And you're young and healthy Peter, so I am not really convinced that it is an evil spirit, though I confess some curiosity as to its true nature." Bob looked up at the clock on the wall over the mantelpiece. "Time for bed, everyone," he said, and they all retired for the night.

JESS OF ROOS HALL

At this time in early October, a family conference had been taking place at the Ringsfield Farm. It was held after supper in the dining room, where the embers still glowed in the hearth and added to the light shed by candles set at either end of the long oak table. Everyone sitting around it had a drink in one hand and dipped into piles of Martha's shortbread with the other. Alf Jarvis and Jim Caldicott had tankards of beer, their wives had glasses of homemade cider, and the two children, Carrie and Hugo, had mugs of warm chocolate. Little Peter was asleep in bed upstairs, and Lucy had been bribed to sit up in the Caldicott cottage reading a book to the older twins and keeping watch over the younger ones.

1793 had been a bad year for the farm. To begin with, the weather had been bad, bad for their crops that is. A cold dry spring had stopped the grain crops from growing lush and tall and the turnips, which were in the Big Field this year, from producing an early crop of leaves for the stock. Even the peas had withered on their stems. Then a hot dry summer had turned unredeemably wet before harvest so that half the grain had perished, diminishing by that amount the income to be had from it. Fortunately the rain had benefited the oilseed, the clover, the late grass, and the turnip roots which would provide ample forage for the coming winter. However disease had got into Alf's precious stock again and had stolen away his profit.

Now Sir Charles had encouraged Alf's plan to cross his Suffolk Dun cows with Tommy, the Norfolk Shorthorn bull, and had even paid the service fees. A fine crop of heifer calves had resulted, there being but two bull calves which had to be sold off for veal. However the hot, dry June and July, before the rains came, had encouraged the rinderpest, and many of the heifers had to be slaughtered. No income was to be expected from the survivors until they were mature enough to be sold. Sir Charles had not permitted cross-breeding of the Norfolk Horn sheep and there had been a severe outbreak of scrapie in the spring which had hit the ewes at lambing time. The orphan lambs from the slaughtered ewes had not all survived hand-rearing, despite the best care that Bill Foster could give them. This meant that the wool crop was seriously diminished and was also poor in quality from those animals which had proved resistant to the disease.

"About the only sickness we lacked this year was the swine fever," Alf Jarvis opened the conference on a gloomy note, "and other farmers have suffered that blight as well. Since we have so many turnips I shall let the pigs into part of the Big Field whilst we pull up the remainder. At least we have profited from the piglets this year. We shall need to keep all the lambs born next spring in order to rebuild the stock. This means that the only sheep we can sell will be some of the older ewes, and they will not fetch much as mutton instead of lamb. I intend to take those to market in Beccles for the Christmas trade. One or two of the dairy cows are drying out from old age and I fear we must send them to the slaughter too. As we have suffered a financial loss I am unable to afford to

replace them, so there will be less milk for sale and we must try to sell more butter and cheese instead, rather than keeping it back for our own use. There is a
dairy shop at this end of Ballygate owned by Bert Sawyer. I have had a chat with
him and it seems there may be business to be done. He informed me that the
two cows in the John Leman School field are to be slaughtered and not replaced,
and the field will be let out a most reasonable rent so that it will continue to provide an income for the School. That field will feed many more animals than
have ever grazed it, especially if we were to supplement the grass with some of
our surplus turnips. They would not sell in the market this year, as everyone has
a good crop after the rain, so we must reckon on using them for feed."

"What are you planning, husband?" Martha broke in, her face flushed with
anticipation.

"I'm planning that I shall take the Sorrels to the fair at St Faith's next week,"
her husband replied. "If they fetch a good price I shall purchase a Lincoln ram
so that next year's lambs will be more resistant to the scrapie. Barney, our
Norfolk ram, is past his best and lost condition whilst struggling against the disease. We can say he succumbed to it, if anyone asks.

"But is that not deception, Papa?" Hugo asked. "What would Mr Ainsworth
say?"

"Mr Ainsworth has raised our rent out of all proportion," his father replied. "I
see it as my duty to protect my family and to ensure that my land remains productive."

"May we go to the Fair?" Carrie asked in order to relieve the tension.

"Indeed you shall," Alf responded, "in fact we shall all be going and shall leave
Bessie and Anna to care for the farm. I have decided to pasture some of those
black cattle from Scotland that are always brought to the Fair. Other farmers
hereabouts fatten them on their fallow fields, especially now that ditches are
being dug to drain the marshes and provide more grazing land. We shall rent
the John Leman pasture quite cheaply, and the extra turnips will see the beasts
through the winter. We also have enough oilseed to keep all our cattle healthy."

"How does that work, Papa?" Hugo asked. "Do we not have to pay for the new
cattle?"

"No, lad, 'tis all done on credit with the banks these days. That's to save folks
carrying about large sums of money which might be stolen or spent before it
reaches its rightful owner. I merely sign a contract and give a promissory note
payable after three months. By the time that is due, in the New Year, we shall
have sold our Christmas stock, and I intend to thresh the wheat early, while
there is still a scarcity of it and the price is high. If necessary the barley can go
to the maltings at the same time to make up any difference.

"What we shall do," Alf continued, "is to fatten the Scottish beasts for the
market next spring. The cattle are driven down from Scotland, from Falkirk or
Carlisle, in vast numbers, hundreds at a time. Some go to each of the fairgrounds
and some go straight down the North Road to the Smithfield Market in London.

Some hundreds are taken to the Fenland fairs, through Spalding and Wisbech, and many are to be found at St Faith's near Norwich, which is where we shall look for them. The Scottish drovers leave the cattle once they're sold and return home. When our cattle have been fattened and are ready for market again, we shall either hire a drover to take them on to Smithfield, or we might realise their sale price more swiftly if we take them there ourselves. At the same time we could dispose of other surplus stock, such as any geese left over from the Christmas trade."

"How will the geese travel all the way to London, Papa?" Hugo asked.

"Ours will go in the waggon, Hugo," Alf replied, "others walk there, some with their feet dipped in pitch and sand to harden them, or some folks even make them little felt shoes to walk upon."

"Now that I would like to see!" Hugo remarked with a laugh.

"Unfortunately, those are not the only changes which I will need to make," Alf announced, and the cheerful faces around the table became more sombre. "I am obliged to dispense with the services of Bessie or Anna, as we can no longer afford to employ both. As they have worked for us so loyally for so long, I have suggested that they share the milking and the dairying for the time being, one working the mornings and the other the afternoons. This will permit them to do turn and turn about at their ease. Neither of them seems about to marry at the moment, so I have proposed that they take care of our wool crop and spin it. That should pay the rent of their cottage as I shall be able to sell the yarn for a much higher price than we receive for the raw wool."

"As for the milking," Alf continued, "I have asked my dear daughter Catherine," and Alf placed his arm around Carrie's shoulders where she sat next to him, "if she will take over milkmaid duties for either of the other girls. As we are losing a few of our dairy herd this may not prove quite so onerous. My dear wife, Martha, will continue to rule house and home as she has always done, and Jeannie here, Mrs Caldicott, will help with the housework and the dairying as she does at present."

"Bill Foster is feeling his age and has approached me to see if he may leave the farm and retire to his sister's house in Northgate," Alf announced. "It was that which encouraged me to think of pasturing the Scottish cattle. We shall take only bullocks, so no milking will be involved, and Bill would be able to watch over them for us from his sister's house which is nearer the water meadows. Also, the field I have rented contains a large shed where we can store the fodder and where Bill can take shelter in foul weather.

"Frank will stay on in the cottage he shares with Bill, and we shall look for a lodger to pay for the spare bed. As there will be only the Fen horses to groom and work, Frank will have more time on his hands, so he has agreed to care for the pigs, whilst Jim here, Mr Caldicott, will care for the sheep in addition to the cows. Responsibility for the hens and geese will be shared by Peter and Lucy," Alf concluded.

JESS OF ROOS HALL

At this juncture Alf Jarvis rose from his seat and walked round the table until he stood behind his elder son, Hugo. "There is one further change which I'm obliged to make," he said, "and which I know will upset all of you, since you will be most sensible of the feelings of the person concerned. I wish Peter to attend the school in Ballygate before he becomes too old to learn. I have agreed with Dr Davey that he may take Hugo's place, and I have also agreed with Lucy, subject to some chosen frippery which she may buy at the Fair, that she will escort Peter to and from school and will call for Miss Jessica as usual. As Lucy is now able to join the Senior Class at her school, that may also prove persuasive.

"Hugo, my dear lad," Alf said, placing his hands on the boy's shoulders, "I did wish to you to complete your education at the John Leman School and go on to higher things, but I regret we just cannot afford it. As it is, I have been paying additional sums for your lessons in Greek and Latin since you joined the Senior School. I need to ask you, Hugo, to make a noble sacrifice by starting to earn your own living. I have been offered a situation for you by Stan Stevenson who owns a wherry on the River Waveney. He travels up and down between Bungay and Norwich or Yarmouth carrying coals, fish, flour, timber and other supplies which he collects form the quays and delivers to the staithes along the river. His current apprentice, Timothy, has completed his indentures and his father is aiding him to buy a boat of his own. Stan needs a new apprentice to help him and said he would be pleased to take you on. I have agreed that you should start work in the New Year, thus allowing you to complete the autumn term at school and to say a proper farewell to your friends. It will also provide time to think about the position, though Mr Stevenson would welcome a quick decision as to whether you would be willing to take it."

"Oh, Papa," Hugo almost sobbed but fought back his emotions as he asked, "May I meet with Mr Stevenson to see how he is?"

"Better than that, lad, I have arranged for Stan to take you on the boat as a passenger, from Beccles up to Bungay, so that you can watch the work that Timothy does, how he manages the horse and the towline and opens the gates to the locks. From Beccles to Yarmouth or Norwich the boat is under sail, so you would learn how to handle a sailing boat. That doesn't sound too disagreeable does it?"

"No, Papa. I'll be happy to try it out," Hugo responded.

"Dear Hughie," Martha added, placing her hand on her son's arm, "we much regret taking you from your school and sending you to work when you have yet to reach your twelfth birthday, but it happens to other boys too."

"Yes, it does, Mama. I've seen boys leave the school early, more particularly when there is a younger brother still waiting for his education. I shall have to make sure I enjoy this last term. One thing for certain, old Davey won't bother me with Latin now he knows I shall not be staying on."

"Keep up your mathematics, Hugo," his father admonished him. "That will assist with what Stan Stevenson has to teach you, for he has sailed the oceans on merchant ships and knows all there is about navigation. You will also need your Accounts to tally up the stores you collect and deliver. Now the Fair does not begin until the 17th of the month, that's Thursday week, so Carrie and Hugo, time for bed. You may tell Peter and Lucy all that has been agreed, for they are uninformed of the details. I declare this family meeting closed." Alf banged the table with his fist and finished his tankard of beer. The Caldicotts returned to their cottage and peace reigned on the ground floor of the Ringsfield farmhouse. Not so upstairs where the younger generation chattered far into the night about all the new developments.

* * *

One further incident occurred at this time in the lives of those at Roos Hall. Mr Ainsworth had now left his bed but still kept to his room, well wrapped in a thick Turkish robe. Woollen rugs swathed his knees whenever he sat reading in an armchair or writing at his escritoire. One evening when Briggs was feeling rheumaticky, Jessica offered to carry upstairs the tray bearing Mr Ainsworth's dinner. Mrs Baines gave her a long look and asked, "Are you sure you wish to do that, Miss Jessica? If Mr Ainsworth is angry or abusive towards you, you leave the tray outside the door and come right back down again. Mrs Jarvis will go to him then, for she does not stand any nonsense."

Jessica happened to know that Mrs Jarvis had already left for the night, so she walked upstairs steadily, feeling the risers with her feet and holding the heavy tray as carefully as she could. She slid it on to a pier table that stood in the gallery outside Mr Ainsworth's room and knocked on the door. "Enter!" a brisk voice commanded from within. Jessica turned the handle until the door was open, then picked up the tray and walked slowly into the room. Mr Ainsworth regarded her with surprise and seemed speechless as she deposited the tray on the table beside him. "Hello, Jessica," he said eventually, "kind of you to think of me."

"I thought I would come to inquire how you are, Mr Ainsworth? Does you head still hurt, and your arm?"

"Yes, they do, Miss, but I think I shall soon make a recovery. Tell me, has Pharaoh forgotten his fright, and is Ted giving him plenty of exercise?"

"Yes, he is, sir, thought he's only riding him around the Park at present as he thinks Pharaoh would be too afraid to go along the lane for quite a while. I talk to him every day whilst I'm grooming James, and I take Arthur with me also, so that Pharaoh doesn't feel lonely."

"You're at ease with those animals, are you not, Miss Jessica? Does you head still pain you these days?"

"No, not now, Mr Ainsworth, but my hair is taking such a long time to grow. Now, eat your dinner, sir, please," she ordered peremptorily, "before it all grows cold." Jessica turned and left the room.

CHAPTER VII
The Fair

The seventeenth day of October had arrived at last. At the Ringsfield Farm, the previous day had been filled with preparations for the journey. The cows had been brought into the byre and would survive on hay, so as to enable Bessie and Anna to milk them more quickly without having to fetch them in from the meadows. This gave them more time to cool and churn the milk, make up any butter required, feed the pigs, the geese and the hens, collect the eggs and to care for the four lively and noisy Caldicott children. Martha had done a huge bake, both for the sustenance of those travelling on the road and for those left behind. A large wooden chest which fitted under the bench of the hay-waggon had been filled with clean kerchiefs, each one individually packed with meats and pastries, together with flagons of ale, cider and milk. This should sustain them until suppertime which they would take at a farm on the outskirts of Norwich where Mr Russell had kindly reserved them lodgings. Although Mr Ainsworth was prevented by his injuries from attending the Fair, Mr Russell, as Sir Charles's Bailiff, would be bound to be there, and whilst Alf had spoken boldly enough at the Jarvis family conference, he still had to ensure that the new ram he meant to purchase was either acquired without Mr Russell's knowledge of else with his full approval.

It was a good twenty-five miles to the fairground north of Norwich on a gently sloping stretch of grassland known as Bullock Hill and which had once belonged to the Priory of St Faith. At the moment the weather was set fair after a wet September and early October, but Jim Caldicott and Frank Briggs had spent the previous afternoon fixing hoops made of hazel stakes to the top rim of the waggon so that a tarpaulin could be pulled over it in the event of rain. There was therefore not much room for passengers, so Jim and Frank were to ride the Sorrels, whilst the children and Bill Foster occupied the remaining floor space, leaving Mrs C, Martha, and Alf Jarvis to perch close together on the driving bench. They set off at dawn with the two Fen Black horses well decorated with jingling brasses and ribbons plaited into their manes. If all went well they could expect to reach the fairground at noon.

From the farm they took the road towards Beccles, then turned left past Roos Hall on the way to Bungay where they would cross the river. Jessica had awoken early and had run to the gate to watch them pass. She had not been permitted to accompany them, as neither Sir Charles, Mr Ainsworth or Mr Russell would have approved. However she wished them an enjoyable outing and Carrie promised that they would purchase some pretty gift for her instead.

From Bungay the road ran across country through Ditchingham and past Woodton Hall where the Suckling family lived that had blood connections with the Rich family and with whose lands the Roos Hall estate had once been united. Three more small villages dotted their route, Kirstead, Brooke and Poringland, before they would reach the outskirts of Norwich at Lakenham. They had gone but a mile or two at an ambling trot when others joined them upon the road. They passed small flocks of sheep, though with no rams among them, a few cattle, and an ox-drawn waggon four storeys high which Alf informed his children was the sort often used to carry poultry to London for the Christmas trade. This one was indeed filled with cackling hens, a noisy cockerel and a layer each of geese and turkeys.

As they neared Norwich, there were hundreds of people walking or riding in the same direction, many landowners and farmers some of whom were known to Alf Jarvis, as well as the shepherds and cowmen who walked with the stock. They also passed journeymen and pedlars bound for the Fair. At Norwich, where they moved through the crowds beneath the city walls at walking pace, they were joined by jugglers and musicians. The children were almost beside themselves with excitement at the noise and colour around them. "Just look at the ribbons on that tray!" Carrie exclaimed as one pedlar snatched off the cloth covering his wares and flashed a smile at the family as they passed. "I shall watch for him at the Fair."

"You'll have plenty to set your heart on, Miss Carrie," Jeannie Caldicott commented as they drove on.

Soon they had left the suburbs of Norwich behind and were out in open farmland again, though the lanes were as crowded as ever. Ahead on the horizon people and animals seemed to be converging from all directions. This Fair was a traditional annual event organised these days by local landowners who lent their stockmen and servants to act as stewards. Thus when the Jarvis party arrived they were directed to one field to park their waggon and to a neighbouring more lush field where their horses might graze when not required. The tarpaulin being spread over the moist ground, Martha and Jeannie swiftly dispensed the picnic refreshments. As soon as they had eaten, Alf directed his staff to their particular tasks. Frank Briggs was to take General and Major to graze in the designated field, where they would be tethered to iron stakes hammered into the ground and well separated from other animals in case of dislike. On his return Frank was to take care of the waggon and protect it from thieves, whilst keeping an eye on the distant horses for the same reason. In due course, Alf said, either Jim or Bill would relieve him so that he might take his turn around the fairground.

Alf Jarvis, Jim and Bill walked off towards the stock enclosures, taking the two Sorrel horses with them. Hugo accompanied them at his own request, while Peter remained with Lucy and the ladies, who followed at a more leisurely pace since it was their intention to tour the merchandise stalls. All the stock for sale had been directed to one end of the fairground, near the wooden dais erected for the auctioneer. He would not function until tomorrow, to allow time for private sales, and then he would deal with the cattle, sheep, pigs and goats in that order, with the horses to be auctioned the following day. This placed Alf in an awkward situation since he would not know what funds he had available to purchase the new ram until the Sorrels had been sold. Meanwhile they had located the steward in charge of the horses and had been directed to one of a number of open-ended pens constructed of hurdles and set up in rows under a few tarpaulins to afford some shelter from the weather. The steward handed them a label bearing a lot number to be tied to the end of the pen, and with his pencil inscribed in a ledger details of their animals, age, sex, provenance, training and experience, for the information of the auctioneer. Should they accept a private offer in the meantime, the ledger entry might easily be deleted.

No mangers or buckets for feed and water were provided, so Bill Foster returned to collect those hanging from the back of the hay-waggon, whilst Alf and Jim moved on to examine the cattle. These were accommodated in larger pens with hurdles used to distinguish the various ownerships. There were lots of healthy Shorthorn heifers ready for breeding and Alf turned to Jim and remarked "This is where I'll bring ours when they are ready for sale. We'll make a better profit here than at Beccles." There was a pen full of Suffolk Dun cattle with their yellow faces and large soft eyes that made Alf's mouth water, and a Dun bull that he might have wished to put to his cows had he not been minded to use Tommy's services once more. They moved on to inspect the black beef cattle that had come from Scotland. These were kept in another field, again with lines of hurdles separating the various herds. They leaned over the entrance gate and Hugo spoke for all when he said, "Don't they look tired and thin!"

"So would you look tired and thin, lad, if you had just walked three hundred miles to be here," Alf responded.

"Is that how far it is, to Carlisle, or wherever it is they have come from?" Hugo enquired.

"Just so," Alf replied, then he turned to Jim and said, "We had better pick our beasts, then see if we can find their drover. How many do you reckon that field would take over the winter, Jim, thirty would you say?"

"That's as many as we have turnips and hay for once the grass has gone," Jim replied. "See there's one group over there seemingly more sturdy than the rest." Bill rejoined them together with the two sheepdogs as they walked round to the far side of the field. A drover, a tall, scruffy fellow with a homespun jacket above his tartan trews, used his shepherd's staff to lever himself up from the plaid on which he had been reclining as they approached. His dogs, a collie and white-haired terrier, glared steadfastly at Pip and Shep, but remained where they lay. The drover introduced himself as Jock McTurk and asked how many head of cattle they were wanting. He had sixty beasts still in his care, he said, of which nearly fifty were bullocks, so they would have a choice. Half a sale was better than none, so Jock urged them to select those animals they desired. He was not a dealer himself, he explained, but merely worked on wages of a shilling a day plus the commission he would receive when all the cattle had been sold. Thus, if they were not yet ready to take their beasts away, for the price of a good pair of boots for his return journey to Scotland, he would be willing to look after their cattle for a day or two until it was time to leave. They haggled and agreed upon a price.

"Have you the contract from their owner?" Alf enquired. Jock fumbled in his scrip and brought out a sheaf of papers. There were several copies of the same document in case the herd had to be split. Alf took one of the sheets and finding he had left his reading spectacles at home, or so he claimed, asked Hugo to oblige and to ready slowly. In the end Hugo completed a copy for each party and Alf signed his name where required. "Just as well you came with us, Hughie, and have had your education too, for we should not have been sure of our transaction otherwise." They watched as blue ribbons were tied to the ears of the animals they had chosen, then walked back to the fairground to look over the sheep.

Pip and Shep, who had already cast a somewhat disdainful glance at the black Scottish cattle, took a far greater interest in the sheep and had to be restrained with leashes. "Don't want them causing mayhem," Bill said, "there's too many loose dogs around already." They found that the ewes had been put in separate pens from the lambs, a cause of much bleating of families parted for the first time. It seemed there were few rams for sale and Bill Foster had not a good word for any of them. Their backs were not straight enough, their legs were too weak, their wool was too coarse or too thin.

Just at that moment a new ram arrived with two stockmen required to hold him as he butted everything in sight with his high bony forehead. "What breed is he?" Alf enquired, looking at the ram's white face and lack of horn.

"He be first cross from a Lincoln, Master, come here from Leicestershire. Very young, though, born late and has yet to see his second winter."

"What does that mean, Papa?" Hugo asked.

"It means that as yet he may not be mature enough, however lively he is, to be put to the ewes this season. However Lincoln stock are known to mature early, so he may just be old enough. Look at the wool on him! That's the longest and finest I have seen in some while. What was his parentage?" Alf asked the stockman.

"The ram was a Lincoln, Master, that's given him his wool and his liveliness, but his shape comes from the ewe. She is a new sort of creature being developed at Dishley, near Loughborough. 'Tis not a proper breed yet, Master, just one of the crosses which Mr Bakewell is trying to create new stock."

"I've heard of him, " Alf commented to the others. "They talk of him at the Norwich market, and even in Beccles too. How much do you ask for him?"

"Whatever the auctioneer can obtain, Master, the highest offer," the stockman replied. "We think he should sell nicely, for the right owner even better than a pure-bred Lincoln."

"Now that's an ambitious animal you're looking at there, Mr Jarvis." Alf turned round smartly to find Mr Russell breathing over his shoulder, the very person he did not wish to meet just then. Had he known it, Mr Russell was a member of the organising committee this year, so his presence at the fairground was inevitable. Introductions were made, including Hugo who was meeting the Bailiff for the first time, having always been at school when he had called hitherto. "I hear you're taking some of the black cattle for fattening," Mr Russell continued. "Had a poor harvest this year?"

"Yes, indeed, Mr Russell, the grain crop has been poor and I've had disease in my animals too," Alf replied.

"Corn prices are high now, but if you lack the grain to sell there's no profit to be made," Mr Russell said. "Whatever wheat you have, I would recommend you thresh it and sell it as soon as you may."

"Indeed, sir, that is what I had determined to do," Alf responded.

"I see you have put your two Sorrels on the market," Mr Russell went on, "they should fetch a fair price as their condition is good and they are not too old for carriage use. I think I may tell you that I know of at least one gentleman who will bid for them. Are you hoping to buy a new ram on the strength of it?"

"That was precisely my thinking, Mr Russell," Alf replied slowly. "Our present ram, Barney, is getting on in years, and although he resisted the scrapie back in the spring, his condition has declined a good deal. I was looking to purchase a Lincoln for its resistance to the scrapie, but none have appeared so far, except this one which I'm told is a first cross with something new."

"If I might say a word to you confidentially, Mr Jarvis," Mr Russell replied, "and this is quite apart from anything Sir Charles or Mr Ainsworth might say, for they do not have the same knowledge of the matter, I believe this ram may represent the start of a new line, and sheep bred from his progeny will have a fair chance of producing fine meat and wool more quickly. It will be an experiment, but it is one I would wish to see carried out, and I would even be prepared to back it with my own money. Would you be willing to make the endeavour, Mr Jarvis?"

"Indeed I would, sir. The problem is that until the Sorrels are sold I do not know how much I may offer for him," Alf replied.

"Let me make a suggestion then, Mr Jarvis. You bid for that ram in the normal way – it is no use my bidding for it since people know me and the price will leap out of all proportion, so bid and secure it. Should your Sorrels not reach the same amount, I will personally cover the difference."

"Thank you, Mr Russell, and for your understanding," Alf responded. "By-the-by, my Catherine has news from Miss Jessica that Mr Ainsworth is out of bed but still keeps to his room with his injuries. Thus we have been unable to consult him on any of our plans."

"I understand, Mr Jarvis. I think you have made a good choice of the black cattle and it must be right to drain some of those marshlands at Beccles and bring them into use. The population of London is increasing at a rapid rate, and they all need to be fed. I'll be there when they auction the sheep, in case you have further need of me."

"Thank you, Mr Russell, thank you, sir," they all murmured.

"There, now we have his approval. I thought we should be honest about it, should we not Papa?" Hugo remarked as they walked away to examine other stock. They checked over the pigs; there were plenty of Suffolk Whites like their own, and lots of black and tan Berkshire pigs which were slightly larger and a popular breed. As Alf had no plans for pigs at present, they moved on to the goats. Here there were some famous-looking billy-goats with long horns, often curving in different directions, and a number of mature nanny-goats obviously intended for milking rather than for the pot. Goats were popular as nibblers of ornamental lawns and could save any scything. However if they escaped their tether and managed to find their way to the vegetable garden, they could do great damage and not every landowner loved them. Bill Foster drew attention to a furious bleating coming from a corner pen. It was a tiny white kid which had perhaps just been separated from its mother and was alone and thirsty. In fact it was too young to lap properly and had upset the dish of water put beside it. "You'll need to put that one to a nanny-goat or it will perish," Bill said to the steward in charge of the goats. He merely shrugged his shoulders and turned away, leading Bill to conclude that the man was a house servant and no farm hand.

They looked briefly at the remaining stock, some exotic ducks and hens, a pair of peafowl, and some retrievers and gun dogs with their puppies. Then they went in search of the ladies in the commercial part of the fairground. Here there were rows of vendors' stalls; at one end a shambles with joints of meat and whole sides of beef or pork, and next to it a series of high wooden racks hung with pheasant, grouse and rabbits. Next came many types of clothiers and drapers offering goods from all parts of the country: rugs, blankets and quilts from Kidderminster; mattress ticking from Wiltshire; upholstery from the Midlands; fustian from Manchester; cottons, organdies, muslins and damasks from Yorkshire and Lancashire; kerseys, baizes and serge-cloth from Devon, together with some fine Honiton lace, and lots of silken and wool fabrics produced here in Norfolk, along with their very own worsted that was just perfect for Sunday suits. Here and there among the throng, pedlars traded their ribbons and boot-laces, and Carrie looked in vain for the man who had smiled at her on the road.

There were stalls selling vegetables, sacks of potatoes, of dried peas and grains, of hops for the brewing trade grown in Essex and brought thence in huge sacks, and there were sacks of wool like those produced on their own farm. Then there were stalls offering hot pies, and places where benches had been set out where one might consume savoury or confectionery treats, along with one's choice of coffee, tea or chocolate, or beer, wines and spirits. One might then be diverted by the troupes of jugglers and acrobats that haunted this fairground as any other, or by the puppeteer who had set up his small red and white striped tent wherein his dolls would act out their cautionary tales for the entertainment of the children. Mid-afternoon a marching band made its appearance, having stepped that way from Norwich, and entertained the idle with a medley of popular airs.

Alf and the others found Martha, Jeannie and the children sitting in one of the refreshment areas drinking tea and consuming large slices of fruitcake. The gentlemen joined them and Peter and Lucy eagerly showed their father their purchases. Carrie and the women had all bought winter bonnets, although Carrie had insisted on selecting a saucy colour as usual.

"I promised to buy something for Miss Jessica, Papa, but we have not seen anything she would wish for yet, have we?" she asked rhetorically.

"I know what she would really like," Hugo stated.

"What is that?" Carrie enquired.

"Some animal that she could treat as a pet. You know how she makes such a fuss of our stock at home," Hugo replied.

"Yes, but we would be obliged to obtain Mr Ainsworth's permission for that," Alf Jarvis interposed, "and we have enough difficulty in dealing with him as it is."

"Perhaps we could keep it for her," Hugo suggested.

"My lad, that would only provide an additional mouth to feed, when I am trying to achieve savings in our expenditure."

"But, suppose we bought something useful, an animal that would be useful to us?" Hugo persisted.

"But then we would be obliged to kill it and eat it eventually," Carrie pointed out, "and Jessica would be most unhappy about that." Nothing more was said and Bill Foster was sent to relieve Frank for an hour or so. Then they hitched up their waggon again and drove to their lodgings at a nearby farm to which Mr Russell had given them directions.

The following morning Alf, Jim and Bill attended the Fair early in order to observe the prices achieved by the stock that went under the auctioneer's hammer. Frank returned with the waggon to collect the ladies and the children. Hugo was supposed to join the other children, but he declined and on reaching the fairground sought the auctioneer's stand, slipping on to the end of a bench not far from his father. The half-sovereign Alf had given him to spend, a princely sum to compensate for the termination of his schooldays, still jingled unspent in his pocket.

The auctioneer had already disposed of most of the cattle by the time Hugo arrived. He could tell by the expression on his father's face that prices here were a good deal higher than those to which they were accustomed at the Beccles stock market. At this rate he wondered whether Alf would be able to purchase a new ram at all. Fortunately the auctioneer started by selling off the ewes and the lambs, which satisfied the needs of a number of purchasers. Now it came to the rams, and half a dozen Norfolk Horn rams were brought in, one after another, the final bids dropping steadily as each sale was completed. At the very end of the morning's business the ram they wanted was brought in and paraded round amid the straw. The ram bounded from side to side, defying the efforts of two stockmen to keep it still so that its conformation might be admired. The auctioneer from his tall desk on its wooden dais read from his ledger the information provided about the creature. Unexpectedly the bidding started low but soon gathered pace. Hugo watched his father who as yet had given no sign of any interest in the beast. Then the price levelled off and Alf raised his forefinger and nodded in the direction of the auctioneer. At once the bidding leapt forward again till there came another pause. Hugo saw his father look across at Mr Russell who was standing at one side of the assembly, and a smile crossed that gentleman's features. Alf renewed his bidding. Suddenly there was silence and the hammer fell. They had their new ram and Bill went to see it returned safely to its pen where it would remain until they collected it on the morrow.

It was noon and everyone made their way to the refreshment stalls. The Jarvis party rejoined the ladies and the children to partake of the pies, pastries and cheeses on sale and quenched their thirst with beer and cider. Carrie informed Hugo that a new bonnet had been found for Jessica which would fit lightly over her tender head and yet was a fetching colour so that she might not hesitate to wear it upon many a social occasion. "So there is no need for you to concern yourself with buying something for her," Carrie told her brother. Bill Foster was sent back to the waggon to relieve Frank Briggs, while Alf and Jim took their ladies to the jewellery stalls so that each might choose a new brooch or pin. The children lingered beside the puppeteer's tent and waited for his next performance.

Presently Hugo slipped away and returned to the auctioneer's audience. He was well through selling the pigs by now and Hugo listened with interest to the respective prices reached by Suffolk Whites and the more popular Berkshire black and tans. No doubt his father would appreciate the information in due course. Then the goats were brought in, by groups or singly in accordance with the owner's instructions. At the very end of the line came the little white kid they had noticed the day before. The stockman carried it under his arm, and when he set it down the little creature collapsed in the straw with only the faintest and most piteous bleat. Hugo, familiar with the lambs which Bill Foster had to hand-rear at home, guessed that the kid had not been fed properly since its arrival at the Fair.

There was scarcely anyone left on the benches now, for most of the farmers had gone for refreshments before the dogs and the birds should be auctioned later in the afternoon. Bidding started at five shillings, and Hugo clutched anxiously the half-sovereign hidden in his pocket. There was no response from the farmers, so the auctioneer dropped his price to half-a-crown. One farmer raised his hand and there was a long pause. "Half-a-crown, I'm bid," the auctioneer called. "Come along, gentlemen, I'm sure you will better that."

"Three shillings, sir," Hugo said quietly.

"Three shillings from the boy at the front here. Did I hear three-and-sixpence?" The farmer who had bid before raised his hand.

The auctioneer looked down on Hugo and asked quite kindly, "Will you go to four shillings, my lad?"

"Yes, sir, thank you," Hugo replied.

A smile crossed the rival farmer's face as he responded, "Four shillings and sixpence."

Hugo looked round at him and then at the auctioneer. "Five shillings," he uttered bravely.

"And sixpence," came the swift reply.

"Six shillings, sir," Hugo added quietly after a short pause.

"And sixpence," came again behind him.

"Seven shillings, I'm bidding, sir," Hugo spoke more slowly this time.

"And sixpence," again the rather jolly voice came from behind him. Hugo turned around and took another glance at the farmer, who pretended not to see him. Was this someone his father knew, someone who had recognised him and was playing a joke? "Eight shillings," he said firmly turning towards the auctioneer again.

"And sixpence once more," the farmer said.

"Nine shillings, sir," Hugo responded with some exasperation.

"Nine shillings and sixpence," the farmer replied. Hugo paused. Did he truly wish to spend the whole of his half-sovereign on a waif of a creature that looked as if it might not survive the journey home? Was he really convinced that this was the pet he wanted Jessica to have for herself, something that belonged to her and not to the beastly Mr Ainsworth or to Sir Charles whom they never saw? He had taken the coin out of his pocket and looked at it, not realising that the farmer behind him was watching intently too.

"Going at nine shillings and sixpence. Do I hear ten shillings, lad?" the auctioneer asked.

"Yes, sir, ten shillings it is," Hugo replied.

"At ten shillings?" the auctioneer looked at the farmer who shook his head with a grin. "All done at ten shillings, done!" and the auctioneer banged his gavel on the desk.

The audience broke for refreshments and Hugo walked up to the auctioneer and asked, "Please, sir, whom do I pay for my animal?"

"Go and find the fellow in charge of it," the auctioneer replied kindly. So Hugo did and found him replacing the kid in its pen. "I've brought the money,"

Hugo said. "May I take the animal now, and can I have a receipt for it please?" A receipt seemed to be beyond the stockman, so Hugo borrowed a pencil from one of the stewards and wrote upon the lot label which had been attached to the kid's pen. Then he asked the stockman to sign it.

Just then a rather unpleasant looking gentleman came up and the stockman handed him the half-sovereign. It appeared he was the owner, for he said, "Is that all, Jackson? The meat alone would almost fetch as much – well, perhaps not ...!" He looked down at the drooping kid, huddled in the straw, then turned abruptly and strode away.

Hugo understood immediately why the creature was in such poor condition. He picked it up in his arms and hurried off to find Bill Foster whom he knew would be sitting beside the waggon, and no doubt whittling some stick or other into a toy for one of the Caldicott children. "Why, Master Hugo, what have you done?" Bill exclaimed as he approached. "Whatever will your father say?"

"I spent my own money on it, Bill. 'Tis for Miss Jessica, if she is permitted to have it, and if not it can eat the grass in our orchard. We never have time to cut it."

"Let me have a look at it," Bill said, and took the kid into his arms. "The poor little thing is starving, if you ask me. It was too young to be taken from its mother. Perhaps she died, or perhaps she had twins and neglected this one." Just then the rest of the family party arrived, ready to leave the fairground for the night.

Alf Jarvis looked at the kid as Bill stood holding it, and then looked at his son. "Oh!," was all he said.

"Please don't be angry, Papa. I bought it for Miss Jessica, if they will have it at the Hall."

"It doesn't seem in very good condition," Alf stated. "I shall not ask how much you paid for it."

"In fact it could do with feeding right away," Bill said.

"Did anyone see goat's milk for sale here?" Alf asked.

"Yes, I did," Martha replied with a chuckle as she explained. "There was some on the cheese stall beside the benches where we sat for our afternoon tea. In fact," she added, "I was wondering at the time whether we should think of making goat's milk cheese for Bert Sawyer's dairy shop. It seems as though Hugo has answered my prayer." Hugo smiled gratefully at his mother.

Frank Briggs, who seeing the family gathered to depart had brought up the horses, was given a penny and sent in search of goat's milk. "Borrow a jug from the stall," Martha instructed him.

"Now I knew I needed to purchase something whilst here at the Fair," Alf said with mock severity, cocking an eye at Hugo as he pulled his driving gloves out of his pocket. "These have become quite worn out. Hand me your pocket knife," he said to Jim who was hitching up the horses. While the family watched with much astonishment, Alf cut off the tip of the thumb of one glove. When Frank returned with a jug of goat's milk, Alf asked him to pour a little into the neck of the glove whilst he held the cut tip firmly between finger and thumb. Then he squeezed the neck of the glove tightly whilst releasing the contents of the thumb into the kid's mouth as Bill held up its head with jaw open. Suddenly the kid realised what was happening and began to suck. They refilled the glove several times and repeated the performance. The bleating eased, the eyelashes dropped, and the kid fell asleep. Frank returned the jug to the stall while Jim remarked that he thought he had seen a goat or two at the farm where they lodged, so they could obtain further supplies overnight. Bill kept the kid beside him on the thick straw as he and Frank passed the night in the barn, and next morning the little creature was already looking more lively. They packed up the meagre possessions they had brought with them and set off again for the Fair, quite early because this was the morning when the Sorrels were to be sold.

When they reached the fairground the steward at the gate warned them that a group of gypsies had arrived overnight, bringing along a herd of half-wild ponies. These had been sent temporarily to the field where the black cattle were gathered and where there was a vacant pen. However the ponies were so unruly that they threatened to kick their way through the hurdles which provided the fencing. Indeed there was a tension in the atmosphere of the Fair today; they had sensed it as they arrived and had already noted the group of gypsy caravans drawn up on the horizon, with smoke rising into the crisp morning air from their cooking fires.

As soon as the hay-waggon drew up in its allotted space, Alf gave orders to his staff. While Frank unhitched and tethered the horses to graze, Bill should keep watch over the waggon, the two dogs and the kid. Once Frank had returned, Bill was to check the well-being of the new ram for which they had yet to pay. "Find out whether he walked here or came by cart," Alf instructed Bill, "because if he is not accustomed to walking you and Frank will need to build a crate for him. Jim," Alf turned to his stockman, "do you take a look at our cattle and make sure they are still safe. I'm off to find the auctioneer to enquire when our Sorrels are likely to be sold. Also to make sure they've not been stolen during the hours of darkness! Ladies," Alf turned to his family, "and children, I propose to depart for home together with all our new beasts around noon. Do not stray from your mother's side, and if you do become lost, please return here and wait beside the waggon. Is that understood?"

"Yes, Papa," they chorused.

"Hugo, you can come with me, if you wish, or you may prefer to help Bill instead."

"I would like to come with you, Papa, to watch our horses sold." Having ascertained that their Sorrels were likely to be auctioned half way through the morning , Alf and Hugo went to visit and feed the horses in their pen. They found the animals restive and nervous, listening to the neighs and screams of the wild ponies half a field away. Captain and Corporal whinnied at their approach and welcomed the presence of those familiar to them. Hugo refilled their buckets from the water-butts set up nearby and fetched more hay from a neighbouring pen. The two horses nuzzled him as he stroked their smooth coats and whispered how sad he was to see them go.

"A pity we have to sell them," his father commented, catching the glint of a tear in his son's eye and the choke in his voice, "but we must keep our land profitable."

They joined Jim at the gate overlooking the black cattle. Fortunately their bullocks, which Jock had been tending with due care, were in an enclosure one removed from that holding the gypsy ponies. These were milling around this way and that, restless and quarrelsome. Occasionally two stallions would rear up and paw at one another, and sometime a red weal would appear on a neck, rump or wither, where a kick or bite had found its mark. "I have established that the existing stock will be sold before those ponies," Alf told Jim, "so we must settle our accounts and try to be away before them. I do not wish to find those travelling before us on the road or we are liable to have some of our beasts go missing."

Alf, Jim and Hugo took their seats on one of the auction benches. The best-bred hunters and carriage-horses were being sold as they arrived. They watched as Mr Russell acquired a jet-black thoroughbred, which they guessed was for his own use, and Jim let out a whistle at the price he paid. Then at last the Sorrels were brought in. The handlers had given them a gloss with their soft leather cloths and Hugo thought they looked quite smart. He heard the auctioneer relate that they had been used for light farm work but were more accustomed to drawing carriages than waggons. As the bidding commenced Hugo looked around to see how many bidders there were and counted at least seven, some farmers but also some smartly-dressed gentlemen. At one point even Mr Russell put in a bid to push the price along, as Alf explained to Hugo later. Finally there were just two of the smarter gentlemen left, perhaps members of the aristocracy, Hugo thought, as the final hammer fell – so Corporal and Captain would go to a good home.

However they were obliged to wait until the purchaser left his seat before they were able to intercept him and obtain payment in the form of a promissory note. Mr Russell came up at that moment and countersigned the note, which would be sure to guarantee its prompt payment. At the same time he handed to Alf in cash the fifty guineas required to reach the purchase price of the ram. Alf paid the fee for the auctioneer's services to his clerk, and they paid for and collected the ram. This they led through the fairground, though with some difficulty, for it bucked and butted the whole way to the waggon. They tied its halter to one of the waggon's wheels and set Pip and Shep on guard. This quietened the ram a good deal and it began to nibble the surrounding grass. Lying underneath the waggon, the little kid let out a bleat at the new arrival and the two animals regarded each other with a look of surprise. The kid watched the ram feeding and hesitatingly took a bite at a blade of grass. "Reckon we'll soon be able to run her with the sheep," Bill Foster remarked as he observed the event.

Whilst waiting for the remainder of the family to return, Bill and Frank had made a crate for the ram out of pieces of hurdle held together with twine. "There's no way he will walk up the ramp into it when we let the tailboard down," Bill declared, "so we shall need to shut him inside it and lift up the whole thing by hand. If he struggles, as he surely will, that will be the devil of a task." Before they were ready to depart Frank was sent to obtain more goat's milk for the kid, Hugo to retrieve the buckets and haynets they had left with the Sorrels – the pen was empty and their horses had already gone, and Jim to find the ladies and the children and purchase refreshments for the homeward journey. Then it took the combined efforts of all four men to lift the ram in its crate into the waggon, and when they had done so it was found that there was little room for any passengers.

"Right, this is the way we shall arrange matters," Alf declared. "Jim and Frank and the dogs are to walk with the cattle anyway, and Bill shall join them until we reach the far side of Norwich. Then I shall call for volunteers among my children. Five miles from each of them in turn." Silence answered him. "I shall toss a coin upon it, then." Alf said, taking a halfpenny from his pocket. "Loser walks but takes the halfpenny." Peter stepped forward immediately and gained the coin, and Hugo offered also and the matter was settled between them. The ladies packed up their purchases and belongings and the tarpaulin was stretched over the hoops as it had begun to rain. Frank drove the waggon to the fairground gate whilst the other men collected the cattle. There was some chaos whilst their new animals passed by the gypsy ponies, but soon they were plodding along in fine style, accustomed as they were to being driven.

It took them more than two hours to reach the River Yare and so to leave Norwich behind on its hill. Alf had realised that the cattle would not be able to walk all the way to Beccles before dark and he doubted whether the horse-drawn waggon could reach home either, although Bessie and Anna were expecting them. They paused briefly for refreshments after cresting the hill towards Arminghall and, looking back, saw the spires of the city gleaming in the light of a late afternoon sun which had stolen out between the clouds. By the time they reached Brooke the sun was sinking fast and Alf decided to press ahead with the waggon in order to seek accommodation for the night, an expense he had hoped to avoid. He obtained lodgings for the family at a hostelry in Kirstead, and called upon a farmer he knew on the Woodton estate who lent him a field for the sake of the manure from the cattle and horses, and a barn where Frank and Bill might spend the night. As Alf remarked to Martha before they eventually slept at midnight, taking the family to the Fair seemed to have much in common with marching an army to war!

Early morning found them on the road again, the ram now most vocal in its protest against captivity, and the little kid kept bleating by way of response. Hugo and Peter both volunteered to walk with the cattle, and after a while even Lucy begged to join them. This allowed the elderly Bill to rest since there would be much for him to do when they reached home. After pausing for refreshments at a hostelry in Ditchingham, the journey began to be tedious, till they crossed the Waveney at Bungay and Beccles was just a few miles away. Jim and Frank were left to drive the cattle straight to their new field on Beccles marshes whilst the waggon proceeded at a trot towards the Ringsfield Farm. When they passed Roos Hall there was no sign of Jessica, so Hugo was unable to show her the kid. "Time enough to have this little one settled in with the sheep," as Bill Foster consoled him. "I've an old lambskin at home. Wrap that around the creature and one of the ewes that lost a lamb earlier in the year might take to it."

Bessie and Anna were busy in the dairy and came out to greet them, wiping their hands on their aprons and with smiles of relief on their faces. "Our apologies for not arriving home yesterday," Alf said, "but it just took too long to bring the cattle. That's the new ram," he told the girls proudly, pointing to the head of the animal peeping out of the crate in the waggon. "Wait till you feel the wool on him. That's what you will be spinning from his progeny. And this is Hugo's little folly," Alf continued, pointing to the creature in Hugo's arms. Anna and Bessie petted and admired the kid which sniffed at the milk on their hands and started to lick their fingers.

As soon as Jim and Frank returned from the marshes they all set about lifting down the crate from the waggon and released the ram, struggling still and as lively as ever, into the security of the pen that had previously contained Tommy the bull. He would not be introduced to the ewes for some while yet. General and Major were munching quietly back in their stable, the hens and the geese had been shut in the barn for the night, and Bill Foster, with the kid tucked under his arm, would spend his last night in the cottage he shared with Frank Briggs. The Caldicotts had been reunited with their four lively children, all safe and sound. It was time for the Jarvis household to climb thankfully into their own beds again.

CHAPTER VIII
The Navigator

Stan Stevenson was a hard man, hard in the sense that he had brought himself up in the school of adversity. Born in Southwold some sixty years since and his father dying while he was still a child, he had joined a merchant ship as a cabin boy at the age of eleven in order to provide a pittance to eke out the existence of his mother and younger sister. Through sobriety unusual in a seaman and the obstinate diligence of the poor, he had risen over fifteen years or so to the position of First Mate. At the end of one voyage he had had the good fortune to transfer almost immediately to another ship and the bad luck to have signed on with one of the most drunken skippers that ever disgraced the merchant navy. They had not long been at sea when a mutiny broke out, and whilst loyally defending his captain against the rebels, a heavy barrel loosed across the deck had pinned his legs against the hatch coaming with such force that one required amputation below the knee by the ship's surgeon. Even when fitted with a peg-leg, Stan had continued to serve, but found his handicap prevented further promotion, and in middle age he had transferred his attention to England's inland waterways instead.

It was the peg-leg which first drew Hugo's eye on that foggy November morning when he walked from the Ringsfield Farm through Ballygate and Northgate to the Quay to join Stan Stevenson and his apprentice Timothy aboard the wherry *Louise*. Stan stood upon his sound leg with the wooden one at an angle of rest as he supervised Timothy's loading of the cargo for the upstream journey. The boat was already well laden with sacks of coal and 'swill' baskets of fresh salted herrings taken aboard at Yarmouth, and to these were to be added a load of bricks from the kiln at Ingate and destined for the floor of a new cottage at Ellingham. The bricks were packed in layers upon wooden pallets and it was Tim's task to secure chain slings under the rim of each pallet, then hop down into the boat to guide the load as Stan cranked the jib crane which lifted and lowered it. Stan's tall frame was almost concealed by the long oilskin coat he wore on this damp and chilly day, but Hugo noted the breadth of his shoulders and his obvious strength as he turned the cranking handle, the metal teeth of the cogs engaged, the pulleys creaked as the ropes slid through them, and the load swung upwards and outwards over the boat. Slowly and steadily Stan let the handle return, his breath a cloud of steam between his red muffler and his much-faded mate's cap, as the pallet entered the main hold of the boat and Tim squared it up with its predecessor and released the chains.

As he swung the chains back to the quayside, Stan turned to the newcomer, cocked a knowing glance out of his blue eyes and wrinkled much-tanned face and said, "You'll be Hughie Jarvis, I daresay. Well, here is your first lesson in loading. Tim, do you stay there in the boat. Hugo will manage this one." Stan showed Hugo how to slide the chains beneath the ridges on the underside of each pallet and to check that they remained in place when the derrick took the strain. "Any slippage and we'd have bricks all over the quayside, or worse still, through the bottom of my boat!" Stan warned him. Once the bricks were settled in the hold and the hatches closed, there was a consignment of timber to be stacked over the top of them, joists, beams and planks cut in the Beccles saw-pit and required for a new building in Geldeston. Tim and Hugo loaded these between them, Stan instructing them to group the planks and beams together by size so that each load represented the same weight for the crane and for balancing the boat.

When all was done, Stan glanced at his pocket-watch and one heard the distant church clock chime the hour as, with a clatter of hooves, a lad from Wilson's Livery Stables appeared leading the tow-horse. This was a Fenland Black like the plough-team at home, and at once Hugo felt a sense of cheer at the sight of the familiar creature. He ran over to it and patted its neck, then held its head as the stable boy handed him the halter. Tim came up and showed Hugo how to attach the towrope to the whippletree and to trail it behind the animal on the side next the water. Then Stan called him to step down the rung ladder on the quayside into the boat. Stan had already lowered himself there using the crane's chains, thus avoiding putting his peg-leg on the slippery rungs.

Stan took his seat by the tiller and motioned to Hugo to sit on the other side of it. Meanwhile Timothy shouted, "Walk on. Heave-ho!" to the horse, and the obedient animal leaned forward into its collar, paused momentarily, and then leaned forward again. Slowly the wherry slid away from the quayside. Timothy guided the horse towards the brick arches of the Gillingham bridge, then detached the tow while the boat slipped beneath it, with a little help from Stan's upraised hands. Then Tim walked the horse over the bridge to the towpath on the far side and attached the tow to the whippletree again. Once the experienced animal was walking steadily along the familiar route it needed no further guidance. Tim nimbly leapt aboard the barge and adjusted the running of the rope so as to keep the bow in the centre of the waterway.

Stan explained to Hugo that his boat was forty feet long and eight feet by the beam, with a load capacity of twenty-nine tons. He had leased and then purchased the *Louise* from Mr Matthias Kerrison, a Bungay merchant dealing in fish and other goods, who had recently pioneered this river route to ensure that his customers received fresh fish from Yarmouth. It also linked his town's industries, such as malting and brewing, with the Waveney waterway and cheap transport for their produce to Beccles and beyond. Unfortunately the upper reaches of the river and the locks Mr Kerrison had built were narrow and resulted in a system of one-way traffic. There were locks at Geldeston, Ellingham, and Wainford, each maintained by a resident lock-keeper. Each keeper's cottage was in sight of the next over the flat marshes and was equipped with a flagpole with wooden arms, those on one side being raised to indicate a vessel ready to ascend through the lock, and on the other depressed to mark a boat waiting to descend. Priority was always given to down-river traffic. The cargoes they carried, Stan explained, often supplied small riverside cottages too, and fires could grow cold or families run short of food should the barges be unable to make their regular journeys up and down the waterway.

Hugo was puzzled; his father had informed him that the *Louise* was a sailing boat, yet he could see no sign of either mast or sails, so he asked Stan. He was rewarded with a deep chuckle. "Ah, my lad," Stan replied, "her mast can be unshipped and left ashore whenever we use the horse to come up to Bungay. That allows us to carry twice as much cargo along the whole deck. The mast is stepped into the tabernacle forward there, and her rigging is rove through the dead-eyes along the rubbing-strake," he said, pointing to the wooden rim that bordered the deck. "We leave the mast and sail in the warehouse on Beccles Quay. You'll not see those in use today."

It was not long before they made their first stop, at Dunburgh staithe, a wooden waterside jetty where a man had come down with a cart for the six sacks of coal which Tim began to unload. The carter saluted Stan and backed his vehicle to the water's edge. Tim laid a plank from the boat's foredeck across to the staithe, picked up a sack of coal, slung it across his shoulders and stepped along the plank to deposit it in the cart. "Now Hugo," Stan said, "can you do that? Walk along the plank first to have the feel of it. 'Tis quite firm, you see." Hugo did as he was bid. Fortunately, riding his father's cart-horses, building hay-ricks and other tasks about the farm had made him unafeared of heights, so although the plank did wobble just a little, he made it to the staithe and back with confidence. Stan put a piece of sacking over the back of his head and clothes, then Tim loaded him with a sack of coal. It was heavy, half a hundredweight at least, Hugo thought. Hugo stepped across to the edge of the deck, paused on the end of the plank to check his balance, and then stepped across to the staithe. Stan Stevenson and the carter applauded.

"Now see if you can throw one upon your shoulders as Timothy does," Stan required of him. Hugo picked up the sack by the 'ears' which protruded at either end of the top edge, watched while Tim hoisted a sack, and then copied his movements as exactly as he could. The sack of coal nestled on his shoulders, though the protective piece of sacking was now over his right shoulder. However he thought his mother probably expected he would dirty his clothes, and anyway Mrs C would run them through the laundry in no time. So he discarded the piece of sacking and hoisted the last sack unaided. A round of applause greeted his efforts.

The carter handed Timothy two large nets of cabbages. "For the White Hart at Geldeston," he instructed.

"Damn!" Stan swore quietly, "that means we must go up the Cut. I had hoped to leave the timber with the lock-keeper." The black horse, as if aware that he was needed again, left his grazing of the lush riverside grass and looked round at the boat. Tim scarcely had to take hold of the tow-rope before the giant quadruped, all of seventeen hands high, leaned into his load again and the wherry moved away from the bank.

From Dunburgh the river curved away gently between its green banks and the eternal flatness of the marshes for a mile or so till it forked at the narrow dyke which led northwards to the village of Geldeston. At the end of it there was a loop of water which allowed the boat to be turned and to head downstream again, but it formed a laborious diversion and added much time to their journey. "I doubt I shall have you home again today, Hughie," Stan commented to him as they drew up to the staithe and the intelligent tow-horse paused to crop the grass again. Tim tossed the two nets of cabbages ashore and shouted their destination to a man who had apparently come to collect them. Two other men then appeared with a long waggon and operated the shoreside derrick to winch off the timber. Timothy and Hugo remained aboard, slipping the chains beneath the ends of each load. A dozen sacks of coal were also unloaded, Hugo taking his turn with Tim.

This time Hugo was given the task of attaching the towrope for the downstream stage as far as the end of the Cut. There the towpath crossed to the upriver bank in order to reach the lock situated in the midst of Geldeston Marshes, but there was no connecting bridge. Bargees had their own ways of handling this manoeuvre: if the water was shallow the horse might be ridden across, but if it was deep, as it was here at full tide, the only course was to use the barge itself as a bridge. This was both awkward and dangerous as it relied on the skill of the navigator in placing his boat against the bank, and the confidence of the heavy horse in stepping onto planks or other support placed across the bow of the boat. Fortunately, this particular tow-horse was well-experienced and stepped almost daintily on to the foredeck via one set of planks and off the far side again as Stan swung the bow to the opposite bank by skilful use of stream and tiller. Tim had led the horse ashore and adjusted the tow-rope on the whippletree as the wherry got under way upstream once more.

Shortly thereafter they reached the first lock and the silhouette of the Locks Inn loomed up in the mist. Stan showed Hugo the sluice gate which regulated the flow of water through the lock system and explained how Mr Kerrison had caused a dyke to be dug running parallel with the river in order to ensure that there was sufficient depth of water for the locks to operate. Stan warned him that the water was their master, and the system could run dry in summer or be flooded out in winter, so that it was important to watch water levels across the marshes. Stan pointed to the signal on the pole which indicated that a barge was expected in the opposite direction and would have priority in passing through the lock. He ordered Tim to moor the wherry fore and aft and take the horse to the water trough beside the Inn. Hugo volunteered for that task and jumped ashore as soon as they reached the bank. He unhitched the horse from the tow-rope, took the end of the halter from its hook on the horse-collar, and the big carthorse ambled trustingly beside him. Locating the horse-trough, he let the animal drink its fill, then spotted a hitching-post next to a patch of dense greensward and secured the halter with the same simple hitch that was used on the farm. Stan, who had come ashore with a basket of herrings in either hand for the Inn's kitchen, nodded his approval as he passed.

As it was long past noon, Stan took advantage of the pause to order refreshments, and paid for bowls of hot soup, bread and a jug of ale for his staff. "Are you permitted to drink ale, Hughie?" he asked kindly.

"Not officially," Hugo replied with a grin. "My mother does not allow it, but then we always have milk to spare, but my father will let me, especially when we're gathering in the harvest or doing other thirsty work at the farm."

"You'll have thirsty work a-plenty with me, all the loading and unloading, and changing tack when we're on the open river." The downstream barge passed through the lock whilst they ate, and Hugo was able to watch it from the window of the Inn. The vessel was a large open spritsail trow with a cargo consisting of marl brought into Bungay from some hillside quarry. "That'll be for Somerleyton Hall," Stan told him, "they marls their fields regular."

"We can only afford to marl one field at a time," Hugo murmured, "which is why I must finish my schooling and seek employment."

They returned to the wherry and Tim re-hitched the tow-line, guiding the horse till the boat had eased into the open lock basin. Then he showed Hugo how to push shut the heavy gate, which took all the strength Hugo could muster, and then to cross the water via the closed upper gate to similarly close its partner. Tim moved the horse forward and ran the tow-line round a bollard. Then he showed Hugo how to press down the lever which operated the paddle-gear and opened sluices in the lower part of each gate, allowing water to flow into the lock basin. Below him, Hugo could watch the barge rising on the incoming flood. Hard work, this canal business, he thought, but he was beginning to enjoy it. When the water reached the same level as the river upstream Tim shouted to Hugo to push on the beam to open the other upper gate. Stan freed the tow-rope and the horse pulled the barge clear. He steered close to the bank, first on one side and then on the other, until both lads had jumped aboard.

At Ellingham there was a large mill with a handsome mill-house. Two fellows arrived with a handcart in which to collect the bricks, which Stan and his team had already unloaded by crane and had left to one side. They delivered a swill of herrings and two sacks of coal to the miller's wife and paid the toll for the next section of the river as far as Wainford. No traffic was signalled in the opposite direction, so they had soon passed through the lock and were on their way. Meanwhile the short winter afternoon was drawing to a close. "We'll not go further than Bungay, I think," Stan told Hugo as he joined him beside the tiller again. "I did warn your father that there might be more than one day's work to this stretch of the river, depending on the number and nature of my commissions. So we'll find you and Timothy a room at the Inn. I shall sleep aboard, as I usually do, and in all weathers. No-one can make off with my boat then, as has happened to other wherrymen in the past!"

At the Wainford lock the lanterns were lit, and Tim placed one at the wherry's bow. They had nothing to unload or take aboard, so did not linger. Beyond the upper lock gates Hugo observed that they had entered a dock basin with channels leading to various parts of the town. Against the paler sky he could see the dark shadow of the maltings to one side, and on the other a quay bordered by a row of inns and shops. It was here that Stan moored the *Louise*. Tim unhitched the horse and took Hugo with him to the livery stable so that he might see where the animal was kept overnight. Four pence changed hands and Hugo had the pleasure of helping to feed and water the horse, even grooming it with brush and curry comb, at which Tim laughed and told him he was making too much fuss of a mere beast of burden.

On their return to the quay they found that Stan had located the owners of the remaining sacks of coal and baskets of herrings which were swiftly unloaded. They all ate a hearty supper, which included some of the herrings, at a nearby inn and when Stan returned to the boat the two lads were shown to their 'shilling-a-night' room. Here Hugo made Tim laugh again by inspecting the bed linen and quilt that overlaid the straw mattress for bed bugs and fleas. "You'll find there have been plenty of those when you wake in the morning with red prickles all over," Tim told him. Hugo found it difficult to sleep. He had seldom known any bed but his own at home, where the mattress was made of good quality ticking, well-stuffed with horsehair, and not with lumpy straw as here, where the linen was washed regularly by Mrs C, the blankets too, at least twice a year, and the quilts were warm with duck-feathers, not thin cotton flock as these seemed to be.

Hugo had noted that the name of the Inn was The Black Dog and that its signboard portrayed the creature's head with a flaming tongue and crimson eyes, a portrait more in keeping with a fiery dragon than any dog. Was this perhaps a representation of Black Shuck that others had experienced but which he had never seen? Then Hugo recalled glimpsing the church tower silhouetted against the evening sky. Was that not St Mary's where, during a violent thunderstorm centuries ago, a huge black hound with flaming tongue and eyes like coals had raced up the nave as the congregation knelt at prayer, scorching the righteous with its brazen breath and vanishing before the altar? Hugo felt a creeping sensation raising the hairs on his legs and arms and those on the back of his neck. Although he could hear Tim's cheerful snores from the other half of the bed, Hugo was sure he could feel a presence in the room. He looked across to the far edge of the bed, beyond Tim's supine form. Was that moonlight stealing in through the attic window? But then the sky had been cloudy all day. Was that the outline of a black dog he could see? A ghostly outline, something resembling a long-eared spaniel rather than a fiery hound, regarded him soulfully out of its golden eyes and rested its paws on the edge of the bed. Hugo dived under the quilt and presently fell asleep.

They were roused by a knock on the door just as the sky beyond the window-panes showed the merest hint of day. Hands and faces were washed in the cold water poured into a basin from a ewer that stood on a bedside chest. A sharp frost and the water would have been topped with ice, Hugo realised, not the warm and comfortable water that Mrs C heated on the kitchen stove first thing in the morning. Breakfast was a slice of ham, a crust of bread and a tankard of hot coffee that burnt one's throat, and then Stan was waiting at the inn door. Hugo was sent to collect the horse while Tim assisted Stan in loading their new cargo.

When Hugo returned to the waterside with the horse, it was to find the *Louise* almost invisible beneath deck cargoes fore and aft, strange bundles wrapped in sackcloth were piled in two heaps, and Tim was busy running ropes across them and roving the ropes around cleats on the rubbing-strake. Stan explained that one pile contained hemp for the rope works at Yarmouth, whilst the other contained flax for the weavers of Norwich. At present the hold was empty and Hugo soon learnt why. Tim threw him the end of the tow-rope and Hugo fastened it carefully to the whippletree behind the horse. Tim guided the horse during the short journey to the brewery where stood a stack of barrels of malt waste destined for the stock-farmers of Beccles. Men from the brewery operated the crane which lifted the barrels aboard in nets. Hugo and Tim had only to slip the barrels out of the nets and slide them into place around the sides of the hold. The central area of the hold beneath the hatches was to be kept clear, Tim explained, for a cargo of flour they were to collect from the mill at Ellingham.

Once the loading was complete, the barge had to be backed out of the brewery quay by the simple expedient of attaching the tow-rope to the sternpost. Then the vessel must be turned on the tiller and the tow attached to the bow again. Stan always checked this himself, since a parted tow could mean a cold swim ashore or a long session of quanting with a pole. They passed quickly through the Wainford lock, then loaded the flour at Ellingham whilst permitting an upcoming barge to proceed. Hugo found that all the lock-gate procedures must be reversed and that the paddle-gates must be opened on the downstream end so that the water level could fall to that of the river beyond. At Geldeston there was nothing to be taken aboard, so they slipped through the lock and then moored to enjoy another bowl of hot soup at the Locks Inn.

JESS OF ROOS HALL

By the Geldeston Cut the horse must be brought across the boat again, this time over the hatches which were free of goods. The horse was somewhat diffident about the hollow sound given by his hooves on the planks, so Stan set Hugo to lead him, since he had observed that the creature felt more confident with someone who smelt of other animals and was used to handling them. Tim guided the horse while the bows were backed out of the Cut and the boat was swung round into the stream again. At Dunburgh there was a pile of turnips contained in nets to be landed at Beccles which they reached in the late afternoon. Hugo helped unload some of the cargo but then Stan sent him to return the tow-horse to the livery stables on his way home. He gave him coins to pay the charge for the extra day's hire, and with a twinkle in his eye included an additional shilling, thanking the boy for his help. "Did you find the work to your liking?" Stan asked.

"Oh yes, Mr Stevenson," Hugo replied, "and I would wish to come another day when you're sailing on the river so that I may learn about that also."

"I shall speak to your father about it," Stan replied, "though I doubt that he will wish you to miss more schooling before you leave."

The word 'school' reminded Hugo that his extra day's absence had yet to be excused there. Once the tow-horse had been returned to the livery stables, Hugo hurried along Ballygate, but found the school closed already and its lights extinguished on this dark winter afternoon. So he continued past it and turned into the Bungay road. At Roos Hall the grounds were deserted and everyone indoors. Suddenly he felt the same creeping sensation that he had experienced during the night, as he remembered the ghostly dog, and this time he knew it was no itinerant flea. Had it been real or only a dream? He turned into the farm track via the wicket gate and ran all the way home.

When Hugo returned to school next day he found himself unexpectedly something of a hero. Even the bullies Mather and Weedon joined the throng of those enquiring details of his experience. For though these sons of professional men thought it beneath their standing to take up such menial work, they were anxious to learn of Hugo's duties for future reference. Apparently Alf Jarvis had already advised Dr Davey that Hugo's absence might extend to two days, so the Head Master treated the boy very kindly when he made his apologies. That afternoon Hugo escorted Lucy and Jessica home as usual. Jessica, who had quite fallen in love with the kid which Hugo had bought for her, which she had named Matilda but which was still being kept at the farm, was full of news from Roos Hall. It seemed that Briggs was to be pensioned off at the year-end. The pension to be paid to him was the merest pittance and Jessica had overheard Mrs Jarvis arguing about it with Mr Ainsworth, to no avail apparently. Fortunately for the old fellow, he had a son and daughter-in-law living in Beccles who had offered him a room now that their son Frank lived in a Ringsfield cottage. Jeb Hanson, the older of the two groundsmen at the Hall, had applied to take Briggs' place. No new groundsman would be employed, since Mr Ainsworth had welcomed the move as a useful cost saving. Jessica felt sure there would be a role for Matilda next spring as trimmer of the lawns at Roos Hall.

Meanwhile Mr Ainsworth, now largely recovered from the injuries caused by his fall, had made his first ride upon Pharaoh since the accident. Jessica related that Ted had told her that the hunter had not taken kindly to being reunited with his master and had positively balked at trotting along the lane towards Barsham. This had obliged Mr Ainsworth to ride over the Ringsfield farmland on the same bridlepath that they used to walk to and from school. Apparently he had had the courtesy to call at the farmhouse to inform Alf Jarvis and had requested that the gates which he was obliged to use might be left unchained. Alf had thought it wise to warn his children of their landlord's presence and to command them to behave with propriety and respect should they encounter him.

However the most fascinating item of news came from Jessica. She had been sitting in the kitchen with Mrs Baines and drinking a cup of chocolate on her return from school the previous day when Lizzie, one of the housemaids, had burst in full of gossip. Jessica's presence there should have ensured restraint, but because Mr Ainsworth had condemned Jessica to taking her meals with the servants and because of his beatings and cruelty to her, which were notorious, the maid felt no compunction in revealing the news that had come her way. "Mr Ainsworth being out riding," Lizzie said, "I thought to clear his luncheon dishes from his study. You remember that he received a letter by the mails today, and Briggs who took it up to him said it must be from Sir Charles since it bore the Rich crest on the cover, well ..." Lizzie paused for breath, "I saw it lying open on Mr Ainsworth's desk and so I took a peek!"

"Oh, Lizzie, you never did, what a wicked thing to do!" Mrs Baines interrupted her. "What did it say?"

"It began, 'My dear Ignatius,' – that's Mr Ainsworth's middle name, isn't it?"

"Yes, called after a saint, so Mrs Jarvis told me, not that any saint would recognise 'is Honour, mind you," Mrs Baines replied. "Go on, Lizzie, what did the rest say?"

"Well, I was reading it quickly in case Mrs Jarvis or someone else should enter and find me, but as far as I can recall it went like this:

'It appears from representations made to me here at Waverley ...

that you have neglected to settle a number of accounts ...

outstanding with persons of means with whom you have played games of chance ...

and have taken it upon yourself to hazard both the income from my Suffolk estate ...

and the allowance I make you for the maintenance of Roos Hall ...'

Here Lizzie paused for an extra long breath and perhaps endeavouring to recollect the precise phraseology that followed.

'In furtherance of this situation I desire that you will immediately ...
repair hither for discussion of your future conduct ...

as soon as you may, and in any event before December 1st next ...
Pray travel by public conveyance so as not to incur unnecessary expense.

Yours, Charles Rich, Bart."

"Now he's for it," Mrs Baines broke in. "That's those gentlemen who came on the day when Mr Ainsworth had his accident, Mr Junkett and Mr Doom, wasn't that what Briggs said they were called? First of December, you said? It will take him two days or more to travel there. 'Tis the end of the month next week, so he had better make haste to do what his guardian wishes. I would not be surprised if Sir Charles detains 'im there at Waverley, where he can keep an eye on him. Then we might have Mr Russell to answer to instead, and he's a much more upright gentleman."

"Who's an upright gentleman?" Mrs Jarvis enquired, entering the kitchen just then.

"I was speaking of Mr Russell, Madam," Mrs Baines replied coolly.

"Miss Jessica, you shouldn't be listening to gossip," Mrs Jarvis said. "Upstairs, please, and change into something more suitable than your school clothes. Your supper will be ready for you when you come down."

"So I had to leave the room then," Jessica told Hugo and Lucy, "but it was my impression that Mrs Jarvis had been standing outside the kitchen door for some time and had heard what Lizzie was saying. That was why she wanted me out of the way while she spoke to the others. Being asked to change for supper, I thought at first that Mr Ainsworth must have relented and meant me to join him in the dining-room, but it appears it was not so."

Mr Ainsworth left Roos Hall the following day. Ted drove him into Beccles where he caught the stage from the King's Head. He did not return to Roos Hall for several weeks, only in the New Year. In the meantime Jessica and the servants had noted a regular correspondence posting back and forth between Sir Charles and Mrs Jarvis, which made them all hope that, save for Briggs' retirement and the promotion of the gardener Jeb Hanson in his stead, life at Roos Hall would proceed with its normal peace and security. In fact it was Mrs Jarvis who gathered the staff together on New Year's Eve to distribute to each their annual gratuity, and who was able to press into the hand of a grateful and somewhat tearful Briggs an extra sum which she had persuaded Sir Charles to supply.

Mrs Jarvis had invited all the staff to supper in the dining-room, a custom which Sir Robert Rich had observed annually, but which had fallen into disuse since his death. She had also permitted Jessica to attend. "Before we sit down to our celebrations," she said, addressing them from the head of the table as they stood by their chairs expecting to hear Grace, "Sir Charles has asked me to inform you that Mr Ainsworth will return to the Hall shortly, but that in future he will only reside here at the weekends. Sir Charles has obtained a place for him at Norwich with Messrs Durrant & Sitwell, a firm of attorneys-at-law. Mr Ainsworth will take the stage to Norwich of a Monday morning and return by the same means of a Saturday afternoon. "Ted," she continued, addressing the stable lad, "you will kindly keep Mr Ainsworth's hunter well-exercised, and Mr Easton, you will keep his guns clean and well oiled, so that Mr Ainsworth may hunt or shoot with his friends at Ilketshall St Margaret's if he has a mind to it. None of you may refer to these arrangements or comment on them in the hearing of Mr Ainsworth, on penalty of dismissal for insubordination, is that clear? Oh, and yes, Mr Russell will ride over from time to time to deal with the business of the Estate. Now, if you are all ready for supper, let us say Grace."

Exactly a week previously the Sir John Leman School had closed for the Christmas festival, and Hugo's schooling had come to an end. At their habitual morning prayers that day pupils had been informed that a further assembly would be held at noon to replace their daily closing prayers. Then the school would shut for the afternoon and pupils would be free to make their own Christmas preparations with their families. At midday, after the prayers had been said, Hugo was most surprised to be called forth by Dr Davey and to be presented with a certificate for good behaviour. Dr Davey spoke briefly about the lad, that he had attended school regularly and punctually, had applied himself diligently to his lessons, had satisfied their Honoured Founder's admonition that pupils 'shall return home quietly and reverently; not making clamour in the streets; not passing by their elders, superiors and betters without due and mannerly salutations', and that he was setting out on a new stage in his life to contribute to his family by taking up employment, and such employment, moreover, as might cause many another lad to quail at its severity and the demands it made upon one's strength and fortitude. In short, Dr Davey concluded, Hugo Jarvis was a good example to them all. After such a eulogy, Hugo could only step out for home with pride.

At the farm he enjoyed one of the happiest Christmasses he could remember. Whilst he had stretched his humble allowance to purchase small gifts for his brother and sisters and his parents, and whilst the school clothes he had previously worn with some care were being cut down to fit young Peter, Hugo was showered with gifts from all directions. Carrie had knitted him a very long muffler for the chilly mornings to come. His father had bought him a seaman's cap that would keep out much of the rain and a long jacket of oiled cloth that would repel most of the seawater he would encounter on voyages into Yarmouth. His mother had made him trousers out of stout linen that would take a knock or two, and Lucy had knitted him a pair of mittens to each of which Bill Foster had attached a leather palm. The Caldicotts provided him with a tin box in which to keep food or other provisions; it boasted both handle and a key, and Frank Briggs generously contributed a pewter flask once owned by his grandfather which would take a pint of ale or other refreshment for use on board the wherry. But it was Jessica's gift which really stole Hugo's heart, for she gave him a small book of poetry that Mrs Jarvis had found for her a year or two past, on the final fly-leaf of which she had inscribed some verses of her own creation.

These read:

> "*I wish you well along your way*
> *Aboard the graceful boat,*
> *And pray God keep you safe from harm*
> *In you new life afloat.*
>
> *I wish you joy, and strength and health*
> *Wherever you may roam;*
> *That you'll recall your loyal friends*
> *Whenever you come home.*
>
> *(sgd.) Jessica A. Rich"*

Childish verses indeed, for the girl was still only ten years of age, but they held a certain sentiment which for Hugo bridged the gap between the security of his childhood and the uncertainty of his future.

The first of January, New Year's Day, dawned crisp and clear but with an icy frost as Hugo left his home at 6.00 a.m. when the sky was still dark and made his way by the road into Beccles and down to the Quay. Stan Stevenson had instructed him to be there by 6.30 a.m. ready to load the boat. It happened that the frost was so severe, following a week of bitterly cold winds and snow that had swept across East Anglia, that parts of the river were frozen over. A message had come from Geldeston that the lock was frozen from bank to bank and that even strenuous efforts with quanting pole and didle, the dredging tool that Bargees used to shift sand and silt when they grounded on a shoal, had failed to shatter enough ice to permit the lock gates to open. In these circumstances Stan Stevenson was now obliged to unload all the cargo destined for up-river and to leave it at the Quay warehouse, to step in his boat's mast and rigging which he had left in the warehouse thinking he would be going up-river, and to load up with such provisions as were already available for a voyage downstream to Yarmouth or up the River Yare to Norwich.

Timothy arrived, blowing on his hands with steamy breath, for he was to continue to work for Stan until Hugo became well accustomed to his tasks. Hugo watched as Stan and Tim carried the heavy mast to the waterside. He noted that the large gaff sail, fully reefed, and its yard were lashed beside the mast, ready for hauling up by block and tackle once the mast and its stays were in place. When the sail was hoisted, since it lacked a boom in order to allow more space for cargo, its tail corner could be secured to a cleat on either aft end of the hatches. Stan stood beside the tabernacle, the strong crossbeam athwart the bows, in order to guide the lower end of the mast between the stepping timbers, while Tim pushed the long pole over the edge of the quay. Once it was home there were metal clamps to hold it upright, and Stan hammered in a couple of wooden wedges for good measure. Tim leapt aboard to secure the forestay at the bow and then the starboard stay while Stan secured the larboard one.

Stan Stevenson had nodded to Hugo on his arrival but was rather more concerned to watch for the availability of suitable cargo. There were a dozen barrels of butter and some cheeses wrapped in sackcloth destined for Lowestoft, more bundles of hemp for Yarmouth, and a substantial load of bricks from the Ingate works in Beccles that were to be landed at Burgh Staithe for refurbishment of the Rectory and the Church of St Peter. "You know," Tim told Hugo, "that old church with the stepped-up tower." Hugo realised how inattentive he had been to his own neighbourhood, for he had often climbed the tall tower of St Michael's Church at Beccles and knew that he must have overlooked the river without noticing its landmarks. Now he hurried aboard the wherry to stow his tin box and flask below the tiller bench where he noted that Stan and Tim always stored their possessions, before jumping ashore again to help with the loading of the bricks.

Presently a waggon drew up nearby with sacks of flour from Walter Green's, the millers, also destined for Lowestoft; they would be lowered into the hold alongside the bricks. Just as everything was tidily stowed another waggon appeared. Accustomed as he was to the strong aromas of the farmyard, Hugo was obliged to hold his nose as this vehicle drew to a halt nearby; it bore a load of cattle hides from the tannery in Puddingmoor. While Stan went to negotiate a compensatory fare from the carter, Hugo enquired of Tim how far they would be obliged to carry such a smelly cargo. "That's leather for the shoemakers of Norwich," Tim replied. "It looks as though we shall sail up the Yare when we're done with Lowestoft and Stan will go on to Yarmouth later. Doubtless there'll be some goods we can pick up at Norwich for the shipyards or the Navy." This was a reminder to Hugo that from now on the *Louise* would be sharing the waterway with other and larger merchant vessels and even the odd Navy warship in search of a refit. It was indeed a new life on which he had embarked.

Once the hatches had closed over the bricks and the flour, Stan had the bundles of hemp brought from the bows and laid over the hatches, under the lee of which he had stored the butter and cheese. This enabled the hides to be laid and lashed down across the bows, whence hopefully their stink would be wafted overboard by the strength of the wind on the sail as they tacked down-river. Hugo was detailed to cast off the mooring ropes and to toss the bow rope to Tim and the stern one to Stan who stood by the tiller and helped Hugo aboard. Then he was sent forward to haul on the halyard with Tim as the reefs were slipped undone and the gaffsail yard rose up the mast, the huge black sail unfolding as it went. The sail billowed taut in a generous curve, slowly drawing the craft away from the Beccles quayside and towards the beckoning sea.

They soon encountered other traffic on the river, long broad trows full of marl or timber and other bulk crops, or wherries similar to their own, some larger, some smaller, loaded with grain for the mills, or sacks of wool or flour for the towns they were to visit. However their first stop was to be at a mere waterside mill which had hung a flour sack at a certain window to indicate to any under-laden wherry that there was a cargo to be carried down-river. Hugo heard Stan swear when he spotted the signal and enquired why the navigator was not keen to collect the load. "Well, young Hughie, do you not see how that Mill is situat-ed on an island at the edge of the higher ground. It has a weir on either side with water to turn its grindstones. To come alongside, those distant lock gates must be closed and the mill dam filled with water from the river until there's clearance enough above the weir for our keel to graze over it, even though we draw merely two and a half feet when laden. We shall need to belay around that capstan on the shore and wait until the dam is full before we can enter the lock. 'Tis a tricky move at the best of times with a fair wind as today, but nigh impossible if there's a crosswind on the river. In summer there's often scarce enough water to fill the dam, and that miller is only still in business, if you ask me, because he's too mean to pay cartage to Burgh Staithe. He'll have to do it one day!"

As Stan was speaking Tim lowered the sail till it rested on the bundles of hemp across the hatches, then jumped ashore and ran the towline astern and around the capstan, using it to hold the boat steady in the current. In front of them, with a wave of greeting, the miller and his assistant hastened to close the lock gates and the water level started to rise. Stan steered the wherry into the basin as Tim released the pressure on the capstan. The sacks of flour were consigned for Norwich and the buyer had specified that they be carried in dry conditions in the hold. This meant that the sail had to be lashed up to the mast again, the hemp moved aside, and one of the hatches opened so that the flour could be lowered within. As each sack weighed a hundredweight, Hugo was too slight of build to lift one, so Stan instructed him to haul upon the mooring rope and keep the boat tight against the bollard on the quay. When all the sacks had been accommodated, the hatches were closed, the hemp replaced, the mooring rope let go and the miller and his assistant opened the lock gates on the far side of the dam. Caught by the enhanced force of the 'flash' current, the barge sped on its way, with Stan steering skilfully between the lock's turf banks. It was only when they were in open water again that Tim could raise the sail.

The *Louise* was obliged to tack twice across the river before reaching their next stop at Burgh Staithe. Stan showed Hugo how to belay the aft halyard around the opposite cleat before releasing the original hitch, so that the sail did not flap wildly and knock anyone overboard as the tiller swept the craft on to the new tack. Once the tail of the sheet did slap Hugo full in the chest as he tried the manoeuvre on his own for the first time, but he managed to pull swiftly and secure the rope, so that only his cap went flying towards the rail, Stan's peg-leg just saving it from going overboard. At Burgh Staithe the sail had to be hoisted up and lashed to the mast again and the hemp moved aside whilst the hatches were opened and the bricks unloaded. Here they collected butter and cheese addressed to Lady Anguish at Somerleyton Hall, and sacks of grain from the

Burgh estate to be ground by the Black Mill, a wind-driven mill standing on the Somerleyton Marshes.

However their next task was to deposit all the goods destined for Lowestoft, tacking across the river from Burgh and navigating a tricky turn into the Oulton Dyke. Here the wind was almost dead ahead and the sail flapped idly, so Stan and Tim took up the long quanting poles kept along the side of the deck, Tim at the bow and Stan at the stern where he could direct Hugo who had command of the tiller. Thus they punted most of the way to Oulton Broad at whose eastern end the Pickford Brothers, long famous for their lumbering oxen-hauled stage waggons which had trundled goods across-country for most of the century, had established a trans-shipment warehouse where goods for Lowestoft were unloaded and cargoes for Norwich, Yarmouth or Beccles could be taken on board. Here they deposited the flour from Beccles together with their first consignment of butter and cheese.

The Pickford quay was stacked high with sacks of coal; obviously a collier had come south from Newcastle and had decided not to dock at Yarmouth where the berths may have been filled by the fishing fleet. As there was then no waterway connection between Oulton Broad and Lake Lothing and the sea at Lowestoft, any collier would deliver its coal in bulk on the dockside by hand, using wooden stretchers carried between two seamen or dockers. In Yarmouth the broad-beamed trows took such cargoes aboard by the same means, scrubbing out the interior of the craft if they were then to carry grain or other 'clean' cargo instead! Such procedures were not so easily adapted to the smaller boats and sailing wherries which dealt mostly with mixed loads. For ease of transport, warehousing brokers such as Pickford's would parcel the coal into sacks, returnable to source when emptied.

Stan was offered, and accepted, a consignment of coal for Norwich which would fill the remainder of the hold. Hugo and Tim were kept busy loading the sacks till mid-afternoon when Stan called for a break for refreshments. Hugo stayed with the boat and resorted happily to the contents of his tin box and flask, home-brewed ale and a delicious crusty pie. He was beginning to feel just a little lonely, never having been so far from home before without his father or some other adult by his side.

Later in the afternoon they called at the Black Mill to deliver the sacks of wheat grain from the Burgh estate. Stan allowed Hugo to enter the mill as its big white wooden sails were in motion, humming and creaking atop the black-boarded column that had given the mill its name. The miller kindly showed him the workings of the huge wooden cogs and axles and the manner of the grinding of the millstones. Tim laughed as Hugo emerged at the end of his visit all white with flour dust. He brushed most of it away before climbing down into the boat as they cast off.

Somerleyton Hall had its own large staithe and there was a man ready to collect the butter and cheese assigned to Lady Anguish. Soon they were sailing down-river again towards St Olave's where Stan had decided they should spend the night. The dying winter sunshine flooded across the marshes as they tacked towards the quay and the long row of old houses that constituted this waterside settlement. A grey mist arose, shrouding the reeds which were still white in places with the morning's frost. Hugo's first day of employment had come to an end.

CHAPTER IX
The Rake

"On one nice trick depends the general fate ..."
From: *"The Rape of the Lock"* by Alexander Pope

A few weeks into the New Year, on a dark morning of unremitting chill, Ted drove Mr Ainsworth into Beccles to catch the morning stage to Norwich. This was the means used by a number of artisans to reach the big city, if they were fortunate enough to obtain employment there. Mr Ainsworth did not wish to be confused with any mere artisan; in fact he would rather not be seen at all. Thus he wore his plainest black topcoat, the most modest of his beaver hats, a high collar and cravat about his throat, and a long muffler which he wound around the gap between the two. He obliged Ted to set him down in Ballygate and to drive on to the King's Head to purchase a ticket for the stage. Mr Ainsworth waited around the corner from the New Market till he saw Ted reappear and drive back towards him – that skewbald pony James was so noticeable and far too well-known in the town.

Ainsworth took an outside seat atop the stage, where only the braver souls sat of a freezing February morning, wound his muffler more tightly, put on his thick gloves, and clasped his coat about his knees which had already communicated to him the inclemency of the temperature. The stage was due to reach Norwich by eight o'clock, the hour when most people started work in winter, unless they were in service, of course. At his interview for the position, Mr Sitwell who, it appeared, managed the small law office that bore his name, informed Mr Ainsworth that if he chose to reside out of town and the stage should be late arriving, he might make up the time lost that day after six o'clock of the Monday evening. Nor need he fear being left alone in the office, for Mr Sitwell himself frequently stayed until well past dinnertime, as was the habit of his profession.

Upon his first arrival at the office in Law Lane, having run half a mile from the stage terminus at the Waggon & Horses, Ainsworth noted that the large office clock, which faced him from the wall as he entered and had a most penetrating tick, registered a quarter to nine. Mr Sitwell nodded that he had noticed it too as he rose to greet his new employee and to show him around the premises. It seemed that Mr Durrant, whom Ainsworth had met on the occasion of his interview, acted as a consultant these days and worked on papers sent round to his home a few streets away. This left vacant his rather elegantly furnished office which Mr Sitwell indicated was now used principally for the interviewing and entertainment of clients, and junior staff were forbidden to cross the sacred threshold. Similarly with his own office, Mr Sitwell emphasised over the top of his wire-framed spectacles, one did not enter without an invitation. Mr Sitwell pointed to the desk where Ainsworth was to sit and where he might hang his coat and hat and place the carpet-bag of spare clothing that he would later take to his lodgings. Then Mr Sitwell introduced him to the only other member of staff, the office boy Snuff. Ainsworth only discovered later that Snuff took his name from Mr Sitwell's habit of indulging in that particular commodity and in calling "Snuff!" loudly through the open door of his office whenever the little tortoiseshell box of the stuff which he kept about his person was in danger of becoming empty.

However "Snuff" seemed to have accepted his appellation well enough, and once Ainsworth had settled at his desk came to introduce himself and to describe his duties. These were to ensure that letters and documents were properly sealed and addressed before he took them to the post office, to collect the incoming mails, to take messages, deliver writs, collect items of property or small debts that were owed, take to Mr Durrant all matters for his consideration and to collect those papers with which he had dealt. Within the office he must light the fire at 7.30 a.m. ready for Mr Sitwell's arrival and boil a kettle of water with which the staff might make themselves a pot of tea – though they must supply their own tea leaves, for those were expensive commodities. For the further maintenance of the office Snuff must bring up coal from the cellar and order more as necessary, fetch fresh water from the pump at the end of the street, and supervise the maid who called one evening a week to sweep and dust the rooms. Should Mr Ainsworth require milk or sugar for his tea, or other refreshment when the weather was too inclement to make a midday sortie attractive, Snuff was all too willing to perform such accommodating tasks, in exchange, of course, for a suitable 'vail' or tip.

Ainsworth sat down at his desk, or rather he slid into it for it was of the tall, upright sort with a long sloping lid and a top shelf equipped with a selection of quills, a knife for sharpening them, an inkwell, a box of sand for drying the script, and sealing wax, a candle and a taper. Snuff provided him with a block of leather covered with parchment on which he advised him to rest his work and Mr Sitwell emerged from his office just then with the first document which required to be copied. Snuff stood at Ainsworth's elbow until he was sure that Mr Ainsworth had sufficient wit and intelligence to produce a facsimile in an acceptable hand, before he retired to his seat beside the stove in the tiny kitchen, there to fortify himself with a sip of brandy from his secret store, after which he would sally forth on his first errand of the day.

When he completed the required copy Ainsworth took it to Mr Sitwell's office and knocked upon the door. Mr Sitwell looked up with an expression of annoyance, his spectacles bobbing up and down on his nose and a wisp of dark hair waving like a reed in the breeze on the crown of his otherwise bald head. "Don't bother me with it, Ainsworth, unless I ask. Put it on the table there and Snuff will sort it out presently. There's a pile of papers on the right-hand corner of the table. Make two copies of each, if you please." Ainsworth took up the papers indicated and retreated to his desk. Already he was being made to feel of very low status indeed, lower even than that of the office boy, Snuff, who it seemed was made responsible for sorting the papers relating to different matters and putting them together. It was not until several salutary days later that as Ainsworth worked on a rather complex conveyance with many sub-clauses and paragraphs, and having cause to ask Snuff a question of office practice, he discovered that the boy could not read! Snuff, of coarse features and rounded shoulders, but of a cheerful disposition provided he had not applied himself too freely to the brandy, Snuff had been born in a workhouse like himself but had not had the advantage of more schooling than Ainsworth had met with at the orphanage. Snuff knew indeed how to read a name or an address that was familiar to him, and if a copy document looked the same as the original, then it was indeed a fair copy. In fact Snuff judged everything by the visual impression it made on his retentive mind.

Ainsworth found himself more at ease after that little discovery, though the job as a whole was devilish boring. At the end of the week, which concluded for him at noon on Saturday, Ainsworth left his desk and caught the one o'clock stage back to Beccles. There was no sign of Ted with the pony-trap, so he walked home to Roos Hall and arrived in a foul temper. Arthur greeted him with joy, but even that failed to soften his mood. He found Ted in the stable polishing tack and Pharaoh ready for some exercise. After a canter around the park he tried to steer the horse towards the Bungay road, but the animal shied and snorted. Ainsworth gave up at that and rode along Puddingmoor Lane among the meadows beside the river. He noted the black Scottish cattle that Alf Jarvis was fattening munching their way through the turnips and hay which had been strewn across the field. Why had he not been consulted before they had been brought in, he demanded to himself, and immediately knew the answer, that Mr Russell had stepped in because he, Ainsworth, had not proved competent, and had been ill or absent at the time when a decision was required.

At Waverley, Sir Charles had informed him of the unfavourable report he had received from his Bailiff, and that to recoup the losses he had caused he must earn his own keep henceforth. Mr Russell was to have charge of the estate and Mrs Jarvis of the 'board' staff engaged to maintain Roos Hall, which it seems that Sir Charles had no inclination to visit. Sir Charles had therefore found Ainsworth the position with Durrant & Sitwell, even advising him to use the name Mr Ainsworth as his identification rather than sully the surname Rich. Sir Charles had added that should Ainsworth neglect his duties or prove unreliable in his post, he would be at risk of forgoing any inheritance at all. Moreover, as Ainsworth muttered to himself, the damned man had still refused to reveal the identity of his ward's father or any of his parentage. Ainsworth thwacked a willow tree with his whip and reaching the outskirts of Beccles rode over the Gillingham bridge to the village there and entered a hostelry where he might drown his sorrows.

At the commencement of his second week of employment the Norwich stage made better time and Ainsworth reached the office at 8.35 a.m. Mr Sitwell looked up and nodded as he entered. Ainsworth handed to Snuff a quarter of tea leaves which he had filched from the kitchen at Roos Hall and Snuff obligingly offered to brew him a pot of the beverage. Ainsworth felt he would soon have control of matters in that department; a person who could not read should be easy to fool. Mr Sitwell had left on the table a number of documents each requiring one or several fair copies, and also a bundle of papers which he requested be placed in chronological order in a file. Snuff, when consulted, produced a cardboard cover and a supply of laces for future use. He showed Ainsworth how the cover should be inscribed in a standard format and where the folders of previous matters were stored. Ainsworth started back in scorn at the thought of being a mere filing clerk, someone of the lowest rank in a shipping or merchant's office, but it suddenly occurred to him that by reading these confidential papers he might learn much about the upper echelons of Norwich society, their scandals and their weaknesses, and that he might thereby establish a social contact or two which would enlighten the boredom of his weekday evenings. Finding a companion with whom he might drink and dine now became a desirable objective, along with persons with whom he might share a hand at cards, for in the cheap hostelries which surrounded Cow Hill, the poor district where he had found lodgings, it was as much as he had encountered to find a game of Shove Ha'penny.

And such lodgings, he concluded grimly when he returned to them on the Monday evening to find the possessions he had left there strewn about and sheets well-rumpled and soiled upon the bed. It seemed that his landlady had not scrupled to let his room to others during his absence at the weekend, and that those others were more in the nature of illicit lovers rather than honest travellers. He was obliged to pay sixpence extra for fresh linen and forced his landlady to supply him with keys to the wardrobe and the chest of drawers so that he might leave behind in Norwich anything not destined for the laundry at Roos Hall.

Ainsworth had sat at his desk for a little over a month when Mr Sitwell actually troubled to speak to him and enquired his familiarity with "accounts". Seeing an opportunity to further his acquaintance with the financial solidarity or otherwise of the prominent citizens of Norwich, Ainsworth hastened to assure Mr Sitwell that the Usher at his well-known private school had been most assiduous at the instilling of the same into his pupils, even at the receiving end of his walking cane. Then Ainsworth realised that Mr Sitwell was merely handing over to him responsibility for the office petty cash! Here were the modest sums Snuff had laid out upon milk and sugar, soap and candles, ink and paper, parchment and postage. There were fees paid to the notaries for formalising documents, an aspect of legal work with which Ainsworth was now making himself familiar. Some of the items were annotated as having been transferred to such and such a client account. Ainsworth made a mental note of the names, and as the past matters had been filed alphabetically he was often able to read up the subject for which that particular client had engaged Durrant & Sitwell's services.

Then one Friday noon-tide, in search of a means of relieving his boredom, Ainsworth entered the Circulating Library and found himself sharing a penchant for the same literature with a tall gentleman, elegantly dressed and sporting a monocle. When the gentleman made to replace on the shelf a book he had glanced at but rejected, Ainsworth held out his hand to see what it was. It turned out to be a volume of poems by Alexander Pope, the brilliant social satirist who had lived much earlier in the century and had verbally dissected the Court of Queen Anne. "You do not find Mr Pope to your taste?" Ainsworth enquired rhetorically.

"One has read so much of his work," the stranger replied. "I must confess I am impatient for a new generation of poets to be born."

"May I take it then that neither Mr Collins nor Mr Dryden are likely to please you? Ainsworth asked.

"No, indeed, nor even does Mr Chatterton, though had he lived longer I think he might have produced verses that I would have found spiritually more satisfying. Excuse my curiosity, please, but I think we have not met before. My name is Gilbert Spencer. Are you new to Norwich?"

"And mine is Ainsworth Rich. I live in Beccles but often visit this city. I'm engaged on business here presently."

"Forgive my enquiring, but have you any connection with Sir Charles Bostock Rich? I am acquainted with his Bailiff, Mr Anthony Russell."

"Oh, yes," Ainsworth gave a nervous little laugh at the mention of Mr Russell, before he added boldly, "Sir Charles is my father." That was the first untruth on the downward path to disaster.

"Where do you dine this evening?" Gilbert Spencer enquired.

"I have yet to find anywhere satisfactory. Which establishment would you recommend?" Ainsworth replied.

"I know a coffee house in Greyfriars, a turning off King Street, near the Cathedral, where one can obtain a decent meal and play a quiet hand of whist at the same time. You do play?"

"Oh, yes, indeed," Ainsworth replied, foreseeing welcome entertainment at last.

"Shall we say seven o'clock, then?" Gilbert Spencer suggested and Ainsworth agreed almost eagerly as they parted. Walking back to Law Lane a distasteful though suddenly occurred. His pockets were empty; only a few shillings remained from the funds he had brought from Roos Hall, scarcely enough to pay for a meal and a pint of beer, but not for a decent bottle of wine. And if they were to play cards for money, as he anticipated, perhaps with other cronies whom his new friend met there on a regular basis, he would be shamed by his poverty. Ainsworth reviewed the meagre items of jewellery he had brought with him to Norwich and realised there was not an expensive piece among them, deliberately so as he had to leave his trinkets locked in the chest at his lodgings every day. Nothing then that he might pledge with a pawnbroker. The week's wages were little enough and he would not receive those from Mr Sitwell till the morrow, just enough then to pay a week's rent in advance and purchase a ticket for the stage to Beccles. He could not simply sign IOUs, for among strangers they would not be accepted. Nor did he think that Mr Russell might be forthcoming, even if he had the means of riding out to the estate to contact him.

Then Fate played into Ainsworth's hands. On his return to the office he checked the petty cash box; it contained less than two pounds. Mr Sitwell, Snuff informed him, had gone out for the afternoon and was not expected to return before five of the clock. At that moment a visitor knocked at the door of the premises and Snuff let him in. He knew the visitor by sight for he was a regular client, and so introduced him to Mr Ainsworth as Mr Tobias Wilmington. Ainsworth asked Snuff to look out the gentleman's file, which he did very swiftly by his own particular means. Then, fancying how it might be to take Mr Sitwell's place for a moment, Ainsworth sent Snuff out to purchase more sealing wax and escorted Mr Wilmington into Mr Durrant's office to enquire how he, Ainsworth might be of help. To his surprise, instead of relating the doleful circumstances of some new business where redress was required, Mr Wilmington announced that he had come to settle his bill. Ainsworth observed that a copy of that Bill, which he had himself prepared at Mr Sitwell's request, together with a note of its brief enclosing letter, lay on the top of the file of papers in front of him. Mr Wilmington placed on the desk a bill of exchange for half the money, payable in thirty days, and a clinking leather bag which he indicated contained the remainder of the charge.

Ainsworth fetched the petty cash box from his desk and for want of other receptacle counted the 210 gold sovereigns into it. Then he took the top copy from a sheaf of receipts and carefully indicated the manner in which the funds had been supplied. This he signed and handed to Mr Wilmington, and having ascertained that there was no further business to be had for the time being, he showed the gentleman out of the office just as Snuff returned with the unnecessary sealing wax. Ainsworth slipped into the petty cash box the change Snuff had handed him without revealing its other contents, and put the box in his desk, pocketing the key as was his duty. He still had the Wilmington file in his possession. Taking his best quill he wrote out a copy receipt and laid it with the bill of exchange and the file on Mr Sitwell's desk. That receipt entirely omitted to mention the two hundred guineas in cash!

Nothing could have been more simple. Mr Sitwell was delayed in his business of the afternoon, Snuff departed at 5.30 p.m. as permitted since his hours began at seven-thirty in the morning, and Ainsworth was left alone with a box full of cash which he transferred lovingly to his own pockets, coin by coin, scattering them about so that they would not chink together and alert either Mr Sitwell as he bade him goodnight, or any pickpocket in the street before he should reach his lodgings. There he paid his landlady a day early for the next week's rent, something that pleased her mightily, and set about dressing for dinner in some of the better quality garments he had brought to Norwich in the hope of making the odd social acquaintance which might assist him to pass the tedious hour until Sir Charles had devised some better opportunity for his future. Had Ainsworth paused to analyse his intentions at this time, it was to make use of the cash for his current needs, take a portion with him to his evening engagement, and to use his well-honed skills to win more so that he might repay his employer by issuing a further copy receipt and producing the cash the moment the absence of Mr Sitwell from the office permitted.

Ainsworth took a cab to Greyfriars, not being sufficiently familiar with the byways of Norwich to walk there in the dark, especially when a purse containing fifty golden sovereigns, which every thief might envy, hung heavily in the inside breast pocket of his overcoat. When he reached the coffee house, also called The Greyfriars and garnished with a wooden signboard bearing the cheerful visage of a jolly monk, he found Mr Gilbert Spencer there before him and engaged in friendly conversation with two other gentlemen, one lean and respectably dressed in a country style, and the other rather more tubby in profile whose prosperous appearance seemed somewhat familiar. Both strangers turned towards him and Mr Spencer introduced him to the lean fellow first, Mr Bannerman of Thorpe, and then to the fatter one, Mr Tobias Wilmington! It was as well that the coffee-house was dimly lit and liberally filled with tobacco fumes, or those present might have noticed that Ainsworth blanched. He was about to play his employer's client at cards with the client's own money!

Mr Wilmington, too, was not a little suspicious. He well recognised Ainsworth, but in respect for the confidentiality of the Law and of his own affairs, forbore to recall their earlier meeting but instead questioned him about his patronym. Ainsworth explained that indeed he was related to Sir Charles Rich and that he resided normally at Roos Hall in Beccles, but had occasion to be spending some time in Norwich. Mention was made again of Mr Anthony Russell, with whom also Mr Wilmington seemed to be acquainted. Then they ordered their meal and two bottles of wine of Mr Spencer's selection and once the coffee had been reached Mr Bannerman brought out a deck of cards. They played whist for shillings at first and Ainsworth was glad that he still had a few of those in his pockets. Suddenly he was none too keen in present company to flourish his purse of fifty sovereigns. Soon, however, good luck eluding him, he was obliged to apply to the barman for change and for another bottle of wine whilst he was about it. His luck continued indifferent, and he was just consoling himself that he had not lost a large sum and might make up the shortfall with funds he might press Mrs Jarvis to release at the weekend, when the game was changed, the stakes were raised, his luck declined further and his skills as a player seemed to pale remarkably compared with those of Mr Gilbert Spencer.

When the fifty sovereigns were exhausted Ainsworth rose to leave the table. He made what sounded a lame excuse, except perhaps to Mr Wilmington, that he had an early appointment in the morning for which he would need to have his faculties about him. With an elegant bow Ainsworth made his apologies and escaped into the street. Then he realised that he lacked even sufficient funds for a cab fare. He could see the spire of the Cathedral silhouetted against a crisp star-lit sky and made his way towards it. Finding himself near the Waggon & Horses he discovered familiar ground and walked wearily back to Cow Hill.

However Ainsworth slept little that night. He had lost nearly a quarter of the sum he had stolen and realised that circulating in Norwich society would not enable him to make up the shortfall with sufficient speed to prevent discovery of the theft. He must seek funds from elsewhere to obliterate his loss. Nor did he believe that Roos Hall could provide enough for his needs. Sir Charles still furnished Mrs Jarvis with an allowance for the maintenance of the Hall, but all the Suffolk estate revenues were borne away by Mr Russell and paid into Sir Charles' Norwich bank account, to which Ainsworth had no access. He did indeed still receive a modest allowance at the Hall, but that was for his personal requirements, for clothes and any entertainment to be had in Beccles, for his Guardian well recognised that no gentleman could live decently upon the petty salary of a law clerk. At dawn he rose, packed up his bags, and sent a message to Mr Sitwell that he had been taken ill suddenly, but hoped that it was of such a nature as to allow him to return to the office at the normal time on Monday next. Then he hailed a cab which took him to the Waggon & Horses, where he caught the stage not for Beccles but for London!

* * *

Hugo had been employed by Stan Stevenson for upwards of three months and Spring was already filling the Waveney valley with greenery. He had made numerous trips up the river to Bungay, up the Yare to Norwich, or along Breydon Water to Yarmouth. By now he was familiar with most of the cargoes they carried, how they should be loaded and stacked, how to work the lock gates, and the names and purposes of all the equipment on board. In addition, Stan had imparted to him the basic principles of sailing a small craft and had entertained him from time to time with tales of his travels aboard the merchant fleet. For his part Stan found he might safely delegate to Hugo all matters concerning operation of the tow-horse, and that as the boy developed in height and strength he would increasingly be able to rely upon him for handling most of the cargo. In fact upon occasions Timothy, who had by now obtained his new boat and was beginning to develop his own business connections, would bring a cargo from one location and transfer it to the *Louise* for onward transportation. Thus Hugo was beginning to make solo trips with Stan and it was on such a day that they set off up the Waveney to Bungay with a cargo of coal and fish for distribution to various waterside staithes and some grain for grinding at Ellingham Mill.

Hugo hastened to meet the lad from Wilson's stable who arrived with the tow-horse and noted that they had not been given their usual wise and experienced animal. It seemed that he had been engaged by some other bargee and they were to be burdened with a novice horse instead. "That's bad luck, lad," Stan said when the situation was explained to him. "We must sail with this fish, for it won't keep fresh till the morrow, and that means you will have to guide him all the way." Indeed it was as much as Hugo could do to persuade the skittish creature to stand still while he attached the tow-rope. Then the horse jibbed at crossing the Gillingham bridge to the towpath on the far side, and Stan was obliged to quant laboriously for a longer stretch than usual till the tow could be attached again. "We've been sent a leery one this time," Stan commented. "I must have a word with Jack Wilson and see what other horses he has."

Fortunately they had nothing for delivery at Geldeston village so did not need to divert up the Cut, but they did need to cross it. This horse had never boarded a barge in its life, and when Stan brought the boat to the bank and Hugo arranged the planks that the animal was to step upon, it simply refused to move. In the end Hugo had to leave the barge behind and walk the horse right along the Cut and down again on the other side of the dyke. This course bargees usually avoided since there were hedges and fences running down to the water. Hugo had not faced such obstacles before, and especially when handling a large and nervous quadruped. Some of the hedges were low and the long-legged creature was able to brush through them, though Hugo had more of a struggle with the thorns. One wooden fence had a removable top bar which Hugo lifted, leaving the horse to step over the lower rail. There were also several ditches to be crossed, one of them quite a deep dyke. To his surprise the horse seemed prepared to swim, so Hugo found a willow stump of the right height, mounted the horse bareback and guided it across with the halter. Thereafter the horse made better progress and soon reached the barge. However they had lost a good deal of time and were glad to pause for refreshment at the Locks Inn.

Presently they set out again. Hugo found that his greatest problem was persuading the horse to stop while he operated lock gates and paddles. Their regular tow-horse would stop automatically and start to graze as each transit point was reached, but this one continued to pull. Stan instructed Hugo to run the tow-rope around one of the waterside bollards, and this prevented it moving forward unasked. At Ellingham Lock they unloaded all the grain which made the barge much lighter, and the horse set off thereafter at such a trot that Hugo had much ado to keep up with him. Nor was it easy to persuade him to stop at some of the wayside staithes where a couple of sacks of coal had to be tipped into each coal bin. It was very late in the afternoon when they reached Wainford Lock and

Hugo hardly had strength enough to operate the lock gates. Fortunately the lock-keeper came out and worked one set of gates whilst Hugo dealt with the other and retrieved the horse. Lanterns were lit and the horse trotted quite eagerly into the Bungay basin, perhaps anticipating a warm stable and its evening feed. As the weather was fine and not too cold, Hugo offered to sleep on the boat, for he knew Stan did not make much profit on these up-river journeys but rather more on the sailing trips. After a good supper they both wrapped themselves in a blanket and a tarpaulin and slept peacefully till morning.

When Hugo went to collect their horse the following morning he was told that it had developed a cough during the night and was not fit to work. Alas, the stable had no alternative available. Hugo returned to Stan with the bad news and received a string of expletives, the precise nature and objectivity of which was known and appreciated only among bargees. Stan stumped up the road to the brewery and asked for the manager. Five men were told off to haul the barge along to the brewery quay where it was to collect a full cargo of beer for the hostelries of Beccles. Two of the men helped Stan and Hugo to load the barrels, first into the hold and then all over the hatches and the deck. They lashed each batch of barrels into place so that they could neither roll about nor fall overboard. Then the brewery-men simply spaced themselves along the tow-rope and began 'haling' the barge down-river. Hugo had watched other vessels proceeding in this way, but hitherto they had always relied on a horse whose hire was so much cheaper. When they reached the Locks Inn Stan was obliged to treat all the men to ale and refreshments, and Hugo knew that no profit was to be made from this trip.

They reached Beccles late in the evening. Stan paid off the brewery-men who would return to Bungay by waggon, no doubt after spending all their pay in one of the many Beccles inns. On the quayside they were met by a disconsolate and bedraggled Tim who confessed that he had suffered a collision in his boat which had been damaged and would take a week or so to repair. It would also cost a deal to mend, so could Stan give him work for a week or two instead? Stan looked at Hugo who realised exactly what he was thinking. "After this trip you deserve a holiday, young Hughie," Stan started to say, but Hugo interrupted him.

"Mr Stevenson, I did not dare ask you before, but now this has come about I'm emboldened to do so. My Papa and our cowmen are about to drive our Scottish cattle all the way to Smithfield Market. It will require a week or so to walk there and a day or two to return in the waggon once they've been sold. I would envy no end to go with them. Could you use Tim in my place until I return? I would take no pay for my absence, of course." Tim looked much relieved as Stan assented. So Hugo ran home through the streets of Beccles, something he only managed now every few days, handed his wages to his mother and declared himself ready to assist with the droving of the livestock.

They set out the following day. Jim Caldicott and Frank Briggs collected the cattle from their meadow. Bill Foster was quite tearful at seeing 'his creatures' depart, but Jim assured him that he was likely to have another herd to care for come the autumn. Bill had also had the cattle reshod. The 'shoes' were shaped like half an orange segment and were fitted to either side of the hoof. One of the blacksmiths at Beccles specialised in such work for all the local graziers. Pip and Shep rounded up the four-legged snorting beasts as if they were no more than sheep and drove them through the gate and along Puddingmoor Lane to the crossroads. Here they met with Alf Jarvis and Hugo with the waggon, duly covered over for protection from wind and rain for some twenty cackling geese. These had not been 'shod' either with pitch or with felt overshoes, but were to graze while the company rested at midday and were to be fattened overnight on bran and grain. Penned in the waggon it was hoped that they would be safe from foxes and guarded from theft by Pip and Shep. All the livestock, including the horses, would pass each night in the same field in the hope of keeping them safe from two-legged thieves also. There were no women accompanying this trip, it being regarded as strictly men's business.

Their way led south through the village of Redisham, among lands that also belonged to the Roos Hall manorial estate but with which they had no family connection. Then they crossed a wide swathe of common land, being careful to keep their cattle separate from those pastured by the villagers. The woods were full of other people's swine too, and Alf instructed his men to steer well clear in case any were infected with the fever. They paused for refreshments on the open turf and Hugo had his first experience of herding the geese with a willow switch in one hand and a mutton pie in the other. He found the birds very obstinate, especially about returning to the waggon when it was time to move on. In the end Alf started the waggon moving without them, at which they 'let out a great noise' as Hugo later described it to Stan and Tim, and ran after the waggon positively clamouring to be allowed back on board. They crossed the River Blyth at Halesworth and shortly afterwards met up with a farmer near the village of Walpole who was prepared to hire them a field for the night and shelter in his barn.

The evening of the second day found them in the vicinity of Saxmundham, where they purchased supplies and moved on to Stratford St Andrew before finding suitable accommodation for themselves and their beasts. At one point they thought of turning out the geese and sleeping in the waggon, but one look at the generous layer of bird-lime which decorated the straw on its floor suddenly rendered that idea most unattractive. On the third day Alf again sought out routes which led through open country where the cattle could graze, rather than leading them along miry main roads which would deplete their food supply and cost a deal in dues at the toll gates. At Wickham Market Alf enquired whether any fair was anticipated where they might sell their beasts without travelling as far as London, despite the fact that the best prices for fattened beef were to be obtained there. Unfortunately they had missed the Shrovetide Fair by no more than a fortnight. Ipswich too did not anticipate any large fairing before the autumn. In three and a half days their journey had taken them halfway to the Capital, though Alf anticipated that progress would become increasingly difficult through mired roads and a press of other travellers as they approached the City. First, though, they must pass through Ipswich in order to reach the marshy ground at Manningtree which would provide good grazing for their stock.

From the peace of the open countryside they entered all the bustle of a large town. None of them was familiar with the layout of its streets, and the High Street being the one likely to be broadest they sought directions and pressed on, only to find themselves in the midst of a street market. It happened that the waggon was positioned at the rear of their little procession rather than leading it from the front. Consequently, and before they were able to prevent it, thirty lowing bullocks were scampering down the street, overturning hand-carts and stalls, hen coops and baskets of eggs, bread rolls and vegetables, all tumbled into a heap on the cobblestones, whilst Pip and Shep were pursued by a host of angry barking local dogs! It was sheer chaos. Alf was worried that the geese might fly out of the waggon and sent Hugo into the back of it to control them. He edged the horses gingerly forward through the crowd, then stopped at the edge of the town centre where the sheepdogs had been able to gather the cattle together. Their only problem was – one of their bullocks was missing.

Leaving Hugo and Frank with the dogs to guard the livestock, Alf and Jim returned to the High Street, each armed with a heavy stick. The stallholders were none too pleased to see them and no one would say which way the stray beast had gone. They apologised to each overset stall owner in turn and paid for some of the broken eggs, but still no information was forthcoming. They had reached the far end of the High Street and happened to look down one of the alleys. There was the missing bullock, standing quietly with a halter around its neck which someone had tied to a hitching rail. Had they not chanced upon it, certain citizens of Ipswich would have dined regally for weeks upon its juicy steaks. Alf and Jim led the beast slowly back down the main street, with all the market dogs baring their teeth and growling as they went. "If this is how we are looked upon in Ipswich," Alf remarked, "whatever will happen when we reach London? I think we must be sure to have the waggon go ahead, so that the beasts have something to follow."

There was much marshy ground around Manningtree, and once or twice they lost their way in narrow lanes that led only to green fields and hedges. Evidently there was something to be said for using the highway. Eventually they managed to ford the River Stour but could obtain no lodgings and were obliged to sleep under the waggon with the dogs. The weather was foggy and they were soaked with dew by dawn. As they approached Colchester Alf decided they should avoid the city centre but sent Hugo and Frank there on foot to purchase supplies. Then they turned aside and joined that great highway the Romans had built which would lead them through Chelmsford to London. Here they found they were no longer alone. Stage coaches, stage waggons full of goods trundling along hauled by ox-teams, mail-coaches, some private coaches, or a smart phaeton, and even the occasional gentleman on horseback passed them by in one direction or the other. Moving in the same direction were other drovers with cattle, sheep or pigs, all sweating their odiferous path along the highway. There were other flocks of fowl too, more geese, coops of chickens, and some fighting cocks destined, no doubt, for the dens of vice in the East End.

In such company herdsmen had to stay alert to prevent their beasts becoming lost or stolen. There was intense competition for every blade of grass to be had along the route, and the highway became a wide miry much-rutted avenue as the herds spread out on either side in search of sustenance. Nor could they be sure of finding overnight accommodation. There were indeed a few farmers who made quite a supplementary living from letting out this field and that for passing livestock, whichever field needed the benefit of their manure. Alf and his team found all the hostelries full before them and were obliged to spend each night under the waggon alongside their stock. On the sixth day they passed through Chelmsford and spent the night at Crow Green. Other drovers had gathered here, both those on their way to the City and some making the return journey. Alf and Jim joined the circle around the large bonfire they had built on the Green and listened to their chat about market opportunities and sale prices. They were within a day's journey of their destination and were anxious to obtain any useful tips for this new experience. Meanwhile Frank and Hugo sat beside a smaller fire of their own, grilled on sticks the sausages they had bought in Chelmsford, drank their ale and thought themselves fine fellows to be engaged on such a venture.

The following morning dawned fine and breezy. Finding their way into the great Metropolis could not have proved easier since all they must do was to follow the crowd. Such was the press of traffic that they encountered many delays as herd after herd funnelled into London along the same route. Romford, Ilford, Stratford, Hackney, places that only Hugo with his wider schooling could have placed in order on the map. Hoxton, Shoreditch and at last into Aldersgate and the eastern edge of the market. The sky was already darkening into a luminous ultramarine as the sun sank in the West, and lamplight twinkled from the windows of house and cottage.

When they reached the fairground it was a scene of total disorder with groups of animals criss-crossing the square as they were driven in or out. Jim Caldicott went ahead to enquire whether he might reserve a pen where their stock could be secured for the night. Space was found but they were obliged to build their own stockade with wooden stakes stored at the site. Once the cattle were within and the waggon placed alongside, Frank and Hugo were despatched to seek out water and fodder for their beasts. They found the price of hay much elevated and were obliged to request extra funds. The geese were fed and bedded down for the night and their horses were freed from their harness and hitched to the waggon along with the dogs. As their stock would require guarding overnight, they could expect to enjoy little sleep. Alf himself went in search of refreshments for all and food for the dogs. They ate and drank where they stood, and slept by turns beneath the waggon which fortunately rested on a fairly clean stretch of hard-standing, and a few yards either way from the stinking offal-filled runnels that ran across the fairground. Nor did they enjoy a peaceful sleep. Apart from all the lowing, bleating and neighing of the livestock, the cackling of their own geese and the frenzied transit of other fowl which had not been so well secured, there was a constant stumbling of drovers and herdsmen to and from the public houses which surrounded the market, and drunken brawls and doltish tricks, such as loosing cattle from their pens and stampeding them through the narrow alleyways between the stalls, kept Alf and his team awake all night. Never had they felt so relieved as when the noises stilled and even the rioters slumbered in the quiet before dawn.

At six o'clock the following morning they were roused from their breakfast beside the waggon by a local butcher. He explained that he owned a shop behind the Shambles where the beasts were slaughtered, over against St Bartholomew-Le-Grand in Long Lane. He had heard that they had some fine geese for sale and was prepared to purchase them all, since he had an order from the Mansion House, no less, for one of the Lord Mayor's banquets. He stepped up on the rail where the buckets hung at the back of the waggon and was much satisfied to be received by a very lively hiss from the geese. A bargain was struck and the butcher promised to return immediately with the purchase price and a couple of assistants to carry the geese, since he preferred not to sully their clean white feathers by walking them through the market and the filth and excrement which covered the fairground. No doubt the feathers were to be sold on for the filling of pillows and cushions. Hugo and Frank decided to lend a hand, having a goose tucked under each arm with their hands clasping each bird firmly by the neck.

Indeed the fairground was literally a stinking cesspit as Hugo crossed it, trying to avoid piles of dirty straw, animal and human excrement, discarded bones, portions of animal bodies, and all the litter left by a vast press of beasts and humans cramped together in a limited space. Nothing more was needed to inform him of his proximity to the Shambles than the smell; the odour of rotting and over-ripe flesh wafted on the cheerful morning breeze. Soon he could see the clusters of ragged stalls hung with tattered sails and tarpaulins for shelter from sun and rain. The overhanging roof of each stall was garnished with a frize de fer of iron meat hooks, each one supporting half a carcass of some unidentified creature dripping a pool of blood. In between hung fleshy scarlet screens of livers, hearts and lights, whilst in front of every stall stood a row of jack-boots, or so one might mistake them at first glance, for they were whole legs of cattle cut off at the knee and complete with skin and hoof. Hugo winced at the thought of their own cattle ending up in such a barbaric display.

When they reached the butcher's stall Hugo saw two ladies sitting on stools beside it and plucking chickens. The birds' bodies were cradled upon their filthy bloodied aprons, whilst the fistfuls of feathers were thrust into a large hessian sack. The women reminded him, as they sat with surly faces and mechanical action, of an illustration he had seen in a recent newspaper, of the French trico-teuses in Paris sitting around the Guillotine at the execution of their King and Queen! Hugo heard a crack, and the butcher had broken the neck of one of the geese. He laid the body on a bench beside one of the tricoteuses; then moved on to the next one which he despatched in the same way. Hugo dared not look to see which one of their birds it was, for he had known them all by name. It was as much as he could stomach to hand over the two he carried and then to return twice with the butcher to transport the remainder.

Freed from this disagreeable task, he and Frank rejoined the others. Hugo found his father deep in discussion with a possible purchaser for their cattle. He hoped they could complete the sale today and return to the open road for the journey home. Hugo glanced over the neighbouring pens towards Farringdon Street and suddenly froze. Staring at him with equal surprise was none other than Mr Ainsworth Rich! Both looked for a long moment and knew instinctive-ly that henceforth they were to be enemies. Hugo wished to draw his father's attention to his discovery, but was unable to interrupt his business chat. When eventually he had an opportunity to tell Alf, his father would not believe him. "Surely you must have been mistaken, lad," he said, "for Mr Ainsworth is employed every day in a law office at Norwich."

"I tell you, I recognised him, Papa, though he looked very pale and not at all well-dressed. The clothes he wore looked as if they had been hired from a pawn-broker."

Later in the day they did manage to dispose of all their cattle to a single buyer and at a good profit, so despite the expenses incurred the expedition had been worthwhile. Leaving Frank and the dogs in charge of the waggon and horses, Alf and Jim took Hugo with them to visit the shops lining Farringdon Street. They purchased trinkets for the ladies and a few luxury spices and fruits that never made their way to provincial towns like Beccles. Hugo kept watch for any fur-ther sign of Ainsworth Rich, but there was none. He remembered Aunt Jarvis telling him that Ainsworth had attended a school hereabouts and supposed that he might be looking up old acquaintances.

As the sun declined over the tumbled roofs and chimney-pots of the Capital, they hitched up the horses and left the fairground, returning the way they had come. That evening they did not pause until they reached the last lighted cot-tage and passed the night on a piece of open ground. As they had swept out their waggon following the sale of the geese they were able to sleep inside it on fresh straw. What a relief, Hugo thought, to be in the fresh air and far away from that foetid and overcrowded atmosphere. Whoever would wish to be employed there for a living?

* * *

Mr Ainsworth Rich had indeed been looking up old acquaintances, or rather anyone who would lend him sufficient funds to enable him to play a decent hand at cards. Having deserted Norwich and leaving the stage at one of the coaching inns in Holborn, he called upon a number of former school friends and former playing partners. Ainsworth found himself much surprised by the coolness of their welcome. This one's wife was expecting a baby, that one's father was seriously ill. It was as much as he could achieve to find any lodging at all amongst them. Then one fellow-gambler did offer him a roof over his head and he secured a few engagements. The funds he had stolen from Norwich, which by now he had not the least thought of returning, lasted just long enough to buy him a new set of clothes and stake money for the first evening's play. His luck in these initial weeks might have best been described as "indifferent" and his skills seemed a little rusty. Curiously his mind seemed to lack that clarity of purpose and that perspicacity of the likely fall of the cards, and that decisiveness of play which had characterised the success he had enjoyed during his first experience of London life after leaving university. Nevertheless his gains sufficed to keep himself in clean linen and to spend liberally on good food and wine when he caroused with his friends. Ainsworth's opinion of himself and his place in the world began to inflate one more.

Meanwhile in Norwich, neither his absence nor the missing guineas were remarked upon at first. When he did not appear at the office on Monday morning, after an hour or two Snuff was sent to enquire at his lodgings. With the week's rent having been paid in advance, Ainsworth's landlady was in no mood to criticise her lodger, and Snuff returned with the message that the poor fellow had seemed quite ill on the Saturday morning when he left for Beccles and was doubtless spending a few days at home to recover his health. It was not until the following week that Mr Sitwell sent a letter to Mr Russell alerting him to the clerk's absence, and not until the week after that did Mr Russell ride over to Roos Hall to enquire news of the absentee. There, of course, the staff had seen nothing of him and had assumed, mistakenly, that the had decided to remain at Norwich for the weekend, perhaps having made acquaintances there with whom he might enjoy livelier diversion than was to be obtained at Roos Hall. To tell the truth they were quite relieved by his absence, for the maids could giggle about their work and Jessica could run up and downstairs, look at the books in the library, groom Pharaoh alongside Ted, and take Arthur for walks in the park without the unpredictable and brooding presence of that unpleasant young man. Indeed Arthur seemed to have transferred his allegiance to Jessica, more especially now that Matilda had been brought to Roos Hall and was busily employed at nibbling the lawns. Arthur was fascinated by the little creature and regarded her as his special plaything. Always a gentle dog, he would crouch on the grass beside her and pretend to growl as she came near. And Matilda, seemingly not one white dismayed, would put her head down and butt at him. Then they would prance around one another, she only limited in her movements by the long rope which anchored her to an appropriate tree or post. When Jessica returned from school each day she would join in their play and began to take Matilda with her when they walked in the park, though she often had trouble in catching the elusive skipping quadruped when it was time to return indoors.

Into this peaceful haven Mr Russell arrived with the unwelcome news that Mr Ainsworth had deserted his employment and his lodgings in Norwich. He discussed with Mrs Jarvis which of them should write to Sir Charles and inform him of this development. It seemed appropriate for Mr Russell to do so, since he had responsibility for the Norwich estates and the business of Sir Charles in that city. A further month passed without any news of the absconder. Then Alf Jarvis happened to mention to Mr Russell during his visit to inspect the Ringsfield Farm, that Hugo averred he had caught sight of Mr Ainsworth only the other day whilst they were selling their Scottish cattle at Smithfield Market.

Meanwhile a more ominous discovery had been made at the office in Norwich. Mr Sitwell had engaged a new clerk and in accordance with good legal practice he was set to go through each of the current files and to bill again all the clients who had failed to settle outstanding accounts after more than 30 days; one of these would appear to be Mr Tobias Wilmington who still owed the sum of 200 guineas. The reminder was duly despatched and immediately upon its arrival in the mails a very indignant Mr Wilmington set off for Mr Sitwell's office, waving aloft the receipt he had fraudulently been given. The conversation which ensued with Mr Sitwell may easily be imagined as the identity of the author of the discrepancy came to light. Mr Sitwell repaired forthwith to the residence of Mr Russell and demanded immediate settlement of the debt, which Mr Russell was obliged to withdraw from Sir Charles's Norwich bank account. He then sat down to write another and even more painful report to Sir Charles, since he was uncomfortably aware that some of the blame might attach to himself for not having supervised Ainsworth more closely, though exactly what he should or could have done he was not quire sure. He also reported that Hugo Jarvis thought he had glimpsed Ainsworth at Smithfield Market and that therefore Sir Charles might wish to initiate inquiries for him in London.

In fact Ainsworth had just previously received an invitation of the sort he coveted most, an evening of cards with three gentlemen of 'the smart set'. Indeed his own friend and host seemed not to have been included which, if he paused to think about it, should have given him reason to ponder. Instead he dressed in his best garb, did not hesitate to conceal about his person all the funds, to every last penny, currently at his command, and set off in a cab to Brooks's Club where the engagement was due to take place. His host for the evening was to be a certain Mr Featherstone, whom his friend and landlord described as a capital fellow, one full of probity and wisdom, so that Ainsworth need have no fear of any card-sharps or of being cheated. Ainsworth had been instructed to ask for him of the doorman and to be sure to give his own name clearly. Both instructions seemed entirely normal and again did not give rise to any suspicion.

"Good evening, sir. May I have your name?" the doorman requested from amid the ample capes of his smart outdoor uniform, for there was quite a chilly breeze sweeping down the elegant street that night.

"Mr Ainsworth Rich," came the prompt reply. "I am engaged to meet Mr Featherstone."

"Would that be Mr Justice Featherstone, sir?"

Ainsworth was surprised and hesitated to make his response. It had never occurred to him that any of the people he was to meet that evening might belong to an older, more respectable, generation. "I daresay it must be he. Please ask the gentleman himself," Ainsworth suggested lamely. The doorman called within to a footman and whispered a message in his ear. Presently the footman returned and Ainsworth was escorted inside. There he was obliged to sign his name and pay a fee for temporary membership, since his former affiliation at the club had long since lapsed. Then he was escorted to a table where three gentlemen were seated. Two of them rose at his approach, one being an elderly gentleman with a slight stoop and a deeply lined face beneath his short wig. That gentleman fixed him with a penetrating gaze from his grey eyes. "Good evening, Mr Rich," he said, "my name is Featherstone."

The gentleman who stood opposite the judge now made his own introduction. A middle-aged and rather corpulent fellow, he was well dressed but by no means extravagantly so, his balding head not bewigged and his podgy hands well endowed with bejewelled gold rings. He said his name was Mr Goldsworthy. The third gentleman, still seated, and dressed in the attire of Legal Counsel, as if he had just stepped that way from the Courts of Law, consented to look up at that moment and to address the new arrival. "Good evening, Ainsworth," he said. It was his old enemy Marcus Todd!

"Sit down, old fellow," Marcus Todd went on. "'Tis good to see you in such fine fettle and I trust that your funds this evening are in equally good shape. You see, Ainsworth, you recently defrauded a relative of mine, a Mr Tobias Wilmington, younger brother of my stepfather, of a trifling sum of two hundred guineas. These gentlemen, my friends and colleagues," he indicated those to either hand, "are fully conversant with your abuse of trust, and should your deportment this evening not give adequate satisfaction we are authorised to issue a warrant for your arrest. Mr Goldsworthy is an officer of the Sheriff of London and Mr Featherstone is a justice the Chancery Division. He will arbitrate as necessary on all matters of play. The game is to be whist. Shall we commence, gentlemen, by each placing on the table a stake of, let us say, two hundred guineas?" All three of them had their stakes ready, each in a plump leather bag. Eyes began to turn their way from the surrounding gaming tables as neighbouring players realised that something unusual was afoot.

Ainsworth had then to confess in public that he had not thought to bring such a sum with him, but he would check his pockets to see what might be found therein and would sign an IOU as surety for the rest. He then had the embarrassment of turning out each of his pockets until, apart from some small change, a sum of 150 guineas had been amassed on his side of the table. Marcus Todd handed a deck of cards to Mr Justice Featherstone which he inspected in detail, and pronounced them to be correct and unmarked. Ainsworth, now watching with eagle eyes, was unable to espy any irregularities upon them. The Judge shuffled the pack several times and returned them to Marcus Todd who dealt each a hand and play commenced.

At first Ainsworth could not stop his hands shaking as the game began. It was such a shock encounter Marcus Todd again and to realise that he was still a sworn enemy, just as he had been at school. He also reflected bitterly that he had not recognised the name of Wilmington when that gentleman had called at the office in Norwich. He should have exercised more caution and awaited a more gullible person. Gradually, however, his resolution steadied, his concentration improved, and for a long while that evening he more than held his own. By this time he was sure that his winnings amounted to considerably more than the two hundred guineas he had stolen. He had realised that this engagement had been a trap set to punish him, surely better than jail, however, or even hanging since he remembered that his offence had been committed by someone in the humble guise of a law clerk. So the gentlemen around him would obviously expect to be propitiated by the acceptance of substantial debts of honour. How much would satisfy them, he wondered? Would they settle for a thousand guineas apiece?

A fresh bottle of wine appeared and then another. Ainsworth drank without paying any heed to its taste or refinement. Were he to suggest playing Faro, for instance, a game of pure chance where one placed bets on the likely fall of the cards, he might easily win from these players all the money he needed to retreat with honour from the situation, being sure to reimburse Marcus Todd with two hundred guineas for his uncle. On the other hand he might lose all and have to promise much in the form of notes for later settlement. At what point might he escape from the trap which had been set him? Whilst Ainsworth pondered, as if reading his mind and growing impatient himself, Marcus Todd suggested switching to that very game. From their present pack he extracted the entire suit of Spades and placed these on the table in front of him in two rows, ace to six nearer him with the seven halfway up alongside, and beyond them eight to king in reverse order. Then he called a footman and announced that they were to play Faro. A tremor of interest turned heads at the surrounding tables.

The footman brought a fresh pack of cards and a wooden box without a lid and having a slit in one side through which a card might be extruded. The Judge took the pack of cards out of their wrapper. These differed from those used for whist in that the picture cards showed their figures at full length, the pip cards lacked numbers and symbols at their corners, and aces counted as low value, having inherited the role of the King's Jester or Fool. Moreover such packs did not meet with the approval of the Worshipful Company of Makers of Playing

Cards, whose motto, "Corde recto elati omnes" – "An upright heart pleases all", scarcely seemed an appropriate sentiment for a gambling den, even one distinguished as a Gentlemen's Club. While the Judge examined the cards as before, Ainsworth realised that he also should be observing them minutely. Unfortunately the predominance of his own cogitations, together with the mellowing effect of several glasses of a claret of excellent vintage meant that his wits were not as razor-sharp as they ought to have been. Nevertheless when the Judge, having shuffled the pack twice, placed it face upwards in the open wooden box, he began to concentrate very sharply indeed.

"I am to be Banker," Marcus Todd announced, "and Mr Goldsworthy here has kindly agreed to record all our bets and whether or not they were successful. Then we may settle up at the end of the game." Marcus Todd waved away the footman's proffering of the rod and buttons which most used to record which cards had already been played. "We are all intelligent enough not to require that," he said with a glance of venom not lost on Ainsworth. However he did allow the players to take some printed cards bearing the numbers of the suits, upon which they might make their own notations, and Ainsworth fumbled in his pocket for a pencil. "Now, gentlemen, place your bets," Marcus Todd indicated the Spades displayed before him and the coloured counters delivered by the footman to each player in two little towers of ten, each counter worth no less than fifty guineas!

The card face-up in the wooden box, and which would presently be discarded by the Banker to reveal the one beneath, on whose numerical identity the bets were being placed, just happened to be the King of Hearts. He had been known as the Pharaoh among the early playing cards which originated in medieval France, and it was after that gentleman that this game had been named 'Faro'. Bets were made by placing one or more counters upon or between the cards of the spare suit of Spades in the hope that the next card when disclosed in the box would make up a numerical pair. A simple game, but one with the odds shortening and the excitement mounting as the cards left in the box diminished. However the Banker is accorded the distinct advantage of raking in all the stakes lost upon the first card of the turn or 'coup' and half the value of all stakes placed upon the second card of the coup if it should bear the same value as the first. Ainsworth groaned inwardly, knowing that Marcus Todd was bent on his complete destruction. Even if they were to play several rounds, Ainsworth knew that they would never let him serve as Banker.

Once the initial bets had been laid, Marcus Todd's hand moved to the wooden box, extruding the discarded King of Hearts and revealing, by strange coincidence, the King of Clubs. "Ha! I play the Lunatic," Marcus Todd exclaimed in an oblique political reference to poor King George III who had recently suffered a period of madness, the King's reputation as a keen gardener being deemed alluded to by the leafy cudgel carried by the King of Clubs. Now bets laid upon a forthcoming king were modest, since the King of Hearts was already a 'dead' card. Moreover Ainsworth had actually bet against a king coming next by 'coppering', that is by placing a copper coin from his pocket atop his counter. It was not a good beginning. Baptised by fire, Ainsworth placed his bets for several turns on a selection of pip cards and managed some modest wins from players who had staked losing counters on the second card of each 'coup'. For a while nothing was heard from their table save low murmurs of 'paix', or 'double paix' as players doubled their existing stakes, while more and more cards were disclosed, extruded and placed on the discard pile. Then someone would cry 'paroli' as a run of wins gave rise to multiple rewards, such that the Banker was obliged to return to the player three or six times the value of his stake, depending on the exact placing of his bets. It was this scenario which Ainsworth hoped to serve on Marcus Todd and which Marcus was equally determined to prevent.

The guessing and the betting continued at a ferocious pace, slackening when a 'missing card' came to light and intensifying whenever a fresh pairing was anticipated. Ainsworth had noted that the Judge had shuffled the pack by splitting the new deck in two halves and merging them twice over, a process which was more likely to leave numbers paired than otherwise. He scribbled a careful note of which cards had passed, though he was beginning to find that the dim light and the excellent claret were making it more difficult for him to decipher his own writing. He staked on a four, left his stake in place and another four came, so doubling his winnings despite the discount paid to the Banker. However in the next two 'coups' he lost heavily, having overlooked the fact that three sevens had already been played and that the only person likely to benefit from the fourth of them was the Banker.

At last the long game came to an end with only three cards remaining in the box. The players had now to calculate the identity of each card and the order in which they would appear. The Judge proved correct and collected the last of the winnings. Ainsworth had felt sure that the Ace of Spades had yet to emerge as he had no record of it. He knew it had been there at the beginning because he had seen it in the Judge's hands when he shuffled the pack. However the last three cards had been a three, a nine and a Knave. Had the missing Ace vanished into someone's palm, or had Ainsworth just been too dull to notice it? But there was no time for wondering, for Mr Goldsworthy, being of a mathematical turn of mind, was reckoning up the player's bets, whether these were successful or not, and how many counters were to be accorded to or deducted from each of them.

A hush descended on the room as Mr Goldsworthy announced the results. He himself had 'lost' forty counters but had won eighty, the Judge had lost thirty-five but had won ninety-five, Mr Rich had lost two hundred and had won only twenty, whereas Mr Todd as Banker had won from twenty of the twenty-six 'coups', taking in a total of two hundred and seventy-five counters and paying out one hundred and ninety-five to the other players in successful bets against the Bank. Ainsworth's stomach turned over and nausea rose in his throat as he realised how hopeless was his position. In terms of sterling he had lost ten thousand guineas and regained only one thousand, which left him owing two thousand guineas to Mr Goldsworthy, three thousand to the Judge and four thousand guineas to the hated Marcus Todd. The latter then unctuously declared that he would retain Ainsworth's original stake of 150 guineas as a down-payment on the sum owed to his uncle and would await settlement of the remainder plus interest at ten percent. Meanwhile, would Mr Rich kindly sign the three ready-prepared promises to pay into which Mr Goldsworthy was presently inserting the relevant sums, to be guaranteed upon Sir Charles Rich's estate. With a blanched face and without being able to speak a word, Ainsworth signed where he was bid, each note being witnessed by the other players. Then he rose from his chair, bowed low, murmured "Goodnight, gentlemen" and left the room to the sound of ribald laughter from all sides. He scarcely remembered to collect his cloak and hat before stepping out into the chilly night.

Ainsworth walked to his lodging, too numb even to search his pockets for the fare for a cab. He doubted that he still possessed coins of any value at all. When he reached the appartment of the kind friend who had given him accommodation he found the door shut against him – the lock had been changed – and his portmanteau and belongings lodged with the porter, so said the note, who had locked his office and departed home to a comfortable bed for the night. Ainsworth found himself obliged to sit on the doorstep until dawn, feeling cold and sick, and to await the porter's return before he could reclaim his goods. Then he took his best studs, pins and jewels to a pawnbroker before throwing himself on the mercy of Mrs Bostock in Bloomsbury, with funds sufficient to pay her a week's rent.

At first, Mrs Bostock, not being apprised of the full circumstances of his appearance on her doorstep and the rent being paid, assumed Mr Ainsworth was merely visiting old friends since he knew London well. It was only when he returned one day having exchanged his elegant clothes for some hired cheaply from a pawnbroker that she suspected the truth and immediately sat down to write to her brother-in-law, unaware that in Norwich Mr Russell had just done the same. It was not long before Mr Ainsworth was safely under lock and key, not at the Fleet prison this time, but at Waverley Abbey in the presence of an incandescent Sir Charles Rich who had just been presented with the three promissory notes!

"If there were a means of having you publicly flogged without sullying the name of Rich, I would surely do it!" Sir Charles broke out in his anger. "Every opportunity Sir Robert or I have given you in life you have thrown away, whether it be at school, university, land management or the law. Were I to hand you over to the Authorities with details of your crime you would inevitably go to the gallows. It is only the magnanimity of Tobias Wilmington and the prompt action of my Bailiff, Mr Russell, in repaying the loss immediately upon its discovery, that has saved your unworthy neck!"

"Mr Russell has paid? But I thought …" Ainsworth started to say, but a thunderous frown from Sir Charles froze his words in mid-air.

"These!" and Sir Charles flourished the three signed notes, "are but a token of the retribution due for such a fundamental disregard for trust. Ignatius, you seem never to have accepted your inferior role in society. You were born in a workhouse, remember, and brought up in an orphanage whence Sir Robert nobly rescued you upon the death-wish of your father."

"Father? But I thought that you …?"

"Were your father? No, I never was, and now I thank God for it. Your real father was a humble man. He worked for Sir Robert in his Government position, defended him loyally and lost his post with the same stroke of the pen as my father-in-law. Sir Robert supported him at his own cost in his last illness and, learning of your existence, had me search you out and bring you to Waverley. Your mother was a lady whose name we shall not mention, for she may be alive still though all trace of her has been lost. So you must appreciate that in your situation you would be wise to be diligent and thankful for the assistance given you. Whilst I can concede that you might find Society dull and provincial in Beccles, you had, I believe, commenced making acquaintances at Norwich and, but for your disgraceful conduct there, might yet have obtained some reasonable diversion. Mr Russell informs me that at both Norwich and Yarmouth there are theatrical and musical performances to be had which would not disgrace the London stage. Success and advancement will not seek you out. On the contrary it is you who must make the effort to find them.

"You should know, Ignatius, that for some time I have been applying to the Foreign Office on your behalf for a position abroad in our Diplomatick Service where you might exercise such talents as you have acquire along with your education. In this matter my efforts have been much inhibited by the fact that you failed to complete your Cambridge degree, since almost every other of our Nation's Civil Servants is similarly qualified. I have it in mind that you might be agreeable to serve in India, for example, where the climate is not entirely intolerable, much of the administrative activity is carried out on horseback, and someone who rides well, is a good shot, can write passable English and can cast up accounts, can become a useful personal assistant to one of our Governors or Ambassadors. That is the stratum which I have in mind as appropriate to your social position. You may take it or leave it, as you decide, but if you were to choose not to accept the post then I would wash my hands of you entirely, including settlement of these notes," he held the papers aloft again, "about which I intend to negotiate with the gentlemen concerned, since my funds cannot stretch to payment of such vast sums."

"You will now be escorted back to Roos Hall, Ignatius, and will remain there until I send for you once I have secured the place of which I spoke. I trust that you will have the good sense not to create fresh scandals there."

Not a word of thanks or appreciation came from Ainsworth's lips, only a frown that he was to be confined again as a dependent rather than living the life of a lord. Instead he enquired, "And what about Miss Jessica, sir? She shares my patrimony there and is a charge upon the revenues of Roos Hall."

"Patrimony?" quoth Sir Charles. "You have none, sir, and Miss Jessica has naught to do with you either. Now, my carriage is already at the door, along with the two footmen who brought you here. Before you join them, however, I wish that you will change those dreadful garments you are wearing for some my manservant has set out for you in my dressing room. Please go there and change at once. The remainder of your luggage already awaits you in the coach."

"Goodbye, Ignatius. Do try to be a credit to our name, and I trust never to find you in such abhorrent circumstances again." Sir Charles turned on his heel and left the room, while a manservant entered and escorted Ainsworth about Waverley Abbey House until he was at last respectably dressed and ready to depart.

* * *

Mr Ainsworth returned to Roos Hall two days later under escort. The carriage was put in the barn overnight and the horses were rested in the stables. The two footmen were well-fed and shared a room in the attics. In all this activity there was ample scope for Ted and all the domestic staff to learn the conditions appertaining to Mr Ainsworth's reappearance, of which the chief from their point of view was that he was no longer in charge. This allowed the maids to giggle and whisk out of sight when they encountered him on the upstairs gallery, and Ted to be laconic about obeying his orders with any alacrity. Mr Ainsworth felt keenly this change of atmosphere, and spent the following morning sulking in his room, while Sir Charles' carriage duly departed on its return journey to Waverley. The weather turned fine and breezy in the afternoon, typical weather for late spring, and Mr Ainsworth thought he would take his gun and go shooting in the park.

Easton brought him his shotgun which he had kept oiled as Mrs Jarvis had instructed. Easton had told him of a fox seen skulking near the hen house and that seemed as good a reason as any to take a stroll about the brushwood and rabbit warrens in the park. He had thought of taking a ride on Pharaoh, but Ted had told him that the nervous animal had kicked out in his stall last night when the strange horses were brought in, and had jarred a fetlock and gone lame. So perforce Mr Ainsworth would take the gun and go on foot. He emerged from the garden door of the drawing room on to one of the main lawns and there beheld an amazing sight; a white kid secured to a wooden stake was nibbling its way across the daisy-studded turf. At once Ainsworth remembered Ted mentioning that Miss Jessica had received the gift of a kid from the elder boy of the Jarvis household. That must be Hugo, the one who had caught sight of him at Smithfield Market, and who had no doubt been prompt to report his sighting.

How dare he make gifts to Miss Jessica, who was part of his, Ainsworth Rich's household here at Roos Hall? She was his creature to beat or smile upon as he chose. None of the household here knew that Sir Charles was not his father; there was no reason why they should have been informed of that most private detail. He repeated the question he had just asked himself. Why should Miss Jessica be beholden to Hugo Jarvis? Hugo was his enemy, just like Marcus Todd.

Ainsworth raised the gun to his shoulder. A shot rang out, echoing from wall to wall of the building behind him. The blazing white bundle of mischievous life crumpled soundlessly to the ground, its blood spattering the daisies. Arthur, who had followed his master to the doorway, rushed to the lawn with all the instinct of a retriever towards it prey. However when he reached the kid he stopped and whined, then started licking the little creature's wounds; it did not stir. Ainsworth stepped forward and made to kick the kid with his foot. Arthur looked up at him, bared his teeth and growled. Ainsworth turned and strode off through the gardens to the park: Arthur did not follow.

Easton and the groundsmen came running up, having witnessed the incident and appalled at what had occurred. Mrs Jarvis also had observed the kid's death from an upstairs window and came bustling down to the garden. It happened that Jessica herself was ill in bed with a severe chill. At all costs she must not know what had happened to Matilda. But Jessica too had heard the shot, for she had been lying in bed reading. She heard steps on the creaking stairway below and ran to her window in time to see Mrs Jarvis hurrying across the lawn to the side of the house. That could only mean one thing – Matilda! She did not stop to put any coat over her night-gown, nor to replace the lace night-cap that fell from her head. Indeed she scarcely remembered to don her slippers as she ran down two flights of stairs and out into the garden. Mrs Jarvis saw her coming and with a distraught face and outstretched arms went to greet her. But Jessica passed her by and threw herself on the ground beside her fallen pet, wild cries and sobs racking her whole body.

One of the ground staff had fetched a clean sack in which to wrap the kid's body. "Are you sure there's nothing to be done for it?" Mrs Jarvis asked Easton.

"No, Mrs Jarvis, the poor little thing is quite dead. He got it right through the heart." Easton wrapped the body carefully in the clean hessian. "I'll lay it in the outhouse for now," he said, "then we can bury it later. No doubt Miss Jessica will want to have a part in that."

Mrs Jarvis took Jessica gently by the shoulders and helped her indoors to the kitchen, where Mrs Baines had already put the kettle on. Arthur, formerly Mr Ainsworth's retriever, followed his womenfolk into the kitchen. When Jessica sat down he put his head in her lap and licked her hand. Arthur knew where his allegiance now lay.

CHAPTER X

The Betrayal

"Often we heard the ghostly ring
of harness passing by us in the night.
The lock pawls clatter ....
Always this presence of some unknown thing."
From *The Spirit of Double Locks* by Martin Hyde

It was a foggy morning in the autumn of 1794. September had been unconscionably wet, and October seemed likely to follow suit. The leaves hung dank and brown on the trees, scarcely bothering to tumble down to join the soggy carpet on the ground. As Stan Stevenson and Hugo Jarvis piloted the *Louise* along the upper reaches of the River Waveney, the summer's vegetation clung in yellow and broken confusion to either half-flooded bank. Floods already lay deep across the marshes, and while the tow-path still stood clear of the water, the overfull dyke gushing through its sluices made it difficult to operate the locks. Fortunately this morning they had been able to hire the steadiest of Jack Wilson's tow-horses, a creature whose experience had taught him to stop if he came upon an unexpected obstacle, and not to panic and jump into or over it without guidance. The landmarks of their route, the staithe at Dunburgh, the Locks Inn at Geldeston, and the Mill at Ellingham, loomed up through the mist like friendly spirits, but as the sunlight faded later in the day strange lights and shapes began to flicker on the marshes.

"They can't be people out there, can they?" Hugo asked. "Those fields are deep in water."

"No, Hughie, it isn't that," Stan Stevenson replied with a chuckle. "That's marsh gas bubbling up through the water and catching fire as it reaches the surface. You watch, lad, and you'll see it flicker up in one place and go out, only to flare up in another." Then, just as they reached Wainford Lock and the evening was closing in, Hugo thought he saw something very strange indeed. One of the shadowy shapes resolved into a black ball, a ball which seemed to have legs beneath it galloping along, and a thick, shaggy coat which floated about it as it ran, and flickering flames that served for eyes, and a burning torch in its mouth. He shouted to Stan, but by the time he did so the shape had vanished. When he described to Stan what he had seen, the latter replied, "Aye, that's Black Shuck a'right, the Harbinger of Doom. You'd best watch out, lad, that he doesn't creep up on you unawares!"

JESS OF ROOS HALL

They slept on the boat that night, well wrapped in tarpaulins, and next morning the fog had lifted. Instead a cheerful breeze greeted Hugo as he ran to fetch the horse from its stable and hitched it to the whippletree for the short haul to the brewery. There he and Stan ate breakfast while waiting for the brewery men to start their shift and bring alongside the load to be taken downstream. The sun shone brilliantly on the flooded marshes, so bright that Hugo could scarcely bear to look at the water, whilst Stan's blue eyes just disappeared within the creases of his wrinkled countenance. The lock gates were still devilish heavy with the press of water, but Hugo managed to find help at each stage and they made Beccles by mid afternoon. Hugo knew that if he hurried to return the horse to Jack Wilson, then ran fast along Ballygate, he might yet to able to meet the girls and Peter out of school and give them a surprise.

And so it proved. Lucy was full of the good marks she had achieved in class, and Jessica smiled as she greeted him but said no more until asked. Presently he did so and received the interesting news that Mr Ainsworth had taken the stage for Yarmouth again. Everyone at Roos Hall was waiting for him to be sent abroad to India or wherever on Government service, so any additional absence in the meantime was most welcome. When he did leave, Mrs Jarvis had promised Jessica that she could return to her childhood bedroom on the first floor of the house, and she was waiting eagerly for that day to come. There was another important development to share with her friends too, although Lucy knew of it already: Jessica's hair had begun to grow again. She took off her bonnet and revealed long fragile curls of the palest gold. "The fire seems to have made my hair curl," Jessica reported with pride. "Now I have ringlets, just as my mother did." Hugo stared at her for a moment, but they stood at the gates of Roos Hall and Jessica waved shyly as she turned and went indoors. Hugo, Lucy and Peter walked on to the wicket gate and went home by the farm track.

The following day the fog returned. This time the *Louise* was to sail downriver carrying goods for Lowestoft and Yarmouth. Stan had to help Hugo carry the heavy mast from the warehouse to the boat. Then he descended into the craft and directed the long pole into its slot as Hugo nudged it over the edge of the quay. This time they had a deck cargo of marble tiles for rebuilding work at Somerleyton Hall, together with the usual order of butter and cheese for a dairy shop at Lowestoft. However the hold had first to be filled to the brim with barrels of salted beef from the slaughter of surplus Galloway cattle brought to the Beccles marshes for fattening. With the premature flooding of the marshes this season there was insufficient keep for all the kine on the hills. The early slaughter of these bullocks in fact suited all, for it transpired that a couple of Royal Navy frigates had come into Yarmouth for repairs and refurbishment after a brisk encounter with a French squadron off Southwold. The two nations having recommenced hostilities some two years since, the North Sea Fleet had a standing order at Yarmouth for supplies of bully beef. Hugo was looking forward to a glimpse of the British warships, something he thought almost as exciting as

'Dutch Sunday' in September when the Herring Fleets of both nations filled Yarmouth Roads for the rituals marking the onset of the fishing season and the North Sea currents wafted thousands of shining 'silvers' to the shores of East Anglia.

The fog thickened and the *Louise* had almost to feel her way downstream, tacking with great caution in an idle wind. They did not reach Somerleyton till the afternoon, exchanging the smart masonry for a whole deckload of pine timber that was needed at Yarmouth for turning into ship's yards and spars. They had eaten nothing since breakfast, so Stan and Hugo walked to one of the Somerleyton farms and obtained a good supper and shelter overnight in a barn. By the next morning visibility had improved again and Stan could guide the now heavily laden and somewhat unwieldy craft safely down-river, through Breydon Water to the Navy saw-pits. After queuing with other craft to await the raising of the cantilever road sections of the Dutch-style Haven Bridge, they sailed on into the long channel of Yarmouth harbour and moored at the Navy Board wharf. Here, whilst the navvies helped them unload the beef, an official in uniform stood by checking each barrel as it came ashore and ticking it off on his list with his pencil. Hugo was impressed. Stan enquired for him the whereabouts of the two Royal frigates. It seemed that their refit had been completed and they had been towed nearer the harbour mouth in order to be able to sail as soon as all their stores and crew had gone aboard.

"If you wish to see those ships, Hughie," Stan said, "I hear they've moved down by the Fort. So why not leave me here with the boat while you run to the end of the Quay to look at 'em. There's an inn nearby called the Herring & Sole. I'll bring the *Louise* along when she's empty and will look for you at the inn," Stan suggested kindly.

Hugo scampered off like a bird released from a trap: sitting or standing about on the boat all day could sometimes seem rather tedious to a growing and energetic lad. In a rush he raced past the vast stands of timber, Baltic pine and Norway spruce brought in by the boatload for the shipyards, and next to them the warehouse of ship-chandling goods and nautical equipment. Now he had reached a plethora of brothels and taverns huddled at the end of the quay, among them the Herring & Sole whose appropriately fishy signboard swung in the wind with a rusty creak. A number of fishing smacks, their catches sold off alongside the jetty by the Denes, and awaiting the return of their crews should the weather improve, lay moored at the quayside. Otherwise the place seemed deserted. At last Hugo espied the frigates, anchored well out in the Roads, with a launch laden with goods and sailors pulling towards one of them even as he watched. He observed the two sets of three masts, their new sails fully reefed on the yards. He noted the cream line painted along the hull of each vessel, against which the gun-ports stood out dark and menacing, but closed tight against the elements as the ships made ready for sea. He could decry the Union flag hanging limply upon each jack-staff and the long triangular pennants which drooped from each mainmast. When Mr Stevenson arrives, Hugo thought, he had a spyglass and would be able to decipher the flags, and perhaps also to read the name of each vessel written across their stern counters where they swung in the river current. The spyglass would also enable him to watch the unloading of the ship's boat, which presently divested itself of its cargo and was returning to shore. Then the fog closed in again and a drizzly rain began to fall. The two ships melted into the mist and Hugo turned toward the inn behind him, deciding to seek shelter until the *Louise* arrived. After all, he might yet continue to observe the ships from a window, and the landlord might well know something of them too.

The inn doorway was low and even Hugo had to bend his head to avoid bumping it on the lintel. Once within, the thick heavy atmosphere of the dimly lit, low-ceilinged taproom almost took his breath away. Sweat, tobacco fumes, bad breath from seamen suffering from the gum-rot of the scurvy, urine from a privy in the wall, liquor fumes from behind the bar, and a patch of vomit not yet cleansed from the floor in front of it – Hugo nearly turned to walk outside again and it was only his sense of loyalty to Stan that persuaded him to follow the instructions he had been given. It seemed that the landlord was a landlady, a vulgar, blousy woman in a stained gown and a filthy fichu, who knew nothing of the ships when asked and merely nodded absentmindedly when Hugo explained that he did not wish to order liquor but merely to await his employer. There were few customers at the inn, and those seamen which sat at the dirty tables laden with uncleared tankards and glasses, soon began to leave one by one. The return of the fog meant that the fishermen would not sail tonight.

Presently just two persons remained, a father and son it would seem from what Hugo could overhear of their conversation. The father was plainly dressed but in good quality Norfolk worsted. The son appeared slovenly, his shirt open at the collar and showing a wide expanse of neck, his jacket hanging off one shoulder, and his pantaloons bearing obvious stains betraying that his bodily functions were not under proper control. Hugo studied the boy's face and recognised the signs of mental disturbance, there having been a similar boy attending the John Leman School. From all that Hugo could learn it seemed that the father was at pains to prevent his son from frequenting the company of some undesirable person. Just then a new figure descended the stairs from the upper regions of the inn. From where he sat Hugo could not see more than the legs of that figure, but the young boy could. He rose from his seat and stepped forward with an expression on his face which Hugo was able only later to describe as that of a dog seeing its master and knowing it was to be beaten yet again! The father stretched out his arm to restrain his son.

Simultaneously, by the low doorway from the quay, two men entered who, from their loose trousers and flapping shirts and jackets, were clearly seamen. They stepped forward to the figure on the stairs. "Your Honour," said one of them, "you promised us five guineas and a boy that would make midshipman.

You wish us to take him off your hands."

At once the father leapt up from his chair and stood in front of his son. "You know who I am, you scum!" he shouted at the seamen, hoarse and breathless with fright. "Don't you dare touch a hair of my son's head!"

The figure descended further down the stairs, perceived Hugo's feet where he sat, and proceeded until his gaze could travel upwards to the face. That figure was Ainsworth Rich! He and Hugo stared at each other for what seemed an age but could only have been a minute. Ainsworth felt in his pocket and brought out a handful of coins. "No, that is the boy I intended," he said coolly to the seamen as he handed over the coins and pointed towards Hugo.

Hugo stood aghast as the sailors came towards him. "No, not me," he said, "I'm waiting for Mr Stevenson, Mr Stanley Stevenson."

"No matter to us," the more vocal of the seamen replied. "We're waiting for our next square meal, and we won't get that till we're back on board with you, youngster." They seized him under each arm, one on either side. Hugo barely had time to snatch from the table his flask and tin box before they lifted him over the furniture and had frog-marched him out of the door and on to the quayside. There Hugo could see nothing in front of him; neither Stan, nor the *Louise*, and even the fishing smacks were wrapped in mist. The two sailors obviously knew the location well, for they threaded through a labyrinth of alleyways among the quay's buildings till they came to a tumbledown warehouse two storeys high. As they paused at the doorway and knocked, Hugo was surprised to find that the boy and his father from the inn had followed close behind them, and all five entered the building together. The large space inside was full of people. At least half of them were seamen discernible by their clothes; the remainder seemed to be ordinary inhabitants of Yarmouth, of all ages and in all stages of attire.

"We have him!" shouted the man gripping Hugo's right arm. "Now we can take him and the other little fellow on board." Hugo had realised by now that he had fallen into the hands of a Press-gang. Stan had advised him about such goings-on, but that account had sounded remote, something from the bad old days, and Hugo serenely sailing up the River Waveney had been able to believe, "It will never happen to me." Well, now it had, and what was he to do about it? It seemed that Black Shuck had been true to his reputation and had caught him unawares after all.

The 'other little fellow', when produced from the upper storey of the warehouse, turned out to be someone Hugo knew, a boy named Gus Mather, younger brother of that Benedict Mather who had bullied him at school. As the sailors roped the boys' arms to their sides and pushed them out of the building, Gus called out in tearful desperation to the well-dressed gentleman, "I am Augustus Mather. Won't you please tell my father where I am?" Then they were hurried back to the fog-enveloped quayside and were marched down some steps into a launch. Other sailors were present who took not the slightest notice of them as they were set down roughly in the bow as if they were parcels of merchandise.

The crew finished loading the boat and then climbed in and slipped their oars into the rowlocks. They pushed off from the quayside and headed out into the fog. Soon there was nothing to be seen all around them. Then one of the crew, who sat in the stern at the tiller and wore a hat, took out a whistle and blew three blasts upon it. From a point in the mist above and beyond them there came an answering note. A few minutes later the exercise was repeated, this time just as a dark shadow loomed out of the mist overhead. The boat drew to the side of the ship and to a wood and rope ladder let down from the deck. All the crew members scrambled up, each carrying whatever was portable from the cargo. Presently a harness with a canvas seat was let down and the petty officer who had stayed behind fastened it around each of the boys in turn. Both were then hoisted up to the deck and deposited at the feet of their captors, who marched them below.

They were taken to a small cluttered cabin in the forward part of the ship where a gentleman sat in uniform with a desk full of ledgers and a large supply of quills and ink. As the group entered and crowded into the scanty floor-space the officer looked up, selected a fresh ledger from the pile, opened it and prepared to inscribe. "Name?" he barked at Gus, and Gus timidly replied. "Name?" he barked again at Hugo.

"No, sir, I'm not giving my name. I was taken by force from my employment, and my employer will even now be looking for me. This boy," he turned to Gus whom he knew to be little older than his brother Peter, "is merely a schoolboy, and his father is an important citizen of Beccles."

"And you, young man, is your father also an important citizen?" the officer sneered.

"My father is a farmer, sir. His name is Alfred Jarvis. Mine is Hugo."

"A farmer, eh? An excellent reason why one of his sons should go to sea," the officer muttered. "That completes our complement, gentlemen. Thank you for your efforts." From a cash box the officer took two silver shillings and gave one to each of the crewmen. Hugo wanted to shout that they had already been paid no less than five guineas by that traitor Ainsworth, but he thought that somehow this would only fall on deaf ears. "Take them to the Chaplain's cabin," the officer ordered "and lock them in. Remember to feed them at mess times, or you'll answer to me!"

Although there was a cot in the chaplain's cabin, once their rope bonds had been removed both boys sat down on the floor. Neither boy spoke for a long while, each being absorbed in his own sense of outrage and shock. Eventually Hugo found the strength to speak to Gus, knowing that if that were Peter, his brother, he would be feeling numb and ill. "How did they catch you, Gus?" he asked.

Surprisingly Gus replied with more aplomb than Hugo expected, for all his nine or so years. "I should not have been at Yarmouth at all really," he replied.

"I've been playing truant from the school. I'm no scholar like Ben or my sister Marion, so when Papa gave me a month's allowance all at once I cut out of school, caught the stage from Beccles and came to see whatever ships were in harbour."

"So did I, Gus. I was working on the wherry today, bringing timber and beef from Beccles to the shipyards. Gosh, this afternoon seems a long time ago already." The cabin had a small window and Hugo had just noticed the growing darkness outside. He hoped that whoever came to feed them would also bring a light.

"I was caught three days ago," Gus went on. "You know that warehouse where they brought you, well there are beds upstairs, and a kitchen through a doorway at the back. I asked one of the sailors where I was and was told it was called a 'crimping house': 'tis a place where they imprison sailors between voyages so that they shall not escape, and the press-gangs bring their captives there too."

"I was taken at the Herring & Sole where I was awaiting my employer, Mr Stevenson," Hugo stated.

"And I was taken from the quayside by the Navy Office where I was watching the loading of the ships. There are two of them, you know. One is named the *Apollion* and the other the *Aetherial*. Gus spelt both names carefully. "I believe we are on the *Apollion*; it was the one nearer to the quay."

"Who was the gentleman in grey whom you asked to tell your father of your whereabouts?" Hugo enquired.

"He's known as the 'crimping-master'. He keeps the warehouse as a lodging place for penniless sailors and a prison for the pressed men. I was told that a ship's purser, I think that's the officer who took our names, he has charge of the running of the ship, takes on the stores for the voyage and such, he sends the crimping-master a message as to how many seamen the ship will need. Then the crimping-master gathers them together and is paid by the press-gangs when he hands them over. So you heard, this ship needs two more boys to become midshipmen, and I suppose that means us."

"Are you acquainted with that gentleman's, the crimping-master's son?" Hugo asked carefully.

"Who? Oh Frank, yes. He's doolally, as I'm sure you will have noticed. By the by, your landlord at Roos Hall, Mr Ainsworth Rich or whatever his name is, well he was on the Beccles stage with me, and he has appeared at the crimping-house too. It seems he has some liaison with Frank, so one of the sailors told me, though I'm not sure I know exactly what he meant by that, do you?"

"No, indeed I do not," replied Hugo, for whom the events that took place at the Herring & Sole had started to make sense. He had begun to feel hungry, but knew there was no food left inside his tin box which by some miracle had survived in his hand through the rough transfer on board. So too had his flask, which he remembered was still half-full of ale. Stan had told him that water on board ship was always full of wriggling things and unfit to drink, so he hoped he would be able to drink liquor like the sailors instead. He unstopped the bung of the flask and took a few mouthfuls, then handed it to Gus who had begun to shed tears. "Don't blubber, Gus," he said, "I'll look out for you."

"Do you think that if we explain ourselves again they will let us go home?" Gus asked.

"I doubt it," Hugo replied. "I think we are stuck here. From what Mr Stevenson, my employer, has told me, they often take on boys of your age and mine to run about the ship doing this job and that. I have always had a dream to join the Navy and now here I am by chance. If it's a long voyage, Gus, you'll be too old for school by the time you return home and will never have to worry over it again!" Gus felt somewhat cheered at the prospect. An hour or so later one of the sailors who had captured Hugo opened the door and brought in some bread and two bowls of broth with pieces of chicken and dumpling floating in it. Two mugs and a jug of water also appeared, together with a lantern which the sailor hung on a hook high overhead where the boys could not reach it and set the ship alight. Before departing he pointed to a bucket concealed beneath the seat of the one chair in the cabin, and told the boys more kindly that they had best get some sleep as they would have a busy day on the morrow. Hugo let Gus have the cot, whilst he took a blanket and slept on the floor, his tin box hidden within his folded coat which he used as a pillow.

Accustomed as he was to waking early, first light brought Hugo to his feet. So did the noises around the ship, on the deck outside the door, along the sides of the vessel and even overhead where he reckoned the senior officers' quarters should be. He walked over to the window and found that he could open it. The fog had lifted: he could see the town of Yarmouth in the distance, and the Denes stretching towards the Fort close at hand above the channel. Even if he could have slid out of the window, he doubted whether he could have swum ashore. Besides, that would mean leaving Gus alone. Presently the same sailor brought them a breakfast of bread and ham, along with another jug of water. As yet Hugo could see no wriggling things in it, so drank some and took a few mouthfuls of his ale for good measure. A little while later their escort of yesterday collected them from the cabin and took them to the Purser's office again. "Come in lads," he greeted them with false bonhomie. "Now that you've had a good night's sleep, are you ready to sign the King's Articles?"

"What are they?" Hugo asked.

"That's the document that says you've agreed to join the Navy, will be loyal to your shipmates, will observe discipline and obey the officers, and in battle will fight to your last breath for King and Country."

"May I read it, sir?" Hugo asked. The Purser looked up at him with a frown; the two sailors nudged each other. The last thing anyone needed in a midshipman was a sea lawyer! Middies were born to come when called, to crawl into small inconvenient spaces to fetch what was required, to keep the guns supplied in battle, and to cause no inconvenience to their superiors. "What happens if we refuse to sign?" Hugo asked. "Will we be put ashore?"

"You'll be put in chains in the foc'sle till you come to your senses!" the Purser thundered. "This is the Navy, not a gentlemen's club!"

"But we were brought here against our will, sir, kidnapped in fact," Hugo responded.

"And so was many a good ship's captain before you that I can recall," the Purser growled with exasperation. "Now I can see you're an intelligent lad that's received a good education. Joining the Navy could be the making of you. As for this boy," he said, pointing to Gus, "I agree he's a little on the small side, but as you'll appreciate from the motion of the ship at this instant, she's hove up her anchor and is under way. I've two score of new seamen to sign on and I cannot spend more time on you two. Sign or be damned!" Hugo put his signature at the foot of the page where indicated, and Gus followed suit, insisting on stating his full name – Augustus Peregrine Mather.

"Mr Jackson!" the Purser called through the open door to another officer who had been hovering without. "This is the Gunner, Mr Jackson. He is in charge of all the midshipmen and will show you to your quarters and your duties. Now don't let me have any more trouble from either of you for the rest of the voyage. Mr Jackson, this lad is Mr Jarvis and the younger one is Master Mather. I'll leave them in your good hands."

The two boys followed Mr Jackson back up the companion-way, past the cabin where they had slept and past other cabins which they were given to understand belonged to the junior officers, to the Gun Room at the vessel's stern. Their first impression was one of a dark space full of dimly discerned clouds. These turned out to be hammocks fastened to hooks in the roof beams. The boys were shown two on the far side to which they were assigned. Hugo was relieved to discover a small locker with sliding doors fixed to the beam beside each hook where books, cutlery and personal items might be stored, and he quickly hid away his precious box and flask. The only daylight emanated from the outline of two gun-ports which would normally be shut tight in rough weather. The whole atmosphere of the space below deck had a strange sweetness which Hugo later came to identify with that mixture of vinegar and Stockholm tar with which the ship had been scrupulously cleansed during her refit; anything to minimise the risk of infection caused by the crowding of so many men into such a small world.

"'Tis a long-standing Navy tradition, gentlemen," Mr Jackson addressed them, "that the newest recruits wait upon the others, so you two will fetch hot water in the morning for the middies' ablutions, and for the older ones who shave, you'll fetch supplies of coffee, serve the rations which will be brought by one of the crew, and you'll wash the mugs and platters afterwards. Then you'll tidy these premises and report on deck in time for assembly, which is where we're heading now and is the reason why none of your companions is here to meet you."

They followed Mr Jackson up to the main deck where the entire ship's company, apart from the Helmsman, had met for the reading of the Articles of War. Captain Sterne stood by the quarterdeck rail, resplendent in his dark blue uniform, gold braid, and white breeches and hose. His shoes had silver buckles but were stout and well polished. Either side of him stood his senior officers, and also the Captain of Marines and the ship's Master being the equivalent of a chief engineer. The junior lieutenants stood in a row behind, with the Chaplain at one end of the line and the ship's Surgeon at the other. Half of the ship's Company of Marines were drawn up on the poop deck and the other half were gathered on the foredeck. In the waist on the main deck stood the crew, grouped by their watches and by their function. The Purser, the Cook and the Carpenter, each with their assistants, stood in one group; the Coxswain who had guided the launch the previous day stood with his team, and so on towards the starboard rail where the Gunner had placed himself amid a dozen assorted fellows, and Hugo encountered for the first time his new companions, the Midshipmen.

Hugo had expected that his fellows would all be young boys. Instead two of them were past middle age, men who had been pressed as boys like himself, but who had lacked the wit and the physical strength to better themselves either at sea or ashore; they were known as 'oldsters'. Then there were several around eighteen years of age, some of them likely to follow the same course as the oldsters, but two who were expected to make officer material when they had completed their training. The other four were lads of his own age or slightly older, and he looked forward to making their acquaintance. Meanwhile Hugo turned his attention to what the Captain was saying, though with some difficulty as a cheerful breeze tended to blow his words away.

The *Apollion* with its muster of some three hundred and fifty souls had been ordered to return to the West Indian Station, along with her sister ship the *Aetherial*, which followed half a mile in their wake. They would take the southern route across the Atlantic, and their first landfall would be at Madeira, a territory which belonged to England's ally, Portugal. As this phase of the voyage was expected to last for ten days or more, depending upon possible delays caused by storms in the Bay of Biscay or further encounters with enemy squadrons, the Captain recommended the new members of his complement to be diligent in their training, so that when it did come to a brush with the Enemy every man would know his station and exactly what was expected of him. At the end of this disclosure the Chaplain stepped forward and said a few prayers, blessing the ship and its crew and leading the company in the Lord's Prayer. Then the Captain called out, "Beat to dismiss, Mr Hunter," and at a signal from the Captain of Marines the drummers of that corps standing along the foredeck rail started up a rousing rat-a-tat-tat and the decks emptied rapidly of all personnel save the seamen on watch and the lieutenant in charge of them.

Hugo and Gus followed the Gunner and the other 'middies' back to the Gun Room. A table which had been stowed away in the ceiling was brought down on supporting ropes, benches were unhooked from the walls and were placed either side of the table whilst Mr Jackson sat on a folding stool at its head. He made each of the middies introduce themselves to the newcomers, stating their names and how long each had served in the Navy. The youngest, it appeared, was a boy of eleven years of age named Philip Harris, known as Pip, and he was detailed to instruct Hugo and Gus as to the duties which he had hitherto performed alone. It was felt unfair to burden Gus with all that was required – many of them had younger brothers of a similar age, so Hugo was to work with him. Any short-comings in their service would be met with the traditional punishments, one of them hinted. Hugo, who had heard from Stan Stevenson of the many types of physical trickery and duress used on shipboard, was quite sure that some unpleasant prank would be played upon them before long.

The stern-ports were wedged open as far as they would go – in a battle the two cannon which occupied much of the deck space in the Gun Room would poke out of those small embrasures. A wide-bottomed rum bottle was brought to the table with a candle stuck in the top of it and now lit. Hugo realised that this was the maximum light available to him and his messmates. After the large windows in his home and the open air of the *Louise*, this place seemed like a prison. Gus was inclined to whimper, but Hugo gave him a stern look and the boy stilled. Mr Jackson brought to the table a large chart, which he unrolled to reveal a diagram of a ship, not their ship but a typical two-decker frigate. He had set Gus on his right side and Hugo on his left with the diagram facing Hugo whom he realised was the one more likely to learn the elements of navigation and seaboard action, and so make himself useful about the ship. Pip Harris sat next to Hugo, a tall slim fellow with brown curls, blue eyes and a merry smile. "Mr Harris," the Gunner commanded, "please name for us every sail rigged on that chart," and Pip obliged. The Gunner proceeded to the next boy along the table, "Mr Thompson, the rigging if you please, and plainly so that our new messmates can see it." Hugo found that much of the terminology sounded familiar from his tuition by Stan Stevenson, but that now masts, standing and running rigging, halyards, dead-eyes and bollards, had been multiplied not just by three but by three again to take in the number of yards on each mast, not to mention the jib-sails, stuns'ls and spanker.

The next young fellow down the line was asked to indicate with his finger the various parts of the ship and to describe their normal functions. Hugo craned his neck to watch the moving finger; he realised that the quicker he learnt his own whereabouts the safer he would be, and the more he could protect Gus whom he observed as being slow to learn and to adapt to the new situation. The Gunner skipped the oldsters and the older midshipmen at the far end of the table and instructed that the chart be passed to the younger ones. "Now, Mr Simpson," said he, "kindly describe for us how the decks are prepared for battle, starting with the lower decks if you please." When it came to the Gun Room, Hugo noted that all bedding was to be stowed neatly within their hammocks which were to be taken down from their clews, tied up with lashings, and run up to the main deck to be stuffed into the nets that hung above the rails all around the ship. "And the purpose of that, Mr Simpson?"

"To save splinters and shards falling upon the crew, Mr Jackson, when the enemy scores a hit on us." As if on cue, a seaman appointed steward to the mid-dies and junior officers entered with the "bedding for the two new young 'uns," as he phrased it, and he dumped a flock mattress, a blanket, coverlet and pillow upon each of the hammocks indicated. When Hugo came to inspect the bed-ding it smelt strongly of carbolic soap, but at least at this stage of the voyage any fleas or lice present were merely dead ones! The steward also informed Mr Jackson that the younger boy, Master Mather that is, was to report to the tailor as soon as the Gunner was through morning lessons, so that he might be fitted out with more suitable clothing from the slop chest. "Those he has will leave him naked in a following sea," as the steward succinctly expressed it. Hugo's gar-ments were obviously considered sufficiently adequate to his task, though what he should do about clean smallclothes he currently had no idea. He would take his chance to ask Pip later.

Meanwhile Mr Jackson proceeded with the drill for battle and the middies' duties thereupon. Hugo learnt that he and Gus were expected to be at the beck and call of the Gunner and his mates to fetch supplies of powder and cartridges for each section of the artillery as required. That was why it was so important to know their way about ship from the very beginning and how to respond promptly to whatever orders they received. Hugo hoped fervently that they would not meet up with the enemy for a long while, until not only had he learnt his duties to perfection, but little Gus had learnt at least the rudiments too.

Presently Gus was dismissed to find the ship's tailor, being reminded from the chart where he was to be found, and Hugo was despatched to the galley for a jug of coffee. On his return Pip showed him where the drinking mugs were kept and explained that afterwards they were to be taken up to the main deck in a bowl and washed in a bucket of sea water – "clean water, if you will get it!" Pip added with a laugh. Hugo found that the two oldsters had departed on watch, while one of the senior lieutenants that had just been relieved from the watch had come to instruct the other midshipmen about the ship's course and how it was to be plotted and logged. The senior middies were obliged to write a log each day and submit it for the First Lieutenant's inspection. Hugo felt he was back at school as he listened and watched while a sea chart was produced giving the coast of East Anglia, which he knew and recognised, and opposite it the coast of Holland. At one corner of the chart the face of a ship's compass had been engraved. The lieutenant had Pip name all the points of the compass and then Mr Thompson all the nautical names of the angles between them. Hugo observed what a lot of learning by rote was involved, but concluded that this was rather more attached to the realities of daily life than sitting in school conning Latin declensions or stanzas from the works of ancient poets. However, as the next set of statistics to be memorised were the calculation of the length of a nautical mile, its subdivisions into cables and fathoms and the passage of time and distance by the use of the sand-glass and the log-line, he began to wish he had paid rather more attention to Dr Davey's mathematics classes during his final term at school. It was as well that little Gus was absent, for calculations of any sort would have passed completely above his head.

The lieutenant then explained for the benefit of all the difference in bearing between Magnetic North and True North and how this was to be calculated in the Northern Hemisphere. On the chart, which used the Mercator projection where all the lines of latitude and longitude are straight and cross at right-angles, he showed with compasses and rulers how the angle of variation was to be plotted and how this had to be set off against the desired course. Today's destination was the North Foreland light-ship which, despite a favourable breeze from the North West, they were unlikely to reach until dark. The officer made one of the two senior midshipmen plot the course on the chart and list the compass bearings to be followed by the steersman as each degree of latitude was attained.

By this time Hugo felt his head was spinning. The lieutenant turned to him and with a sympathetic glance bade him take the drinking mugs up to the main deck to be washed. Hugo did so, standing by the rail for a few moments to breathe in the fresh air which was so lacking below deck. The ship was sailing steadily under her main course and topsails with a jib set to the foremast and a spanker aft on the mizzen, a sail which reminded him all too sadly of the *Louise*. Hugo wondered whether Stan Stevenson was still searching for him at Yarmouth, and how he would manage to crew the *Louise* without him. Then he turned and observed the buckets of sea water set about the deck and immediately understood why Pip had laughed as he urged him to find a clean one. The men of the watch, when taken short, did not resort to the latrines down below in the beakhead, but merely relieved themselves overboard when aloft in the rigging, or when on deck into the nearest bucket! Hugo made sure to draw fresh water from the sea pump and realised that he had many adaptations to make in his new career.

In the days that followed the middies were kept well-employed with 'reefing practice', where a yard and sail were rigged some twenty feet above the main deck and they were ordered to scramble up the ratlines and along the hawser that served as a footrope, then reach over on command to take in the reefs, one at a time. Hugo was nimble and not unduly concerned about standing on a swaying rope and holding on to a buffeting sail, while many feet below the large wooden box of the ship seemed to describe a giddying circle. Little Gus, however, was petrified of heights and Hugo realised that sooner or later Gus would be forced aloft at the end of a cat's tail. He asked himself what he might do to postpone that event.

Then there was gunnery practice where the gun ports were opened and the guns run out, each station at a time in order not to disturb the balance of the ship. Gun teams were drawn up, and wads, sponges, cartridges, powder and lin-stocks, buckets of water, and all the other items necessary were laid out in dummy fashion so as not to waste ammunition, and the new crewmen were familiarised with their tasks. Little Gus proved more adept at filling cartridges and got praised for his pains, which was a blessing since at night in his hammock Hugo could hear the lad sobbing away. Hugo himself felt homesick from time to time, conscious of the anxiety and uncertainty his parents must feel, and wishing he could let them know of his whereabouts and welfare. When he did have an idle moment and some daylight, it became his custom to open his tin box and to read the book of poems Jessica had given him, and slipped within it the letter of apology and grief she had written to him after Mr Ainsworth had shot and killed Matilda. Yes, that fellow had a lot to answer for. Hugo had learnt that when they reached Madeira there would be an opportunity to send a letter home together with official despatches. He knew exactly what he wished to say about the wretched Ainsworth!

CHAPTER XI
The Bay of Storms

Stan Stevenson watched Hugo run along the quay in search of the Royal Frigates, and wished to himself that he had two sound legs again. Then he turned to the Shipping Clerk who was about to tick off the last batch of salt beef. He handed down the document to Stan and asked him to sign it. It took the form of a receipt for so many barrels, and then Stan noticed that it included an amount for "Carriage from Beccles". He pointed out to the Clerk that carriage on his boat had been paid for by the consignee at Beccles, and the Navy therefore had nothing extra to pay. "No matter," came the reply. "Please sign it and have done."

"But there's no need to charge the Navy for something it has not purchased," Stan protested. "'Tis defrauding the Service in time of War, and I'll not have it!"

"In that event," came the smart response, "I'll just put a cross there and print your name, so folks will think you cannot write," the Clerk told him with a sneer.

Stan looked around him; the fog was closing in again. He would have some difficulty to manoeuvre the *Louise* to the end of the quay where Hugo should be waiting for him and he would need as much visibility as available in order to reach the pick-up point quickly. He signed the fraudulent statement and handed it back to the Clerk, resolving to mention the matter to the first naval person in authority who crossed his path. Then he cast off the *Louise*, hoisted her gaff sail and pushed off from the quay. The wind had dropped with the return of the fog and in order to avoid the fishing smacks moored alongside Stan was obliged to tack out into the harbour and then set a course for the concealed end of the quay. His navigation was perfect; he threw the mooring ropes over a couple of bollards and stumped up the steps towards The Herring & Sole. As he did so he heard the sound of oars in their rowlocks creaking away into the invisible distance.

The tap room at The Herring & Sole proved empty, save for the landlady who was even now clearing away the dirty tankards with a slovenly air. Stan enquired whether she had seen a boy sheltering there whilst waiting for him. "Which boy?" she replied with a knowing leer, "the one that went away with two men, or the one that went away with one?" Stan, at a loss how to reply, described the clothes Hugo had been wearing and the hat on his head. "Oh, the one wi' a 'at, 'e went off wi' two fellows. They'll all be at No. 51 by now." Stan's heart sank. He knew of 'No. 51' as a euphemism for the port's crimping-house. It would take a constable of the watch with a writ from a judge to extract someone from the clutches of a Press-gang. Where was he likely to obtain such authority at this time of day? Besides, with two frigates in port, each doubtless short of a crew, speed was of the essence before the boy could be taken out to the ship. Moreover Stan was in some danger himself as a former mariner. His discharge papers were at home at his cottage and it was only his peg-leg that might serve as a deterrent to the press-gang.

Stan knocked at the door of No.51 and was somewhat relieved when it was opened by the crimping-master's son. "Frank, have you seen a lad of your age dressed in a seaman's jacket and cap?"

"I seen plenty, Mr Stevenson, the docks is full of them."

"He was supposed to meet me at The Herring & Sole."

"Oh, that one. 'Is Honour was going to send me away to the ship, but 'e saw this boy and sent 'im instead. So I get to stay ashore with my father like always."

"Who's His Honour?" Stan enquired; thinking there might be a witness he could consult.

"'E's a gentleman what comes Yarmouth sometimes and pays me do things for 'im," Frank stuttered over the reply. Stan concluded that no help was to be obtained in that direction.

"Is the boy still here, Frank, is he within?" Stan pressed him.

"No-o-o, Mr Stevenson, he be gone to ship." Stan did not know what to do. Should he insist on searching the premises for his employee? That would only stir up the animosity of the crimping-master and of all the other sailors whose raucous chatter he could overhear. Besides, he was more than conscious of the danger in which he stood. He knew Frank well enough by sight and reputation to believe he was telling the truth, however twisted the version which came from his lips. Stan thanked the unfortunate lad and hurried back to the *Louise*. He tacked across the harbour in the growing gloom and moored again at the Navy Board quay. There he climbed painfully up the iron ladder attached to the wall of the quay, cursing his wooden stump as it slipped on the rungs and nearly precipitated him into his boat. He saw the Clerk with whom he had had the argument over the shipping receipt and enquired where he might find someone in charge.

"That's me. I have sole responsibility for the goods shipped in and out of this warehouse," the Clerk replied jauntily.

"Is there no Navy Board officer or naval captain to whom I could speak?" Stan asked with desperation. "The lad who works for me has been seized by the Press-men and taken out to one of the frigates."

"Oho, no remedy for that, Grandpa," the Shipping Clerk replied, "no remedy at all. Still, it will save you the cost of burying him," he added callously. "If you had not spent so long refusing to sign my receipt, you might have caught up with him yet." The barb was below the ribs and doubled Stan's anxiety. He hurried down the slippery ladder into his boat and hoisted sail, but in the light wind, the growing darkness and the fog-hidden presence of other craft he had great difficulty in finding a place to moor on South Quay near the centre of the town. Once on land he went in search of the Mayor – the County Sheriff was based in Norwich, the Lord Lieutenant on a distant estate, the law offices and the courts were closed for the night, and he could not think of any other person who might rouse out the Port Authority to rescue young Hugo. He knocked at the door of the elegant mayoral mansion in King Street and a black servant in livery answered him. It seemed that Mr Mayor was in the process of dressing for a very important Aldermen's dinner and was not to be disturbed. If Mr Stevenson wished to pursue the matter he should return in the morning – the late morning!

Stan walked back to his boat and wrapped himself in his usual tarpaulin but slept scarcely a wink. Whatever was he to tell Hugo's father? Even more pressing how was he to sail the *Louise* back to Beccles with a pre-arranged cargo of fish and coal without assistance? Then, like an answer to his prayer, as a reluctant sun transfused the lingering mist, he observed Timothy's boat moored only a cable's length away. With a hoarse voice he hailed the lad who hoisted sail immediately and came smoothly alongside. Tim readily agreed to leave his own boat at Yarmouth, helped Stan to load up as quickly as they could and set off up-river for a straight run to Beccles. Fortunately the tide was now flowing rather than ebbing, so that the force of tidal water as well as a somewhat fitful breeze impelled them more rapidly. As soon as they reached Beccles Quay, Stan scribbled a note to Alf Jarvis requesting an urgent meeting and asked Tim to deliver it. Tim ran all the way to the Ringsfield Farm and was quite breathless by the time he knocked at the door.

Jeannie Caldicott opened the door, having been engaged in laying a fire in the parlour. She recognised Tim as Stan Stevenson's erstwhile apprentice and called over her shoulder, "Martha, I think you'd best come to the door. It may be bad news."

Martha appeared, her hands covered with cream which she wiped with a cheese cloth. "What is it, Tim?" she asked. "What's happened?"

"I don't rightly know the details, Mrs Jarvis, but it seems Hugo has been taken by the Press-men. Mr Stevenson asks if Mr Jarvis could kindly meet him at the Quay so that they can decide what's to be done about it."

"Oh, my goodness, Hugo, my poor boy! Quick, Tim, go to the barn. I think my husband is there. Come this way through the dairy, 'tis shorter." She showed Tim through the house and into the yard. Once Alf Jarvis had read Stan's note he decided to use his pony-cart to drive into Beccles. The Fen Blacks were in the midst of ploughing the Big Field so he would not disturb their labours. Instead he sent Tim over to Roos Hall to borrow James and to bring him back by the bridle path. This was done, Tim riding rather uncomfortably bareback since he was used to a different form of transport. Thus Roos Hall had the news as soon as the farm. Mr Ainsworth was still away from home and moreover an important-looking package had arrived for him which Mrs Jarvis was fairly sure contained instructions about his outward voyage and his posting abroad. She hoped fervently that Mr Ainsworth would return home in time to meet those commitments.

Alf Jarvis took Tim with him back to the Quay and left him in charge of James and the cart whilst he accompanied Stan to the Maltings Inn where coffee was served, or something stronger if required. Both men were distressed at what had occurred. Stan described in detail what had happened, the information given him by the lad Frank and the efforts he had made to find someone in authority who might be able to rescue Hugo. Alf Jarvis had news of another disappearance too, several days since, of young Gus Mather. Peter had reported his absence from school, and Lucy had obtained further details from his sister Marion. The family had no reason to suppose he had done more than play truant, till someone at the King's Head happened to mention a boy of that description buying a ticket for the Yarmouth Stage. Surely the Navy was not so irresponsible as to kidnap a schoolboy well under the age of ten? Stan had obtained the names of the Royal Frigates, but which one were the boys on, and were they together? Stan had learnt that the frigates had sailed with the tide early that morning, their destination unknown due to that secrecy normal in wartime. He handed to Alf Jarvis the humble wages due for Hugo's employment, and with a tear in his eye said how much he wished that instead he might bring him his son.

Alf Jarvis bade Stan Stevenson goodbye and drove to the offices of Messrs Mather & Weedon, a Beccles firm of attorneys-at-law, both of whom cherished hopes that their respective sons, now enjoying their first term at university, might succeed them in their profession. Gordon Mather was an impatient man who did not favour being disturbed when conducting an interview with a client, particularly when that client was an important gentleman of property whose business he had only secured after much effort and by temporarily undercutting the fees charged by his competitors, and more especially by those of Norwich. So he frowned deeply when his Clerk had the temerity to enter and to whisper in his ear that he had a visitor outside with news of his missing son. "Let him come in, then," Mr Mather replied grumpily, begging the pardon of his client.

Alf Jarvis entered, hat in hand, and wished "Good-day" to Mr Mather and to his client whom he also knew quite well. He described rapidly Stan Stevenson's loss of Hugo and his visit to the crimping-house where he learnt that the boy had already been taken aboard ship. He added that Mr Stevenson had not been aware that another Beccles boy, Augustus Mather, was also missing or he would have enquired after him too. Mr Jarvis wondered whether in view of these circumstances Mr Mather would be willing to obtain a writ from a judge for a constable of the watch to enquire after both boys at the said crimping-house, and if this proved negative, to make such further inquiries in the town of Yarmouth as Mr Mather should deem appropriate.

"I have already had a search made of Yarmouth town," Mr Mather responded, "but without success. I would not have commanded a search of the crimping-house because I would have assumed my son too young for any role in the Navy, but I shall set that in hand immediately."

"If they have already sailed with those frigates, of which you have the names, I believe, you should refer to the Admiralty," said a voice from the depths of the client's armchair. "I can give you the address of Sir Henry Martin who is Sir Maurice's present successor as Comptroller." The client was none other than Mr Robert Suckling of Woodton, the gentleman farmer on whose land the Jarvis family had lodged their stock overnight a year past when returning home from St Faith's Fair. His well-known relative, Sir Maurice Suckling, had led a distinguished career in the Royal Navy which had concluded with his appointment to the position of Comptroller. That gentleman had died sixteen years ago in 1778 and had been buried in the chancel of the Church at Barsham where his father had served as Rector. A much younger Alfred Jarvis and his new bride Martha had attended that interment as a tenant of the linked estates of Suckling and Rich. "You have a relative of your own in the Navy and in a senior position, do you not, Mr Jarvis?" Robert Suckling continued.

"Yes, a Rear Admiral currently serving in the West Indies, so my Uncle Robert informs me," Alf replied, twisting his hat rather shyly in his hands. "So, if your inquiries come to naught, Mr Mather, I would be much obliged if you would advise me, so that I may write to both of those gentlemen to let us know which ship our boys are upon and that both are safe from harm – that is," he hesitated, "as safe as one can be in a Navy at War!"

Of course Alfred Jarvis did not write himself to such distinguished people. As a tenant farmer and the son of a tenant farmer, his book-learning had been limited to the basic rudiments of reading, writing and enough arithmetic or "accounts" to work out the amount of seed required or the percentage profit to be had per acre from his farm. So he called upon his valued Aunt Jarvis who visited on a Sunday afternoon with her husband Robert, and the whole family sat around the dining table and contributed their ideas and phrases, while Jeannie Caldicott kept them well stimulated with cups of tea and Martha's legendary shortbread. Peter was the one who 'dropped the pebble in the pool' when he demanded, "Why does the Admiral spell his name with an 'E' when we spell ours with an 'A'?"

They all looked for response to Uncle Robert as their elder statesman. "Bless me, young Peter," he replied, "Sir John Leman himself would be proud of you. However, I believe the difference is regional, the 'E' being a Welsh rendering, whilst the 'A' is more English, especially here in East Anglia. The early Jervises owned lands along the Welsh border and in later centuries they have dispersed southwards and eastwards at a time when spelling was not as exact a knowledge as it has now become with the likes of Dr Samuel Johnson and his famous Dictionary."

"So long as he really is our relative," Peter pronounced. "I mean, it would seem foolish to write to him if he is not."

"Quite right, Peter," Alf replied, rather gratified at the erudition shown by his second son. "So far as your Uncle Robert and the gentleman concerned are able to discover, they are cousins about five times removed." So they composed the following letter to Sir Henry Martin, Comptroller of the Royal Navy:

"Your Honour,

"We are anxious to establish the whereabouts of our son, Hugo Jarvis, aged twelve years, who was detained by Press-men in the town of Great Yarmouth on Thursday, 9th October last, and was taken aboard either H.M.S. Apollion *or H.M.S.* Aetherial," [they had some difficulty with the spelling of the names], *"both ships being then at anchor in Yarmouth Roads. We seek information also about a neighbour's child, one Augustus Mather, who disappeared from Yarmouth town at about the same time, and he but a schoolboy of nine years.*

"Should Your Honour be unable to assist us from the muster records not yet being deposited with the Navy Office, we beg you will kindly forward the enclosed letter making the self-same inquiry to our esteemed tho' distant relative, Rear-Admiral Sir John Jervis, presently believed to be serving His Majesty in the West Indies.

"We trust that Your Honour will kindly forgive our forwardness in thus addressing you, but the sudden removal of our eldest son has caused our family much distress.

"We should be gratified for your kind acknowledgement of this present, and until then remain,

Your Honour's most obedient and humble servants,

Alfred and Martha Jarvis."

* * *

Meanwhile the *Apollion* and the *Aetherial* had steered a stately course down the English Channel, dipping their colours in acknowledgement to other royal Navy vessels and to Navy-escorted homecoming convoys of East Indiamen. They enjoyed fair weather and a little excitement when they chased a French corvette inshore on the Cotentin Peninsula. In the Gun Room, Hugo was applying himself to the jargon and mathematics of navigation. He learnt that shipboard time ran from noon till the following noon, and that therefore a ship's daily log was half a day behind the date on land. The boys were set tasks of finding the position of the ship by taking compass bearings at regular intervals from landmarks on the shore, such as church steeples and prominent headlands. Hugo observed as his elders worked out the mathematics and plied dividers and rulers to establish latitude and longitude. He was becoming familiar with the names and functions of such instruments as the sextant and Hadley's quadrant. Also Harrison's chronometer, that rather recently patented invention which at last enabled the navigator to compute his longitude with certainty, by reference to the time at the Meridian and the observed time at his location, taken from the declination of the sun. Thus, when the *Apollion* had gained the latitude of Cape Finisterre and stood but a few sea miles off that great foreland, Hugo knew something of the means with which the First Lieutenant had calculated that Madeira was still seven hundred nautical miles distant and that the ship's bearing towards it should be South Sou'West and half a point Westerly.

Unfortunately for the *Apollion* and her crew, rounding the Cape proved to be like opening the door of a cupboard into which a thousand demons had been crammed. She had sailed into the teeth of a Biscay Storm! The ship's Master and the old hands had already noted that halo around the sun in the forenoon when the watch had taken its sightings form the Cape, and that the sea, silky grey, had a swell running in two directions at once. Now as they left the shelter of the land a wall of water rose up in front of them and the first blast of a squall hit the sails with such force as to send them all aback against the masts. This put the masts and rigging under the greatest strain. The Bosun piped all hands and, "Reef the main course. Shorten those tops'ls," came the urgent command.

Everyone was sent aloft, Hugo and Gus included. Hugo was ordered to help rein in the main topsail. He had climbed that high before, though never with his body beaten with gusts of icy rain and with the ship bucketing about beneath him as she met the confused swell. He clung on where he could, blinking the stinging raindrops from his eyes, his breath coming in short sharp painful gasps as he balanced on the footrope and leaned over the yard, reaching for the reefing lines that fluttered so far below. With numbed fingers he grasped the hard heaving canvas, gathering it up and securing the lashings at last.

Below him on the main yard Hugo glimpsed Gus squashed between two gigantic sailors who had decided to ignore him and who with steely muscles and huge bony hands were grappling with the main course as it flapped and billowed like a soul possessed. As the wind increased in strength, the main yard itself was lowered to the deck, the t'gallant masts stood down, while Master and Helmsmen fought desperately to lay the vessel on a starboard tack, away from the headland and its fringe of dangerous rocks. The topsail yards having been hauled right around, at last the sails caught enough wind to send the *Apollion* veering westwards into the open Atlantic and a tumultuous swell. Yet still the storm increased, and a bitter wind blew all before it. Eventually a single reefed topsail on the foremast and a close-reefed triangle of a jib was all that provided them with steerage-way in the raging elements. All the rigging creaked and groaned and howled and whistled in the wind, and the mainmast was as taut as a drawn bow before the shrieking blast.

When much later Hugo descended form the rigging, there was no sign of little Gus. In his soaking wet clothes and with shivering limbs, he made his way round the deck, clinging to ropes and rigging as each icy wave swept aboard. He rescued a coop of half-drowned hens that no one had had time to carry below, and wondered what had happened to the ship's two goats that had provided milk for the officers' coffee. Between the waves he glimpsed something small and white lying like a discarded shirt in a pool of water by the gunwale. It was Gus, pale as a ghost and icy cold to the touch. Another sailor ran to help him and they carried the boy below, struggling to keep the wave that followed them from sweeping through the open hatchway. The seaman led the way to the sick berth forward in the tossing foc'sle, and Hugo ran for the surgeon. While he waited the seaman had stripped off Gus's wet clothes and had found a couple of blankets in which to wrap his tiny form.

When Hugo arrived with Mr Dunstan, the surgeon, who had been assisting one of the officers injured by rigging and tackle which had swept him across the deck in a foaming torrent, the seaman returned to his duties and the surgeon felt young Gus's pulse. "He's barely alive, Mr Jarvis, barely alive. Will you go to the galley and fetch a bucket of water as hot as can be, and ask the cook for a tankard of tea, strong and sweet." Once Hugo had departed the surgeon located his hip flask, took a swig from it himself, then dribbled a little between Gus's lips. He rolled the boy on his side but no sea water emerged, so he applied a little brandy once more and Gus coughed. Then he vomited sea water all over the deck. By the time that Hugo returned with a bucket in one hand and a lidded tankard in the other, Gus was sitting on the edge of a cot.

"Oh, Gus!" Hugo exclaimed as he staggered across the swaying deck with his burden. The surgeon made Gus sit on a stool with his feet and his hands in the hot water whilst he sponged his body with the warming fluid. Then he rubbed him well with a towel, wrapped the blankets around him and gave him the tea to drink. Hugo swabbed the boards with the rest of the bucket of water, then returned to his duties on deck. It was dawn the following day before the ship outran the tail end of the storm and encountered a brisk north-westerly breeze which blew them back to their course.

Hugo had been able to change his soaking wet clothes for those just a little less damp in the canvas bag which he had hired from the slop chest on the strength of his meagre wages, and had snatched a couple of hours sleep, when the drums of the Marines parading on deck summoned them all to assembly. Each of the ship's functionaries made his report to Captain Sterne on the state of the vessel and its crew following the storm. Thus the First Lieutenant announced the *Apollion's* present location, her distance from her destination and the revised route thereto. The Master reported on the state of the ship's masts, rigging and sails, those which had split or been damaged by the storm, and when the carpenter and sailmaker could provide replacements. The Surgeon reported about the injuries he had treated, including the saving of the boy Gus. "He failed in his duty, did he not?" Captain Sterne enquired of the Bosun.

"Yes, sir, worse than useless on the mainyard. Lucky there were good men either side of him who took his place."

"Mr Dunstan," the Captain turned to the Surgeon, "have the lad sent up on deck as soon as he can stand."

"And the boy who carried him below?" Captain Sterne continued. Hugo flushed bright red. "He left the deck without permission and must also receive punishment." The officer of the watch stepped across the deck and stood beside Hugo, obviously intending to prevent him escaping his fate. Hugo gave scarcely a thought for himself but knew that Gus would be feeling weak and empty after his ordeal. Whatever were they going to do to him?

With assembly over, the First Lieutenant, a Mr Barber, strolled across to the quarterdeck rail and summoned Hugo and the officer of the watch to approach. The lieutenant had a reputation for bullying; his fellow officers called him descriptively Barbarossa – 'Redbeard', from the colour of his locks, but Hugo soon learnt that the nickname apparently referred also to a tyrannical Tunisian pirate of past centuries. All the signs indicated that he should expect the worst.

"I'm told you're a farmer's son, Mr Jarvis, is that so?" the First Lieutenant asked.

"Yes, sir," Hugo replied.

"Good with animals, are you? Know how to milk a goat?"

"Yes, sir, indeed I do."

"Right, well you'll find our goats and hens in the hold. Bring them up on deck. Mr Smith," he pointed to the officer on the watch, "will show you where to tether them under the foc'sle till the Carpenter has time to make them new pens. You can look after them till we reach Madeira, unless they're consumed beforehand. They're to be milked fresh for the Captain's breakfast every morning, Mr Barber commanded.

"What about my duties in the Gun Room, sir?" Hugo queried.

"You work that out, Jarvis, with the other lads."

"Yes, sir."

Hugo escaped below feeling he had been let off very lightly indeed. But had he? He was obliged to disturb a couple of seamen resting off-duty in their hammocks to help him remove the hatch over that part of the hold where the animals had been taken during the storm. The perfume that struck his nostrils was a mixture of death and muck. He found that half the chickens had expired, so transferred all their limp corpses to one coop whilst he made his way up to the main deck with the other and the officer showed him where to stow it. Hugo later discovered that the dead birds had all reached that day's cooking pots! Then he descended again to bring up the goats. There was no way he could carry a large struggling animal up the ladder that led out of the hold. He noticed a derrick and pulley lashed to one of the posts that supported the deck, found a piece of canvas of the right size, wrapped it around the bleating and butting animal and fastened it to the hook on the end of the tackle. Then he ascended the ladder, aided by a butt from the goat that was nearest him, and heaved the creature on to the deck. He released the canvas wrap, took a firm grip on the halter and pushed and pulled the goat between hammocks and cannon and barrels and benches and all the impediments that bestrew the 'tween-decks of a fighting ship at sea. The companion-ways were the worst as goats and stairs were never meant for one another. If he pulled, the goat would not budge; if he pushed from behind, it pushed back. It was like trying to lead a donkey without a carrot, Hugo thought.

Eventually he succeeded in tethering both goats on deck and covering himself in bruises. Back to the hold he went for fodder for the goats and feed for the chickens. Then to the galley for bowls to hold their water, filling each sparingly lest the precious liquid slop over as the ship rose up and down the now steady ocean swell. Finally he returned to the hold with a broom and swept all the muck the animals had left into the bilges. He replaced the derrick in its lashings, fastened the hatch so that it could be slid aside when he needed fresh fodder without troubling the rest of the crew, and yet the hatch would not cast loose if the shop took a roll. He was learning to pay attention to such details, and to think ahead. Finally he returned to the main deck and reported to Mr Smith.

The latter was about to dismiss him so that he might attend morning classes in the Gun Room when Gus appeared in the doorway, pale as a little ghost. Mr Smith ushered him aft towards the First Lieutenant, who observed the movement and glanced down with a frown. "It's up to the masthead with him, Mr Smith. That's the normal punishment for failing one's duty in the rigging. No special treatment because he may be young," he said as Mr Smith hesitated.

Hugo rushed forward, shouting, "Oh no, please, sir, Gus gets vertigo when he's sent up any height. He'll just sicken, sir. Can I not do his punishment for him?"

"That's enough, Mr Jarvis. Kindly go below as ordered or I'll have you flogged for insubordination!" Reluctantly Hugo turned away and went below. The last thing he saw as he did so was Gus kneeling in a sobbing heap at Mr Smith's feet crying piteously, "Don't make me go up there, please sir, don't." But sent up he was, to the crow's nest above the topsail yards with Big John, one of the more burly Able Seamen, climbing the ratlines behind him and swishing a rope's end against Gus's bare ankles lest he should falter.

When Hugo returned to the main deck later in the day he could see Gus's shadow still in the crow's nest. There was not a sound from him, but a trickle of vomit was making its way slowly down the mainmast. The punishment period ended at eight bells of the afternoon watch. Mr Smith hailed the crow's nest and ordered Master Mather to make his way down. There was no response. Big John was sent up to investigate and found the boy collapsed face down, his bare legs and arms red and swollen with sunburn and exposure, and not a sign of life left in him. Big John descended with the burden over his shoulder and his voice was unusually gruff as he reported to the officer. He was instructed to return the lad to the sick berth and see what the surgeon could make of him.

A few days later the *Apollion* sailed into harbour at Funchal, Madeira. There was no sign of the *Aetherial*, either among the ships already in port or upon the ocean behind them. They had lost contact with her in the storm, and Captain Sterne could only hope for her reappearance during the few days they must spend in port before setting out again. However there were many other vessels present, and the low grey hills that surrounded the harbour formed a background to a forest of masts and yards dimly glimpsed through the pink mist of dawn. Most of the ships were either Portuguese or British, save for an American frigate of a rather rakish rig that was making its way seaward as the *Apollion* approached, and which declined to dip its colours in response to the usual greeting from a vessel of one friendly nation to another. Whilst some of the Portuguese ships were men-of-war, set to guard the islands against any territorial ambitions to which the French might aspire, others were trading vessels en route from the East Indies and West Africa with cargoes of spices, silks, carpets, fine timbers such as camphor, sandalwood and ebony, and of precious jewels and ivory too.

The British ships anchored there, in particular a large convoy of East Indiamen, were laden with similar goods, though some had brought tea and porcelain from China, expensive and fashionable items which fetched a high price upon safe delivery to London. Some British ships were outward-bound, and of these two were of particular interest to the crew of the *Apollion*, for they were to escort them across the Atlantic, first to Barbados and thence to Port Royal in Jamaica. These ships were merchant vessels, only lightly-armed but carrying a number of rich English families, together with their fine furniture and household goods, to the elegant mansions their husbands had built for themselves among the sugar and cotton plantations of the West Indies. It was Hugo's first experience of prosperity above and beyond the rather spartan economy of board-waged Roos Hall, and the idea of providing an armed escort for such people rather fascinated him.

However his more immediate concern was his own liberty. The *Apollion* had anchored within the shelter of the harbour but several cables' lengths offshore. Hugo had assumed they would moor alongside the quay and that he would be able to take a turn ashore along with the rest of the crew. It seemed that the choice of an offshore station was deliberate in order to prevent desertion by the crew and by the pressed men in particular. Thus Captain Hunter and the Marines went ashore in all their finery and could be heard drumming and piping their way up the long incline to the Fort, where their Portuguese allies had prepared for them a fine reception of fresh food and much good wine. Captain Sterne and his lieutenants, save for the officer of the watch, had departed in the launch on a round of visitations to the other British ships in harbour, beginning with a Royal Navy schooner on loan to the Portuguese fleet, and ending with the much feasting aboard the two merchant ships they were to escort.

Upon the *Apollion*'s arrival in port a number of bum-boats had come alongside full of showily-dressed doxies. Some of these had been permitted to climb aboard to entertain the crew, as well as a few rather older and uglier women who had cargoes of cheap trinkets for sale. None of this interested Hugo who had observed similar goings-on during his brief visits to Yarmouth. He was far more intrigued to have his first experience of a foreign land with a part-European, part-Creole population and strange dishes and customs new to his tastes.

Time hung heavily on Hugo's hands at present. Morning lessons had been suspended until the ship was under way again. The goats and hens that had been his charges had all been eaten and their replacements had not yet come aboard. Most of the crew were about their own business and his fellow middies had been assigned the privilege of accompanying the Captain and officers in the launch, primarily as oarsmen though they would be permitted to climb aboard the other vessels. Hugo descended to the sick berth and looked in on Gus, its only occupant on this peaceful and sunlit morning. Gus lay half-asleep but turned towards Hugo with a wan smile as he entered. Big John, the rough and burly Able Seaman, had whittled the end of a broken spar into a model boat, complete with tiny oars and a sail made of cloth torn from someone's shirt tail, and he had given Hugo strict instructions what he was to say when he presented it.

"Gus," Hugo began, "this is for you. Big John has made it for you while you've been ill. He's asked me to tell you he has no hard feelings, and he hopes very much that you have none either."

"Thank you, Hughie. I'm feeling a lot better today. Now that the ship is at anchor I don't get so sick. They brought me a good breakfast this morning and I have it still." He patted his belly. "The ship is very quiet of a sudden. Where is everyone?"

"Mostly ashore, the lucky fellows. We are not allowed to land, Gus. 'Cause we were pressed they think we'd try to escape," Hugo replied.

"Well, we would wouldn't we?" Gus responded.

"Madeira is only an island, Gus," Hugo replied, "and we would have to persuade some sea captain to risk his own career by taking us home. Even if we could reach another ship by ourselves, there is no guarantee that another captain wouldn't just use us for his crew instead."

"Oh, then we are bound with the Navy, as you said, Hughie. I seem to remember you telling me you would have the chance to send a letter home when we reached Madeira. At least you could tell them where we are."

"Why, so I was told, Gus. I will enquire of one of the officers about doing so."

"Will you tell them about me too, Hughie, and apologise to my parents for playing truant that day. I would not have been taken otherwise."

"Of course, Gus. I'll make sure your parents are given all our messages." It was thus that Hugo sat down at the Gun Room table and in the absence of his noisy companions wrote the following lines:

"Dear Miss Jessica,   *Funchal, Madeira, 25 Oct. 1794*

"I am sending this letter to you at Roos Hall in the hope that your name and address will provide a better guarantee of its delivery than one directed to an humble farmhouse. The enclosed sealed note is written to my parents. It relates the circumstances of my arrival aboard this ship, H.M.S. Apollion, *and describes my daily duties, which will doubtless much divert my brother and sisters. In short, I am not displeased with my situation since I have long had a yearning to enter the Navy, though I have sent my apologies to my former employer, Mr Stevenson, for the accident of Fate that brought me here.*

"However I have to relate that young Augustus Mather is here with me, taken by the same means as myself. He is not fitted for a life aboard ship since he suffers from vertigo on being sent aloft. I wish you would kindly hand both letters to Mrs Jarvis upon receipt, so that she may notify our respective parents of our whereabouts, and situation.

"I wish you well and trust that you may have found another creature to take the place of the dear departed Matilda.

My humble respects,
Hugo Jarvis."

After addressing the cover carefully to Miss Jessica A Rich, care of Mrs E Jarvis at Roos Hall, Beccles, in the County of Suffolk, Hugo delivered his precious missive to the Purser's offices. The incumbent indicated the sack set aside for despatches from officers and crew. Believing that the communication could contain no more than childish trivia from a young boy to his sweetheart, who was perhaps better able to read than his parent could, the packet was left unopened by the security officer aboard the *Apollion*. It passed with similar immunity through the Admiralty system until it reached its destination towards the end of the year. There its arrival caused no little consternation and prompted Betty Jarvis to pen yet another indignant missive to Sir Charles Rich about the now absent Ainsworth.

CHAPTER XII
The 'Ebony' Trade

The *Apollion* slipped down the trade winds towards Barbados as sweetly and swiftly as fine weather and a moderate sea permitted. The *Aetherial* had managed to rejoin her sister-ship at Funchal. A Navy frigate from the Mediterranean Fleet, calling at Funchal for news and despatches from the West Indies, reported that it had espied the *Aetherial*, dismasted and crippled by the storm, which had treated the slower sailer more harshly than the *Apollion*, creeping into Gibraltar for running repairs. She arrived at Funchal a week late but just in time to fulfil her orders and set sail again.

Although the *Apollion* had eventually docked alongside the quay in order to take on bulk supplies, Hugo had obtained no closer acquaintance with Funchal. Instead he had again been placed in charge of the ship's "menagerie", as Mr Barber described it, namely two more goats, a dozen geese instead of hens, and six pigs, though Hugo scorned to compare these scrawny creatures with the plump Suffolk Whites on the farm at home. The geese had had their pinions clipped, and when the weather was fine they were permitted to leave their pen and take a little exercise about the deck. However Hugo was aware that on one of the birds the clipping was incomplete, and sure enough when he went to confine them again at dusk one day that particular goose proved elusive. It ascended to the poop deck and when Hugo pursued it there, much to the amusement of the officers on duty, it flew up in the air again and plopped down in the ship's wake. Hugo was at a loss what to do. To cry "Goose overboard!" would seem ridiculous and the Captain would scarcely order the ship be hove to and a boat lowered just to rescue a goose. So he ran back to its pen and seized the juiciest looking piece of green fodder he could find, held it over the stern for the bird to see and shouted at it with all his strength. The goose, finding the water around it salty and barren, and observing its fresh water and food supply disappearing into the distance, with a great effort rose up again from the waves and landed upon the main deck with a thump, having broken its good pinions against the rigging on its way. Hugo seized the bird with much relief, since he knew that its value would have been deducted from his wages, together with some other punishment, no doubt, if the recapture had failed.

The fresh greenery enjoyed by the menagerie was one of the benefits of calling at Funchal where ships on long voyages would take aboard several tons of vegetables and fruit, in particular lemons whose juice would be mixed with the daily ration of grog, that unpalatable blend of rum and water, in order to save the crew from developing scurvy. Hugo had learnt all about that common seafaring disease from Stan Stevenson and had even encountered the odd scorbutic sufferer stumbling painfully along the quays at Yarmouth. He knew that crews could be decimated below viable strength by this debilitating condition, with its bouts of lassitude, sores and pains in the limbs, and gum rot and foul breath in the head. So he made sure young Gus drank his full ration of lemon juice, even though he was made to take it just with water and was inclined to spit it out. Hugo was much relieved to learn that Captain Sterne had now decreed that Gus was to be assigned to deck duties only and was not to be sent aloft. Even then, those on watch or his messmates had him running from this errand to that, such that, when eventually he climbed into his hammock, he slept from sheer weariness and had no time to sob his homesickness into his pillow.

During assembly one peaceful morning Captain Sterne ordered that gunnery practice would commence at noon and continue until eight bells. To everyone's surprise they were soon engaged in the real thing, for over the horizon there hove in sight two fat French merchant ships heading for home with a single warship for escort. She, however, was fully armed with sixty-four guns and two carronades, weapons whose deadly task was to sweep the enemy's decks clear of living beings. Captain Sterne immediately ordered the decks prepared for battle and asked his signal officer to run up the mizzen mast, unseen by the French, flags confirming those tactics which he and Captain Whitton of the *Aetherial* had agreed previously to use in such circumstances. Enemy French merchantmen were highly valued as productive of prize money for officers and crew and any French warship which could be sunk or disabled was one less for the British West Indies squadron or her Channel and Mediterranean Fleets to overcome.

The two fleets were approaching one another at some four to five knots in a brisk north-westerly breeze, but it would be an hour or so before they came within firing range. Captain Sterne ordered the British merchant ships to slacken speed and allow the *Aetherial* to overtake them to follow the *Apollion* in line astern. Unbeknown to the French captain, he was seriously outgunned, for though the *Aetherial* was a standard frigate of thirty-eight guns, including two carronades, the *Apollion* was larger and more heavily armed. Built in the 1760's for the East India Company, her lines had been considered too sleek for the carriage of goods and she had been converted into a fifty-gun warship with two full decks of guns and two carronades. Her speed and capacity had rendered her ideal for her rôle as armed escort for valuable cargoes.

On board the *Apollion* the main deck was cleared all unnecessary equipment, including the remaining animals from the menagerie which Hugo, with Gus to help him, had to hurry below decks. It was difficult to carry a struggling pig down to the hold with a procession of hammocks, trussed-up for stowing in the netting, coming in the other direction! Then the boys helped their fellow-middies to lay out powder and cartridges, swabs and sponges, for the gun crews. All buckets had to be filled with sea water to dowse fires caused by the passage of cannon-ball and shot. Down in the orlop well, beside the hatches that covered the hold, the Surgeon, Mr Dunstan, was laying out his implements, including bone saws and cauterising irons. His two assistants donned their dark red canvas aprons, coloured thus so as not to emphasise the blood which would soak them soon enough, and filled the water buckets for washing out wounds and sluicing down to the bilges the runnels of slippery blood. A cauldron of hot coals was brought down from the galley and hung on a hook from an overhead beam, and the instruments to be heated were laid on a shelf beside it. Nearby was the surgeon's operating table, the only piece of furniture in the ship that was actually nailed to the deck and not stowed away in time of battle. On a shelf stood the flasks of diluted vinegar used for cleansing wounds of dirt and splinters, as well as bottles of smelling salts, ointments, salves, and flasks of rum and brandy for anaesthetising or reviving the hapless victims of battle. Back on deck, Mr Hunter had his Marines fully-armed and ready for boarding as soon as the ships converged close enough for grappling irons and boarding ladders to be slung across the gaps between their hulls. Aboard the *Aetherial* the same routine was being followed.

The French warship, faster and more manoeuvrable than her merchant companions, interposed herself between them and her enemy as the *Apollion* approached, the British ships taking the opportunity to seize the weather gage. Both sides opened fire as the vessels came within range, but to little effect. For Hugo and Gus it was their first experience of the hot blast of cannon-shot hissing overhead and plunging sizzling into the sea on either side of their ship, whilst casually punching holes in canvas and rigging if they happened to encounter any on their way. Then, at a given signal, the yards of both British vessels were swung round to catch the breeze more fully. As one the *Aetherial* and the *Apollion* tacked hard to port, one in front of and the other behind the French merchant ships and their escort. The French warship's captain could only strike his fist angrily on the quarterdeck rail as he realised he had been tricked, and ordered his carronades to fire a burst at the *Apollion* before she vanished beyond the French merchantman's unprotected stern. Soon the British ships were loosing their cannon into the unguarded starboard flanks of the lightly armed merchantmen, the *Aetherial* first and the *Apollion* thereafter since she had perforce to tack twice before she could come alongside. Well-aimed gunfire had brought down a good deal of the French merchants' rigging and the British ships closed in, slackening their own sails and waiting for the breeze to drift their prey within grappling distance. Then the Marines rushed across the boarding ladders followed by a number of able seamen armed with pike and cutlass, whilst Captain Sterne awaited calmly the reappearance on his beam of the discomfited

French warship. To give her Captain credit, he did try to force the bows of his vessel between the two merchantmen, but Captain Sterne had foreseen this and had grappling hooks slung between the French ships, linking them together with heavy cables.

Next the French captain thought of attacking the British merchant ships, though he appreciated that they too were armed. Even if he did capture them, he would still be court-martialled for the loss of his own charges, so he decided to sail around the bows of his fleet and attack the *Apollion* again from the lee-ward side. Here he was faced with another quandary, for the decks of the French merchant ships were covered with struggling men, half French, half English. If he used his carronades he would give as much grief to his own compatriots as he would to his enemy. His only option was to aim for the British rigging in the hope of disabling his foe. His misfortune was that his ship rode higher in the water than the British vessels, and that the breeze had now stiffened, heeling over his vessel so that his first broadside sailed over the masts of the British ships and did further damage to the French ones! At this a cheer went up from the gun decks of the *Apollion* whose shots had been aimed low, sometimes even skipping from wave to wave. After the recoil, whilst the gun was being swabbed and reloaded, Hugo and his fellow middies could peer through the vacant gun port and observe the trajectory of each shot before scampering back to their duties, choking on the thick fumes of gunpowder and cordite and brushing sparks from their clothing. Now Hugo knew why the gunners always stripped to the waist for battle.

Suddenly there came a shout from one of the gun crews. They had noted that the bows of the French warship seemed lower in the water. There was a report like a gunshot as her main topmast split and collapsed, sending a welter of canvas and rigging over the port beam, steepening her previous list. Captain Sterne ordered the fore and aft deck guns of the *Apollion* to be cranked up to their highest elevation and several shots plunged into the stricken enemy's hull. Then came a reverberating boom of an explosion and flames burst out amidships. The French sailors and militia on the merchant vessels, aghast at the fate of their warship, surrendered at once, and the British Marines were given the task of sorting out the living from the dead, imprisoning the surviving Frenchmen in the holds of their own ships, posting armed guards and clearing their decks so that skeleton crews could be sent aboard to sail the prizes into port. By now the French warship had vanished below the horizon. Captain Sterne sent the launches away to search for any survivors, but they found only flotsam and bodies. All trace of the enemy had vanished beneath the waves.

Hugo found the aftermath of the battle more trying than its progress. Being given rapid orders by one gun team after another to supply this or that left him no time to think of himself. Now that he had every opportunity to do so his legs trembled as he descended into the hold to feed the menagerie which he had been instructed should remain below for the time being in case there were other

French convoys to contend with. Beside the hatches he found Mr Dunstan and his assistants still tending the wounded, and their horrible groans and cries reminded him of farm animals, particularly cattle, which had suffered broken limbs or had otherwise injured themselves falling into ditches and the like. He hated to see animals in distress and shuddered at the sounds. There was a pile of corpses laid to one side, waiting for burial on the morrow, and one of the surgeon's assistants asked him to fetch more buckets of sea water for sluicing down the blood-soaked orlop deck. Hugo watched fascinated as Mr Dunstan, sweat pouring from his brow, continued to cut, cleanse, cauterise and patch like some diabolical cook, the brandy and rum going as often to his own lips as to those of his patients!

Hugo retrieved his hammock from the netting and found it embedded with splinters of wood and even a spent French sharp-shooter's bullet. It would take him a while to sort that out and he felt so weary that he could have slept where he stood. Instead every hand had plenty to do. The Master had inspected masts and rigging and had given orders as to what needed to be taken down and replaced. Spares were brought up from the hold and the Carpenter and his assistants were already busy with hammer and saw. Fortunately there had been no damage to either British ship below the waterline, nor any leaks provoked by the vigorous activity of the guns as they thundered back and forth on their carriages. The Bosun was reorganising watches for the night since some of his best crewmen had had to be spared to man the French prizes. Half of the Marines had returned aboard, some to have wounds dressed, while the remainder stayed behind to guard the prisoners. The Purser was sent over in the jolly-boat to make a list of the French merchantmen's cargoes so that a decision could be made whether both ships were worth escorting to port, now expected to be Carlisle Bay at Barbados, and the prizes were inspected for leaks for the same reason. It seemed that one of the ships was full of sugar, partially refined, and the other was laden with sacks of coffee beans, both worth a considerable amount on the London market. Their best solution would be to find a British convoy homeward bound, so long as the prizes were properly registered at the Navy Office in the names of their respective British captors so that prize money could later be claimed.

The following morning, while the French prizes were being jury-rigged for the voyage, Captain Sterne on the *Apollion* and Captain Whitton on the *Aetherial* held short burial services for the men who had died. Damaged hammocks and torn sails served as shrouds as the bodies were wrapped and sewn in as decently as possible, weighted, and were slid overboard from a stretcher made of two planks knocked together. Hugo felt sad to see such a sight and grasped the hand of little Gus who was standing shivering behind him. For both of them it was their first real contact with human death, each having come from a healthy family without infant mortalities, though at this point a vision crossed Hugo's mind of that young woman who had come to the farm to help his mother – that was before the advent of the Cadicotts – and who had died in mysterious circumstances after giving birth to a child. Idly he wondered what had been her name. He was sure he should remember it if he tried. Meanwhile the drums had beaten to quarters, the ships got under way, *Apollion* leading, then the British merchantmen guarding the prizes between them, and the *Aetherial* bringing up the rear.

They reached Bridgetown, Barbados, quite quickly and without further incident. There they found a British convoy ready to escort their prize cargoes home and were able to dispose satisfactorily of that responsibility. One of the French merchantmen had developed a leak, or some member of her erstwhile crew had used his exercise period to carry out a little sabotage. The coffee beans she carried were transferred to a British ship, such of those beans as were not ruined by seawater, and the French ship was taken out of harbour and scuttled. Hugo being free of other duties was permitted to take an oar in the launch that carried out the order and thus had an opportunity to observe how it was done with fuses and powder blowing holes at strategic places in her hull. It seemed a shame to sink the whole vessel, but he understood these exigencies of war.

One of the British charges carried families destined for plantations in Barbados, so once the fine furniture and the elegant ladies and children had gone ashore, to the accompaniment of much ribaldry and crude but accurate comments from the frigates' crews, she was able to receive the sacks of coffee beans to add to her new cargo. Their remaining British charge was to be escorted onwards to Port Royal by another convoy, for Captain Sterne had received orders to report to the Admiral-in-Command at Government House, St Christopher (now St Kitts) in the Leeward Islands. On their way the *Apollion* and the *Aetherial* were to search for a Spanish pirate that had captured a fast American frigate and was preying on merchant shipping in the Caribbean. At this time Britain was at peace with both those nations following the conclusion of the American War of Independence and negotiation of the Treaty of Versailles in 1783. Why Royal Navy frigates should be ordered to perform a favour for these two nations, their crews were at a loss to understand. Either some very rich pickings or some vital diplomatic objective had to be involved. When they learnt that the American frigate concerned was the U.S.S. *Beacon* out of Boston, that same ship which had snubbed the British colours on its departure from Funchal, even more speculation was rife among the crews as to how such a fast-sailing and elegant vessel should have been captured so easily.

Meanwhile, seeking out one particular ship in a stretch of ocean as wide and diverse as the Caribbean was like looking for a needle in a haystack, and odds were laid on the main deck as on the quarterdeck as to the likelihood of their success. Of course one should also take into account the fact that Captain Sterne had served in these waters for upwards of a dozen years and had earned his gold braid under Admiral Rodney at the famous Battle of Les Saintes off Guadeloupe in 1782. Moreover Captain Sterne's orders instructed him to avoid contact with enemy shipping and warned him that the recent British conquests of the islands of Guadeloupe and Martinique had just been overtaken by the French. Enemy naval forces were believed to be concentrated off the Atlantic coast of those islands and therefore Captain Sterne should be advised to take a more prudent westerly course to his destination. He should also bear in mind that the said Spanish pirate had last been sighted heading north-west from the coast of Venezuela.

The two British frigates were ready for sea again within a few days. Just time for restocking and provisioning with supplies and spare yards and rigging for what could be a contentious voyage. As at Funchal, none of the pressed men were permitted ashore at Bridgetown and in fact they were kept busy, Hugo and Gus included, taking the fresh supplies aboard and storing them in the appropriate locations in the ship with which both boys had become familiar. They had been at sea for little more than six weeks since leaving England, but already their homes seemed an unfamiliar dream from the past. The outward voyage from Bridgetown, through the St Vincent Passage and under the sombre shadow of the 4,000 ft volcano Soufrière, was rough and stormy since they had to contend with both adverse winds and currents, and once again the sleeker *Apollion* showed herself the better sailer, closer to the wind and faster than the more plump *Aetherial*.

When clear of the islands they turned north, as it were along the string of the bow formed by the Lesser Antilles. Once they spotted a French squadron half a dozen strong, hull-down on the horizon, but Captain Sterne ordered the helm turned away. His crew glanced at one another with surmise; it was unlike their captain not to pick a fight with the enemy, even if they were outnumbered. None but Captain Sterne himself knew the precise content of the secret Government mission upon which they were engaged. It seemed that the Spanish pirate, Manuel de Silva, was no ordinary freebooter but a refugee from justice, having failed in an attempt to assassinate the King of Spain. If the British could return him to Spain and the due process of Law, it might help to persuade that country not to join France in its Revolutionary War with Britain. As for the American frigate which he had captured and had made his flagship, it appeared that it was of a rather advanced design, and the British Government wished the Navy to take a good look at it before handing it back to its rightful owners. They had even despatched a naval surveyor for the purpose, a Mr Mackenzie, who was quietly residing aboard the *Aetherial* as Captain Whitton's "guest".

Captain Sterne's objective was Isla de las Aves, Bird Island, a speck of land in the midst of the ocean that had once formed the base of a now extinct volcano. It was a well known pirate haunt, seldom visited by others because of its remoteness and the likelihood of receiving an unpleasant reception at the hands of its transient inhabitants. But it was endowed with freshwater springs, various tropical fruits and groves of coconut palms, such that it provided a useful point of replenishment for those who dared not anchor in more civilised harbours. On nearing the island, both captains exercised extreme caution, approaching it by daylight and with every topmast manned by lookouts. It appeared deserted. The *Aetherial* was despatched to circumnavigate the isle, with instructions to fire her cannon in the event that she needed aid, whilst Captain Sterne sent the launches ashore with Mr Hunter and a large party of Marines to look for signs of occupation. As the boats reached the shoreline some large birds, which occupied many of the trees and had been flying about in a desultory manner, suddenly flew up in a great flock.

"What birds are they?" Hugo enquired of Big John who happened to be standing on watch beside him.

"They're Frigate Birds, Mr Jarvis. Huge fellows those, more'n two yards across, big as an albatross. You'll find them on many a tropical island but they're not good eating, tastes foul they do. Strange they should fly up so; they don't usually do that 'less you're up in the trees trying to rob their nests."

An hour or so later Mr Hunter and his party returned to report that the island's landing-place was a scene of utter devastation with much of the light timber cut down and carried away and all the coconut palms felled to rob them of even their greenest nuts. A great number of the Frigate Birds had been shot and their eggs taken, since the remains of this activity were strewn across the beach. Strangely though, it would seem that no fires had been lit. Captain Sterne remarked to Mr Barber on hearing this news, "It appears that our Señor da Silva, if indeed he did pass this way, must have been in a devil of a hurry and with many mouths to feed if he has taken all the nuts and the bird's eggs too. He must have captured several ships and needs to make port without delay." As soon as the *Aetherial* reappeared with a negative report as to other signs of life, the two ships got under way again. Since the devastation of the beach appeared recent, there was a possibility that the pirate might not have travelled far, though Captain Sterne realised that in a straight race the *Beacon* could far out-sail the *Apollion* – hence the Navy's interest in her design. He reckoned that Señor da Silva would be heading for a Spanish-friendly port such as Santo Domingo on the island of Hispaniola and asked Mr Barber to plot a course in that direction.

Captain Sterne's prediction proved absolutely correct for on the following day, in the middle of the ocean, they came across a most curious sight. Two ships lay side by side, almost motionless in the water. The nearer one, the *Beacon*, appeared unharmed, but the rigging of the other ship was a mass of sailors and carpenters making running repairs to masts, spars and sails. "Evidently Señor da Silva was in too much of a hurry to carry out his repairs at Bird Island but must needs make them whilst under way, " Captain Sterne commented to Mr Barber from the quarterdeck. "The other vessel looks sound enough in her timbers. Portuguese by the cut of her, wouldn't you say, Mr Barber?"

"Indeed, sir, I think she's a négrier, a slave ship, and that is why he needed all those coconuts. The *Beacon* must have captured her on her way to Brazil and he has hundreds of slaves on board dying of thirst and starvation," Mr Barber responded.

"Yes, and must carry his cargo to port, and a slave market too, most speedily or they will all perish. Well, I'm sure we British can show him a better way of handling things. Clear the decks for battle, Mr Barber." The Bosun's pipe was heard, the rat-a-tat-tat of the Marines as they paraded on deck, and the terrible but inevitable routine commenced as the two British ships bore down on their prey.

Señor da Silva was caught nicely in a dilemma. The better part of his crew was aboard the slaver engaged in repairs. By the time they had all climbed back aboard the *Beacon*, the British ships would be firing broadsides which as like as not would damage further the prize he was busy re-rigging. His only alternative was to cut his cables, hoist sail and hope to draw off the British ships in chase, then to disable them in combat and return to collect his prize. He had one other problem, which he momentarily ignored, he himself was no professional sailor but rather a political activist, a scribbler of pamphlets and news-sheets by vocation, who had taken objection to the ineptitudes of his monarch, Charles IV of Spain. As the cables linking the two ships parted and the breeze filled the sails being hoisted on the *Beacon*, he stared across the widening gap and realised that his First Mate had been among those left aboard the slave ship. He was the only one who knew how to trim the *Beacon*'s cordage so as to give the sleek frigate that extra turn of speed. Moreover looking at the number of sailors which Da Silva had left behind, Captain Sterne reckoned that there would not be sufficient manpower left aboard the *Beacon* to fire a complete broadside. Therefore the obvious tactic would be to engage and board the vessel quickly with a British ship on either side. Ordering the *Aetherial* to crowd on all sail, the *Apollion* did likewise and was soon within gunshot range of the *Beacon*. Captain Sterne ordered his gun crews to aim high, their object being to disable the *Beacon* and not to sink her.

Señor da Silva, however, was not a man without resources. Secured and guarded with the foc'sle of the *Beacon* were a dozen members of her original American crew whom the Spaniard hoped to ransom at the American Consulate at Santo Domingo. These men were manacled, so he swaggered through the doorway and asked for volunteers to man both the ship and the guns.

"Who're we fighting?" the American captain asked immediately.

"Two British warships," the Spaniard replied.

"Much as I disdain the bastards, my Government is at peace with England right now," the American captain responded. "I'll be hanged as a pirate if I help you. And that applies to all my officers too."

"What about these men?" the Spaniard demanded, kicking one of the American sailors with his foot.

"What's in it for us?" the seaman regarded him with a beady eye.

"Good food, plenty food," the Señor offered.

"In that case we'll eat first," the seaman replied, "then we'll help you. No point in dying hungry if we don't survive the battle."

"All right, but you hurry, yes?" The Spaniard yelled to his cook to bring a bucket of the stew upon which he had recently dined, as well as bread and water. The cook and his assistant delivered the food promptly; each sailor took a bowl of stew, a portion of bread and a turn at the flask of water. You have never seen food consumed more slowly by starving men!

"Hurry, hurry, I need you on deck," the Spaniard reappeared and urged them. The seamen, each reaching the halfway stage of consumption, handed his bowl and crust to one of the officers and stood up. The cook's assistant unlocked each shackle in turn and the man was taken up on deck. When he came to the last seaman the assistant was seized and never left that cabin with the key. At this moment the first cannonball from the *Aetherial* thudded aboard the *Beacon's* decks. Simultaneously the *Apollion* swept across the *Beacon's* bows. She had two carronades mounted on the foredeck and filled with lethal grape-shot. The American sailors saw it coming, and knowing its potential each flattened himself on the deck. Those of the pirate's motley crew that remained standing were simply mown down. The American Captain and his officers, bursting forth from the companion-way armed with such weapons as they had found en route, surrounded and secured the Spanish captain who stood dumbstruck at the devastation caused to his crew. One of the American sailors hauled down the pirate's colours; a tree, leafed and fruited proper upon a field argent, and thought to replace it with an American flag till his Captain restrained him. Then the American crew reefed the *Beacon's* sails until she came to a standstill with the British ships on either side of her. A party of Marines boarded the American craft. The Spanish pirate was taken captive aboard the *Aetherial* whilst the American captain and his officers were brought to the *Apollion* where Captain Sterne and Captain Whitton were already conferring on the quarterdeck.

"You had better send Mr Mackenzie aboard the *Beacon* together with the prize crew," Captain Sterne had commanded. "He must make his measurements as we sail, for it will be difficult for us to detain the *Beacon* once we have reached port. The American Consul will have all the documents ready for signature as soon as we arrive, and with the Captain present we will be unable to refuse to let her go."

The American captain and his officers were escorted to the quarterdeck where Captain Sterne and Captain Whitton introduced themselves. "Captain Anderson of the U.S.S. *Beacon* of Boston," the American replied with a hurried salute. He continued, "I would demand that you release my ship and my men immediately, so that I can return to the Island of La Blanquilla where that damned pirate has marooned the rest of my crew. I would be grateful also to borrow some of your sailors to assist the few American seamen who remain with me."

"One thing at a time, Captain Anderson," Captain Sterne interposed calmly. "Firstly we must return to the slaver and persuade those aboard her to surrender."

"She was our prize, you know," Captain Anderson insisted. "We had come upon her anchored off La Blanquilla, that's an island off the north coast of Venezuela ..."

"I am aware of that," Captain Sterne murmured somewhat impatiently.

"She appeared to have been abandoned. My crewmen found no one aboard, but a hold full of starving slaves crying with thirst, some hundreds of them – a valuable cargo. So I ordered a few of my crew to take charge of the slaver and the rest to go ashore for water and food to feed the slaves, otherwise we would simply have had to throw the lot of them overboard as they died. No sooner were my men ashore than Señor da Silva appeared aboard an old Dutch hulk towed by boats full of cut-throats. Their presence had been concealed from us by a lofty rock formation. We were taken completely by surprise. They boarded my ship and raised sail immediately, leaving the bulk of my men stranded ashore. Then they had the effrontery to use my ship's cannon to sink their Dutch hulk as they departed. I must return and search for my men."

"I regret that will not be possible yet awhile," Captain Sterne replied. "I have urgent orders to proceed to St Christopher, where I will deliver the slaver as a prize of the British Navy, and having duly recorded our capture of the *Beacon* it will no doubt be possible to return her to you without delay through the good offices of your country's Consul."

"You British! You're all too concerned with your wretched formalities and with claiming your prize money!" Captain Anderson protested, quite overlooking the fact that it had been his intention to dispose of the remaining slaves for the benefit of his own pocket at some convenient American slave-market, such as Charleston in South Carolina.

"However, it puzzles me, Captain Anderson, how Da Silva could have brought the slaver so far north without first repairing her rigging?"

"Oh that damage was done in a storm two night ago," Captain Anderson replied. "We were struck by a severe squall and the dolts Da Silva had put on board lacked the skill to save her. The *Beacon* had no similar problem. Even a fool can sail her."

"So it would seem," Captain Sterne commented dryly. The American failed to grasp the double entendre. As they were speaking the Portuguese slaver appeared over the horizon. Mr Barber reported that she seemed already to have struck Da Silva's personal colours and to have replaced these with an American flag instead. Everyone had the tact not to mention that the flag had been hoisted upside down! In any case, it was soon hauled down again when Da Silva's First Mate, who had no particular gripe against any nation save his own, observed that the British had taken the American ship and not the other way about.

A British crew from the *Aetherial*, together with Mr Mackenzie, were put aboard the *Beacon*. To have left any American seamen aboard her would have risked her giving them the slip and outsailing the British ships during the night.

Besides, they would surely have reported to their officers the suspicious nature of the activities of Mr Mackenzie.   Instead the American seamen were sent aboard the slaver, a huge vessel, together with selected crewmen from the *Apollion* and a few of the best of Da Silva's men. A large party of Marines guarded each ship, including the remainder of Da Silva's crew who were divided up and imprisoned, some on each vessel. There being no British casualties from the brief action, the dead among the pirate crew were despatched overboard without ceremony, though the British naval surgeons did treat a number of wounded sailors.   Meanwhile launches from both the British frigates were loaded with casks of water, and some mandioca found aboard the slaver was hurriedly cooked when it was learnt that the slaves, originally some 400 in number, had neither been fed nor watered since the night of the storm.   Among the crews of the *Apollion*'s launches were Big John and young Hugo Jarvis, together with most of their midshipmen, though not little Gus.

Even as he pulled on the launch's oar, Hugo could smell the stench emanating from the slaver. He could identify by now those seaboard stenches deriving from sweat, urine, faeces, wounds which were suppurating, scurvy and some of the other diseases to be found upon any ship. This stench was one he was quite unable to compare. He thought of the tannery on the corner of Puddingmoor Lane in Beccles and decided that this was far worse. He thought of raw flax as it lay soaking in the Fenland ditches around Norwich before being woven into linen, and decided again that this was much worse than that. Whatever would he find aboard this ship? He had heard about the slave trade, of course, for Stan Stevenson had described to him many of its features. Moreover Hugo's great-uncle Robert, learning of his interest in the subject, had saved for him extracts from the newspapers reporting some of the fine speeches made in the Houses of Parliament against slavery by such eminent gentlemen as Charles Fox, Edmund Burke, William Pitt and William Wilberforce. Uncle Robert opined that, despite the growing moral doubts among the British public, the Trade was far too profitable, too necessary for the running of Caribbean and American plantations, and too entrenched among the bigwigs and influential persons of all the nations engaged in it, for legislation to ban or control it to stand any chance of success. Hugo's only personal knowledge of black people was of the footman of the Mayor of Yarmouth who stood behind his carriage dressed in smart livery when that important gentleman rode about his business.

The launches came alongside the slaver and their crews scrambled aboard. They were met by some of their Marines, already there on guard duty, who helped them hoist up the casks of water. "We've opened up the hatches," one of them said, "or you would all have been asphyxiated. We've also found some flagons and jugs which can be filled from your casks when we lower them into the hold."

"What will they drink from?" Big John enquired.

"So far as we can see," the Marine replied, "they all seem to have half-coconuts to serve as cups and dishes, and some even have spoons, but the rest must do as they can. I think that there are many dead among them and many that were sick in the storm. There's piss and shit everywhere. We started to swill the deck beneath them but they're so tumbled about that we couldn't get in among them. That's why we've asked for the Middies – they can climb over the bodies with less damage to them than heavier persons such as yourself."

"Let me go down and take a look," said Big John. The first cask was sent down with a mallet to strike out the bung. Hugo and Pip followed carrying some of the jugs. The stench was so overpowering that both boys tied their kerchiefs around their faces.

"We need lanterns down here, can't see a thing," Big John shouted to those on deck. Indeed the only thing Hugo could see by daylight filtering dimly through one or two half-open ports, was the whites of hundreds of eyes, shining like glow-worms in a dark cavern, eyes that seemed frozen in their sockets by fear.

Suddenly a voice, croaking and hoarse, came out of the darkness, whispering in broken English, "You throw us in sea?"

"No," Big John replied gruffly. "We've come to give you water and food."

The voice croaked again, "You fatten us for eating?"

"No," Big John replied, "we'll take you to land."

Once more the voice demanded, "Then you sell us for slaves?"

"Yes, I daresay that will happen," Big John replied as he filled some of the jugs and flagons.

"That a pity," the voice spoke again. "We are free men, but our chief have quota supply Portuguee," and the voice lapsed into silence. More jugs and some lanterns came down and now the boys could see the scale of their task. In a deck space a little less than six feet high there were platforms at knee height along the sides of the deck, and more running down the centre and almost touching the others. There was also a half-deck each side at about the height of Hugo's shoulder. These platforms were almost invisible beneath a heaving mass of black bodies jammed shoulder to shoulder and head to feet as far as they could go. Those on the outside faced the sea with one leg and one hand shackled alternately to the man next to him. Those in the centre sat up permanently and could only lie down when those on the seaward side sat up. Having lain there untended through a storm and its aftermath for more than two days, the system had collapsed and the sick and dying lay higgledy piggledy over each other, some suffocating from the weight of those above. Hugo's glance fled in horror from those below to those on the half-deck, rough shelves made of spars and timbers, beside him. Hundreds of diminutive black forms stared back, some faces wet with tears, other too frightened to cry.

"Why, they're only children!" Hugo exclaimed to Big John as he picked up a flagon of water.

"Yes, they seize them also to work on the plantations, or to train as house-boys," the bluff seaman replied with a tone that almost implied shame. "Now take that jug down that far side and come back when it's empty." Hugo did as he was bid, climbing over the prone forms, sorting out heads and shoulders, lifting those too weak to help themselves, gently filling coconut shells held in trembling hands. Some clutched at him out of turn and he was obliged to push them aside. Some failed to move at all. If he could Hugo tried to dribble a little water between their lips as he had seen Mr Dunstan revive wounded seamen with a drop or two of brandy. Sometimes the trickle resulted in a choking and the 'corpse' came to life; sometimes it remained prone. It was difficult for Hugo to tell where he had stopped serving when he returned with a fresh jug, and he found he could only do so by counting bodies as he crawled over them. Behind him he was aware of Pip and the others helping the children to water and sorting out those in the centre of the hold. He had come across one man who was not only dead but also decomposing fast. His skin had turned a curious yellow colour and a haze of flies hovered about him much more thickly than over the rest who were still sufficiently alive to wave them away. Hugo shuddered and crawled on to the next man. He did not feel the bite of the insect which stung his bare neck as he passed.

"There's quite a few dead amongst them," Hugo reported to Big John as he returned for a refill, "and one that is really being eaten by maggots."

"Aye, lad, but we'll have to leave him till daylight. Then we'll sort them out and have them up on deck in batches for some exercise. Then we can swill down their quarters. They'll help us, those that have the strength."

"I've counted nearly seventy men up to the partition where the foremast comes down," Hugo continued, "I can hear voices on the other side of the bulkhead. What goes on there?"

"That's the women slaves," Big John replied. "There's some as have given birth, sights not fit for young eyes to see, so the Marines are dealing with those."

"Oh," Hugo replied, thinking to himself that he was quite accustomed to birth scenes, living on a farm, but he took another jug and willingly crawled down to the far end of the hold to serve the last few on his line. Then it was a matter of distributing the mandioca, which had been cooked in the slaver's galley by its own cook, well-supervised by a couple of Marines. British sailors lowered the concoction down into the hold in steaming buckets and half-coconut shells appeared, converted into handy scoops. Again the Midshipmen crawled along the hungry lines, thrusting a warm and mushy bowl into each pair of upraised hands. At this stage it was almost dark and time for the boat crews to return to their respective ships.

Next morning, the wind being fair and the sea benign, the four ships set a course for the island of St Christopher, *Apollion* ahead, keeping pace with the *Beacon* under reduced sail, and *Aetherial* chivvying along the Portuguese slaver which was the slowest of the fleet. Those Marines not on guard duty were now aboard the slaver helping the British crewmen unshackle the slaves a score at a time and bring them on deck to be sluiced down with sea water, given a fresh strip of canvas to serve as a loin cloth, and be fed and watered once again. A huge cauldron had been set up on deck in which the seamen were stewing beans brought over from the *Apollion*. The slaves eyed the big cooking-pot askance, wondering once more whether they too were to be cooked and eaten.

As the platforms were progressively cleared, some of the more healthy slaves took brooms and buckets of sea water to sluice their fellows' uncleaned body fluids into the bilges. The platforms upon which the slaves had lain were scrubbed down with vinegar before the cleansed were fastened there again. It took all day to move progressively from one end of the hold to the other. The children were found to have been lying upon mats woven from coconut fibre which were now soaked with faeces and urine. These were thrown overboard, some of them being used to wrap the dead, including two mothers and their stillborn infants that had not survived the trauma. The sharks, which habitually followed the slave ships with their stinking bilges, had tender eating that day!

Two days later all four ships anchored in Frigate Bay, St Christopher, and Captain Sterne went ashore to deliver his despatches, together with Captain Anderson to intercede on behalf of his lost ship and crew. Captain Sterne was ready to let the *Beacon* go now, for Mr Mackenzie had already delivered his report on her dimensions and capabilities. Her speed, he opined, came partly from her slim lines and partly from the cut and trim of her rig, with its slanted masts and greater use of triangular sails which could be hauled closer to the wind. For these latter measurements Mr Mackenzie had been obliged to climb the rigging himself, disguised as a British seaman so as not to attract the suspicions of the American sailors working aboard the slaver. His ineptness above deck level would still have attracted their attention, though, had they been close enough to observe it. As for Señor da Silva, a force of British officers from the fort at Basseterre was sent out to escort him to military confinement, whilst the survivors of his motley crew were hustled ashore by the Marines, since their labour could readily be employed in quarrying rocks to lay down a road around the island. The usual port doxies soon appeared and clamoured to come aboard. Hugo fancied a turn ashore and this time Mr Barber was prepared to permit it. He and Master Mather might accompany the Purser, Mr Iver, in the jolly-boat, provided they each took an oar and assisted Mt Iver in his business of re-provisioning the ship.

Now Mr Iver had missions of his own in mind, for which he had not the least desire to be accompanied by two inquisitive young boys; in short, Mr Iver 'had a lass in every port'. He therefore instructed the boys on landing that they might amuse themselves for an hour or two, provided they returned to the Market Square by the time the clock there showed six, so that they might all row back to the ship for the night. Hugo skipped with glee at the unexpected freedom, though in truth he did not feel very much like skipping. For the last two days he had suffered a headache. Moreover his back felt sore and his tongue clove to the roof of his mouth.

Hugo presumed he must have swallowed to much bad air while aboard the slave ship and that if only he could empty those foetid vapours from his lungs and replace them with clean fresh air, he would soon feel normal again. He was also very conscious of the movement of the ship as it slid over the waves, and again thought that a walk on terra firma would help restore a sense of normality. Not so, for when he had secured the jolly-boat painter and had walked up the steps to the cobbled street, he found that his legs trembled and his swimming sensation was worse than ever. His eyes stung too, and shrank from the bright sunshine of the port and its whitewashed buildings. Suddenly he felt very sick indeed and vomited all over the pathway.

"Hughie, what's wrong? What's the matter with you?"

"I don't know, Gus. I've never felt like this before."

"Shall we return to the ship?" Gus asked.

"We can't do that, for Mr Iver is expecting us. Let me just rest awhile here in the shade. Oh, wait with me, please, I'm going to be sick again," and he was, a long jet of yellow liquid laced with bile. Gus was now becoming rather alarmed. They were walking in a quiet residential street with whitewashed cottages all shuttered against the light. No one else seemed to be about in the blazing sun. Opposite their patch of shade was a smart-looking residence, its plaster walls painted pink, its roof tiled with grey slates rather than timber or palm thatch, its eaves corniced in a convoluted pattern which, had Hugo known it, had just become the rage among the Arrivistes, those enlightened beings who had replaced the aristocracy as the leaders of fashion in Revolutionary France. The door, which was made of polished wood and varnished like the panelling of the Captain's cabin on the *Apollion*, bore a large brass knocker. Gus ran across the street, lifted it thrice and let it fall.

The door was opened by a black servant with a mop in her hand from dusting the hallway. "What you want?" she demanded. Gus, being non-plussed by the appearance of a black person, was struck dumb. Another larger black figure appeared behind the servant, a majestic figure swathed in bright orange and red cloth, and with a smaller cloth tied about her head in the form of a turban, with the two fringed ends reaching up like wings towards the sky.

"What's wrong, boy?" the tall lady demanded, coming forward with a smile. "Why have you come here?" she enquired in perfect English and revealing two rows of exceedingly white teeth.

"Please, Ma'am, my friend here has been taken ill in the street and I don't know how to help him."

"Have you come from a ship?" the lady enquired again.

"Yes, Ma'am, from the frigate *Apollion*."

"Is that the one that arrived yesterday, along with the slave ship?"

"Yes, Ma'am. We captured her from a pirate and brought her to port.

"Oh, you did. And did you go aboard that ship, young fellow?"

"No, Ma'am, but Hughie here did. He took water and food to all the slaves..."

His voice tapered off at the realisation that he was addressing a black person likely to have pronounced prejudices against those who dealt in slaves.

However, she said, "You bring him here and let me look at his eyes." Gus aided Hugo across the street and up the steps into the shaded hallway. "Yellow and much inflamed, I thought so. My lad, you've caught the Yellow Jack, yellow fever."

"Is that very bad?" Gus asked. "Will he die?"

"As he is young and healthy, likely he will not, but one can never tell. Certain it is that he will not be allowed back on board like that. How did you come ashore?"

"In a rowing boat with Mr Iver, the Purser."

"Mr Iver? Just the very man. Bring Hughie, if that's his name, in here. I've a comfortable bed he can lie on. He must eat nothing, but drink liquids all day. I've some special receipts of my own which will bring down his fever – see how he's perspiring already. He'll be very ill for a week or so, but should start to recover after that. Why don't you – what's your name?"

"Augustus, Ma'am."

"Why don't you Augustus, go find Mr Iver and tell him what has happened. Say that your friend Hughie has been taken in to be looked after by Madame Joly. Can you remember that name and pronounce it just so?" Gus nodded. "And that Mr Iver should send me enough from Hughie's wages to keep him for the next two weeks until he's better. Can you do that?"

"Yes, Ma'am," and Gus returned to the sunlight, now waning in the West, and with some difficulty made his way to the square where the Purser had told him to wait. Fortunately Mr Iver was prompt to time and Gus duly explained what had happened. That of which he was unaware was that Madame Joly was well-known in the port as the keeper of the best quality brothel! Her girls were carefully chosen and schooled, and served only the senior officers from the many ships that called. Of British officers she was very fond, for many of them were gentlemen, she maintained, though a little over-addicted to their liquor. Indeed Mr Iver himself did not qualify and was obliged to seek his pleasure elsewhere. He listened to Gus's tale with a gloomy countenance.

"That's most inconvenient," was his first pronouncement. "With both ships due to sail in a couple of days he will not be well enough to come with us. We must leave him behind, and you too, Master Mather, just to keep a watch on his recovery. Does Madame Joly think he will, recover I mean?"

"Yes, sir, she says he's young and healthy, and she also has special medications of her own to treat him."

"Oh, yes, she has a reputation for it. She often cares for officers who fall sick, and their wives hate her for it! Look, Master Mather, you had better return to the ship to collect your kit and Mr Jarvis's personal possessions too, and I'll pay you what you're owed by way of wages. That should be enough to see young Jarvis through. The *Aetherial* is off to Port Royal, Jamaica, to dispose of the slaves. There a British Agent, Mr Thomas Dolbeare, will handle the sale for us and will see our credit transferred to the Navy Office in London. Meanwhile the *Apollion* has been ordered to join the British squadron to harass French shipping off the island of Guadeloupe, to see if we can starve the Frenchies into surrendering the island to us again. There's no knowing when we'll return here. So if neither ship has arrived by the time Mr Jarvis recovers, and if you do not take the fever yourself, you must report to Government House – you see that large stone building on the far side of the square? That's where the Admiral has his office. You must say you are ready to go aboard another ship. I'll furnish you with a form of honourable discharge, and one for Mr Jarvis too."

It was dark by the time Gus returned from the *Apollion*, escorted by Mr Iver and another seaman who both raised their hats respectfully when Madame Joly herself answered the door. Gus spent a wakeful night on a pallet on the floor beside Hugo's bed. He decided it was not as comfortable as his hammock on board ship. As for Hugo, he tossed and turned all night, groaning and muttering in his sleep. So far as Gus could make out, that concerned the horrors Hugo had observed aboard the slave ship. Madame Joly appeared from time to time to sponge Hugo's chest and forehead and to dribble liquid into him in the form of a warm infusion made up in a teapot. It smelt foul so Gus did not enquire what it was made of. Next day Hugo's condition was even worse. He had ceased to mutter and was semi-conscious. Madame Joly had her servant strip off his clothes and she sponged him all over with cold water, Gus helping her to turn his body on its side. She left Gus to continue the spongeing whenever her business called her away.

This procedure continued for three more days, while Gus observed that Hugo's body had turned a strange yellow colour and that the inflamed pink circles around his eyes had become purple and sunken. Gus had seen that symptom among the sick and dying on the *Apollion* following her action against the French warship. He knelt at Hugo's side, applying the cold sponge vigorously, trembling as he felt Hugo's limbs go rigid and then collapse again. "Oh, Hughie, please don't die. Please God, don't let him die," he muttered. "Else how shall I manage on my own, in a strange country and so many miles from home?"

When Gus awoke on the seventh day of Hugo's illness, everything in the room seemed strangely quiet. He found the sponge still moist in his hand and realised that he had fallen asleep whilst tending his friend. He leaned over and felt Hugo's brow; it was cold to the touch and his eyes were closed. The purple circles had turned grey. Gus could not hear Hugo breathing and let out a great yell. Madame Joly's servant entered the room. "Hughie's dead!" Gus cried, breaking into uncontrollable sobs.

The servant bent down and took Hugo's wrist. "He's not dead, Master Gus, he sleeping. Fever's gone. You come have breakfast. He be awake by then."

And so it proved. Hugo was blinking at the daylight by the time Gus returned, and pulling a blanket over his nakedness. "Hello, Gus. How long have I been ill?" he asked.

"'Tis seven days, I think, since we came here."

"Have you been caring for me all this time?"

"Yes, but Madame Joly too. She has shown me what to do and has made you drink lots of awful stuff, her special medicine, she said."

"Well, whatever it was it's done the trick. I'm hungry but feel very weak. I think my head will be dizzy if I try to get up."

"Don't you dare try to get up, Master Hughie," Madame Joly said entering the room at that moment. "You'll be as limp as a blossom out of water. You had your breakfast, Augustus?" Gus nodded. "Then you take this bowl of broth and you kneel down beside Hughie and feed him one small spoonful at a time." She handed the bowl and spoon to Gus, then brought cushions and pillows which she placed behind Hugo's shoulders. He did feel very dizzy when he sat up and was glad to have Gus hold the bowl because his own hands trembled so.

It took several days before Hugo was well enough to get out of bed and sit about the house or in the small shaded garden that lay beyond it. In the meantime a strange event had occurred. One day a footman from Government House called with a message for Madame Joly. He was not sent by one of her usual customers, of whose comings and goings Hugo and Gus were now vaguely aware, but the note he carried caused Madame Joly to sit down with the boys and her servant Melissa in the candlelit kitchen one evening and to inquire more closely into the identity of her visitors. "I have been requested to send you two young gentlemen up to Government House as soon as Hughie is well enough to walk there. Who are you? You're English but where are you from, and how did you come to be aboard that ship?"

"We were taken by a press-gang, Madame, both of us at the same time," Hugo replied, "from a town named Yarmouth on the east coast of England."

"Ah, England," Madame Joly responded with a heavy sigh. "I've often heard about it from my gentlemen, all green with grass or gold with corn. Everyone has plenty to eat and is very rich. Fine houses and fine furniture. I would love to see that place, that's my dream."

Hugo was laughing by this time. "Oh no, Madame, there are many poor and hungry people there too. My father is a farmer, but I had to leave home and start to earn my living. I was helping on a boat, a small boat carrying goods up and down a river."

"What is this 'press-gang' then? I have heard it spoken of before but I do not understand."

"'Tis a means of forcible recruitment for the Navy," Hugo replied. "Groups of sailors go about looking for citizens and even for young boys and take them by force to work aboard the ships. In my case I was waiting for my employer and Gus was standing on the quayside watching the ships being loaded. He should have been at school and is far too young to be a sailor."

"If I could go home," Gus murmured, "I swear I would go back to school and never play truant again, never!"

"And you were taken by force from the quay?"

"Yes, Ma'am," Hugo replied.

"Then you are also slaves," Madame Joly commented softly. She continued, "You saw the conditions on that slave ship, Hughie? Augustus told me you were helping to feed those poor people. Were you shocked by what you saw?"

"Oh yes, Madame, I have never seen anything more horrifying in my life. On our farm, the animals are given gentle care, space to move around, good fodder or as much as we can afford, until the day we sell them or send them to the slaughterer. Indeed I am always sad to see them depart. But the conditions on that ship, chained up like convicts in a jail, with no chance to move or take care of themselves except in rare moments of exercise, and the children also, so many children I could not believe it. They should have been in school like Gus. I've heard about the slave business before, but I never realised it could be so brutal."

"There now, so you saw how they are kept on the ships, but do you know how they are taken from their homes, whole families or sometimes just men or women or children, whatever the slavers want. The Arabs are the worst; they kill whom they do not take and burn their houses. But others make contracts with the village chief to provide so many people the next time the ship returns. The Portuguese do that, so do some of the other Europeans, the British too. That boat was Portuguese; at least they give the children mats to lie on, but the food is poor and they seldom permit much exercise. The English are better at that; their crews are more disciplined so they can permit more exercise, and they tend to feed the slaves better too."

"Yes," Hugo responded, "I remember one of them asking when we fed them whether we were fattening them for eating! It was horrible that the poor souls should think that. What will happen to them now?"

"Mr Iver said that the 'Aetherial' would escort that ship to Port Royal in Jamaica," Gus intervened. "Will they be sold there? It seems a frightful thing to do, as bad as the gentleman who sold Hughie to the press-men for five guineas."

"Did he now?" murmured Madame Joly with interest, turning to Hugo again.

"After they are sold, Madame, what will then be their fate?" Hugo asked.

"Most will go to the plantations to work with the sugar cane," Madame Joly responded. "The work is dirty, dusty and hard; they don't survive for long, so more people are sent for to take their places. They have no freedom, no wives or families; their original African families were parted from them or killed before their eyes. Then they were forced to march long distances to the sea-port, chained together in the burning heat. Many do not survive that either. A sea voyage of many weeks or months follows – that Portuguese ship would have taken at least a month to cross the ocean. Then, as you know, it was captured by a pirate off Venezuela, so I hear" – Madame Joly obviously had her own sources of information – "then it was brought here by your captain and now sent on to

Jamaica. That means two or three months of unhealthy and miserable confinement in strange surroundings. Do you not agree that this crushes the human spirit? What memories do those cane workers have that they should wish to continue living?"

"What happens to the women and children we saw?" Hugo enquired.

"Oh they work in the cotton fields, as often as not, though some of them are taken as house servants, like my Melissa here," and Madame Joly patted the arm of her servant as they sat around the table.

"Did you also come here from Africa, Madame?" Hugo asked with some temerity.

"Yes, young man, I did. I was a pretty young girl, the beauty of our tribe and as yet unwed. An English captain came and selected me to be his personal companion. No doubt he paid my parents handsomely – I was the chief's youngest daughter, and the Captain promised to marry me when we reached a Christian church on this side of the Atlantic. In fact he was very kind; in the few months we were together he taught me to read and to write a little, and for that I shall always be grateful. When we arrived here I was with his child and he established me in a small cottage near the harbour. Then he sailed away and I have never seen him since. Maybe he is dead; maybe he was never ordered to come here again, for he was a Royal Navy captain. My baby was born, a beautiful daughter, but she caught typhus as a child and died. That is why I have taught myself about medicines for fevers and other diseases and why I look after young sailors, if they happen to catch the fever as you did, Hughie. You will have realised how I lived my life until I was able to purchase this large and comfortable house. That is why I take care of my girls, for each of them is the daughter that I lost and the other children I could not have."

There was a pause before Madame Joly continued. "Now that you have my life story, young fellows, I want you to make me a promise, especially you, Hughie, who has seen that slave ship. Whenever and wherever you are given the chance, will you speak out against the Trade and its dreadful consequences?"

"I certainly will, Madame Joly, indeed I will," Hugo promised.

"And you too, Augustus?"

"Yes, Ma'am."

"There must be some reason why someone has asked to see you at Government House," Madame Joly surmised. "One of you must be an important person."

"What, us?" laughed Hugo, "when we were pressed into the Navy as the least of the Midshipmen, to wash dishes, swill down the heads and fetch the powder for the guns? The letter I wrote home form Madeira telling my family where I was, I doubt that it will even have reached its destination yet, so there cannot have been a reply. So far as I am aware, neither Gus nor I have committed any offence."

"Well, do not fret about it. Time alone will tell," Madame concluded.

A few days later Hugo and Gus set out for Government House, Hugo walking slowly and carefully, Gus skipping along with a happy anticipation that some pleasant surprise might at last be at hand. At the entrance Hugo showed the guard on duty the note written to Madame Joly. It had been signed by a Mr Edward Talbot, so they asked for that gentleman by name once they found that the guardsman could not read. They were escorted into a large ante-room, wood-panelled, cool and dark after the hot sunshine outside. Hugo was glad of the respite. A clerk sat writing busily at a desk and two copyists sat equally busy beside him. The clerk enquired their names, which Hugo gave, holding out the note for the clerk's inspection. He nodded and said, "Unfortunately Mr Talbot has gone down to the ship this morning, but he warned me to expect you and that if the Rear-Admiral were available he would wish to see you."

"The Rear-Admiral wants to see us?" Gus squeaked, whilst Hugo felt sure there must be some mistake.

"Yes, which of you is Mr Jarvis?"

"That's me, sir."

"You've to enter first alone, and Master Mather you'll be called for when the Rear-Admiral's ready." The clerk knocked at the door and entered, saying to the person within, "Mr Hugo Jarvis is here, Sir John. Shall I send him in?" A murmur of assent came from the depths of the room beyond and Hugo was ushered inside. He found himself in a large chamber with a high ceiling and dark wooden panelling as before, but this time there were portraits on the walls and flags and standards were swung out from them, angled as if upon bowsprits. He noticed that all were naval flags, some grey with age, some even torn by a lucky shot. His attention was drawn swiftly to the gentleman seated in the centre of the room on the far side of a long wooden table surrounded by chairs. He wore a frock coat of a dark blue cloth that contrasted nicely with the white ruffles at throat and wrist, and a white waistcoat that matched with his stockings and breeches. His Admiral's costume with its large gold epaulettes, gold braided sleeves and buttons, hung on a stand in one corner of the room. He would appear to be a man of middle height, but lean and not corpulent as many high officials were in Hugo's limited experience. His face was angular, rather thin and pale, and his grey hair was cut short on the crown of his head but curled and powdered at the sides. Hugo marked the man's nose, which was long and high-bridged and reminded him of someone he knew but could not at this moment identify, whilst his lips too were those of a plain man rather than an aristocrat.

"You wished to see me, sir," Hugo began tentatively as he approached the table.

"Hugo Jarvis, please take a seat," and the incumbent pointed to a chair on Hugo's side of the table. Hugo sat and placed his seaman's cap on his knees. "Well, young man, it would appear that we two are related." As Hugo's eyes grew wide the incumbent continued, "I am Sir John Jervis, Rear-Admiral in command of the British West Indies Fleet, and I have reason to believe that we are distantly related. You see, when I stood as the Member of Parliament for Great

Yarmouth," and Hugo almost started out of his chair at the mention of that name, "I used often to visit Beccles where I had some business to transact." Tears came to Hugo's eyes as he listened to the familiar names. "On those occasions I would often sample some of your uncle's, no, your great-uncle's fine wines at the Bear & Bells, I think it was. One day we fell to talking over our similar surnames, mine spelt with an 'E', I believe because originally it was Welsh, and how it has become anglicised and is now commonly spelt with an 'A'. Your Uncle Robert and I suddenly discovered we had several relatives in common living in Staffordshire, London and East Anglia. So far as I can compute it, your uncle and I are cousins four or five times removed."

"Oh, I know who you are now, sir. Uncle Bob's told us a great deal about you and has always followed your career from the newspapers," Hugo broke in enthusiastically.

"Has he, indeed. Well, the gentlemen of the Press have not always been as complimentary as one might wish. However, I digress. I understand that you, Hugo, are barely recovered from the yellow fever. I suffered the same myself a few months ago and feel its effects still. They never leave you entirely, these fevers, and seem to recur along with increasing age. I am now nearly sixty years old, and feeling it, so applied to the Admiralty for leave to retire. Unfortunately at the time there was no officer of sufficient seniority available to replace me and I was obliged to continue in command. During that time the French over-whelmed us in the islands of Guadeloupe and Martinique. Your ship, the *Apollion* I have despatched there now to stiffen our blockades. Last month a fast frigate left Spithead with despatches from the Admiralty advising me that Vice-Admiral Caldwell had already left England in H.M.S. *Majestic* and that I might anticipate his relieving me some time in November. In fact the *Majestic* has but now arrived in port.

"I bore you with much detail, Hugo, but now I come to the nub of my tale. Included with the despatches from London was a note from the Navy's Comptroller-General enclosing a letter personally addressed to me by your parents, Alfred and Martha Jarvis."

"But how did they know where I was?" Hugo asked bewildered.

"They had discovered you had been pressed aboard the *Aetherial* or the *Apollion* but did not know which ship, nor to what destination she had sailed. Instead they urged me to inquire through Admiralty channels, little guessing that we should encounter each other upon this distant island. When I read their letter both the *Aetherial* and the *Apollion* had left port although the *Apollion* was scarcely out of the bay. I hastily scribbled a message to Captain Sterne and sent out a local fisherman in his light craft with a signal flag at his masthead order-ing the *Apollion* to heave to. Captain Sterne was most surprised, but imagining that his orders had suddenly been changed the *Apollion* cast anchor. He met my messenger as he came on deck, turned over the note I had written and inscribed on the back his reply indicating that you were to be found care of Madame Joly, along with young Mather whose whereabouts were also inquired after.

"Now, speaking of young Mather, I know his father well for the several pieces of business he did for me when I stood at Yarmouth. It would appear that he is rather young to be at sea on naval service."

"Indeed he is sir, and not well adapted to it either, since he suffers sickness and vertigo if sent aloft."

"So Captain Sterne relates. He speaks differently about you, though, Hugo."

"I'm gratified that he has noticed me, sir. I have always dreamed of going to sea, especially of joining the Navy. I only objected to the manner of my seizure."

"So, if we were to regularise your post as Midshipman and I were to recommend you to another ship, of even to the *Apollion* should you wish to remain with her, would that content you?"

"Indeed it would sir," Hugo replied.

"And would you be willing to study and take the examination to make Lieutenant?" Sir John asked gravely.

"Yes, I would, sir. I've been attending lessons with the other middies already."

"Indeed. 'Tis good to see another of my family following in my wake, as it were. If you pass the examination, Hugo, advise me of it. It would please me to follow your progress. If you wish it I could have a deed drawn up that you might spell your name with an 'E'. That would prevent the Admiralty treating you with disrespect, I think."

"I should be honoured, sir," Hugo replied quietly.

"As for young Mather, I could take him home with me on the *Boyne* which is due to sail for England in a few days. How would that suit him, d'you think?"

"I would think he will be overjoyed, sir."

"Very well, let us have him come in and ask him, shall we?" Hugo rose and opened the door, calling in as solemn a voice as he could muster that Master Augustus Mather should enter at the command of Rear-Admiral Sir John Jervis.

At this Gus entered, shivering with much trepidation, then observed that both the Rear-Admiral and Hugo were smiling broadly, and suddenly the morning's optimism returned.

"Take a seat, Augustus," Sir John told him. "I have news that I know will delight you. Captain Sterne advised me where to find you after I had received a letter from Hugo's parents – you should know that we are distantly related – asking me to establish what had happened to you. I am acquainted with your father who has done business for me in the past and I know he would wish to have you safely home in England and completing your education."

"Ooh, sir," Gus squeaked, "if only I could go home sir, I would never play truant from school again, never, sir, and I would really apply myself to my lessons."

"I am glad to hear it. Captain Sterne is ready to release you from your duties on the *Apollion* and as I am leaving for home on the *Boyne* – she's moored alongside in the harbour now taking on supplies – how would you fancy sailing with me as my cabin boy?"

"What would be my duties, sir? I mean, would I have to trim the sails?" Gus enquired solemnly.

"Not at all. Hugo has told me that you suffer from vertigo. No, you would wait upon me, serve my meals, hang up my uniform, send my smallclothes to be laundered, and keep my cabin and papers tidy. How would that suit?"

"Oh, sir, that sounds fine to me. But what about Hughie, is he to go home too?"

"No, Hugo wishes for a career in the Navy. He is to remain here at present and to await a position on another ship. I shall write a letter to his parents which you may carry with you and deliver when you reach Beccles."

"I shall be sad to leave him behind, sir," Gus said, "because he has saved my life more than once."

"And you have taken care of me, Gus, when I was ill," Hugo replied. "There's one more matter, sir," he said, turning to Sir John. "Are you still a Member of Parliament?"

"I did resign my seat, Hugo, when taking up this command, but I hope to serve there again upon my retirement."

"I caught my fever on that slave ship, sir, the one that the *Aetherial* is escorting to Kingston. I saw the terrible conditions on board. Would you be willing to speak against the Trade, sir, on your return home?"

"I will give that issue my best consideration, Hugo, I promise you," Sir John replied with a smile. "Now, young fellows, I have much to do, so I suggest you make your way to the *Boyne* and ask for my Secretary, Mr Talbot. He will show you both over the ship, where you will sleep, Augustus, in an alcove beside my cabin, and where you will mess with the Midshipmen for company. As for you, Hugo, I'm gratified to have met you and wish you well in your career. I will have the letter of recommendation you need sent round to Madame Joly's house tomorrow. Please give her my compliments."

"Yes, sir, and thank you for everything, on behalf of both of us," Hugo said as he stood up and led Gus from the room. After that Gus skipped all the way to the quayside, running back when Hugo paused in the shade of a building from time to time. The 'Boyne' was a fine vessel, a three-decker of ninety-eight guns, and they felt very distinguished being taken on a guided tour of it. Word had already preceded them that Hugo was a relative of the Rear-Admiral, so every seaman stood to attention as they passed, and all the functionaries, the Cook, the Surgeon and the Carpenter, were eager to display their tools and the application of their skills. Hugo also borrowed a telescope from one of the officers in order to examine the *Majestic*, Vice-Admiral Caldwell's flagship, which was anchored in the bay. She had seventy-four guns, but he thought he preferred the sleeker lines and lighter, more flexible, armament of the *Apollion*. That was the type of vessel on which he wished to serve, he decided.

It was all such a far, far cry from being press-ganged on Yarmouth Quay!

CHAPTER XIII
The Unseen Hero

The *Boyne* anchored at Spithead in February 1795 and Rear-Admiral Sir John Jervis sent his Secretary ashore to carry his despatches to the Admiralty in London. With him went Augustus Peregrine Mather, at last returned to terra firma and to the prospect of a reunion with his anxious family. Mr Talbot escorted him to the Norwich stage and paid for his inside seat, leaving him a few guineas extra for the overnight stay at Ipswich and for transport between Norwich and Beccles, which Gus assured him he could arrange for himself. Tucked away in the modest portmanteau which Gus used as a convenient footrest because his legs were too short for the seat, were three important letters, two from the Rear-Admiral to Gus's father and Hugo's parents, and one from Hugo himself to his family, reassuring them that he was enjoying a fine recovery from the fever and that he wished to make a career in the Royal Navy.

It was early evening by the time Gus reached Beccles, for he heard six o'clock chime from the church tower when he arrived in New Market Square. Nevertheless, as it was not a Saturday, he felt sure his father might yet be at work in his office, and he preferred to face his father alone before arriving home and being smothered by all the womenfolk there. He stood on tiptoe to peep through a gap in the drapes that covered the office window, observed the candelabra still lit on his father's desk, and with a choking feeling in his throat timidly reached up and tugged at the bell beside the street door. Gordon Mather gave a snort of annoyance; it was doubtless some street ragamuffin pulling his bell for a lark at this time of night. He then wondered whether it might be some client with urgent business for him to attend, and only then did it occur to him that it could be someone with news, whether good or bad, of his long-absent younger son. He pushed aside the drapes and looked out into the street, but could see no one at all standing on the kerb. Nevertheless he ought just to make sure; he could not have imagined the sound of the bell, could he? He drew back the security bolt and turned the key, still expecting to find an adult standing before him. It was quite a shock to find a child there, not a street urchin but one wrapped in a warm overcoat and muffler and whose features were concealed beneath a stylish cap.

"'Tis me Papa, home at last!" Gus managed to exclaim. Gordon Mather, a gentleman of great dignity, probity and reservation whenever he addressed a magistrate or judge, felt his knees buckle beneath him as he knelt on the threshold to embrace his child. Nor did he pause to return to his papers and to tidy them away as he usually did at the end of the afternoon's business. He merely ensured that the fire in the hearth was all ash and embers, blew out the candles, then locked the office door, took his son by the hand and marched proudly with Gus at his side down Blyburgate and all the way home. It was only around midnight, when the family's excitement had diminished and they were making their way to bed, that Gus remembered the letters he carried and delivered them to his father's hands where his parents sat alone by the last of the parlour firelight.

Early next morning Gordon Mather sent a messenger over to the Ringsfield Farm. Remembering his own joy of the previous evening, his note gave no hint of the reason for his request, but he simply asked whether he might present his compliments to Mr and Mrs Jarvis at, say, eleven o'clock that morning, if that would be convenient.

"Gordon Mather? Whyever is he coming here?" Martha enquired with a puzzled frown. "Have you some business with him, husband?"

"No, not that I know of, Alf replied. "Depend upon it, though, he wants to sell something and cannot find a buyer!" Thus, by the time Mr Mather drove up to the farm in his pony-trap with Gus beside him, and Gus at his father's bidding ran to stand quietly on the doorstep till Mr Mather had rung the bell, Ringsfield's best parlour had been tidied and dusted, a generous fire graced the hearth, and Alf and Martha stood in the hallway, stiffly starched in their Sunday best. As the front door opened Mr Mather raised his hat, bade them good morning and said, "May I present my son, Augustus?"

"Come in, sir, do," Alf cried with a broad smile. "You have news of Hugo?"

"Indeed I do," Gordon Mather replied. "As you can see, Augustus has returned home safely and can relate presently all their adventures. In the meantime," he added as Carrie took their hats and coats, her eyes wide with anticipation, "I have two letters for you both." They took their seats in the parlour and watched breathlessly as Mr Mather unwrapped the oilskin package in which the letters had travelled. "This one, which you had better read Mr Jarvis, is addressed to you both by Rear-Admiral Sir John Jervis, responding to that inquiry which you kindly addressed to that gentleman on my behalf. And this one, which I am sure that you as his mother will wish to study first, Mrs Jarvis, is from your son."

At Mr Mather's invitation Alf was able to open and read (he managed to disguise how slowly), the letter from the Rear-Admiral. It informed him that Sir John had encouraged Hugo in his choice of career and had furnished him with the necessary introduction to whatever suitable ship might be available. It concluded by stating that Hugo had made a favourable impression upon him and that seamanship must run in the family, for all that Sir John himself had been born in the Midlands with never an ocean in sight. The letter ended with expressions of greeting to Robert Jarvis and a promise to sample his best wines again whenever business should next draw Sir John to Beccles. Martha could see that Hugo's letter was quite a long one, so she reserved reading it until the company had departed.

Carrie entered just then bearing a tray of coffee. There was milk for Gus, which he scorned and informed them that on shipboard he had drunk wine with the officers and rum like the seamen, though he then confessed this his 'grog' had been made with lemon juice and water since he was considered too young to take strong liquor. Other titbits emerged from Gus's chatter, but nothing by way of a comprehensive account, so Martha enquired whether Gus might come again at the weekend when all the children would be able to question him about his and Hugo's adventures. While she would have rejoiced had her son also returned home, Martha had already gathered from Hugo's one previous letter received in December that he had taken a liking to the Navy. Alfred too thought Hugo should stay there, since it offered a rather better avenue to success than helping Stan Stevenson in his boat on the river. So long as their boy was safe and well, his parents were content to abide by his decision. Besides, the position with Stan Stevenson had now been retaken by his former apprentice, Timothy, who had been unable to make a profit from the carriage of goods in his own small boat.

When he had finished sipping his coffee and had demolished yet another portion of Martha's shortbread, Mr Mather had further news to relate. It seemed that the Crimping-Master at Yarmouth had been brought to book by legal actions on behalf of his own and some poorer families, whose fees, incidentally, he had foregone, for permitting the forcible removal of very young children by the Press-gangs he serviced and supervised. In a case brought at the Norwich Assizes which had only recently concluded, the said rascal had escaped the noose but had been condemned to forcible abduction himself, namely transportation to the convict settlement at Botany Bay in Australia. The felon, still all impudence despite his conviction, had thereupon asked the judge if he might take his wife and child with him, as fare-paying passengers if you please, thus disclosing that he had made a tidy income from his obnoxious occupation. However, it was but yesterday morning that one of Mr Mather's clients had brought him the latest gossip, that Frank, the Crimping-Master's simple minded son, had developed a bad case of consumption, so that his father would depart alone to serve his sentence.

Meanwhile, in the distant island of St Christopher, Hugo had completed his convalescence. This had been much aided by the due receipt of the promised letter of recommendation from the Rear-Admiral, and in practical terms by a gift of twenty guineas which enabled Madame Joly to ensure that her young gentleman, as she now distinguished him, benefitted from the very best of her cuisine. The *Aetherial* had returned to the island after an absence of nearly two months, having concluded with gratifying results the disposal of the slaver's cargo. Hugo sought out the Purser and finding that she had orders to rejoin the *Apollion* and the rest of the West Indies squadron off the Leeward Isles, applied to sail with her and to transfer to his own ship if there were still a vacancy on board. The letter of recommendation received from Sir John Jervis and which most casually disclosed a kinship, seemed readily to open all doors, and he was welcomed to the Gun Room, given a uniform and some very light duties. He bade a grateful farewell to Madame Joly before he sailed and promised to call upon her again whenever he should return to that port.

The *Aetherial* encountered her sister-ship along with others of the British fleet cruising off Guadeloupe, escorting home-bound convoys past the islands and intercepting as many French vessels as their lookouts could decry. Hugo's former shipmates welcomed his return and he had a personal interview with Captain Sterne. That wise gentleman advised Hugo that he should not allow, and as his captain and superior officer it was not his practice to permit, connections between members of his crew and persons of rank to influence his professional judgement, and that the first duty of all sailors was the safety of the ship and the valour and success of its crew in battle. A timely warning, Hugo thought, as he lay in his hammock – now one centrally placed in the Gun Room and not at one side where he and Gus had suffered all the beam-end motion of the ship. He opened his tin box, one of the few items that reminded him still of home and family, and took out the book of poems which Jessica had given him. He ran his hand over her signature and again observed the initial 'A' of her middle name. In his mind he went through all the girl's names he could remember beginning with 'A'; there was Ann, Anna – though more often that was spelt Hannah, Augusta, like his friend Gus, Amelia, Angela, Annabel, Amy, Ada, Adele, Alice … Oh, and yes, Alicia, he had forgotten that one. That woman who came to the farm, supposedly to help his mother though she had not seemed a very practical person at the time, her name had been Alicia. He could recall it now that his mind was relaxed and content. She was some sort of relative, he believed, and had died in childbirth. She had been buried in Beccles churchyard and he remembered that his mother had visited the grave a couple of times, taking Carrie and himself with her. He wondered again what was Jessica's second name and resolved to write her another letter next time he was able to send mail home, so that she might have something of his to cherish, just as he had of hers.

As for Jessica, she had passed her twelfth birthday and had begun to consider herself a young lady. Her gowns and costumes, of which she had acquired several new ones with the help of Mrs Jarvis, now came down to the ground and no longer had the above-ankle hems of boisterous childhood. With her school friend Lucy Jarvis, she of the somewhat frivolous mind, she discussed bonnets, ribbons and gloves, and when alone agonised over which exact pattern of lace cap would best set off her still scanty golden ringlets. Everything at Roos Hall seemed so much more pleasant and orderly now that the dreadful Mr Ainsworth had left for foreign service. His hunter Pharaoh had had to be sold to recoup that good-for-nothing's gambling debts, as had the family carriage that had remained in the barn unused since Sir Robert Rich's last visit. Ted, the stable lad, had obtained a position in a more aristocratic household, and the dog Arthur now slept in the stable to keep the skewbald pony James company. Tom, one of the groundsmen who had taken on the role of gamekeeper, now cared for both animals.

Jessica had buried the goat Matilda in a secluded corner of the grounds and from time to time would place a small posy on her grave. She had thought about selecting a new pet, but had decided to wait until her schooling came to an end in a year or two so that she might then choose a suitable dog as a companion. Meanwhile a school friend had urged upon her a tortoiseshell kitten named Selina which she had house-trained and which slept upon her bed at night now that she had been able to return to her former large bedroom on the first floor of the Hall.

With Mr Ainsworth's departure Mr Russell had felt able to visit Roos Hall and Ringsfield more easily. It seemed he was an artist of quite passable talent and had been pleased to sit with Jessica and assist her whilst she made pencil sketches and water colours in the park and gardens. Unbeknown to her, or indeed to Mrs Jarvis who had arranged the lessons, Mr Russell himself was engaged on a portrait of Jessica executed in oils, which he had placed in an elegant frame and presented to the two ladies one evening before departing for his home near Norwich.

Jessica was quite overcome and thought this no ordinary compliment. Brought up as an orphan, she had expected little of life, courtesy of the modest allowance that had been regularly diminished by the extravagances of the dreadful Mr Ainsworth. Then he had killed the pet goat which Hugo had given her, the only creature she had been able to look upon as exclusively her own. Now, a fine gentleman who held a prominent position , who rode to hounds and did so many other things well, had taken the time and trouble and generosity to present her with her portrait. She felt overwhelmed, carried the portrait upstairs in its wrapping and set it up on the couch on the far side of her room where she could lie and look at it at night, before blowing out her candle – oh yes, and after saying her prayers as Mrs Jarvis had taught her.

When Jessica eventually extended news of this private event to her school companion, Lucy, she was at first non-plussed by Lucy asking did she not consider Mr Russell a most handsome-looking gentleman. She pondered over Lucy's reaction later that evening as she lay in bed stroking Selina's ample fur. Yes, she did suppose him to be handsome, and in any event she would look forward to his next visit. Apart from Mrs Jarvis, whom Jessica knew was paid to look after her, this was the first kindness she had received from an adult, and Mr Russell became something of an object of adoration. Mrs Jarvis, meanwhile, became alarmed at the fervour with which Jessica demanded news of Mr Russell's next visit, and tartly reminded the girl that the gentleman was a happily married per-

son of more than forty years with two grown-up daughters older than Jessica herself. Jessica went into the sulks for the rest of that day, but brightened on receiving an invitation from the parents of one of her classmates to join them on
Saturday afternoon for a family picnic.

*　*　*

And what of that awful fellow Ainsworth? In fact that gentleman was nearing
the end of his voyage to his next destination, the City of Calcutta. He had sailed
on an East India Company vessel from its London Dockland base at Poplar, a
run-down suburb of the sprawling capital, beyond the City's eastern gates and
surrounded by marshes and scrubland. It was the haunt of thieves and criminals
of every description, yet the place where the most delectable and expensive cargoes – sugar and coffee from the West, spices, silks, cottons and calicoes form the
East, tea and porcelain from China, were transferred to river tenders for their
journey into the heart of the metropolis.

Contemplation of the end of his voyage reminded Ainsworth that he only
knew two things about India, the first being that somewhere in that vast Sub-
Continent his former school friend Richard F. was still serving with the Light
Dragoons and the second was a play he had once dozed through at a London
theatre during one of his sojourns in the Capital. Entitled "The Nabob" (which
Ainsworth understood to be the anglicised version of the Indian princely title
'Nawab') and written by a well-known English satirist Samuel Foote, or some
such name as Ainsworth could remember, for the fellow was long since dead,
the piece concerned one Sir Matthew Mite who, having prospered by underhand
dealings and much chicanery in the service of the East India Company, on his
return to England sought acceptance in Polite Society and a seat in the House of
Commons, something which would cost him a few thousand pounds in bribes
to electors. The play related Sir Matthew's humble origin and that as a dissolute
schoolboy he had thrown a barrow-woman from Smithfield Market into the
Fleet ditch. Ainsworth had sat up and paid attention at that point, for there was
a tradition of such a prank at his own school, and he wondered whether the
author had had any connection with St Peter's-atte-Aldersgate. The drama then
related how Sir Matthew had fooled the Society of Antiquaries into thinking him
an expert on antiques, and how he had scandalised his acquaintances by propos-
ing to set up a harem of young women whom he would 'forcibly imprison'.
Having failed to obtain a seat in the Commons by legal means, Sir Matthew
adopted fraudulent practices, learnt, he claimed, in India, to force an existing
Member, Sir John Oldham, to resign. This provoked Lady Oldham to declare,
"With the wealth of the East we have imported the worst of its vices!" Features
of this play were considered to make libellous references to the hero of British
India, Robert Lord Clive, though others maintained that the model for Sir
Matthew Mite was quite another gentleman.

Sir Charles Rich had obtained for Ainsworth a position as a "writer" in the Calcutta office of the Governor-General, Sir John Shore. It sounded a grander placement that it was, and Ainsworth had already realised with some asperity that he was about to become a copy-clerk again, much as he had been in the Norwich law office. However he had also learnt that the great and distinguished Lord Clive, victor of the famous Battle of Plassey in 1757, and Governor-General and administrative reformer until his retirement in 1767, had also started his career in India as a humble "writer", an accounts clerk for the East India Company. Thence by judicious financial dealings and by the demonstration of an unexpected but instinctive military courage and flair, Robert Clive had rendered his services indispensable.

The East India Company had traded in India almost since its foundation under Queen Elizabeth I in the year 1600. It soon developed its own warehouses and trading stations at strategic locations, of which the most important were those at Bombay, Madras and at Calcutta, a settlement on the banks of the River Hugli, a deltaic tributary of the mighty Ganges in the rich and fertile province of Bengal. Britain's habitual enemy and colonial competitor, France, through its trading equivalent, the Compagnie des Indes Orientales, had a parallel interest in India. It had developed trading stations at Pondicherry, near Madras, and at Chandarnagore, near Calcutta. In the middle years of the eighteenth century the French General Dupleix had made great efforts to secure French political, financial and military supremacy in India, to the detriment of British interests. It was at that stage that Robert Clive entered British history by successfully resisting the French siege of Arcot in 1751 and going on to relieve that of Trichinopoly.

Bengal's well-irrigated fields produced cotton, sugar cane, indigo, rice, cattle, mulberry bushes full of silkworms, and the drugs betel nut, opium and cannabis. The peasant farmers, or 'ryots', owned smallholdings which they ploughed with their own oxen and employed poor villagers to pick the cotton and to process the other crops. Fine cloths, silks, brocades, muslin, calico and cotton were all produced in mud-walled, palm-thatched cottages, providing extra income for the villagers. There was also a tradition of metal working, particularly in iron for, contrary to its reputation, India had few mineral reserves of silver and gold. In fact it was through trading with the Europeans that the Indian Mughal Emperors in Delhi and the provincial princes supplemented their supplies of those precious metals, for they obliged the Europeans to pay for their cargoes with bullion.

The Indian Emperors and the princes kept control of their possessions by the extensive use of tax collectors or 'zamindars', and even humble ryots were able to mortgage their forthcoming crops in order to pay off their rents. Favours were granted to friends or creditors in terms of local rents and mortgages, until there was one vast structure of interwoven financial obligations between peasant and landlord. Robert Clive in his junior administrative capacity had bought into this system and had learnt how to manipulate it to his advantage and enrichment. Nor was he alone in this, for the East India Company had developed its own army to defend its forts and trading posts, and every officer who knew a thing or two made sure to benefit by tapping into the trading and taxing systems.

The complex nature of relationships among the princes and their frequent internecine quarrels and assassinations led them to hire troops from the East India Company to stiffen their own battalions of sepoys. If victorious, and they usually were with the Europeans' superior discipline and fire-power, with musket and field gun as opposed to matchlock and spear, the Europeans could expect to receive favourable revenue concessions by way of remuneration. Thus the British in particular began to play an increasing role in the revenue collection system, to the point where they were able to decide which princely candidate to support for any throne which might become vacant. Once their nominee had been enthroned they could then expect a handsome retainer for their military services.

Thus in Bengal, when one Mir Jaffar sought to overthrow Siraj-ud-Daula (the prince who had captured the fort at Calcutta in 1753 and had imprisoned one hundred and forty-six of its garrison in the infamous "Black Hole", an enclosed room where all but twenty-three had perished during the night), Robert Clive seized this opportunity to ensure that Mir Jaffar received the Company's support. Robert Clive himself led the force that recaptured the fort, aided by gunfire from five British warships anchored offshore under the command of Admiral Charles Watson. Later, in 1756, with France and England engaged in the Seven Years War, Clive led a force which captured the French trading station at Chandarnagore situated upriver from Calcutta and which he maintained constituted a threat to British interests. Clive went on to defeat Siraj-ud-Daula in a pitched battle at Plassey in 1757, the ousted ruler being assassinated by the brother of Mir Jaffar without Clive being able to bring him to trial. This campaign gave Britain the balance of power over France in rich Bengal and laid the foundation of British imperial supremacy in India.

Back in England once more, Lord Clive's financial activities in India, and in particular the generous subsidies he had received from Mir Jaffar, became the object of much vituperation and of inquiry by a formal Committee of the House of Commons. Clive was exonerated in the end, but became depressed and committed suicide in 1774. Meanwhile the Houses of Parliament, realising the scale of profits to be made out of the business of the East India Company, obtained from it an annual subvention of £400,000, then a colossal sum, ostensibly to off-set the costs of providing military and naval support such as Admiral Watson's warships. A Parliamentary committee recommended "harmonisation of the administration of Bengal with the spirit and principles of the British constitution", though ten years later the orator Edmund Burke was still making the same plea when he and Charles Fox introduced an India Bill. This was thrown out by the House of Lords who considered that such measures were inappropriate for the protection of Britain's private interests.

One Act which did pass both Houses of Parliament in 1773 established an administration led by a Governor-General and having a Council in each of the three main 'Presidencies' of Bombay, Madras and Bengal. This Act also established a Supreme Court in Calcutta staffed by British judges, with appeal available to the Privy Council in London. Significantly the Treasury also gained access to the East India Company's accounts! A further Act of 1793 dealt with the system of land revenues and forbade private financial transactions by the Company's officials. This followed a spate of alleged self-enrichment by the Governor-General Warren Hastings who was dismissed in 1782 for 'exceeding his remit'. His impeachment by the House of Commons was still in progress in 1795 when Ainsworth Rich left London for Calcutta, though Hastings was eventually acquitted.

By this time yet another Act of Parliament had created a Board of Control sitting in London to supervise all aspects of Britain's dealing with India's princes and merchants, and the position of Governor-General had become more of a political and military post than a commercial one. The Company was beginning to lose its supremacy in Indian affairs, and Ainsworth had been recruited as a civil servant working for the Government rather than as an employee of the East India Company as Robert Clive had been. It was in this changing atmosphere that Ainsworth arrived in Bengal, still expecting to make his fortune and position through intelligence and bravado as his predecessors had done, but also aware that he was entering a new world as yet totally unfamiliar to him. Indeed Sir Charles had been kind enough, when sending Ainsworth the ticket for his passage, a passport obtained on his behalf and a bond for several hundred pounds with which he might obtain lodgings and servants appropriate to his needs, to enclose some account of the political structure of Bengal, together with one of the many handbooks produced for the guidance of young officers and administrators making their first incursion into the business of Empire.

At this time Calcutta boasted a population of more than four hundred thousand, spread out along the River Hugli's banks in little wooden huts thatched with palm reed, or with any alternative material that might have obligingly fallen into the water from a passing ship. A strip of torn hessian or sail canvas covered the doorway at night but was left open by day, for he who owns nothing never fears a thief. Cooking was carried out in the open in the shade of a building or a tree, and the last meal at suppertime was consumed by the family seated on the ground beside the cooking fire in the darkness with only their faces aglow from the flames, talking in low tones or passing on some oral legend, occasionally to the accompaniment of cither or pipe. Narrow muddy corridors led between the houses to the nearest dusty street that was always a sea of people and traffic, children, ox-carts, litters and animals. The river's bank was punctuated by frequent small timber landing-stages, many of them in a state of gradual disintegration, and the river's surface was peppered by a sprinkling of diminutive craft, all rushing hither and thither by oar or sail, like demented insects on the surface of a pond. Along either bank, lone fishermen cast their nets into the water or swung them aloft on long poles before plunging them into the flood. Among the wooden jetties, men and boys stood at their ablutions, or women stooped to wash dirty dishes or clothes.

All this Ainsworth observed with a curious gaze as his ship sailed upriver. Here and there amid the huts of the poor rose clusters of taller buildings, the intricate gates and cupolas of Hindu temples, the red minarets and colourful domes of a mosque, and the shining stonework of St John's Church, newly completed. For this was a city where worshippers of many faiths and cultures of many styles already dwelt together cheek by jowl. In the distance, amid the heat haze and through the swarms of hovering mosquitoes, he could make out the massive bulk of Fort William, and beyond the wharves and warehouses, a long Esplanade full of elegant buildings which he presumed housed the Government. As the ship moved slowly to its mooring in the Garden Reach, Ainsworth studied the assorted crowd on the quayside waiting to greet the new arrivals. There were purveyors of fresh fruit and cooling drinks, and there were carriages, carts, and means of transport of various descriptions, among which Ainsworth noted many in the form of old-fashioned litters known hereabouts as palanquins. Ainsworth resolved that he would select some other more manly means of reaching his destination, the Governor-General's Office, till he observed that the people of quality who had travelled with him and were the first to be escorted ashore, immediately reserved the most elegant and luxurious of the palanquins. One other observation struck him as curious and different from the other ports where his ship had called; there were no port doxies or prostitutes to be seen, for here loose women did not exhibit themselves in public, being kept behind closed doors by their pandars for private entertainment only.

The moment Ainsworth reached the end of the ship's gangway he was approached by a slim-limbed fellow in a soiled dhoti who, in surprisingly passable English, offered his services a s a porter. As his trunks were yet in his cabin, Ainsworth clutched only a modest portefeuille containing his documents and the more instant of his personal requirements. The porter explained that he would await the unloading of the gentleman's trunks and would convey them to the Government compound, whence the sahib would be able to make his own arrangements for their removal to his lodging when he had established that particular necessity. It occurred to Ainsworth that such porters must be accustomed to meet every ship and to transport the luggage of generations of merchants, soldiers and administrators whose business had brought them to India. The porter enquired how he might identify the trunks, and Ainsworth, concerned lest his surname encourage the uninformed to treble their charges on mistaking him for a prince, remembered that the labels on his luggage were embossed with the Rich coat of arms. He recalled that the fly-leaf of his pocket book also bore the same design and tore it out. He handed it to the porter together with a shilling from his pocket. To his embarrassment, the porter returned the shilling, stating that such coins were worthless in his country, but that he would expect to receive a silver rupee for each trunk safely delivered.

If English currency was not acceptable here, Ainsworth realised, he had better amend his priorities and instruct his palanquin bearers to take him straight to the East India Company's bankers, whose address he had carefully recorded in his pocket-book. There he was made extremely welcome on presentation of Sir Charles' bank draft, and it was made clear to him that credit and other financial services would be available to him whenever he wished. Furthermore, the Bank's Manager, a Mr Seth, informed him of the street where he would be best advised to take lodgings and the name of the agent who would help him to find them. Moreover the said agent would also put forward suitable persons to be engaged as servants and to guide him about the city as required.

Duly impressed, and furnished with a purse full of silver rupees to pay off the palanquin, the porter and any other initial expenses, Ainsworth proceeded to Government House and enquired after the Governor-General's Secretary with whom he expected to undergo an interview. Indeed Ainsworth had given time and thought to rehearsing what he might say to account for some of the more disagreeable facts of his past life. However he was informed that the Governor-General, Sir John Shore, his Secretary, being his brother-in-law Hubert Cornish, and the Head Clerk, one Henry Bonnay who was Ainsworth's immediate superior, and a number of other gentlemen from the Establishment had gone up-country on a hunting expedition. Since Ainsworth was expected and his recommendation had been approved, he might spend the rest of the day seeking out and settling into his lodgings and then should report for employment the following morning at say nine-thirty a.m. When Ainsworth looked surprised, having anticipated a starting hour of eight as in England, or perhaps even earlier, it was explained that most of the young gentlemen employed here, whether in a civil or military capacity, cared to utilise the cool morning hours to exercise their horses and themselves, then to take a leisurely breakfast before appearing at the office. He could own a horse here? A successor to his beloved Pharaoh of whose disposal into other ownership he had been made aware before his departure from England? Suddenly Ainsworth was beginning to come around to the idea of life in India.

Leaving his portefeuille with the guard at the gatehouse for a few small coins, Ainsworth took a link-boy to seek out Mr Biswas, the recommended lodging agent. He found the latter most accommodating since there was, it seemed, an excellent cottage available in Chowringhee Road, and just vacated by a young family widowed during military action in Rajasthan and returning to England on a ship that his own would have passed while entering port. They had employed one Anando as their 'khidmutgar' or steward-cum-butler, who must be trustworthy since the Major had retained him for some ten years. If he were acceptable to Mr Rich, and Ainsworth noted that the English meaning of his surname was not lost on Mr Biswas, then Anando would supervise the rest of the staff and save the sahib the bother of dealing with them. Mr Biswas advised that Anando should be paid at least eight rupees per month, the cook Davi Das, who was by all accounts a painstaking fellow since the Major's two small children had thrived on his cuisine, should receive some six rupees monthly, as should the 'dhobi' or laundry-boy. Anando would engage a new one as the previous incumbent had returned home to tend his dead brother's farm upriver. There was also a 'bhisti' or water-carrier, whose expense could be delegated to Anando since he served several households.

The 'cottage' to which Mr Biswas escorted Ainsworth turned out to be a Georgian-style town house of modest proportions with one large room at the front overlooking the street, ideal for entertaining one's colleagues or fellow -officers, as Mr Biswas made sure to point out. Behind this was a dining-room with a table and chairs already in position, a fair-sized kitchen and scullery, and a wing of staff cabins on one side of the shaded garden, well-screened by flowering shrubs. Upstairs there was a large bedroom equipped with a marital bed, again overlooking the street, and behind that two smaller rooms that might be used for guests or for storage, together with a dressing-room provided with a hip bath and drainage trough, and a bucket-sluiced latrine – quite a luxury for an incoming junior "writer", as Mr Biswas was not slow to imply. After a long and not uneventful voyage from England, any place within four walls that bore the slightest resemblance to the comforts he had left behind, seemed a haven to Ainsworth. He made the necessary payments, signed the deeds and shook Mr Biswas by the hand. Anando was introduced and was pleased to escort him back to the compound gatehouse where, to his pleasant surprise again, the porter stood waiting with the correct luggage. It seemed churlish to give the fellow only two rupees, so Ainsworth added a third, watched with interest by Anando as he loaded the trunks on a donkey-cart. Ainsworth perched atop one trunk clutching his portefeuille, which he realised from the fresh fingerprints upon its brass fittings had been scrupulously examined by the gatehouse guards during his absence. Everything had been replaced in perfect order, but Ainsworth had learnt yet another lesson of what he should expect in his new location.

Next morning Ainsworth entered the Government compound at the appropriate hour, having been furnished with a pass at the gatehouse. He was shown to the new Writers' Building, designed and built in the 1780's by Thomas Lyon. From the exterior this huge block of neo-classical architecture looked rather daunting, and Ainsworth wondered whether he would find it a palace or a prison. He was conducted to a large room painted white and furnished with wooden desks and chairs. A leather-topped desk and table at one end of the room were set aside, it seemed, for the absent Head Clerk. To Ainsworth the scene resembled nothing so much as a schoolroom of his earlier years, and he groaned inwardly as a dozen curious faces turned towards him.

"Ainsworth Rich," he said, thinking he should make the first remark.

"Ah, yes, we had been told to expect you," one of the young gentlemen, slightly older and more mature than the rest, said, coming forward to shake hands. "I'm Timothy Fairburn, the Head Clerk's Deputy in his absence. This is your desk and I'll introduce you to these others."

"No, you will not, Tim. We're quite capable of speaking up for ourselves," said one fellow with a cheery face full of mischief and an unruly mop of blond hair. He then introduced himself as David Lambton, not long previously of Oxford University and he named his college. All the others followed suit, indicating their provenance in terms of military or educational establishment.

"And what about you, Rich, where did you graduate?" David asked when his colleagues had had their way.

"I was at Cambridge," Ainsworth began, foreseeing the trap into which he had fallen as one who had never graduated but had left in disgrace. He then mentioned his college, which resulted in a hoot from David who exclaimed:

"I thought I knew the surname. Don't say you're that awful chap who led a riot and imprisoned one of his professors in his lodging?" The answer was plainly visible in Ainsworth's face. David Lambton continued, "Professor Sharp was my cousin's grandfather. The old man committed suicide, you know, couldn't obtain another position and had no resources to fall back on. His life savings were in that strong-box which the students found, and by the time the College authorities had sorted out how much belonged to the College, which in fact was but a small portion, and how much rightly belonged to the Professor, the old fellow had died. So, you're a cad, Ainsworth Rich! Better not try any high-handed stuff on us. We have our own means of reprisal, have we not?" He glanced around at his colleagues and as he did so gave a large and very pronounced wink.

Ainsworth suddenly felt rather ashamed of himself and appalled that at least one of the darker secrets of his past was already known on this very first day in his new position. How much more might come to light? Tim Fairburn came to his rescue, bringing him some copy-work on which he might practise his orthographic style, so that it might be corrected to conform with Government and Company service rules. This was definitely a shade too close to the Norwich law office for Ainsworth's comfort, but application to the task saved him for the time being from the obligation to answer any further questions about his past. At midday cakes and coffee were served, the coffee in silver cups on silver trays and out of a tall, steaming, silver coffee pot. The fragrance wafted across the room and the writers gathered around the Head Clerk's table to enjoy their refreshment.

At a pause in their conversation, just as Ainsworth feared that some other probing question might be forthcoming, he decided to raise a matter of his own and enquired where he should go to purchase or hire a suitable riding hack for early morning exercise. There was just a fraction of a second's hesitation before Tim Fairburn answered that he would be recommended to try such and such an address, and to ask his khidmutgar to escort him there first thing in the morning. The clerks returned to their work, broke for refreshment in the form of coffee again, or tea as one wished, some time after two in the afternoon, and then for "tiffin" at four o'clock. This was a substantial meal, a sort of high tea with cold meats, curries and desserts, which seemed to have replaced the old-fashioned English "dinner". Everyone then worked quietly for another hour or so until sunset, when the office closed and they were free to return to their lodgings or to seek out an evening's entertainment.

Ainsworth found Anando waiting for him at the compound gate. He lit a resinous torch from the guards' brazier and they set out. Ainsworth mentioned to Anando, as he hurried after him through the narrow ever-darkening streets, that he wished to purchase a horse for riding and that his new colleagues had informed him that he should call in the morning at such and such an address. At this Anando collapsed into such a fit of giggles that he nearly dropped the torch, and he continued laughing almost hysterically until they reached the cottage. Once indoors Ainsworth faced Anando and asked him why he was laughing. With tears in his eyes, Anando replied, "That address they gave you, Sahib, that is the knacker's yard! It is indeed very full of horses early in the morning, but they are worn out ones ready for slaughter! I, Sahib, will show you the right place. We go to livery stables, you choose horse, try him out and if you like him you make purchase. Livery stables keep horse for you and you ride him every day."

So that's how 'tis done, Ainsworth thought to himself as they set out at dawn the following morning. The air was cool and fresh, lightly perfumed with the nectar of frangipani and oleander, for the noisome daytime odours of the gutter had not yet had time to mature and surge upwards into the sunshine. The distance involved was short, which pleased Ainsworth who hoped to dispense with the services of a guide in due course. The stable was owned by Mr Biswas, who was of course a brother of that same Mr Biswas, the letting agent. He greeted Anando with enthusiasm and obviously knew him well. Ainsworth studied a selection of animals, some of them already in private ownership and merely for hire, before his eye fell upon one standing in a shaded corner and he enquired its antecedents. "He very high-spirited animal, Sahib," Mr Biswas spread his hands. "He captured by Army from dead Rajput warrior, Sahib. He firstborn of French cavalry mare by Indian stallion of Rajasthan." Ainsworth was sufficiently familiar with the racing fraternity on Newmarket Heath to know a French thoroughbred when he saw one; he had yet to meet the more upright, arch-necked and short-backed Royal horses of Rajasthan. He asked the stable lad to bring forth the animal for his further inspection.

The stallion was a bright chestnut, and when the sunlight caught its coat it shimmered with flames like a mirage in the desert. The boy turned the horse around and Ainsworth saw that it had a long white stripe right across one flank. He enquired the origin of the mark and was told it had resulted for a sabre slash in battle which had healed and the hair which had regrown over it had been white instead of chestnut. This was why the animal had been sold, since it was unsuitable for ceremonial purposes. Still, that would hardly matter in relation to casual hacking. Ainsworth ordered the horse be tacked up and the boy gave him a leg into the saddle. He found the Indian saddle a different shape from those used in England and the Indian gait adopted by the horse was also quite different. Yes, this was most certainly a spirited creature, he thought, as he felt its muscles bunch under him like an archer drawing his bow. He walked the horse slowly round the stable yard, guiding it firmly with his knees when it seemed inclined to prance and sidle along. He tried a trot, but the horse's different gait made the timing of the rise and fall much more rapid than that to which he was accustomed at home. "Indian officer ride very straight, very upright," Mr Biswas offered by way of explanation.

Ainsworth felt that he might well adapt to the new pace in time. Such a pity there was insufficient room in the yard to try a canter, but he was assured that there was plenty of open space nearby, the threadbare turf around Fort William for a start, or further down river beyond the town. Anando would be able to guide him to a suitable area where his previous master, the Major, used to ride, Mr Biswas suggested. Ainsworth enquired the price of the horse, and translating rupees into sterling was surprised to find that it amounted to two hundred pounds, much the same as in England. Caution suggested that he might hire the horse for a few mornings before deciding to purchase, but caution had seldom been one of Ainsworth's characteristics. He signed a promissory note on the spot, paid for the creature's keep for the month, and with Anando leading the way on a donkey kept at the stable, he set out on his first ride in India. A week later he was in love with the creature and had learnt to master its paces, while the horse for its part appreciated a talented rider and the extended gallops that they both enjoyed. Ainsworth named his steed 'Mughal' after the imperial dynasty of India which still resided at Delhi, and soon did not hesitate to ride it along the Strand below Fort William where the ground had been cleared of slum housing to prevent the possibility of another surprise attack.

Thus, with a few days of his arrival, Ainsworth had already spent most of the funds which Sir Charles had supplied, on his lodgings, his horse and his staff. Anando had demanded to be paid a month in advance and had insisted that ten rupees monthly was the correct remuneration for his services. The other staff should receive half in advance and half in arrears, in accordance with their lower status. Ainsworth realised that he was almost out of funds already and that he himself had yet to receive any recompense for his labours; nor would he do so until the end of the month. It occurred to him that perhaps he should take up again his ability to win at cards as a means of recouping some cash. He had played, of course, with the other passengers aboard ship, but the stakes had been low and he had made scarcely enough profit to settle his bar bill. He enquired of his colleagues what social opportunities might be available but found their responses evasive. Eventually Tim Fairburn obtained for him an invitation to a card party at a senior army officer's lodgings. The accommodation there appeared rather similar to his own and Ainsworth realised that in Calcutta one's choices were limited by availability rather than rank. This was obviously not the place to make one's fortune and he must seek opportunities to move about the country if he were really to prosper at last. Meanwhile there was the humble problem of petty cash, and he concentrated his attention on the run of play.

Even though beer, wine and spirits were circulating among the tables, Ainsworth resolved to drink little and to study the Society into which he had been thrust to see how he might benefit from it. He had noticed, for example, that there were few ladies present, and learnt that this being the hot season, those who could afford to do so had deserted their husbands for the hills upriver. Those who could not afford European luxuries took Indian mistresses, and at least settled domesticity restricted drunkenness, vice and absenteeism from their labours. However those Indian wives or mistresses did not often appear in Calcutta Society, such as it was, and nor did the East India Company permit them or their children to accompany their employees to England for home leave or retirement. It seemed rather a harsh regime applied in such hot and uncomfortable circumstances – for Calcutta was still seething with memories of the infamous 'Black Hole', and some of the survivors were still spoken of by long-standing residents of the town.

At the conclusion of the evening Ainsworth's winnings showed a profit of one hundred rupees in cash and two modest promissory notes. At least he would be able to pay his staff at the end of the month, he concluded, as he put the cash in his purse and the notes in his pocket-book. At a stroke he had doubled his income, for a junior writer, so he had been informed, could expect little more than the same sum by way of salary. He was fortunate in that the "tiffin" served to all personnel at the Compound six days out of seven was a substantial meal, so that he was unlikely to starve. However Davi Das always cooked him a generous breakfast, and was on hand to turn out a tasty delicacy for supper if he so required. Some time or other he would be faced with a grocery bill, even though he was aware that rice and vegetables came cheaply in fertile Bengal.

On Sundays, attendance at morning service at St John's Church was compulsory for all service personnel, the Governor-General proceeding thither in a palanquin with extra bearers running alongside and a mounted military escort, even if it was a journey of only half a mile! Ainsworth had never been one for religion – his memories on the subject consisted of church parade from the orphanage with an armed escort provided by Mr and Mrs Bulstrode, and obligatory attendance at St Peter's reinforced by Captain Tanner's cane in the event of non-compliance. At Roos Hall he had been free from any such obligation, even though the staff there had customarily walked to the church at Barsham, except for Mrs Jarvis who had insisted on accompanying her husband to the larger establishment in Beccles. That good lady had done her best to encourage him, but he had resisted all her endeavours. So compulsory attendance here was irksome, especially as he would rather be riding the elegant and energetic Mughal instead. However this did provide a further opportunity to study the congregation, a different mix from the colonel's card party, for there were a few women and children too, as well as one or two youths who caught his eye.

The end of Ainsworth's first month of employment came at last, and in the continued absence of the Head Clerk it was Tim Fairburn's task to obtain the pay due to his young colleagues from the Treasurer's Office nearby. Tim returned with a sheaf of papers in his hands, which he distributed by name, Ainsworth's coming last. On the elegantly embossed Company notepaper he could make out the following words: "Pay to Bearer within thirty days from the date hereof the sum of One Hundred and Ten Rupees ..... less any discounts applicable." "What's this?" Ainsworth cried aloud and looked to his colleagues for a response.

"What else do you expect?" David Lambton told him. "We all live on credit here, the whole crumbling structure is built upon it, and we clerks are at the bottom of the pile. As to our pay, if we're in funds we bank it, and if not we give it to the tradesman who has presented the largest bill!"

This was a fine state of affairs, Ainsworth muttered to himself as he left the Compound that evening. Sir Charles had assured him that he would find him a place in "the Diplomatick Service", and that though he must start at a low level, with his intelligence, if properly applied, he should soon make his way to the top. Yet Tim Fairburn still occupied a subsidiary position after five years in the post. How then had the 'Nabobs' made their fortunes? For a start Ainsworth paid a call early the following morning on his banker, who explained that as his account was still in funds – just – he could advance him cash on his Company note straight away, subject to the usual discount of twelve per cent. However, if he cared to wait a month until the bond was due, he would be able to obtain almost the full amount. As to the promissory notes which Ainsworth handed to him at the same time, he would retain those for encashment should the opportunity or Ainsworth's need arise, but he regarded such paperwork as worthless.

Finally Ainsworth asked Mr Seth if he might recommend him a tailor. The dhobi Anando had employed made a good show of beating his linen and small-clothes to death, but was not to be trusted with outer wear. Anando himself was more competent, since he must have kept the Major's uniform in good order. However Ainsworth had found on opening his trunks that a damp voyage had played havoc with his smartest outfits and that a local tailor or 'darzee' who could produce lightweight attire for the hot summer season was an absolute necessity. Mr Seth knew just the man and Anando, who awaited him outside the bank, could take him there immediately. Mr Seth gave him brief instructions in Bengali which Ainsworth did not understand at all except that he caught the name of the tailor – Biswas, yet another Mr Biswas!

Ainsworth had realised that he had had the misfortune to arrive in Calcutta during the burning heat of summer and that in the cooler months of winter when the families returned from their country retreats, when games were played and balls given, and when the open ground where he exercised Mughal became a racecourse, then his social life should improve and his opportunities for advancement might increase. In the meantime he had no choice but to apply himself to his job and see if skilful labour made him more eligible for promotion or reward. Indeed the solid masonry of the Writers' Building provided the best of sun-shields through the unforgiving heat, for with windows open on both sides of the Head Clerk's Office, an odiferous breeze cooled by its association with the river and wafted along the room by a coolie's rhythmic application to a row of dangling punkahs, kept the temperature just within the range of tolerability. Moreover Ainsworth's duties now extended beyond mere copying. Sometimes he was given documents to draft, and he actually began to wish he had spent longer in the Norwich office and had learnt more of such useful legal practices. At other times he was asked to prepare a schedule or a summary of a number of documents relating to a particular subject. Then there were statistics to be marshalled into good order and Company format, such as the rice harvest for the province of Bengal and how much of it had been sent upriver to the various forts and strong-points owned by the Company and garrisoned by British troops on its behalf. It was through this means that he learnt that a regiment of Light Dragoons was stationed at Lucknow and wondered what chance he had of accompanying some visiting patrol so that he could seek out news of his boyhood friend Richard F.

The hot season had broken at last and the South West Monsoon troubled the swelling waters of Ganges and Hugli. The Governor-General, Sir John Shore, had returned from his hunting trip, his bearers laden with elephant ivory and no less than five tiger skins whose heads would be stuffed to gaze up at generations of his descendants at home in England. On the morning following his return he had the garrison drawn up in the Compound yard at dawn, and having inspected them, all the clerical and administrative staff were invited to join the concourse at seven. Having been forewarned of this possibility, Ainsworth and his colleagues had been obliged to forgo both their morning rides and their breakfast. Sir John then delivered an address in which he outlined the principles of morality and behaviour which he expected to have observed by those under his command, "Englishmen," he went on, ignoring the fact that numerically speaking the larger part of his audience consisted of Indian Sepoys, "are to be expected to display a Sense of Honour and Virtue, as well as a Reputation for Bravery, Clemency in Victory and Good Faith in their business transactions."

On their dismissal from what David Lambton labelled "Morning Prayers", the clerks filed to their office where the Head Clerk, Henry Bonnay, joined them for the first time since Ainsworth's arrival. A large amount of correspondence addressed to him in person, such that it could not be opened in his absence even by Tim Fairburn, awaited him on the large table beside his desk, in neat piles according to its origin and likely nature. Tim Fairburn stood at Mr Bonnay's elbow and assisted him with a flick of the wrist and the exercise of a chased and worked silver paperknife. A number of items required instant copies to be made for the attention of the Governor, and some for the Commandant of the Garrison. Ainsworth was handed a batch for his attention and started upon them, despite a feeling of grievance at having missed his daily contact with Mughal. A serving of coffee accompanied by sugary biscuits and muffins presently put him into a better mood. At the end of the day Mr Bonnay asked Ainsworth, to whom he had earlier been introduced by Tim Fairburn, to stay behind after the other clerks had left the building.

"Mr Rich," his superior addressed Ainsworth. "I have examined the work you have completed today and have found it consistent with the high standards set by this office. I trust you will continue to serve us as well. I have also to inform you that, even though your recommendations to this service came from no less a person than Mr Henry Dundas as President of the Board of Control, the Governor is aware of the undesirable reputation which surrounded you in England and which caused your Guardian, Sir Charles Rich, to despatch you abroad so that he might obtain relief from your debts. I can assure you that we in the Indian service will take much the same attitude towards riotous living, indebtedness and vices, and any repetition of the reputation here, such as to bring dishonour on the Governor's office and the Company's administration, will be forcibly dealt with. It is probable that you would lose your position without being provided with the fare home. Do I make myself clear?"

"Yes, sir, indeed so," Ainsworth replied, horrified to find that his Fate was stalking him still. As he left the Compound, Anando awaited him as usual, but Ainsworth did not even have the courtesy to give him a word of greeting. When he reached the cottage he was obliged to change quickly for an evening engagement for which he was already late. He did not want the company to make up tables without him, for his chance of winning any meaningful sum to assist his finances would have vanished. When he found that the dhobi had torn the ruffle of his best shirt, which he had then hidden at the back of the wardrobe, Ainsworth strode out into the garden to where his servants sat around their evening cooking fire, seized the fellow by the arm and gave him a beating with his cane. When he went indoors again to change the offending shirt, Anando followed him. "You not beat Indian servant, Sahib," he said. "Not allowed. Beating contrary to human dignity, Sahib. Make Indian lose caste. Is looked upon as very bad thing. Not Company practice. I no take you to card party tonight, Sahib. If you go you take Link-boy, not me." Of course to attend a social event without one's smartly-uniformed khidmutgar would not only cause much European loss of face, but no link-boy would stand by and defend one against robbery in the street.

A few weeks later, in the autumn when the South West monsoon had run its course and the air was clear and fresh again, a somewhat bedraggled cavalry detachment of Company troops clattered up to the gateway of Fort William and were there kept waiting whilst the Garrison Commandant was fetched to verify the bona fides of their mission – the troops of Siraj-ud-Daula had overwhelmed the Fort's garrison by a ruse, and since then no one took any chances. The young clerks observed the new arrivals from those windows which overlooked the Fort and much avid speculation ensued. They were to know soon enough, for Henry Bonnay was summoned to Sir John's office and returned an hour later with a request for two volunteers. It seemed that there was a 'strike' at the East India Company's 'factory' or warehouse, three hundred miles upriver at Patna. This was the gathering and storage point for the Company's rice harvest, among other commodities, from most of its land-holding in Bengal. It appeared that the harvest, having been safely garnered in prior to the monsoon, was now locked within the warehouse and that local dacoits (robbers) had joined with the Company's workers to refuse to handle the shipping and distribution of that crop down-river to Calcutta and upstream to the British fortifications, of which the chief ones were Benares (Varanasi) on the Ganges and Lucknow on the River Gomti.

Lucknow was the capital of the province of Oudh whose Nawab, Asaf-ud-Daula, was a valued commercial ally of the Company, and the presence of a British-led garrison at Lucknow was at the Nawab's own request to enable him to establish law and order in his lands and to prevent incursions by others, whether led by princes or by criminals. It was the Nawab who had learnt, no doubt through his network of spies, that the rice crop was besieged in its warehouse at Patna and who had requested the Garrison Commandant to send a detachment down-river to ascertain the true state of affairs. The troops had travelled by water, making use of the flooded river and taking their horses with them, but they had run out of supplies and due to the floods had been unable to obtain either food for themselves or fodder for their horses. Thus all were in a muddy and half-starved condition by the time they reached Calcutta. They had been prevented from landing at Patna, though as the floodwater swept them past they had observed that the Residency and its warehouses stood above water-level and that the buildings were surrounded by a large crowd of people, but whether they were strikers or merely refugees from the floods, the soldiers were quite unable to tell.

Henry Bonnay, a man of some length of service in the East India Company and much experience in dealing with Indian workers, together with a colleague from the Treasurer's Office in case questions of finance should be at issue, had instructions to take with them to Patna a couple of reliable clerks to draw up any documents or agreements. Bonnay himself spoke Bengali, Hindi and Persian, and there were personnel at the Patna Residency who could help with additional interpretation. As escort they would have the detachment of troops from Lucknow, as soon as these had rested, and an equal number from the Calcutta Garrison. Bonnay asked for two volunteers 'who could defend themselves in a scrap and knew how to use pistol and sabre'. David Lambton volunteered immediately and turning to Ainsworth asked, "How about it, Rich? How're you with small arms?"

"I shoot quite regularly," Ainsworth was glad to reply, "and I learnt to fence at school, though I've had no cause for it since."

"Precisely," David continued, "but these other fellows," and he indicated with a sweep of his arm their colleagues in the Head Clerk's Office, "they're peaceable gentlemen without military ambition."

"I had thought myself too newly-arrived to qualify," Ainsworth responded with unaccustomed modesty, "but if Mr Bonnay approves I would willingly go."

Henry Bonnay sent the pair of them over to the Barracks at Baraset, a training ground for Company troops situated some sixteen miles from Calcutta. Ainsworth rode there on Mughal, but David took an Indian cavalry horse from the Garrison. "Don't use your own horse for expeditions like this, " he advised. "The Indian horses are willing mounts but they don't last long, so the Company always provides replacements. Your Mughal is too fine an animal for that. I wish we could bring more European stock over here. I'm sure it would improve Army efficiency." They spent three days training hard with sword, pistols, and with the new Brown Bess musket, a smooth-bore, muzzle-loading weapon that could outshoot the Indian matchlock. They passed the test, were approved and despatched, along with fifty mounted Sepoys, five British officers and five ox-drawn waggons loaded with supplies.

It was a good three hundred miles to Patna. They would have travelled by river had the Ganges not been in flood and the downstream currents presently too strong. Progress would be faster by road, say thirty miles a day, provided their route was now free of floodwater and the track had not been washed away. They rode north out of the city, passing the turning to Baraset, and continued along the eastern bank of the river as far as the town of Hugli, where the Company owned a warehouse. This had preceded Calcutta as the Company's principal trading station in Bengal, but the silting-up and shallowing of the river had rendered it less useful, although some of the Company's crops and revenues were still collected there. While Henry Bonnay and the Treasury Officer went to inspect the warehouse, David and Ainsworth watched with admiration as the Sepoys supervised the ferrying of the whole party across the river to its western bank. Their chosen route had enabled them to pass by without incident the French trading station at Chandarnagore, which had been released to its original owners after the Seven Years War, and the Dutch station at Chinsura. Settling a workers' strike at one's warehouse was not worth an international crisis!

Once across the river tiffin was served and the horses rested. They did not set out again until the sun had begun to decline and then travelled for a couple of hours until dark, still alongside the river, watching the ryots planting rice in their newly-flooded fields, or reconstructing their mud-walled houses where these had been overwhelmed by the monsoon. On one occasion they helped the local people lay planks and stones across an erosion gully so that their waggons might pass, and sometimes their horses would be used to drag aside a fallen tree.

At dark, camp was pitched, fires lit and supper was cooked and served to the sound of jackals howling from a distant grove. David and Ainsworth enjoyed each other's company and Ainsworth thought it was the grandest time he had had in his life, save perhaps for those wonderful summers at Waverley.

On the second day they rode through the town of Mayapur with its many Hindu temples, and passed bands of pilgrims making their way thither. Next evening they camped not far from the island City of Murshidabad, once the capital of Siraj-ud-Daula. Ainsworth had hoped to visit the tomb of that tyrant in its "Garden of Happiness" on the river-bank, but again their small military force turned aside, not wishing to trouble the serenity of that ruler's more compliant successor. So they rode along farm tracks among the mulberry bushes on the low rounded hills and left the Ganges valley behind, so cutting off a vast riverine curve before rejoining it again at Bhagalpur. "The trouble with hills is that, instead of mosquitoes, they tend to host other pests in the nature of dacoits," Henry Bonnay warned his assistants. Indeed they saw several groups of tribesmen who appeared over rocky ridges. A round of musket fire usually sent them scurrying for cover, and David and Ainsworth discharged their pistols for good measure. At night double guards were set over waggons and horses in order to deter such thieves. By the time they reached Patna they were all very weary, but put on a good show of riding into town and drawing up the now-empty waggons before the massive Golghal (granary) and the Residency. A crowd of people milled around in the afternoon sunshine, but parted to let them pass.

However word of the arrival of a troop of soldiers whistled its way round the town of Patna like a forest fire, and soon the nearby Maidan (square) was filled with a muttering crowd. Henry Bonnay and his Treasury colleague ascended the steps of the Residency, presented their credentials to the guards, and were ushered inside. They were met by Mr Henry Lushington, a high-ranking Company man who in the old days of East India Company trading would have been known as a "senior merchant" but now enjoyed the title of "Resident". His function was to oversee the collection of all revenue due to the Company from the surrounding valleys of Bihar and Bengal, whether in money or in kind, to maintain good diplomatic relations with the relevant princes, and to sit as a judge in any disputes arising, whether among individuals or systemic as reflected in the workers' strike. It is to be noted that the Resident himself had not requested assistance and was probably rather embarrassed to find a delegation from headquarters arriving before he had completed the delicate negotiations necessary to resolve the problem.

The Golghal, a large domed building eighty feet tall which dominated the Patna skyline, was a huge grain silo having a circular staircase winding up the exterior so that rice could be emptied in at the top and shovelled out from shutes at the bottom as required. It had been constructed as the brainchild of a Captain Garstin at the behest of Warren Hastings, then the Governor of Bengal, following a severe famine in 1769-70 when the rains had failed and ten million

Bengalese people had died of hunger. However the monster silo was never full and this it seemed was the origin of the discontent among the people. Fearing a repetition of the famine a quarter of a century before – and it is true to say that the monsoon had been somewhat lighter this year, though its floods seemed to have caused the usual disruption – they were refusing to allow the East India Company's workers to remove grain from the silo or to send upriver those barges which had already been loaded with grain, until the silo itself was full, something which would have required many harvests.

Whilst their superiors were accommodated comfortably inside the Residency, David and Ainsworth were obliged to remain outside in the hot sunshine along with the military escort. As it seemed likely to become an extended sojourn, the Sepoys set up camp in the Maidan, drawing up their waggons in the shape of a pentagon, and hitching the horses in the shade beside the oxen under some oleander trees. Then they lit a fire, made coffee and started to prepare tiffin. At this point it was amazing how many traders from the town emerged from the crowd with goods for sale, water, fruit, live chickens, vegetables, spices, "enough for a fortnight of tiffins", as David Lambton remarked.

"I would have suggested that these people could be bought off, you know, for a little extra money to provide security against their rents," Ainsworth commented. "I suppose they are aware of that within," and he jerked a thumb in the direction of the Residency. The following day the Resident and his colleagues called upon the leaders of the local communities, Hindu, Buddhist and Jain, and a settlement was duly brokered involving the slightest of temporary rises in the price to be paid for future crops of grain. A document was indeed drawn up to finalise the matter, Henry Bonnay being responsible for the Hindi version of it and David and Ainsworth producing copies in English for Henry Lushington's retention and for Sir John Shore in Calcutta. As the barges laden with rice set off upstream, the ox-waggons and the Sepoys from Calcutta were loaded on rafts for their return trip down-river. The detachment from Lucknow had the duty of escorting the grain up the River Gomti to ensure that it reached its destination. Henry Bonnay was minded to go with them, but was also aware that a speedy return and response to Calcutta was equally desirable.

Ainsworth was all too conscious that his dear friend Richard was stationed at Lucknow. He had confirmed that with the officer commanding the detachment of troops. Ainsworth searched his brain for any reason he might make that would take him to Lucknow when he was already half-way to that desired destination. Then Henry Bonnay decided he should despatch his two juniors up to Lucknow with the grain, so that they might report to the Resident there and bring back any correspondence. They could then return to Calcutta entirely by water in order to save time and expense. Like the Lucknow troops, David and Ainsworth took their horses with them on the barges, since Lucknow was situated on an escarpment above the river, and in this country it was wise never to be separated from one's means of transport.

Each barge had a single mast with a huge spritsail on a long yard. The hold had been filled with grain and the hatches closed over it. Straw was spread over this and the horses stood upon it, being tethered to a rail. An awning was stretched aft above the tiller, and stools were available so that the young gentlemen might sit with the helmsman, or if they preferred they might move forward to where his assistant stood in the bows, spotting the many shifting shoals in the river. The voyage of some four hundred miles to Lucknow was expected to take a fortnight, the water route being easier and safer now than by horseback. At dusk they would draw in to the river's bank and David and Ainsworth messed and slept with the soldiers on sleeping mats placed around the embers of their camp fires.

At last they glimpsed on the distant horizon Lucknow with its silver domes and the minarets of the mosque built by the Mughal Emperor Aurangzeb, and the newer mosque just completed by the Nawab, Asaf-ud-Daula, beside his Imambara or mausoleum. This the Nawab had commenced building after the great famine, on the same principle as the Golghal at Patna, to give employment to the starving, and which would soon house this personal shrine and tomb. For the Nawab's health was failing and his concern for the welfare of his people would have been quite touching had Henry Bonnay not opined that the Nawab's spies had been given instructions to inspire the strike at Patna in order to force up the price for grain!

David and Ainsworth made their way to the Residency, which occupied an elevated position not far from the cantonment where the Regiment camped and trained. The Residence itself was a relatively modest mansion, having pleasant gardens with trees and fountains, where the Resident came out to meet them on their arrival. He received Henry Bonnay's report, together with a copy in Persian of the Agreement concluded at Patna, which would be copied again at Lucknow before being presented to the Nawab. The Resident informed the clerks that his own despatches would be prepared on the morrow. He then offered them hospitality at the Residency and suggested that they might next day wish to take a turn about the City – his servant would conduct them to all the sights – and meanwhile, would they care to join him at a Regimental dinner planned for this evening? It was just the opening Ainsworth desired, an opportunity to meet Richard socially and to ascertain why the letter he had written to him all those years ago had been returned unopened. During the voyage he had spoken to David Lambton about his school friend and how he hoped to renew his acquaintance with him, so that his colleague had offered him every support.

David and Ainsworth were without suitable clothing for such an event, as all the Regimental guests would be garbed in their smartest uniforms, but the Resident's khidmutgar came to the rescue with borrowed breeches, waistcoats and cut-away evening coats. A darzee was employed for several hours to make the final adjustments, so that the two clerks felt quite at their ease when they joined the throng in the Residency's dining-hall. First, though, there were drinks to be had in an anteroom, and Ainsworth eyed the company eagerly, searching for his friend. Indeed he had difficulty in recognising him, for Richard had grown tall and square with the most military-looking of moustaches. "Richard!" he said, his voice almost breaking with emotion as he reached the man's side, then found he had been conversing with none other than the Resident. The latter turned with some surprise and asked, "You know Major F., I see."

"Yes, sir, we were at school together many years ago," Ainsworth replied hastily.

"I'll leave you to your reminiscences, then," the Resident said and moved away.

"Ainsworth? Whatever bring you here?" The Major turned towards him in astonishment.

"May I present my colleague, David Lambton. We are both employed in the administration at Calcutta, and have been assisting in the resolution of the dispute over the distribution of rice from Patna."

"What resolved the situation?" the Major asked. "Rupees?"

"As usual," David Lambton chipped in. "Look, I'll fetch myself another beer and leave you two to chat."

After the normal polite enquiries into each other's health and fortune since leaving school, Ainsworth, who found the Major's attitude more reticent than he expected, dared to ask, "Did you receive a letter from me some four years ago now, and why did you return it to me unopened?"

"Yes, I did receive your missive, even here in India. I was stationed at Fort St George at Madras in those days. Why did I send it back? Firstly because my father had instructed me to have nothing more to do with you, or he would even now cut off my allowance. However the main reason is that it was handed to me by my then Commanding Officer, Major Todd, Leonidas Todd, the elder brother of your old rival Marcus."

"Marcus Todd!" Ainsworth exclaimed. "That fellow's family haunts my life. On several occasions I have lost heavily to them at cards, and on the last occasion I know it to have been a trap."

"I think there is another factor which you should understand and which has come to my knowledge among the instructions given me by Major Todd. A senior member of his family was instrumental in pressing for and obtaining the dismissal of Sir Robert Rich from his Government post. It seems likely that there has been ill-feeling between the two families dating back several generations. You may not be aware that Sir Robert Rich was thought to be responsible for writing the "Letters of Junius" that were published in the newspapers and were so damaging to Lord North's Government, though afterwards more likely culprits emerged. A member of Major Todd's family was recruited by the Government to lead their inquiry."

"Well, they need pursue me no further!" Ainsworth declared with surprise. "Neither Sir Robert Rich nor his son-in-law Sir Charles had any blood relationship with me at all, so I have eventually discovered. It appears that I am the illegitimate offspring of some clerk or other person who assisted Sir Robert in an administrative capacity and who bequeathed me to his former superior on his deathbed. My mother was apparently a lady whose identity has yet been withheld from me, even though I have her likeness in this locket, as you know."

"Perhaps her family name was Todd," the Major suggested gently.

"Yes, or Wilmington," Ainsworth added under his breath.

"And perhaps Sir Robert was unjustly blamed for the deed?" the Major added. "Come, there's the gong for dinner and we should be going in. The ladies, such of those as are courageous enough to share our lives here, are probably seated already. Ah, yes, Ainsworth, may I present to you my wife Amelia. This is Ainsworth Rich, an old school friend."

Ainsworth bowed low over the hand of the most dainty, petite and attractive young lady in order to hide a surge of jealousy, which he knew had flushed his features. Richard had been his friend, the love of his life, the one whose absence he had mourned ever since, and who was now no longer his, no longer the same. He had matured and had changed, had taken on responsibility, had two small children too, as Amelia was quick to inform him when Richard had sat him down beside her. Richard placed David Lambton on his other side and commenced an avid conversation with him about the Company's business in India and the roles of British civil and military personnel.

* * *

Ainsworth Rich and David Lambton left Lucknow two days later and with their horses boarded a light craft which would take them down-river. It had a small sail, and a thick layer of khus grass served the horses as straw. No Indian servants went with them, only the boatmen who spoke no English and communicated by sign language. Each evening they would draw in to the riverbank and take the horses ashore for exercise. The boatman would light a fire and they slept around it on sleeping mats. Their food was the small amount of provisions supplied to them at Lucknow, and when those were exhausted there was rice and yet more rice. They had landed at Patna and had obtained fresh food and litter for the horses, but that evening, just as the boatman was steering the raft towards the bank, it snagged on a fallen tree hidden underwater and rolled over.

David and Ainsworth were precipitated into the flood. Ainsworth surfaced quickly, being a strong swimmer, and remembering thankfully that the despatches he carried were wrapped in oilskin. However of David there was no sign. Could he be trapped beneath the tree? Ainsworth dived under the water, which was filthy with mud thrown up by the tipping of the boat and the plunging of the frightened horses. Ainsworth felt the offending tree trunk rather than saw it, and worked his way along it, hand over hand. Suddenly he sensed clothing swirling about his feet and leant down. Ainsworth braced himself against the tree trunk, but it took both hands and much effort to pull David free. He held David's head above the surface and with powerful strokes swam backwards to the shore. He found that the boatman had righted the raft and having moored it came to help him drag David from the water. They laid him face down on the bank, with his feet up the slope, and pumped his lungs hard. David began to stir, and having made sure he was conscious Ainsworth went in search of the horses.

These he found grazing peacefully in some poor peasant's garden half a mile away, and managed to retrieve them without incident. Returning to the river-bank he saw that a fire had been lit, and David was already stripping and drying his clothes. Evidently he was a survivor. Alas, their provisions had not survived the upset and so they slept on the bare ground without any supper. Neither of them had much money in their possession, and now that the gunpowder for their pistols was soaking wet they could not even defend themselves if dacoits came to steal their mounts. Next morning David was awake with the dawn and had raided a nearby field where a crop of young maize stood ripening in the sun. They would be obliged to forage similarly every evening when they drew to shore.

By this time Ainsworth was feeling rather hazy in the head. He preferred to sit on the deck of the raft rather than perching upright on a bench near the boat-man, where a scrap of canvas served as an awning and provided partial shade. Two days later, as the little craft neared Calcutta, Ainsworth was seriously ill of a fever, with vomiting and diarrhoea, and David was at his wit's end spongeing him with a wet cloth and finding enough clean water for him to drink. Once they reached the docks, David commanded a palanquin, raided Ainsworth's pockets and his own to tip the boatman, and ordered a link-boy to take them to Ainsworth's lodging. Fortunately the link-boy had guided Ainsworth in the past and knew his address. There he handed his friend into the care of Anando, returned the horses to the Fort and reported to the Compound.

Ainsworth had caught cholera, a frequent experience in a land where running water was often heavily polluted with organic matter. Anando had nursed the Major through just the same illness, so he knew exactly what to do. The Major had returned to duty before he had properly recovered, Anando recalled, so it was no wonder he had lacked the strength to defend himself in battle. That would not happen this time, he resolved. Presently David Lambton returned. Having delivered the despatches to Henry Bonnay, he had collected his overdue pay, had cashed it at his own bank and had brought half the proceeds to Anando to fund the medicines and the care that Ainsworth would need. He promised to call back in a day or two to see how his colleague fared.

Ainsworth hovered between life and death for all of three weeks. When at last he regained consciousness and the use of his faculties he was surprised to find himself lying comfortably in his own bed with his own faithful servant tending him, since he had in delirium imagined himself cast adrift on the boat in the swirling river. He learnt that David Lambton had not suffered similarly from his dip in the river, but on the contrary had financed his friend's care and recovery. He sent Anando to the Compound with a message that David should collect all the pay owing to Ainsworth for the last two months, take the bonds to Mr Seth, and bring him the resultant cash. This enable him to repay his friend with gratitude, and to settle what was owing to his staff, particularly to Anando and to the dhobi who had patiently washed all his soiled bed linen.

Ainsworth's next thought was for his horse Mughal, but for many days he lacked the strength to walk to the stable. Eventually he hired a palanquin. To his relief Mughal was in good shape and welcomed him. Ainsworth learnt that Mr Biswas had hired out the horse for others to ride during his absence, so that it had earned its keep – just, for its irritable temperament when deprived of its skilful owner had made it more risky to hire to anyone not an expert rider. The horse nuzzled Ainsworth as he tried to explain to the creature his inability to ride that day. Somehow the animal seemed to know that he was sick and when Ainsworth had left it returned to its hay-rack with an air of resignation.

Last of all, Ainsworth went to visit Mr Biswas, the letting agent, to settle the rent now owing after an absence of over two months. His landlord's attitude seemed surprisingly reasonable, considering that at any time during his journey Ainsworth might have been killed, leaving his debts unpaid. The reason for Mr Biswas's amicality then became clear when he took Ainsworth into his inner office and closed the door. "I have two sons," he said. "Elder one is clever, he want to be babu." Ainsworth knew what the word meant; it was the term given to Indian members of staff working in the Writers' Building, either as translators or, if their English was good enough, performing much the same functions as Ainsworth himself. "My second son, Ajoy, he much younger, very handsome, pretty boy. He like to work for you. Make very good house-boy. Clean and very smart in uniform. You have first son made babu, I send you second son. You like him."

Ainsworth feeling rather faint from his illness and wondering how Mr Biswas had divined his proclivity, hastily promised to give the matter his earnest consideration, and departed for the Government Compound in his palanquin.

CHAPTER XIV
The Royal Service

Hugo had spent almost two years at sea in the West Indies following his recuperation from yellow fever at St. Christopher. He had applied himself to his Midshipman's duties and diligently to his studies. It was not the mathematics of navigation that he found difficult, for he had learnt geometry and long division and multiplication from Dr. Davey, but it was the matter of knowing what step to take next and when, and how to recognise those adverse conditions, the waves and currents, the winds and squalls, which required constant amendment and adjustment to the trim of the ship and its course: that was the true art of seamanship. He learnt that the Caribbean experienced storms of unusual force every summer and autumn, known as hurricanes, and that losses to shipping could be severe unless there was time to seek shelter among the bays of the Leeward Islands. By contrast the spring season was often balmy, with light winds which made it difficult to pursue their quarry, even under full sail, and as often as not the boats had to be manned to tow the ship into the wind, or seawards round a headland in order to face the enemy.

By now he had plenty of battle experience and had learnt to take the place of any member of a gun-crew who should fall injured beside him. He must just drag the body, or what was left of it, out of the way of the motion of the gun. Then he must secure the tackle after recoil to gain access to the business end of the smoking barrel, poke in the 'worm' to remove the remains of the previous cartridge, swab it down with a wet sponge on a pole from the nearby bucket of water, and feed in the new cartridge containing gun-powder, jam in a wad to hold it in place and then lift into the barrel the shot that was to be fired. The size, weight and type of shot varied on command, and it was the Middie's business to understand thoroughly which was which. A further wad, made of old rope or suchlike, was jammed in after the shot to keep it in place as the ship rolled. The gun was hauled back to protrude through the gun-port and her elevation raised in accordance with instructions. The cartridge was spiked through the touch-hole and further loose powder added from the gunner's powder-horn to make a train. Then the gunner's mate, upon an order given by Mr. Jackson, or by an officer from the hatchway above, would take a heated linstock tipped with a slow-match and apply it to the touch-hole. The guns were seldom fired all at once, since that destabilised the ship, but in turn as the ship passed by her target or drew alongside it for boarding.

Hugo had taken his turn on watch, had become accustomed to clambering aloft, even amid the shrieking furies of a hurricane. He knew how to reef topgallants and topsails, how to bring down the yards or stand down the topgallant masts and brace the rigging with chains, the same chains that in battle were used to secure the yards abaft so that the sails remained slack whilst the vessels pounded each other to destruction. He had stood on deck with his fellow middies learning to use the sextant, then plotting the course on paper and checking it by the chronometer and by the ship's compass set in the binnacle beside the helmsman. He had learnt the meaning of each flag and the signals that might be run up the rigging to indicate identity or give a message or an instruction to another ship in the fleet. He could also recognise the flags of various nations, and especially the dreaded Republican tricolour of France, dreaded because England might at this moment be under invasion by the Force being amassed on the French Channel coast by the Revolutionary Generals in Paris. Hugo knew that his task on this distant shore was to keep as many French warships and merchantmen as possible blockaded in the Leeward Islands, and to sink or disable any that might be encountered at sea. It was frustrating to be so far from home, and whenever there was an opportunity to send despatches Hugo would write a letter to Jessica at Roos Hall and enclose a separate screed for his family. On these occasions, however, he informed Jessica that she was not obliged to show his letter to Mrs. Jarvis. Instead he pictured her having the excuse to saddle James and ride along the bridle-path to take good news to the Ringsfield Farm.

On blockade-duty, conditions aboard ship became as irksome as those of the besieged. Supplies of fresh food quickly perished or ran out, the availability of fruit, particularly of lemons or limes, was irregular, and some of the crew began to show symptoms of scurvy. Petty squabbles and quarrels among the seamen or the Marines became magnified into open hostilities. Trouble arose from cases of theft or jealousy, or even from a bad hand at cards in the games of Euchre and Seven-up which were common among the crew, and from the bets taken at Whist among the officers. Hugo did not much care for cards, thinking the enthusiasm with which they were played a waste of energy. He would rather have read a good book, but apart from the Bible there were few on board and those mostly in the Captain's cabin.

When tempers really became frayed and violence or dishonesty, non-performance or insubordination were involved, the Navy had an array of ingenious punishments it was entitled to inflict. Transgressors could be 'mast-headed' as little Gus Mather had been, 'keel-hauled' and dragged beneath the ship or 'dipped' at the yardarm - though these were somewhat controversial in shark-infested waters, flung into the foc'sle in chains, or simply flogged. Mr. Barber, or 'Barbarossa' as the First Lieutenant was known, favoured the latter above all else since it broke a man's spirit and rendered him less likely to cause trouble in future. The fact that he then deserted at the next port was not Mr. Barber's concern because the press-gangs could be relied upon to bring in fresh recruits. However this was not so upon an isolated naval station, although the West Indies squadrons did welcome aboard the odd runaway slave. After all, one could always hand him back with an apology in the event of pursuit and identification, having obtained some work out of him in the meantime, and without the least obligation to add him to the ship's muster or to pay him any wages!

Captain Sterne's attitude to punishment differed somewhat from that of his second in command, in that he was inclined to give greater consideration to the value of the man to the ship and whether he was capable of good work when required. He thought it counter-productive to break a man's spirit if the next moment his strength would be needed to reef sails in a storm or to heave shot into the mouth of a cannon. Consequently, when the ship's company gathered to see punishment administered, the Captain ensured that punishment duly took place and in public, but he limited the number of lashes applied or the duration of uncomfortable exposure to the tropical sun. Indeed there was one occasion where a man was bound and stripped ready for flogging fifty lashes for attempting, when in a drunken rage, to throttle a fellow-seaman. A sudden breeze sprang up which obliged the crew to wear ship. When all the excitement had died down, it was noted that the seaman was still standing there, waiting for the Bosun's lash to fall, and having been swamped repeatedly by incoming seas whilst the *Apollion* was changing tack. The Captain took one look at the seaman whose trousers were by now heavily soiled, and not only with sea-water, and said, "Seaman Jones, do go and change those disgusting trousers. Cut him down, Bosun."

Nor was that the end of the affair, for Captain Sterne then started a practice of rotating the stewards or 'captain's servants' who waited upon him, his officers and upon other sections of the crew. He had Seaman Jones made his personal steward for a fortnight, and the poor fellow was so grateful for his missed flogging that he was forever in the galley seeking out the best titbits for the Captain, a process which allowed him to purloin unnoticed the second-best for himself! It was the Captain's policy to ensure that every seaman understood the operation of other sections of the ship and that he, the seaman, was an integral part of a team with one double objective, the defence of England and the defeat of France.

It was as part of this policy that Captain Sterne followed the usual Navy practice of inviting the Midshipmen, or at least those who were studying to become officers, to dine at the Captain's table in the Ward Room on the Quarterdeck. They were invited two by two, in order of seniority, and only on Sundays, provided the ship was free of emergencies. Thus Hugo eventually had his turn, along with Pip Harris with whom he had developed a particular friendship since the lads were close together in age and who with Gus's departure shared the middies' chores aboard. The boys were seated either side of the Captain so must take care not to drink more wine than was seemly, for Captain Sterne favoured sobriety among his officers as setting an example of reasonable behaviour to the rest of the crew. It was noted that Captain Hunter had rather more trouble with his Marines and that they were habitually confined to quarters for misbehaviour.

Captain Sterne enquired of each of the lads in turn his progress in his studies. Pip confessed that he found studying tedious and wished that he might take a more active rôle, such as fighting alongside the Marines when they boarded the enemy. Hugo replied that just as he thought he had mastered a subject he discovered there was yet more to learn, though he too found the blockade tedious and would like to have books to read to while away the time. Captain Sterne immediately offered Hugo the run of his own library, which Hugo ventured to consult one day when he knew the Captain to be well-occupied on the quarter-deck. To his surprise and regret he observed that half of the Captain's 'library' consisted of those classical texts which he had scorned at school. However from among the rest he selected a modestly slim volume which he thought might be of interest. Entitled "Reflections on the French Revolution", it was by Edmund Burke, a Parliamentarian with whose name Hugo was already familiar from Uncle Bob's references to the movement against slavery. On deck he approached the quarterdeck rail and asked Mr. Barber whether he might transmit to the Captain his wish to borrow the book. The Captain gave his assent with raised eyebrows. "If he can read that text and reason from it, we'll have a man for Parliament in the Gun-Room!" he said.

Pip Harris's wish for more active training was also fulfilled. Captain Sterne had expected to receive orders to land the Marines on one or other of the British-owned Leeward Islands, either to relieve the existing garrison or to participate in military action upon one of the many islands which the French had conquered - St. Lucia, Tobago, Guadeloupe or Martinique,among others. However such orders were not yet forthcoming and Captain Sterne was obliged to feed Captain Hunter and his men, still one hundred strong despite much sickness and some injury, and to keep them occupied within the confines of a modest fighting vessel for long periods of sea-watch between brief excursions ashore. It had been his normal practice in the past, a policy he recommended following Pip's request, to have the Marines train the Midshipmen as well as other members of the crew in the use of small arms, pistol, pike and cutlass. Most of the pressed men and some of the younger middies had never handled weapons before. After training they should at least be able to pick up a weapon and defend themselves if their ship were boarded. Moreover, pistol-fire offered the amusement of hanging an old tin tray at the yardarm and holding a heated contest to see who could score a hit as it bobbed and spun in the wind.

Whilst on patrol too, the men were able to amuse themselves with singing and dancing. Concert parties were held on deck where some of the seamen would don pantomime costumes or even masquerade in officer's uniform and ape their betters, to the entertainment of all, the officers concerned not excluded. When patrolling in company with other vessels, exchange visits took place in which the Middies were sometimes included. However sounds carry a fair distance at sea and it was always necessary to keep a careful watch for the Enemy and not to alert him to one's presence until one was ready for the scrap.

In the autumn of 1796 a severe storm, some called it a hurricane, struck the West Indies and did particular destruction among the Leeward Islands. French shipping suffered equally with British, many merchantmen and supply ships were sunk, often even at their moorings. Captain Sterne, who knew the Caribbean well, had observed its development in advance and had conveyed his concerns to the rest of the squadron. His advice was accepted and the signal given that the fleet might disperse and seek shelter among the bays of the nearest friendly islands. The *Apollion*, being a fast sailer, soon reached the shelter of a headland, stood down and secured all yards and rigging, and kedged out its anchors fore and aft. Such precautions were timely, for the storm blew over the crest of the headland and thrust high waves ashore on the far side of the bay. However the tormented sea was progressively sucked away from beneath *Apollion*'s keel such that it was doubtful whether the anchors would hold. A thunderous drenching downpour made labour on deck a martyrdom and the water, both salt and fresh, percolated all corners of the ship, so that it became necessary to work the pumps continuously, as well as to cast overboard weighted grappling hooks and nets, and any other heavy obstacle to the fury of the waves.

When the storm finally ended, the vessels that had survived crept out of their havens in search of the rest of the fleet. It took many days for them all to assemble at the agreed rendezvous of English Harbour in the island of Antigua. A further week passed before the British sloop *Desire* brought news of their casualties and fresh orders for some of the warships. The *Apollion* received instructions to land her Marines at last at St. John's, Antigua. She was then to proceed to St. Christopher to collect troops from its garrison who had been relieved and were due to be sent home. No, they were not going home themselves, at least not yet, for the *Apollion* was to call at Funchal for fresh orders as to whether she was to be assigned to the Mediterranean Fleet. It appeared that Spain had joined the French coalition against Britain and every vessel that could be spared was required to patrol the coasts of France and Spain to warn of the sailing of an enemy fleet. The saddest part of the news brought by the sloop was of the complete loss of the *Aetherial*, Captain Whitton and his officers, the crew and the Marines. Those aboard the *Apollion* were particularly affected by this, since the two ships had kept company over several years and they had had so many joint adventures, experiences and entertainments as to have become almost of the same family, a small village, as it were, cast adrift amid the temperamental elements.

Captain Sterne ordered a funeral service to be held the following Sunday morning before the Marines were landed at St. John's. They paraded in their finest uniforms and officers and crew all donned their 'Sunday best' insofar as they possessed any, much borrowing and helping out preceding this below decks. The ship's tailor had sorted out some black "crape" and had made arm-bands for all the officers and the Marines, and black ribbons with which the crew might tie their long hair. The drums and pipes played the traditional slow marches and laments for those lost at sea, the Chaplain made a fine sermon about the valiant now resting from their labours, and Captain Sterne took the opportunity to inform all his crew of the latest political and military develop-ments in Europe which had necessitated their new assignment.

He reminded them of the summer of '94, before they had left England, when Lord Howe had defeated the French fleet from Brest off Ushant on the "glorious First of June". England had hoped then that such a victory would keep the Channel inviolate from military invasion from France. But that had proved a vain expectation, for during their absence from home the government of France had reorganised itself after the Terror of the Revolution, and the Directory now in charge had set out upon a steady military conquest of the Continent. The Austrian Netherlands had been overrun and defeated at the Battle of Fleurus, Prussia too, and Spain had been obliged to make a non-offensive alliance with France under the Treaty of Basle. During the military campaigning season which had just ended, French armies had achieved outstanding successes against Austrian territories in Northern Italy under a young Corsican general named Napoleon Bonaparte. He seemed destined for national eminence and the public in England had begun to fear that he might soon turn his attention across the Channel. Meanwhile, in order to fund her military expansion, France had come to rely upon revenue from the valuable sugar and cotton crops grown in the West Indies, hence her capture of some of the islands, Captain Sterne explained, bringing his commentary back to that theatre of war with which his crew were already familiar. That was what they respected and admired about their captain; he treated them as intelligent beings, wise enough to understand such develop-ments and to appreciate their importance now that Spain had placed the servic-es of her not inconsiderable navy at the disposal of France. Evidently the *Apollion*'s capture of Señor Manuel da Silva and his return to judgment and exe-cution in Spain had not proved sufficiently persuasive after all!

Once the Marines had been landed at St. John's, Antigua, the *Apollion* turned north towards St. Christopher. The ship felt curiously naked and vulnerable without the noisy and quarrelsome Marines in their red and white uniforms. Captain Sterne had set double lookouts at the mastheads, for he did not wish to be caught unawares. Although his crew had received some training in the use of arms, he felt that he could not be confident of their success if confronted with trained enemy forces. However when the lookouts spotted a French schooner of half the armament of the *Apollion*, and with no sign of soldiers aboard her, Captain Sterne did not hesitate to attack, conscious of his ship's superior gun-nery and that this prize would make a useful addition to the depleted West

Indies fleet. The guns were run out and loaded, including the two carronades set up on the foredeck, and the *Apollion* began firing as soon as her weapons were within range.

Captain Sterne had reckoned without the enthusiasm of his own crew, for all along the decks pikes and pistols had been laid by and the seamen were eager for the fray. Hugo was supervising the supply of ammunition to some of the guns on the main deck, and Pip stood beside him ready to fetch from below whatever was required. Pip too was thirsting for battle and had fastened on his sword-belt, something he should not have done before the order to board was given, as it would encumber him in his gunnery duties. The *Apollion* had loosed her first broadside, gun by gun, and was rapidly closing to board. Hugo was helping the gunner's mate to ensure that the elevation was correct; their target was the rigging of the French ship, while those on the gun-deck below would concentrate upon blasting the enemy cannon into silence, muzzle to muzzle. "I'm looking forward to a scrap, Hughie, aren't you?" Pip shouted as he drew his weapon, climbed on the netting and flourished his sword at the sky. A cannonball flashed past his head, took off his arm and his sword and deposited them in the sea on the other side of the ship! Pip's body fell insensible at Hugo's feet.

For a moment Hugo closed his eyes. Then he remembered his training. 'Move aside any body or wounded man which might impede the action of the gun and the crew'. With a gulp, he took hold of his friend by the legs and moved him into the shelter of the gunwale. Then he returned his attention to the firing of the guns. The *Apollion* was now abreast of the French vessel and preparing to tack across her bows. Suddenly, out of her foc'sle arose a wall of blue-coated men of the Garde Nationale of France, in transit, no doubt, from one Leeward Island fortress to another. Swiftly Captain Sterne ordered the carronades to be loaded with grape shot and fired at point-blank range, even as the French soldiers were aiming their muskets at the quarterdeck of the *Apollion*. Which guns could fire first?

The two detonations were simultaneous. Both Captain Sterne and Mr. Barber fell to the deck wounded, the Captain in the shoulder, the First Lieutenant in the leg. On the French vessel ragged gaps appeared in the ranks of the Guardsmen who were busy re-loading their muskets for a second shot. At that moment a broadside from the *Apollion*'s lower deck slammed into the timbers of the French ship and sent her juddering sideways over a wave. The movement spoilt the Guardsmen's aim and a second round from the carronades did even more destruction amongst them and the rest of the French crew. Their Captain, also wounded in the leg, immediately ordered his colours struck and his ship hove to. Aboard the *Apollion*, the starboard gun-crews, who as yet had taken no part in the fight, were ordered to take their pikes and board the French vessel to secure their prisoners, the Bosun and Mr. Jackson to lead them.

Meanwhile the oldsters among the Middies were detailed to form stretcher parties to take the *Apollion*'s wounded below. Hugo watched as they collected Mr.

Barber and delivered him into Mr. Dunstan's care. Captain Sterne insisted on remaining on deck to supervise the capture. He unfastened his sword-belt and used it as a sling for his wounded arm. At long last Hugo was able to give attention to his friend, for the port gun crews had been ordered to remain at their stations in case there should be further resistance from the enemy. He looked round at the place where he had dragged Pip's insensible form but could find only a large pool of blood on the deck. Had they taken Pip below, or had someone concluded he was dead and had slipped his body overboard without waiting for permission to do so?

Hugo dared not leave his post: he would be flogged for insubordination if he did. It seemed to take an age for order to be imposed on the French ship. The surviving Guardsmen were chained up in their own foc'sle, the wounded were sent down to the care of their own surgeon, and the French captain was swung aboard the *Apollion* in a canvas sling. Captain Sterne accepted his sword from Capitaine Dufresne, then courteously sent him below to be treated by Mr. Dunstan, all this before he accepted any assistance on his own part. He sent Mr. Smith, the Second Lieutenant, to take charge of the prize along with a hand-picked crew and ordered the Master to command the *Apollion* while he went below to have his wound treated.

Not till the port gun-crews were stood down and allowed to take refreshment before watches were set for the night was Hugo able to seek news of Pip Harris. He crept down to the orlop deck, dreading what he might find. He was just in time to observe the French captain, his wound having been cleansed and dressed, being carried to the Second Lieutenant's vacant cabin under guard. Hugo learnt that their Captain and Mr. Barber had been similarly attended to, and now there was a line of seamen with flesh wounds awaiting Mr. Dunstan's care. Some slumped on the blood-soaked planking; others were well enough to assist by fetching fresh buckets of water or heating the cauterising irons. To Hugo it seemed a scenario from Hell, and there was no sign of his friend. As he turned away sadly, one of the Surgeon's assistants said, "You looking for Mr. Harris?" Hugo nodded. "You'll find him in the best bed in the sick berth. Mr. Dunstan dealt with him first. Had to stop him bleeding to death, you see."

Hugo ran to the sick-berth and opened the door. All the cots were occupied by moaning and tossing forms. He wondered how many of those poor fellows would be dead by morning. Pip was at the far end, pale and unconscious, his body reeking of alcohol, his face lathered with camomile ointment where the cannonball had scorched his flesh in passing. The eye, too, on the same side, appeared to have been bruised, for its rim was turning a vivid shade of purple. There was nothing Hugo could contribute to his friend's care, so he snatched some food from that supplied to his mess-mates and returned to his duty on deck.

A few days later both ships anchored off the island of St. Christopher. The French commander, Capitaine Dufresne, was escorted ashore to be detained at His Majesty's pleasure until a suitable exchange could be established. Those that remained of his manifest were sent to work with the road-gang, life expectancy among the existing labourers being somewhat short. Their ship, the *L'Aurore*, was refitted and manned by a volunteer crew of seamen, supported by a few soldiers from the Fort who had no particular wish to return to England where they might have to account for their misdeeds. Renamed *Aurora,* the schooner was despatched to rejoin the Leeward Islands squadron in a scout and intelligence rôle. Captain Sterne and Mr. Barber, meanwhile, were both having their wounds tended ashore where fresh water and good food were abundant, and the Master and the Purser, Mr. Iver, had charge of procuring supplies and spares for the trans-Atlantic voyage.

Pip was still seriously ill in the sick-berth, drifting in and out of consciousness, and his severe wound, though the break had been clean, showing signs of infection. Hugo thought of Madame Joly who had tended him with such care. Would she be able to help his friend? He decided to ask Mr. Iver who responded, "I daresay she might, Mr. Jarvis, but why don't you come ashore with me and put it to her?" Hugo felt a strange sense of time departed as he walked along the once-familiar street and knocked on the well-known door. He thought of little Gus and though he knew from the one letter he had received from home that the boy had returned safely, he hoped that he had kept his promise to study hard at school.

Hugo raised the big brass door knocker and let it fall. The door opened upon the wrinkled face of Melissa, a brilliant smile spreading across her cheeks as she called within, "Madame, 'tis your young gentleman."

"My young gentleman? Which young gentleman is that?" Madame Joly responded as she came to the doorway. "Oh, Master Hughie, what a pleasure to see you. Your ship just got in? Do step inside and tell me all your news."

"Good afternoon, Madame Joly," Hugo said formally, removing his cap, but a broad grin developing across his face as he stepped over the threshold. "Thank you, but in fact I have come to ask a favour."

"I know, one of your shipmates is wounded and you want me to care for him," Madame Joly guessed. "What does Mr. Iver say, if you're still aboard the same ship, that is?"

"It was he who suggested I might venture to ask you," Hugo replied.

"Who is the fellow in question, and what has happened to him?" Madame Joly enquired as they made their way into the shady garden and Melissa brought drinks of pineapple juice and slices of water melon.

"His name is Philip Harris, Pip for short, and he is a year or so younger than I. A cannonball took off his right arm near the shoulder and burnt the side of his face. The wounds are not healing well and Mr. Dunstan, our Surgeon, says he does not consider Pip could make the voyage across the Atlantic."

"Poor boy," Melissa murmured, "to lose his right arm. How he ever going to do a job of work like that?"

"You sailing home, then, Hughie?" Madame Joly asked.

"We don't know yet," Hugo replied. "We are ordered to call at Funchal, in Madeira, and then we can expect to find out. Our Captain and First Officer are wounded too, but they are to spend only a few days resting ashore. Pip would have to stay here until he could obtain passage on another ship. We can pay for his care, of course. Mr. Iver will arrange it," Hugo hastened to assure her.

"That is of secondary importance," Madame Joly murmured in reply. "What really matters is whether I can take sufficient care of him with my special receipts in order to save his life."

"Can you, Madame?"

"Yes, I think so. Have him brought here on a stretcher as soon as the ship comes alongside the quay for loading, beforehand if you may. Mr. Dunstan always was a good butcher, but he's not so soothing at the bedside. Now, tell me about yourself. Have you had any news from England?" Madame Joly yet remembered her English lover with nostalgia.

"Yes, I've received one packet from home," Hugo replied. "Young Gus arrived safely and has returned to his school. My family is well, but my mother's father, my grandfather whom I had never met, has died. He lived in the West Country, the other side of England from my home. He was a farmer too but had no-one to take over his farm since his only son was in business. Thus the farm had to be sold, but my father wanted to acquire grandfather's Devon Red cattle for crossing with our Norfolk breeds. The cattle had to travel to us by sea, all around the south coast of England, then north to Yarmouth. They were put on a ship normally used to transport troops and were fired upon by the French who mistook it for a gunboat! Luckily a fog came up in the Downs and the cattle were saved from injury, but our stockmen who travelled with them had quite a tale to tell when they reached home."

Hugo omitted to mention that he had also received a letter from Miss Jessica, mostly relating details of the cat Selina, the painting lessons she was receiving from Mr. Russell (much surprise), and the fact that a pianoforte had been acquired at Roos Hall upon which the church organist from Beccles, no less, was teaching her to play. Surely such news could not have slipped Hugo's mind? Nor her postscript that there had been no tidings at all of Mr. Ainsworth who had departed for India? Maybe Hugo had just become a little shy about having a young lady of unknown parentage but living in a fine mansion write him letters?

Pip Harris was put in a sling, the same canvas sling that had been used to transfer ashore Capitaine Dufresne, and by that means was lowered into the launch. Once ashore he was placed on a stretcher and delivered into the care of Madame Joly. They laid him gently on the bed she had prepared, and Hugo remained behind to ensure that the likely costs of Pip's treatment could be met. What he did not disclose, to Madame Joly or to anyone else, was that as well as bringing the wages owed to Pip for his last two years of service, Hugo had contributed all of his own, less his expenses concerning the Slop Chest. Madame Joly quickly lifted Pip's bandages to examine his patched and scarred shoulder. She pursed her full lips and gave some rapid orders to Melissa in their own tongue. Then she laid a hand on Hugo's arm, as Pip writhed uneasily in his half-conscious state. "I'll do my best for him, Master Hughie," she said, "indeed I will."

When Hugo returned to the *Apollion* he found she had been towed to the quayside and the garrison relieved from the Port was being brought aboard. They sounded noisy and unruly, half of them unsteady on their feet from the effects of a more than adequate application of alcohol, and the rest brawling and shouting like children let out of school. Hugo was unaware whether this was their normal state of behaviour or whether it was the result of some over-generous farewell celebration, but he knew that such disorder would not be to the liking of Mr. Barber or the Captain. It seemed likely to prove a rough voyage.

On their first day out of St. Christopher Captain Sterne assembled the whole company on deck and pronounced a severe lecture on the discipline and good order he expected to be observed aboard any ship he commanded. He praised his own crew for their loyalty and good service and told the military men that he had anticipated better of them than a drunken rabble! He would not tolerate such uncouth behaviour corrupting the general orderliness of his seamen. Thus, for the time being, supplies of alcohol to the military officers would be strictly limited to that required to maintain good health, and there would be daily exercise at arms on deck in which such seamen as could be spared from other duties would also take part.

By the time the *Apollion* arrived off Funchal, Madeira, towards the end of January 1797 the soldiers were better disposed towards the Captain and his crew. Floggings had been kept to a minimum, extra duties being the more usual punishment for minor infringements of discipline, and a cheerful attitude prevailed. This was as well because at Funchal the soldiers learnt that they were not yet to depart for England but were urgently needed to supplement those already serving on the island in case of enemy attack. Nor was the *Apollion* to be relieved of her command, even though she had spent more than two years continuously at sea. Instead Captain Sterne had received personal instructions from Sir John Jervis, now promoted full Admiral and placed in charge of the British Mediterranean Fleet.

These informed him that he should not proceed to England since sailors aboard ships stationed over-winter in some Southern England ports had become mutinous, demanding a doubling of their pay, resolution of other grievances and better working conditions. "Since the *Apollion* is undoubtedly untainted by such indiscipline," Sir John had written, "I wish you will take her to Gibraltar for any urgent attention she may require before joining my command, presently at anchor in the mouth of the River Tagus. Should you not find me there, then you may look for me seeking to engage the enemy between Cadiz and Cape Spartel," (Morocco). "Lord Spencer," (First Lord of the Admiralty), "has given me leave to recruit whom I may among our support vessels, since he is unable to send me enough warships to match the enemy's numbers, and the ships of our

Portuguese ally are quite unsuited to the task."

Sir John then added by way of postscriptum, "If by chance my young kinsman Hugo Jarvis is still aboard your vessel, I beg you will grant him no special favours, but the best training you may, always ensuring that he performs all his duties with the utmost respect and diligence." It would seem that Captain Sterne and the Admiral had much in common when it came to the governance of those under their command. Captain Sterne took the opportunity of Hugo's next invitation to the Ward Room to impart the Admiral's message, not omitting to quote the provisos. "Thank you for telling me, sir," Hugo replied modestly with a catch in his voice.

The Admiral had also given Captain Sterne instructions to retain fifty of the best soldiers aboard his ship, or to recruit that number from the Fort at Funchal, so that if boarded the *Apollion* might give a good account of herself. Captain Sterne interviewed several officers personally, of which he selected five and asked each to choose nine of the best men known to them for their loyalty and courage. This was to be no freebooting expedition but the protection of the lifeblood of England, for the Admiral's mission was to prevent the main Spanish fleet based in Cadiz from joining forces with its sister fleet based in Cartagena, and the combined armada sailing north to swell the French Channel Fleet based at Brest. This overwhelming force would then be able to escort the fleet of troop transports necessary to carry out an invasion of England, or alternatively to attack her 'back door' in Southern Ireland.

Hitherto the Admiral's fleet had been able to blockade the main French fleet in its Mediterranean base of Toulon. British capture of the Corsican fortresses of Bastia and Calvi had enabled the fleet to keep watch on French activities conveniently from the Bay of San Fiorenzo. However Napoleon's military success in Italy and the declaration of war by Spain on 8 October 1796 had completely transformed Sir John's task. He had been obliged to evacuate the Mediterranean and to concentrate instead on patrolling the Atlantic coast of Spain. He had left behind in the Mediterranean a small squadron under a certain Commodore Nelson in the *Agamemnon*, one of the Admiral's most trusted commanders, to collect from their refuge at Porto Ferraio in Elba the British Governor of Corsica, Sir Gilbert Elliot, and his staff. Nelson was then to rejoin the Admiral's fleet in the Atlantic in the region of Cape St. Vincent, bringing whatever news he could of naval movements at Toulon and Cartagena.

Once the *Apollion* had taken aboard at Funchal the supplies she required, including a consignment of onions (also used as an effective antiscorbutic treatment whenever lemons or limes were not available), and the detachment of soldiers under their officer Captain Alastair Macdonald, she set sail for Gibraltar. However there was a violent easterly gale blowing through the Gut, as the entrance to the Mediterranean was known, so Captain Sterne decided instead to locate the British fleet first before proceeding to Gibraltar once the bad weather had amelioriated. Arriving off the mouth of the River Tagus, he was informed by the commander of a British sloop left there in an intelligence capacity, that Sir John Jervis had sailed thence southwards on 18th January, with his force reduced to only ten ships of the line by the *St. George* grounding on a sandbank. Moreover he learnt that a squadron of seven ships sent from England previously to reinforce the Admiral, had missed the rendezvous, misunderstood their instructions and, reaching Gibraltar without making contact, had simply turned around again and sailed home! The Admiralty had now despatched a second squadron of just five ships under Rear-Admiral Sir William Parker which expected to find Sir John and the Fleet off Cape St. Vincent. Evidently any additional assistance by the *Apollion* was likely to be most welcome.

It was 13th February by the time the *Apollion* had taken on fresh water at Lisbon and had left the Tagus, turning south along the coast of Portugal. Having explicit orders to make for Gibraltar for a much-needed careen and re-caulking, since good seamen were having to be detailed to man the pumps, Captain Sterne ignored all temptations posed by passing Spanish merchantmen, even though any one of these might have been carrying a cargo of bullion from Havana or Manila. Instead he ordered his crew to crowd on all sail, though the easterly gale still blowing out of the Gut made navigation in a southerly direction rather difficult. That same gale, blowing hard throughout the Mediterranean, had sped Commodore Nelson westwards past Toulon and Cartagena where he had been unable to observe any signs of naval activity. He called in at Gibraltar for news and learnt that the Spanish Cartagena fleet had sailed for Cadiz under a new supreme commander, Admiral Don José de Cordova. Nelson hastened to follow but found Cadiz harbour empty and continued westwards, still propelled by the easterly gale that had driven the Spanish fleet far to the west of its destination. Unbeknown to the Spaniards, the British fleet now sailed between them and the safety of their home port.

On reaching the British Fleet off Cape St. Vincent, Nelson found Sir John Jervis closeted with Sir William Parker and others of his captains aboard his flagship *Victory* where they discussed possible tactics for the forthcoming battle. The gale had now died away and a light mist had settled over the ocean. They were all aware of the proximity of the Spanish Fleet, but without being precise as to its numbers or its exact location. Indeed, Nelson claimed to have seen ships engulfed in the mist on his way to the rendezvous, but once again they were hampered by a shortage of frigates to despatch as scouts. It was not until after nightfall that Sir John, wide awake as ever on the eve of battle, heard the signal guns fired by the Spanish Fleet, and a Portuguese frigate arriving during the night reported the presence of enemy ships some fifteen miles to the south.

As the morning mist lifted in a light and now westerly breeze the situation became clear. The Spanish Fleet, consisting of twenty-seven warships, against the British fifteen ships of the line, was split into two divisions, with eighteen vessels in one and nine in the other. Sir John's objective was to prevent the two groups joining forces against him. Accordingly, he decided that the British Fleet should pass between the two groups and should concentrate its fire on the larger force. This group included the Spanish Admiral's flagship, the *San Josef* (112 guns) and a giant four-decker battleship of 130 guns called the *Santissima Trinidad*. The Admiral formed his ships into a single line led by the *Culloden* (74) under Captain Troubridge, another of Sir John's most reliable commanders. He placed his flagship, H.M.S.*Victory* (100 guns) in the centre of the line. Nelson, now transferred to his own warship, the *Captain* (74) was in 13th place, with the last ship being the *Excellent* (74) under Nelson's friend Captain Collingwood.

As the British Fleet passed close to the Spanish ships there was a brisk exchange of broadsides. Then Sir John signalled to his fleet to tack in succession and to close with the enemy as they came alongside. Commodore Nelson in the *Captain* anticipated this signal, fearing that if the Spaniards were given time to manoeuvre their groups could join forces. The *Captain* wore ship very sharply and headed straight for the enemy, in particular for the group of vessels surrounding the *Santissima Trinidad*. The *Culloden* swiftly came up to join him, supported by the *Blenheim* (74), and Captain Collingwood in the *Excellent* also tacked sharply to bring his guns to bear on the core of the Spanish Fleet. Soon the *Captain* lost her fore topmast and many of her sails, becoming almost unmanageable, but Nelson's colleagues crowded in to assist. The *Captain* collided with the stern of the *San Nicolas* (80 guns) and Nelson personally led a boarding party into the Spanish ship through its quarterdeck gallery windows, meeting pistol fire all the way. When that ship surrendered, Nelson continued, climbing across the tangled wreckage that linked the *San Nicolas* to the *San Josef* ahead of it, and that too surrendered. As night fell, both fleets drew apart,   the British Fleet with the four prizes it had taken, though not alas the *Santissima Trinidad*. In the morning the Spanish Fleet, though still far more numerous, fled towards the safety of Cadiz and any possibility of conjunction with the French Fleet at Brest had been thwarted.

The *Apollion* did not take part in the famous Battle of Cape St. Vincent, but she came upon the scene the morning afterwards. In the distance Captain Sterne identified the orderly masts of the British Fleet, with much of the rigging repaired overnight, and nearer at hand the shattered and disorderly retreat of the Spaniards heading for home. Having the advantage of the wind and no orders to the contrary, Captain Sterne decided to tack along the western flank of the retreating ships. He ordered the *Apollion*'s guns loosed in succession as she passed, bringing down a good deal of rigging with some well-aimed fire. Then she joined the British Fleet and her captain reported to Admiral Jervis. Captain Sterne had ordered the jolly-boat lowered from the davits for his transfer to the *Victory*, since he observed that a general signal had been hoisted inviting all captains to 'come aboard'. In fact there was quite a crowd of boats about the lofty warship. When he reached the flagship and had climbed aboard, Captain Sterne was puzzled to find the whole ship hushed in silence. His first thought was that his veteran Commander-in-Chief might have suffered some accident and had died, but then he realised that all the *Victory*'s crew were lined up in formation, the Marines too, and they were listening hard. On the quarterdeck of his flagship the Admiral was making a formal presentation of the sword surrendered by the Spanish admiral, De Cordova, to Commodore Horatio Nelson who had led the victorious boarding of the *San Josef*. Then Captain Halowell, Sir John's flag captain, called for three cheers for the British Navy and their glorious achievement. When these had died away, every seaman returned quietly to his task, as if victory were the business of every day.

Sir John greeted Captain Sterne warmly and congratulated him on his gunnery. "Mr. Jackson," (Master of the *Victory*) "tells me you have knocked down as many yards with one broadside as we did in an hour's hot work yesterday," he said with generous exaggeration. After enquiring of Captain Sterne the state of affairs in the West Indies station, Sir John instructed him to proceed to Gibraltar as required and not to take excuses from the shipwrights that the job could not be done in a month. "My first destination will be Lagos Bay," said Sir John, "so as to carry out our more serious repairs in sheltered waters. Then I return to keep watch on Cadiz. All Spain will be in a tizzy as a result of our success. It is likely they will dismiss De Cordova and must seek his replacement, so we shall have no action there for a month or two. Do you look for me at either location upon your return."

"Thank you, Sir John, and may I too offer my felicitations on your splendid victory. By-the-by, young Hugo Jarvis is indeed still aboard my ship. He makes much progress and should become a good officer in due time. I have a mind to recommend him whenever we return to England. I did not bring him with me today - you instructed me not to show him favours but I ordered my First Lieutenant, Mr. Barber, to invite him to the quarter-deck and to lend him his spyglass!" Sir John chuckled and nodded his approval. The two men raised their hats, shook hands and parted.

Then the Admiral penned a brief account of the battle and sent the despatch to the Admiralty by Captain Calder, his Chief of Staff. Despite its modest brevity a grateful nation, freed for the time being of the threat of invasion, honoured the victor by creating him Baron Jervis of Meaford (his birthplace in Staffordshire) and Earl of St. Vincent, a title by which he was known ever after. That other hero, Commodore Nelson, was created a Knight of the Bath, and received promotion to Rear-Admiral. He was later granted the Freedom of the City of London. Others of the captains involved also received recognition, though not Captain Sterne and the *Apollion* since that vessel had arrived a day too late to claim battle honours.

But Hugo had witnessed the ceremony aboard the flagship, courtesy of Mr. Barber's telescope. Since the departure of little Gus Mather, Hugo had never disputed any issue with the First Lieutenant, now made all the more irritable and impatient by the pain in his wounded leg and the limp it had imparted to his stride across the quarterdeck. Nevertheless Hugo was surprised to be called from his duty of supervising the guard of honour as the captain left the ship. Hugo anticipated that Barbarossa had some onerous task in mind with which to challenge his diligence and endurance, as he often did, for Mr. Barber was something of a bully in the style of Benedict Mather and Martin Weedon and did not permit his juniors to outshine him in performance. Hugo had to restrain his delight and keep all his emotions to himself as he watched every detail of the ceremony of the sword and then his captain being greeted by the Admiral. He noted that Sir John would raise his hat even to a junior officer who approached him with a message. He felt exceedingly proud of his family's esteemed tho' distant relative.

Of course it did take longer than a month to careen and recaulk the *Apollion*, scraping two years' growth of seaweed and barnacles from her underside, repairing any coppering damaged through contact with reefs and sandbanks, replacing rotten tree-nails, stuffing oakum into any unfilled cranny and covering it with a generous coating of pitch, and then repainting the hull in accordance with Navy Board regulations. In fact very little of this activity could be carried out at all, for the simple reason that the dockyard workers at Gibraltar had downed tools and gone on strike. Such had been the infiltration of their ranks by mutinous crews arriving from England that, once the *Apollion* had been divested of her cannon and ballast so that she might be heeled over against the Mole and that a working platform of planks could be lowered over her seaward side, she seemed likely to stay there for the duration of the War!

It appeared that the situation had worsened considerably from that which Sir John Jervis had encountered there earlier in the winter in that, whilst he had described their performance as "dilatory", hence his warning to Captain Sterne, now it could only be termed "complete inaction". Moreover other ships awaited attention besides the *Apollion*, in particular some of the smaller sloops and snows that transported messages and intelligence between the various squadrons of the Fleet.

Captain Sterne called upon the Navy Board's Commissioner and then upon the British Governor-General who received him very cordially but confessed that he had neither men nor financial inducements which he might impose on the undisciplined workforce. Indeed he had remonstrated with their supervisors personally, but to little avail. The chief grievance, it appeared, was the low pay provided exceedingly tardily by the Navy Board for what was an unconscionably filthy occupation where hands were easily calloused, blistered and cut by the sharp edges of barnacles and scrapers, the continuous rubbing of unrewarding surfaces, and the staining of fingers, faces and clothes with the scorching hot pitch. These men had learnt of the various stoppages which were taking place in English ports and even on individual ships where captains and officers had been forced to accept the rebellious actions of their crews at the end of pistol or pike. In the Gibraltar yards the workers wished to ensure that their function and needs were not overlooked in any settlement awarded to sailors and shipyards at home in England.

Captain Sterne returned from his visit to the Governor and conferred with Mr.

Barber. They had several times inspected the labourers working on the *Apollion*. These had studiously picked up their tools and proceeded whilst the officers were present, whistling tunelessly as if unaware of their presence. As soon as the officers moved on the tools were laid down, a deck of cards would be spread on an upturned barrel and someone would fetch a jug of wine. Obviously the representations made by a Captain with a crippled shoulder and arm and his second in command with a pronounced limp were having little effect. In desperation Captain Sterne assembled certain members of his crew which had been billeted ashore whilst the repairs were taking place. He selected those Able Seamen who had served him longest, together with some of the Midshipmen of whom Hugo was one. Captain Sterne explained the matter and that no official help could be obtained from the Navy Board Commissioner or the Governor-General. He told them he was confident that they were as anxious as he to have the ship cleaned and repaired so that she might rejoin the Fleet and show the Enemy her customary turn of speed. He then made an unusual request: rather than idling their time away ashore among the port's tawdry amusements, would they be willing to take turn and turn about among the workmen surrounding their ship, talking to them and encouraging them to perform their tasks?

To Mr. Barber's surprise, Big John was the first to volunteer, the others following where he led. "After all," as Captain Sterne had declared, "your lives depend as much as mine on the good quality of the work carried out in this shipyard." Self-consciously at first, but then with greater confidence, the Able Seamen and young Midshipmen moved among the dockyard workers, asking questions and lending a hand here and there. Hugo had his hands stained brown with pitch and splashes of paint over his shoes and stockings as he and Big John walked and talked among the dockers. They came upon one group playing cards and waited quietly beside them until the game had ended. As one of the players made to shuffle the pack, Big John's large heavy hand descended upon his shoulder and squeezed hard. The players looked up. "Will you not now return to your work?" he asked.

"Your wives and children, and your parents at home in England, are in danger of invasion by the French who will surely slaughter them. England cannot defend herself without her Fleet," Hugo added. "We need every ship."

"Then they should pay us a decent wage to do this filthy job," one of the workers spoke up boldly, and all his companions chorused, "Aye!"

"If you will finish our ship so that we can rejoin the Commander-in-Chief, I will ask our captain to put your grievances to him in person," Hugo offered, having knowledge of the people involved. "I cannot say fairer than that."

The workers stood up slowly, as if with great reluctance, pocketed their cards, picked up their tools and resumed work. "Did you see that?" Mr. Barber commented to Captain Sterne. "Young Jarvis there said something to them which has persuaded them back to work. He'll make a good officer one of these days, I'll warrant it."

"Or a good man for Parliament," the Captain added drily, "as I've remarked before."

When the *Apollion* sailed from Gibraltar and joined Admiral Jervis blockading Cadiz with the British Fleet, Captain Sterne duly supplied his Commander-in-Chief with a report on the conditions he had experienced in the Gibraltar ship-yards. He found that the Admiral had already written to Lord Spencer at the Admiralty of his concerns about the mutinies, and especially those occurring on individual ships. He blamed these to some extent on a lack of good leadership among the officers, these often being recruited from the younger sons of the nobility, rather than rising with experience through the ranks as he and Horatio Nelson had done. Lord Spencer had replied giving details of the action taken by the seamen at Plymouth and Portsmouth, and his conclusion that the Government had no choice but to accede to at least some of the sailors' demands, in particular, those concerning failure to supply them with full rations of good quality food, no pay for men wounded in action or struck down by sickness, late payment of wages and prize money, and insufficient shore-leave due to the practice of sending press-gangs aboard incoming merchant vessels.

Lord Spencer went on to say that the Admiralty had decided to despatch Lord Howe, popularly known as "Black Dick" by the sailors who had served under him, to Spithead with instructions to reach a settlement with the seamen's delegates and to arrest for trial any ringleaders who still offered resistance. Britain could not afford to indulge any form of revolt in an age when Revolution across the Channel had taken on such a bloody guise as the Terror, more especially after the National Convention in Paris had issued a Declaration vowing to assist other nations to overthrow their monarchies in a "democratic revolution".

Unfortunately mutinous activities continued throughout the summer of 1797. On 20th May, only a few days after the dispute at Spithead had been settled and the Channel Fleet had been able to put to sea at last, one Richard Parker of the *Sandwich* led a serious revolt among the British Fleet anchored in the Nore, off Sheerness, in which a dozen warships blockaded the Thames estuary and plundered home-coming merchant vessels for their supplies. Admiral Buckner went aboard the *Sandwich* but failed to obtain a settlement. The government hastily passed two emergency measures through Parliament condemning the actions of the mutineers, and shore batteries were set up with permission to sink the country's own warships if necessary! These ships included H.M.S. *Agamemnon* (64 guns) upon which Horatio Nelson had achieved so many recent successes against French forces in the Mediterranean. Realising now that their cause was lost, on 9th June the rebel force began to disintegrate with ships slipping away one by one and surrendering to the nearest naval authority. Even then, some were fired upon by those rebel crews who remained loyal. Eventually Richard Parker was court-martialled and hanged at the topgallant yardarm of the *Sandwich* "for having been the Principal in a most daring Mutiny on board several of His Majesty's ships at the Nore, and which created a dreadful alarm throughout the whole Nation."

That same month Admiral Jervis had to deal with a mutiny aboard the *Romulus* when she rejoined the Fleet on watch off Cadiz. Her crew had been in contact with mutinous ships stationed in the Azores. The Admiral divided the crew of the *Romulus* between two loyal warships and ordered five of the ringleaders to stand trial "in order to put an end to these attempts to carry (take over) His Majesty's ships wherever it pleases a few ruffians who keep the rest in awe and fear." In July another mutinous rising occurred on the 98-gun warship *St. George*, one of Jervis's own fleet. The disturbance was prompted by the Admiral's sentence of execution against two homosexuals, witnessed *in flagrante delicto*, on the grounds of "going into another man's hammock." The leaders of this mutiny were tried aboard ship of a Saturday and hanged on the Sunday, thus causing outrage in religious circles. However they were punished by their own shipmates, on the Admiral's specific orders, and delegations of crews and marines were sent to watch the hangings from all the other ships in the Fleet. Sir John also sent the popular Rear-Admiral Nelson, accompanied by Captain Miller and selected members of his crew from the *Captain*, aboard the 74-gun warship *Theseus* in order that he might impose strict discipline on seamen affected by insurrection arising mostly on ships fresh out from England.

Admiral Jervis decided that the best remedy for indiscipline in his tedious blockade of Cadiz would be to despatch some of the more lively vessels on a special mission of their own. The Canary Islands constituted a Spanish territory where her merchantmen and their escorts were likely to call on their way home for fresh water and supplies. Such vessels could be laden with anything from bullion and jewels to valuable timber, and cargoes of sugar and coffee. In short, they made highly desirable prizes and a chance for underpaid and troublesome seamen to enhance their pay. In addition, the squadron might fire upon several forts and demolish their defences so as to deny their strategic value to the enemy. Of these the most heavily fortified location was Santa Cruz in the island of Tenerife. Here, as well as the castle of San Cristobal, a curtain wall furnished with sixteen stone towers flanked the seashore. British frigates had enjoyed previous successes on this coast, and recently had captured the French corvette *La Mutine*, leaving her hundred-strong crew stranded on the island.

Now there was news of the arrival at Tenerife of a bullion cargo from Manila in the huge armed merchantman *El Principe d'Asturias*. Admiral Jervis instructed Rear-Admiral Nelson to take possession of the port and the town of Santa Cruz and of any Spanish vessels he might find there. With the *Theseus* as his flagship, Admiral Jervis assigned to Nelson four ships of the line, the *Culloden* under Nelson's friend Captain Troubridge, the *Zealous* under young Samuel Hood, and two others of which one was the 50-gun *Apollion*, upgraded to bear the Rear-Admiral's pennant in view of her fine armament and reacquired turn of speed. Three ordinary frigates and a cutter called the *Fox* famous from her long service in the Mediterranean, were added as support vessels.

It took six days of hard sailing for the ships to reach the latitude of the Canary Islands, six days in which their commander, Admiral Nelson, had all the crews and the marines on deck, training at the guns and at the use of pikes and small arms. The squadron anchored just out of sight of the isle of Tenerife and its selected landing-parties were sent aboard the frigates who crept inshore, the larger vessels following behind. Once near the shore the men would be transferred to their own boats which had been towed behind the frigates. Hugo was a member of one of the landing parties; it was to be his first shore battle and he felt somewhat nervous as he clutched sword and pistol. Here his actions would be watched and commented upon not only by his own superiors, but they would be judged by the standards of their valiant chief, Rear-Admiral Nelson, with his battle-hardened status newly enhanced by his bravery at the Battle of Cape St. Vincent.

The first attack, by night, failed, for the boats were swept aside by a strong offshore current of whose existence Nelson had been unaware. The second attack, following on by daylight and supported by bombardment from the British squadron, also made little impression on the fortifications of Santa Cruz, and the boats' crews were now too exhausted to think of invading the town. The British forces were recalled and the squadron withdrew over the horizon and out of range of the Spanish guns. Nelson decided to attempt a third landing, by night and from the boats as before, but this time striking the shore beside the town and its mole rather than beneath the fortified towers to the west. In addition, with their scaling ladders they would attempt to overwhelm the Citadel whose garrison was thought to number only three hundred souls and poorly-led. Against this Nelson could pit a force of nearly a thousand seamen and marines.

The boats were divided into groups according to their ships' companies and were linked together by ropes so that they could not become separated in the darkness. Big John muttered to Hugo as they sat at their oars that he did not think such linkage served a useful purpose, since if one boat were sunk by a lucky shot they would all be thrown into the water before they could cast off the ropes. Hugo replied that he had espied the Rear-Admiral himself taking a place in his own leading barge and accompanied by his stepson Josiah Nisbet. Captain Sterne had remained aboard the *Apollion* both because the injury to his shoulder still prevented him from using his sword and because the commander had left him in charge of ensuring that every ship in the squadron maintained its allotted place in the plan of attack. Mr. Barber had accompanied them, however, and the dark silhouette of his bicorne hat could just be glimpsed at the bow of their boat.

On the fortifications ashore, a wide-awake sentry on the Paso Alto battery glimpsed foam from a splash of oars and alerted the Commandant-General, Don Antonio Gutierrez, a seasoned commander who had anticipated just such an attack. Aboard the huge bullion ship from Manila, which still lay at anchor in the bay, the Spaniards quietly primed their guns. The Paso Alto battery had the honour of firing the first shot, and the cutter *Fox* received a direct hit as cannon and musket fire thundered down upon the British forces from all sides. Nelson ordered his boat to land at the Mole and that all others should follow him. The Admiral scrambled ashore, drew his weapon, and was immediately hit in his sword arm. He reeled backwards, his stepson catching him as he fell. Josiah realised that his stepfather had received a serious injury and that he required immediate surgical treatment if his life was to be saved. He made a tourniquet out of his own stock and ordered the barge to pull away from the Mole. All around them the sea, lit up by flashes of cannonfire from ship and shore, seemed full of struggling figures, many from the *Fox* which had now sunk. Nelson, still conscious, insisted that any live casualties they encountered be pulled aboard his boat.

Josiah had the barge creep along the shoreline and out to sea until they reached the nearest ship, which happened to be the frigate *Seahorse* upon which the Admiral had dined with his captains just a few hours before. However Nelson knew that the pregnant wife of his friend Captain Fremantle was also aboard the vessel. He declared that he would not wish to scare her and that Josiah should seek out the *Theseus* instead. Maybe he also realised that the surgeon aboard the *Theseus*, Thomas Eshelby, would make a far better job of treating his shattered arm. The surgeon diagnosed "a compound fracture above the elbow caused by the passage of a musket ball". Painful amputation followed and opium was afterwards administered, being repeated nightly for some while.

In the meantime Hugo and the other members of the boats' crews were scrambling ashore wherever they could, some on the Mole and some on the beaches. The surf was strong and so was the offshore current. Confusion reigned since orders could not be heard amid the constant rattle of musket fire from the fortifications. Some took shelter among the port's warehouses where they were fired upon by the local residents - a much warmer reception than had been planned. Some boats were simply swept out to sea again, where they were vulnerable to cannon-fire from the guns of the Spanish militia, and also from French artillerymen still smarting from the loss of their ship *La Mutine*. The Enemy, now known to be some eight hundred strong, was hardly the weak force that Admiral Jervis's informants had promised.

Captain Troubridge led a group which took over a convent with thick inpenetrable walls, and from there attempted to negotiate with the Spanish Commandant. Then daylight revealed streets strewn with British dead and wounded, and a line of shattered boats still lying offshore where they had attempted to make a landing. Now it was a matter of seeking terms of surrender, to return to their ships with honour by promising not to attack the Canary Islands again. This being accepted, the seven hundred or so survivors were obliged to empty their weapons of ammunition and to apply for Spanish assistance in reaching their ships! The Spanish Commandant even entertained the defeated British captains to dinner; surely a doleful occasion!

And where was young Hugo Jarvis amongst all this mayhem? Big John, himself limping from a wound in his leg, searched for him among the alleys and squares of the town, to the accompaniment of loud hisses from the inhabitants lurking in their doorways and on their balconies. Then he searched along the shoreline where again he came upon the corpses of many fellow-seamen whom he recognised. Some of them moaned as he turned them over and Big John would then shout to the stretcher parties that had now been formed. The Spaniards insisted that the British clear their town and seafront of these unsightly corpses, so that those that had not already drowned in the bay were taken aboard and quietly weighted and slipped into the sea. Over one hundred and fifty men and officers had died, and others would not survive among the hundred or so wounded. Finally Big John, failing to find his protégé, made his way back to the Mole in order to embark in one of the borrowed Spanish boats along with others of the survivors. At the seaward end of the Mole there was a pile of corpses, among them those of several young lieutenants, Captain Bowen of the frigate *Terpsichore* and Captain Alastair Macdonald of the *Apollion*'s Marines.

A bare arm stretching out from beneath the pile caught Big John's eye, the fingers clutching at the wet seaweed that covered this part of the Mole. He ran to the spot as fast as his injured leg would carry him, and with all his strength turned over the pile of corpses, muttering apologies to his superior officers as he did so. He discovered young Hugo, intact but unconscious, and with a head wound acquired from a musket ball that had ploughed along his temple but had not penetrated his skull. Big John picked him up in his strong arms and carried him to the boats. Then he supervised personally the young man's return to the *Apollion* and safe delivery into the care of Mr. Dunstan. "And what about yourself, John? Are you not hit in the leg there?" the Surgeon asked. "Let me take a look at it." Indeed Big John had scarcely noticed the wound, so great had been his concern for the lad.

On the following morning, as the British fleet prepared to leave Tenerife, the body of Captain Bowen was lowered into the sea with full military honours, drums a-rolling and a salvo fired from the guns; it was a last token of respect for all those who had died. Admiral Nelson even exchanged diplomatic gifts with Commandant Gutierrez and offered to take his despatches to Cadiz! This was perhaps a measure of the guilt Nelson felt for proceeding with a land attack once the intelligence concerning the Enemy's strength and state of preparation had proved false.

As soon as Big John could free himself from his duties, he sought out Hugo in the sick-berth and found him sitting up in bed, pale and much bandaged, and rather depressed. Enquiring whether he was in pain, Hugo replied, "Not much, thanking you, but I am despondent indeed. When I came to myself after being hit, I found my pistol in my belt undischarged and my sword still in its sheath. John, I believe I had not struck a single blow for King and Country, but was thrown down as soon as I climbed up from the boat and never fought at all."

"Leastways, you're in good company," Big John replied, "for the very same thing happened to the Admiral. He got hit by a musket ball the moment he stepped ashore and has had to lose his right arm, poor devil."

"Oh, just like Pip Harris," Hugo murmured. He could not help remembering Melissa's words, 'To lose his right arm - how he going to do a job of work like that?' To lose a limb as a seaman was bad enough; Stan Stevenson had shown him that such a loss could be overcome, or at least survived, but a one-armed Admiral seemed to stretch the imagination a little too far. Indeed, in his cabin aboard the *Theseus*, Rear-Admiral Nelson's thoughts ran along much the same lines. After dictating his formal despatch to his secretary, he started writing painfully in a spidery left-hand script the accompanying personal note to Admiral Jervis in which he declared, "I am become a burthen to my friends and useless to my country" and felt that he should "make room for a better man to serve the State".

Admiral Jervis sent Nelson home to recuperate on the *Seahorse*, together with the wounded Captain Fremantle and his pregnant wife. No such pleasant denouement awaited young Hugo, for as soon as he was able to stand on his feet without feeling dizzy he was recalled to duty, bandages and all. In this he was one of many aboard the *Apollion*, both seamen and Marines. Even Mr. Barber had acquired additional injuries at Santa Cruz in the form of sabre cuts and slashes, so that he too was scarcely fit for duty.

The Tenerife squadron had rejoined the main Fleet outside Cadiz, but soon Admiral Jervis led them back to the mouth of the River Tagus, leaving Captain Collingwood in the *Excellent* and just a few support vessels to continue on watch. This move had been prompted by the unwelcome news that Portugal, Britain's last ally, had sued for peace with France and had been served with terms which the Portuguese government had yet to ratify. The Admiral's strategy was to be able to threaten a bombardment of Lisbon and its home fleet if ratification took place. At this time Britain faced attacks at sea not only from French and Spanish shipping, but also by the navies of all those European territories which had already submitted to the Revolutionary Army of France. For instance a Dutch fleet, hostile to Britain, was being equipped in the mouth of the River Texel and preparing to sail. Admiral Duncan, in charge of the Channel Fleet in the Downs, had his force reduced to only two ships of the line, the *Venerable* and the *Adamant*, due to the mutiny taking place at the Nore. With these two ships he tacked up and down off the Texel, making elaborate signals to an imaginary squadron such that he deterred the Dutch from putting to sea. Eventually the former mutineers sailed forth to join him just in time to defeat the Dutch in the Battle of Camperdown on 11 October 1797 and to send the Enemy scuttling back to port.

News of this victory reached Admiral Jervis in November at the same time as the less welcome tidings that Napoleon's defeat of the Austrians had led to the signature of the Treaty of Campo Formio and confirmation that the Austrian Netherlands (Belgium) now belonged to France. Britain was becoming increasingly isolated. It was in that month too that, while Admiral Jervis was awaiting the outcome of the possible defection of Portugal, a large fleet of East Indiamen, both British and Portuguese, appeared at the mouth of the Tagus. They were escorted into sheltered waters by two British frigates whose captains sent their respects to the Admiral and sought permission to proceed inshore. It seemed that the Portuguese convoy had been attacked by Spanish vessels off the Cape Verde Islands. The Spaniards had sunk or disabled the Portuguese escort ships and had carried off two of the Portuguese merchantmen with the most valuable cargoes. The British convoy had then appeared over the horizon and the Spaniards had withdrawn, though not before being chased and fired upon by the British frigates. The British commanders had offered their protection to the Portuguese ships and the combined fleet had reached the Tagus safely. Perceiving an excellent propaganda opportunity, Admiral Jervis welcomed the Portuguese captains aboard his flagship and made sure they informed their Government of the vital assistance rendered them by the British Navy.

Then the Admiral visited each of the escorting British frigates. The better one he decided to retain to support his Atlantic Fleet, after which he ordered Captain Sterne to take that frigate's place with the *Apollion* and to escort the British East Indiamen back to England. They were going home at last! All their Marines were due for home leave anyway, said Admiral Jervis as he welcomed Captain Sterne aboard his flagship and informed him that he was putting aboard the *Apollion* those of his officers and sailors who had been seriously injured at Santa Cruz or elsewhere and had not yet been able to resume their duties. The Admiral was sending them home as a hospital ship rather than as an object of glory! They would shepherd the East Indiamen into the Thames estuary and leave them to make their way to Limehouse where the Company was building extensive new docks. The *Apollion* would slip into Chatham Dockyard whence the sick could be tended, the disabled pensioned off, and the able could claim the back pay and prize money due to them after their long voyage.

Hugo knew exactly what he wished to do, to make a brief visit home to see his family, and then to return to sea again as quickly as possible. Captain Sterne invited Hugo to his cabin as the *Apollion* moved slowly landwards from Sheerness. He enquired Hugo's age and when told that he would soon celebrate his sixteenth birthday, replied that he thought him sufficiently skilled and experienced to take the examination to make lieutenant, even though he was officially short in years, though not in physical strength and appearance. The rule laid down by the Navy Board, as Captain Sterne reminded Hugo, was a minimum of six years at sea, but this could be and often was varied when a candidate was put forward upon a strong personal recommendation. Hugo already had a letter of recommendation signed by Admiral Jervis with whom, Captain Sterne indicated, with just the merest hint of exaggeration, he had discussed his plan to furnish Hugo with a substantial recommendation of his own detailing Hugo's extensive and varied experience at sea aboard the *Apollion*.

Captain Sterne pointed out that once Hugo gained the qualification he would face a much better prospect of a career in the Navy and would have some element of choice of the vessels upon which he served. In fact. Captain Sterne told him gently, it was unlikely that either of them would serve on the *Apollion* again, and that he should say farewell to her and to his shipmates. Hugo took his Captain's advice.

CHAPTER XV

The Tiger's Lair

"It is better to live a day as a lion, than a lifetime as a sheep."
Tipu Sultan, Seringapatam, India, 1799.

In the City of Calcutta it was the middle of April and the hot winds of the dry season had begun to blow. It was a Sunday afternoon, a day of rest for European civil servants, and Ainsworth Rich was stretched out at full length upon the large sofa in the front room of his lodging. The windows which faced the street and the oven-hot breeze were closed, as well as the louvred wooden shutters outside which let in the merest modicum of daylight. Ainsworth's chemise was open wide at the neck above the loose white nankeen trousers which he and many others in the Indian Service had adopted for summer wear. His shoes and stockings lay upon the floor where he had thrown them, and the cushion beneath his head was moist with sweat. He had taken an opium pill and had reached "that happy state of inanition that is the only resource for hastening the lagging foot of time," as Mary Sherwood was to express the matter some years later. Above his head a punkah, operated by a silent coolie, waved back and forth, wafting in water-cooled air from the street doorway which was open and equipped with a tatti or mat of khus-grass kept wet by yet another coolie seated outside in the shade of the porch.

And there was the rub - Finance. Each of the coolies, though Anando had hired them just for the day, would expect a few annas upon his departure at night, and Ainsworth doubted if his purse contained even sufficient coins to pay them. His journey to Lucknow and back, and his resultant fever, had allowed his salary to accumulate such that he had been able to manage most of his expenses except part of the rent, and for that he still owed Mr. Biswas an ever-increasing amount. On his return to the Writers' Building he had been interviewed once more by Henry Bonnay who, after congratulating him on his recovery and on his rescue of David Lambton, which had by then become common gossip, informed him that the Governor, Sir John Shore, had discovered that Ainsworth had never been obliged to pass the accounting examination that was the basic qualification for employment in the Civil Service of the East India Company. Due to Ainsworth's superior age, and because Sir Charles Rich had been able to obtain for him a personal recommendation from Henry Dundas as President of the Board of Control, he had been placed in the Head Clerk's office rather than among the juniors and apprentices in the rest of the huge Writers' Building. These were no more than eighteen years of age, or younger, and yet had all passed the same examination in England before despatch to India. It happened that David Lambton was in the same position as Ainsworth, having travelled to India directly after graduating from Oxford and before deciding to seek employment with the Company. The pair of them were sent to receive tuition from a Senior Clerk in another part of the building. Both passed the test easily and were gratified to find their pay advanced to one hundred and fifty rupees per month as a result.

That had helped a little, Ainsworth mused, but it had not solved the problem. Moreover Henry Bonnay had said that if they wished to progress in their careers the Governor required them to start learning some of the local languages, Hindi - or Hindustani as it was known then, Bengali which was spoken in business and commercial circles in Calcutta, and Persian which was the language of the Moghul princes and the nawabs with whom the senior officers of the Company were used to deal and negotiate. As yet there was no language school provided in Calcutta, though there was talk of a need for one. Instead, back in the 1780s Sir John Shore had been one of the founders together with Sir William Jones of the Asiatick Society of Bengal, a philosophical and philological gathering of intellectuals interested in the study of Indian cultures and religions. Henry Bonnay informed Ainsworth that the Secretary of that Society, the painter Robert Home, held a list of recommended munshis or teachers who would impart to the more aspiring among the young writers a working knowledge of the required tongue. But which to choose and at what expense? Should he study Persian, the language of princes, when it would be years before he would be permitted to deal with them, or Hindi which was the common language of large sections of the population and in particular of the Sepoys of the Company's army with which as yet he had no connection but which might be useful in the event of further expeditions like that to Lucknow, or Bengali which would at least permit him to give more precise attention to Anando and to communicate more effectively with his Banker, his Landlord and, in his mind most importantly, with his Tailor! Ainsworth decided upon the last one and would share his lessons with his friend David who had come to the same conclusion.

But there was still the expense of tuition and the interruption of his leisure hours, those evenings that he valued for their social opportunities, the soirées of the cool season where he was beginning to meet some of the leading administrators and their wives, and some of the local characters, such as William Hickey, Attorney to the native citizens of Calcutta. He had buried his English wife years ago in the nearby cemetery and now consorted with an Indian lady called Jemdanee, who was merry and bright, and scandalously sat and joked with the gentlemen after dinner whilst they drank port and smoked cigars or the hookah bubble pipe with its fragrance of rose-water and cinnamon.

There was backgammon, and board games galore, for everyone played, the ladies usually preferring five-card Loo, whilst the gentlemen, especially the officers of the garrison at Fort William and their current Commander-in-Chief, Colonel George Harris, usually favoured Tredrille, a gambling game which had many similarities with Faro. Ainsworth was still cautious about gambling for high stakes; he had taken Henry Bonnay's warning about indebtedness to heart, and often preferred to listen instead to Colonel Harris's tales of the battles he had fought in the South alongside Lord Cornwallis against Tipu Sultan, "The Tiger of Mysore", and how at his defeat in 1792 the Sultan had delivered up to his Lordship his two young sons as hostages for his future good behaviour. To listen to Colonel Harris one would think he had won all those battles single-handed, rather than fighting alongside a galaxy of other distinguished military figures, some of whom visited Calcutta from time to time.

Then there was the consumption, at others' expense, if Ainsworth could arrange it, of good British beer, bottled and shipped out from England, of malmsey wine at one rupee the bottle, or even claret at a rupee and a half, (there were approximately 8 rupees to the pound sterling). Ainsworth particularly enjoyed riding out to Baranset of a cool Sunday in winter where the military cadets had set up a drinking and gaming club. He had negotiated a favourable rate with his landlord, Mr. Biswas, whereby he might use the services of his younger son Ajoy to run with his horse as he rode, as every other gentleman did. Ajoy would then take care of the creature while he played cards, not winning much for the stakes were low, and then, when he was almost too drunk to keep the saddle, Ajoy would see him safely home.

There was also the occasional ball given during the winter season, as well as theatrical performances now and again, but the latter were put on only by amateurs from among the European staff where the most attractive young male writers took the female parts. The balls were for meeting and dancing with young ladies who were the daughters of his superiors, and Ainsworth had little fancy for that anyway. As for young Ajoy, he had not yet taken him into his household, though there were times when he was tempted to do so, but in truth he could not see how he might bribe someone in Company service to employ Ajoy's elder brother as 'babu', even though Mr. Biswas had become quite pressing on the matter. Ainsworth wondered whether he might eventually persuade Mr. Biswas to forgo his debt, or even to agree to a reduced rent in future, in exchange for finding the right opening for the landlord's ambitious son.

Meanwhile public events were developing in Bengal and other parts of India which were soon to shape Ainsworth's life and to draw his thoughts away from personal minutiae to the wider scene. Sir John Shore, the present Governor-General of British India, had himself joined the East India Company's service as a 'writer' in 1769 the year of Ainsworth's birth. There he had become fascinated by the revenue system, had profited from it like Robert Clive, but had also written copiously to the Company's Court of Directors at Leadenhall Street, London, recommending its reform. This had earned him a place on the governing

Revenue Councils of several districts, including that at Murshidabad where he served as Persian translator at the court of the Nawab of Bengal, and in 1775 on the Supreme Council at Calcutta under Governor-General Warren Hastings who despatched him to make revenue settlements in Patna and Dacca. John Shore returned to England when Warren Hastings was recalled in 1785 and he later spoke in his Governor's defence at Hastings' trial for impeachment.

However when Lord Cornwallis, a military man with no special knowledge of the complex revenue systems of India, was appointed Governor-General in 1786, the Company requested that John Shore be sent out to assist him. He returned to India in April of that year, leaving behind his new bride, Charlotte Cornish of Teignmouth, Devon. Whilst working for Lord Cornwallis, John Shore reorganised and simplified the revenue systems of Bengal, giving primary responsibility to the traditional zamindars and avoiding such complexities as making direct arrangements with the individual ryots. He had a reputation for integrity, and it was perhaps of his prompting that the Regulating Act of 1793 forbade private trading by the Company's employees. Having returned to England in 1790 with a comfortable pension, John Shore was surprised to be asked to go back again in 1792 in the supreme position of Governor-General. The request came from Henry Dundas himself, accompanied by a baronetcy. This must have been one of the reasons why Sir John took note when the same source recommended to his service one Ainsworth Rich.

In fact Sir John had returned to Calcutta but two years before Ainsworth's arrival. He was much interested in religion and something of an evangelist. Of the close friends he had made in India, one was Sir William Jones of the Asiatick Society, whilst another was Charles Grant who, in the following century, was to arouse much antipathy by his campaign to evangelise the Indian nation, this being one of the many causes behind the Great Mutiny in the middle of that century. Sir John himself, after his eventual retirement as Lord Teignmouth, became President of the British & Foreign Bible Society. Thus it was no wonder that he had insisted on attendance at church by the Company's staff at Calcutta, Ainsworth Rich and all the junior writers included.

Once installed as Governor-General, Sir John had continued with the revenue reforms instituted under Lord Cornwallis. One of the guiding principles he followed in order to reduce financial corruption was to separate the zamindars from their judicial functions as local justices. Under the previous Indian justice system, the accused would pay a large bribe to the judge, as would his accuser, and the judge was obliged to return the bribe given by the losing party! Such a system had given the zamindars extensive powers of life and death over those ryots in their debt. Sir John's policy, backed by Lord Cornwallis in the 1780s and by the Board of Control under Henry Dundas in the 1790s, was to agree clear and permanent tax arrangements with the zamindars and to install senior civil servants as magistrates, where they wielded absolute but impersonal power, often merely assisted by an interpreter.

As with any 'new broom', Sir John created enemies, and in the period follow-ing Ainsworth's arrival in Calcutta there surfaced a rumour amongst the officers in the Company's army that the corrupt means whereby they had subsidised their pay hitherto were to be swept away. Mutinous action seemed imminent when Sir John improved army pay and permitted the officers to continue to apply for extra expenses. The rumour died away and the Board of Control in London, which had been about to send out Lord Cornwallis to restore order, was duly satisfied. By this time Ainsworth and his friend David Lambton had perfect-ed their studies in Bengali to the point where Ainsworth was given such tasks as translating into that language Government instructions for the information and guidance of the general public. Their fluency allowed them to travel widely with-in Bengal and to participate in the settlement of disputes involving the various native zamindars. They wrote their own despatches and yes, they collected their own fees. Suddenly life for Ainsworth was a little easier. He had paid off his debts and now Mr. Biswas would be obliged to make him an offer!

Late in the autumn of 1797 news reached Calcutta of the death at Lucknow after a long illness of the Nawab, Asaf-ud-Daula of Oudh, he who had been such a loyal ally as well as a fruitful source of revenue for the East India Company. The Nawab had been buried in his spectacular Imambara mausoleum with great cer-emony, a procession of a thousand trumpets, a hundred elephants complete with lofty howdahs and trappings of gold, of wives and dancing girls, some of whom then immolated themselves in despair at his death, and much genuine sorrow since it was felt that he had been a father to his people. The Company's Resident at Lucknow had previously reported that Sa'adat Ali Khan, the Nawab's younger half-brother, had seemed likely to succeed as Nawab and was the most suitable person to do so. Moreover, although many royal children claimed Asaf-ud-Daula as their father, including Wazir Ali Khan whose extravagant wedding in 1795 had alerted the Company to his unsuitability as a potential successor, it had been widely known in palace circles that a devotion to the effects of powerful drugs and an excessive attention to sexual activity in his younger days had rendered Asaf-ud-Daula impotent. This last opinion emanated from one Major-General Claude Martin, formerly a French cavalry officer, who had entered the service of the East India Company and who had long been installed at Lucknow as the Nawab's Superintendent of Artillery. He had even obtained the Nawab's permis-sion to build himself a palace and had had constructed a vast castellated man-sion which he called 'Constantia'. So when Claude Martin sent word that Wazir Ali Khan was about to seize the throne, Sir John Shore took this news very seri-ously indeed.

Earlier in the year Colonel George Harris, the great raconteur, had been pro-moted Major-General and moved to Madras. In his stead had arrived Sir Alured Clarke, previously Commander-in-Chief at Madras and already a military leader of repute, in that on his way out to India in 1795 he had assisted Lord Keith in wresting the Cape of Good Hope from the Dutch, thus safeguarding Britain's sea route to India. Sir Alured had been appointed Commander-in-Chief, initially for Bengal, though later for all British India, and a member of the Supreme Council in Calcutta. His appointment owed much to a general tightening up of British control not only through Lord Cornwallis's reforms, but also militarily due to the increased threat from France to Britain's trade and territories. Sir Alured had therefore just the qualities of courage and sound military leadership upon which the Governor-General might rely to accomplish a difficult and dangerous task, namely to depose Wazir Ali Khan and to replace him with the Company's choice as the next Nawab of Oudh.

In order not to deprive Fort William entirely of its military garrison and Calcutta of its protection against, say, a French attack from the sea, only a small force of one hundred mounted Sepoys could be spared for the task, together with their complement of European officers. It was estimated that Claude Martin would be able to call upon similar forces among native troops at Lucknow likely to be loyal both to the Company and to the memory of their dead Nawab. To create as strong an impression as possible, the leaders would ride upon two elephants, Sir John and his secretary Hubert Cornish in one char-jarma or travelling howdah, and Sir Alured Clarke with his secretary Neil Edmonstone, a senior Persian translator from the Calcutta secretariat, in the other. Henry Bonnay was also to be of the party as the best all-round linguist in the Calcutta service and because of his experience in negotiating with all degrees of persons from peasants to princes. Mr. Bonnay would travel in one of the ox-drawn supply waggons due to a recent leg injury and was to bring with him those secretarial and scriptorial necessities likely to be required, as well as any assistants he needed, so long as they were able to defend themselves against hostile attack. Who was he to choose among the more senior clerks but Ainsworth and his friend David Lambton? They had visited Lucknow before and knew its lay-out in the event of ambush; they had met Claude Martin on that occasion, as well as many of the British officers; they had recently returned to the Baranset barracks for further military training; and they were learning Hindi,in addition to their competency in Bengali, which was spoken by most of the bearers and servants who accompanied the force. They would ride on horseback, along with the soldiers, and could keep an eye on Sir John's twenty-one year old nephew, also called Hubert Cornish, who was fresh out from England and would be left at the Residency in Benares (Varanasi) on their return journey where he was to start work as a writer. Taking into account their supply waggons and a large number of remounts to replace the Indian horses every few miles, it was an impressive cavalcade which left Calcutta that November, after the end of the rains and in the cooler weather of approaching winter.

Their route along the eastern shore of the River Hugli followed that with which Ainsworth and David were already familiar from their previous journey to Lucknow. At the town of Hugli camp was made, and while tiffin was served to the troops and the junior staff, the Governor, the Commander-in-Chief, their respective secretaries and Henry Bonnay were ferried across the river to the Residence. It had been decided that the column would not cross the river here, but upstream at Murshidabad where they would need to visit the Nawab of Bengal in his island city. What Governor-General could dream of passing by without paying the Nawab a courtesy call? However the fact was that the Nawab owed the Company a considerable amount of revenue. Now Nujam-ud-Daula was famous for the quality of the fighting elephants which were bred and displayed at his court. The Governor planned to offer His Highness a discount on his debt if he would supply him with a pair of magnificent tuskers, docile enough and fit enough to be ridden to Lucknow, where the Governor might present them to the new Nawab of Oudh, without mentioning, of course, whether that was to be Wazir Ali or anyone else.

The City of Murshidabad occupied an island in the middle of the Hugli. The waters surrounding it ran into broad lagoons and shallows, one of these being so still and reflective as to be known as the Lake of Pearls. It is a place of legends and an abode of spirits, but at the time of Ainsworth's visit the town was a citadel of small houses and narrow streets, save for the one broad avenue leading up to the old palace. It was here that the Nawab would greet his guests. An encampment was set up on the banks of the Hugli and Henry Bonnay, who knew the Nawab of old, was sent across the river like a medieval herald to announce the Governor's approach, even though the Nawab was able to observe it quite plainly from the palace window where he had set up the telescope the Governor had presented to him on a previous occasion. It was important to follow all the usual diplomatic niceties, especially when asking a favour. This also gave the Nawab time to make his own arrangements, to have his wives dressed in their best, and sumptuous dishes prepared for his guests' repast.

Thus by the time the Governor and the rest of his party, as well as the cavalcade of troops and the baggage train, had all crossed the river, the avenue was crowded with people. Girls threw handfuls of rose petals from balconies draped with swathes of silk, and banners flew from every turret. A company of uniformed drummers and pipers met the visitors at the waterfront and filed beside them along the avenue, protecting them from the enthusiasm of the crowd. Then the Nawab actually descended from his throne and met them upon the steps of the Hall of Audience with mutual bowing and shaking of hands, a signal mark of friendship and respect. "Gosh, the Governor must have promised him a sizeable rebate indeed," was David Lambton's whispered comment to his friend.

The Nawab led the Governor back to the Throne Room, seated himself cross-legged on the scarlet cushion that filled the chair, and allowed the Governor to introduce to him Sir Alured Clarke as his new military chief. In turn the Nawab called forth his senior wife, his newest wife and his eldest son. Henry Bonnay and his assistants stood immediately behind the Governor, together with the two secretaries and the Governor's nephew. All were introduced, the senior employees by name, the assistants by their function, save young Hubert Cornish who was given special mention. The Nawab's Vizier, who had been supervising the preparation of the feast, then appeared to announce its completion. He too was introduced to the guests so that he might conduct them to the appropriate seating upon the many cushions that surrounded the rows of long low tables. Ainsworth noted that whilst he and David had been placed sympathetically among the damsels of the court, the Governor's nephew had been seated beside the Nawab's son, who was presently overheard enquiring about the education that Hubert had received at his English school and at university. It was a splendid scene, the laden tables, the courtiers in their swathes of brilliant silk and satin contrasting with the Company personnel in their dark blue cutaway coats with gilt buttons, or gold buttons and gold epaulettes in the case of the Governor, and the dark crimson of Sir Alured Clarke's uniform with the its gold braiding, and white waistcoat, shirt and breeches common to all the Company's officers. Behind the guests stood the waiters in their flat turbans and pale kaftans with bright silk sashes. Beyond them again stood the torchbearers, lighting up the lofty walls of the damask-draped room.

The refreshments ended, the central tables were borne away and hookahs appeared in the carpeted circle between the male guests as the ladies of the court withdrew. Ainsworth and David drew at the hookah with the rest, but it was young Hubert's first experience of the article and the others looked on with amusement as he choked upon it to begin with. Half an hour later there came a blast of distant trumpets from the end of the Palace garden. A host of glowing torches led the way through the formal garden with its clipped bushes, pools and fountains, to the balustrade on its far side overlooking the river. Here the resinous torches were slid into iron sconces set upon stone pillars so that the leaping flames could light up the shoreline below. The Nawab's elephants were about to fight!

In the silence that followed a fanfare of trumpets, there came a shuffling of cushioned feet upon the path beside the gardens. The torchlight disclosed dim forms in the shadows as a long line of elephants came through the high arch at one end of the courtyard and exited through the arch at the far end which led down to the shore. The beasts wore trappings from head to tail, with saddlecloths, and head-shields of gilt metal which reflected the golden glow of the torchlight. Each carried two mahouts, one on the neck of the elephant and one on the saddlecloth, each with his feet hooked through the trappings, and each carried an ankus or goad, a spiked metal rod hooked at one end. The elephants paraded several times before the audience, the Nawab and his honoured guests seated upon a dais, the rest, women as well as men, pressing forward to peer over the balustrade.

Then the elephants formed up in two lines stretching from the wall of the garden to the river, their headshields twinkling like rows of lamps in the darkness. These, Ainsworth deduced, were to constitute the borders of the battleground.

Then he noticed that part of the shore beneath them was occupied by a wall constructed of mud bricks, stretching again towards the river from the place on the balcony where the Nawab sat, though there were gaps in it at either end through which the elephants had paraded, and a smaller gap in the middle whose significance he had yet to appreciate.

There came another fanfare of trumpets and two more elephants appeared, but separately so that when paraded on the shore they passed by at opposite ends of the mud brick wall. These were Koomeriah elephants, the Nawab's son whispered to them as he sat watching with Ainsworth, David and Hubert standing beside him, princely elephants bred specially for royal festivals and for the fight. They were to be distinguished by their size and bulk, he continued, their shorter back legs denoting forward strength, and by their heavier trunks which formed a valuable weapon. These two were exceptionally well-bred, he told them proudly, the backs of their ears being marked by many pink and white blotches. These elephants wore neither saddlecloth nor head-guard, and the purpose of the spare mahout, the prince explained, was in case the first one fell off and was trampled to death!

The two beasts were brought to a halt, one either side of the gap in the centre of the low wall. Both threw up their heads and trumpeted loudly, then tried to thrust at one another through the narrow gap. Their tusks, which had been trimmed at the ends and bound with bangles of gold, now served as formidable slashing blades. The huge uplifted trunks pressed forward against each other as both animals strove to push through the gap, goaded on by their shouting mahouts and encouraged by the partisan crowd who had taken bets on the outcome. Suddenly the bricks of the wall began to give way and one of the tuskers pushed himself through. The other resisted him still, though blood ran down his legs from several slash wounds in his chest. Then he turned and ran into the river. The victor would have followed him but was held back at the shoreline by elephants from the edge of the 'ring'.

There was a round of shouts and applause, then sweetmeats and fresh juices were served whilst the mud bricks were replaced and two new contestants were selected. Ainsworth thought privately that the scene had reminded him of some fat Japanese wrestlers he had watched in the East End of London. By contrast David Lambton remarked to the prince that he thought it a shame to see such noble beasts made to fight, and was told that they were chosen to do so when in musth and were well-primed beforehand with opium and with arrack, the intoxicating palm wine. Two more contests followed before the evening's entertainment concluded. Ainsworth and David took their leave of the prince and looked for young Hubert who had slipped away upon the arrival of the second pair of fighting elephants. It seemed he had been quietly sick.

Next day Sir John and his party were taken to visit the elephant stables and various Koomeriah-bred beasts were paraded for the Governor's selection. Ainsworth noticed that none of the creatures exhibited bore signs of the evening's injuries, so he concluded that either those contestants had been slaughtered or they were kept elsewhere. Two of the largest elephants were chosen for Sir John and then it was merely a question of the price. The Governor, Sir Alured and Henry Bonnay retired into a small saloon to discuss Company business with the Nawab, whilst his son escorted the younger members of staff across the river to the Garden of Happiness to inspect the tomb of Siraj-ud-Daula, he of the Black Hole of Calcutta. Ainsworth could not suppress a shiver at his proximity to the last resting-place of the tyrant, but the prince was proud of his father's predecessor and disclosed that the Nawab proposed to be buried beside him. The Nawab also planned to build a new palace upon a nearby hill, though at present the project was stalled for want of funds.

The Governor's cavalcade left Murshidabad the next day and proceeded to Patna via Bhagalpur. There they renewed their supplies, left the most worn of the horses in exchange for some fresh ones, and halted for two days of rest and entertainment for the troops and of wining and dining at the Residency for the officers and staff. This time the force did not proceed up the River Gomti to Lucknow, but continued along the banks of the Ganges to Benares (Varanasi) in order to collect the latest despatches sent there by Claude Martin. Ainsworth suspected that the Governor also wished to give his nephew a chance to inspect his new workplace so that he could decide upon acceptance whilst riding on overland to Lucknow.

At Benares the Company staff were taken to the Residency whilst the military contingent organised the crossing of the river by raft with their horses, oxen, waggons, servants and finally the four elephants. The last caused the most trouble, refusing to swim as was usual, or to board any vessel where the deck was not covered by a thick mat of earth and rushes. In the end a boat laden with fruit and sweet things had to be towed across the river ahead of each raft and the elephant rewarded when it reached the far bank. At the Residency the Governor was greeted warmly by the incumbent, Mr. George Cherry, who already knew Sir Alured Clarke since both had previously served in Madras where Mr. Cherry had been Persian secretary to Lord Cornwallis. Sir John was familiar to him for the same reason. The secretarial staff were new to him, however, as was young Hubert Cornish, and the meeting would provide both of them with an opportunity to assess suitability. Mr. Cherry then introduced the visitors to Mr. Samuel Davis of the Bengal Engineers who was serving as a district judge under the new system developed by Sir John. He and his family were presently lodging at the Residency whilst more suitable accommodation was being prepared for them in the town.

After refreshments Mr. Cherry took the Governor and Sir Alured into his office to show them the despatches received from Lucknow. Those from Claude Martin disclosed that Wazir Ali Khan was indeed 'already disporting himself upon the Nawab's throne' - the exact import of his choice of words would later become clear, whilst the Resident there added that he had been approached direct by

Sa'adat Ali Khan with an assurance of his loyalty to the Company and a request for any help which that body might provide, whether by military assistance or diplomacy, that might restore him to what he was convinced was his rightful inheritance.

Their onward journey to Lucknow was much disturbed by banditry. Night after night the howling of the jackals or the cough of a leopard betrayed the presence of dacoits and they had to contend with several ambushes in which bullets flew and many Sepoys and some officers were wounded and one killed. Henry Bonnay opined that Wazir Ali Khan had got word of their arrival and intentions and had sent out agents provocateurs to harrass them. When they reached Lucknow there was no fanfare of trumpets to greet the Governor-General as there had been at Murshidabad. Instead the Company garrison led by Major-General Martin appeared to escort them to the Residency and to the cantonment grounds. A similar local troop was detailed to escort Mr. Bonnay to the palace where he was to present the Governor's compliments to Wazir Ali Khan and request an audience.

Claude Martin had noted the two Koomeriah elephants which the Governor had brought and as soon as the staff were within doors at the Residency, he drew Sir Alured aside and murmured, "I doubt that Prince Wazir Ali will be much impressed by a gift of elephants, even of prime fighting ones. You must know that some twelve hundred elephants were assembled for the man's wedding, and a hundred of those bore howdahs covered with silver. The prince himself rode upon the neck of a huge Koomeriah all decked out with solid gold!" Claude Martin also had messages for Ainsworth and David from the friends they had made during their previous visit, and a farewell note for Ainsworth from Richard F., whose regiment had just been posted to Delhi and replaced by one from Hyderabad. Thus the Company's Sepoys available at Lucknow to carry out any military operations were new and untried; it was not certain that they would back the Company's choice of Nawab rather than this showy Prince.

News of the Governor-General's arrival was despatched to Sa'adat Ali Khan at the same time as Henry Bonnay returned from the palace. He had been informed that 'His Highness is sleeping', even though it was well past midday and had been met only by the Vizier. However he was advised that an entertainment was planned for that evening, and if the Governor were agreeable he might care to attend, accompanied by just his senior staff. Sir Alured thought there was a risk that the Prince might have arranged an ambush, so had the Company's troops placed on alert in their cantonment. He had the five secretarial staff carry pistols concealed at the back of their waistbands, and took along two very tall turbaned Sikhs from his own personal bodyguard. The guards at the palace gate looked up at the tall Sikhs and allowed the group to pass unmolested. They approached the steps of the Hall of Audience but found the Throne standing empty and with various courtiers lounging here and there in attitudes of boredom and listlessness. The Vizier appeared and hurried towards them. "His Highness begs you will excuse him," he said. "He plans to take part in the entertainment himself and is completing his toilette. His Highness requests that you please be seated upon the dais at his right side," he continued, motioning them towards the seats in question.

Henry Bonnay had already informed his colleagues that the entertainment was to be a "nautch".

"What is a nautch?" Hubert whispered as they sat.

"A performance by dancing girls in pretty costumes," David Lambton replied. "You will find that very popular at most of the Mughal courts." Ainsworth had just resigned himself to an evening of incomparable boredom when the dancing troupe entered and he sat up very straight indeed. As the musicians at the far side of the hall struck up a rhythmic melody, a troupe of gaily-costumed figures tripped lightly forward to take their places before the Throne. There were the flowing skirts, the gauzy scarves, the beading of tinkling coins, the painted toes and hands beringed with jewels, the high headdresses and the flashing dark eyes. The leader of the troupe was especially agile, leaping from one flexible ankle to the other, the hands and wrists weaving an intricate dance of their own above the head. Suddenly the leader broke from the rest of the troupe, ran lightly up the steps and leapt upon the Throne. As one, the Europeans suddenly realised that this dancer was Wazir Ali himself, dressed as a woman, and as one they rose to make him a formal bow. In reply, Wazir Ali Khan parted his garments before them and exposed his genitals.

Sir John Shore, shocked and insulted, sat down rather sharply, his cheeks flushed. The others followed and returned their gaze to the dancing girls. "Gosh!" David Lambton exclaimed quite audibly, "they're all fellows!"

It was not a pleasant evening for most of them, except perhaps for Ainsworth who might have confessed to some tingle of excitement at watching these lithe young men perform their intricate movements. Refreshments followed, but Wazir Ali had vanished and it was left to Claude Martin to escort them around the public rooms of the Palace and to introduce to them the few of Asaf-ud-Daula's staff who remained in place. The Governor was visibly upset, and Claude Martin murmured to him, "Well, I did use the word 'disporting' in my despatches, and took it that you would understand what form of debauchery was intended. I should warn you that no-one has set eyes on Wazir Ali's bride since the day they wed, but palace rumour has it that he beats her every evening before retiring to bed with one of those dancing boys."

"We must consult urgently with Sa'adat Ali Khan," the Governor replied, "so let us ensure we may visit him tomorrow."

In order to disguise their intent the following morning, the Company personnel walked as a group towards the Palace compound, as if they were merely sightseeing in the cool of the morning air. The subsidiary palace where Sa'adat Ali Khan lived was within sight of the Royal Palace, but its street door lay on the far side. As that doorway was reached the Governor, Sir Alured and Henry Bonnay

slipped inside, being almost pulled within by the sentries who had been instructed how to recognise them. The remaining staff continued nonchalantly upon
their way, presently being joined by three British officers from the cantonment,
also dressed in dark cutaway coats, one even bearing gold epaulettes, so that to
the casual observer the group remained identical to that which had passed by the
Palace gates. After resting awhile at the river bank and taking refreshment there,
they strolled back again and spent the rest of the day among the Sepoy troops
where the young secretariat put in some target practice. It was not until after
dark that their seniors rejoined the group and all returned to the Residency with
an escort from the Regiment.

None but the three participants knew the content of their counsel with
Sa'adat Ali Khan, but the Regiment were given orders to strike camp before dawn
and that Claude Martin would supply a special escort of loyal Sepoys to guard
their progress as far as Benares. Major-General Martin left them after supper, and
rumour had it that it was his intention to guide the forces of Sa'adat Ali Khan
through the intricacies of the private quarters of the Palace. It was not until
Claude Martin's fusilliers joined them in the twilight before dawn on the road
out of Lucknow that the junior staff realised that the hooded figure, hunched in
the saddle with his feet shackled to the girths of his mount, was in fact the prince
Wazir Ali Khan!

Behind them the city was awakening to a chaos of rumour and confusion, as
people thronged the streets demanding to know what had happened. Sounds of
lamentation were to be heard emanating from the Palace, but nobody knew who
had died. There were no guards at the gates, so the citizens began to wander into
the Palace grounds. Here and there they found a discarded sandal or turban, a
broken talwar, a pool of blood. Closer they pressed to the royal buildings. Bodies
lay strewn in the Hall of Audience. These were turned over and were soon identified as guards or eunuchs. Had there been a Revolution? Who would give them
an answer? It seemed that all not dead had fled, and they pressed on through the
empty rooms, picking up a jewel here, a bauble there, a fine stool overturned in
the way of someone's flight. The sounds of lamentation came from the Harem,
it would appear, but who would dare to enter and discover what had happened?
Then they found the double doors of the Harem standing open, a huddle of wailing women inside, and in the middle of the floor on a raised slab of cold marble
the body of a young woman, face down and naked. From the stripes of raw flesh
upon her back it would appear that she had been beaten, often and with violence, and from the bruising of her buttocks anyone wise enough would realise
that she had been cruelly buggered to death!

But who had done such a thing? What criminal had slain the princess? And
where was her husband? Not the most meticulous of searches could discover
him. The crowd moved on, seeking to exit from the Palace on the far side of its
courtyard. There the gates lay open wide again, and beside them another body.
They turned it over; it was the Prince's Vizier. Now there was no-one left in

authority, none to guide them and serve as 'the father of the People'. But wait, another royal figure lived nearby, Prince Sa'adat Ali Khan, he who had been half-brother to their beloved Nawab, Asaf-ud-Daula. Perhaps he would take charge of the situation and give them guidance. The mob turned the street corner and gathered outside his doors. These were locked and barred, and two very tall guards armed with British muskets stood impassively before them. One of the crowd stepped forth and enquired for the Prince. "His Highness is sleeping, shh!" the guards commanded, rattling their muskets as they made to push back the crowd.

Then a figure appeared on the balcony. It was Sa'adat Ali Khan himself, dressed in a European night-shirt - no one was to guess that beneath it he was fully clothed and ready to fight or flee as the occasion offered. Instead he hushed the crowd and asked would someone please inform him what had occurred that they should disturb his peace so early in the morning. Some tried to describe what they had seen, but as if he could not make head nor tail of it he offered to dress in a hurry and come with them to the Palace. They bore him with them, chattering away as they went. He observed each scenario as if it were news, and when they came to the Harem, whose doors still stood wide open, he refused to enter. Instead he sent for his senior wife and her ladies, and his own Vizier who had followed the crowd in order to protect his master, began organising the retrieval and identification of the bodies and the cleansing of the Palace yard. In the afternoon Sa'adat Ali Khan found himself installed as the new Nawab by popular acclaim, and that evening, after supper, he had time to inspect the Royal Stables and the two huge Koomeriah elephants which had just been delivered there from the cantonment over by the Company's Residency.

Meanwhile the Governor's cavalcade was riding briskly through the hills towards Benares. The ox-waggons full of supplies had been sent ahead by a few hours but were soon overtaken. In fact the threat of ambush by dacoits inclined them not to separate themselves too far from their commissariat, for these were barren hills where no other food source was available. Indeed they were followed and harrassed, but to little effect for their number being swollen by the additional troops from Lucknow deterred such attacks. More worrying was the reaction to be received from Claude Martin's native troops and from the Company Sepoys fresh from Hyderabad upon learning that their hooded captive was none other than Wazir Ali Khan. Sir Alured posted his guards very carefully each night and himself hardly slept at all. Every mile they advanced towards the banks of the Ganges increased their safety, but it was a nerve-racking journey.

At Benares the prisoner was locked in a tower forming part of the city walls near the Residency. The troops were encamped nearby and the staff were once again accommodated in the house. It had been decided that they would return to Calcutta by river, leaving the troops to travel by road, bringing the remaining supplies and the prisoner with them. It soon became common knowledge that while at Lucknow the Governor-General had received a letter, forwarded from

Calcutta, from the Court of Directors in London, informing him that his services had been terminated and that Richard Wellesley, Lord Mornington, was being despatched to India in his place. Faced with such a cold response at the end of thirty years' hard work in the Company's service, Sir John had no wish to linger up-country but wanted to return to the Bengali capital by the quickest route possible. There was also news of trouble brewing further south in Hyderabad and Mysore which would demand the attention of Sir Alured Clarke as Commander-in-Chief, so no delay could be permitted. Henry Bonnay, Ainsworth, David and Neil Edmonstone took ship with their superiors next day, having said a cheerful farewell to young Hubert Cornish whom they were leaving behind at the Residency in Benares. He had decided to accept the position offered there and would receive his training from a senior writer already employed who bore the elegant name of Mountstewart Elphinstone.

* * *

On their return to Calcutta, Sir John immediately set about the sad task of putting his papers in order for his return to England. Even though he had been informed that the King proposed to create him a Baron of a location of his own choosing (Sir John had in mind his wife's home town of Teignmouth), he resented this abrupt termination of his services and the offhand manner in which it had been communicated to him by means of a messenger who, but for a stroke of good fortune, might easily have been slain en route. He felt it a snub to the policy he had long followed under Lord Cornwallis' rule and later upon his own volition, that of maintaining good relations with the Indian princes and their zamindars and only interfering, as in this last case, when the choice of a successor seemed likely to cause real damage to the local population and also to the Company's coffers. Sir John supposed it was merely the matter of the Company's coffers which had moved the Court of Directors to require his dismissal.

Meanwhile the remainder of the cavalcade had also returned to Calcutta overland, bringing with them their distinguished prisoner who was deposited into the comfort of the best prison cell in Fort William (where he remained until his death seventeen years later). The same means brought some unexpected despatches from Benares, amongst which was a personal letter of gratitude from Hubert Cornish addressed jointly to David and Ainsworth for having served as his companions and advisers during the expedition to Lucknow. Part of the text read as follows:-

I scribble this in haste, dear friends, that it may travel to Calcutta with the troops and reach you as soon as Mr. Davis's official despatch reaches my uncle, the Governor. You missed all the best excitement! The morning following your sailing from Benares the detachment was astir before dawn preparing for its own depar-

ture. At the Residency, Elphinstone and I had determined to take a ride before breakfast. We were dressed and our mounts stood waiting in the courtyard. All at once we heard strange and stealthy noises in the corridor outside our room, and opening the door perceived the shadowy figures of some half dozen Sepoys led by Prince Wazir Ali who had evidently escaped from confinement. They crept into Mr. Cherry's room and we heard him cry out in alarm. Guessing only too well what was happening, we closed and locked our door, slid up the sash and climbed, or rather fell, out of our window into the yard. We leapt on our horses, snatching the reins from the servants' hands, and rode hell for leather till we had put a good distance between ourselves and the house. Finding no pursuit behind us, we circled round to the cantonment and roused the first British officer we could discover. He called upon a dozen others to join us, and with some loyal Sepoys and the two tall Sikhs Sir Alured had ordered to return with the troops, we rode and we ran to the Residency.

"There the front door stood open wide and at our approach the disloyal Sepoys melted away like shadows through the servants' exits. Entering the hallway we came upon a fearsome sight. Wazir Ali stood upon the staircase, one arm upon the balustrade, the other held his talwar which he brandished high. At the head of the stairs stood Mr. Samuel Davis in his nightcap and dressing-gown, holding the villain at bay with a long spear which he had snatched from its display on the wall. Behind him, their eyes wide with terror, stood his wife and two small children clutching at their mother's skirts. Our two Sikhs merely stepped forward and passed their long sabres under each armpit of Wazir Ali. One of them removed the talwar from his hand, throwing it down the stairs, and then both picked him up by his garments, twisted him around and frog-marched him back to the ground with a shining sabre blade either side of his ears. There he was swiftly shackled and returned to the cantonment, whilst we accompanied Mr. Davis into Mr. Cherry's room. We found the poor man stretched out on the floor with his throat cut. Mr. Davis nevertheless sent for the physician just to have a witness of Mr. Cherry's fate. Mr. Davis is to take charge of affairs here until a replacement is appointed, and I have had my first lesson in the treachery that can attend our tenure in this country.

"I trust that you both returned safely to Calcutta and that it will not be long before we may renew our acquaintance.

Your sincere friend, Hubert Cornish.

Richard Wellesley, Lord Mornington, the new Governor-General, did not reach Calcutta until 17 May 1798, four whole months after Sir John Shore had received news of his dismissal. By that time Sir John and his brother-in-law, Hubert Cornish senior, had long since left for England and Henry Bonnay, though dubious about his own position under what promised to be an entirely new regime, had struggled to keep control of the vast amount of correspondence and business that seemed to surge through the portals of the Writers' Building. However Ainsworth was already familiar with the kind of personality with whom they had soon to deal, for his Lordship's brother, the soldier Colonel Arthur Wellesley, had already visited the City and had been available to meet Calcutta Society at the house of William Hickey. Ainsworth had been present at a soirée there and had been introduced to the Colonel as one of a number of Company employees. Later, after the Colonel had returned to his regiment at Madras, William Hickey opined to Ainsworth that if the incoming Governor was anything like his brother, he would be "endowed with an uncommon share of vanity".

Ainsworth was to remember those words and the uncomfortable feeling they gave him, for even though he had now spent three years in India, anyone from the crème of London Society would be bound to be aware of the reason for his banishment. He was scarcely surprised, therefore, when Lord Mornington called together the entire staff of the Writers' Building one day in the cool air of the marble hall on its ground floor and addressed his employees for the first time. He introduced to them his brother Henry Wellesley, Lord Cowley, who would act as his Political Secretary and deputy in all matters, and Major William Kirkpatrick, the former Resident at Hyderabad, whom he had recruited as his private secretary for his intimate knowledge of princely politics in India. Ainsworth learnt subsequently that Lord Mornington had encountered Major Kirkpatrick at the Cape of Good Hope when both were on their way to India, and his Lordship had been much impressed by Mr. Kirkpatrick's perspicacity regarding certain rumblings of trouble brewing in Mysore, the realm of Tipu Sultan.

Lord Mornington continued that it was his first impression of the British administration, as he found it in Bengal, that its officials were "corrupted by sloth, indolence, low debauchery and vulgarity." Now that the Company's officials performed judicial as well as commercial and military functions, he went on, it was incumbent upon any Governor-General to "secure to the people of this Empire" (it was the first time his listeners could recall such a word being used in connection with the Company's activities in the Sub-Continent) "the benefit of the ancient and accustomed laws of this country, administered in the spirit of the British constitution." David Lambton, standing beside Ainsworth, whispered to him sotto voce, "I bet that's pure Edmund Burke. He's always preaching about ruling India as if it were a corner of England. You may read of it in the newspapers that arrive from home, if you care to."

To that end, the new Governor intended to reform the Secretariat entirely so that better-educated and more learned administrators and judges would be available to govern the territories which Britain controlled. "Here it comes!" Ainsworth murmured back to David as he listened. Lord Mornington began with the so-called 'writers' whom he considered unfit for such a rôle. Their work, he said, was "menial, laborious, unwholesome and unprofitable, the duty of a mere copying clerk." Ainsworth thought that actually he could scarcely agree more. What then did the Governor propose? Lord Mornington went on to compare the

Writers' Building to a boarding school, where boys as young as fifteen had come out to India totally inexperienced in the ways of the world and had been lodged there by the Company whilst they acquired the tools of their profession. In future, he said, the minimum entrance age would be raised to eighteen, and entrants would be expected not only to have taken the standard accountancy examination in England but also preferably to have spent some time at university. Personal recommendation from a family member or from an existing officer of the Company would no longer be taken as sufficient for acceptance. At this announcement, a large proportion of his audience was obliged to take due note.

"In future," the Governor continued, aspirants for employment in the Indian Service should have "a general knowledge of those branches of literature and science which form the basis of the education of persons destined to similar occupations in Europe. To this foundation should be added an intimate acquaintance with the history, languages, customs and manners of the people of India, with the Mohammedan and Hindu codes of law and religion, and with the political and commercial interests and relations of Great Britain in Asia." "Finally," he said, "their early habits should be so formed as to establish such solid foundations of industry, prudence, integrity and religion, as should effectively guard them against those temptations and corruptions with which the nature of this climate and the people of India will surround and assail them in every station, especially upon their first arrival."

The Governor went on to say that he had in mind founding a college where all young civil servants coming to India should receive their first year of training. This should include an intensive study of the languages and customs used in India, and that Sanskrit and Persian should become compulsory subjects in addition to Hindi, and Bengali, Urdu, or whatever local language might be appropriate to the duties to which officials were seconded. Moreover, all the present staff who had not served for three years, whether in a civil or a military capacity, were to attend the same educational courses, at the end of which they were to take examinations in each subject which would have the same value as a university degree in Europe. To achieve the funding and approval necessary for this project, Lord Mornington was preparing a detailed paper for submission to the Court of Directors of the East India Company and to the Board of Control in Parliament.

In the meantime, his Lordship continued, there were many practical improvements to be made which were already within his control. Henceforth the daily hours of work would be standardised for the whole Writers' Building at between seven in the morning until four in the afternoon, when tiffin would be served for those who required it, particularly among the resident juniors.

Ainsworth groaned aloud at this, and Lord Mornington, sensing the direction whence the murmur had arisen, glared at him and held up his hand. "Yes, I am aware that certain of the more senior writers and members of the garrison here take a morning ride before presenting themselves for their labours of the day, but in future they must either ride before dawn or in the evening after their work is done."

Ainsworth had realised immediately that he would be obliged to sacrifice either his daily contact with Mughal or else his long evenings at cards endeavouring to supplement his meagre income. His Lordship's next statement proved of even greater interest, for he said that he proposed to review all the salaries of the Company's staff in order to make them more compatible with the degree of responsibility expected of them, and more practical for the surroundings in which they were required to live. Some of the very routine copy-work, he added, would be taken over by Indian clerks who could display a good command of spoken and written English and had a fair hand at transcribing it. Was there hope here for Mr. Biswas's elder son, Ainsworth wondered? Perhaps he would be able to resolve his landlord's persistent whining at last.

Then the Governor added, as it were, a postscript. Of course, he said, those senior writers who had left work incomplete upon taking tiffin would be expected to return to finish it before nightfall. Thus, as in many a commercial venture where the hours for attendance are brought forward, the dutiful employee is thereby pressed and persuaded to make a further sacrifice! Ainsworth felt angry and depressed. Just as he had managed to rise above the abject poverty associated with the position into which his Guardian had thrust him, the pleasures he had achieved by his own efforts were being denied him once again. However his attitude softened a little when he learnt what level of salary he could now expect, especially if, having already spent three years in India, he were adjudged fit, under the new system, to carry out those special envoy and settlement tasks to which he had been assigned recently under Henry Bonnay's guidance.

Of the latter there was different news. Henry had become somewhat withdrawn of late. Tim Fairburn had departed on home leave and Henry had been obliged to cope single-handed with the interregnum between Sir John's departure and the arrival of Lord Mornington. Having limited resources, he had turned to Ainsworth for assistance, their task bringing them closer in a paternal relationship which Ainsworth found gratifying after his own lack of parental input. This also had the effect of making him privy to a great deal of the confidential correspondence flowing through the Head Clerk's office. He had learnt, unexpectedly, that his chief was actually a Breton, though he had been in the employ of English people so long as to have completely lost any French accent. Now that the Terror in France had subsided and the Directory had been established and was beginning to govern the country like a regular European cabinet, Henry Bonnay had turned his mind to the question of taking some long overdue home leave or even of retirement. With the French Army under General Napoleon Bonaparte beginning to dominate Europe, the correspondence he had seen had led Henry to believe it was only a matter of time before the French General would turn his attention to India and the vast riches to be sought in this nation. Besides, Henry Bonnay said, the French Navy was seeking to blockade British trade to India in the same way as it already controlled that of much of Continental Europe. Ainsworth would have gathered, had he not, from the letters passing through his hands, that some of the Indian princes, on whom Britain relied for stability in India, were secretly pursuing negotiations with the French government with a view to obtaining large subsidies in the event of French success, or at least keeping their own channels of trade open should the European blockade interrupt trade with India.

Of the Indian princes, the chief villain at this time was Tipu Sultan, the "Tiger of Mysore". His father had been one Hyder Ali, the Nizam of the large Central Indian province of Hyderabad, a very intelligent and talented man who, in alliance with his son, had defeated British armies in battle and had caused some hundreds of prisoners to be entombed for several years under conditions of torture and slavery. Hyder Ali had died and Tipu Sultan had been defeated near his palace of Seringapatam in 1792 by Lord Cornwallis. A peace treaty had been drawn up by Sir John Kennaway, the first British Resident permitted to set up business in Hyderabad. He had been succeeded in 1794 by Major William Kirkpatrick who, when departing on home leave in 1797 had left in charge his brother James who eventually succeeded him in this key position.

Now that William Kirkpatrick had been brought to serve in Calcutta, Henry Bonnay confided, he believed that his own days as confidant to the Governor-General were over, and that when Lord Mornington implemented his promised reorganisation of the Political and Foreign Sections of the Secretariat, he would be dismissed. He informed Ainsworth that he had discussed the situation with Claude Martin during the expedition to Lucknow, and he too had come to the same conclusion, that there would be conflict on Indian soil between the armies of England and France. Major-General Martin had opined that he was unsure which side the new Nawab of Oudh, Sa'adat Ali Khan, would support. At present he was still beholden to the British, but Henry knew that some of the Indian princes, particularly the Maratha ones of the central provinces to the north of Hyderabad, were not happy with the high-handed action just taken by Sir John Shore in replacing Wazir Ali. Such princes were ready to listen to any subversive proposals which Tipu Sultan might make. Moreover, the army of the present Nizam of Hyderabad was actually led by French officers under a General Raymond, and Sir John Shore had exacerbated that weakness by having one of the two British regiments stationed there sent up to Lucknow instead to support his plan to bring about the overthrow of Wazir Ali.

This was the situation which William Kirkpatrick had disclosed to Lord Mornington when they met at the Cape en route to India. Lord Mornington had appreciated immediately what a disaster it would be for Britain, her trade, prosperity, and prestige as a nation, should the French take over Southern India. The new Governor-General had landed at Madras in April 1798, his first task in his new position being to visit the Nawab of the nearby province of Arcot (where

Robert Clive had famously resisted a French siege by General Dupleix and had installed a friendly ruler). Lord Mornington intended to collect a large sum which that gentleman owed the Company by way of revenue dues. The Nawab refused to comply; it was the nadir of Britain's influence. Nor would he agree to certain amendments to the terms of the Treaty of Seringapatam which Henry Dundas, now also Minister of War in William Pitt's cabinet, regarded as harmful to Britain's interests. The chief amendments required were that the Princes' private armies should not be staffed by French officers, and that they should have no diplomatic dealings with France. It was known that Tipu Sultan had written to the Directory in Paris offering it his services. By the same post Tipu had written to the new Governor-General, care of the Calcutta office, congratulating him on his appointment and trusting that relations might continue on the same friendly basis as they had under Sir John Shore! Henry Bonnay turned over in his hand as he spoke the file copy of that letter which Ainsworth had made from the original which had been inscribed in the fair script of Tipu Sultan's English secretary.

On being apprised of the new situation at Hyderabad, Lord Mornington had immediately despatched there Sir Alured Clarke with a detachment of the Calcutta garrison and with Neil Edmonstone to act as his secretary and interpreter. The Nizam was to be urged to dismiss the French officers commanding his fourteen thousand strong army. If he agreed he was promised four additional British battalions instead, those presently threatening his northern frontier under the command of Lt. Colonel Roberts. His task was made easier by the sudden death of General Raymond, some said by poisoning. A new treaty was signed by the Nizam, he was agreeably impressed by the forced march which Lt. Colonel Roberts led to his capital without robbing the countryside, and promised to persuade the Peshwar of Poona, a state on his North-Western frontier, to agree to a similar arrangement. The superfluous French officers were returned to France by means of a slow British troop transport that bore them first to England and long delayed their return to the battlefield!

By this time also Henry Bonnay had departed and the former Head Clerk's office had become the Foreign Section ruled by the eagle eye of Major William Kirkpatrick. That gave Ainsworth the privilege of learning of the latest developments in Britain's fortunes around the world, though Major Kirkpatrick regarded all the Company's previous employees with equal suspicion. He also ensured that the new Governor-General's rules concerning business hours and the studying of languages and other matters were strictly adhered to. Thus a somewhat Presbyterian gloom had spread over the functions of the young writers and Ainsworth had begun to feel bored and frustrated. Attendance "at the Kirk" had also been enforced, and King George's birthday had been about the only jolly occasion Ainsworth could remember, and that merely because he had enjoyed getting horribly drunk.

On 18 October 1798, despatches much delayed in arriving from London contained the devastating news that the French Fleet had slipped out of its port of

Toulon unobserved and that Rear-Admiral Nelson, Commander-in-Chief of the British Mediterranean Squadron, anticipated that because General Bonaparte was aboard with a large army their likely destination would be to land in Egypt. From Alexandria they might then march overland to Cairo and thence to the Red Sea where they might possibly embark for India, a voyage of just three weeks. Nelson was reported to be in hot pursuit, but would he reach the French in time to thwart their plans?

At this news, what may be termed a sense of panic gripped the Residencies of the East India Company. Who were their friends? Who their enemies? Where would the French army land? The nearest viable port to the Red Sea was probably Bombay, where Jonathan Duncan had served long and loyally as the Company's Resident. To the north, Surat had been the site of the Company's first Factory in India and its Nawab was presently an ally. To the South-West was Poona whose Peshwar, Daolat Rao, had just concluded a treaty on the same lines as that agreed with the Nizam of Hyderabad, in particular there were to be no French officers in the private armies and no diplomatic ties with France. The Company's spies had established that Tipu Sultan was in correspondence with many of the Indian princes, including the Peshwar of Poona, the Scindia of Gwalior, the Holkar of Indore, the Gaekwar of Baroda and the Bhonsla of Berar, and was seeking their military aid against the British. Tipu was also known to have approached Zaman Shah of Afghanistan, and to have sent a fleet of merchant ships as far as Mauritius for the purpose of transporting French troops to India. Was there a fleet already stationed in the Red Sea and waiting to receive Napoleon's army, they wondered?

Anxious weeks passed and then a further despatch from London reached the Foreign Section in Calcutta. As far back as 1st August 1798, Admiral Nelson had gained a famous victory at Aboukir Bay, near Alexandria, sinking all but two of the French warships. It appeared that there was no onward transport lurking in the Red Sea and that General Bonaparte's army was now stranded in Egypt. India was safe and the Governor of Bombay sent a reward of a lakh of rupees (worth about £10,000) to Admiral Nelson for his fine achievement.

Lord Mornington thereupon dictated a letter to Tipu Sultan giving him news of Admiral Nelson's victory and the destruction of the French fleet. His Lordship indicated that it would be an opportune moment for Tipu to settle his differences with the British and to agree the desired amendments to the Treaty of Seringapatam. Ainsworth learnt of this correspondence from his friend David Lambton who had been seconded to the Political Section of the Secretariat, the one dealing with relationships within India and with its ruling princes. David had learnt Persian fluently and had passed the examination, being now engaged in translating some of the more delicate diplomatic exchanges. Ainsworth's own progress with the Persian language was slow, he had failed the examination, and as for Sanskrit, he regarded that as a subject fit only for Brahmin priests and fakirs and saw no reason for trifling with it himself.

No reply was received from Tipu Sultan, so his Lordship wrote again in January 1799, with an ultimatum that Tipu's failure to respond, coupled with his previous refusal to negotiate, constituted a breach of the terms of the Treaty and thereby Britain considered herself free to take whatever remedial action she might determine as necessary to protect her interests. A few days after the despatch of the above epistle, David Lambton stepped into the Foreign Section of the Writers' Building with a personal letter in his hand. It emanated from Neil Edmonstone at his new base at Fort St. George in Madras. He informed them that his services had been seconded to Colonel Arthur Wellesley, youngest brother of the Governor-General, who was engaged in fitting out a military expedition in the South. "Tipu Sultan," David and Ainsworth exclaimed together. Apparently the Governor had deputed his younger-brother, Lord Cowley, to take charge of the general management of the campaign, General George Harris had the supreme military command, and Arthur Wellesley was responsible for the readiness of the troops, their commissariat and equipment, and for other logistics such as the secretariat. The last he had delegated to Neil Edmonstone, begging him to recruit a deputy skilled in Persian as well as someone with a knowledge of French, since there would be an urgent political need to learn of any planned invasion by the army of France.

"My French is practically non-existent," David Lambton told Ainsworth. "Did you not say that you had a good knowledge of it?"

"I can read it quite fluently, that's true," Ainsworth replied. "At university I read Voltaire, Descartes, Rousseau and whatever French romances my fellow-students brought back from France after witnessing the fall of the Bastille prison, anything in fact rather than study the Classics of ancient Greece and Rome which I had always loathed."

"So you could take a diplomatick text written in French and make good sense of it?" David asked.

"Yes, provided it were not written in cipher."

"Well, then, would you care to come with me, first to Madras and then into battle Heaven knows where? Neil did say I should pick someone who knew how to take a stand on the battlefield, and it would be good to be working together with him again."

"A welcome diversion from my drudgery here, that's certain," Ainsworth replied, feeling rather more cheerful. "We shall need the Major's permission, of course."

Major Kirkpatrick proved unexpectedly malleable, even providing them with good quality side-arms and a month's pay in advance to meet their initial expenses at their destination. They took ship on a troop transport along with detachments from various regiments who had been selected for the purpose. Britain could not afford a failure.

On reaching Madras David and Ainsworth realised why Major Kirkpatrick had been so helpful; his brother James was the current Resident and lived in

Government House on the outskirts of the city. The British administration there, it seemed, was petrified at the prospect of any military action by Tipu Sultan, especially if it were backed by efficient French contingents. They remembered the victories of Hyder Ali in 1780, how Colonel Baillie's force was overwhelmed at Perambakan, and how a larger British force encountered a further bitter defeat later that year at Seringapatam. Among the military leaders gathered at Fort St. George was an irascible Scot named David Baird who had been imprisoned at Seringapatam for three and a half years in appalling conditions, being chained up all day except when required to carry out slave labour. It was a brutal memory, even if David Baird's mother had been heard to remark that she "pitied the man chained to our Davie!"

Major-General Baird, however, was feeling a grudge of a different sort. He was of the opinion that George Harris should have called upon him to organise and command the expeditionary force. He resented the sudden arrival in India of three brothers of the name of Wellesley, each filling a key position to which others might aspire, and in particular that Colonel Arthur Wellesley had been despatched to Hyderabad with his 33rd Infantry Regiment to organise and equip the force of sixteen thousand Sepoys and cavalry which the Nizam, now a firm ally on promise of some territorial gains, had hastened to provide. Colonel Wellesley's personal intervention had been rendered all the more necessary because the leading British officer of the Nizam's army, a Major Aston, had foolishly got himself killed in a duel. The one good result was that the Colonel inherited the Major's grey Arab stallion, Diomed, a fine animal, whose stamina served as a timely reminder to Arthur Wellesley that he meant to secure the introduction of Arab and European blood into Indian army cavalry stock. For instance, Indian horses lacked the strength needed to drag field guns, and these had either to be harnessed to slow-plodding oxen, or taken apart and loaded on elephants where they would not be available for repelling a sudden ambush. Indeed the Nizam had pressed upon Colonel Wellesley the services of his battle elephants and camels, together with hundreds of pack mules to carry their tents and supplies over the rough terrain - quite a menagerie!

When Ainsworth and David Lambton reached Madras they learnt that Neil Edmonstone had already accompanied the 33rd on its journey north to Hyderabad. They were instructed to join other recent recruits and march towards Bangalore where they would meet up with the Nizam's army on its way south. Though their detachment numbered several hundred men, Bangalore was in enemy territory and there were spies and traps everywhere upon their route. Wells were poisoned, horses and oxen died in mysterious circumstances, rocks and boulders detached themselves from the hillsides to fall upon them or bar their path, and if any looked up at the skyline or into the bush they were sure to catch the flash of a turban or sandal crouching back out of sight. At the end of their two-hundred mile journey when they joined the main force, it was to find that it too had suffered setbacks, and that oxen had proved no more robust than

Indian horses at drawing field guns and heavy equipment.

Neil Edmonstone greeted Ainsworth and David warmly and while the tents were being erected took them to meet some of the senior British officers. Ainsworth was surprised how many of them he had met already at entertainments in Calcutta. As they passed General Harris's tent he caught a glimpse of them and called them in. "Who have we here?" the General enquired, "I seem to recognise this rascal," he said, pointing a stubby finger at Ainsworth. "Likes a game of cards and took a tidy sum from me the last time we played. We must remedy that whilst you're here." Neil explained that David Lambton had been brought in to assist with Persian translation when dealing with Tipu Sultan, whilst Ainsworth would cover the French. A tall shadow filled the doorway; it was Colonel Wellesley mounted on his new acquisition Diomed.

Neil Edmonstone did the honours again as the Colonel slipped down from the saddle.

"Splendid mount, sir," Ainsworth said with a glance full of admiration.

"Have we met before?" the Colonel asked. "I think we have."

"Yes, sir, at William Hickey's house at Chinsura."

"You ride, of course?"

"Yes, indeed, a stallion from a Rajasthan sire and a French mare."

"Any good?"

"Indeed, sir, furious and very fast," Ainsworth replied with pride.

"Good, then we must race them when I am next in Calcutta." The Secretariat withdrew to permit the military men to confer in private. Neil Edmonstone had managed to secure a rather large tent on grounds that the important documents he would be required to handle needed secure protection from sun and rain. Even the sleeping mats that David and Ainsworth had brought with them, and their modest baggage from having to travel light overland from Madras, did little to diminish the available floor space. For a moment that first evening, after a good meal accompanied by a reasonable bottle of claret - somehow strangely not lacking among the regiment's officers, no matter under what strenuous and remote circumstances - there was almost an air of civilisation about the encampment.

So far neither party had encountered serious military opposition, but that situation was about to change. They left the vicinity of Bangalore, then a small provincial town, and proceeded towards the capital Mysore. It was General Harris's intention to encircle and besiege Seringapatam where Tipu Sultan was ensconced in his fortified palace and to cut him off from any communications or reinforcements. They rode through hilly, well-forested country, sometimes on tracks that were scarcely discernible as they crossed the hills. The Nizam's Sepoys appeared to Ainsworth to have brought with them a great deal too much baggage - ox-waggon wheels creaked and shattered and became detached from their axles, gun-trains became stuck in the ruts and had to be extricated, the camels would eat the wrong foliage in the stretches of jungle and made themselves sick, and the elephants were so easily spooked by gunfire that Colonel Wellesley regretted that he had been obliged to please the Nizam by bringing them along.

In the neighbourhood of a little place known as Malavalli they had emerged from the jungle and were about to tackle a grassy hillside, when the troops at the front of the column came to an unexpected halt. They pointed upwards to the crest of the hill where the horizon bore a strange and unusual outline - war elephants! A whole line of them, and behind and between them the bristling glint of spear and talwar. About two thousand of them was Colonel Wellesley's estimate as he quietly gave orders for the 33rd to form a front and wait for his signal to fire. The cavalry he massed on either flank, with the camels and elephants further back with strict instructions to defend the baggage.

With the discipline imbued from their French officers, Tipu's forces advanced en masse. The 33rd held its fire and its breath. When the enemy was no more than sixty yards distant the signal to fire was given, the front rank kneeling, the line behind standing, and each replacing the other as they reloaded. A marvellous precision. Shattered gaps appeared in the enemy ranks and confusion broke out. Their elephants ran about quite out of control and trampled more men underfoot than had been felled by British bullets. As the firing eased and hand-to-hand combat began, Colonel Wellesley called upon his cavalry who swung into action and chased the last stragglers from the field. Pleased with the result of their first action, General Harris's forces completed their encirclement of Seringapatam by 5 April 1799.

However there were still some obstacles to be cleared before siege works could begin. The surrounding countryside was full of Tipu's loyal supporters who sought to harass operations in every way, laying traps, cutting away bridges, digging ditches in roads, and even firing rockets into the tented encampment. The British troops learnt to regard every thicket with suspicion lest it conceal a sharp-shooter or a booby-trap. The movement of troops by night was severely curtailed by these tactics, and Colonel Wellesley learnt the sad and painful way through the loss of friends and comrades, as had Admiral Nelson at Tenerife, the inadvisability of making night attacks. After one such skirmish, twelve British soldiers were carried into Seringapatam as prisoners and had nails hammered into their brains by way of punishment. (Their bodies were discovered later, thrown into a ditch.) At the same time Tipu Sultan was still sending correspondence to Lord Mornington in Calcutta, protesting his innocence and hoping to have "many happy letters" by way of reply. Instead Lord Mornington gave instructions for the siege to proceed.

Batteries were placed, ditches were dug, with zig-zags and enfilades connecting these works, all in the best style of the French expert Vauban who had successfully fortified some one hundred and fifty castles in France. Nothing was left to chance. Then the British guns opened up, and one by one the enemy guns fell silent. Suddenly, on the morning of 2nd May, a huge explosion shattered the eardrums of besieged and besiegers. Black smoke billowed into the sky above the high white battlements and ramparts of the fortress, and fragments of bodies and timbers covered the glittering tiles of the Sultan's palace. What had happened? A rocket magazine had received a direct hit. The explosion created a breach in the walls which the British immediately enhanced with further gunfire. After dusk they silently placed scaling ladders in position, and by daylight the storming party surged into the attack. Major-General David Baird had been accorded the honour of leading it through those ramparts where once he had known Hell. Shouting to his four thousand troops to follow him, he leapt from concealment in a ditch and crossed the dry bed of the River Cauvery that surrounded the fortress. Behind him his men swarmed into the breach and planted the British flag on the rampart. Thousands of Tipu's defenders simply turned and fled, leaving all the outer works undefended. The British troops fanned out and on the far side of the fortress there was fierce resistance by the Northern Gate. Here there were some casualties, but soon all resistance had been quelled and ten French officers, they who had drilled and trained the Sultan's army, surrendered and asked for quarter.

But where was the Sultan himself? Had Tipu escaped? By the Northern Gate where the fighting had been bloodiest, they turned over a pile of corpses, and by the amulet on his arm, that of the sacred "Uma" bird that also graced the pearly canopy of his tiger-striped throne, they identified the body of the tyrant. Tipu's corpse was still warm and the eyes open but lifeless. The body was taken with some respect to the Hall of Audience in the Palace and there laid upon a gun-carriage. General Harris's A.D.C., Lieutenant Jeffrey Prendergast, together with three companions, had the honour of keeping guard over it by night. Next morning it was buried beside the tomb of his father, Hyder Ali, in the Loll Baug garden, shaded by mourning cypresses. The Tiger was no more.

*   *   *

Meanwhile Ainsworth and David had remained with Neil Edmonstone in the British encampment as non-combatants. Indeed they had had occasion to use their pistols from time to time to shoot refugees from Tipu's fortress foolish enough to choose this route through the British lines. When the battle was over and the Union flag flew proudly above the battlements, they received a summons from Colonel Wellesley and made their way through the breach in the walls to the Sultan's Palace where the British senior staff were taking breakfast. Despite their victory the atmosphere around the table was tense; it appeared that the Colonel had been appointed Governor of Seringapatam in preference to Major-General Baird,who had thought the position his by right of both seniority and sufferance. Colonel Wellesley had the tables cleared, and set his clerks to work as he dictated despatches to his brothers in Calcutta and Madras. As they worked, the Secretariat were conscious of a constant background of shouts and hammering as the Palace was looted of all valuable objects; jewels were snatched from bodies and prised out of walls. From Tipu's own office a pile of correspondence was brought forth, some received and some yet to be despatched. There were many communications with the French Government and its War Minister, Talleyrand, and Ainsworth was set to work to translate them. One message in Persian from Tipu to the Maratha princes, dated in April but never sent, read, "Oh happy moment. The time has come when I can deposit in the bosom of my friends, the hatred against those oppressors of the human race. If you will assist me we will purge India of the villains." Colonel Wellesley enclosed the translations of both French and Persian correspondence with his despatches.

To halt further looting, the Colonel gave an order that looters would henceforth be severely punished, and hanged several as an example. Tipu's robes and turbans were sent off to Calcutta where they would be auctioned, together with his horrible musical toy in the shape of a tiger devouring an employee of the East India Company complete with dark coat and beaver hat, accompanied by much growling and melody produced by devices in its stomach*. The Secretariat had the task of packing these articles which were brought to them by orderlies. At dusk they were at last free of duties and wandered through the empty Palace room by room. It was eerily silent and smelt of death. They observed the damage caused by the looters and that only fragments of ornamentation remained. Ainsworth stepped into one room alone and saw a curious sight. A scarlet waistcoat of quilted satin, much embroidered and bejewelled, hung upon a projection high up on one wall, as if it had waited in vain for someone to snatch it down when making his escape. A talwar with its tip broken off lay upon the floor and with this Ainsworth was able to reach the garment. Into his mind there came a vision of Ajoy wearing it; he was such a graceful youth. Quickly Ainsworth folded the waistcoat and thrust it inside his shirt. No need to declare such a personal item, he concluded, as he concealed it within his baggage back at the encampment.

It was not until July that General Harris and the Nizam of Hyderabad's troops departed northwards and Colonel Wellesley returned to Mysore with the 33rd Regiment. His friend, Colonel Barry Close, had been appointed Resident at Seringapatam and the five-year old Rajah of Bangalore, the last of a line of Hindu kings ousted by Hyder Ali, was restored to his throne. Or rather, what was left of it, for the northern half of the province had been transferred by treaty to the Nizam for his assistance, and Daolat Rao, the Peshwar of Poona, claimed the other half, although he had merely remained neutral. That dispute was still for future settlement when Ainsworth and David Lambton were relieved of their extramural duties and travelled with some of the returning troops, and much baggage addressed to Government House, to Madras where they took ship for Calcutta.

On his return to the Writers' Building, Ainsworth learnt that Major Kirkpatrick had become a Colonel, and the Governor-General a Marquess under the Irish peerage for his services in the defeat of Tipu Sultan. Ainsworth himself was greet-

* Now at the Victoria & Albert Museum, London.

ed by nothing more than a pile of work. He collected the usual Company bonds in respect of his back pay and deposited those with his banker. However he did not pause to take tiffin at the Compound since he had come in straight from the docks in Garden Reach and he rather wanted to inspect the state of his lodgings by daylight. He took a palanquin to Chowringhee Road so that the bearers could also carry his luggage. As he walked in through the door he could see layers of dust and unattended dirt everywhere, shining in the beams of the late afternoon sun. He shouted for Anando and the old man appeared, rubbing the sleep from his eyes. "You return safe, Sahib?" he asked with a bow.

"Yes, Anando, and I find my house full of dirt and dust. There will be no back-pay until every bit has been cleaned up."

"Yes, Sahib, I understand. I call servants." With a clap of his hands he summoned Davi the cook and the dhobi and a flurry of activity ensued, whilst a group of lay-abouts who had been using his house and garden as a bivouac during his absence quietly slipped over the garden wall into a passageway that ran behind the houses. Ainsworth left them to it, depositing his bags in his room for Anando to unpack. He badly needed to bathe after his long day from ship to home, but supposed that to be out of the question for the next few hours, so he decided to visit Mughal. He reached the stable at dusk and looked to the stall in the corner where Mughal normally stood. The stall was empty. Ainsworth snorted with annoyance at the thought of someone else being out riding on his elegant horse. The sound brought Mr. Biswas to his side. "Pleased to see you returned, Sahib," he said, "but have bad news, very bad news indeed. The Sahib's horse, Mughal, he die. He get colic disease and fall down dead. You pay his keep, Sahib, then I find good new horse for you."

Ainsworth turned away as for a moment tears stung his eyes: another friend he valued had vanished from his life. Had Mughal really died of the colic, or had he received such severe mistreatment from some careless rider that he had become ungovernable and had had to be destroyed? He would never know. Meanwhile the fellow had the cheek to demand payment for the horse's keep when, for all Ainsworth knew, Mughal might have died the day after his departure for Madras. Ainsworth waved Mr. Biswas aside, telling him that he would return another day to settle the matter. Then he walked home.

Anando did not seem surprised, but shepherded his master upstairs to his bedroom which had now been cleaned and the unpacking done. The waistcoat of scarlet satin that Ainsworth had purloined at Seringapatam was spread very carefully upon the counterpane of his bed, together with other items of attire which Anando had assumed Ainsworth might require for his evening's entertainment. Anando reported that the dressing-room had also been cleaned and the bhisti-wallah had supplied water for a bath which was even now heating upon the kitchen stove. Ainsworth asked Anando to order a palanquin to take him to William Hickey's town house and made a leisurely toilette. Tonight he intended to celebrate the victory at Seringapatam, even if no-one else seemed inclined to enquire his part in it.

When Ainsworth returned home in the dawn, dead beat and dead drunk, such that he rather fell out of the palanquin and up the steps of his lodging, he found the house clean and the little scarlet waistcoat just where he had left it on his pillow. He brushed it aside and sank on to the counterpane without removing either topcoat or shoes. Yes, he would give the jacket to Ajoy, who would look smart in it, for the last offer of his father in that respect had been made the day before the departure for Madras: five thousand silver rupees in cash if Ainsworth would obtain for his elder son one of the special civil service positions now on offer for Indian babus. It was an offer Ainsworth could no longer afford to refuse, for at William Hickey's he had just given assurances for a total of Rs4,500. He was falling for his old vices and temptations all over again.

CHAPTER XVI

'The Nelson Touch'

The boy stood on the burning deck
Whence all but he had fled;
The flame that lit the battle's wreck
Shone round him o'er the dead. ...

The flames rolled on - he would not go
Without his father's word;
That father, faint in death below,
His voice no longer heard.

While o'er him fast through sail and shroud,
The wreathing fires made way.

They wrapt the ship in splendour wild,
They caught the flag on high,
And streamed above the gallant child
Like banners in the sky.

There came a burst of thunder sound..."

From "Casabianca"
by Mrs. Felicia Hemans
(1793 - 1835)

Hugo Jarvis took the river ferry from Chatham Dockyard to Temple Steps and the Norwich stage from Holborn. He had chosen an outside seat both because it was less expensive and because as a sailor, weather-hardened after three years at sea, he expected to find the English country air no more than mildly bracing. He had reckoned, of course, without the fact that most of his time at sea had been spent in the Tropics, which as everyone knows has the effect of thinning the blood, and without the low temperatures to be encountered on a frosty December night near the coast of East Anglia. In short, he was freezing! He comforted himself with the thought of drinking warm punch at the next inn where they would halt to change horses, and that the portmanteau strapped beneath his seat held a handful of gifts carefully selected for his family.

There was a bottle of French brandy for his father, some fine Honiton lace for his mother to remind her of her childhood home county, good quality writing paper scented with orange blossom for Carrie, who was the only member of his family to have written him, a book of puzzles for young Peter who enjoyed them so, and a commonplace book for Lucy who might thereby be encouraged to write something in it. His portmanteau also contained the pewter flask which Frank Briggs had given him before he had joined Stan Stevenson on the canal-boat *Louise*, and which he now had every intention of returning to him filled with brandy or some such other equally acceptable potion. Similarly carefully packed within was the tin box the Caldicotts had given him and the book of poems which it contained along with Jessica's letters.

JESS OF ROOS HALL

There was one further most important gift, and that was a novel which he had selected for Jessica. A romance written by a well-known authoress, Fanny Burney, it was entitled "Evelina" and sub-titled "The History of a Young Lady's Entrance into the World." Hugo had chosen it with the assistance of a bookseller in Charing Cross Lane who informed him that it concerned a young lady sent to live in an aristocratic household in order that she might learn the ways of Polite Society. Hugo had thought of Miss Jessica growing up in isolated seclusion at Roos Hall and that the book would help her acquire the etiquette required in a person of her position, that is if her Guardian Sir Charles Rich ever ceased his neglect and sought for her a suitable situation in life. Little did Hugo realise how significant his choice was to prove.

The stage coach rolled on. Hugo wound his muffler more tightly about his cheeks and pounded his gloved fists together whenever he dared detach both of them at the same time from the rails of the lurching vehicle. He realised that three years had passed since his abduction and that many changes would have taken place at the farm without his hearing of them. For instance, Carrie was now a mature eighteen years of age, Lucy over fourteen, like Miss Jessica, and even young Peter was a fellow of twelve, the same age as Hugo had been when he had left school. He wondered how tall his brother had grown and whether he had proved an apt student. Then he thought of the Caldicotts and realised that the boys, the older pair of twins, were now some seven years old and the younger girls were four! Hugo reckoned that made for a rather noisy and lively household He had brought Jim Caldicott a bottle of his favourite tipple and some lace for his wife, though not quite so fine a piece as that chosen for his own mother. He had brought lace for Bessie and Anna too, but nothing yet for the Caldicott children. He would purchase them toys at Beccles once he knew what would suit.

It was all very well having a numerous family, Hugo thought, but the gifts had cut into the meagre savings from his service, even though when at Chatham he had been ale to pick up from the Navy Office some prize money for the time he had spent in the West Indies. It struck his conscience that the sale of the slaver and its cargo had probably accounted for a large portion of his income, and he wondered whether Admiral Jervis had kept his promise to speak about the abuses of the slave trade in Parliament. Now that he was the Earl of St. Vincent, Hugo supposed that entitled the Admiral to a seat in the House of Lords, and he questioned whether such issues were of greater concern there than in the Commons. He must speak to Uncle Bob who would have kept up-to-date with the newspapers. He must also speak with him about Admiral Jervis's offer to let Hugo spell his name with an 'E' now that he had passed his lieutenant's examination and was hoping for assignment to a ship of the line.

Hugo had written from Chatham estimating the date and timing of his travel to Beccles, so that his arrival was not unexpected. In fact the Caldicott children had been sent into the front parlour to keep watch for hours from the windows that overlooked the drive, and Lucy and Peter had rushed home early from school enquiring at the tops of their voices whether Hugo had yet come. Hugo strolled up the lane in the dusk, a tall, slim figure, his portmanteau balanced casually upon one shoulder as if it were a barrel of beef or a sack of coal to be loaded on the *Louise*.

Alfred Jarvis opened the door to his elder son and there were tears in his grey eyes as he folded Hugo in his arms. "Hello, son, welcome home," was all he said, but it was the first time for a long while that Hugo could remember an embrace from his father. His mother came next, more tears than words as she took his arm. Then it was the turn of Carrie and the other children, of the Caldicotts, of Bessie and Anna who had both found excuses to linger in the dairy after the milk had been cooled, and even of Frank Briggs who had spent the last part of the afternoon giving the harness in the stable an extra spit 'n polish. Eventually family and employees all ate supper together, squeezed around the big table in the dining-room, and nobody remarked at what late hour the children went to bed after Hugo had finished relating all his adventures, or at least all he judged fit for the younger ones to hear.

Yes, there had been many changes at the Ringsfield Farm during his absence and several more were planned. The most significant news was that the Caldicotts would be returning to their original home in the Lowlands of Scotland, in Galloway to be precise, where Jim had inherited a property most suitable for the rearing of black cattle. These he would send annually to Ringsfield to be fattened, courtesy of the services of Jock McTurk, who would later take them to market. Extra grazing would be needed for the beasts, in addition to the meadow on the marshes where Bill Foster still presided, though a little more frail these days. This pasturage appeared to be forthcoming on the almost contiguous acres of unimproved grassland owned by Jake Martin at Ilketshall St. Andrew. Indeed that gentleman had some difficulty in managing his smaller farm single-handed, the living being too poor for him to afford hired help. Jake's younger son Luke was still at school, and his elder son Benjamin had just finished his studies in accountancy and had set up his business in Beccles with a view to assisting local farmers and tradespeople to manage their accounts, pay their taxes and invest their savings.

Now it so happened that Miss Carrie and Mr. Benjamin had taken quite a fancy to one another so that there seemed a possibility that the two farms might become united, even though they belonged to different landlords, Jake Martin's forming part of the Suckling estates around Barsham. An agreement had therefore been drawn up along the following lines, that the Galloways would be pastured on Jake Martin's land after the marshes had flooded in winter, that Frank would be sent over with the horses to plough Jake's remaining acres and would sow them with crops which were not to be sown that year at the Ringsfield Farm, so that each tenancy could expect to obtain a better price for its crop, and Ringsfield manpower would be available to assist Jake with the harvest. In due course Carrie and Benjamin would take over the Caldicott's cottage, while Luke would inherit his parents' farmhouse where he had been born and raised. Young Peter too was thinking seriously about following his father's profession, which made Hugo glad that he had determined on a career at sea. He enquired about Gus Mather, but the family had no particular news other than that he was away at boarding school. However Gordon Mather had been grateful for Hugo's care of his son and had drawn up the agreement with Jake Martin for a very reasonable consideration. Hugo told his family that he intended to call upon Gordon Mather personally and also upon Stan Stevenson if he were still to be found plying the River Waveney with the *Louise*.

On Sunday afternoon Uncle Bob and Aunt Jarvis arrived with the skewbald James and the pony-trap, and Hugo was obliged to tell of his adventures all over again. He had hoped they would bring Jessica with them but they did not; in fact Aunt Jarvis had emphasised that this was "a family occasion". Hugo indicated that he wished particularly to thank Miss Jessica for receiving and forwarding his mail care of an important address such as Roos Hall, so Aunt Jarvis suggested he make a formal visit to the Hall the next Saturday afternoon at three o'clock and afterwards take tea. Uncle Bob, on learning of Hugo's contacts with Admiral Jervis, suggested he call at the Bear & Bells one day during the week so that they might discuss such matters together, away from all the noise and disturbance of the family, whilst Alf interposed that if Hugo had any time to spare, his assistance around the farm would be more than welcome!

It was the middle of the week, after Market Day, when Hugo eventually walked into Beccles to make his various social calls. At the Quay he enquired after Stan Stevenson and learnt that the *Louise* with Tim and his employer on board had gone up-river to Bungay yesterday and might be expected back later in the afternoon if the young man would care to return then - evidently Hugo's respondent no longer recognised him for Stan's former assistant. Hugo called on Bill Foster and his sister at Northgate, taking them gifts which his mother had parcelled up for them. It was obvious that they were very poor and only just making ends meet, so a few comforts were most welcome. Then Hugo knocked at the door of Mather & Weedon's premises. It was opened by a Clerk who showed him within. However it was not Gordon Mather who rose to greet him but his son Benedict, the one who had bullied Hugo at school!

"Hugo Jarvis! Heard you were expected home. Good to see you," said Benedict, coming forward. "Listen, I'm sorry I was hard on you at school. Silly thing to do really, and you did such a great job looking out for Gus. Shall we shake on it?" he suggested, holding out his hand.

Hugo was glad to take it. "How is Gus?"

"He's at Eton and takes to it very well, or so he assures us."

"But is he learning anything?"

"Good Lord, I wouldn't know. I hear you're related to Admiral Jervis, the Earl of St. Vincent as he is now, and meeting up with him in the West Indies all that way from home. That must have been a surprise."

JESS OF ROOS HALL

"We are but distantly related," Hugo replied, "but he was very kind to us and he's a good commander, strict but fair."

"Gus speaks highly of him in any event. I'm sorry my Pater is not here," Benedict continued. "Did you wish to see him over something particular? He has done work for your father recently, so you're a client now."

"No, thank you. I only came to enquire after Gus. Please give him my best regards and tell him I have made lieutenant. I hope that he too is fulfilling his promise to the Admiral," Hugo said, shook Benedict's hand again and allowed the clerk to show him out.

As he left the office of Mather & Weedon Hugo glanced across the road at the Church tower, that stocky independent structure, and then at the graveyard beside it. It occurred to him to try to identify the grave which his mother used to bring him and Carrie to visit when they were tiny children. He tried to remember where it was - over in the far corner, he thought. As it was a weekday there was no-one about in the churchyard, and nor did any persons hurrying about their business in the street, or strolling up and down peering in shop windows, pay him any heed. The grass was long and wet and squashed easily underfoot, those weak green blades of winter. He walked along the path beside the row of tombstones nearest the far wall, muttering each of the surnames aloud as he passed. When he saw it, he was equally surprised by the posy of fresh flowers that graced it as he was by the names it bore. "Alicia Elizabeth Jarvis", the epitaph read, "Beloved daughter of Robert and Elizabeth Jarvis", and then no other message than the dates,"12 February 1762 - 20 May 1783".

Poor girl, to die so young, was his first thought, and then 20 May 1783, why that was only five days after Jessica's birth. Hugo had since remembered that Alicia had been the name of the woman who had briefly stayed at the Ringsfield farm and had given birth there. So she was Uncle Bob's and Aunt Jarvis's daughter, and never had he heard her spoken of since. Very curious, if she had been their only child. And who was it who had placed the fresh flowers there? Who but Aunt Jarvis who attended that church so frequently. Was this, then, the riddle of Jessica's parentage? He must seize the opportunity of his visit to Roos Hall later in the week to enquire, very casually to be sure, what the 'A' stood for in Jessica's middle name.

Saturday arrived at last, and of course his father would ask Hugo to give a hand with raking over the muck heap that very morning. He asked to be excused from luncheon with the family but helped Mrs. Caldicott fill the outhouse bath with hot water instead and jumped in, being especially careful to soap his hair well, for both ships and farms were alive with ticks and lice. When he left the comfort of the warm bath it was to face the freezing December air whistling under the door of the outhouse with only a bath towel of threadbare cotton to defend his bare torso. Conditions he had endured stoically on board ship did not seem quite fair in this context! Returning to his bedroom in his underwear he found that his mother had already laid out on his bed all freshly laundered the best among the clothes he had brought home from the sea. They were not exactly smart, but they were clean and honest. He dressed and combed his unruly hair. Now, should he wear a hat? Might it be expected of an afternoon visit? He thought it so, tried on the new cocked hat which he had bought in London as part of a lieutenant's uniform, looked in the mirror and practised raising it up and down, and bowing with it in his hand. If Jessica were like Lucy, and they were together in their final year at school, she would probably collapse in giggles at the sight, and how would he feel then? Hugo's new-found self-respect seemed ready to be wounded.

Hugo set out in plenty of time, scarcely being able to wait until the tall creaking pendulum clock in the hallway had struck half-past two. He took the track past the meadows to the wicket gate, realising too late that it was thick in mire at this time of year. He should have taken the longer route by the lane, but then in December that was probably just as muddy. When he reached the Hall he spent some minutes removing as much of the mire as he could on the boot-jack beside the front door before ringing the bell. It was answered by Betty Jarvis who had been quietly watching his approach through a window.

"Good afternoon, Aunt Jarvis," Hugo said, raising his hat. "I fear I have mired my boots a good deal walking through the track."

"Come in Hughie. Miss Jessica will be down in a minute. I've told her to put on a warm cloak. As the weather is fine I suggest you take a turn in the garden and then into the park where the path has been newly gravelled."

"Thank you, Aunt Jarvis, that sounds fine," Hugo felt somewhat relieved that his aunt did not appear about to act as chaperone, since he rather fancied being free to converse with Jessica on his own, especially as he had in mind one particular question which he wished to insert into their conversation. He felt in his pocket for the book "Evelina" which he proposed to give Jessica and which Carrie had carefully wrapped for him in pretty paper tied with a pink ribbon. Then he heard a step on the stair and looked up. Jessica was silhouetted against the window, her cloak billowing about her and long ringlets escaping from beneath the rim of her bonnet. When Jessica eventually arrived before him, a little breathless, he found her taller than he remembered and quite beautiful to look at, her delicate features flushed with pleasure, her complexion as fine as bisque porcelain, and her eyes bright and merry. For a moment Hugo was speechless as Jessica held out a tiny gloved hand and said, "Hughie! I'm gratified you could come. You'll take a turn with me in the garden? Thank you, Mrs, Jarvis," Jessica said as she stepped out of the doorway into the cobbled yard.

"Delighted to see you, Miss Jessica," was all that Hugo could manage as they turned the corner of the building into the garden.

Jessica's "Thank you, Mrs. Jarvis" had suddenly reminded him of her superior social status and the fact that he was merely a farmer's son. Behind them, before the front door shut, the dog Arthur slipped out, appointing himself to join the party, as did the housemaid Lizzie, warned by Mrs. Jarvis to maintain a discreet distance from the young couple and not to attempt to overhear what they were saying. Betty had a duty to Sir Charles to keep Jessica safe from harm, and she certainly did not want her charge to follow in the ways of her own daughter Alicia.

"Your hair has grown such a deal since the fire," was the first thing Hugo found to say. "It looks very pretty," he continued, with an attempt at teenage gallantry.

"Thank you. I do all I can to encourage it. I have Lizzie brush it for me every night before I go to bed. That is considered to help it to grow thick and strong," Jessica replied,

"I have Lizzie brush it..." and there again the social differences between them had been made evident. The fact that he, Hugo, would soon be ordering crewmen and midshipmen about on the deck of a battleship in the midst of fire and flying missiles did not yet occur to him as offering a parallel route to distinction.

"What about you, Hughie?" Jessica said as he shepherded her through the wrought iron gate at the far end of the garden and leant down to give a pat to Arthur as he followed them. "You must have many stories to tell which you could not include in your letters."

Which could he tell her, about the dirt aboard ship, the smells, the rotten food, the stinking bilges, the bad language, violence, drunkenness and filthy habits, the chafing of one's hands and the freezing of one's feet on the yards, the deafening noise of gunfire, the smell of gunpowder and cordite, the shaking and reverberation of the guns, and that horrible fear of masts, yards, men, missiles, bullets, blood, body parts, breaking through any defensive nets erected and falling upon one as one stood sweating at one's duty? No, he could only tell her of the beauty of sea and sky on a clear day, of dolphins and whales swimming alongside in their mysterious fashion, of sheltering from storms, of the lush vegetation and richness of the West Indian islands, of the kindness of their inhabitants such as Madame Joly, of laughter at the pantomime rôles performed by the sailors at play, their music and their dancing, their comradeship (and he remembered for a moment Big John who had befriended him and whom he was unlikely to encounter again) and of some of the distinguished people Hugo had now met, such as Admiral Jervis and Rear-Admiral Nelson. Jessica seemed to show little interest at this point, for all that Nelson was a Norfolk man and related to their neighbours, the Sucklings.

They had managed to put quite a distance between themselves and Lizzie who was absorbed in lifting her skirts and shoes clear of the muddy patches underfoot. It was time to bring out his gift, Hugo decided. "Jessica, I thank you most heartily for the notes you have sent me along with Carrie's letters, and thank you once again for the book of poems you gave me long ago. They were of much comfort after I had been seized at Yarmouth and had no idea what would become of me. May I return the compliment?" and he handed her the pretty pink package which Carrie had devised for him.

Jessica undid the ribbon and opened the wrapping. "Evelina," she read out,

"The History of a Young Lady's Entrance into the World." She laughed a little archly and then said, "I can quite see why you thought such a tale might be applicable to me, Hughie, but you should know that my Guardian, Sir Charles, has arranged for me to attend a finishing school near Ipswich from September next until I reach eighteen. I am to board there and have every intention of making amends for my solitude here at Roos Hall. However, I shall read your book with interest, rest assured, for it may well contain hints as to my behaviour when I meet my new companions."

"Her new companions," Hugo thought bitterly, realising that in future Jessica was unlikely to place as much reliance on his friendship and that of his sisters. "Shall you continue to write me?" he enquired tentatively. "I would be much gratified to know how you go on. You may find your new school as different and amusing as I consider my existence at sea."

"Oh yes, I do hope so," Jessica smiled.

"By-the-by, " Hugo continued in as casual a tone as he was presently able to command, "I note that you sign your letters with your full name but for the middle initial 'A'. What does that stand for?"

"Alicia," Jessica replied without a moment's hesitation. "I have often asked whether either of my names is derived from my mother or from some other relative, but no-one seems able to tell me. So I have resigned myself to being a nobody until someone informs me otherwise." Suddenly the wistful tone of her childhood had returned to Jessica's voice. Hugo recognised it, took her hand and gave it a gentle squeeze.

"You know you always have many friends at Ringsfield," he said. "I hear that you do not ride over as often as before. You must make amends for that. Do you help with the harvest again next year?"

Jessica nodded, "I expect so," then asked, as might any member of his family, "Will you be home again soon, Hughie?"

"I have no idea, I regret to say. The minimum period of enlistment is six months, and that is only for the ranks. As an officer, I may not return to England within two or three years, depending upon the actions in which my ship is engaged and the state of peace or war with France and her allies. So you see how much I shall value hearing from you."

"Hughie, the path ahead appears very muddy. Shall we return now? I am beginning to feel the chill." They were soon back in the warmth of the house where Jeb Hanson had set a fire crackling in the grate, and Mrs. Baines had supplied cakes, scones and jellies enough to feed an army. Mrs. Jarvis presided over the teapot and Selina appeared around the door, tail in the air, ready to take a cautious sniff at Hugo's ankles and to accept any sweet offerings which might find their way to her from the table.

Hugo walked home along the farm track, not caring now about the mire adhering to his boots. Instead he tramped on in the darkness, thinking about what he had learnt. If Jessica was the child of Alicia Jarvis then Aunt Jarvis was her grandmother and yet why was she not acknowledged as such? And was Uncle Bob her blood relative too, or only related to her by marriage? If she were a second cousin then she was a member of his family, but if only related by his great aunt's marriage then she was not a blood relative at all. Was her Guardian, Sir Charles, her real father? Was there much inconvenient scandal? He did not think he dare ask even Uncle Bob upon his next visit to the Bear & Bells. With that he reached the farmhouse door and made his way into the brightness within.

*　*　*

The New Year, 1798, was just a few weeks old when Hugo received a summons to return to Chatham as there was a vacancy for a junior officer aboard a ship recently arrived at the dockyard for repairs. When he reached Chatham it was to discover quite a different situation. It appeared that his ship had sunk at its moorings, being rather more extensively invaded by the shipworm than her previous crew had realised. The ship was an old warrior from the past built earlier in the century during the Seven Years War with France, and she had served in various British stations around the world. Now, however, her days of active service had come to an end. She had been dragged hastily into a vacant dry berth and the offending timbers replaced, but the verdict was that she must be taken to Gravesend to serve as a prison hulk. Hugo supposed that if she then sank at her moorings again the loss of a few convicts awaiting transportation would scarcely be mourned!

So there was Hugo left to kick his heels at Chatham on half-pay, which meant that he sometimes had to choose between his food and his lodging. Gone were his dreams of fitting himself out smartly for his new position, instead it seemed he would be lucky to obtain any officer's berth at all. Then he was informed that H.M.S. *Vanguard*, a fine two-decker of 74 guns and a 'ship of the line', was fitting out at Blackstakes, near Sheerness, and that if he were to present himself to the Purser along with his lieutenant's certificate, he might well be taken on. He took the Medway ferry to Sheerness, her rivers being England's most frequented highways. The ship looked beautiful in the morning sun as he ascended the ladder from the small rowing-boat which had taken him alongside.

Mr. Sheppard, the Purser, looked him up and down, then asked upon what ship he had served his apprenticeship.

"The *Apollion* with Captain Sterne, sir," Hugo replied.

"And you've passed the examination already at sixteen years of age?"

"Yes, sir. I was taken by the Press-men at the age of twelve."

"So you've had four years before the mast." Hugo did not correct him, for he went on immediately, "Can you cox a launch? What do you know about loading supplies?"

"I've done it before, sir, many times. Also I served on a wherry previous to joining the Navy, so I know how to sail a boat and how to handle and pack goods, sir, and the use of pulleys and a derrick."

"Well, I'm short of midshipmen for they're all to join us at Portsmouth along with the Admiral. I've plenty of seamen but no-one to put in charge. The men are on the main deck. I'll take you up and introduce you. The boat is by the stern and here's a list of the stores that should be at the warehouse on the quay there, and if not call on Mr. Sparrow, the Shipping Clerk in charge, and ask him where they are." The Purser was obviously having a trying morning. "Put your bag down there, Mr. Jarvis. You'll need a uniform from the slop chest too, but at present I've no tailor aboard. I've no cabin space for you either. The Admiral will wish to house some of his own recruits in the junior officers' cabins, so if you don't mind you'll be obliged to hang your hammock with the Midshipmen, and to mess with them too for the time being."

"I'd still like to sign on, sir, for I'm anxious to get to sea again," Hugo replied. "By the by, what is the name of the captain?"

"Captain Berry, Edward Berry," the Purser replied as he brought forth a copy of the Ship's Articles and showed Hugo where to sign. Suddenly Hugo remembered the similar scene aboard the *Apollion*, how he had refused to sign at first, and he let out a sigh for his old shipmates. He had heard of Captain Berry, a senior ranking captain of considerable experience. He thought he should be in good hands here, but who was the Admiral the Purser had mentioned? Unlikely to be his relative Admiral Jervis, for that distinguished commander had been last seen on guard duty between Cadiz and Cape Spartel. Thinking it impertinent to ask, Hugo followed Mr. Sheppard on deck.

The men Hugo was to work with gave him a very casual glance. Some he could see were experienced sailors, and they looked the most sceptical. Others the purser had told him were landlubbers and knew not a thing about ships, but then England was at war and could not be choosy whom she recruited. The Purser introduced him as Lieutenant Jarvis and among the seamen there was an intake of breath, no more. "Do you follow me into the boat," Hugo said as he slipped neatly over the taffrail, long legs being of much assistance, and stepped down into the boat, then held it steady by the ladder until the first man came down. This was a seaman and he took the other side of the ladder. Both of them had to reach up to assist the landlubbers with their footing and then help them to a place in the boat. Most, fortunately, understood how to use an oar, and with less difficulty than might have been they reached the quay where there were steps leading up to the top. Hugo made sure the boat's painter was properly secured, then went to check over the cargo. Some categories were complete, some not. He had to decide which should be loaded first and how much the boat would carry. For a veteran of sailing on the *Louise*, Hugo thought, this should not be too difficult.

When all the goods had been safely transferred to the *Vanguard*, after Hugo had shown several of the landlubbers how to shoulder a sack or a keg, and one or two seamen how to stack them in the launch, and all the personnel were back on deck, one of the sailors turned to Hugo and said, "Purser says your name is

Jarvis. You be the grandson of the Admiral then?"

"No," Hugo replied with a chuckle, "I'm but distantly related to him."

"Leastways you take after him then, the way you checked over those stores. I've served under him and very strict he is. You met him, have you?"

"Yes," Hugo replied, "just once, in the West Indies." A ripple of interest went around the seamen.

"You'll be telling us about that, some time, then?" the spokesman asked.

"Yes, some time," Hugo said over his shoulder as he went below to report to Mr. Sheppard. He knew that he had already won a little respect from the new crewmen. That might be valuable in the days to come.

Gradually the ship's crew, her stores, ammunition, guns and equipment came to the waterside at Blackstakes and were loaded aboard, though the senior officers and the captain did not take up their posts until later. In the meantime Hugo had had his own choice of hammock-space in the gunroom and had struck up an acquaintance with the Cook's chief assistant in the galley who happened to hail from Lowestoft. Thus he was not short of sustenance and the only dishes he was obliged to wash were his own. Moreover, a ship's tailor had been engaged who fitted him out very neatly in the white breeches and stockings, and the dark blue cutaway coat that had become the standardised uniform for officers in the Royal Navy - the tricorn hat he had acquired already. As the crew came aboard, Hugo noticed many new faces who, observing his uniform, asked for directions about the ship. He also found on returning to the gun-room one day that three oldsters had arrived, had moved his hammock and had replaced it with one of their own, but upon his appearance and his quiet uttering of the greeting, "Gentlemen?" it was swiftly put back in its original position!

Finally the captain and his senior lieutenants came aboard and everything was all at once a-bustle. Captain Berry was, it seemed, a stickler for good order, so that the first day of his presence was spent in a thorough inspection of the ship, its contents and its personnel. Hugo was detailed to conduct the Captain around the ammunition stores, indicating the location of each type of shot, whilst the Purser stood in the doorway with the keys in one hand and the relevant manifest in the other from which he read out the quantities available.

When they had done and the Captain was eventually satisfied, he turned to Hugo and asked, "Are you from Norfolk, Mr. Jarvis, your accent would indicate it?"

"From the county border, sir, between Bungay and Beccles," Hugo replied. "My father's a farmer."

"You're on Suckling land, of course?"

"No, sir, but they own neighbouring properties."

"I'm a Norwich man myself," Captain Berry revealed to Hugo's surprise. "I ought to be better acquainted with that part of the county," he added and accompanied Mr. Sheppard on the next stage of his inspection.

On a bright, breezy morning in March, H.M.S. *Vanguard* hoisted her anchor and sailed out of the Thames, through the Downs and thence into Portsmouth Harbour a day or two later. The next morning Hugo accompanied Mr. Sheppard, who had by now become a familiar acquaintance, and two seamen in the launch to the dockside in order to collect a group of young men who were to serve as midshipmen aboard the warship. The Purser was evidently privy to what was proposed but seemed remarkably reticent about divulging the details when Hugo enquired.

It appeared that these were all young men of good family, mostly from Norfolk and Lincolnshire, the sons of the gentry and of merchants and professional men, who had been invited or persuaded by the Admiral, whose identity was yet to be kept secret, to experience and share with him the bracing life to be had aboard ship at sea. When they reached the quayside they encountered a vast pile of personal baggage all addressed clearly to H.M.S. *Vanguard*, but no sign at all of the young men in question. One of the seamen who pulled the oar beside Hugo in the launch muttered, "They'll be babes in arms they'll be sending us. We shall need to be teaching them everything!" Hugo, remembering his own first days aboard ship, could see himself engaged in the Middies' chores again, simply because the young gentlemen would expect to be waited upon!

Enquiries of some dockside workers led Hugo and Mr. Sheppard to a nearby public house where the Purser was obliged to shout very loudly indeed to make himself heard above the drunken rumpus within, and obliged to dodge very smartly a number of missiles once he had managed to do so. Half the miscellany then followed the Purser outside, only to find that due to the large amount of baggage, which the two seamen had now loaded into the boat, there was space in it for only two of the young men, and another journey back and forth would be necessary.

"I shall take the two oldest of you," and Mr. Sheppard called out two names, "Giles Spencer and Nicholas Wilmington." One was present, the other still at the inn whence he was swiftly retrieved by one of the younger boys. Both had to be assisted by the seamen to take their places in the boat, and the long row back to the *Vanguard* proceeded.

Once aboard, the Purser told the young men to pick out their personal luggage from the pile which the seamen were bringing aboard and to follow him. He did not offer to carry any of it for them, but left them to struggle with their overweight belongings. Mr. Sheppard conducted them to one of the junior officers' cabins, the one which Hugo should have shared with the Fifth Lieutenant. Over his shoulder as he went he instructed Hugo to take two more seamen with him and to retrieve the remaining youngsters - names as per list - from the distant quayside. It was thus that Hugo had an opportunity of observing the newcomers before the remainder of his shipmates. They were aged, he judged, mostly between thirteen and fifteen years, the first two having been perhaps a year or so older than himself. They were no more than schoolboys, Hugo thought, with pale hands and fair skin now flushed with drink. Most would be seasick for the first few weeks of the voyage, and here was the *Vanguard*, so ship's rumour had it, about to rejoin Britain's Mediterranean Fleet keeping watch for the enemy off the coasts of Spain and Portugal, scarcely a rôle for amateurs.

On the morning of 30th March, Captain Berry had everyone assembled on deck, Marines, seamen, officers and the motley Midshipmen, some of them distinctly pale of countenance. Hugo was one of the junior officers forming a guard of honour by the ship's rail and a hush fell over the gathering. The Admiral's barge had been sighted and he would be piped aboard. Captain Berry himself stood at the head of the gangway to meet him. Hugo's view was obscured by the presence of his superior officers standing beside him, so it was not until a left hand grasped one side of the taffrail without a right hand to accompany it that Hugo realised that their secret commander was none other than Rear-Admiral Sir Horatio Nelson! Hugo's next thought was of Pip Harris with his similar handicap and then of Stan Stevenson who had lost half a leg. Seemingly once one reached the rank of admiral one could still be expected to function!

A few hours later the *Vanguard* was warped up to her anchor and then slipped down the Solent. At the eastern end of the Isle of Wight, off St. Helen's, she awaited that favourable easterly breeze which would speed her down-Channel and into the Bay of Biscay. The fair wind arrived on 10th April and by the end of the month *Vanguard* had joined the Earl of St. Vincent and his fleet on patrol once again off Cadiz.

Hugo had watched with interest the differences between life aboard the *Vanguard* and his previous experience on the *Apollion*. The crew, he noted, were of mixed ability and he thought a little short of experience. The Marines, on the other hand, appeared well-disciplined by their captain, William Faddy, and better-behaved than those he had known in the West Indies, for all that they consumed as much liquor, and he felt one might rely upon them when boarding the enemy. The senior officers appeared competent and inclined to take after their captain, very fussy as to detail. Maybe that was because there was an Admiral on board.

And such an Admiral, one with a brilliant reputation for personal courage and for demanding high standards of seamanship and initiative from others, but one who for the moment kept often to his cabin, wrestling as a recluse with the physical handicap which Fate had thrust upon him. One of the oldsters had had occasion to wait upon the commander with his dinner one afternoon when the Admiral's own servant, Tom Allen, had fallen sick with the ague, and thus Hugo learnt of the little gadget, half fork and half knife with which the valiant man tackled his food. Hugo wondered how the Admiral managed to write with his left hand and whether he would practice with pistol and sword. There would be no more leading of boarding parties, he realised, as Admiral Nelson had done at the Battle of Cape St. Vincent.

After a few days, however, the Admiral duly appeared on the quarterdeck as gunnery practice was taking place. Hugo had long since noted that the

Vanguards' cannon were fitted with flintlock detonator mechanisms, set off with a mere tug at a lanyard, and more modern than the linstock system still in use on the *Apollion*; this made for a much more rapid rate of fire. The Admiral watched the crews at work on the main deck for a while, then stepped down and walked from one gun team to another, having a word with the gunner's mate and sometimes with individual seamen if their technique required correction. He followed the same procedure on the foredeck, then went below where for some moments he stood behind Hugo's team while Hugo showed one of the landlubbers and some of the watching midshipmen just how priming and loading should be done. "I came to see how my boys were getting on," was all the Admiral murmured as he ducked under the beams to where the next gun-team were sweating away. Later the Admiral had all the gun crews assembled on deck and informed them that he expected them to increase their rate of fire to one every ninety seconds if they hoped to overcome the French.

The Admiral's "boys", as he called them, were about as nimble at adapting to life aboard as bulls in a cornfield, Hugo thought. Firstly, they refused to accept that in the Navy they are the least important of those on board, receive the same food as the crewmen, sleep in the same comfortless conditions and are often required to dirty their hands at the same tasks. Also in any emergency they will be ordered about, sometimes punished, facing the same perils and receiving the same injuries as anyone else. Sharing their accommodation Hugo found particularly trying, since their excess baggage took up valuable living-space and he was sure it would all be thrown overboard once the decks were fully cleared for action; and they persisted in thinking him their man-servant, despite his uniform. Hugo was even more shocked to discover that the Admiral had been so tardily recompensed for his services by the Navy Office that he had been obliged to accept payment from the fathers of the said "boys" for the privilege of bringing them along - only some of the fathers had yet to pay! If an Admiral had encountered such difficulty in receiving his just reward, what chance had he, Hugo Jarvis, of earning a gentleman's pension out of a career in the Navy? Perhaps those shipwrights in the Gibraltar yards had good reason for their actions after all. Someone should take up their case in Parliament!

Admiral Jervis, the Earl of St. Vincent, gave Horatio Nelson a very warm welcome upon his arrival among the British Fleet off Cadiz. This time Hugo was on duty on the quarterdeck when the event took place and had no difficulty in viewing matters through a telescope as Rear-Admiral Nelson was updated on the local state of affairs. The position of Portugal as Britain's ally was still extremely nebulous and weak, whilst there was news that the French Fleet, together with thousands of troops and the necessary transports and support vessels, were massing in the Mediterranean under the command of General Napoleon Bonaparte. No-one knew where they intended sailing, nor what was their objective. It could be to take action against the Austrians in Northern Italy, or against the Kingdom of the Two Sicilies (Naples, Southern Italy and Sicily) whose monarchs, King

Ferdinand and Queen Maria Carolina, the sister of France's tragically guillotined Queen Marie Antoinette, had so far presented an obstacle to the Corsican General's plans to conquer the whole of Italy. The friendly island of Malta, owned by the Knights of St. John and a stepping-stone between the western and eastern basins of the Mediterranean, would no doubt fall a victim to the French. Alternatively, the British base at Gibraltar could be their objective and the French could spill into the Atlantic with Lisbon or the sugar trade in the West Indies as possible destinations.

However, if the reported size of Napoleon's army was correct, the large number of transports required would seem to indicate a projected landing within the neap-tidal waters of the Mediterranean. Could the Corsican be thinking of Egypt, and - oh horror! of the land route to India and all the revenues and the riches that country exported to Britain's shores? French control of India, the Cabinet in London realised, would grant the enemy World Domination and such absolute economic power that England would be quite unable to resist now that she had lost her American colonies. Who better could Admiral Jervis send to spy upon the French, who was intelligent, intuitive, and acted with speed and initiative, than the charismatic Rear-Admiral Nelson? In fact Lord St. Vincent had received just that instruction already from Lord Spencer at the Admiralty.

Scarcely were the civilities of reunion completed before the *Vanguard* put to sea again, accompanied by two other 74-gun warships, the *Orion* under the command of Sir John Saumarez, and the *Alexander* under Captain Alexander Ball. As scouts, Admiral Jervis spared Nelson three of his precious frigates, and the small squadron set off southwards. They were barely over the horizon before Lord St. Vincent received further despatches from London with additional news about French military activities. It seemed that French soldiers were massing not only in Toulon but also in Marseilles and Genoa, so that a destination in the Eastern Mediterranean appeared more likely. Moreover the French army was estimated at 35,000 strong, numbers which indicated plans for a substantial land campaign. Egypt now seemed a more likely destination and the route to India a real possibility. London was aware of signs of restlessness among erstwhile friendly Indian princes, and, wrote the Lords of the Admiralty, one Tipu Sultan was known to have contacted Citizen Robespierre of France during the Terror and to be sending merchant ships to Mauritius for use as troop transports. It was vital, therefore, that Sir Horatio Nelson be supplied with a force large enough to attack and disperse the French fleet and to destroy as many as they could of its transports. Lord Spencer was sending Admiral Jervis, under the command of Sir Roger Curtis, eight ships of the line from the Fleet protecting Ireland to assist with Cadiz patrol duties, so that the Admiral might despatch all his most trusted captains and their warships to accompany Nelson into the Mediterranean.

Admiral Jervis lent Nelson ten of the best, all of seventy-four guns, plus the *Leander* with fifty guns, but there was a crucial delay before they were able to catch up with their new commander. Instead Nelson's small squadron crept past

Cadiz, observing as it did so no sign of unusual activity. Hence Admiral Nelson became ever more sure that Napoleon's target was within the Mediterranean. At least Lisbon was safe for the time being, Nelson mused, and his Commander-in-Chief could await the promised reinforcements with equanimity. Nor did Nelson allow his crews to forget the significance of their mission. Every day was consumed with gunnery practice, and slowly the speed of fire increased as Nelson had each gun fire in turn, station by station. The Marines were drilled too, the young Norfolk middies being sent to them to learn the use of small arms and sword. Then it was the turn of the seamen with pike and cutlass, often with the Admiral himself watching and picking out any defaulter for additional training. No wonder they said the Admiral was the best in the Fleet, Hugo thought, as he turned into his hammock one night and instantly fell asleep.

As the squadron approached Toulon where the French battle fleet was known still to be lurking, one of the frigates, the *Terpsichore*, formerly a French vessel, deceived a French corvette fresh out of port into thinking her friendly and so captured her quite easily with no loss of life. Hugo watched enviously as the prize was towed alongside the *Vanguard* where the Admiral had been holding a meeting with his captains. Sir John Saumarez, being a Guernseyman and familiar with the French tongue, was called upon as interpreter, and went aboard the French vessel to question its crew. It seemed that General Bonaparte himself was due to sail from Toulon with a fleet of fifteen warships commanded by Vice-Admiral François de Brueys, a veteran of the French contribution to the Americans in their War of Independence against Britain. Thus there would be no love lost between the English and French commanders. Moreover the transports gathering at Toulon had already embarked twelve thousand troops, said the Frenchman, and thousands more were expected.

In his cabin Admiral Nelson hastily wrote with his spidery left-handed script a despatch to Lord St. Vincent with all the details he had learnt, and adding that he anticipated a land destination for such a large body of troops within the Mediterranean. A prize crew was put aboard the French corvette with orders not to delay in delivering the news to the Chief and the French crewmen to Gibraltar, whence they might make their own way home!

One evening a few days later when the squadron had taken up its surveillance position between Toulon and the island kingdom of Sardinia, Hugo Jarvis had been assigned the second Dog Watch. It was an important occasion for Hugo, for should the French fleet slip out of harbour unobserved on his watch, shame and dishonour would fall upon him, his commander and the rest of the crew. Hugo had therefore resolved to give attention to every detail of the scene around him. He noticed, for instance, that the setting sun held a halo, that the sea looked grey and silky and that the ripples upon its surface seemed to be running in two directions at once. He recalled seeing similar conditions once before, a long time ago, then remembered that it had been when the *Apollion* on her outward voyage from England had first rounded Cape Finisterre into the teeth of a storm. The wind too was rising, and when he checked the glass by the helms-man it was to find the mercury falling. All his superior officers were at dinner with the Admiral and Captain Berry, and when he sought out the Master, a Mr. Clodd, to inform him of the likelihood of a hard blow before morning, Hugo was told he was not yet due for duty and should not be disturbed. Hugo did manage to alert the Bosun, who paid him rather more heed, but it was only on comple-tion of his watch at eight o'clock that Hugo was able to locate the First Officer, Edward Galwey, and to advise him of his opinion.

Hugo went below to his supper and sat chatting with some of the "Norfolk boys" till after midnight. Scarcely had he reached his hammock when a violent blow shook the *Vanguard* as if she had crashed into a precipice beam ends on. Hugo could hear objects crashing about on the deck above him, and without waiting for the Bosun's whistle he thrust his feet into his sea-boots, grabbed the seaman's cap that he had saved from his canal-boat days, and raced up the com-panionway to the after hatch. He arrived on deck just as the main topmast went over the side of the vessel. Hit by a violent and sudden squall, all the sails still worn by the *Vanguard* had gone aback without anyone being ready to reef them, despite the earlier warnings he had given. The noise he had heard when below was the main topsail yard and its complement of men crashing to the deck amid the billowing canvas. The mizzen topmast was the next to go, followed swiftly by the foremast which split in two. The ship began to swing around uncontrol-lably, swept along by the welter of ropes and spars hanging over her port beam. Hugo seized an axe and began chopping away at the broken rigging, trying to free the ship of its burden. Above the shriek of the wind he could hear the roar of breakers and knew that *Vanguard* had dragged her anchors and must run upon the rocky shore if she could not be righted and steered in time. Beside him other seamen were pulling on board crew members entangled in the fallen rigging and throwing ropes to the pairs of upraised hands that here and there rose above the waves.

Hugo moved to the foredeck and began to cut away at the cables holding the broken foremast, hoping that some poor sailor whom he could not see in the darkness was not trapped amid the welter of sinking canvas. As he paused, soaked to the skin and breathless, a long rope snaked over his head, missing him by inch-es. He looked up to see the *Alexander* bearing down on the *Vanguard* and shoot-ing across her bows. Seizing the rope, he hauled upon it till the end of an anchor cable came aboard, then ran that twice around the capstan and secured its lash-ings to the bitts. Behind him, under almost bare poles, the *Orion* stood by, watch-ing like an anxious hen. Both sister ships had fared better in the blast, had already shortened sail to a minimum and had set a course away from the shoreline. Now the *Alexander* pulled the stricken flagship very, very slowly away from danger. Other seamen joined Hugo to heave upon the life-saving cable, working the cap-stan to bring the ship around and upright now that she was free of the wreckage.

Hugo left the foredeck and went aft to help sort out the fallen yards and the wet and tangled sails. He helped below a number of injured sailors with broken bones and many cuts and bruises. Mr. Jefferson, the Surgeon, would have a busy night of it. Reaching the quarterdeck stairway he found himself confronted by Lieutenant Galwey who shouted at him, "Mr. Jarvis, you're not wearing regulation uniform,"

"No, sir, I was off-duty when the squall struck."

"Then go below and change it," was the reply. Hugo struggled down the companion-way of the bucking ship and met the Second Lieutenant, Nathaniel Vassal, who told him that Mr. Jefferson was short of an assistant since one of them had been concussed by falling rigging. It was not a task which Hugo favoured, having seen it all before in the orlop well of the *Apollion*, but he fetched buckets of water, found himself winding bandages around the arm of one of the oldsters who were now his friends, and watched with fascination as the Surgeon set broken limbs.

It was almost noon before Hugo was dismissed to his bed, and he was summoned on deck again mid-afternoon when a roll-call was held. It seemed that there had been but four fatalities, two among those who fell with the main topsail yard; three of these were seamen and the other Thomas Meek, one of the Norfolk Midshipmen. Hugo pictured the Admiral having to write slowly and painfully to the young man's parents with the sad news of the loss of their son, and he hoped they had other children at home. It was not what would have happened on the *Apollion* as she had weathered similar incidents in fine style, as had the *Orion* and the *Alexander*. H.M.S. *Vanguard* was a disgrace and Hugo felt ashamed for her. The *Alexander* had continued to tow her for many hours until they reached the shelter of the Isle San Pietro off the south-west tip of Sardinia where substantial repairs could be effected. The *Alexander* was lashed alongside the stricken warship while the stump of the foremast was winched out and new timber stepped in. To provide new sails and rigging the three ships pooled all their stores. Moreover, during the tempest all the accompanying frigates had vanished. No, they were not sunk, for the lookout on the *Alexander* had observed them making off with lanterns bobbing in the direction of Gibraltar. "I had hoped they had better faith in me," was the Admiral's sad comment when he heard the news.

Once the *Vanguard* could sail again the squadron crept back slowly towards Toulon, hampered by light winds and by the need to complete the re-rigging of the flagship. It was Hugo's impression that no-one aboard had slept for days with the constant banging and sawing by the ship's carpenters and by the experienced crewmen running up halyards and rigging and bending on a new set of sails. Once they reached the vicinity of the French port it was clear from the lack of naval activity that the great Fleet had sailed already and that Nelson now had the problem of finding it. In the late afternoon of 5 June 1798, Admiral Nelson entertained his three captains and the senior officers of the *Vanguard* at dinner to consider where the French Fleet might have gone and what course they should take to locate it. Naturally their first conversation concerned the aftermath of the bad weather and the Admiral again thanked Alexander Ball in particular for towing the *Vanguard* to safety.

Captain Ball responded, "You may thank the young fellow who stood in the bow of your ship, Admiral, caught that cable we threw and rove it round the capstan with the speed of lightning. He was alone there at the time, though others soon joined him. He wore a merchant seaman's cap, if I observed him correctly."

"What, on my ship?" Captain Berry interposed, all indignation. "Never would I permit it!"

Lieutenant Galwey broke in, "I think that may have been young Mr. Jarvis, Captain. I caught him coming aft and sent him to change into regulation wear. He claimed to have been off-duty when the squall struck. He never did reappear though."

"That may have been my fault," Second Lieutenant Nathaniel Vassal interposed quietly. "I regret that I detained him below and sent him to help Mr. Jefferson whose assistant had been hit by falling yards. To my knowledge Mr. Jarvis was engaged there till morning."

"Jarvis? Any relation to the Chief, Edward?" Sir John Saumarez enquired of Captain Berry.

"I have no knowledge of it," Captain Berry replied. "He hails from Norfolk, though, and has his lieutenant's certificate at the age of sixteen!"

"Ah, we Norfolk lads, Ed'd, I believe we have a natural affinity for the sea," the Admiral interposed. "Where is his home?"

"Near Beccles, Admiral. His father's a farmer, not on your cousins' land, however. My Purser tells me he writes letters to Roos Hall."

"I know it well, Ed'd. You'll recall that my mother was born just along the lane there at Barsham Rectory. Roos Hall estate was indeed Suckling land once and should have been returned to my family under an old agreement." Sir Horatio Nelson seemed well informed about his cousins' affairs. "In any event, Ed'd, please give the young fellow my compliments for his prompt action."

Mr. Galwey took a long draught from his glass of wine and thought it unwise to mention at this point that the same young gentleman had also warned him of the likelihood of extreme bad weather overnight, and that the Master, Mr. Clodd, had not thought it necessary to take more than the minimum precautions against it. Fortunately for him a diversion was caused by a message brought from the officer of the watch that a sail had been sighted to the West in the direction of Gibraltar. The ship appeared to be a French corvette but was flying a white ensign.

Lieutenant Galwey rose immediately to verify the observation. He returned some minutes later and announced, "She could be the *Mutine*, Gentlemen. I have signalled both our sister ships to remain alert."

"That will be Captain Hardy," Admiral Nelson murmured. "I wonder what tidings he brings? Perhaps he has seen my frigates, or he may even have news of the French Fleet." The Admiral was silent for several minutes, for the newcomer was *La Mutine* that Captain Hardy had captured from the French, leaving her artillerymen stranded ashore at Tenerife where they had contributed much to Nelson's own disaster there.

Dinner had long finished and the Admiral and his three captains sat alone with the port and cigars when Captain Hardy was piped aboard more than an hour later. He did indeed bring exciting, and in fact unexpected, good news. Though he had seen nothing of the *Terpsichore* and her companion frigates, he had made contact, however, with a merchantman sailing westwards who had espied the French Fleet passing to the North of Corsica. Better still, he was the herald for a British Fleet of ten of the best of the Chief's seventy-fours, as well as the *Leander* with her fifty guns. These were but three days' sailing time behind him, Captain Hardy told them, and had express orders from Lord Spencer and the Government to engage the French Fleet wherever they might find it. Captain Hardy reeled off a list of the ships which Admiral Jervis had made available.

Then the Admiral spoke again, "It seems that Fate has delayed us here for a purpose. The Chief is sending me a Band of Brothers. Now we shall surely have the better of General Bonaparte."

Admiral Nelson now had at his disposal a fleet of fifteen vessels, all but two of them heavily-armed warships. He divided his force into three squadrons, detailing that if the enemy warships and transports were located together, one division would attack the transports whilst the other two would break up the French line of battle and aim to sink or capture at least one third of Napoleon's forces.

The next news Nelson had of the French came in the middle of June, that some ten days earlier their Fleet had been sighted off the North-Western tip of Sicily and heading eastwards around the northern shore of the island. There was still a possibility, then, of an attack upon the Kingdom of the Two Sicilies, but Nelson was increasingly inclined to the view that the French objective was Egypt, the port of Alexandria and the land route to the Red Sea and India. The Admiral sighed that though his fleet had crowded on all sail, they were still too far behind the French to be sure of reaching them before landfall. Nelson called briefly at Naples but did not personally go ashore, sending two of his captains with despatches for Britain's Envoy, Sir William Hamilton and his wife Lady Emma, and to beg for frigates from the King's First Minister, Sir John Acton. However Sir John refused to assist, for the excellent reason that his monarch feared to attract adverse attention from the French.

Nelson set sail again immediately, passed the Straits of Messina, and present-ly encountered another friendly merchantman whose captain confirmed that the French had taken Malta. There they had looted the treasures of the Knights of St. John at Valetta and had already set sail again, heading further east. Nelson consulted his leading captains and then prepared a memorandum for Lord St. Vincent, setting down his decision to proceed to Alexandria, since he foresaw that once the French army landed there they could "with ease" reach the Red Sea, "and if they have a concerted plan with Tippoo Sahib" (sic) "to have vessels at Suez ... our Indian possessions would be in great danger."

As they approached Alexandria, Nelson regretted again his lack of fast frigates and sent the *Mutine* ahead, that being the only vessel whose loss or capture his force could sustain. When the *Mutine* reached Alexandria it was to find that port empty of all save Turkish and Egyptian vessels and basking in its innocence under the tropical sun. Thinking that Napoleon must have landed further east or even in the Levant instead, the British Fleet sailed on. In actual fact they had outsailed the French and were now ahead of them!

Fearing that Napoleon might have landed at another Mediterranean island, or indeed that he had missed them off Sicily, Nelson led his force all the way back again to the eastern shore of that isle, but found that too basking peacefully under the blazing sun of mid-July. "It must be Egypt'," he said and struck the table with his one remaining fist as he called his captains around him once more. Nelson was conscious of the crucial delay caused by the lack of reliable information and agonised over the thought that if Bonaparte had reached Egypt, say, by the end of June, he could have arrived in India by the time his British Fleet could reach Alexandria again, sailing time from Suez to Bombay being a mere three weeks.

At the Gulf of Coron in Greece, Nelson at last obtained news of the passage of the French Fleet sailing southeast towards Egypt a whole month previously. Were they too late? Had the opportunity been missed? Had the French Army been landed and were their warships and transports now snugly in port? The Admiral was still haunted by that failed attack at Tenerife when he had completely underestimated the strength and determination of the gunnery trained upon his men. To lose again would shred his reputation and his self-respect. Approaching Alexandria once more they found the harbour full of French ships, but these were only the empty transports. The French flag flew above the citadel and there was no sound of warfare in the vicinity. The French Army had evidently long departed on its march into the interior. Nelson's only quarry now must be the French warships, but who knew where they were, perhaps even safe in harbour at Valetta under the massive walls of that city's fortress?

It was now the morning of 1 August 1798 and the British Fleet sailed on slowly eastwards to check the Nile Delta and the Levant once more for traces of the enemy. Lookouts had been sent to the topmasts of all the ships for the purpose of overlooking the sand dunes and reed beds that marked the Egyptian shore. As they approached the fortified headland above Aboukir Bay, a signal appeared at the masthead of the *Zealous* at the head of the British column; it was the longed-for message, "Enemy in sight!" Hugo would only remember the mad scramble that ensued to clear the decks for battle, even their live bullocks being thrown overboard, and then an eerie silence that followed as the British Fleet waited for the wind and for the leadsman taking soundings to sing out the all clear as they edged tediously around the shoals of Bequier Island that guarded Cape Aboukir.

The French Fleet lay in line astern, curved like a crescent moon in the shallows of Aboukir Bay. They made a fine silhouette against the setting sun, sinking all-aflame in the West. Their bows faced towards their enemy, but the British noticed immediately a number of weaknesses in their position. The French vessels were not close enough together to prevent the British breaking through their line; they had fitted no springs to their anchor cables which would allow them to swing round and fire their port guns as well as their starboard ones. Moreover, it soon appeared that they had not even bothered to run out those guns which faced the shore.

Admiral Nelson had instructed his captains to take the initiative in placing their ships alongside the enemy and to make for the Van and the Centre of the French line. With a north-westerly breeze now filling its sails, the British Fleet nosed into Aboukir Bay. At first the French Admiral de Brueys had thought of putting to sea as he had more ships with greater fire-power, but then he remembered that he had sent foraging parties ashore and lacked sufficient men left on board to man all the guns. It was the classic catch situation, one which reminded Hugo of Captain Anderson's tale of how the U.S.S. *Beacon* of Boston had been caught out by a Spanish pirate off Venezuela.

Admiral Nelson had his eye on the breakers on the far side of the French line and he tried to gauge the depth of water in which the French were anchored. Captain Samuel Hood of the *Zealous* and Captain Thomas Foley of the *Goliath* coming up fast astern and positively racing to be the first to attack, were blessed with exactly the same inspiration. The *Goliath* sailed around the bows of the leading French ship, *Le Guerrier*, and leaving her to the *Zealous* lined up alongside the second French warship, *Le Conquerant*. The *Orion* under Captain Saumarez found her way around the two of them and gave her attention to ships further down the French line, firing broadsides as she went into the empty gunports of the French vessels. H.M.S. *Audacious* under Captain Gould broke through the French line and was joined by the *Theseus* under Captain Miller in an attack on the third and fourth French ships, *Le Spartiate* and *L'Aquilon*. Captain Berry placed *Vanguard* on the seaward side of *Le Spartiate* so as to pummel her from both directions at once, while H.M.S. *Minotaur* swung in astern of her and attacked *L'Aquilon*. Captain Darby of the *Bellerophon*, seeing the van of both fleets well-engaged,broke through the French line astern of them, but being rapidly dismasted by some accurate fire from the French flagship *L'Orient* (120 guns), drifted back through the French line again, causing much confusion to his colleagues until he was able to steer his way clear of the combat. Captain Peyton of H.M.S. *Defence* picked out *Le Franklin*, a vessel of American origin acquired during the French participation in the American War of Independence. Captain Ball in the *Alexander* swept under the bows of the giant French flagship and directed his gunfire against her and her neighbour, *Le Tonnant*, whilst the *Swiftsure* and the smaller *Leander* bravely faced starboard broadsides from

JESS OF ROOS HALL

L'Orient. H.M.S. *Majestic* was the last of the British Fleet to enter the conflict as she fired on the *Tonnant* from the seaward side. Only the *Culloden* under Captain Troubridge was unable to take part, having grounded herself on the reefs of Bequier Island, right under the guns of the French fort!

Aboard H.M.S.*Vanguard*, Hugo had been assigned the task of standing beside the aft hatch to shout to the gunners below deck instructions on their target and the particular shot to be used. He had tied his kerchief about his face to stop himself choking on the cordite and gunsmoke that swirled about the main deck in front of him. When he received an order from Captain Berry or one of the officers on the Quarterdeck above him, Hugo would uncover his face and bellow through his megaphone till he felt his lungs would burst. From the news relayed on the quarterdeck, Hugo had overheard that four ships of the French Van had already surrendered and he heard the Admiral himself call to Captain Berry that he thought the *Spartiate* must yield soon, when the latter gave one final burst of gunfire and a fragment of shell struck the Admiral's right temple, detaching a flap of skin which fell over Nelson's good eye, as did torrents of blood. Hugo saw the commotion just as he stepped out from beneath the quarterdeck seeking his next instructions. In fact one rather large fragment of shell-casing bounced on the deck quite near him and he had to jump sideways to avoid it. He was in time to see the Admiral being carried below, and Hugo's heart sank within him. This was Tenerife all over again and with the commander wounded and withdrawn from the combat. He returned to his post and presently Captain Berry's precise tones were heard with fresh instructions. Shortly afterwards *Le Spartiate* surrendered.

Warping her anchors, *Vanguard* was slipping down the French line towards De Brueys' flagship, *L'Orient*, Nelson just before he was wounded having instructed Captain Berry to commence attacking the centre and rear of the French column. Night had fallen, but a pattern of stern lanterns and the flashes of gunfire, as well as flames from the fires that often were started among the tangles of fallen timber and canvas, allowed the crews to distinguish friend from foe. One particular fire seemed to blaze more brightly than the rest, and that was aboard *L'Orient* whose elevated decks shed flames like a gigantic beacon and illumined the whole of the battle.

Captain Berry leaned over the quarterdeck rail and seeing Hugo on duty there ordered him to seek out the Admiral and inform him that the French flagship was on fire and seemed likely to blow up. Hugo ran down the aft companionway and, dodging the recoiling guns and their toiling crews, made his way forward down to the orlop deck where Mr. Jefferson was busy plying his grisly trade. No sign of the Admiral there, and when he enquired he was told the commander was resting in his cabin. Hugo knocked timidly on the door and a voice, stronger than Hugo expected, bade him enter. The Admiral's cot was empty, but by the light of a flickering lantern he could be seen sitting at his desk with a blooded bandage draped around his head. Using his left hand, the Admiral was trying to hold paper and pen together against the juddering of gunfire from the ship. That took courage and determination, Hugo thought. "Message from Captain Berry, sir," he said. "French flagship's on fire, sir, and may even blow. Captain thought you would wish to know, sir."

"Indeed, thank you," the Admiral replied. "Tell Captain Berry I will join him as soon as I have finished this note. You're young Jarvis, aren't you?" Hugo nodded. "Any relation to the Chief?"

"Only distantly, sir," Hugo smiled.

"But you're a lieutenant now?"

"Yes, sir, but I was pressed into the Navy from Yarmouth."

"Indeed, Yarmouth," there came a hint of a nostalgic sigh from the Admiral. "Thank you, Mr. Jarvis," he said to terminate the encounter. Hugo returned to his duty on deck and presently a slight figure, deathly pale under the red and white linen that covered the upper part of his head like an Egyptian fez, moved slowly and silently as a wraith up to the quarterdeck whence all the ship's officers were staring at *L'Orient*. Both British and French vessels were being warped away from her proximity, since once the flames reached her powder magazines she would blow to smithereens and send huge fragments of timber and ammunition over the surrounding sea. Not till much later would they learn how Admiral de Brueys, having had his legs shot away and tourniquets tied around the stumps, had thrust both of them into a barrel of sand to keep himself upright on deck whilst continuing to direct his gunners. Nor that the ship's flag-captain, Casabianca, having been seriously wounded and taken below to the surgeon, had left his young son Giacomo waiting on deck for his father's return, whilst the great vessel burned above and below him and finally exploded, blowing all to fragments.

There was an awed pause in the fighting then, the explosion so vast as to be heard in Alexandria, fifteen miles away. In the temporary silence, Admiral Nelson was heard to ask Edward Galwey whether any of the *Vanguard*'s boats being towed alongside were intact, and being informed that only his personal barge was still seaworthy and not stove through, he said, "Then send it to search for any who may still be alive." Mr. Galwey leaned over the quarterdeck rail and seeing Hugo nearest to hand bade him take four seamen and the Admiral's barge to search for survivors from the explosion.

"What, French ones too?" Hugo asked.

"Yes, even those poor devils," the wounded Admiral replied.

So Hugo spent the remainder of the battle trawling around in the black waters lit by moonlight and by the fitful flashes of gunfire. Bodies and bobbing heads and arms formed black silhouettes against the glitter on the waves. He sat in the boat's stern and steered it towards the debris whilst the seamen rowed, and when they came across anything soft they jabbed it with an oar to see whether it responded. They did not find many, and when taking those they did to the nearest British ship had to run the gauntlet of splintered masts, yards, sails and missiles that came raining down from above.

The first person they hauled on board the barge was a French sailor, probably from *L'Orient* for he was covered with black powder and looked like a black-amoor. He had received a blow on the head and was concussed, but otherwise seemingly in one piece. For a while they found nothing but bodies and wreckage. The first British ship they came upon was the *Bellerophon*, still trailing one of her masts over her port side. They heard a cry and pulled out from a tangle of canvas and ropes a British sailor from the ship. He had a broken arm but apparently no other injury. Hugo hailed the vessel but the losses she had sustained were such that Captain Darby, himself injured, would accept his own ship's wounded but could not cope with any prisoners. It was the same state of affairs at the *Majestic* for her commander Captain Westcott had been slain, the most senior officer to be killed on the British side.

Hugo perceived that they were now approaching the remaining French vessels. First the *Tonnant*, now a hulk with her guns silent, had slipped her cable and drifted out of line. Others of the French rearguard had followed suit but were not so fortunate, for two had been set on fire and another run ashore. Two of the last ships in the French line did make sail and move away, despite the valiant efforts of the *Goliath*, the *Zealous* and the *Theseus*, the only British ships still fit for service, to stop them. These were *Le Guillaume Tell* and *Le Genereux* bearing Rear-Admiral Pierre Villeneuve. Together with two French frigates, these were the only enemy vessels to escape the complete destruction of that night. (Both warships were subsequently captured by Captain Berry a year later, one while Nelson was aboard.)

Hugo returned to the *Vanguard* with the Admiral's barge and a total of sixteen French seamen that no other ship seemed inclined to accept; it appeared that they had more than 3000 French prisoners already, of which a thousand were wounded, from the seven ships that had struck their colours and were still afloat. Back on board the flagship, Hugo could survey the battle scene. It was one of utter desolation. Smoking hulks from both fleets lay listless upon the idle water, while between and around them all the refuse of warfare swirled sluggishly with the tide. Hugo was allowed no rest, for the Admiral's barge was much in demand for transport, carrying the British captains back and forth from the *Vanguard* as they reported their casualties, the state of their vessels and those of their prizes, congratulated the Admiral on his outright victory and enquired after his injury. Some even brought him souvenirs, swords and medals from the captured Frenchmen, and Captain Benjamin Hallowell of the *Swiftsure* surpassed all by towing to the *Vanguard* a large section blown out of the mainmast of *L'Orient* which he told Admiral Nelson would provide suitable timber for a coffin!

"I thank you," said the Admiral with some surprise. "I trust you will not wish me into it betimes!"

That morning Admiral Nelson completed his despatches, borrowing Captain Ball's secretary, John Tyson, to replace his own who had been wounded early in the battle - which was why Hugo had found the Admiral writing in his own hand. Now he was able to list the British casualties as 218 killed and 677 wounded, whilst the French had suffered some ten times as many fatalities. Six out of seven French vessels captured and not sunk Nelson considered could be converted for use by the Royal Navy, and these were sent to Gibraltar for repair, along with a squadron of British warships under Sir John Saumarez. The *Goliath*, the *Zealous* and the *Swiftsure*, together with the missing *Terpsichore* and her sister-frigates which had now arrived, were detailed to blockade Alexandria and prevent any of Bonaparte's troop transports escaping to sea. Nelson's immediate problem was to send news of the victory and the defeat of the French Fleet to London as swiftly as possible to relieve the Government's anxiety. One copy of his report was dispatched with Captain Berry on the fast-sailing *Leander*, first to Earl St. Vincent and thence to London. For safety, a duplicate was dispatched on the *Mutine* with one of Nelson's "boys", Thomas Capel, as acting Captain, who sped to Naples and then overland to London.

A third despatch involving some more intricate instructions was sent with a Lieutenant Duval, a former diplomat and a foreign linguist, who was to travel through Egypt and if he found that Napoleon's army was still encamped in the interior, with no fleet awaiting it at Suez, he was to proceed to India and inform the Governor of Bombay of the victory which had rendered that country safe from invasion. That establishment of the East India Company was to respond with its gratitude and a lakh of rupees.

Meanwhile the *Vanguard* would head for Naples as her starboard timbers had been so battered by the bombardment as to require radical overhaul. Before she sailed, Admiral Nelson commanded the Chaplain to hold a service of thanksgiving on the main deck. As the personnel assembled, the gaps in their ranks left by victims of the battle, such as the death of William Faddy, the Captain of Marines, became obvious. Two more of Nelson's Norfolk "boys" had died, one of these being Giles Spencer from the junior officers' cabin, and his companion Nicholas Wilmington, a tall, broad-shouldered fellow with curly blond locks, could not restrain his tears as the Chaplain preached of the valour of the departed and their just reward in Heaven. They sang a hymn together, some of their voices cracking with tears and others hoarse with the smoke and fumes of the guns. This ceremony completed, Captain Berry departed aboard the *Leander* and Captain Thomas Masterman Hardy from the *Mutine* took command of the *Vanguard*.

Hugo was at last dismissed for food and rest after forty-eight hours of strenuous and stressful activity, but on his way to his hammock he was met by Mr. Sheppard, the Purser. "That cot in the junior lieutenants' cabin that Mr. Spencer, God rest his soul, used to occupy, it's yours now if you wish it," he said. "I've told Mr Wilmington you'll be joining him and have asked him to pack up Mr. Spencer's belongings and send them to the hold for storage till we reach England again." Down below, Hugo found the gun-deck in such chaos with some of the guns still run out,and airy gaps in the timbers where cannon shot had ripped through, that he was glad to snatch up his few belongings and head back up the companion-way.

Hugo knocked respectfully on the cabin door and a voice within bade him enter. Nicholas Wilmington sat on the edge of his cot, his head in his hands and his shoulders shaking with what sounded suspiciously like sobs. "I was grieved to hear about Mr. Spencer," Hugo said to open the conversation. "How did he die?"

"He was shot to pieces by cannon fire," Nicholas replied. "It came right through the top of an open gun-port and hit him midriff. I was standing next to him at the time and was covered with his blood. I just stood there all-agape till some of those oldsters came by, picked up the two halves of him and stuffed them out through the open gun-port. I shall hate them for ever for doing that. How shall I face his parents when I go home? - if ever I get there, that is?" Remembering his somewhat similar experience with Pip Harris, Hugo felt that a little manly encouragement was required, and seeing a brandy bottle and two tankards still resting on a shelf where they had been left two days before, he poured a tot for Nicholas and one for himself.

Presently the young man calmed a little and started telling Hugo about his friend. Hugo was desperately tired and would have fallen asleep where he sat had Nicholas's words not begun to interest him. "Giles and I were at school together," he related, and mentioned the name of a distinguished educational establishment for young gentlemen in the City of Norwich. Hugo knew of it by reputation, some pupils from the Sir John Leman School having been fortunate enough to transfer there. Moreover it appeared that the two families also knew one another well, the fathers Gilbert Spencer and Tobias Wilmington both being merchants of Norwich, though dealing in different commodities. Hugo was sure he had even seen the name 'Wilmington' written in large letters on the wall of a warehouse in the dock basin when he had sailed up the River Yare in the *Louise*.

What Nicholas said next had all of Hugo's attention. "I was in the Purser's office the other day when you brought in your correspondence for inclusion with the despatches. I noticed that you had addressed your letter to Roos Hall at Beccles. That belongs to the Rich family, and I wondered what was your connection with them?"

"The Housekeeper there is my great-aunt," Hugo replied, hoping that Nicholas had not noticed that the first line of the address had read "Miss Jessica Rich". It appeared he had not, or discounted it, for Nicholas continued, "There is quite a scandal between that family and ours. Shall I bore you if I go on?"

"Not at all, please do," said Hugo through his weariness, thinking that he might learn something of relevance to Jessica and her paternity.

"My Uncle, Sir Everard Wilmington," Nicholas continued, "married his second wife quite late in life. My Aunt Marianne was a young widow living at Brighthelmstone when my uncle met her whilst taking the sea air there following a severe bronchial infection. I believe my aunt took it upon herself to look after him and nurse him until he was quite recovered. He then brought her back with him to London and married her very shortly, his previous wife having died some years before. They had had no children, nor has my aunt borne him any, but Uncle Everard, wishing to have offspring to inherit his estate, and perhaps for comfort in his old age, took upon himself responsibility for Aunt Marianne's two stepsons, Leonidas and Marcus Todd."

So far there seemed nothing particular in Nicholas's recital, and Hugo was dying to yawn but thought it much too impolite to do so. Then Nicholas said, "Leonidas was the elder and his father, a retired Brigadier living in Brighthelmstone in much reduced circumstances, had managed to purchase him a commission in the Army - I believe he is now serving in India. But Marcus was much younger, conceived in the Brigadier's retirement, and when his wife, their mother, died he felt he could not cope, so placed the boy in a private orphanage in the town. He then took my Aunt into his household, first as a housemaid, since she was but nineteen at the time, and then he married her. At some stage or other of their marriage my aunt must have confessed that she had had a child by a previous relationship, and that the illegitimate consequence was still living in the workhouse at Lewes where he had been born. Imagine the horror of the respectable though poverty-stricken Brigadier on receiving such a revelation. He instructed his wife immediately to transfer the said infant to the same private orphanage in Brighthelmstone where he had placed his son Marcus. None of this was known to my Uncle Everard when he married Aunt Marianne and it only came out much later.

"Even so, no-one is supposed to know the identity of her illegitimate lover, but my mother has it that Aunt Marianne, having been betrothed as a young child to someone much older, was seduced at the age of sixteen from the bosom of a genteel family living in the village of Kensington. She is said to have eloped with a handsome government inspector many years her senior. That government employee was either Sir Robert Rich or one of his staff. My mother says he had a Chief Clerk who was exceptionally good-looking by the name of Ralph Ainsworth. However, you are younger even that I, so that the tale may have no significance for you. It merely explains why there is no love lost between your landlord Sir Charles Rich and my relatives in London and Norwich."

Nicholas had gone rattling on with his tale, his eyes upon the floor and his expression still downcast. When he glanced up it was to find Hugo looking at him fixedly as if he had seen a ghost. In the course of the last few months Hugo had happened upon the secret of both Jessica's and Ainsworth's births, information which could be of vital importance to his family and to himself. Ainsworth Rich, he who had always claimed he was the son of Sir Charles, 'Well well! Whom should he tell? How might he reveal it, and to whom?

"What?" asked Nicholas, suddenly observing Hugo's expression.

"Oh, nothing. Should I come upon any information of relevance when next I return home I shall be sure to tell you. By-the-by I hear we are heading to Naples for repairs. That should provide us with a chance to explore the city."

"I have been there before," Nicholas said, then his expression clouded over again as he continued, "with Giles and his family. They took us in vacation time when we left school. But then, instead of sending us to university as we had expected, our fathers thought to make men of us by sending us to spend a year at sea." Hugo could observe tears welling in Nicholas's eyes again, but he mastered them and instead added brightly, "Naples is a magnificent city. I should be delighted to show you around." They both turned in then and soon were fast asleep.

CHAPTER XVII

The Forbidden Fruit

"I am full of sin; Thou art a sea of Mercy.
Where Thy Mercy is, what became of my sin?"
Tipu Sultan, from his pocket-book
found at Seringapatam, India, 1799.

Ainsworth Rich awoke suddenly with an urgent need to relieve himself. As he swung his feet from the bed to the floor, the room swirled around him, and the rising sun,which gave him sufficient light to wander into his dressing-room, seemed to leap up and down like a yellow indiarubber ball. His brain thumped against his temples, and his eyes felt as though they had been heated with smoothing irons. He had told himself during the course of the previous evening that he ought to indulge less in William Hickey's best claret. Or was it brandy? He couldn't remember. Returning to his bed, he saw that the little scarlet satin waistcoat, his souvenir of the fierce battle at Seringapatam, had fallen to the floor when he had brushed it impatiently from his pillow. He picked it up, and as he did so found that the lower edge of the garment felt very hard and sharp. He supposed that it was due to the raised embroidery, but then something seemed to sparkle through the lining inside it. Ainsworth's hands trembled, and he knew that this tremor did not arise from his state of inebriation.

He took his pocket knife and carefully cut a stitch or two that hemmed the lining in place. Then he cupped his hand beneath the slit. A pile of small grey stones, then some larger blue, green, red and purple ones, filled his shaking hand. Diamonds! probably from the famous Golconda mines in South India, and no doubt the rubies, emeralds, sapphires and amethysts emanated from Benares. He held in his palm half a fortune, but he could not convert it in India. Trading in precious gems was forbidden to East India Company personnel unless they were departing on retirement when they could be used to pay for their passage. In any case Ainsworth was unsure of the value of such uncut stones on the English market. For a moment he had a vision of a terrified official in Tipu's burning palace, leaving his most precious object, his ready money, where only he could retrieve it, judging correctly that the rest of the world would pass hurriedly by without observing the little jacket on its lofty hook.

Then Ainsworth dragged his thoughts back to the present. Wherever might he hide the stones without Anando finding them? Those secret compartments in the existing furniture would all be known to him. There was a secret inside pocket in his portefeuille, but he carried that with him whenever his occupation took him to different districts of Bengal. He opened a drawer of the dressing-table and came across an old coin purse, the one he had last used in England and which bore the Rich coat of arms. That was a start, and he tipped the stones carefully inside it. Then he found an old pair of stockings which he had thrown into a corner of the drawer one evening and had forgotten to ask Anando to have them mended. He tucked the purse inside the stockings and buried them under a neat pile of shirts that the dhobi had carefully laundered and pressed. He must find a better hiding place, but where? He could not trust his banker; people would talk. The stones were spoils of war, and those from Seringapatam had been divided up between the Wellesley brothers and the military commanders involved. Some larger items had been sent home to England for the benefit of the Company and the State. Then Ainsworth recalled that many of the soldiers had taken personal souvenirs from the Palace, even breaking off carvings from the walls, so perhaps his theft was not so heinous after all. He comforted his conscience with this thought and fell back to sleep.

Ainsworth should have paid heed to the expression on Anando's face, the sneer of his curling lip and the glitter of his eye, when he brought Ajoy to live at the "cottage" a few days later. Ajoy was wearing, of course, the little scarlet embroidered waistcoat, white loose trousers and tunic with embroidered bands at ankle and cuff, smart new sandals and a sash about his waist of the finest silk. At this time, being no more than a young teenager, his head was bare and his curly locks cut short so that they framed the smooth beardless complexion and the generous features of his face, his fine dark eyes and his full lips. Anando realised that never again would he accompany his master to an evening of music, dancing or cards, where he would stand with the other servants and deliver food or drink as required, and then afterwards would half-carry his master home. Instead he had been demoted to house-steward, whilst all the glamour of these European occasions and the generous tips that were often forthcoming for a khidmutgar, would fall into the hands of this inexperienced but handsome youth. A further insult to Anando's dignity and pride was caused by the fact that Ajoy was to sleep in the little spare room in the cottage, whilst he, Anando, the senior servant in age and ability, would continue to use one of the servant's cabins in the garden; this amounted to a severe loss of face. The possibility that Ajoy and his master might sleep together did not disturb Anando one whit. Such experiences were a daily part of the kaleidoscope of life in India. Anando would have been most surprised to learn that in the British Navy two sailors had just been hanged for 'visiting with another in his hammock'.

The appearance of Ajoy beside his master at one of Calcutta's fashionable soirées that autumn, and then at a winter ball, caused quite a stir among the expatriate community of Bengal. Comments were most ribald at the barracks at Baranset where Ainsworth still rode from time to time, but these days on a hired hack. Of greater significance was the remark made by Colonel Arthur Wellesley to his brother the Governor-General that "It seemed that Mr. Rich might have succumbed to the Italian vice." However, the same gossip-monger failed to transmit the Governor's reply.

Ainsworth, feeling bored and frustrated after five years in the Company's service without notable promotion or any indication of future distinction, hardly cared what his neighbours or his colleagues might think. Of more immediate concern to him was the effect that Ajoy's handsome appearance was having on the eligible daughters of the Company's magnates, and even more upon their matronly mammas! Ainsworth began to experience pangs of jealousy as the whirling dancers turned to feast their glances upon Ajoy, or one of their parents called upon him to circulate with a tray of sweetmeats. Nor did Ajoy hesitate to return the eager glance or to collect the generous tips. Even more galling was the cost of the liberal supplies of rosewater which Ajoy lavished on his own bathing as well as that of his master, and the perfumes with which he scented his breath.

The dawning of the new century had caused Ainsworth to review his position in more detail. Colonel Kirkpatrick still ruled the Foreign and Political Departments with an iron hand, giving Ainsworth little opportunity to stir from his Writer's desk. His former colleague, David Lambton, had become a revenue collector in a distant part of Bengal and made infrequent visits to Calcutta. Colonel Wellesley, conferring with his brother about the minor brigands he was pursuing among the plains of the Deccan, had no further need of a French linguist. That gentleman's only acknowledgement of Ainsworth's acquaintance had been to express disappointment at the death of Mughal and to race Diomed against other well-bred mounts instead. Indeed Ainsworth was developing quite a paunch now that he no longer rode on a daily basis. He was thirty years old, only just out of debt by the merest margin, and totally bored with his existence. This was not, most certainly not, what Sir Charles had promised him.

On 10 July 1800 Fort William College opened its doors on the Governor-General's express orders, despite the discouragement he had received from the Court of Directors in London. Dr. John Borthwick Gilchrist, a medical doctor trained at Edinburgh, was appointed its first Principal. He was a scholar of Sanskrit and Persian, and had already published a Hindi dictionary. He was to be assisted by a Persian specialist named Charles Stewart, and Charles Theophilus Metcalfe, a then undistinguished young fellow barely half Ainsworth's age, was enrolled as the College's first scholar. All Company personnel in the Writers' Building who had not passed the examinations set in four of the required languages, were ordered to attend extra lessons at the College. Ainsworth had been sent back to school yet again!

However he did not have to suffer long, for a few months later Colonel Kirkpatrick was sent to Poona to assist in finalising a Treaty with the Peshwar, Daolat Rao, and he remained there to serve as Resident. In his place Neil Edmonstone returned from Madras and was put in charge of the Foreign Department as Chief Clerk. The two friends were soon parted again, however, perhaps even with Neil's collusion, for a bright young recent recruit to the Writers' service by the name of John Ravenshaw, ten years younger than Ainsworth and with the minimum of five years in the Company's employment, was appointed chief tax collector or diwan for the South Cunara district of Bengal, and Ainsworth was to accompany him as his assistant. It was a position of trust, the young man Ravenshaw lacked worldly experience, though he could read Sanskrit and could converse nonchalantly in Persian with the local princelings, their poets and their courts. Ainsworth, with his good command of Bengali and Hindi, his years of experience, and the expeditions to Lucknow and Mysore to his credit, found himself able to guide his superior with very little trouble at all. Due to the manner in which he exercised his function some rich pickings came his way, although he felt a sufficient sense of loyalty to the Company so as not to defraud it altogether.

Chief among the collector's duties was to summon each of the local zamindars and to negotiate with them the revenues due to the Company. Naturally every zamindar would approach wringing his hands and pleading beggary, but it was the collector's task to investigate the situation, to establish how far the zamindar's claims were justified, and to secure as much revenue for the Company as possible without depriving the ryots of their next season's harvest. In the ryots' hand-to-mouth economies, poised on the edge of poverty, the precept of saving for future contingencies had never been adopted. In a good year the ryots would count their blessings, pay their debts, and make additional sacrifices to their gods for their good fortune; in a bad year, a time of flood or famine, they simply learned to starve.

By the Bengal Settlement of 1793, Lord Cornwallis and John Shore had separated the system of Zamindars and Talugdars, tax-collectors and landlords, from any judicial function, henceforth to be carried out by senior civil servants at district courts, and responsible to a British-run Supreme Court sitting in Calcutta. The zamindars, who were often landlords in their own right, formed a tradition inherited from the Moghul emperors and princes, and whilst India was no more than a trading partner there seemed little need to impose change. But Robert, Lord Clive, had made the Company itself a landlord over a large tract of Bengal, and the territorial expansion, which began through rivalry with the French in the second half of the eighteenth century, created a more pressing need for collecting revenue on a regular basis. The zamindar system was a clumsy tool, encouraging corruption, lack of investment in agriculture, and social disorder and cruelty among the Indian peasantry.

Leaving his colleague, John Ravenshaw, to interview the zamindars and to discuss terms and conditions as well as overlooking whatever accounts and records they maintained, Ainsworth took their escort of twenty Sepoys and toured the surrounding villages, all those that he could ascertain fell under the control of the particular zamindar in question. He found their interrelationships most complex, since few were direct tenants, there were no formal deeds or leases, and the most useful person to consult was usually the village headman or patel. Ainsworth knew that if he was welcomed to a village it was either because there had been a good harvest and the ryots had confidence that their zamindar would successfully conceal the extent of their good fortune, or it could be that the zamindar had been exceptionally avaricious or cruel and they wished to lay complaints against him. On the other hand, if Ainsworth found the road barred by a group of peasants armed with spears, talwars, bows and poisoned arrows, and a few matchlocks for show, it could mean either that the villagers were determined not to be asked to pay more, or that they were so deprived that there was no more to be had from them.

Each ryot's smallholding of three or four acres, known as a 'bigha', could be defined as sufficient land upon which to support a family of his particular caste. There was no standard land measurement, no fencing, and no common land for grazing as there was in England. Instead there were constant arguments between zamindar and tenants, and much litigation. As a rule of thumb, the poorer the ryot the worse his fate. If he fell into debt to the zamindar because his crop yield was poor, there had been fire or flood, the monsoon was late or non-existent, the ryot could then seek a loan from a manwari or moneylender at twelve to eighteen per cent, he could mortgage the next season's crop or his land, sell his oxen, his goods and chattels, his wife or his daughters. Beyond that, if he remained incapable of paying, there was a tradition in India of physical torture to the point of death.

Wherever Ainsworth went, he heard tales of ears, noses and limbs being hacked off, eyes and genitals stuffed with peppers, and lashings and beatings of all kinds. He observed the results of such treatment as he rode, the beggars in the streets, the one-legged man with his crutch making for the nearest town to beg a bowl of rice, scars and deformities such as he had seldom experienced elsewhere, save briefly at the Battle of Seringapatam. Nor were these punishments confined to just the menfolk. A peasant would invite Ainsworth to step inside his mud-walled hut where his wife would unfasten her garments to reveal two ugly purple weals where nipples had once graced her breasts; these had been tweaked off by a cleft stick of bamboo. "My wife is expecting our next child," the ryot would say, "How shall we feed it if my wife cannot do so? I have no money for a wetnurse." Infanticide was prevalent, and disease often killed what penury spared.

Ainsworth would return of an evening to the lodgings he shared with his colleague. "What did you discover today?" John Ravenshaw would enquire. Ainsworth would inevitably respond that it was better not to know until one had spent many years in India and could understand its ways. John, for his part, would relate his assessment of the character and trustworthiness of the zamindar he had interviewed, the financial formula agreed upon for settlement, and whether this was to run for three years or ten, in accordance with the rules laid down by the Company. The usual formula was to allow the ryot to retain some forty to fifty per cent of the value of his crops as the cost of continuing his cultivation, with fourteen per cent being allowed for the cost of fresh seed, but both them were aware that a vindictive zamindar could confiscate up to eighty per cent of a ryot's production, leaving him barely sufficient for subsistence and nothing for planting again.

It was a vicious cycle and it sickened Ainsworth who so far in life had paid little heed to the feelings and sensibilities of others. He looked forward to his return to Calcutta at the end of his three-month tour of duty. On reaching the cottage he found it strangely silent and shrouded in dust as before. He gave a shout and Anando appeared but failed to greet him with the same courtesy and willingness as he had always done hitherto. Indeed his servant would not even meet his gaze. The cook Davi appeared next, followed by the dhobi, and a bhisti-wallah appeared at the garden-door as if summoned by a genie. Ainsworth did not enquire this time how many of their respective acquaintances had been camping out in his property during his absence. Instead he asked, quite naturally, of the whereabouts of Ajoy. "He not here, Sahib," Anando replied, "he return to father." Ainsworth was hot and weary, having been riding all day and only taking a palanquin to return home after leaving his mount with the Sepoys at the Fort. He would visit Mr. Biswas in the morning and find out what had occurred.

Ainsworth called upon Mr. Biswas early next day before continuing to his office. A servant ushered him within and Mr. Biswas himself came forward to greet him, extending both hands. Ainsworth realised straight away that something serious had happened as, with all a father's indignation, Mr. Biswas hastened to furnish the details. It appeared that immediately following Ainsworth's departure for Cunara, Anando had driven Ajoy from the cottage and had obliged him to lose face by returning to his father's house. Then one afternoon Ajoy had returned to the cottage in the absence of Ainsworth's servants. In the kitchen he had heated water for a bath and having carried it all upstairs, had sat himself in the bath surrounded by Ainsworth's soaps and remaining supply of rosewater. Anando had returned to the house and, seeing signs of activity, had at first assumed that Ainsworth himself was present. However, recalling that Ainsworth had departed on what was expected to be a long tour of duty, Anando armed himself with a poker and crept upstairs, surprising Ajoy naked in his master's bath. He seized the young miscreant and then did that which he had blamed his master for doing, beating the boy with the poker. Then Anando pushed Ajoy downstairs and into the street stark naked, throwing his clothes to him from the upper storey. After such treatment and such loss of caste, Ajoy dared not return. If Mr. Rich desired to secure his son's services, Mr. Biswas concluded, he would be obliged to hire him for one day at a time.

At that juncture Ajoy himself entered the room. He took one look at Ainsworth and rushed across the floor to embrace him by the knees. Much surprised, and embarrassed before the boy's father, Ainsworth patted Ajoy's head and enquired what injuries he had received. Ajoy showed him a number of horizontal weals that were still livid on his legs and complained that he had received two black eyes and a split lip from contact with the stairs indoors and more bruises from those at the front of the house, whilst he had had to endure the shame of covering his modesty in the street in front of a crowd of curious passers-by.

Ainsworth took from his portefeuille a silver-gilt casket studded with semi-precious stones that had come his way during his tour of duty. Its value was not so great but he could not have sold it without raising comment. Better by far to give it to someone whose father would easily be able to realise its worth when required. "Ajoy," he said, "I have brought you this small gift from my travels and I regret that you must receive it under such poor circumstances."

"Oh, Master, I thank you, most generous of masters," the boy exclaimed, and showed the trinket to his father. On his return to his lodging that evening Ainsworth decided to say nothing to Anando about the matter but just to wait awhile until normal relations with his staff had been resumed. Before retiring to bed that night he sought a clean shirt for the morrow in the chest of drawers and looked into the corner to check whether the stockings and the hidden gems were still safe. He found that the stockings had been washed and mended, rolled up in exactly the way he had left them and with the coin purse and stones tucked inside. Anando had discovered his treasure! Suddenly Ainsworth sensed that his days in Calcutta were numbered.

It was now the hot season and the monsoon was expected at any moment. At Government House tempers were frayed for the Governor-General was having one of his periodic disagreements with his brother Arthur, with his other brother Henry, Lord Cowley, acting as a reluctant go-between. At the request of Henry Dundas, Minister for War, the Governor had authorised the despatch of three thousand Indian troops to the Red Sea for the purpose of assisting General Abercromby to defeat Bonaparte's army which was still stranded in Egypt following the Battle of the Nile. What more natural than that the Governor should wish to give the supreme command of the force to his brother Colonel Wellesley? Then it was realised that the Colonel had insufficient military rank to lead such an important campaign, and that there was no more senior contender for the post than Major-General David Baird, he who had been worsted of command at Seringapatam. General Baird had presented himself at Calcutta, loud in his complaints, and after some resistance the Governor had yielded to his request. Arthur Wellesley was not amused.

Moreover, despatches had arrived from London informing the Governor that in February (1801) William Pitt had resigned as Prime Minister, due to the King's refusal to grant Catholic Emancipation in Ireland. Pitt had been succeeded by Henry Addington, a rather pompous individual lacking real distinction as a statesman. At the same time Henry Dundas had taken retirement, becoming Viscount Melville, and Lord Castlereagh had succeeded him as President of the

Board of Control of British India. The new Government ushered in a totally different atmosphere from the previous situation where the Wellesley brothers had been able to hold all the reins of power. Henry, Lord Cowley, was recalled to England. Expenditure was to be more rigorously controlled from London, additional troops and armaments were no longer forthcoming, and territorial expansion would no longer be approved. Worst news of all was the instruction the Governor-General received from the Court of Directors, and fully endorsed by Lord Castlereagh, to close down his cherished Fort William College with immediate effect. Neil Edmonstone considered the new policy most short-sighted when Ainsworth joined him at one of the many Calcutta taverns one evening, and he opined that the Directors and the Board of Control both were simply uneducated about practical conditions on the ground in India, and that delays in communication between the two countries made such far-flung territories impossible to govern, as it were by remote control. The word in Europe was, Neil advised Ainsworth, that peace was likely to be concluded with France very soon, since Henry Addington would never make a minister for war. And so it proved, for the Peace of Amiens was signed in March 1802.

By the time this news reached India the Wellesleys had troubles of their own. The Peshwar of Poona and the Scindia of Gwalior had been defeated by the Holkar of Indore, and the Peshwar had sought refuge in the Company's Residence at Bombay. In December 1802 Arthur Wellesley, now promoted Major-General, on his brother's instructions concluded a Treaty with the Peshwar at the town of Bassein near Bombay. Since the Peshwar was the leading sovereign among the Maratha princes, his conversion to having his sovereignty protected by force of British arms was quite a feat of diplomacy. The Peshwar was subsequently returned to his throne at Poona, and General Arthur Wellesley could turn his attention to dealing with the remaining Maratha princes. Ainsworth listened to the almost daily news of the Wellesley triumphs with a sense of bitter gloom; Neil Edmonstone had accepted an invitation to accompany the new Major-General on his military travels and had taken David Lambton with him. It seemed that only Persian linguists were required on this campaign, and in Calcutta Ainsworth was left to the boredom of routine correspondence and Company accounts.

It was in an effort to relieve this boredom that Ainsworth took Ajoy Biswas back into his household, but only on those occasions when he was sufficiently close at hand to ensure that the boy came to no harm. Never would he depart on field duty again leaving the boy a victim to the jealousy and spite of his fellow-servants. Indeed the cook Davi, probably at Anando's instigation, had more than once tried to poison Ajoy, whose traditional duty it was at mealtimes to taste each dish first before presenting it to his master. It was such a pretty sight, Ainsworth thought, to watch Ajoy on his knees, licking the last traces of his tasting from his lips as he lifted the dish with his white-gloved hands and presented it to his master. Anando had always served his master's meals with courtesy and respect, but would have considered it beneath his caste to kneel to this junior representative of a foreign race.

Whilst Ainsworth toiled all day at the Writers' Building, Ajoy, having escorted his master to his dawn ride and then run beside his palanquin to the Esplanade, would attend his father's business in another part of the City, and would reappear like a genie from a bottle in time to take a torch and escort Ainsworth home. If he went out for the evening, Ajoy would run beside his master's palanquin if the journey were long enough to warrant one or would otherwise accompany Ainsworth on foot. On one occasion, Ajoy had discovered a snake lurking in the waiting palanquin - again Ainsworth had cause to suspect one of the servants - and on another evening when Ainsworth had returned home very drunk, Ajoy had chased away a cobra found curled up beneath Ainsworth's bed. It belonged to a snake-charmer who worked the Chowringhee Road, for the fellow had had the unwisdom to leave the basket in which the snake normally resided upon the chest in the hallway downstairs. Anando, on being loudly summoned by Ainsworth, had appeared fully-dressed and ready-armed with a forked stick by which the creature had been secured and returned to its normal abode.

There had been other changes made to Ainsworth's routine. When he rode to Baranset of a Saturday or Sunday afternoon, Ajoy was no longer obliged to run every mile there and back, but sat feet-a-dangle upon the donkey kept at the stables for which Ainsworth paid an additional hire. At Baranset Ainsworth could indulge his passions for cards and gambling, but not that of dalliance with his handsome lover. Nor was he free to do so in daylight hours in his own home, for did he dare to do so his servants would be bound to interrupt him, someone would call at the door, or, by some devious arrangement which Ainsworth again accredited to the baleful influence of Anando, a band of local musicians would suddenly appear and shatter all romantic and poetic thought by blasting away with pipes, trumpets and drums beneath his bedroom window, thereby ensuring that many heads emerged from all the neighbouring doors to enquire the cause for celebration. Nor was Ainsworth free to dismiss and replace his servants; they went with the lodging, courtesy of Mr. Biswas, and besides, Ainsworth would have had difficulty in locating and selecting reliable alternatives.

The Governor-General, now the Marquess Wellesley, on the announcement of his elevation to the peerage, albeit to the peerage of Ireland, the land of his birth, had considered Government House in Calcutta a structure all too plebian and functional to provide an adequate complement to the dignity of his office. Consequently he had purchased an estate fifteen miles north of the City and removed from its polluted airs at a place known as Barrackpore. Here he might spend weekends and any other intervals which might occur in his duties. The spot was pleasantly rural, lightly forested and well-provided with game for hunting. There his architect created a Palladian mansion Indian-style, with cool floors, doors and windows which opened so as to direct currents of cooler air through its salons, and wide shady verandahs on all sides. The grounds were landscaped and furnished with sculptures and fountains, and were planted with the most colourful and languidly perfumed of the Sub-Continent's myriad vegetation.

The Governor decided that he would mark the completion of this project with a grand ball to be held at New Year when the cool dry season left the roads moonlit and clear of mud. All the senior staff connected with the governance of Bengal were invited, together with those members of the Ton who happened to be resident in or visiting Calcutta at the time. Military men from the British regiments serving in India, the Judges from the Supreme Court at Calcutta, naval captains from the Far East squadron patrolling the Indian Ocean guarding Company merchantmen between China and the Cape, the Company's Bankers and some of the City's leading businessmen, all were invited. So too was Ainsworth Rich, much to his surprise as he did not believe himself greatly in favour with the Governor-General. Rather did he attribute it to the influence once more of Neil Edmondstone who had just returned briefly to Calcutta with the Governor's brother, Major-General Wellesley, in an interlude of his campaigns against the Maratha princes.

Carriages, waggons, pony-carts, dooleys and palanquins galore, as well as cavalcades of horsemen, bearers and runners with torches, crowded the road to Barrackpore that evening. The grandest social occasion that Calcutta had seen in years was anticipated, and every participant had made sure to garb himself in his finest costume, whilst their ladies had been planning their couture for weeks beforehand, and every darzee of repute had been obliged to resort to a strict appointment system to manage his queue of clients.

Of the ladies, all were exclusively European, Indian wives and mistresses not being included. The Indian merchants and bankers who attended were accompanied by neither wives nor daughters, though sometimes by their sons. There was just one exception to this practice made for everyone's favourite host, the prominent lawyer William Hickey. During his military campaign in the Northern Deccan, General Wellesley had taken into protective custody the beautiful widow of a Hindu rajah at the instant when the lady was about to commit suttee (suicide by burning on the funeral pyre) in respect for her dead husband. On reaching Calcutta the General had asked his friend William Hickey to take the lady into his household which had remained desolate since the death in childbirth in 1797 of his lively consort Jemdanee. However, once dinner was concluded and the dancing and cards had commenced, The Ranee, as she was known, began to feel out of place and retired to sit at a table close to where the Indian servants gathered awaiting the orders of their masters. The Ranee knew several of the servants by name and some, conscious of her isolation, took turns to stand beside her and to converse, though their stance was awkward since none might dare to take a seat. Ajoy was among those the Ranee called to her side, though he was soon commanded to circulate among the card tables and to take orders for wine and refreshments.

Ainsworth had been placed at dinner between two daughters of the Ton whose education in matters of taste, art, music, and poetry might have achieved the highest standards, but whose knowledge of life, and life in India in particular, he found sadly lacking and naive. Moreover their physical charms moved him even less. Resisting, for once, the temptation of gambling at the card tables, and even more firmly an invitation from a group of elderly ladies to partner one for backgammon, Ainsworth wandered among the group of gentlemen standing at one end of the ballroom. His own banker introduced him to several acquaintances and he met again some of the officers he knew from the campaign against Tipu Sultan, including General Harris who gave him a friendly nod. Then he glimpsed among the crowd a head of unruly blond hair whose profile was both dear and familiar. David Lambton was making one of his rare visits to Calcutta and the two fell into instant and welcome gossip.

Meanwhile, at the other end of the ballroom The Ranee still sat alone and unattended. Ajoy having completed his round of serving refreshments made to pass her table when she called to him. The next event that Ainsworth observed, as the dancers cleared momentarily from the floor, was his own servant and the object of his passions seated upon The Ranee's lap with her hands and arms caressing his lithe and faultless complexion. Breaking off his chatter with David Lambton in mid-sentence, Ainsworth strode rapidly across the empty ballroom floor, causing many heads to turn at the disturbance, and seizing his servant's arm with the merest inclination of his head towards The Ranee, he dragged young Ajoy after him through one of the exits. Supposing there to have been some domestic misbehaviour on the servant's part, or that his master was merely departing in a huff, no-one gave a further thought to the incident.

How dare Ajoy allow himself to be pawed over by another, Ainsworth fumed furiously as he dragged the boy after him. Ajoy was his creature, his plaything to treat as he fancied, to beat or caress as he chose, the source of his own titillation and comfort. How dare he besmirch his purity with the sensual favours of others, of strangers, and of those Ainsworth considered to be of lower social status? From the sconce-lit corridor Ainsworth dragged Ajoy into a darkened room and turned the boy round to face him. Then the softness and the perfume of the being he held in his grasp overwhelmed him. He murmured in Bengali an apology for his own brutality and began covering the boy's face and neck with his own passionate kisses. He ran eager hands over the lithe limbs within their cloaking of flimsy garments. Suddenly Ainsworth observed in the moonlight flooding through long windows that the centre of the room was occupied by a bed of kingly proportions covered by satin damask drapery. He gathered up Ajoy in his arms, deposited him in the midst of the softness, and flung himself upon him, scarcely bothering to kick off his trousers or his shoes.

Presently there came a click as the door handle turned and a tall square figure stood in the doorway, observing with astonishment and incredulity how the surface of his bed rose and fell in the moonlight. The humping did not cease, for his entrance went unperceived. A house servant, previously commanded, arrived with a lantern and the Governor-General of British India was suddenly presented with the spectacle of his own place of repose, lonely for want of a wife left in England, being defiled by an humble amanuensis from the Writers' Building in the City!

"Mr. Rich, kindly leave my house at once and take your servant with you!" the Governor shouted in a voice that cracked with affronted indignation. With a white face Ainsworth adjusted his smallclothes, slipped his now shaking legs into his trousers, retrieved his shoes and fled from the room, with Ajoy stumbling after him. There was an exit at the end of the corridor and the Governor's servant showed them outside into the cold night air.

At first Ainsworth could not stop trembling. Why did it have to be the Governor's own room that he had violated? If he had chanced to enter a servant's room instead, none but the servant would have paid him heed. How was he to return home? He had travelled to Barrackpore in a carriage with some others from the Writers' Building, and obviously he could not deprive them of their transport. "Do you need a horse, sir?" It was a sergeant in attendance upon one of the cavalry officers who had been seated around a brasier with his fellows, whilst the Indian bearers and drivers sat about another fire close by. Ainsworth accepted the offer and had Ajoy helped up behind him. "Just leave the horse at the Fort," the soldier instructed him as Ainsworth thanked him and picked out the road ahead.

It was a long and lonely ride, just the two of them in the moonlight. Ainsworth found the presence of young Ajoy's thin arms around his waist a comfort as he strove to determine the track. Like most of his fellow-guests he had left all his weapons at home in Calcutta and out here in the darkness he could fall prey to dacoits, or even to a hungry leopard. He felt no guilt for any offence he might have caused, for feelings of guilt had seldom featured in Ainsworth's mentality. That which he desired and decided upon, he thought, must always be his by right. Nevertheless he anticipated some cause for complaint by the Governor upon the morrow and concluded that it would be prudent to return Ajoy to his father's house. Dawn was breaking by the time his weary mount clattered over the cobblestones of the causeway at Fort William and he was able to leave the horse at the gatehouse with details of its provenance. Then he took Ajoy by the hand, and led the sleepy and reluctant boy to his father's doorstep where once again his presence at the unusual hour needed to be explained.

Half an hour later Ainsworth entered the cottage alone and disshevelled and clapped his hands for Anando. As morning had broken his servant was already astir. Coffee was brewed and the bhisti-wallah furnished the wherewithal for a cleansing bath. Ainsworth found his dresser drawer full of clean linen and chose his most sober attire for a reluctant appearance at the Writers' Building around noon. He found the office deserted by all save the more junior of its employees and tried to put his mind to his task as he audited yet another pile of Company accounts. Afternoon tea being delivered at the usual hour of two-thirty and just as Ainsworth was wondering whether his presence was at all necessary that day, when David Lambton strolled in through the doorway of the Foreign Department.

"I'm afraid you're in trouble, old fellow," was his greeting, "and a great deal of it too. The sound of the Governor shouting at the top of his voice reached the ballroom last night at a pause in the dancing. His anger was clearly audible, though not the words he used. He did not reappear with his guests for some time, and then only to have a word with his brother and after that with Charles Metcalfe, his private secretary," David Lambton told him. "Everyone was conscious of a change of atmosphere, and even though the entertainment continued, the heart had gone out of one's enjoyment, you know. The party began to break up and by dawn everyone had gone home, except for myself and a few of the soldiers from the 33rd Foot, Arthur Wellesley's regiment.

"Suddenly we observed a column of black smoke rising from behind the Governor's mansion, and supposing the house to be on fire we ran to take a look. Imagine our surprise to see the Governor's servants casting upon the flames drapes and bedding of the finest quality. Sheets and pillows as well as the mattress were all consigned to the flames. At the last came to the bed itself, which was a shame as it was that finely-carved one made of heavy walnut wood which we had such travail to transport from the ruins of the Palace at Seringapatan, the one that was said to be Tipu Sultan's own. As we stood observing the scene with some bewilderment, one of the Governor's servants informed me that his master had discovered one of his guests upon it 'in flagrante delicto' with an Indian servant boy," David Lambton continued. "Remembering how abruptly you had deserted our conversation, and knowing your preferences in these matters, I had no difficulty in establishing the identities of the persons concerned, and your name is likely to be circulating all round Calcutta by now. You will be cut dead by everyone," he concluded.

"What do you think will happen?" Ainsworth enquired, somewhat abashed at his friend's intimacy with what he considered to be his private existence.

"I think you may need to visit your banker and settle up your affairs. Do you have many debts?"

"Only minor matters at this time, but little credit either."

"I would resolve my assets in such a situation," David Lambton advised.

Ainsworth put down his coffee cup, took his hat and cane and departed for Mr. Seth's establishment before the hour of tiffin should bring an end to business for the day. Ainsworth informed his banker that he needed to take some home leave immediately - 'family business' was the excuse he used. Mr. Seth proved very understanding. Had he perhaps heard news of last night's escapade? He promised to render Ainsworth's accounts, including the presentation of any promissory notes deposited with him in the past, within twenty-four hours, but

he would, of course, demand a discount of twenty per cent for this special service. Ainsworth had no recourse but to agree. Then he hurried to the home of Mr.
Biswas to enquire after his rent. Mr. Biswas spread his hands eloquently as he
explained that while no rent was due for the cottage for another fortnight, his
son Ajoy was much bruised and should Mr. Rich wish to make use of his personal services in the future he would be obliged to demand a hire fee of say --- Rs.
per day. Ainsworth realised that the sum requested was identical with the fees
applicable to the most sought-after City prostitutes!

Ainsworth then recollected that he had left instructions with his darzee for
the making up of a new cutaway coat and two pairs of nankeen trousers. If the
clothes were ready, which he doubted due to competition from preparations for
the Governor's ball, he would be obliged to pay for the order; if not he would
cancel it. The coat, for which Ainsworth had already had a fitting, was indeed
ready for collection, and if Mr. Rich would care to try on the trousers and would
pay for them at the same time, they could be sent round to his lodging later in
the evening when the last stitches were complete. Ainsworth paid the sum
requested, overlooking any of the accustomed bargaining, and departed for the
cottage. There he laid out the new coat on a chair in his bedroom, checked in
his drawer that the precious gems were still hidden in the corner - at least, the
coin purse still rattled - changed into evening wear and went downstairs.

Anando and his other servants were nowhere to be seen, so Ainsworth walked
down the road till he could summon a link-boy to guide his way with a resinous
torch. He called at the Blind Beggar Tavern, a dockside inn situated near Garden
Reach, the haunt of sailors and of thieves. He had chosen it because news of his
misdeeds were unlikely to reach its clientele and would be greeted by no more
than a shrug of the shoulders if they did. To his chagrin the bar was tenanted by
soldiers from Major-General Wellesley's 33rd Regiment who hailed him upon his
entrance with a mighty shout. "Here comes the gentleman who sullied the
Governor's bed," cried one, "and caused him to light a big bonfire," finished
another.

Ainsworth backed out of the door and turned away from the inn. He had
already dismissed the link-boy, thinking he would not need him again for an
hour or two, especially if he had chanced upon a game of backgammon which
might have detained the idle moment. Now he was alone in a vice-ridden district with only his walking cane for company. He grasped it more firmly as shadows loomed up before him, and he swung round abruptly if he fancied he heard
a footfall behind him. By night these alleyways were full of cut-purses and cut-
throats, and with a rapid stride Ainsworth headed for the distant light shining
from the windows of the Fort, and beyond them from the buildings that lined
Tank Square. As he reached the Strand and then the Esplanade, Ainsworth began
to feel bolder. He sought out another tavern where he was known to the barman, only to retire baffled when he received the same reaction from an assorted
clientele. As David Lambton had warned him, his name and his misdeed was all

round the City by now. He returned to the cottage, drank a whole bottle of brandy and sank into his bed, still protesting inwardly at the unfeeling world about him.

Ainsworth awoke late the next morning, his head still reeling from the brandy. He hurried into his clothes, those that he had worn the day before, drank some scalding coffee that Davi had prepared, and departed on foot for the Writers' Building without awaiting the services of a palanquin. Neil Edmonstone looked up from his desk as soon as Ainsworth entered the Foreign Section. "Ainsworth," he called, "I regret to say that you are required to present yourself at the Governor-General's office immediately upon your attendance here. Charles Metcalfe has sent me a note timed at seven o'clock this morning."

With a mere "Thank you," to his superior, Ainsworth turned on his heel and crossed the compound to Government House. There he was shown into Charles Metcalfe's office and was made to wait an hour and a half before the Governor was willing to see him. The Marquess Wellesley kept him standing, and when Ainsworth thought it diplomatic to make some apology for his error in desecrating the Governor's own boudoir, he held up his hand. "I wish to hear no more about it," Richard Wellesley said. "My hospitality and goodwill have never been so insulted. I trust that you realise, Mr. Rich, that in England you would have been tried and hanged for such an offence, whether it was in a private bedroom or in a public place. Had that offence taken place here within the Government's premises you would also have hanged, for this is Crown land. However my own mansion is not so designated and I must abide by the custom of the country in which I serve. Its legal codes do not consider such activity a crime unless accompanied by brute force, the which I am reliably informed was not present in this case.

"However, your crime is a mortal sin in the eyes of God and in the teaching of the Christian church, and your actions have brought desecration upon my house and dishonour upon the good name of my administration and that of the East India Company. In these circumstances I have no alternative but to dismiss you instantly from your employment here and to demand that you remove yourself entirely from this City and from British jurisdiction in Bengal. On my orders Mr. Metcalfe has kindly sought out a position for you wherein you may earn your passage home to England. The East Indiaman *Beaumaris Castle* is due to sail for the Cape and thence to London tomorrow and its officers have need of a steward to serve them at table. With your experience of good wines I should imagine you to be most suited to the task. Your servants are packing your trunks as we speak, with orders to deliver them to the docks. You may return to your lodging to collect your personal papers, pausing on the way only to settle such debts as you may afford. There have been more than sufficient occasions when persons dismissed from the Company's employ have departed leaving ourselves to bear the brunt of their financial incompetence.

"Mr. Rich, your reputation preceded your arrival here, and it has not improved since. I have written a personal note to your Guardian, Sir Charles, which goes overland, and may advise him of your return. I bid you goodbye, then, and please, on your way out, do thank Mr. Metcalfe for the arrangements he has troubled to make on your behalf."

Ainsworth stood, pale and shattered by this tirade, though in truth if had had any humility to recognise his own faults he should have expected it. "Goodbye, sir," was all he could murmur as he walked unsteadily to the door of the room and turned to close it behind him. Then he was obliged to face young Charles Metcalfe and the smirk of the younger man at the disgrace of his senior. Instead of giving the secretary his own thanks, Ainsworth had spirit enough merely to pass on those of the Governor. He returned to the Writers' Building to find that his portefeuille, his hat and his cane had been deposited with the caretaker at the door. Then he remembered his diamonds and wished that he had put them in his pocket when he had dressed this morning, as he had half a mind to do. If only he had not consumed quite so much brandy! Losing all dignity he ran for his lodgings, receiving cat-calls from the bearers of passing palanquins who concluded Ainsworth had gone mad by ignoring their services during the heat of the day.

Ainsworth rushed into the cottage, nearly colliding with Anando in the hallway. "Trunks gone, Sahib, already gone to docks," the old man told him. Ainsworth ran from room to room; in the sitting-room his drinks cabinet had been cleared - he had no idea where the contents had gone. Such books and papers as had lain about, Anando assured him, had been packed in the trunks and he would find them on board ship. Ainsworth rushed upstairs to discover his bedroom and dressing-room completely empty, nothing in the wardrobe or chest of drawers, on the dressing-table, in his dressing-room, beside the bath,and nothing in that drawer where his diamonds had lain hidden for so long. Anando assured him that all his belongings had been carefully packed by the dhobi and himself. Ainsworth looked the old man in the eye; his glance did not waver. Taking out his purse, he felt he should not leave on a discordant note with the people who had served him well, within their limitations, for the seven and a half years he had spent in Calcutta. Accordingly he gave Anando twelve rupees for himself, six for the dhobi and six for Davi the cook. Anando was agreeably surprised, thanked Ainsworth most humbly and wished him a safe voyage home.

On foot once more, and ignoring the heat of the day - it was the cool season anyway - Ainsworth visited first his darzee and enquired after the two pairs of trousers for which he had already paid. It appeared that the tailor had only just completed his work upon them and they were now ready for collection. The tailor obligingly wrapped the garments in a parcel and Ainsworth departed for the office of Mr. Seth. The banker handed him the final account of his deposits and some small percentage of the debts he was owed by his fellow gamblers. Ainsworth was beginning to feel grateful for any rupees which still jingled in his pockets. He asked Mr. Seth if he might take the balance in gold, and another huge discount was thereby deducted. Still, remembering the lost diamonds, Ainsworth thought that gold of any sort might buy him a night's lodging or two when he arrived in London.

His last call was at the store run by Mr. Biswas with the aid of his son Ajoy. Ainsworth confirmed that he was obliged to leave for England immediately and expressed his regrets. He said that he would have liked to have given Ajoy a parting gift to thank him for his loyal service, but that the suddenness of his departure had robbed him of the opportunity of doing so. "It is of no matter, Sahib," Mr. Biswas replied. "In fact my son has something he wishes to give you." At this moment Ajoy, who had hovered at the rear of the shop unsure of his welcome, ran forward and threw his arms about Ainsworth who felt tears springing to his eyes. Without a word, Ajoy drew out of Ainsworth's embrace and taking his master's hand palm upwards he placed in it a modest leather object. It was the coin purse in which Ainsworth had hidden his diamonds!

"Look inside, Sahib," Ajoy urged him. "All the stones are there, every one." Ainsworth shook the purse which rattled and then opened it carefully. The gems glinted within.

"How did you come by this?" Ainsworth demanded.

"He did not steal it," Mr. Biswas hastened to intervene, "my son is not a thief."

"Sahib," Ajoy began, "I met the servant near your doorstep who had been sent to order Anando to pack your trunks. He told me you were being sent away, and I knew that those stones which were precious to you might not be safely included in your baggage. I therefore ran into the house and up the stairs and seized the purse before anyone could stop me. You see, I had found the stones and had touched them many times without your knowledge. Sahib, please forgive me."

"Forgive you, Ajoy? You are my salvation," Ainsworth exclaimed, "for indeed I shall have little else to live on when I reach England. Come, let me spread the stones upon this table and you shall choose one to treasure for your own."

It seemed no coincidence that Ajoy should select the biggest and best ruby, already partly cut, and translucent with flashes of purple fire. Ajoy clutched it in his small elegant hand, "May I have this one, Sahib?"

"Indeed you may, one red as blood and with it, dearest boy, you have my heart." Ainsworth gathered up the remaining stones, put the purse in his pocket, shook Mr. Biswas by the hand and gave Ajoy a final embrace, and a wave as he walked away down the street, blinking tears from his eyes as he went. This was the closest Ainsworth had come to an emotional relationship since his boyhood passion for Richard F. With unwilling steps he made his way to Garden Reach and the bulky presence of the *Beaumaris Castle*.

Once aboard, Ainsworth was directed to the Purser's office where he was instructed as to his duties, and a seaman was detailed to show him to his cabin which he would share with the Captain's valet. Once there and he observed the limited space available between the cots hung against each wall, upon the seaman's suggestion he packed one of the trunks with the clothes and belongings he expected not to need before he reached England, and allowed it to be taken down to the hold. As the trunk could be locked, he had included with its contents the little purse with its hoard of precious stones. Kept in his cabin, he thought, such valuables would be no safer than a ripe banana in a cage full of monkeys!

The following day, the remaining crew and cargo came aboard, the hatches were closed, the mooring ropes cast off, and under tow by her own launches the *Beaumaris Castle* edged out of Garden Reach into the main stream of the Hugli River. Once her sails filled and the boats were hoisted back on board, the pilot who had guided her upstream from Fulda took the helm once more and eased the bulky craft downstream towards the Ganges Delta, eighty miles distant. There she would await her sailing companions, perhaps other East Indiamen from China and South East Asia laden with tea, porcelain, more silks and more spices, together with a proportionate and well-armed naval escort.

As the ship reached the Delta Ainsworth observed the crew pointing towards a sandbank into which a freshly-wrecked vessel was slowly sinking. The place was a quicksand surrounded by a treacherous maelstrom into which any vessel careless of her navigation could be sucked willy-nilly to her grave. It was known as the 'James & Mary' from a famous ship which had sunk there in 1694. Once the vessel had been caught in the fatal current there was no escape for ship or crew, since no boat could be launched or line thrown aboard which would not also be sucked down into the maelstrom. Any passing crew had simply to watch helplessly whilst their fellow-mortals drowned before their eyes. The present wreck appeared hull-down and lifeless.

Watching this scene as his ship passed by and learning of its history, Ainsworth could only compare the wreckage before his eyes with the wreckage of his career in India, and he saw his own vessel as a prison within which he must live out his sentence without any certain hope of a future at the other end of the voyage.

CHAPTER XVIII
The Yarmouth Connection

Naples, 1st October 1798

Dear Miss Jessica,

I thank you most gratefully for the news of home which I received upon our landing here a week ago. By the time this reply reaches you, England will surely have learnt of our recent Victory over the French Fleet which we encountered at Abu Qir Bay, not far from Alexandria, Egypt. I have to tell you frankly that, like all great battles, it was a scene of immense destruction, especially among the French whose casualties far exceeded our own, particular devastation being caused by the complete explosion into fragments of their flagship, 'L'Orient'.

"My own ship, the 'Vanguard', the flagship of our commander Rear-Admiral Sir Horatio Nelson, saw much heavy action and sustained great damage as a consequence. This made us in dire want of materials so that, along with some other ships of the British Fleet, we sailed slowly towards this City where we might obtain respite and repair. Upon our approach on 22nd September last, when we were no closer than the island of Capri, a great flotilla of the citizens of Naples came out to greet us, together with their King Ferdinand, whom I think a tall, ugly fellow but very jovial, and their Queen Maria Carolina, who is also jolly but no longer youthful. Accompanying them was the King's First Minister, Sir John Acton - an Englishman who has made a place for himself in a Foreign State - though I should mention that this Kingdom of the Two Sicilies is presently, as I understand it, Britain's only ally in the Mediterranean Sea. Thus good mutual relations have much importance. Britain's Envoy here is Sir William Hamilton and his wife Lady Emma, with whom I observe that our Admiral is already well acquainted from the way that they greeted one another upon their coming aboard from the Royal Barge. We have all been received as heroes, even the humblest sailor, for our destruction of the Enemy hath been so complete as to prevent any French attack here from the sea for the future.

Once the ship was safely berthed, all the officers were sent ashore, apart from the Master, the Purser and the Carpenter, as those who must supervise our repairs. The Admiral, who sustained a flesh wound to his head during the battle, is entertained by the Hamiltons at their elegant Palazzo Sessa in the City, and not far from the Palazzo Reale - there is much to and fro-ing between the two households. For the rest of us, there seems no end to the celebrations, and we are fêted wherever we go. One has only to mention that one has taken part in the battle from the deck of the 'Vanguard' and free food and wine, and even lodging, is urged upon us. Indeed, the streets here are decorated with blue 'Nelson' banners bearing the Admiral's name and many gold anchors, and every street musician is singing songs in our praise, some of them in the most atrocious English you may imagine. Even the Town Band in our honour has learnt to play 'Rule Britannia' and 'See the Conquering Hero Comes'!

"I have a new companion from among our crew. His name is Nicholas Wilmington, a native of Norwich. He is a year or more my elder, but joined our ship at Portsmouth at the invitation of our Admiral, along with a group of youths from Norfolk and neighbouring parts whose fathers sought to give them the experience of a year at sea. Alas, such is the peril of our profession that three of them have perished during this voyage - not quite what their parents had expected, I think.   One of these was Giles Spencer, another Norwich fellow and a family friend of Nicholas. In some ways I have taken his place in that I now share Nicholas's cabin and that he, having visited Naples on a previous occasion, has been my guide against the misfortunes that may befall one in a strange city. For instance, I verily believe there are more thieves and pickpockets here than there may be in all of London. There are also many fine buildings with much ornate sculpture, marble floors of many hues, and portraits and busts set about the walls of every publick building. Nicholas has some little command of the Italian language so that we manage quite well, but this does not prevent our getting into numerous misadventures, some of which I may be persuaded to relate when next I am home!

"I am sensible that you may presently be attending the school at Ipswich of which we spoke at our last meeting. I trust that you find it to your liking and that it fulfills the expectations you had of it. I suppose that my Aunt Jarvis will forward this letter to you if it would otherwise delay your receipt of it, and be sure that any correspondence you are kind enough to send me will in future be delivered post-haste after our famous Victory!

Your humble servant and friend,
Hugo Jarvis.

P.S. I enclose, as usual, a separate note for my mother to reassure her that I am still alive and in good health."

Repairs to H.M.S.*Vanguard* completed, the ship left Naples on 15 October with her Admiral back on board and Captain Hardy in command. Promotions took place to fill the gaps left by the casualties of war and Nicholas Wilmington was made 'acting lieutenant' on promise of his continuing his training and taking the examination upon his next return to England. As Nicholas was eager to learn, he sought Hugo's assistance and they worked together to improve their knowledge and their skills.

The Admiral's objective was to inspect the blockade which Captain Ball of the *Alexander* had been despatched to carry out at the port of Valetta where the French had left a large garrison. This proved effective, though the more limited French forces isolated on the small island of Gozo among a hostile native population did surrender. Somewhat to Hugo's surprise, the *Vanguard* returned to Naples again, but then he learnt that the British Fleet was to support a military campaign by the Austrian General von Mack to recapture Rome from the French, a campaign to which King Ferdinand was to contribute some four thousand Neapolitan troops and six hundred cavalry, all to be landed at Leghorn (Livorno) from Nelson's ships.

By the time that *Vanguard* reached Naples again, despatches had arrived from London and elsewhere reacting to the news of the Nile victory. Captain Capel had arrived first, for Captain Berry and the *Leander* had been waylaid at sea by the French. From the Admiralty Lord Spencer sent word to the Lord Mayor of London and church bells were rung all over the capital, with salutes fired by guns at the Tower and in Hyde Park. Crowds gathered and poor Captain Capel was followed by hundreds everywhere he went. Lord Spencer sent the news to the King, who was taking the sea-air at Weymouth. That messenger was also waylaid - by a highwayman who, learning of the content of the despatches, wished the messenger well on his way and without harm. Celebrations also began in Norwich, where Captain Berry was well-known as Nelson's flag captain, and a Victory Ball was held at the Assembly Rooms. The same example was followed at Swaffham, the nearest large town to Burnham Thorpe, Nelson's birthplace and some-time residence.

At Beccles the news was received via the stage coach coming flying down the road from Norwich with flags fluttering from its roof and windows and the driver more than merry from the many inns and hostelries at which he had paused on his way to share the good tidings. Robert Jarvis immediately had Peter swathe the Bear & Bells in bunting, hoping with all the faith he could muster that young Hugo had survived the battle without injury and that some personal missive from him would soon be forthcoming to confirm that outcome. The fact that his great-nephew was serving on the *Vanguard* brought Uncle Bob such a flood of customers that he was obliged to take on an extra barman for a month or two, and he had the great satisfaction of drawing the clientele away from his rival, the King's Head.

At the Ringsfield Farm, however, they durst not celebrate for fear it might be too soon, but awaited the news from Hugo himself - a long endurance, for it took several more weeks for his letter from Naples to arrive, and then a further twenty-four hours passed before Aunt Jarvis dared to open a cover addressed to Miss

Jessica, even though she recognised the handwriting well enough. Such was the force of habit in service, even to one's own secret granddaughter.

King Ferdinand's troops had been duly delivered to Leghorn at the end of November, whilst the Austrian troops had marched there overland. There had been but little resistance from the French forces in Rome and King Ferdinand was able to send an invitation to the Pope to return to the Vatican since the heretical enemy had fled. Nelson, his task complete, led his fleet back to Naples, and talk among every crew was the expectation of sailing for England, home, to share the festive season and their own triumph with their loved ones. Nicholas Wilmington was especially anxious to console the family of his friend Giles Spencer over the loss of their son.

Instead, just two weeks later, the Palazzo Reale was obliged to receive back its monarch as a fugitive, with news that the French Army had routed the Neapolitan forces and was marching on his Kingdom. Sir John Acton and Sir William Hamilton advised the Royal Family to take flight to Sicily, the presence of Nelson's fleet providing an obvious escape route. Even then, time was wasted on packing up and loading aboard, covertly via the Palazzo Sessa, all the royal treasures. Artistic and archaeological works which Sir William Hamilton had spent a lifetime collecting were also shipped abroad, and H.M.S.*Colossus* later sank in a storm off the Scilly Isles with a full cargo of priceless classical vases. Hugo and Nicholas played their part in this shipping process, each taking an oar of the *Vanguard*'s boats, and Hugo's loading and stacking skills being much in demand in the transport and storing of these delicate artifacts.

Nelson's greatest problem was how to spirit away the King and Queen and their children against a background of increasing social unrest, with only part of the population remaining loyal to the Crown and the rest more ready to welcome the French and much-needed political reforms of the kind recently introduced in Paris and Washington. Cover was to be provided by a reception given by the Envoy of the Sultan of Turkey, he who had presented the now Baron Nelson (of The Nile and Burnham Thorpe) with that diamond cockade that used ever after to decorate the Admiral's tricorn hat. Nelson had all his boatmen dress in dark clothes and boat-cloaks and to wait at the quayside whilst he made his appearance at the Reception, along with the Hamiltons and Lady Emma's mother. Then, while the rest of them crept aboard one of the British boats, Lord Nelson quietly walked along the quay and was shown through the cellars and undercroft of the Royal Palace to where the King and Queen awaited him.

To Hugo at an oar of the Admiral's own barge, waiting for the Royal Party with bated breath, it reminded him of that dark and dreadful night at Santa Cruz, and he found himself shivering a prayer that the episode would not end in the same way. There was a rumour that rebellious factions had taken over the waterside batteries which guarded the City, and gunfire from either of those could sink their little flotilla in an instant. The fugitives reached the boats without incident, and several long pulls at the oars took them quickly away from the shore. As a precaution Nelson had had the carronades unshipped from the decks of his fleet and loaded into reserve boats in order to provide protective fire if necessary.

On board the *Vanguard* all the senior staff cabins had been vacated for their Royal and distinguished guests, and Hugo was able to welcome Nicholas to the dubious distinction of a midshipman's berth on the Gun Deck! Two days of contrary winds prevented the British ships from leaving port. During this time General von Mack appeared to report on his own defeat, and he was roundly ordered to make a stand before Naples with all the troops he could muster before he could think of retreating to Sicily. However, once out of port, the *Vanguard* and its companion Neapolitan warships and merchantmen were met by a violent storm which tore sails to tatters. Nicholas scarcely had time to complain about the discomforts of sleeping in a hammock, for he and Hugo spent so little time there. Every hand was on deck engaged in damage limitation, whilst Emma Hamilton ministered to the Royal Family who were overcome with seasickness and fever. Their youngest child, six-year old Prince Albert, actually died during the course of this brief but apocalyptic journey.

The *Vanguard* docked at Palermo on 26 December 1798. The Queen, prostrate with grief at the loss of her child, was driven straight to the Palace in a closed carriage, whilst the King gaily made preparations for hunting! The Hamiltons were obliged to rent a villa outside the town, unheated and devoid of all the elegant existence they had left behind in Naples. The ship, freed of its unexpected guests and their voluminous baggage, was in dire need of a good cleansing, and Nicholas had the pleasure of joining Hugo and the rest of the crew at soaking and scraping the decks and disinfecting all surfaces from stem to stern with Stockholm tar and vinegar.

For Lord Nelson himself there were other concerns. He had still not fully recovered from the wound he had received at Aboukir Bay, and he now had political responsibility for the safely of the Sicilian Royal Family in case that island too should rebel against them or should fall to the French. Nelson had transferred his flag to a small craft moored in Palermo harbour in order to keep a close watch on such issues, as well as on his own developing relationship with Emma Hamilton. But news came of a revival of Italian fortunes in the South of Italy which might even result in the recapture of Naples. To support this movement, Nelson despatched Captain Troubridge in the *Culloden* with the *Vanguard* under Captain Hardy and two others of his fleet to blockade the port of Naples and prevent the French garrison being re-supplied by sea. The British Marines and seamen swarmed all over the outlying islands of Procida and Ischia, being welcomed by the local populace and enjoying the beauty of the Maquis in full flower at the end of April. The *Vanguard*'s Purser also availed himself of the opportunity to bargain for fresh fruit and vegetables.

However the triumphant little force was soon recalled to Palermo on receipt of bad news from Gibraltar where illness had forced Admiral Jervis to take refuge and to hand over his command to Lord Keith.* It seemed that twenty-nine French ships of the Brest Fleet had passed Cadiz unseen and had entered the Mediterranean. Lord Keith relinquished his blockade of Cadiz to pursue the French, only to be followed out of Cadiz by seventeen Spanish warships. Suddenly the Mediterranean was full of enemy shipping again and the outstanding victory of the Nile would be voided should the French and Spanish contingents manage to join forces. There was also the matter of the French needing to rescue its numerous army still stranded in Egypt, something that Britain was most eager to prevent.

Nelson responded by sending ten of the best of his Band of Brothers to join Lord Keith in the defence of Minorca and the continued watch on Toulon. Then, learning that the French had already passed Minorca, he recalled Captain Troubridge's force from Naples and Captain Ball from Malta to reinforce the defence of Sicily in case the French fleet should intend to land there. It was all very confusing, Hugo thought, for the crew who, robbed of their anticipated voyage home, were now expected to defend foreign interests with the same valour as they did those of Britain.

Lord Keith sent Nelson two more warships with news that the French Fleet had been able to reach Toulon and the Spanish had slipped into Cartagena without any British interception taking place. Admiral Jervis also sent Nelson further reinforcements under Rear-Admiral Sir J. Thomas Duckworth, who brought the sad tidings that the Admiral was obliged to retire due to ill health and that Lord Keith was to succeed him as Commander-in-Chief, Mediterranean. The Admiralty's orders to Lord Nelson were that he should use his Fleet to patrol the Eastern Mediterranean so as to prevent the French from making a landfall at Malta, Sicily or Egypt. Naples too was a possible target, Nelson thought. There, according to despatches from captain Edward Foote of the frigate *Seahorse* whom Captain Troubridge had left on watch, the Royalists under the command of Cardinal Ruffo, a politician, were regaining the upper hand. Timely support from a British Fleet at this stage, Nelson believed, might just swing the balance of power and enable the Sicilian Monarchs to regain their rightful throne. At this point, it seems, Nelson decided to ignore the requirements of the distant British Admiralty and to give priority to the needs of his friends.

Among the freshly-refurbished warships which had accompanied Sir Thomas Duckworth was the *Foudroyant*. A three-decker of eighty guns, she was taller, longer and carried a more powerful armament than the *Vanguard* so Nelson transferred his flag to her, along with Captain Hardy and several members of the *Vanguard*'s crew. Hugo felt a vivid sense of disappointment and almost of desertion at the Admiral's departure. He had enjoyed his moments of proximity to the great commander, and much though a new captain and officers might be made welcome, it was not quite the same thing as having Britain's Hero aboard. Lord Nelson had also taken the Hamiltons into the *Foudroyant* with him, to act both as his interpreters and as envoys on behalf of the Sicilian Monarchs.

* *George Elphinstone, Lord Keith, was an uncle of Mountstewart Elphinstone, the East India Company's Resident at Benares, India.*

JESS OF ROOS HALL

Cardinal Ruffo had negotiated an amnesty with the rebels which would permit them and the French garrisons to depart unharmed if no French fleet appeared within twenty-one days. Nelson did not approve of such deals with the Enemy, especially remembering the presence of a French Fleet at Toulon which had already eluded once Lord Keith's vigilance. Moreover, King Ferdinand and his bellicose Queen, left behind in Sicily, most emphatically disagreed that any clemency should be shown to the rebels, and commanded that examples be made of all the ringleaders. At the time of the receipt of this instruction, embodied in a letter addressed by the Queen to Lady Hamilton, the rebels and their families, as well as the French garrisons from the two waterside forts at Naples, had embarked on Neapolitan coasting vessels known as polaccas, anticipating a voyage into exile at Toulon. Lord Nelson immediately placed the polaccas under armed guard, and Sir William Hamilton notified Cardinal Ruffo in writing that there had been a change of plan.

Arrests were made, among them notably Commodore Francesco Carraciolo, formerly the commandant of the Neapolitan Fleet and already known to Nelson, but who had since changed sides. A court martial composed of eminent Neapolitan Royalists was convened aboard the *Foudroyant* and Carraciolo was condemned to be hanged. Nelson had the sentence carried out at the yardarm of the Neapolitan's own flagship, a scene eagerly watched by the crews and marines of the British Fleet, crowded upon the decks and manning all the yards. Hugo viewed the event with distaste as the Italian Count was hanged on high like a common criminal and his body was then cut down and allowed to fall into the sea. Whilst he acknowledged that rebels deserved punishment, he also realised that those who had taken places aboard the polaccas had in fact surrendered their persons into their enemy's care, and he thought that they should have been treated honourably as prisoners of war. Besides, hanging was no decent end for a gentleman, and was it not Lord Nelson himself, when aboard the *Vanguard* and dealing with the poor French fellows who had been pulled from the sea after the explosion of *L'Orient*, who had spoken of "humanity in victory"? Hugo was sure he had heard the Admiral say as much more than once.

Presently King Ferdinand himself arrived from Sicily and was lodged in the Admiral's cabin aboard the *Foudroyant*. The trials and executions continued, on board ship and in the City, and gunfire now resumed from the Fortress of St. Elmo above the town whose French garrison had not been so easily persuaded to desert their strong position for the comfortless polaccas. Hugo and Nicholas had to take their turn on guard with the rest, and found that women as well as men were being brought aboard *Vanguard* in chains and then sent for execution. Hugo both saw and heard executions taking place by beheading or hanging, and learnt that the prison of Naples, and another in Sicily, were full to overflowing with so-called "Jacobins" accused of taking up the libertarian ideas of the French Revolution.

It was against this obscene and disturbing background that the anniversary of

333

the Battle of the Nile was celebrated with illuminations and music, and Hugo could not help recalling with regret, as he chatted with Nicholas, their innocent pleasures of a year before. However worse was to come, for King Ferdinand, rising early one morning and going on deck, found himself confronted by the decaying corpse of Count Carraciolo floating head uppermost in the water, ghastly and bloated by its long immersion! Who is to say that this was not the verdict of Fate upon the King's unmerciful treatment of his foes? Nelson had the corpse dragged ashore and buried without ceremony.

Eventually the French garrison of Fort St. Elmo surrendered to a force commanded by Captain Troubridge, and along with the remaining refugees aboard the polaccas they were permitted to sail for Toulon. Lord Nelson escorted the King and the Hamiltons back to Palermo, leaving Captain Troubridge in charge of matters at Naples with the acting title of Commodore. At Palermo Nelson received indignant despatches from Lord Keith complaining that he had been obliged to follow both the French fleet from Toulon and the Spanish one from Cartagena back into the Atlantic to Cadiz, not having sufficient forces to intercept them without Nelson's assistance. Lord Keith insisted that Nelson detach squadrons to patrol all possible sources of French activity in the Mediterranean. Prom Palermo Nelson sent orders to Sir Thomas Duckworth to patrol the Strait of Gibraltar, four warships were set to watching Minorca in case the French decided to sail out of Toulon, three were assigned to aid a Portuguese squadron to pin down the French garrison at Valetta, and Sir William Sidney Smith was to sail east to make sure the French Army did not escape from Egypt in its transports. Sir William then committed a tactical blunder. He forwarded to General Bonaparte newspaper cuttings detailing some minor French defeats in Italy and the Netherlands which caused the 'Monster of France' to realise that he was wasting his opportunities whilst stranded in Egypt. He boarded a small ship at Alexandria which slipped past the British blockade and safely landed the General in France. Scarcely a month later, in November 1799, the Directory in Paris was overthrown and replaced by a cabinet of three Consuls, of which Napoleon was one. A few weeks later he had established himself as the First Consul and had become the Dictator of France.

In England the Admiralty realised that the naval and diplomatic situation in the Mediterranean had become unsatisfactory. Sir William Hamilton, at the age of nearly seventy, was to be replaced as Envoy, and Nelson's health having deteriorated, Lord Keith ordered him home. The Admiral escorted Queen Maria Carolina and her children to Livorno whence she would travel overland to her home city of Vienna, and had sought Lord Keith's permission to transport himself and the Hamiltons back to London in the *Foudroyant*. This was denied, since the warship was in good shape and too powerful a ship to be spared from the Mediterranean Fleet. His Lordship must perforce also travel overland! Instead it was the *Vanguard* that upon his review Lord Keith judged most in need of careening, re-ballasting and refurbishment, having been at sea continuously for the better part of three years. So he ordered her home to Deptford where she docked in October 1800.

The crew were paid off, collecting prize money in respect of the vessels captured at the Battle of the Nile, as well as medals of honour for their valour. Gold medals were reserved for captains and admirals, but all the senior officers were awarded silver ones, junior officers medals of silver gilt, and all the crewmen and Marines were granted copper medallions. As a junior officer Hugo was entitled to a silver gilt medal, but when he discovered that Nicholas would receive only a copper one, plus a second copper piece which he might deliver to the parents of Giles Spencer along with the Admiralty's compliments, Hugo requested that he might take a copper medal instead. He excused this publicly by declaring that he had spent most of the voyage serving as a crew member anyway, and privately, that he did not wish to laud himself over his friend's tragically lost companion. Nicholas was much moved by Hugo's generosity and vowed they should seek to serve together on their next ship, since they had found each other such good company. Both took the Norwich stage together and parted in that city, Hugo catching the conveyance for Beccles with every intention of making his home leave long enough to celebrate both the Christmas season and his own nineteenth birthday in the middle of the month.

*   *   *

Beccles, 1st January 1799

Dear Hugo,

As I write to you from my room here at Roos Hall on a morning crisp with frost, fresh air steals thro' my window, which is open so that I may hear the bells ringing in the New Year from Beccles Tower on the distant hill.

I thank you for your kind letter written from Naples, but must tell you that I was unable to receive it until I returned home for the Christmas vacation. This was because at my school - of which more anon - there is no privacy of either one's person or one's possessions, and one's most intimate details are held up for publick inspection. Thus I had instructed your Aunt within a few weeks of my arrival there, that she should retain all correspondence for my return. Fortunately Mrs. Jarvis had the good sense to open your letter and remove the note within addressed to your family. They were still awaiting anxiously news of your safety, and dare not rejoice at the Fleet's famous Victory upon the Nile until your letter arrived and allay'd their fears.

"Indeed we are all rejoicing still. Your heroic Commander's name is everywhere written upon banners, many publick places have sprouted flags and bunting, there are Victory Balls put on at every Assembly Rooms, and many new songs have been composed which are passed around and sung among any family of a musical inclination or provided with a pianoforte. Even the organist at Beccles Church has

made a collection of them and has brought me some that I might improve my skills during the Christmas vacation. This reminds me to tell you that there is to be a special thanksgiving service this evening at which I shall attend with your Aunt and her husband. I should add that Barsham Church is also in the midst of its celebrations, both Church and Rectory being much be-flagged, and the Suckling family not in the least reluctant to remind the rest of us of its close connection with Lord Nelson, the Hero of the Nile.

"I turn now to some less palatable news and furnish you, since you were kind enough to inquire about it, with a description of my school, so that you may appreciate why I take care to keep at a distance from it all those matters I hold dear. It is situated at the outskirts of Ipswich, beside a small village by the name of Faithful Street. This curious title derives, they say, from a Puritan community of Weavers which inhabited it at the time of the Civil War in the middle years of the last century. Indeed, I think it very 'puritan' still, tho' its economy is much declined, I am told, due to the superior quality of woven cloths now produced in mechanical factories.

"The Street consists of two long rows of thatched cottages either side of a gravelled lane, much rutted and mired in winter. The cottages appear to have been neglected since the day they were built and are fallen into decay, some of the thatched roofs collapsing so as to resemble a line of hills. This, however, is in complete contrast with their inhabitants whom we pupils have every opportunity to examine when we are marched thrice to Chapel of a Sunday. On each occasion the same faces sit in the same places, each with the same uncharitable expression framed either with many masculine whiskers or by the narrowest strip of starched muslin within a black bonnet. Black is the general colour of their costume for both men and women, and even the few children that appear among them, unnaturally silent so far as I can tell, are similarly garbed. There, I have described first our one weekly entertainment and have not yet provided you with a sketch of the school itself.

"This is housed in large premises known as Faithful Park Mansion, and is enclosed within private grounds at one end of Faithful Street. The Schoolmaster and his wife, Mr. and Mrs. Plowright, are of the tall, thin, mealy-mouthed variety, also garbed in their black and white costume for seven days of the week. You may imagine that I was much put out to discover this as I have always loved fresh colours and Mrs. Jarvis had packed my luggage with several of my favourite gowns. When I arrived at the school I was informed that these were not at all suitable for my decency and that new attire would be made up for me in the village. Well, it was, and poorly made and uncomfortable to wear it is too. Besides, there is the extra expense which Sir Charles must now bear. Mrs. Jarvis has informed me that my Guardian had not visited the school personally, but had relied upon a recommendation from a friend. I should wish to know who that friend may be and whether he has a daughter at my school, for if he thinks it a fit regime for genteel young ladies, he is much mistaken.

"*The food here is very plain. I have heard you complain often enough of the lack of quality of the provisions supplied to the Navy, but I believe that you fare better than we with our plain rye bread,little butter, thin gruel, vegetable soup which we girls have labelled 'cabbage water', no meat, since that is 'of the flesh', but minute portions of fish, potatoes and vegetables, and next to nothing by way of desserts or preserves, since those too are considered sinful. Similarly, we may eat cheese, but not eggs, since those are 'the produce of lust'!*

"*We rise at six, wash in cold water, and assist the one housemaid to lay the fires and dust the furniture. Then we breakfast whilst the Bible is read to us by Mr. Plowright or his wife, this being preceded and followed by several prayers. At nine of the clock we proceed to the schoolroom, formerly the ballroom of the mansion, I would surmise, and a teacher appears. There are five of them, instructing us in Elocution, Deportment, Art, the French language and Geography. All are male, of no great distinction of face or figure and no more cheerful than are their employers. Each travels from his dwelling in Ipswich and returns there at noon.*

"*After refreshments we may take a turn in the Mansion's grounds if the weather is fine, and at two o'clock we are summoned by a bell and may either labour in the garden growing vegetables for the table, or may be assigned similar domestic tasks within the house, cleaning the silver, putting away the pots, shaking the carpets, or carrying out any of those domestic activities normally performed by one's servants. I am sure that such duties are not those that my Guardian intended me to fulfill.*

"*We dine at five, again with the same litany of prayers and Bible readings, and then must spend two hours of what is known as 'silent study' by which is meant either conning lessons for one of our teachers or reading from a long list of what Mrs. Plowright terms 'improving works' but which I consider entirely boring and devoid of any amusement or spirit of generosity. I had taken 'Evelina', the book you had given me, in the expectation of being able to read it of an evening. Alas, Mrs. Plowright has described it as 'shockingly fast' and 'written by a woman, too,' who must therefore be held a person of the most dubious morals. So I have been obliged to devour its text in secret and to lock it away in my trunk to which I pretend to have lost the key, but which I hang on a string about my person. This is yet by no means so secure, for Mrs. Plowright has a habit of visiting our rooms whilst we are dressing, and though my room-companion is pleasant enough, I fear she would betray me if pressed.*

"*I am conscious that your choice of this work for my instruction was due to the resemblance it bears to my own life, in that Evelina is sent to live with a noble family in London where she is taught fine manners. I must relate to you that my fellow-pupils, numbering nineteen, being all daughters of the landed gentry, one would expect them to have been raised in disciplined and well-behaved families. I find this not so, many are quite hoydenish in their conduct, and the manners which your good Aunt has taught me seem far superior to anything I have experienced at Faithful Street. There is one other similarity which I bear to Evelina, how-*

ever, and that is her lack of confidence and self-respect due to ignorance about her birth. I am still not convinced whether Sir Charles Rich is in fact my father, and as to the identity of my mother I am entirely ignorant. This situation has its consequence at Faithful Street where I am looked upon as a 'charity girl', and therefore experience spite from the other girls and a larger share of household duties. In the book, Evelina's birthright is disclosed and she is enabled eventually to marry a pleasing suitor. I can only hope that the same Fate may one day befall me.

"One other aspect of my further education which I ought to mention is the matter of music, which you will note that I have not listed among the subjects taught us. That is because music for pleasure is here held to be 'the work of the Devil'. Indeed a musician does call upon us weekly of a Saturday morning, but he is permitted to instruct us only in the descants to the hymns we are to sing at Chapel the next day, along with some knowledge of the works of Mr. J. S. Bach, not even those by Mr. Handel who is considered entirely too jolly!

"Thus, to return to Roos Hall and to find awaiting me your letter, as well as a batch of patriotick songs and melodies in honour of your Admiral and the British Navy, provided me with much pleasure and relief. Pray do go and fight some more battles, Hugo, so that I may have more of such diversions upon my next returning home!

Your sincere friend
Jessica A. Rich"

* * *

The British frigate bearing this and other family communications had ploughed back and forth twice between Palermo and Naples in search of Lord Nelson, and it was only after it was discovered that he had taken his flag to the *Foudroyant* that mail for the *Vanguard* was separated and delivered. His post reached Hugo in Naples in July 1799, in the midst of the grotesque Neapolitan-style hangings and beheadings taking place in the City square. Hugo felt that he dare not even open his letters to read of home, the farm, Roos Hall, Jessica and innocent youth, amongst the human degradation which surrounded him. How could he sully the lives and minds of his dearest ones with tales of his every-day tasks, the guarding of prisoners in chains, women as well as men stinking in their own natural filth, then rowing or steering one of the ship's boats with a group of supposed Revolutionary felons destined for the grisly procedures taking place ashore? Hugo had learnt by now that many of the prisoners in the gaols and the victims of the scaffold were from the noblest Neapolitan families, one victim even being the Royal Family's own physician whom sir William Hamilton knew for a fine botanist and naturalist. The scenario in Naples, Hugo thought, must be no better than that which had surrounded Madame Guillotine in Paris. When he discussed such matters with Nicholas, they marvelled that their much-respected Commander could assent to these practices. Did this anti-'Jacobin' panic apply everywhere in Europe, under every Monarchy, they wondered? Might they expect to see similar scenes unfold in England too? There had of course been the naval mutinies, but it may be that their swift repression had of itself helped to curb such Republican tendencies.

It was only some months later that Hugo penned two notes to his family, one to his sister Carrie and the other to his Aunt Jarvis. In both he urged them to keep Miss Jessica occupied and amused during her school vacations as she seemed to have been condemned to such a dismal scholarly establishment. Not till December 1799 did Hugo find sufficient courage to write to Jessica and to send her his best wishes for the turn of the new century and the year 1800. He wrote again as soon as the *Vanguard* was ordered home, knowing that the busy frigate bearing the mails would arrive in England long before his warship with three years' growth of barnacles and kelp beneath her keel.

* * *

When Hugo reached Ringsfield early in October 1800 it was to find the whole household a-bustle with eager discussion, and it was some minutes before he could discover the reason for it. In fact this should have been a period of peace and calm in farming life with the grain harvest long since stored, the turnips lifted, the wool gone to the spinners and not quite yet time to start fattening the geese for Christmas. On the water meadows, Jock McTurk had just delivered a herd of sixty Galloway cattle, personally selected for Alfred Jarvis by Jim Caldicott who had returned with his family to the Scottish Borders. It was true that the byre at milking-time was part-occupied by Devon Red cows and partly by Alf's treasured Suffolk Duns, and that a new young Devon Red bull filled the pen that Tommy, the Norfolk Shorthorn, used to grace. It was also true that the sheep now looked fatter and woollier following Alf's introduction of a Leicestershire cross-bred ram into his old Norfolk Horn stock. But the pigs looked the same and nothing else had changed, or had it?

And then it suddenly dawned on Hugo what all the fuss was about -Carrie's wedding to Benjamin Martin of Ilketshall St. Andrew. "I'm glad you're come, brother," Carrie greeted him with a hug and a kiss at the front door of the Ringsfield Farm. "I told Papa I would not marry until you were home, until all the family could be together. Come, now, Hughie, you must help us decide at which church we should be wed. Ben's father, Jake Martin, wants us to wed in his village, but St. Mary's is on the top of a windy hill and half a mile of mud from that horrid little ale-house which is the only place where one might lay on a wedding-feast. I do not wish to be wed at Ringsfield Church, for it is too dark and gloomy, all tombs and monuments. I would prefer the Barsham Church which can be reached by road much more easily. Then we could hold the feast in the grounds of the Rectory as Marion Mather did when she married Martin Weedon last year. I am sensible that neither Ben nor I have attended the Barsham

Church as we ought, but as Mr. Horace Suckling is the Rector there on Mr. Robert's behalf, I thought that Papa could be persuaded to ask Mr. Robert Suckling's permission since he knows him quite well. As it is to be a winter wedding, the weather is bound to pour with rain, so I propose to ask Marion if we may borrow or hire that tent they used to such effect last year. What do you think, Hughie?" Carrie concluded the long catalogue of her concerns.

Hugo set down his luggage in the hall, now contained in a sea-chest rather than the mere portmanteau which had several times been washed over by the ocean during his last voyage. He walked through to the dairy to greet his mother - looking a little older and more frail, he thought, and then his father who came in from the yard rubbing his grimy hands on his breeches as usual. "There you are, son," Alf said, "you hear all this to-do about weddings? I keep out of it as much as I can. Come into my office and we'll share a jug of ale, or something a little stronger," Alf added with a wink as he collected two glasses from the dresser in the dining-room. "Lucy's gone into Beccles with Bessie to do some shopping. I'm surprised you did not see her on the road, but maybe she's chatting to that young man of hers again. She's been most impatient for her sister to marry so that she may follow on in the Spring when she reaches eighteen."

"Who is she walking out with, Papa?" Hugo asked. "Do I know him?"

"You should do, he went to your school. His name is Daniel Mackenzie."

"Oh yes, but he was one of the seniors, Papa, much older than I."

"Precisely, but he has qualified as an engineer and Lucy has the idea that she'll accompany him all around the world whilst he builds bridges and canals and so forth. That is what he's doing here in Beccles, studying whether it would be profitable to widen the locks on the Waveney up to Bungay, since old Matthias Kerrison only made them single-track. You should go down to the Quay and meet Daniel. He has a small office in the warehouse where your former employer, Stan Stevenson, leaves his gaff when he goes up-river."

"Where's Peter, Papa? I suppose him to have finished school by now."

"Well, so he has, leastways he has left the John Leman School. He's studying in Norwich these days, at that agricultural college where I sent Frank Briggs. Frank manages most of the farm now and I'm content to take life more leisurely. Frank will be back this afternoon, come milking-time, as he is over at Jake Martin's this morning giving young Luke a hand. Oh, that reminds me to tell you, one of our horses died. You remember General? Well, he was all of thirty-one years old. He just stopped in his tracks with the plough one day and could go no further. We managed to finish the field with Major, who's still going strong at twenty-five. I've commanded Peter to accompany Mr. Russell to St. Faith's Fair in a fortnight in order to purchase a replacement which your brother will ride home. As you see, we're not yet sure of the date for the wedding and will need to have the banns read once your sister has her way with the choice of the church, so I presume it will take place around the end of the year. Do you expect to be home for long?"

"I cannot really say, Papa," Hugo replied. "They may send for me as they did before, or I may just make my way to a port and offer my services. Yarmouth is much used by the North Sea Fleet, so I hear, though there are less chances for promotion in these waters than there are with the Channel or Mediterranean Fleets."

"Why not apply to our honoured relative, Lord St. Vincent?" Hugo's father suggested.

"I understand that he has been invalided home and is in retirement, though now that I have qualified as a lieutenant I recall that he did ask that I keep him advised."

"Well, there you are then, should nothing better turn up," Alf replied.

"I aim to stay through Christmas, Papa, with your blessing. No doubt the ladies will need assistance at the wedding, setting up the tent, if there is to be one, and Mama will be bound to bake too many pies that will all need transport to the event. If there are tasks you would have me perform around the farm, please do say, but otherwise I propose to stretch my legs around the countryside as 'tis a long while since I had the opportunity to admire it."

The following afternoon Hugo took a stroll into Beccles and called at the Bear & Bells to chat with Uncle Bob. Hugo had noted the bunting that still swathed the hostelry, now much faded after two years of fluttering in the wind and rain, and suggested to his uncle that he help Peter Jones to take it down. "I do not expect that we shall have another victory like that to celebrate," Hugo said, "at least not for a while. Besides," he added, "the last I saw of our Commander he was heading for Leghorn and intending to travel to England across the Continent. Until Admiral Nelson is back aboard ship somewhere, I doubt there will be much excitement." Having shared a jug of beer with his uncle and the removal of the bunting with Peter, Hugo expressed his intention of walking down to the Quay and of introducing himself to Mr. Daniel Mackenzie whom he understood was courting his sister Lucy.

"If you're going that way," Uncle Bob responded, "like as not you'll see your old employer, Stan Stevenson. His shipmate Timothy caught his foot betwixt boat and quay last week and broke his ankle. Stan cannot manage without him, and he and his boat are at the Quay awaiting Timothy's return."

Indeed Stan Stevenson was the first person Hugo encountered the moment he turned out of Fen Lane on to the Quay. Stan greeted him with the greatest of pleasure, the wrinkles on his weather-tanned face crinkling into the broadest of smiles. "So you be home again, boy," he said, "and safe with it. I hear you've been sailing with Admiral Nelson himself and took a hand in the famous battle that we're still celebrating in these parts."

"Yes, Stan, so I did," Hugo replied. "Have you time to join me for coffee, or some brandy if you prefer?"

"Aye, lad, I've only been stamping up and down here on my peg-leg, trying to keep it warm in this cold wind. You shall tell me all your tales."

An hour or two later Hugo remembered to enquire the whereabouts of Mr. Daniel Mackenzie, the engineer. "Ah, he's in a little alcove along the Quay, in the warehouse where I store my gaff, you'll remember Hughie. I'll take you to him and introduce you."

In a dimly-lit office, with a lighted lantern hung permanently on the beam overhead since only a modicum of daylight, much shaded by the neighbouring building, struggled in through the cobwebby window at his right hand, Daniel Mackenzie stood at a large table covered with maps and drawings to which he added precisely scored lines with the aid of various instruments and the sharpest of pencils. A tall, spare fellow, he looked up as his visitors entered and removed his wire-framed spectacles. He held out his hand to Stan. "Morning, Mr. Stevenson," he said. "What can I do for you?"

"Morning Mr. Mackenzie. This is Mr. Hugo Jarvis, that's brother to Miss Lucy."

"Good to meet you, Hugo. So you're the famous sailor from the Nile that Lucy chatters on about. Didn't you attend the John Leman School, as I did?"

"Yes, I did," Hugo replied. "Now I recognise you, but I thought your name was Tomlinson?"

"That's probably because I lived here in Beccles with my aunt, Betsy Tomlinson. My parents are Scottish but moved to London when they were first married. My father wished me to grow up in the fresh country air, away from the smoke of the capital."

"Tell me, your father isn't by chance a marine architect?" Hugo enquired.

"Yes, he is," Daniel replied. "How did you know?"

"I sailed with him in the West Indies. He lodged aboard our sister ship, the *Aetherial*. Your father was employed by the Government to take the measurements of a fast American frigate we captured called the *Beacon*."

"Why, that's so," Daniel Mackenzie replied eagerly, "and you should see the vessel now being built to her proportions at the Blackwall yard. Actually, though, we should not speak of such things as officially 'tis a secret project of the Government."

"Are you employed by the Government yourself?" Hugo asked.

"Indeed no, not at present, though I have hopes in that direction. This study of the canal and the cost of widening it is a private contract for the Maltsters. They are the only merchants with business enough to profit from such a scheme. I was hoping to go up-river to view the working of the locks and Mr. Stevenson was to take me, but he cannot work his boat on his own. I've walked along the towpath, of course, but then I came upon the Geldeston Cut ..."

Hugo smiled knowingly and Stan leapt at the opportunity. "I suppose you wouldn't consider giving me a hand, Hughie, like the old days, just till Tim's ankle has healed? Three more weeks the doctor said it would take."

Thus it was that Hugo strode home that evening, sorted out his oilskin and his old merchant seaman's cap from his sea-chest and joined Stan, Daniel Mackenzie and a cargo of timber from the saw-pit and a tow-horse from Jack Wilson's yard, gliding up-river in the well-remembered and familiar wherry *Louise*. The trip took two days, and Hugo kept Stan company on the boat at night, leaving Daniel to seek a bed at the Inn at Bungay. Next morning, as they voyaged downstream with a hold full of beer kegs from the brewery, Daniel, who had lodged at the Black Dog Inn, enquired if either of them had ever seen that notorious manifestation.

"Why, yes," Hugo replied, "just out there on the marshes," he pointed. "It was my last voyage on this boat and I remember you saying, Stan, that I should watch out that Black Shuck, or Fate or Bad Luck, or whatever the black dog stands for, did not catch me unawares. But it did, for that's when I was taken by the Press-Gang."

"I hope to goodness, then, that I do not see the creature," Daniel commented. "Its visage on that inn signboard was surely grim enough."

Hugo laughed and said, "By-the-by, I forgot to mention that our sister ship, the *Aetherial*, was afterwards lost with all hands in a hurricane. Your father may wish to know of it. We held a funeral service for our friends among her crew."

"I thank you," Daniel responded, "that news cheers me vastly this cold grey morning." However, they returned to Beccles without incident.

A few days later, on Thursday, 6 November 1800, Stan Stevenson and Hugo happened to be at Yarmouth delivering a cargo of pinewood to the naval timberyard at Southtown, when Hugo observed the arrival in Yarmouth Roads of the Mail Packet, the *King George* come from the Continent, to be precise from Cuxhaven in Germany. He noticed its arrival in particular because it was accompanied, quite exceptionally, by a number of fishing smacks and small pleasure boats, quite a flotilla in fact. Whatever could be happening?

"Stan," Hugo called down from the quayside to Mr. Stevenson who stood in the boat facing sternwards and wrestling with the last of the deck cargo of the *Louise*, "do you still have your spyglass? Will you hand it me, if you please?"

"Aye, lad. Here it is. What have you seen, Hughie?"

"The flags on the *King George*, there's the Union flag at her maintop as usual, but there's a blue pennant on her mizzen and a group of signal flags run up between her masts." In fact there were four signal flags, the outer two being chequered blue and white, the middle two firstly blue and yellow quarterly and then a white flag bearing a blue rectangle in its centre. "N.L.S.N." Hugo read off quickly, squinting through the telescope. He turned to Stan, his expression a mixture of amusement and awe. "I think the Admiral himself is on board, Stan. That is why the other boats are following him."

"Well, fancy that! But he's a good Norfolk man," Stan replied, "returning to this county for his first home-coming. Look, the Packet is drawing in near the granary next to the Southtown wall. Looks like his Lordship means to make quite an entry to Yarmouth."

By this time both Stan and Hugo could observe people gathering on both sides of the river. On the Southtown bank all the warehousemen, timber and dockyard workers were downing their tools and swarming to the quayside. On the Town Quay people were rushing out of their houses and running on foot or climbing into their carriages, since in this naval city many could read the flags and anticipated an occasion, a great occasion. About the Town Hall - Hugo could see its portico as he turned to use the spyglass on the scene up-river, there seemed to be a tremendous bustle. He spotted the Mayor's black footman running here and there at top speed and clutching in vain at his neat little wig which kept falling from his head. Soon the Mayor's coach and horses appeared in front of the Town Hall and robed and hatted figures gathered around it. There was obviously to be an official reception for England's Hero. "Don't you heed me, Hughie," Stan said, "I'll see what I can from here with my spyglass. But you run and watch it all whence you can. Looks as though he means to come ashore and go through the Southtown Tollgate and along the Turnpike to the Haven Bridge. He must pass over the bridge, and that might be your best point for hailing him, especially as there's already such a press of folks gathered this side of the river."

It was quite a distance to the Haven Bridge, and although Hugo ran along the quay as far as he could, then made his way through one of the dockyards to the turnpike from Lowestoft, it took him valuable minutes to reach the suggested vantage point. When he did he found that the seaward side of the bridge was already well-occupied by spectators and he was obliged to stand on the north side and towards the Southtown end. Then Hugo noticed there was a milestone beside the bridge giving the distance to Lowestoft and that by perching atop it he discovered he could see over all the heads in front of him. Meanwhile the carriages, official or merely self-important, passed continuously over the bridge towards Southtown at such a rattling pace that spectators, dogs and children alike were in peril from the flying hoofs.

There was then a long pause, whilst the Mayor and Corporation waited and chafed beside their carriages. Word on the street was that the Admiral was putting on his dress uniform, complete with honours and decorations. Having only one arm to assist him, one could understand that the gentleman would have some difficulty. At last he was ready and descended the beflagged and bunting-garlanded gangway to the quay, the first passenger to be permitted ashore that day. Behind him came two other grandly-dressed figures, Sir William Hamilton and his wife Lady Emma, as Hugo later related to Stan Stevenson. Mayor Samuel Barker stepped forward with his mace-bearer on one side and his sword-bearer on the other. They all bowed low together and the Mayor made a speech of welcome, not so well-made since he had been obliged to construe it in a hurry. But the gist of it was warm and sincere and informed his Lordship that he and the Corporation had long-since passed a Resolution to offer his Lordship the Freedom of the Borough of Great Yarmouth, if his Lordship would be pleased to accept. According to the next day's newssheets, his Lordship had replied that he would be most gratified to accept such an honour. He then asked to be taken to the most convenient inn, along with the friends of his party, since they all wished to rest for a day or two to recover from their voyage across an habitually stormy North Sea.

An open carriage awaited nearby into which stepped Lady Hamilton, handed up by her husband, and then an elderly lady whom one might have suspected of being Sir William's wife,except that those in the know were able to whisper that she was merely Lady Emma's mother. Lord Nelson placed himself facing forwards on the near side of the vehicle, so that his remaining arm and his good eye could be directed towards the welcoming multitude. At the Southtown Tollgate Lord Nelson presented the Toll-Keeper with a golden guinea, which that delighted fellow would no doubt treasure for the rest of his life, and the carriage was then allowed to pass. The procession proceeded at a trot up the Turnpike road to the Haven Bridge where it came to a complete halt, there being such a press of people on the bridge that there was insufficient passage for the horses, never mind the weight of so many being too much for the wooden drawbridge. At that moment a number of sailors stepped forth, gathered no doubt from the crews of the sundry naval vessels then in port. Lengths of cable soon appeared, the horses were taken out of the shafts, and with a hitch or two here and there the vehicle could be haled forward in true Norfolk waterman's tradition.

It was at this pause of motion that Hugo, elevated on the milestone, found himself close to the Admiral and almost face to face. "Why, Mr. Jarvis," Lord Nelson said, noticing a friendly and probably a welcome face among a crowd of strangers, "I trust that you will join me when I take ship again?"

"Yes, sir, I should be honoured to do so," Hugo replied, almost falling off his perch with surprise and gratification.

"Brave fellow!" the Admiral commented as his carriage moved on.

The crossing of the bridge completed, the procession headed towards North End and turned up Fuller's Hill to Church Plain, opposite the Gothic arches of St. Nicholas. It came to a halt before the Wrestlers' Inn on the south side of the square, an elegant building in the Georgian style of early in the previous century. The distinguished party went within and their baggage followed presently borne on a drayman's cart. The carriages dispersed, but the crowd lingered, anticipating further attention from their hero. Nor were they disappointed, for soon a sash was thrown up in one of the bay windows that graced the first floor of the Inn. The Admiral leaned out, resting his good arm upon the sill, and addressed the breathless crowd. He reminded them that he was a Norfolk man by birth and proud to be so. The crowd returned with three cheers and a verse of 'See the Conquering Hero Comes'. Then the window was closed and none but the town's notables now entered the Inn, the Mayor, the Aldermen, and some of the town's leading merchants and professionals to whom scribbled invitations had hurriedly been sent.

Hugo, standing among the crowd outside the Wrestlers', had been joined by Stan who had accepted a tow under the Haven Bridge and the *Louise* was now moored beside the Norwich Warehouse, ready to take a cargo up the Yare next day. Naturally Stan was full of questions about Lord Nelson's entourage, not omitting the delicate matter of his relationship with the Hamiltons. Stan had noticed through his spyglass that Lady Emma was rather stout, and from the manner in which she held herself he opined that she was 'expecting a happy event'. However her husband appeared very elderly and somewhat frail. Hugo thought Sir William was at least seventy, but felt a loyalty to his commander which made him loath to criticise. Stan's expression was a picture of creases and wrinkles as he declared sagely that there were, after all, advantages in living the single life and being one's own master, for he would not fancy to be nearby when Lord Nelson took the Hamiltons home to meet his lady wife at the new house he had purchased at Roundwood, near Ipswich!

* * *

For the remaining events of the two days which followed until Lord Nelson and his guests left by coach for Ipswich, Hugo like most of the rest of the population was obliged to rely on the local newspapers which his Uncle Bob had always saved for him. When eventually he called on his uncle on his return to Beccles several days later, he was met by an indignant accusation. "You insisted on taking that bunting down! Said we would hear no more of the Admiral for a long while," Uncle Bob remonstrated.

"He didn't drive through here from Yarmouth, did he Uncle?" Hugo asked surprised.

"No, I'm told they took the coast road through Lowestoft, but the whole of Beccles was buzzing with the news and this time 'tis the King's Head that's been able to corner the trade when the Yarmouth stage arrived."Hugo's uncle continued, "If you wish to see what a mess the Yarmouth Town Clerk made of the rules about granting his Lordship the Freedom of the Borough, just read that paragraph there, the one I've marked for you. He told Lord Nelson that he must put his right hand on the Bible when taking the oath, and again that he must sign receipt of the grant with his right hand. Twice the Admiral had to remind him that his right arm reposed in the sea somewhere off the island of Tenerife! Then there was Mrs. Suckling that owns the Wrestlers' Inn - possibly she is a relative of his Lordship, though I know not of it, asked him whether she could change the name of the place to 'The Nelson Arms', and again the poor man had to remind her that the plural would be contrary to fact! You'd expect folks to be more sensible of the limitations of the famous, would you not?"

Some three weeks later, when Tim had recovered from his injury and could work with Stan Stevenson again, Hugo, left in idleness, borrowed James from Roos Hall and used their own pony-cart to take his sister Carrie into Beccles to purchase provisions for the wedding feast, as well as more trimmings for her own and the bridesmaid's gowns. Hugo had understood that Lucy was to be the sole recipient of that honour, but he wondered whether it would provide an opportunity to bring Jessica into the family now that he was aware of her blood relationship with Aunt Jarvis. He tried to broach the subject as they drove into the town, but Carrie was adamant about it. "I've already promised Lucy that she will look as becoming as the bride, and that I will throw her my bouquet for luck. If I go back on that decision you know what a fuss Lucy will make, and none of us will hear the end of it."

When they had left the pony-cart hitched outside the Bear & Bells and Carrie was walking along the street past the Church with much determination, her basket in one hand and a long shopping list in the other, Hugo said to her, "Carrie, come with me a moment. I wish to show you something." He took her across the churchyard to the corner where he had discovered Alicia's grave.

"What's this, Hugo? Why have you brought me here?" Carrie then read 'Alicia, dearly beloved daughter of Robert and Elisabeth Jarvis,' and the answer dawned upon her. "This is the tomb Mama used to bring us to visit when we were children, only she stopped doing so after a short while and we never came again," she said. "Alicia was the name of the lady who stayed with us to have her baby. We never were told what happened to the child. Perhaps it died, like its mother, only a few days after it was born."

"Carrie," Hugo said gently, "I think that Jessica Rich may be that child and that Sir Charles may be her real father. Look at that death date and you can work out that it was only a few days after Jessica was born."

"But that would make Aunt Jarvis her grandmother. Why has she not said so?"

"Perhaps Sir Charles ordered her not to. He wishes to avoid the embarrassment and calls himself her Guardian instead," Hugo replied.

"But poor Jessica, believing all these years that she has no family when she is really part of ours."

"She may not be, Carrie, not if Alicia was born to Aunt Jarvis by a previous marriage and Uncle Bob took her on when they married. After all, they have had no other children."

"Yes. Look, I will try to involve Jessica in my wedding. She would have been invited anyway, but you will have to help me with Lucy. I do not think we should tell her about this, for she can never retain a secret. In fact we had better not tell anyone for now. No wonder you wrote asking me to keep Jessica amused. Have you known about it all this time?"

"Yes, ever since my previous leave."

"You're a kind fellow, Hughie, and you deserve well," Carrie finished, giving him a sisterly pat.

Carrie's wedding took place early in January 1801, by good fortune on a clear frosty day with some early sunshine. True to her word Carrie had thought about inviting Jessica to be a second bridesmaid, but had decided that the aisle at the Barsham Church was not wide enough for two fully-gowned ladies to proceed up it side by side. So she arranged for Jessica to wait at the church door and take their cloaks, and then to sit in the family's pew. The days preceding the wedding had been full and busy with baking and brewing and making paper garlands for the marquee borrowed from the Mathers. They kindly lent some of the decorations which Marion had used for her wedding, ceramic vases and dried flower arrangements and suchlike. With so much concoction and confection in progress it was easy for Hugo to ensure that Jessica was involved, and indeed Betty Jarvis brought her over in the pony-cart every day. Aunt Jarvis assisted with the baking and Jessica with her artistic flair designed much of the decor. Hugo himself was kept busy helping his father, Peter, and Frank Brigg s to manage the farm and its livestock, and to ensure that their home-brewed ale would be of the finest quality for the wedding guests.

When they all sat down to meals together, Hugo often entertained them with some tale or other of his adventures, usually carefully selected. For instance, he made much of his first visit to Naples but never the subsequent ones. Let the family think his ship had spent its days cruising randomly about the Mediterranean Sea questing for those elusive Frenchmen. When he had a chance to sit next to Jessica and to encourage her to speak, she told Hugo more about her bleak school life and that she was hoping to leave it for ever in a few months, for she would celebrate her eighteenth birthday in May. She said that Mrs. Jarvis had written to Sir Charles reminding him of the situation and enquiring his plans for Jessica now that she was quite grown up. Apparently Betty Jarvis had also hinted broadly that a visit from Sir Charles and his family would be most welcome so that everyone might be advised of his intentions.

In return Jessica had taught the younger members of the family to play cribbage. It appeared that one of the senior girls at her school had smuggled in two packs of cards and two crib-boards which the formidable Mrs. Plowright had yet to discover, and surreptitious card parties by candlelight had helped to enliven the recent months. Hugo allowed Jessica to correct his errors of play and it was his impression that his Aunt Jarvis regarded this family scene with especial pleasure. Would Aunt Jarvis lend her support to his growing friendship with Miss Jessica Rich?

After the wedding service was over and the newlyweds had signed the Church register, all repaired to the Rectory via some freshly-gravelled paths, and via some strategically-placed duckboards to the marquee. This had its own canvas floor, in this season concealing a deep layer of straw supplied from the farm and laid down with the help of Easton and the servants from Roos Hall. Indeed all the Roos Hall staff had been pressed into service, Mrs. Baines baking a number of dishes which the maids had delivered on their way to the church, and they helped too at the Rectory, making cups of tea and chocolate and glasses of warm punch to keep the wedding guests content on such a cold day.

Among these guests were the Mathers and the Weedons, strangely now friends of the family, and more than that for their firm had occasion to use Benjamin Martin's professional services. Augustus Mather was home from Eton College, looking very smart and mature, and Hugo had much ado to recognise him. Gus was one of the few people to whom Hugo could describe most of his experiences, since the boy had seen enough of sea-life to understand the rest. Benedict Mather was there too, still a bachelor, in his mid-twenties and well enough set up now in his father's profession to be seeking a wife. Hugo was somewhat concerned to observe how much time Benedict spent chatting to Jessica, and presently he moved across to offer both of them another glass of punch. At that Jessica excused herself and Benedict, taking his opportunity, commented, "She's a pretty little thing, isn't she? Maturing nicely," he went on as if discussing the progeny of one of his father's horses. "Such a shame that no-one knows anything about her origins or her parentage. I mean, is Sir Charles perhaps her father, and is that why he does not bring his family to Roos Hall? And Lord knows who was her mother. Do you know anything more, Hugo?"

Hugo knew the answer, or most of it. Was he justified in pleading ignorance? Was he being discreet for Jessica's sake, or merely being selfish with an eye to his own interests? "No, Ben, 'tis still a mystery to me, to all of us," he corrected hastily, and went on to speak of politics, the war with France, the chances of invasion and the strengths and weaknesses of the British Navy, which were matters of equal interest to a businessman such as Benedict Mather.

Presently it was time for the bride and her husband to depart for the briefest of honeymoons beside the seashore at Southwold, a honeymoon limited by available funds as well as by the fact that cold and stormy onshore winds would hardly be conducive to long walks on the sands or a venture into the bathing machines that had begun to appear on seaside beaches. The family had thought it fine that the pair should spend awhile together before they returned to live in the former Caldicotts' cottage and took on the responsibilities of the farm.

Not long after the wedding, Uncle Bob's partner Peter Jones came trudging up the lane to the farm with a message for Hugo. "Your Uncle says you should take a look at the notice-board outside the King's Head," he told Hugo. "There's an advertisement for sailors wanted to man the Fleet gathering at Yarmouth," Peter said. "They would appear to want officers also, for it mentions all ranks."

"Thank you, Peter. If you care to wait I shall take my hat and coat and walk back with you," Hugo replied.

The advertisement did indeed seem promising, but Hugo remembered the pact agreed with Nicholas Wilmington that they would make their next voyage together. So he hitched a lift on a carrier's waggon heading for Norwich and after several inquiries located Nicholas at the riverside warehouse where he remembered having seen the family name painted on the wall. Nicholas too felt enthused about returning to sea. Having missed commencement of the University year and his father not able to anticipate the date of his return home, he had been helping out in his family's warehouse in a rather junior capacity. Nicholas had become completely bored and life at sea again seemed likely to provide much more excitement. They agreed to meet up on the morrow in Yarmouth, each travelling there by the morning stage. Hugo's family felt saddened but not surprised when he returned from Norwich, packed his sea-chest and announced his imminent departure.

* * *

Early in 1801 Lord Spencer had resigned his position as First Lord of the Admiralty and John Jervis, Earl of St. Vincent, had been persuaded out of retirement to take his place. Admiral Jervis had been living at Tor Abbey, Devon during his previous command of the Channel Fleet which had recently arrived home for the winter from the blockade of Brest. Internationally, a quarrel had arisen with Russia whose mad Tsar Paul I had claimed sovereignty over the island of Malta. As titular head of the Order of the Knights of St. John which owned the island, the Tsar considered he should be granted annexation of Malta as a result of aid which Russian ships had given the Royal Navy in defeating the strong French garrison left at Valetta. In December 1800 Russia had entered into an alliance with Denmark, Sweden, Norway and Prussia, just those countries which supplied the British Navy with vital ship-building materials - timber, cordage, pitch and iron. Their objective was to resist Britain's claim to the right to search passing vessels for war supplies on their way to France. Sweden, Norway and Prussia took little note of this requirement, but Denmark denied British ships entry to her ports and sent troops to Hamburg to close off similarly the mouth of the River Elbe. The British Government concluded that Denmark needed to be taught a lesson.

The Admiralty placed command of the North Sea Fleet in the hands of Admiral Sir Hyde Parker, and in February 1801 he sailed into Yarmouth Roads aboard H.M.S.*Ardent* to take charge of the squadron already gathering there. But Sir Hyde was a man in his sixties and fond of the softer pleasures of life. These did not include spending winter months in the cold draughty cabin of a British warship when he could just as easily manage affairs from the comfort of the Wrestlers' Inn and the charms of his plump new young wife, known to the Press as the Admiral's 'sheet anchor' and to sailors and officers alike by the nickname of "Batter Pudding". Lord Nelson, now promoted Vice-Admiral but otherwise in disfavour following his enforced overland return from the Mediterranean and the scandal surrounding his private life - he had parted from Lady Nelson and had spent Christmas with the Hamiltons at William Beckford's vast Gothic folly of Fonthill Abbey - was summoned to Torbay by Earl St. Vincent and after some discussion was appointed Sir Hyde's second in command.

Lord Nelson had little respect for Hyde Parker's abilities as a warrior and considered that his new Commander-in-Chief would be likely to cramp his own normal daring and initiative. Sir Hyde Parker's reactions to this appointment were not recorded, but cannot have been enhanced when Nelson insisted on calling upon his superior at his hotel very early in the morning and disturbing him in bed. This followed his arrival in port on board the *St. George* (98 guns) under

Captain Hardy. Nelson had chosen the *St. George* since her draught was relatively shallow and he knew that success in this enterprise could well depend on accurate navigation in estuarine conditions.

The North Sea would be a fresh battlefield for Hugo. His only voyage in those waters had been aboard the *Apollion* following his seizure by the press-gang. He had of course listened to the tales of others, from Stan Stevenson and more recently from the fishermen at Yarmouth who sailed forth in almost all weathers to search for "silvers". However he was conscious of his own inexperience, realising that in a new vessel he might have more responsibility for matters of navigation. At the time when he and Nicholas reached Yarmouth neither commander was present, and the Navy Office was merely recruiting manpower among those who knew how to load a ship. As yet officers had not been appointed to specific vessels, for the very reason that there were few officers present. Not wishing to return home or to survive in Yarmouth without employment, the two young men signed on and were kept busy supervising dockers and sailors as the ships already in harbour were loaded with solid stores - spare yards, spars and sails, shot and cannon balls, hammocks and bedding, barrels of bully beef and ship's biscuit, in fact most of the provisions that were unlikely to spoil or to walk off the ships by themselves!

When Sir Hyde Parker appeared in February there was scarcely a ripple in the pace of port activity, but with Lord Nelson's arrival a month later it was as if everyone in the harbour had stood to attention. Stores were completed, new sails bent on, rigging checked and repaired, sailors arrived in increasing numbers, then the Marines, whilst Lord Nelson himself had brought along a detachment of infantry commanded by a Lieutenant-Colonel Stewart. Most crews were nearing completion by the time that unassigned personnel were sent to fill vacant places. Hugo and Nicholas had stressed that they wished to be appointed to the same ship, and so they were, to one called the *Glatton* under Captain William Bligh. Nicholas was to fulfill the duties of a junior lieutenant, whilst Hugo with his greater experience and his qualification became "acting Second Lieutenant". The terms of his appointment troubled Hugo and he mused upon them overnight. Then he suddenly recalled the identity of his new commander. Captain Bligh was the fellow who had sustained a mutiny aboard a ship called the *Bounty* and who, being set adrift in mid-Pacific Ocean with eighteen of his crew who had not joined the rebels, had navigated nearly four thousand nautical miles to make landfall at Timor (Indonesia). With such a brilliant by-the-stars navigator aboard, Hugo thought he should have to look to his laurels, but surely other seamen should flock to the standard of such a talented commander? Then Hugo remembered that Captain Bligh also had a bad reputation for harshness of discipline. Was this why others hesitated to serve under him? Nicholas opined that as 'regular fellows before the mast' he and Hugo should have nothing to fear from a tough taskmaster.

Lord Nelson found preparations so far advanced at Yarmouth that he expected Sir Hyde Parker to depart immediately. Then he learnt from his dawn call upon his superior that the Admiral planned to transfer his flag to H.M.S. *London* which had only just arrived in port and needed time to take on provisions. One other point which Sir Hyde mentioned was that his dear young lady wife had reserved the Town Hall and had employed the services of an orchestra for a Grand Ball so that she might thus introduce herself to the upper echelons of Yarmouth Society and expect return invitations from all of them,and so relieve the boredom of her husband's absence! Lord Nelson, aware of the necessity to surprise the Scandinavians before their ships could be refitted after the winter's freeze, and also anxious, one might suspect, to return to Lady Emma whose daughter Horatia had just been born, objected strongly to the proposed delay. He wrote a letter of complaint to his old colleague Captain Troubridge, who had been appointed to assist Admiral Jervis at the Admiralty. A sharp reply to Sir Hyde from the First Lord himself caused the said Grand Ball to be cancelled, "Batter Pudding" to be despatched back to London, and the Fleet to be at last ready to sail.

It was not a pleasant voyage. The weather was rough, and ice and snow greeted the vessels as they sailed north. The squalls required much reefing of topsails and the bringing down of t'gallant masts and their yards. Ice gathered on the rigging, freezing the halyards and making them snap, causing immediate injuries and further chafing and cuts during their repair. To add to these general discomforts, the *Glatton* with only fifty-four guns was shorter in the keel than either the *Vanguard* or the *Apollion*, so that her motion was decidedly vertical in these abrupt choppy seas. Nicholas was violently seasick and Hugo, who shared his cabin, had to minister to his friend as well as catering for his own needs. So far they had seen little of their notorious commander, since he had kept to his quarters and had left much of the navigation to the Master and the First Officer, both of whom had sailed with him before.

Having left Yarmouth on 13th March it was the twentieth before the Fleet rounded the north of Jutland and anchored in the Kattegat, not far from the Fortress of Kronborg which guarded the entrance to the Sound leading south to Copenhagen. There they awaited a report from a British diplomat, Nicholas Vansittart, who had been sent ahead to offer the Danish Government an ultimatum, either to withdraw from her alliance with Russia and rescind her embargo on British ships, or risk the destruction of her Fleet as it lay moored beneath the walls of her Capital. Nicholas Vansittart returned with a refusal of Britain's ultimatum and with details of the ships and shore batteries the British fleet would need to face. Sir Hyde Parker held a conference aboard the *London* to which he was obliged to invite Lord Nelson, much as he disliked the man.

Copenhagen was a walled city, its defences enhanced by ravelins from which cannon might fire in two directions at once. The harbour, which led into the heart of the capital, was defended on one side by a double wall of fortifications and on the other by a citadel whose star conformation lent it much fire power with little damage in return. Either side of these structures several gun batteries had been set up along the shore, and a further set of strong defences known as the Trekroner (Three Crowns) Battery guarded both the channel into the harbour and the deep-water route further into the Sound. Against this wall of protecting guns the Danish Fleet of eighteen warships had been moored bow to stern with floating batteries anchored between them and no gaps left to be exploited as had happened at Aboukir Bay. Moreover the central area of the Sound, known as the Middle Ground, was a vast mudbank which severely restricted freedom of movement of any vessels advancing to the attack. As a further deterrent to their foe, the Danes had carefully removed from the Sound all the buoys which marked the deeper water.

Learning from Nicholas Vansittart that the larger Danish vessels were moored near the Trekroner Battery, Nelson suggested that he leave those for the attention of the Commander-in-Chief whilst he took an attack squadron down the eastern channel of the Sound near the Swedish shore. As soon as the wind turned favourable his vessels would sail north and commence firing upon the tail end of the Danish forces, thus taking them by surprise.

Sir Hyde Parker reluctantly agreed this plan and assigned to Nelson a dozen warships and half a dozen sloops and frigates, all with their shallower draught. For this reason Admiral Nelson transferred his flag to the *Elephant* (74 guns) under Captain Thomas Foley, he who had eagerly led the *Goliath* into battle at Aboukir. With these provisions made, the British Fleet sailed safely into the Sound to the northern end of the Middle Ground without any reaction from the Swedish shore and with Danish defensive fire from the Kronborg Fortress falling far short of the British ships.

On 1st April Nelson's squadron sailed south and anchored after night-fall at the southern end of the Middle Ground. Overnight neither leader was idle. Lord Nelson himself took a boat, a leadsman and a store of buoys and personally re-buoyed the deeper water channel. It was a skill which the Admiral had acquired from his earliest years at sea. From the *St. George*, left behind with Admiral Hyde Parker, Captain Hardy did the same and discovered deeper water nearer the Danish fleet which would allow Sir Hyde's squadron to advance and attack the formidable Trekroner Battery.

This was one battle where the smaller vessels of Nelson's fleet led the way into combat. In pride of place the *Arrow*, a mere sloop of thirty guns, was followed by her sister vessel the *Dart*. Then came three of the frigates with the *Amazon* upon whose deck that morning Admiral Nelson had personally re-checked the overnight soundings. All sailed to their allotted anchorage beneath the ominous Trekroner Battery, firing their port guns in succession as they went, and repeating rapid broadsides once on station. Next came the seventy-four gun warships, led by the *Defiance* bearing the flag of the third in command, Rear-Admiral Thomas Graves. Nelson placed the *Elephant* opposite the Danish flagship *Dannebrog* and had the *Glatton* tucked in just astern, much to Hugo's satisfaction.

A mixed group of warships followed and spread out along the remainder of the Danish lines. The two forces were a mere cable's length apart, little more than two hundred yards!

Whilst the guns were being run out on the port side, facing the enemy, the crew on the starboard side had not been idle. The leadsman was busy taking one sounding after another as the British force inched its way forward. Aboard the *Glatton* Hugo had the duty of supervising this vital task and of making sure that the measurement was clearly understood by the ship's Master who instructed the helmsman and supervised the trimming of the sails in the favourable south-easterly wind which followed astern. Hugo's function became all the more important once the noise of gunfire began to drown out all other sounds, including that of the human voice. From his viewpoint in the bows Hugo could glance back along the line of battleships. He noticed already that the *Russell* and the *Bellona* were no longer moving and that half a mile away the *Agamemnon*, Nelson's favourite ship, also seemed to have wedged herself upon the Middle Ground. Three powerful warships were denied their rôle, and Nelson their support, leaving the tail end of his squadron to bear a greater burden of enemy attack.

Following the soundings taken by Captain Hardy, Sir Hyde Parker's squadron was free to move forward to attack the Trekroner Battery and to support the British sloops and frigates which were taking a pounding from it. Alas, the wind that favoured Admiral Nelson's squadron was not so generous to his Commander-in-Chief whose force was obliged to tack and tack about over the dangerous shoals before it could come within firing range of the enemy. Having reached his battle station at last and finding little diminution in the fire-power of the Danish batteries after three hours of British attack, Sir Hyde Parker was becoming somewhat sceptical of the final outcome of the battle. Moreover he had as his flag captain one William Domett, a Job's comforter to any struggling cause, whose lugubrious "Do you really think so, Admiral?", repeated often, was enough to set the seal of disaster on any venture. Sir Hyde Parker had come to the conclusion that he should fly the signal for retreat and have the rest of the British fleet sail towards him and out of danger.

Meanwhile Admiral Nelson, pacing his quarterdeck in the company of Colonel Stewart, was enjoying what he habitually described as "warm work" when a shot from the *Dannebrog* hit the mainmast of the *Elephant*, sending splinters and fragments flying. A second shot from the *Dannebrog* intended for the *Elephants'* mizzen mast flew straight over her stern and took off the fore-topmast of the *Glatton* instead. Mast and sails came ballooning down on the main deck, enveloping Hugo as he supervised the gun-teams as to load and elevation, in accordance with instructions from the quarter-rail where Captain Bligh stood conferring with his First Officer. Hidden under a welter of spars and canvas, Hugo almost suffocated before he was able to burrow his way out and to help the seamen drag the wreckage clear of the guns. As the situation calmed he faced towards the quarterdeck and gave a salute to indicate that gunfire could now continue. The *Glatton*, a converted East Indiaman like the *Apollion*, was mostly equipped with heavy-shotted carronades and incendiary shells, so her gunfire was particularly important and effective at close range. Hugo was quite unaware that behind him his Captain had responded to his salute with a "Carry on, Mr. Jarvis." Hugo would have been surprised that the captain, and such a much-feared captain at that, even remembered his name.

It was at this point that Sir Hyde Parker had his signal officer run up to the maintop of the *London* Signal No.39, the instruction for disengagement and recall. It is claimed that at the same time he remarked to William Domett, "If he (Nelson) is in a position to continue the action he will disregard it," but hindsight in the wake of success says much it dare not utter in the face of disaster. The sloops and frigates, already heavily battered by the Danish guns, obeyed the signal, weighed anchor and moved on. Rear-Admiral Graves aboard the *Defiance*, the leading warship, observed the signal and turning to his flag captain enquired what signals the *Elephant* now flew. "Still No.16, to engage the Enemy more closely, Admiral, and he's just put up a pennant acknowledging the Chief's signal" Admiral Graves told his signal officer to repeat Signal No.39, but only at the yardarm where the instruction was not mandatory, and ordered his flag captain to carry on firing. He was unaware that behind him Lord Nelson had famously said, "I see no signal," applying his telescope to his blind eye!

Admiral Nelson, surveying the scene of battle between the palls of smoke, knew that accurate and heavy firing from the British guns had silenced many of the Danish floating gun-platforms into smoking ruins. Of the Danish warships, by this time only four were undamaged, but even when the defeated vessels struck their colours as a signal of surrender, he noticed that they were being re-supplied from the shore with fresh men and ammunition. No sooner did boats from the British ships pull towards them, full of Marines ready to take possession of the Danish hulks, than they started firing all over again. This infuriated Nelson, for he was confident of the superiority of his British gunners. When the *Dannebrog* continued to fire in this way he had the *Elephant* and the *Ganges* immediately ahead of her train all their guns upon the Danish vessel until it caught fire, drifted out of line and later blew up. Captain Fremantle of the *Ganges*, one of Nelson's 'Band of Brothers', came aboard presently to ascertain his Commander's view of the battle. Lord Nelson told him he was anxious to bring fighting to an end for humanitarian reasons, since unlike the French the Danes were not normally sworn enemies of Britain. To this purpose he had written a note which he proposed to send to the Trekroner Battery under a flag of truce, stating that if the Danes continued firing he would burn all the craft captured, together with all the Danish sailors who had bravely defended them. Captain Fremantle approved the text and it was re-written by the Admiral's secretary on his headed notepaper and taken ashore by Sir Frederick Thesiger, a diplomat fluent in Danish and Russian.

Whilst Admiral Nelson and Captains Foley and Fremantle awaited a response from the Danes, the advance of Sir Hyde Parker's squadron in force had caused the vessels still firing among the Danish van to strike their colours. However gunfire still came from the four intact Danish vessels and from the Trekroner Battery where, unknown to Lord Nelson, the Danish Crown Prince Frederick and the Commodore of the Danish Fleet, Admiral Fischer, were studying his note. They sent back a request for clarification to which Nelson replied with a further note indicating that his objectives were humanitarian, that he proposed to cease firing and suggested that the Danes retrieve their wounded from their burning ships. He added a final sentence expressing a wish for future friendship between the two nations. The Trekroner guns ceased firing then and a Danish diplomat was sent aboard the *London* to negotiate a truce with Sir Hyde Parker as Commander-in-Chief.

As the guns finally fell silent, Admiral Nelson signalled to his battered fleet to weigh anchor and proceed, but the tide having fallen several vessels were stranded on the Middle Ground and had to wait for the tide to rise again. The *Glatton* had no such problem, partly because she was a smaller vessel and partly because Hugo was again hard at work with the leadsman to ensure that she nudged her way to safety. It was soon realised that had Lord Nelson not ignored Sir Hyde's signal and continued firing, and had he not then negotiated a truce with the battle won, all the stranded vessels would have served as sitting targets for the Danish guns.

The British Fleet took possession of the Danish 60-gun *Holstein* and two smaller Danish vessels made their escape. The remainder were emptied of prisoners and burnt. The grounded British ships were freed, though the *Agamemnon* spent four days hauling the frigate *Desirée* from the Danish mud. Punishments were meted out for cowardice and failure of duty among the British crews. True to his reputation, Captain Bligh had one man flogged aboard and another sent by boat to be flogged from ship to ship. Hugo had the details later from Nicholas who had witnessed both incidents while supervising gunnery on the lower deck. One was a landsman who had fled from the firing of the guns after a shipmate had been killed beside him, after the manner of the death of Giles Spencer, and the other had half-throttled the gunner's mate as he reproved him for incorrect loading of a gun. Tensions run high in time of war; neither man survived his flogging and added their corpses to the pile to be quietly buried at sea. There were more than two hundred and fifty dead, together with a further six hundred and ninety wounded, of whom many would not survive. The Danes had lost many times more, including two hundred and seventy killed when the *Dannebrog* exploded.

The *Glatton* had suffered thirty-four men wounded and seventeen killed, of which one was William Tyndall, a junior lieutenant. Nicholas was unharmed but saddened by the loss of another colleague; Hugo was much-bruised from the rigging that had fallen upon him but unbowed, especially when he witnessed Captain Bligh called aboard the *Elephant* to be congratulated by the Admiral on the accuracy of his gunnery. Lord Nelson later supplied Captain Bligh with an indemnity for continuing to fire in contravention of Sir Hyde Parker's signal.

Much to his surprise, his Commander-in-Chief sent Admiral Nelson ashore to negotiate terms of peace with the Danes. His Lordship did not vaunt himself as a diplomat, but perhaps Sir Hyde thought that the Admiral in full dress uniform, complete with all his decorations and titles, would create a greater impression. He was accompanied by Sir Frederick Thesiger and by Captain Hardy, since Nelson had immediately after the battle returned to his cabin aboard the *St. George*. In the end all that was agreed was an armistice of fourteen weeks. Sir Hyde Parker sent Colonel Stewart back to England with the news, together with three warships full of wounded, the captured *Holstein*, and the *Isis* and the *Monarch*, both of seventy-four guns. The latter having lost her Captain in the battle, William Bligh was promoted to take his place. At Yarmouth the numbers of wounded overwhelmed the small military hospital that formed part of the barracks near St. Nicholas Church and extra surgeons and nursing staff had to be called in from London to care for them. Those sailors who did not survive their wounds were buried in the Sailors' Burial ground within St. Nicholas Churchyard.

Although the *Glatton* had received some damage to her timbers and guns by shots from the Danish batteries - the Danes had aimed low with a view to penetrating the hulls of the British vessels and sinking them - she was nevertheless able to accompany Sir Hyde Parker and the rest of the British Fleet further into the Baltic with the object of impressing the Swedish and Russian navies with their victorious fire-power and deterring them from taking further action against British merchant shipping. Lord Nelson also emphasised the importance of reaching the enemy fleets before the melting ice would allow them to provision and set sail. It was anticipated that the Swedish Fleet would be found at Karlskroner, and a false rumour that it had already sailed caused Admiral Nelson to have himself rowed for six hours between the *St. George* labouring over the shallows with her deeper keel, and the *Elephant* which was twenty-four miles ahead. As the journey was made without the Admiral having the benefit of his boat-cloak, the freezing temperatures caused one of his recurrent bouts of malaria.

News had now reached the British Fleet of the assassination in March of the mad Tsar Paul I and Sir Hyde Parker received a note from the Russian Ambassador at Copenhagen that the new Tsar, Alexander I, had reversed his father's policy and would henceforth regard Britain as a friendly nation. If true, such news negated the whole rationale for the Battle of Copenhagen and all the mutual destruction caused. At the same time instructions were received from Lord St. Vincent at the Admiralty recalling Sir Hyde into retirement and leaving Admiral Nelson in command of the Baltic Fleet. He, more sceptical than others of Russia's intentions, decided that the presence of a British Fleet off the Russian naval base at Reval (now Tallinn, Estonia), might deter any Russian reluctance more forcibly. Leaving the *Agamemnon*, the *Glatton*, four other warships and a frigate to continue a blockade of Karlskroner, reinforced by an ultimatum that any Swedish ship leaving port would be treated as hostile, Nelson sailed to Reval with the remaining squadron. The Russians were duly alarmed at the unexpected and uninvited arrival of eleven British warships which they protested was not the act of a now-friendly nation. Lord Nelson, no doubt with tongue-in-cheek, replied with a note stating that he had merely come to pay his respects to the new Tsar and intended to set sail again immediately, which he did. Not long afterwards, the political alliance which had caused the problem was dissolved and Sweden and Russia released the British merchant ships they had held in their ports.

Whilst Admiral Nelson's squadron had departed for Reval, the ships left on watch before Karlskroner had scarcely been idle. Much damage from the Battle of Copenhagen had received only temporary repairs, so that this presented an opportunity for further carpentry and re-rigging. The *Glatton* which fortuitously had received less hits than most, perhaps because the enemy's fire-power had been concentrated upon the Admiral's flagship immediately ahead of her, found herself distributing her spare stores of timber, sails and food as these were required. Among the stores transferred, Hugo, supervising the lifting and loading as often before, noted with approval the inclusion of a barrel or two of lime juice, that useful remedy which he had been taught to respect aboard the *Apollion*. He still missed his first ship and often thought wistfully of her. The pause was also another opportunity for punishment, one flogging for theft and another for neglect of duty, being carried out aboard the *Glatton*. Then, too, it was a time for celebration when news arrived that Lord Nelson had been created a Viscount and Rear-Admiral Graves a Knight of the Bath. Captain Fancourt of the *Agamemnon* was moved to order a salute of twenty-one guns.

When the rest of the Fleet returned from Reval it quickly became known that Lord Nelson had applied for shore-leave due to illness. This being granted, he sailed for Yarmouth in one of the Fleet's messenger brigs, the *Kite*, as soon as his successor Admiral Sir Charles Morice Pole arrived aboard H.M.S.*Aeolus*. It was only later that the Fleet, remaining on patrol in the Baltic, learnt that on reaching Yarmouth the Admiral had ignored a welcome reception which Mayor Barker had arranged at the Town Hall. Landing instead at the humble fishermen's jetty on the main beach, and walking over the Denes between their tiny cottages, he visited the hospital at the Barracks where the wounded from the battle were still being cared for. When the Admiral eventually reached London there was little public rejoicing, for the Danes were not regarded as inveterate enemies, and no medals were struck for valour at the Battle of Copenhagen.

Patrol work in the Baltic Hugo found colder and duller than he had in the West Indies, so he was glad when the Fleet was ordered back to England in October without taking part in any further naval actions. They had been at sea a mere nine months, so there was little pay to be collected, and the *Holstein* having been the only prize, a junior officer's share thereof would be minimal. Hugo and Nicholas had discussed the situation at length whilst they were sailing home. By the time they arrived, once again Nicholas would have missed commencement of the academic year. Besides, at the age of twenty-two he now felt himself far too old to return to serious study of the Classics or any other subject of which his father might approve. Hugo, needing to earn more than his keep, and requiring promotion and prize money if he was to aspire to the hand of Miss Jessica Rich, had determined upon taking another voyage as soon as a ship might be available. He had one minor satisfaction on being signed off by the Purser aboard the *Glatton*. Opposite his name on the Muster Roll that would later be filed at the Admiralty, he was shown that the prefix 'acting' had been crossed out, and that after it someone had inscribed "Cool and efficient under fire". "Whose hand is that?" he enquired of the Purser.

"That's Captain Bligh himself, son. You're a lucky fellow. Will you be sailing again?"

"Yes, indeed, as soon as I may find a place."

"I wish you luck, then, Mr. Jarvis," the Purser said and shook him by the hand.

Some of the Baltic Fleet returned to port at Yarmouth and some to the Thames for refitting and paying off. Hugo and Nicholas were relieved that they were sailing into Yarmouth Roads, since they could both make visits to their families before seeking their next berth either at Yarmouth or in London. As the *Glatton* passed the Fort at the southern tip of the Denes, and then the village of Gorleston on her port side, the warehouses about Southtown hove into view and Hugo on the foredeck, whence he had been relaying the soundings over the shoals to the ship's pilot at the helm, suddenly glimpsed a familiar silhouette; the *Apollion* was in harbour, here in Yarmouth!

The moment the *Glatton* had docked and her officers were free to go ashore, Hugo and Nicholas strode along the quay to where the *Apollion* was berthed. It was almost exactly seven years since Hugo had first been so ignominiously hoisted aboard her, yet he ran up the gangway with an eager stride. Like a rabbit into its burrow, he made his way to the purser's office, and who should be sitting there but Mr. Iver, a little greyer, a little more rotund in his person, but overwhelmed with delight at the sight of a shipmate lost to view for the last four years. Hugo introduced Nicholas, exhibited his lieutenant's certificate, and enquired whether the ship had a full complement of officers.

"Yes, we have, Mr. Jarvis. You see, we were ordered here to guard the port whilst every other vessel that could be spared was sent to join the Fleet in the Baltic. I suppose you to have heard what happened to the *Invincible* that was also ordered north? On her way out of harbour she grounded on the Haisbro Sands and was lashed to pieces by the sea. Only a third of her muster of six hundred were saved from drowning. Now that your Fleet has returned, we shall be heading south again and paying off at Chatham. The word is that we shall be sent on escort duty then, taking a convoy of East Indiamen to Funchal, or else across the

Atlantic. There will be places to be filled then, for I know at least one lieutenant that's headed for home. If you care to sign on here, I will have a word with the Captain and see if we can offer you a pick of the hammocks in your old Gun Room till the new crew is made up. As for you, Mr. Wilmington, we are due to remain at Blackstakes some three weeks taking on a new crew and stores for our next assignment, plenty of time I would say for you to do as Mr. Jarvis has done and take your certificate. Then you'll be a true naval man and not just a gentleman volunteer."

Hugo enquired after Captain Sterne. "Oh, he has retired long since. He never did recover from that shoulder wound he took in the 'Windies'. The bullet lodged in his shoulder-blade, you know. They couldn't get it out for fear of cutting an artery and it left him with a crippled arm for life. Mr. Barber's gone too. He died in a skirmish on our next voyage."

"And Big John?" asked Hugo.

"Ooh, he's in Portsmouth. He got gangrene in the leg he wounded at Santa Cruz and is stumping around on a peg-leg these days, doing a little fishing and telling a lot of yarns. Our Captain now is a Devon man, name of Devereux, Charles Devereux, well-connected I believe but leaves all the navigation to the First Lieutenant Jonathan Salmon - known as Mr. Fish among the crew. He's a man of great experience - you could learn a lot from him, Mr. Jarvis, that is ..." Mr. Iver coughed, "if you haven't learnt as much already sailing with the great Admiral. You'll be the envy of the quarterdeck and the crew will not tire of the telling of it."

"When do you sail?" Nicholas asked, thinking of his promised visit to his family.

"In just a week. We're to board some wounded from the Barracks and take them to Chatham for the winter. They've had to be bedded in tents here in Yarmouth. Can you two be back here in say three days?"

"We will, I promise you," Hugo replied. They returned to the *Glatton* to collect their belongings and set out for home.

CHAPTER XIX
A Strange Encounter

The *Beaumaris Castle* left Calcutta on 4 January 1803. She sailed in the company of four other East Indiamen coming from China and Malaya, and one more which joined the convoy off Madras. Two Royal Navy frigates escorted them, and though they encountered a cyclone in the southern Indian Ocean, which caused much discomfort but fortunately not much damage, all the vessels having experienced navigators, they reunited thereafter and reached the Cape of Good Hope in fine order.

Alas, Ainsworth Rich had not enjoyed the voyage. He was horribly sea-sick during the cyclone and could only remember with nostalgia his outward voyage eight years before which had seemed so tranquil and full of optimism. His sickness had left him with an unpleasant cough - in Calcutta he had suffered with it for years if he cared to acknowledge it, worse in the rainy season but scarcely noticeable when the weather was crisp or hot and dry. His sickness prevented him from fulfilling adequately his shipboard duties, which were otherwise not too disagreeable, being those of manservant and butler to the officers. However the Captain, whose surname was Foreman, recognised in Mr. Rich an aristocrat fallen upon hard times and revelled in his situation, never ceasing to remind him of his reduced circumstances by an acerbic or sarcastic commentary exchanged with his First Officer, Mr. Fullsham. Each sally would be followed by a snort from Captain Foreman as he took a pinch of snuff, and a cackle of high-pitched laughter from his lieutenant. The most humiliating moments of Ainsworth's daily routine took place when the Captain dined with his officers, and the Master, the Purser and the Physician, or he who represented himself as one, for whatever he had prescribed for Ainsworth's sickness seemed to have done him no good at all. Arrival at a port, and one with as fair a landscape as that surrounding the Cape, seemed likely to offer a welcome avenue of escape, and Ainsworth could scarcely await permission to go ashore.

Captain George Elphinstone had captured the Cape for Britain from the Dutch in 1795. In the previous century and a half the Dutch had built a fortress at Cape Town and had developed a harbour for the refurbishment and re-supplying of passing merchantmen, a facility which the ships of other friendly nations were permitted to use. However when the French overran the Netherlands in

1795, Britain quickly realised that her valuable shipping route to India could easily be severed and decided upon conquest of the Cape. By this time the Prince of Orange had sought refuge in England and Britain hoped that the Dutch Colony would submit without a fight. Captain Elphinstone, aboard H.M.S. *Monarch*, had moored in False Bay and opened negotiations with the Dutch Governor. However the latter received news that the French Revolutionaries had absolved Dutch citizens from allegiance to their sovereign and the Governor decided not to cooperate. Captain Elphinstone ordered a bombardment of the Dutch military camp at Muizenberg and then landed seamen and marines who occupied the settlement. Shortly afterwards a second squadron of British warships appeared off Table Bay and the Dutch Governor tendered his submission. When Captain Elphinstone sailed home to Spithead in January 1797, he was rewarded with a barony of the Irish peerage and became Lord Keith.

By the time that the *Beaumaris Castle* arrived off Cape Town six years later little had changed. Most of the local inhabitants were still Dutch farmers along with their black servants and labourers. English forces occupied almost exclusively the Fort and the harbour, as well as one or two strong-points along the southern coast designed to deter unwanted visitors. This was the first glimpse Ainsworth had had of the Cape settlement and its tabular guardian mountain, for his voyage out from England had taken place during the hostilities and his convoy had been obliged to water elsewhere at friendly West and East African slave-ports.

However when the *Beaumaris Castle* and her companions rounded the Cape of Good Hope and approached Table Bay, they found the anchorage already full of merchant shipping headed for Europe, in particular a Portuguese fleet of five East Indiamen and a British frigate dutifully guarding the merchandise of her remaining European ally. Thus the new arrivals were obliged to anchor offshore in waters where they would be extremely vulnerable should any storm blew up from the West. That is exactly what occurred a few days later, so that they were forced to seek shelter in the lee of a low island that stood offshore. It amused the convalescent Ainsworth to observe Captain Foreman quite pale with agitation at this juncture, for the captain knew well that the island had an evil reputation as the Dutch had been using it as a leper colony, and there was the West wind blowing all their iniquitous vapours straight into the open windows and hatchways of his ship!

When the storm had subsided, a messenger was sent from one of the accompanying frigates to the frigate of the inshore fleet, suggesting that the two fleets exchange anchorages to permit the second convoy to reprovision, and that they should then proceed up the West African coast together, the better to defend themselves against pirates or a renewal of warfare between the European nations. Although peace between France and England had been declared a year before by the Treaty of Amiens, its ratification had thrown up a number of problems causing delays in implementation of the terms. One of these was that the Dutch should regain possession of the Cape, but as yet no Dutch garrison had been sent out to do so, and the Fort and harbour facilities were still under British control.

In port at last and able to appreciate at first hand the statuesque beauty of Table Mountain and its flanking hills, Ainsworth fell into step with a detachment of marines from one of the frigates who were marching to the Fort where they were to be billeted for the duration of their stay. There he called upon the Commandant, introduced himself by reference to Sir Charles Rich, and asked if he might borrow a horse to go riding into the hills. The Commandant warned him that he could easily be set upon and robbed, since the Dutch were very aggravated about their continuing loss of sovereignty and looked forward to having their colony returned to them. In addition, the Commandant told him, there were vagrant groups of freed slaves and also Bushmen hunters in the hills who would not hesitate to attack him if they thought he was worth robbing. Ainsworth, who had left his steward's uniform on board ship and had come ashore dressed in the nankeen trousers, loose shirt and simple jacket that he had worn in his leisure hours in Calcutta, showed the Commandant the pair of handsome pistols that he carried in his belt. The property of the East India Company, they had been lent to him by Colonel Kirkpatrick and never handed back on his departure, since Anando had already packed them in his trunk. The Commandant grinned, shouted to his orderly to find Mr. Rich a decent horse and to order Samuel, his black houseboy, to accompany his guest on a donkey to ensure he could not become lost.

Like a bird freed from a cage, Ainsworth set his mount at a trot and looked down at Sam and the donkey pacing along beside him. Sam's ankles swung wide over the animal's belly, just as Ajoy's had done when they had ridden out to Baranset together, Ainsworth remembered with a catch in his breath. The few streets of the town with their low-lying whitewashed and tiled or thatched cottages were soon left behind and the lane, still clearly defined, wound gradually upwards. In the fields grain crops and maize were ripening fast in the autumn sunshine and Ainsworth noted the presence of vineyards hung with generous bunches of still-green grapes. The farm buildings were set back from the road, and if the occasional grizzled farmer or hooded farm-wife did glance in his direction there was little to distinguish him, Ainsworth felt, from one of their own. Besides, had he not ridden into many an Indian village, often with little real protection by his Sepoys, and had he not faced quite a few hostile reception committees single-handed?

The farmland had come to an end now and he was riding more slowly up the scarp of a grassy hill. The lane had become a path, one used by other riders though, for he could see hoofprints ahead of him in the sandy soil. Presently the path forked. "This way, sir," Sam told him. "You want get to top, I show you way. I show you where we leave horses, then walk to top." Now they were moving through light deciduous woodland. Birds he did not recognise and butterflies he wanted to stop and admire fluttered away before him as he rode. When the trees thinned out and ended Sam dismounted and led the way to a stream. He tethered their mounts to a thicket there and bade Ainsworth drink deep. "You not bring hat or water flask, sir. You get very hot in shining sun." This was true, Ainsworth reflected, and with his training in the Tropics he ought not to have overlooked those simple precautions.

They started to climb a path, at times steep and rocky, at others meandering gently along the slope before it zig-zagged and ran back along itself a score of feet higher up the mountain. The grass beside them was the long yellow grass of early autumn, the late flowers blooming or wilting in the sun. Several times Ainsworth, who was leading, came across a snake lying in the pathway, stamped his foot and waited until it slithered off, as he had been accustomed to do in India. Sometimes there was only a mysterious rustle in the grass. Rock hyraxes, on guard beside their burrows, perched atop the scattered rocks to observe the pair as they passed. Ainsworth thought of taking a pot-shot at them but reflected that it might draw undesired attention to their passage. Now they were about half-way to the summit, Ainsworth estimated, as he paused to mop his brow with his neckerchief and also to catch his breath. Evidently he was not as fit as he had expected. He reasoned that it must be due to his recent illness and to that lingering cough.

Ainsworth pressed on, the path becoming steeper and more rocky the higher they climbed. He found that he needed to pause time and again to breathe more freely and to still his beating heart, till eventually Sam said, "You let me go first, sir. Then I pull you in bad places." The sun, moving into its zenith, shone on the broken sand-coloured rocks with blazing intensity. Ainsworth half-closed his eyes against the brilliance, then found himself stumbling dangerously. Pausing again, he viewed with satisfaction the lion-shaped outlying hill which was set out clearly below him. How far was the summit now? A thousand feet above him, perhaps?

The path became steeper, more steps than slopes, and he found himself using his knees to clamber up. Sam, all of fifty feet above him let out a chuckle. No doubt he had guided many a stumbling visitor along that same route. As they reached the boulders that marked proximity to the summit, the rocks turned grey and weather-beaten. Moss and lichens encrusted them, the long grass vanished and the fynbos flourished in every gully. The spiky flowers of the Protea contrasted nicely with their dark green leaves. The bushes and their flowers diminished in height, the herbage grew rougher step by step as they ascended. Finally a narrow footpath led up a green valley and over a dip in the mountain's rim. The summit at last!

Ainsworth threw himself down on the short turf of the tableland and panted for quite half an hour before he had the strength to sit up and look around him. He had taken off his kerchief and had laid it over his burning forehead. Now Sam drew his attention to a boulder whence he might enjoy the most precipitous yet magnificent view. Looking down upon the harbour and the modest settlement that surrounded it, Ainsworth was amazed at the delicacy created by height and distance. He, Ainsworth Rich, stood upon the Roof of the World, like an eagle, or even like an angel, gazing down at fragile humanity isolated below in a green and blue cushion of space. He felt his own breath still caught in his lungs, his own fragility, and knew he would never reach the Roof of the World again.

As the afternoon's shadows deepened upon the lion-shaped hill below, Sam called to him and told him that they must descend now in order to regain the fort before dark. As they started down over the tumbled rocks, the lowering sun blinded Ainsworth and he began to stumble. Sam removed his own wide-brimmed hat and donated it, saying sagely, "You sho' bring hat, sir. Water bottle too, next time maybe." But Ainsworth knew that there would never be a next time. This was his moment, when time itself had stood still and he had touched, for an instant, that Heaven in which he had never had any belief.

Two hours later they found their mounts grazing peacefully and Ainsworth could lie down upon the grass and bury his burning head in the stream. Then he dried his face with his kerchief and mounted his horse. When eventually at dusk they reached the Fort, he dismounted, gave the bridle to Sam and tipped into the boy's cupped palm the last of his silver rupees, the only coinage he possessed. Then he returned to his ship and resumed his duties. The next day the *Beaumaris Castle* and the remainder of the fleet weighed anchor and sailed north up the long West coast of Africa.

The voyage passed almost without incident save those of normal seaboard life, more rough weather till they reached the Tropics, the crews cleaning the decks and repairing the rigging, a flogging or two for some infraction or other, the ships almost running out of water, though never it seemed out of liquor, and putting into a West African slave port for fresh supplies. For Ainsworth this was a renewed encounter with the slave trade, since his previous ship had visited the same port on its outward voyage to India. He observed the wretched creatures as they stumbled along chained together and were herded aboard a slaver which happened to be in port at the same time, but it did not occur to Ainsworth that in a moral world human beings should not be treated thus. To him it was all part of the natural order of things; those who had reason to be superior, such as the richer, more fortunate or better-born, had a right to expect a more comfortable and privileged existence. It was not in Ainsworth's nature to sigh over the misfortunes of others.

As they approached the Cape Verde Islands in the month of March 1803, the shipping lanes became more frequented and they encountered a French squadron and then a Dutch one, both of which maintained their distance. There was no dipping of colours at the British mastheads and no corresponding friendly signal from the foreign ships. Everyone, it seemed, was anticipating a renewal of hostilities. Around the Canary Islands there was a great deal of Spanish shipping to be seen, but Lord Nelson when at Tenerife had given an undertaking that there would be no further attacks on those islands, so the British frigates of their escort kept their gun ports closed and hastened on towards Madeira and the port of Funchal. When they arrived it was to find two important pieces of news awaiting them. One was that the Dutch squadron they had passed had been heading for Cape Colony intending to take repossession of that territory, using force if necessary. The second item of news was that their fleet would now be divided, the Portuguese vessels sailing home to the River Tagus under escort by their own countrymen, whilst the British frigates which had guarded them so far would be returning south with another eastbound convoy. Their own protection would be handed over to two other British frigates already in port. One of these was the *Aeschylus* of thirty-six guns, and the other a larger vessel of fifty guns, H.M.S.*Apollion*.

* * *

Hugo Jarvis and Nicholas Wilmington had lodged and messed with the midshipmen aboard the *Apollion* until the ship docked at Chatham and the medical cases she had brought from Yarmouth had been delivered to the military hospital. Then the ship sailed down the Medway to Sheerness where she was to be refurbished and re-provisioned. As active young fellows they had assisted with these tasks, but as their new convoy would not be ready to sail until after Christmas, and the politicians were engaged in formalising a peace anyway, they begged some leave, planning to sample the delights of the Capital. Nicholas celebrated the festive season with relatives having a town house in Mayfair, where Hugo was also invited. However Hugo had errands of his own. His sister Lucy and her suitor Daniel Mackenzie had decided to postpone their wedding for a year, and Alfred Jarvis had asked his elder son to visit and report upon the family of his future son-in-law.

So Hugo called upon Daniel and his family whom he found living in pleasantly rural Kensington. The total loss of the *Aetherial* made a suitable opening topic of conversation, whence the subject matter might move more easily to the technical improvements being incorporated into the new frigates being built at the Blackwall docks, east of the City. Hugo had noted that the *Apollion* had updated her cannon since his previous voyage in her, so that detonation by flintlock hammers enabled a faster rate of fire. Hugo was curious as to what other improvements might be introduced or being investigated for the British Navy. For instance, he had heard that in France there was a project to build a submersible craft that might blast a hole in a warship from beneath her keel! At this Mr. Mackenzie senior enquired whence Hugo had heard such news and made a careful note of his source - a Danish officer captured at Copenhagen.

Hugo then went on to discuss the changes he had noted in the nature of shipboard warfare, just in the course of the few major battles with which he was acquainted. He recalled that at the Battle of St. Vincent, Commodore Horatio Nelson had personally led a boarding party which had captured two of the four prizes taken that day. At Aboukir Bay on the Nile, however, little boarding had taken place until enemy vessels had either struck their colours or had been too damaged to offer much resistance. Off Copenhagen, by contrast, there had been no boarding at all until the enemy vessels had struck their colours, and even then boarding parties had had to hold back until any renewed firing had ceased. Was this to be the pattern of future warfare at sea, Hugo enquired, with vast gun platforms battering each other into destruction and surrender, leaving sailors and Marines with less hand-to-hand fighting and relying much more on the technical qualities of the guns? Hugo's hypothesis provoked such long and detailed discussion among the three men that poor Mrs. Mackenzie and Daniel's younger sister Harriet were obliged to enter and remind the gentlemen that dinner awaited them in the dining-room and would spoil unless they afforded it their most earnest and immediate attention. Hugo was able to despatch to his father a most advantageous assessment of the standing and suitability of the Mackenzie family as future in-laws for his pretty sister Lucy.

When Hugo returned to Chatham he found the *Apollion* almost ready to be piloted out of the Long Reach to join her new convoy, along with a frigate of thirty-six guns, the *Aeschylus,* commanded by Captain Edrington. As Second Lieutenant Hugo found himself lodged next to the Chaplain's cabin where he and Gus had spent their first bewildered night aboard more than seven years ago. Nicholas, having duly obtained his certificate, was already accommodated in a cabin he shared with another junior officer. Accompanying Mr. Iver on a tour of inspection, Hugo found many of the staff unchanged; Mr. Dunstan and his assistants still officiated in the orlop well and the cockpit, and Mr. Jackson was still responsible for the guns. However the *Apollion* had a new Master, a Mr. Brightman whom Hugo remembered serving as Bosun on another ship at Aboukir Bay. They recognised each other and shook hands. It made a reassuring commencement to Hugo's new posting.

By the time the convoy sailed for Funchal in January 1802, the legal right of the escorts to secure enemy ships as prizes was already highly debatable, for official peace negotiations had commenced as long ago as the previous September. Nevertheless, Hugo and his fellow-officers still felt their hackles rising when sailing through the Downs and close to the French port of Boulogne where Napoleon Bonaparte had added daily to a vast military encampment and to a flotilla of brigs and gunboats with which he hoped to achieve a successful invasion of England. Hugo had gathered from discussions with his Uncle Bob, from the newspapers and from his shipmates on the *Apollion* that whilst he had still been with the North Sea Fleet in the Baltic last summer, Government and country had gone through a period of panic. The 'home guard', the Volunteer Sea Fencibles, had been called up and had paraded and practised their gunnery, and when Lord Nelson had returned early to England from the Baltic in July 1801, he had been ordered almost immediately to supervise defensive preparations in the Downs. Eventually the Admiral had decided to attack the barrier of blockships before Boulogne Harbour in the hope of destroying its strategic value. He planned an action by night, as at Tenerife, but as before Santa Cruz advance warning had allowed the Enemy to improve its defences. Chains had replaced anchor cables which could be slashed with a cutlass, and nets had been hung between the French gunwales and the yards so that boarding sailors and marines would be fired upon before they could gain access to the decks. Also, once the mayhem had commenced, in the darkness there was no means of coordinating such an attack. The British vessels retired with their wounded and it seemed that Peace would be welcome. It is true, however, that Nelson's actions had at least kept the French in port.

Hugo's renewed service on his old ship was not without excitement. In mid-Channel they encountered a strong South-Westerly gale and a French brig dismasted and in distress. They took her in tow, Hugo being sent aboard with a prize crew who, once the weather had eased, had her jury-rigged in a few hours. Hugo then had the honour of commanding her as she sailed into Portsmouth where he handed her over to the Harbourmaster and was rowed back to the *Apollion* in the Captain's gig. Captain Devereux regarded the incident with satisfaction and Hugo knew that his skills had been noted for the next opportunity of promotion. Besides, a small and fast-sailing boat like the brig was in short supply in the Royal Navy - 'the eyes of the Navy' Lord Nelson called them.

The convoy reached Funchal without further incident but found no frigates there able to supply an on-going escort to the Cape and India. Instead there was a Portuguese convoy of three ships heading initially for the Cape Verde Islands, though Captain Devereux suspected that they were engaged in the slave trade and intended to make further landfall on the West African coast. He agreed, for a fee, to add the Portuguese vessels to those already under his protection and a new convoy was formed. The faster British merchantmen were to follow their lighter sister-ship, the *Aeschylus*, with the heavier-armed *Apollion* sailing astern of the slower Portuguese vessels. By the time they passed the Canary Islands early in March 1802 their line of sail stretched over three miles, and the *Aeschylus* was often lost to sight below the horizon.

It was in these circumstances that the watch aboard the *Apollion* heard the sound of gunfire ahead. Hugo was in charge at that moment and immediately sent word to his captain who thereupon ordered all sail set. Leaving the convoy aside the *Apollion* leapt through the water. A seaman sent up to the maintop reported two strange sail, both firing on the *Aeschylus*, though the leading British merchantmen were advancing to her support. As they passed their Portuguese convoy Captain Devereux sent a signal that they should fly British flags, that being the surest way to impress any enemy. Hugo, still holding the telescope from his watch, volunteered to climb to the maintop with it to see what flags the intruders carried. He found every step of the way up the high swaying rigging as familiar as of old. He had sufficient sighting of the strangers to be able to report that one was a Spanish warship of some eighty guns, a three-decker anyway, and the other, though flying a Spanish flag, he was sure it was a Portuguese slaver. Hugo remembered all too well that previous capture off the Isla de las Aves in the Caribbean which had caused him to catch yellow fever.

When Hugo returned to the deck he found it already clearing for action, the Bosun having roused all hands; hammocks were being thrust into the nettings, sand was sprinkled on deck to give a better footing, buckets of water were stood by or carried below to the orlop deck, the gun ports were opened, the tackles secured, wads, sponges, cartridges and gunpowder were brought up and checked over by the busy middies, of whom Hugo was glad he was no longer one. Instead it was his duty to tour the ship with the Captain and ensure that all preparations had been made correctly and that the crew knew their work, for unlike Captain Sterne, the present commander had only given the gunners a couple of practice sessions, and some of them were landsmen and novices. With this dearth of practice in mind, Hugo suggested to his captain that he take the more exposed position beside the forward hatch, whilst Nicholas Wilmington, who had also supervised a gunnery station at the Battle of Copenhagen, stand by the after-hatch to ensure the correct response was transmitted to the gun-teams. Captain Devereux agreed and the *Apollion* was ready to fire.

As the *Apollion* hove in sight of the battle, it became obvious that the *Aeschylus* was already severely damaged. Her foremast had been shot away, her mainsail was in ribbons and not all of her guns were firing, some having received direct hits from the Spaniard's cannon. Her boats had been lowered and her captain was obviously trying to warp her round into a position where she could fire her port guns instead. At the moment she was bows-on to her enemy. The leading British merchantman, on her way eastwards with a cargo of manufactures destined, no doubt, for India or China, had paused within firing range of the second ship and had aimed several broadsides at her rigging, to some effect, but being armed only with six-pounders there was little more damage she could do. She received a desultory fire from the enemy in return, leading her officers to suppose that she carried only a skeleton crew.

By this time the *Apollion* had overtaken all the slower Portuguese merchantmen and was to windward of the British ones whose crews gathered on deck raised a cheer, any noise to frighten off the enemy. Captain Devereux guessed that the *Apollion*'s appearance to windward of the battle scene would cause the Spaniard to break off the action and attempt to escape. He therefore had the Master set a course which would intercept her as she tried to leave the scene. The port guns were primed and ready to fire, the aim being to approach near enough to loose a powerful broadside which would thud into the ship's towering stern and immobilise her rudder, despite the enemy being a much taller and heavier vessel. On the quarterdeck the order was given to fire, Hugo and Nicholas transmitted it on deck and below with the speed of lightning, and the whole ship shuddered backwards as the heavy guns bellowed. From the foredeck and the poop her carronades sent grape shot ploughing through the gilded stern quarters of the enemy and over her decks as the *Apollion* swept past and with pinpoint accuracy from Mr. Brightman she drew alongside. The seamen were ready with grappling hooks and ladders to clamber up the Spanish ship's side, helped by the shallow slope of her tumblehome. *Apollion's* detachment of Marines overtook the seamen en route and a brief hand-to-hand combat took place. It did not last long as the Spanish ship was undermanned, and the Marines soon had her colours lowered, the Union flag raised in their place, and could begin sorting out their prisoners.

Half a mile away the three British merchantmen had surrounded the second ship and had taken her prisoner. As Hugo had guessed, she turned out to be a Portuguese slaver with a full cargo of blacks from West Africa whose pitiful cries could be heard now that the gunfire had ceased. The leading British East Indiaman, named the *Beaumaris Castle*, took on board the Spanish crew from the slaver and imprisoned them in her foc'sle. Having few injuries to her own men she made up a prize crew and sent them aboard the slaver, along with a medical assistant to bind any wounds. Some few members of the original Portuguese crew were discovered below decks and released on promise of their cooperation in sailing in convoy.

Meanwhile the crew from the Spanish warship, the *San Barnabo*, being more numerous, had been divided up between the *Apollion* and the other British ships. Having few injuries of her own, the *Apollion* was able to lend Mr. Dunstan's services to those Spanish wounded likely to survive, and he went aboard with one of his assistants to treat them. Now the crippled *Aeschylus* slowly came up to join the group. She had suffered considerable damage and loss, with two officers and seventeen men killed, and her gun-deck a shambles since one of her cannon had exploded and two others had been thrust off their carriages by some accurate Spanish gunfire. The cannon had rolled about the deck and had caused further broken limbs before they could be secured. Since their barrels were red-hot from firing, they also caused burns and fires until they had been sufficiently dowsed with sea water. Mr. Dunstan was retrieved from service aboard the Spanish ship and taken to the *Aeschylus* to assist its surgeon who had many a broken bone to set.

As the weather was calm and balmy in this tropical latitude, the convoy cast anchor and Captain Devereux ordered all their captains to supper aboard the *Apollion* so that they might decide what to do with their prizes. The leading Portuguese captain, João de Pereira, made it very clear that he and his colleagues would be eager to take charge of the Portuguese slaver, and this seemed appropriate. But her cargo was extremely valuable, such of it as survived. The Marines had already confirmed that the slaves seemed mostly to be suffering from fright, so Captain Devereux required some form of compensation for himself and his crew if he were to forgo the prize money which would have been available had he delivered the capture to a British Government agent in a friendly port. As the Portuguese Cape Verde Islands were no more than a hundred miles distant, it was decided to take the captured ships to Antao, the nearest of the larger islands, and to decide what financial compensation might be available to Captain Devereux when they reached their destination. Meanwhile Captain Devereux had asked Hugo whether he had any experience of sailing upon such a slaver, and on receiving a positive reply sent Hugo to command the ship the next morning, along with two score of the *Apollion's* more competent seamen. His instructions were to feed and water the slaves, inspect the prisoners and send back the surgeon's assistant if he were no longer needed. "Do you, Fish, take command of the Spaniard," he told his first Officer, Mr. Salmon, using that gentleman's familiar name.

About noon next day they set out and two days later the whole convoy had arrived in port, the jury-rigged *Aeschylus* last of the column. There a surprise awaited them, for the local Portuguese authorities had impounded a French warship which had attacked some of their merchant vessels. Named *La Belle Helène*, she had sixty-four guns and was a beauty. Captain Devereux, whose family had been in shipping since Francis Drake had sailed from Plymouth to defeat the Spanish Armada, could not take his eyes from her.

He asked the Portuguese Governor if he might inspect her straight away and suggested that an exchange of the slaver for their French captive could perhaps form a basis for agreeing compensation. Besides, Captain Devereux pointed out, should peace be declared shortly, the Portuguese might be obliged to set their captive free without any form of compensation at all. This was accepted and Captain Devereux, mindful of likely political developments, had some ingenious documentation drawn up by the Portuguese Governor's lawyer. There was one deed by which the British East India Company acquired ownership of the French vessel, and another, also with a translation into English, by which *La Belle Helène* was to be leased to the service of the Royal Navy. Captain Foreman, having authority from the Court of Directors in London to charter such additional vessels as were needed to carry available cargoes, had no hesitation in signing where required, in return for an equal share of the generous bribe which accompanied the sealing of the agreement!

Another British convoy of five East Indiamen accompanied by two frigates now arrived at Antao. These were all homeward bound to London, though the frigates being in good shape they were persuaded to accompany the *Beaumaris Castle* and her two companions southward to the Cape in order to free the *Apollion* and the now-repaired *Aeschylus* to accompany the northbound vessels and the prizes back to England. The Portuguese took charge of all the Spanish prisoners, promising to give them 'a long voyage home' and Captain Devereux shared out the French crew from the captured ship with much the same objective in view. Mr. 'Fish' continued to command the large *San Barnabo* and Hugo was given charge of the beautiful French warship. Now he had real responsibility, and chose his prize crew with extreme care, making sure there were no landsmen among them.

The new fleet left Antao for Madeira at the end of March 1802. When they reached Funchal some three weeks later they learnt that the Peace had been signed at Amiens, France, a month since on behalf of Britain, France, Spain and Holland, though the Portuguese would appear to have been overlooked. Under the terms of the Treaty, the British Cabinet led by Henry Addington had agreed to return to their previous owners all the conquests Britain had made since war was declared in 1793. This meant that the Dutch would receive back Curaçao and the Cape of Good Hope, the French would regain or keep those hard-won West Indian islands, Guadeloupe, Martinique and the others, and Malta would be returned into the guardianship of the Knights of St. John. Of all her many military gains, Britain would only retain Ceylon, and the island of Trinidad which she had taken from Spain. For the thousands of sailors, soldiers and marines who had taken part in fierce actions over the past decade, and the many who had lost their limbs or their lives, it was a disappointing result. Moreover the Royal Navy would now be stood down, along with the Volunteer Sea Fencibles, the Dragoon guards, the regiments of foot and all the artillery battalions, with every man paid off and the many surplus officers retained on half-pay. Hugo was so glad he had chosen to sail with a merchant escort vessel, whose rôle as a defence against piracy would continue in peace-time, rather than seeking a place on a ship of the line when he and Nicholas had parted from the *Glatton*.

However Captain Devereux was not so happy. Peace meant that no more captures could be made, and that any prizes still in enemy hands had to be relinquished by the date of the Treaty's ratification. "We had better hurry home, Fish," he told his First Lieutenant. "I shall go into Spithead with the Spanish vessel and young Jarvis with me on the French one, while you and Captain Edrington deliver our ships and the rest of the convoy to the Thames. There's bound to be a Court of Inquiry set up over these two prizes and that means weeks of delay."

Hugo Jarvis had the honour of delivering a second and more splendid vessel into the hands of the Portsmouth Harbourmaster, and his Captain after him on the larger but slower *San Barnabo*. They made a spectacular sight as they rounded Spithead together and swung across to anchor a cable's length from the Harbourmaster's Office. The pilot on each vessel insisted that the officer responsible for these foreign arrivals accompany him inshore in the pilot boat. A crowd had collected on the surrounding docks and fish wharves, hissing at first as they thought these were foreign ships come to crow over a craven England that had made such a poor peace, then cheering as the whisper went round that these were foreign prizes brought home by British sailors.

Captain and officer were treated rather like schoolboys caught out in a prank as they stood before the Harbourmaster and were informed that their arrival had been anticipated by a nosy British schooner who had apprised herself of the situation when at Funchal and had brought the news to Portsmouth along with her despatches. An Admiralty Court had already been convened to hear the matter. Now that they had arrived it would sit next day and meanwhile they would spend the night at the nearby White Hart Inn, and they and their ships would be put under guard till the matter was resolved. Naturally Hugo felt extremely nervous at this, his first 'brush with the Law', but he looked across to Captain Devereux who gave him the slightest of winks.

Next morning, after being woken by their guards and taken down to the inn's parlour where they breakfasted splendidly on bacon and eggs with a pot of good coffee, and all at the Navy's expense, ("No point in going to the scaffold on an empty stomach," as Captain Devereux whispered to his young companion), they were taken to Admiralty House and into a large, gloomy, wood-panelled room hung with official portraits of past Lords of the Admiralty. They sat on benches and were instructed to rise when their Lordships were brought in. There were three chairs placed on the far side of the table in front of them, and a desk to one side where the Clerk sat already busily scribbling away. The Usher asked them to stand as two gentlemen entered in the naval uniform of Commodores. They took the outer two chairs behind the table, leaving the larger middle chair empty. Hugo recognised one of the officers at once; he was Captain Thomas Troubridge, last seen wielding cutlass and hangman's noose among the rebels at Naples. He doubted whether the captain would recognise him. The second person was presently introduced as Captain John Markham, and like his colleague he served as Executive Officer to the First Lord of the Admiralty, currently the Earl of St. Vincent.

With his colleague's consent, Commodore Troubridge began to speak. "This morning's meeting is merely one of inquiry," he said. "Our purpose is to ascertain the facts in order to decide whether there is a legal case to answer. The charge, if justified, would be one of piracy upon the High Seas, in that vessels had been taken in violation of the terms of a Treaty of Peace signed at the City of Amiens upon the twenty-fifth day of March last and ratified by His Majesty's solemn Declaration this past twenty-sixth of April, such subsequent acts being contrary to the Articles of War. This is not yet a Court Martial, and if the holding of such a judicial procedure proves necessary, you will of course be at liberty to choose your own Legal Counsel to speak on your behalf. Now, Captain Devereux, do you hold Letters of Marque?"

"Yes, your Honour, I do."

"Do you have them here with you?"

"I regret they are in my cabin aboard ship," Captain Devereux replied.

"We may have them brought here later, then, if we have reason to doubt your word," Commodore Troubridge continued. "Now, which ship did you capture first, and upon what date?"

"It was upon the twenty-first of March, your Honour, in the afternoon. The Spanish vessel, the *San Barnabo* fired upon our sister ship, the *Aeschylus* under Captain Edrington. My ship, the *Apollion* was aft of the convoy, about three miles adrift of the head of it, when we heard the sound of gunfire. We put on all sail, overtook most of the convoy of three Portuguese merchantmen and three British ones of the East India Company, and came upon the Spaniard having done so much damage to the *Aeschylus* as to render her unable to manoeuvre. On appreciating our stronger presence, the Spaniard sought to escape, but we fired a good broadside into her stern and then boarded her. Here is a copy of my Log for that day, your Honour, witnessed by the Purser, Mr. Iver, since my officers were engaged aboard other vessels, and there's a copy of the Log of the *Aeschylus* signed by Captain Edrington and witnessed by the Master of his ship, since both his First and Second Lieutenants had been killed in the action. In addition he lost seventeen men killed and more than a score wounded. Here is a copy of the Muster Roll which indicates the injuries caused."

"I distrust all these copies," John Markham intervened. "Why do we not have the originals?"

"Because, your Honour, they are still upon the ships to which they belong and will be duly delivered to the Navy Office when they arrive at Chatham," Captain Devereux replied smartly. Commodore Markham asked the Clerk to make a note that the copies should be compared with the originals.

"This log entry of Captain Edrington refers to there having been a second vessel in the company of the Spaniard. What ship was that?" John Markham asked.

"It was a Portuguese one, your Honour, which the Spaniard had captured. You will recall that my convoy included Portuguese vessels as well as British ones, and Portugal being an ally of Britain in the War which has just ended, I was unable to take her as a prize."

"No, I understand, a pity," Commodore Troubridge commented. "Did she take any part in the affray?"

"Yes, your Honour. She exchanged a few shots with the leading British East Indiaman, the *Beaumaris Castle* of Captain Foreman, but there were few injuries and little damage on either part."

"What did you then?" John Markham asked sharply.

"We were but a hundred miles from our next destination, the Cape Verde Islands, which the Portuguese vessels were anxious to reach and my British ships were in need of fresh water and supplies, so we decided to sail for Antao Island and to repair the *Aeschylus* and see to other matters once we reached port."

"And I suppose that entering into a friendly port you came upon the French vessel and decided to take her as well?" Captain Troubridge asked with something of a sneer.

"Your Honour, she had already been captured by the Portuguese," Captain Devereux replied quietly, though Hugo glancing sideways at him could see that the trim moustache and small goatee beard that he wore were trembling dangerously. This red-haired man of Devon, this heir of Drake, Hawkins and Raleigh, was beginning to lose his temper.

"On what date did you reach Antao?" John Markham enquired. "The twenty-fourth of March, your Honour, in the afternoon."

"And I suppose you have made a copy of your Log to prove it?" Commodore Troubridge demanded with a sneer.

"Yes. Here it is, your Honour," and Captain Devereux produced another page from his sheaf of documents.

"There is no mention here of any French ship?" Commodore Troubridge asked.

"No, Your Honour, but upon seeing the French vessel in harbour, lying there empty, Captain Foreman of the *Beaumaris Castle* went ashore and enquired of the Portuguese Governor of the place whether he might purchase it, if it would suit his purpose," Captain Devereux replied.

"Captain Foreman did? Why ever should he want a French warship?" John Markham demanded,

"I understood from him that he has authority from the Court of Directors of the East India Company to purchase or otherwise obtain ships suitable for his Company's needs," said Captain Devereux.

"So the French vessel now belongs to the East India Company?" John Markham asked.

"Yes, your Honour, but Captain Foreman has leased her to the British Navy for such purposes as the Admiralty shall decide," and Captain Devereux produced the last two of his remaining documents, the purchase Agreement with the Governor of the Cape Verde Islands, and the leasing Agreement to the Royal Navy, all dutifully signed and sealed by Captains Foreman and Devereux and the dates entered most carefully as the twenty-fourth of March, 1802, just one day before the Peace Treaty had been signed.

"How fortunate and convenient for you, Captain Devereux, that you were able to place such a date upon these documents. Pray where was that done?" Commodore Troubridge sneered again.

"At Antao, your Honour, the same day," the Devon man replied.

"And where is Captain Foreman now that he may confirm these matters?"

"I left him sailing for the Cape of Good Hope, when I departed north homewards, your Honour."

Unseen by them all a door at the back of the courtroom had opened, and the person standing behind the curtain which covered it and which bulged not a little in the draught, had overheard much of these interchanges. Then the curtain was pushed aside abruptly and an old man entered, of average height, portly, distinguished-looking, his naval uniform grand with epaulettes, the star of his knightly order on his breast and a gold medal upon a blue ribbon nestling in the folds of his white lace stock. It was only the expression of glad recognition on Hugo's face that made the two commodores turn round; the newcomer was the Earl of St. Vincent, First Lord of the Admiralty.

John Markham shot out of his seat and pulled out the middle chair so that his superior might ease himself into it. St. Vincent put up one hand to silence his assistants. "I have already overheard most of what has transpired and wish but to pose a few supplementary questions," he began. "You should know, Gentlemen, that this young man before you, who has navigated hither a fine French warship of some sixty-four or so guns, if I count them correctly, Lieutenant Hugo Jarvis, is a kinsman of mine, for all that he will spell his name differently. Thus I have every expectation of hearing from him nothing but the truth, is that not so, Hugo?" he said, looking straight into the younger man's eyes.

"Yes, my Lord, indeed so," Hugo replied, barely repressing a stutter.

"Then tell me, pray," Lord St. Vincent continued evenly, "all these facts given to us by Captain Devereux, are they true to the very best of your knowledge?"

"Yes, my Lord, as I witnessed them myself," Hugo replied.

"And the capture of the Spanish ship, did that take place on the date Captain Devereux indicated?"

"Yes, my Lord, it did."

"And what was in the Portuguese ship, Hugo, what cargo did she carry?"

"She was a slaver, my Lord, with a full cargo."

"I surmised that might have been the case," said the wise old Earl softly. "And you with Captain Devereux thought that such a cargo should be delivered to a suitable haven quickly before it spoiled? Were they in good order when you took them, Hugo?"

"Yes, they were, my Lord. Captain Devereux put me in charge of the slaver since I was familiar with such a ship. The slaves were a little seasick and frightened by the gunfire, but otherwise in health. Perhaps they had not long been embarked, my Lord, from the shores of Africa."

"Perhaps so. Captain Devereux," the Earl turned to the older man. "You're something of a buccaneer, are you not, living up to the reputation of your Devon countrymen? So you saw that trim French warship and longed to strut upon her quarterdeck, and you had a full cargo of slaves to sell for profit, but suitable purchasers were an ocean away, and slaves chained in the hold of a ship can so easily depart this life, a shipful of troubles in short. No doubt your Portuguese companions nudged at your elbow suggesting a deal might be done to your mutual benefit. So, fearing that peace might already have been declared, you hatched this scheme with Captain Foreman, whose acquaintance I confess never to have made, whereby he would purchase the French vessel from the Portuguese for a consideration, which is not mentioned in this document and which may thereby be illegal, the said vessel then to be conveniently leased to the Navy so that you might claim prize money in her respect or at least compensation were she reclaimed by the French. And this convenient date of twenty-fourth of March last when supposedly you arrived in Antao and immediately concluded this deal, when was that document dated, Hugo?" he turned to the young man again.

"We arrived in port on the twenty-fourth, my Lord, as Captain Devereux has averred," Hugo responded. "I did not witness the signing of those documents, indeed I knew nothing of them until this moment, but I do recall that all the ships' captains spent a very long evening ashore being entertained at the Governor's mansion."

"Very well, gentlemen," the Earl concluded, "I think we have the information we require and talk of courts martial would seem unnecessary. Your Clerk, gentlemen, will nevertheless write to the Navy Office at Chatham and request verification of the appropriate log entries and muster records. Both ships will be impounded by His Majesty's Government for the time being, but their crews may be landed and paid off here. Those that wish to embark again upon the *Apollion* or the *Aeschylus* may obtain travel warrants from the Navy Office, and you two gentlemen," he said, addressing Hugo and his Captain, "are free to travel when you will, but I beg that you, Hugo, will come with me to my office. I have a paper to give you."

Captain Devereux told Hugo that he would take the pilot boat back to the *San Barnabo* and would have a seaman bring Hugo's sea-chest ashore from *La Belle Helène*, and they would meet up at the Navy Office building. Hugo followed the Earl of St. Vincent into a small office which the Admiral excused as temporary accommodation whenever he needed to visit Admiralty House, Portsmouth. He had, he told Hugo, just set his staff to carry out a very thorough investigation into corruption and mismanagement in the Navy under the terms of a Royal Commission. Their aim would be to propose remedies for many of the practices and abuses which had provoked the infamous mutinies at Spithead and the Nore, which mutinous spirit still haunted the Navy, its ships and its premises. "That being so," he said, "when I learnt of the forthcoming arrival in port here of some rather post-Treaty prizes, and your name was mentioned, Hugo, I had to ensure personally that all was done in accordance with the Law."

"What will happen to the vessels now, my Lord?" Hugo asked.

"Well, the Spanish one is a large vessel, and you were lucky to take her so easily?"

"She was undermanned at the time, my Lord."

"Spain may well seek her return and may offer us some of their prizes in exchange. The French one will be put to good use once hostilities are resumed, as I am sure they will be. This Treaty is but a sorry truce, giving back the conquests we made in the 'Windies' and at such cost indeed! It was a good ruse of your captain to put her into the name of the East India Company. I doubt that Leadenhall Street would approve of it, but maybe they will not learn of it either. I am sure that Captain Foreman received his just reward, your captain too, for a valuable cargo of slaves."

"I know nothing of that, my Lord, but we haven't been without a flagon of port wine ever since!" Hugo replied.

Earl St. Vincent laughed, opened a file from his portefeuille and took out what appeared to be a legal deed. "I promised you this when we first met years ago, for the day when you passed your examination and made lieutenant, yet you never returned to me for it. Since then I have learnt by a side wind that you served on the *Vanguard* at the Nile under my dear friend and colleague Lord Nelson, and just astern of him on the *Glatton* before Copenhagen. Tell me, how did you find Captain Bligh? Some hold that he is often enraged to madness and that it caused the famous mutiny of Fletcher Christian and his fellow-ruffians in

1789, but I think that an excuse concocted by friends of the mutineers that seek their return to this country."

"He was perhaps a trifle morose, my Lord, kept to himself, and inclined to flog for the sake of maintaining discipline. But I found him fair, and he was very fair to me."

"I am glad to hear it. This is what I wanted to give you, Hugo. 'Tis a Deed of Poll allowing you to call yourself by the name JERVIS spelt thus, the same as mine, if it would please you. I have just recommended my nephew Thomas to a new post, and I see no reason why you too should not benefit from my position. Given that the facts set out today prove true, I shall recommend you to the first lieutenancy of a ship of the line the moment we are at war again. In a twelve-month you should make post-captain."

"Thank you, my Lord, for your kindness, and for your timely intervention today," Hugo said, accepting the document.

"Oh, a trifle. I feared my colleagues might be too harsh with you. We must preserve the brave ones who will sail into battle with eagerness and enthusiasm, not smother them with tedious controls."

Hugo, knowing that the Earl was thinking again of the courageous initiatives taken by Admiral Nelson, smiled and bade his great-uncle four or five times removed farewell. Then he ran to the docks, collected his sea-chest from a ship-mate, queued with the rest of them at the Navy Office for his travel warrant and his pay, booked his place beside Captain Devereux on the next day's post-chaise to London, and spent a jolly evening of celebration at the White Hart Inn.

* * *

The next voyage of the *Apollion*, across the Atlantic and back, and accompanied by the well-repaired *Aeschylus*, was quite unremarkable, save for the weather on the return leg of their voyage between Port Royal, Jamaica, and Madeira. With some storm damage to be repaired, they and their convoy spent longer than usual in the port of Funchal, and were still there when a fresh convoy of five Portuguese ships and six British ones arrived from the Cape of Good Hope. Their escort of three British frigates would now return south with an outward-bound convoy, whilst the *Apollion* and the *Aeschylus* would escort all the northbound vessels. The leading and largest vessel of the new convoy was greeted with pleasure on the quarterdeck of the *Apollion*, and indeed the gratification was mutual, for the new arrival was none other than the *Beaumaris Castle*. It was the custom of the East India Company that the captains and officers of their escort be invited to dine aboard the leading vessel upon the first evening of their engagement. Captain Foreman expressed himself as delighted to renew his acquaintance with Captains Devereux and Edrington, and would be most gratified to receive them and their officers aboard the *Beaumaris Castle* at four o'clock of the afternoon. Captain Devereux passed the invitation to Lieutenants Salmon and Jarvis as a matter of course, but Hugo asked if his friend Nicholas Wilmington might accompany him to provide the poor fellow with a diversion since his mood was somewhat despondent. Captain Devereux, ever grateful that Hugo's connection with the First Lord had saved him from suspicion of piracy and the risk of the hangman's noose, had no hesitation in granting his request.

Captain Foreman and Lieutenant Fullsham greeted their guests in the ante-room that preceded the officers' ward-room in the rather palatial after-quarters of the large, broad-bellied East Indiaman. Two stewards, both in immaculate uni-forms, enquired what liquid refreshment they might wish for, indicating a wide choice of alternatives, some from the most exotic of sources. Hugo, who drank for his health when at sea but otherwise abstemiously, accepted a glass of red wine and stood listening to a conversation between the captains. Nicholas Wilmington was nearby, chatting with some of the East Indiaman's other offi-cers. Hugo's attention strayed for a moment to the person of the second steward, the one who had not served him. The fellow was tall and thin, and rather pale for a steward on such a well-stocked ship. There was something familiar about him, but he could not think what it was.

As Hugo's glance returned to his colleagues, the steward's glance fell upon him. His hands paused in mid-air, his legs seemed rooted to the deck, and his expression froze, his eyes becoming quite glassy. He could not be sure of it, eight years and more had passed since last he saw the fellow, then a mere youth, but he could swear that the person speaking now to Captain Foreman, a person wearing, moreover, a naval officer's uniform, was none other than his old enemy Hugo Jarvis! Suddenly the steward found himself able to move. His feet detached themselves from the floor, he put a few full glasses of various liquors upon a sil-ver tray and advanced across the carpeted deck towards the group of gentlemen. Hugo, sensing the merest rustle of movement behind him, turned round abrupt-ly and found himself staring into the face of Ainsworth Rich!

"Why, Mr. Ainsworth, what brings you here?" Hugo asked, startled. Ainsworth, who had been planning to spill wine on Hugo's uniform so as to spoil his evening, was so surprised by the sudden movement that he spilt the wine on himself instead and slopped much of the rest on the tray.

"Oh, Mr. Rich, now see what you've done!" cried Captain Foreman as he paused with a pinch of snuff twixt box and nostril. "You have quite ruined your uniform. You're such a clumsy fellow. Do go and change it at once." As Ainsworth turned away his breath seemed to catch in his throat, and he doubled his confusion with a fit of coughing. "And do take some physic for that cough you have. We don't want your malodorous airs breathing all over us at table. That scoundrel," Captain Foreman continued once Ainsworth had gone, "goes by the name of Mr. Rich, but he ain't, or if ever he was he ain't now. I picked him up at Calcutta and surmise he was thrown out and told to earn his passage home. He has a shifty look about him, did you not say so, Mr. Fullsham?" he demand-ed of his lieutenant.

At the name 'Mr. Rich' Nicholas Wilmington turned and made his way swiftly to Hugo's side. "I heard the name 'Rich'" he said, and you called that steward 'Ainsworth'." Nicholas dropped his voice to a whisper. "Is he the one, the child my Aunt Marianne had with Ralph Ainsworth, or with Robert Rich, we never have known the truth of it?"

"It seems likely that he is," Hugo replied.

"I was not aware that you knew him. You have never told me before," Nicholas protested.

"Well, I did not see a need for it. He used to live at Roos Hall. The fellow had been sent to India to make his fortune, since Sir Charles Rich, his guardian so-called, had refused to settle any more of his gambling debts. I have not set eyes on the man for upwards of eight years, but he was the one who sold me to the press-gang."

"What a bounder! Did you realise that he was about to spill that wine on you, and when you turned around he spilt it on himself instead?"

"Nicholas, he will no doubt serve us at table also. Should you wish me to introduce you to him as his step-cousin?"

"That will indeed give him a shock, but wait until I have my napkin well-placed over my uniform so as to catch any further spillages! By-the-by, I should explain that my family's purpose in excluding Aunt Marianne's 'misfortune' from our circle is naturally the matter of avoiding any call upon our financial resources. I hope your introduction will not furnish him with any such ideas?"

So it was, half an hour later, when Ainsworth, in a clean uniform once more, approached Hugo's chair with a silver tray bearing a pair of exquisitely engraved glass decanters, Hugo turned towards him and stated, "I thought you to be in India, Ainsworth." (No 'Mr.' this time.) "May I introduce my friend and fellow-officer, Nicholas Wilmington. I think you may discover that he is related to you, a step-cousin in fact." The effect upon Ainsworth of the dreaded surname Wilmington was quite spectacular.

He had gone as pale as a ghost long before Hugo had finished the sentence. He took a step backwards, nearly tripped over the carpet and just managed to deposit the tray and the expensive decanters upon a sideboard, before he covered his face with his hands and fled the room.

"Tut, tut, whatever is the matter with the fellow?" Captain Foreman exclaimed. "I declare he grows worse in his attentions every day. Whatever did you say to him that scared him so?" he asked Hugo.

"I reminded him that it was he who betrayed me to the Press-men when I was a boy," Hugo lied, knowing that Nicholas would not wish him to reveal the other business.

"Well, that seems to have done you little harm, from all that Captain Devereux tells me, with you an officer now and a kinsman to the First Lord, very handily as he related it."

Hugo blushed, thanked the Captain for his invitation and offered him the gravy-boat by way of concluding the conversation. A full two courses had been completed before Ainsworth reappeared, his fellow-steward having become quite aggrieved at having to fulfil his colleague's duties as well as his own. The next time Ainsworth came to serve Hugo and his friend, he pressed a small slip of paper into Nicholas's hand. It read, "May I speak with you, if you please, before you leave. I beg you will concur." It was signed "A.I.R.".

"Should I speak with him, do you think Hugo?" Nicholas asked.

"Ainsworth has always been an insufferable fellow," Hugo replied. "He boasts that Sir Charles is his father and that he is the heir to the Manor of Roos Hall. If he is not aware of his more humble origin I think it will do him good to learn of it."

When Hugo returned aboard the *Apollion* in the early hours of the morning, he did not go to bed, for all the weariness he felt. There was a schooner due to leave next day with despatches for London and Hugo wished this message to catch the mails:

23rd April, 1803

"Dear Jessica, (he wrote - no "Miss" this time, for Jessica herself had so permitted him during the preparations for Carrie's wedding). *"I am writing this urgently from Funchal (Madeira), in the hope of its inclusion in tomorrow's mail that will reach England long before our slow and stately convoy heads up the Channel. I have just come from dining with my Captain and other officers upon the foremost among the East Indiamen of our convoy, the* Beaumaris Castle. *She is quite luxuriously appointed when compared with our more plebian and practical establishment. At table we were waited upon by two stewards, one of whom I recognised to be Ainsworth Rich!*

"Apparently he is on his way home from India and is earning his passage! Thus I fear he may have fallen upon some misfortune and may even have left large debts behind him. I do wish you will warn my Aunt Jarvis so that she may advise Sir Charles and Mr. Russell as she deems appropriate. Beware of him, Jessica, for I do not believe that experience has made him change his ways.

"I hope you are in excellent health, as you always assure me you are. Should the movements of my ship permit me sufficient shore-leave to travel home, I hope to call and pay my respects in person.

Your sincere friend,
Hugo Jarvis.

The *Beaumaris Castle* docked at Limehouse on 11 May 1803, thus arriving safely before England declared war on France again a mere seven days later. Unaware of such developments, Ainsworth disembarked with his two trunks and the ungenerous wages which had accrued from more than four months of labour aboard the East Indiaman. Having insufficient funds to travel to Waverley or to Windsor in search of his Guardian, and not expecting any welcome there as a result of the warning letter which the Marquess Wellesley had sent overland, Ainsworth decided upon taking a cab to the only refuge he knew, Mrs. Bostock's boarding-house in Bloomsbury. When her maid opened the door to his knock and the lady of the house could see him framed in the doorway, she let out a cry of alarm and rushed forward.

"Oh no, Mr. Ainsworth, you cannot come here. My brother-in-law has forbidden it!" and she shut the door in his face. Fortunately he had not dismissed the cab since his two trunks remained perched behind the vehicle, so he asked the cabbie to drive on to the address of a friend. Once again he was turned away, and then a second time. In the end in sheer desperation he returned to the Bloomsbury district and booked himself into a modest hotel. Ideally he needed a room where he had space enough to unlock his trunk and take out the coin-purse containing the diamonds. The hotel porter swore loudly at having to carry upstairs two such heavy burdens, and Ainsworth was obliged to pay the man a double tip. It being already late in the day, he proposed to leave the matter of exchanging his precious stones for some rather more precious funds until the morrow, dined cheerfully at his hotel and slept long and somewhat fitfully, disturbed by that rocking and sliding sensation of a ship that is no longer there.

Next morning he took a cab into the noisome East End of the City, to the premises of a moneylender he had known in his gambling days. He showed his contact some of the stones and enquired where best he might go to obtain a fair price for them. "Oh no, you cannot sell those here," the moneylender told him. "They're illegal. You will need to take them to Amsterdam and have them cut properly. Then you can sell them in this country. Did they not tell you that when you purchased them in India? You did say you had just returned from that country, did you not?"

Furious and disappointed, Ainsworth caught yet another cab to his hotel - he would have walked had it not been for a fear of footpads robbing him of the wretched gems. He had a fortune he could not touch, and another one that would never be his, from what Nicholas Wilmington had told him about his mother's situation. Nicholas had said that Ainsworth's birthright would never be acknowledged, and that his Aunt Marianne had no desire to make the further acquaintance of the illegitimate infant she had borne. There was only one place in the country where, by chance, his humble origin might not have percolated, and that was Roos Hall. The staff there still believed he was the son of Sir Charles Rich, or if not that then of Sir Robert, and Ainsworth saw no need whatever to advise them of anything different.

* * *

By misfortune the schooner that had taken aboard mails and despatches at Funchal in April had encountered a severe storm in the Western Approaches and had been lost with all hands. Thus no-one at Roos Hall or Ringsfield had received

Hugo's warning. Sir Charles, too, had yet to open the Marquess Wellesley's missive which awaited his attention upon his next residing at Waverley, an event of little frequency these days when his domestic joys and his duty to his King caused him to trot endlessly betwixt Windsor Castle, Kensington Palace and Buckingham House next St. James's on the outskirts of London.

At Roos Hall there was a bustle of preparations for a celebratory event to which the Ringsfield family and other acquaintances from the town of Beccles , the Mathers, the Weedons, and several others, including the neighbouring Sucklings, were to be invited. The fifteenth of May would be Miss Jessica's twentieth birthday and Betty Jarvis had saved sufficient funds from Sir Charles's allowance and from her own salary to make a memorable occasion for the poor girl who was still obliged to live in isolation in the gloomy old mansion, and in ignorance of her relationship to Sir Charles and to the Jarvis family.

These days Betty Jarvis no longer walked to and from her home at the Bear & Bells to her employment, but with or without Sir Charles' knowledge used the pony-trap with James the skewbald, the outfit being left at Jack Wilson's livery stables overnight. On special occasions, or at times of domestic crisis, she would stay at the Hall, using one of the vacant staff bedrooms. Today was such an occasion, the eve of her granddaughter's party, for she needed to be up early in the morning to assist Mrs. Baines and the two housemaids with the laying out of the downstairs rooms and the arranging of plates, cutlery and dishes. The marquee had been borrowed again from the Mathers, and Easton had set it up on the lawn, just in case it rained, for this was only May and the Spring had been a cold one. Peter Jones was to leave care of the Bear & Bells and of Robert Jarvis who had taken to his bed with a bad cold to his new young wife, Margaret, and to bring a dray loaded with kegs of beer, ale and brandy, and not a few flagons of wine. The gardens looked fresh and tidy; the walks in the park had been gravelled over anew after the winter's mud. Musicians had been hired for dancing, and of course Miss Jessica herself would give a performance at the pianoforte.

All these arrangements were being ticked off in Betty Jarvis's mind as she drove back to Roos Hall that Sunday after attending evensong at Beccles Church and bidding goodnight to her sick husband. James, the pony, knew his way well enough, so the first thing Betty noticed as the vehicle turned towards Bungay was that the cart had come to a complete halt and that James was trembling from head to foot. It was dark in the Bungay road. The tall overhanging trees lent extra gloom to the misty dimness of the dusk. Betty thought she could see something ahead of her, moving between the trees, but the shape was vague and her eyesight these days not what it used to be. She peered again through the twilight, and there it was, a black shape that resolved itself into a carriage, trundling along the lane, swaying from side to side, with clusters of black plumes at every corner that nodded up and down. Curiously she could hear no sound of hoofbeats. Then the carriage turned in through the gates of Roos Hall and she could not see the coachman, just a bundle of clothes swaying in time with the vehicle. That was IT! ... The Apparition of Death! Whatever had happened at the Hall?

Betty urged James forward, and at last he did so though with great reluctance, still bucking and shying as she turned him between the gates and along the drive. As she drew up in the yard, Betty could see no sign of any carriage and knew that it had been the Death Coach she had witnessed. She found lights in the house and the kitchen door standing open, so something must have happened, for the other servants would normally have gone to their beds. At that moment Jeb Hanson emerged from the Hall's front doorway and ran to James's head. "Oh Mrs. Jarvis," he said, his voice breathless with alarm, "you'd never believe it but Mr. Ainsworth is here. He's come back!"

CHAPTER XX

A Visit to Waverley

For Betty Jarvis 1803 had been a dreadful year. It had begun well enough but matters had taken a terrible turn for the worse that night when she saw the Headless Coachman turn his horses towards Roos Hall and she learnt that Mr. Ainsworth had returned. Betty had hurried into the kitchen where she found Mrs. Baines still busy with party preparations. "Well, I was interrupted earlier, you see, when Mr. Ainsworth arrived all unexpected," Mrs. Baines said. "I asked Jeb to light a fire in his room that's so damp since no-one has slept there for all these years, and then Jeb had to help him unpack the two big trunks he brought with him. Nothing much in them, Jeb says, except strange clothes. I had cooked him a supper by that time and had Jeb take it up. That's what he'd been doing when you arrived."

"Thank you, Mrs. Baines. I shall go up and speak to him once I've taken off my hat and tidied my hair," Betty Jarvis replied. "Who does he think he is, arriving without any warning? You may be sure neither Sir Charles nor Mr. Russell knows of this. Still, we must keep civil tongues in our heads until Miss Jessica has had her happy day. I do hope that Mr. Benedict Mather or another of those young gentlemen makes an offer for her soon, or I really do not know what will become of her."

"'Tis a pity Mr. Hugo isn't here to cheer her," Mrs. Baines responded, "They look right together, those two."

"Yes, it is a pity, but I doubt poor Hugo will ever have standing enough to impress Sir Charles." Betty had left the kitchen then, had gone upstairs to the room she was to occupy, had stoked up the fire which Jeb had lit for her, and laid out her nightdress and her brush and comb. Then, donning her firmest expression, she had descended to the first floor and had knocked upon the door of Mr. Ainsworth's room. His voice was weaker than she expected as he bade her come in.

"Good evening, Mr. Ainsworth," she said as she entered.

"Mrs. Jarvis!" he said, turning to her with some surprise. "I would have expected you to have left for your home by now."

"As it happens, Mr. Ainsworth," Betty continued, resolved not to address to him any reverential 'Sir', "I am staying here overnight since we have a special celebration planned for tomorrow. It is Miss Jessica's twentieth birthday."

"Oh, is that so. I wondered what all the decorations were for in the hallway as I came in, and the big tent I saw in the garden. Is my father expected?" he enquired with pretended nonchalance, though the possibility had alarmed him.

"If you mean Sir Charles, Mr. Ainsworth, then he will not be here, though Mr. Anthony Russell will, and so will many of the friends Miss Jessica has made among the residents of Beccles. I have come to ask you to be civil to her tomorrow, since we do not need to have family business aired before Mr. Robert and Mr. Horace Suckling and their ladies who are also expected."

"Where is Jessica?" Ainsworth asked.

"She is resting in her room presently and I intend to apprise her of your arrival," Mrs. Jarvis replied firmly.

"I trust that she still sleeps in the garret upstairs with the other servants," Ainsworth stated haughtily.

"Indeed she does not and has not done for years. You must understand, Mr. Ainsworth, that many things have changed since you went away, and without specific orders from Sir Charles they will remain as they are!" Full of indignation Mrs. Jarvis turned on her heel and left the room. As she had suspected, Mr. Ainsworth's return posed a threat to them all and to their way of life. Betty Jarvis walked stiffly along the corridor and knocked on the door of the room at the end of it. The young woman's voice within said, "Come in?" ending with a question.

"Oh, 'tis you, Mrs. Jarvis," Jessica said. "I know already, Mr. Ainsworth has returned, and I heard the two of you having words. How tiresome of him to arrive just before tomorrow's event. I do hope he will not cause an upset."

As Betty had entered a huge dog, jet black with long hair and erect ears, had risen to his feet, his ears cocked, his eyes bright. Then, seeing Mrs. Jarvis sit upon the chair beside Jessica's bed, he knew that the two human beings he loved most were about to chat, so he let out a sigh and lay down on the rug at the foot of the bed. He was of a type of shepherd dog popular among aristocratic families on the Continent. Some of the emigrés from France and her Revolution, and refugees fleeing the fighting in the Netherlands, had brought their pets to England with them, and though British-born he was nevertheless a thoroughbred. His name was Horatio, a name much in vogue at this time, especially in Norfolk where Admiral Nelson was such a hero.

"I cannot understand why Sir Charles or Mr. Russell even has not forewarned us of his coming," Betty Jarvis grumbled. "He seems to think he is still in charge here, despite all that has happened. He even expected you still to be sleeping upstairs in the attic! Jeb, who unpacked his trunks, says he saw nothing of any consequence among the contents, so he cannot have made his fortune in India, as the saying has it. Well, I for one am not showing him any particular courtesy, at least not until I have had time to write to Sir Charles and obtain his instructions. And Horatio, I think you should keep him with you at all times, Miss Jessica. We cannot be sure that Mr. Ainsworth will not repeat what he did to Matilda."

"Oh I hope not, Mrs. Jarvis, I do hope not, but now that I am grown up he may not dare to take such liberties. I would wish to rest now, so I will see you in the morning."

Mr. Ainsworth slept late the following day, fortunately for all the staff at Roos Hall with their many tasks still needing completion. Peter Jones arrived at noon bringing with him the mails which he had picked up from the Beccles post office. Among these was a letter addressed to Jessica concealed within a covering note from the Admiralty. Mrs. Jarvis, fearing that it might bring bad news about Hugo, took it to Jessica and stood beside her while she opened it. The covering letter merely explained that the mailbags from a lost Navy schooner had been washed up on the coast of Cornwall and that some of the packages enclosed in oilskin had still been legible. Jessica's letter was one of the fortunate ones. With trembling hands she opened it and read Hugo's warning of Ainsworth's return. "How nice that it has reached me on my birthday," Jessica said warmly, "and look, Hugo says he met Mr. Ainsworth aboard ship where he was earning his passage as a steward! Something must have gone very wrong for him in India."

"Indeed it must, Miss Jessica. If he dare step out of line today I shall challenge him with it, for all that I am only the Housekeeper!" Mrs. Jarvis declared stoutly and left the room.

But of course Ainsworth did disgrace himself, almost progressively, and with all members of the company in turn. It began when Jessica first descended the staircase, her toilette complete, in a gown of sheer white muslin bound with blue ribbons that set off to perfection the pale gold of her hair. This she wore in curls upon the top of her head with a blue ribbon around her brow to keep the curls in place, whilst other curls and ringlets fell upon her shoulders. Ainsworth paused and looked up at her, at the pearls and beads about her neck and the fashionable cockade à la Nelson in her hair. "How much did my father pay for all that?" he demanded by way of greeting.

Horatio, like a black shadow, moved out from behind Jessica's skirts and growled. "Hello, Ainsworth," Jessica said. Like Mrs. Jarvis, there would be no 'sir' from now on.

"I see there is a new dog. What happened to Arthur?"

"He died, three years ago. He was twelve years old, you know. This is Horatio, and he is mine," Jessica said quietly with a hand on the dog's collar.

"I see you are having an entertainment. Is that allowed?" Ainsworth demanded again.

"You must speak with Mr. Russell when he arrives, Ainsworth. I have nothing more to say," and Jessica with Horatio as rearguard stepped through the drawing-room and into the garden to where Peter Jones and the servants were arranging decorations and drinks in the marquee.

The next person Ainsworth accosted was Easton, the groundsman. He demanded access to his guns, but Easton, still remembering vividly the death of Matilda, had scarcely needed a prompting from Mrs. Jarvis to remove the guns from their cabinet and to lock them in the outhouse. He told Ainsworth that they had gone to be repaired, since none of them had been used for so many years. Next Ainsworth wandered across to the marquee, helped himself to a glass of wine and managed to spill it all over a damask tablecloth, which had then to be changed and put in soak, and a fresh one turned out to replace it. That put him in the black books of the domestic staff.

Presently the guests began to arrive, and Jessica had placed herself at the front door waiting to greet them. Imagine her annoyance when Ainsworth pushed past her and stood out in the courtyard, introducing himself as Sir Charles' son and the new Lord of the Manor in a loud and slightly intoxicated voice. Fortunately Mr. Russell was among the first to appear, took in the situation at a glance as he handed over his horse to Jeb Hanson, and holding Ainsworth by the elbow, invited him to accompany him within. One glance at the expressions on Jessica's and Betty Jarvis's faces had told him all that he needed to know. How much of the reason for Ainsworth's return to England Mr. Russell managed to extract from him he did not disclose, but both gentlemen reappeared more than an hour later and Ainsworth, now drinking heavily, henceforth introduced himself to all and sundry by his full name, Ainsworth Ignatius Rich, not omitting to add that Sir Charles Rich was his guardian.

This caused much consternation among the guests who chattered avidly about Ainsworth for the rest of the afternoon, quite placing Miss Jessica in the shade, whilst Benedict Mather actually took Mrs. Jarvis aside and asked who the fellow was and what was his kinship, if any, with Miss Jessica. Mrs. Jarvis, being unaware of the true facts herself, could only respond that she hoped it was not so and that this uninvited guest was not expected to remain long at Roos Hall. When all the guests trooped indoors and sat to listen to Jessica's performance upon the pianoforte, followed by duets and solos by the contrasting soprano and contralto voices of Mrs. Carrie Martin (née Jarvis) and Mrs. Marion Weedon (née Mather), they observed Ainsworth sound asleep and snoring noisily in a corner, which quite disturbed the atmosphere of the proceedings.

It is sometimes said that dogs have no ear for what we humans call music. Some will slink away and rest somewhere else; others will sit by the source of the sound and howl, much to the embarrassment of any live performer. Horatio was one of the first kind and when Jessica played upon the pianoforte he was accustomed to retreat to the furthest part of the room, so long as his mistress remained in sight. Horatio, retiring to the corner of the drawing-room beneath the window, whence he might glance along the gap between the wall and the chairs for the audience to watch Miss Jessica as she played, found he had an equally clear view along the other wall of Ainsworth as he sat lolled upon a chair in the opposite corner of the room.

Now, people who have fallen asleep in an upright position have a habit of nodding, either forwards or sideways, and when they lean too far in one direction or the other, their sense of imbalance wakes them sufficiently so that they restore themselves to the vertical. And so it was with Ainsworth. Young Horatio found this a source of much interest and amusement, and had he not been so well-trained by his mistress, would no doubt have growled or barked at the jerky movements the sitter made from time to time. By the end of the concert programme, however, Ainsworth's centre of gravity was dangerously far from the vertical and the final round of applause brought him half-way to his senses. Beginning to open his eyes he beheld sitting in front of him a large black hairy dog, with a mouth full of shining white fangs lubricated by a dangling and very pink tongue. Ainsworth let out a fearsome yell and struggled to rise from his chair.

"Black Shuck! Tis Black Shuck come to haunt me!" he cried. As all the audience turned in horror and apprehension to look at him, Horatio improved the resemblance by leaping up on his hind legs till he stared Ainsworth full in the face. "Get away, you horrible creature!" Ainsworth shouted, flailing his arms. Then he fell flat on the floor in a dead faint.

Disturbed and embarrassed by the scene they had witnessed, the guests filed into the hall, decided not to linger for the dancing, and started to leave. Jessica had just enough self-control to bid them goodbye at the front doorway, along with an apology for their unexpected house-guest. "Just returned from India," she said, as if that might explain what appeared to be a large dose of insanity. Then she turned back to the Jarvis family and a few other close friends who had remained behind and burst into tears in Carrie's arms. "It's too bad of him to spoil my birthday. Everything else want so well. Why did he have to come back to Roos Hall? Why did he not go and find his father, if Sir Charles really is that?"

Mr. Russell, who had remained quietly behind the other guests, then gave a slight cough and came forwards. "So far as I can gather," he said, "but Mr. Ainsworth tries to conceal everything, so we may never be sure of the truth, he arrived back in this country so short of funds that this was the only place to which he might travel. Even Mrs. Bostock, Sir Charles's sister-in-law, who keeps a respectable boarding-house in Bloomsbury, apparently refused to take him in."

Mr. Russell turned to Mrs. Jarvis who had returned from supervising Easton and Jeb Hanson as they carried Mr. Ainsworth to his bed. "Mrs. Jarvis," he said, "I promise to send word to Sir Charles tomorrow. I shall post it to Waverley Abbey and ask his steward there to forward it by special messenger to wherever Sir Charles may be found. We must have his instructions on this matter. Mr. Ainsworth is a disrupting influence and it is not right that his unfortunate presence should disturb the happiness of others, especially on the charming Miss Jessica's birthday." Mr. Russell bowed low and kissed Jessica's rather shyly outstretched hand, then mounted his horse and rode back to Norwich.

Next day Mr. Ainsworth kept to his bed. "A great pity he had not done that to start with," as Mrs. Jarvis and other members of the Roos Hall staff commented. Jeb, who had been set to wait upon Ainsworth, reported that he appeared to be asleep most of the time. Everyone assumed that this was the result of his long journey back to England and the troubles he had encountered in reaching Beccles. The following morning when Jeb entered with Mr. Ainsworth's breakfast, he found the fellow in a fever, and his bed soaked with perspiration. Also a cough, which they had scarcely noted before, had become more pronounced. Dr. Crowfoot was sent for. Stout and spindly-legged now, he puffed up the stairs, having aged much in the decade since Ainsworth fell from his horse as a result of an apparition of Black Shuck on the Barsham Marshes. Dr. Crowfoot spent a long while over his diagnosis. It may be that he deduced that which Ainsworth had successfully kept from Mr. Russell, since he must have enquired into Ainsworth's lifestyle in India. When Dr. Crowfoot emerged he refused to speak to anyone save to Mrs. Jarvis, and he remained closeted with her in the office designated as the Housekeeper's Room for a good half hour.

After Dr. Crowfoot had left, Mrs. Jarvis joined Mrs. Baines in the kitchen. "What did the doctor say? Not good, was it?" Mrs. Baines asked.

"A touch of pneumonia," Mrs. Jarvis replied steadily. "Good broth and fresh air, Dr. Crowfoot said. Thank goodness we have the summer to look forward to. I've a prescription for cough elixir from him. I'll have Lizzie take it into Beccles when she goes home, and ask for it to be ready for me to collect in the morning."

The following day Mr. Ainsworth was well enough to leave his bed and to sit in a chair reading. There had been a few books among the belongings he had brought home from India and he asked Jeb to place them on a bookshelf near his chair so that he might take his choice from them. Jessica asked Mrs. Jarvis whether she should visit Mr. Ainsworth to enquire after his state of health. "You'd best keep right away from him, Miss Jessica," Mrs. Jarvis told her. "What he has is infectious if 'tis not handled properly. We must await Sir Charles' instructions. I daresay though that Mr. Ainsworth will be sitting reading in his room for some days. Jeb says he has brought back a few volumes from India, but I expect he will have read those before. If you mean to be kind to him, why not look in the library for some suitable works he might not have studied?"

Jessica loved books, and in the two years since she had left her schooling behind she had sampled the contents of most of the shelves in the quite comprehensive, if a little out-of-date, library at Roos Hall. Thus she knew her way about it and easily picked out half a dozen titles in which Mr. Ainsworth might possibly express an interest. Quite forgetting Mrs. Jarvis's instruction about keeping her distance from Ainsworth, and not understanding exactly in what context that was meant anyway, Jessica carried the books upstairs and knocked on Mr. Ainsworth's door. Asked to enter, she commanded Horatio to 'Heel' and then 'Lie down' and the obedient dog dropped to the floor, though nevertheless watching his mistress anxiously.

Ainsworth, sitting in an armchair with his back to the doorway, and thinking the newcomer was merely one of the servants, did not turn round until he heard her speak to the dog. "Why, Jessica, good of you to visit the invalid," he said in a half-jovial voice. "Some books for me, too."

"I thought you might tire of those you had brought home with you, Ainsworth, so I have made a selection from the library downstairs. Pray tell me if they are not to your taste and I will look out some others for you."

"I thank you for your kind thought. By-the-by, I apologise for mistaking your dog for Black Shuck the other day. I must have given your guests quite a fright," Ainsworth said, a most rare apology coming from him.

Much mollified, Jessica asked, "But you did once see Black Shuck, the real one, did you not? I remember I was at school at the time and so missed all the details. What did he really look like?"

Ainsworth, pleased to be asked for his recollection, told Jessica, "I was riding along, minding my horse, when this huge dark creature wrapped itself around me. I could not breathe, for it choked me. I could not see, except that there were flaming eyes like live coals amid the blackness, but I could feel a hot hairy prickling sensation all over me, and a terrible stink - I remember that most of all. You wait, Jessica, until your dog leaps into a bog on the marshes and you must groom the mud from all that long hair. Then you will know what I mean by that particular odour. Thank you again for the books," he said by way of dismissal. Jessica turned, called to Horatio and left the room.

Later that day Mrs. Baines remarked to Mrs. Jarvis, "Did you know that Miss Jessica took some books from the library up to Mr. Ainsworth's room? Jeb saw them there and asked him. Didn't you tell her to avoid going near him?"

"Tut, tut. Yes, I did. I hope the window was left open, as I told Jeb it should be, and that she took Horatio with her for her own protection."

A few days later Mr. Ainsworth could be seen walking about the gardens at Roos Hall, well wrapped-up in overcoat and muffler, even though it was late Spring and the weather becoming quite warm. His pace was slow and hesitant. Jeb had asked if he required an elbow to lean upon, but he refused it. Ainsworth had his walking cane, of course, but somehow it no longer seemed adequate to the task. He remembered how briskly he used to walk along the Strand and the Esplanade at Calcutta during the cool season when he had no need of a palanquin. He wished he were there now, feeling the heat boring into his bones, soaking up the sunshine. Then he wondered why there had been no word from Sir Charles. Perhaps the Governor-General's letter had not yet reached him, or had perhaps gone astray. No doubt Mr. Russell would inform Sir Charles of that which he had found out upon his visit to Roos Hall, but Ainsworth had managed to keep from that gentleman the most prominent of the reasons for his dismissal, so that he might be suspected rather of theft or embezzlement, still a matter of disgrace but not one which would call forth as much moral opprobrium. Ainsworth's thoughts were interrupted by a bout of coughing and he made his way indoors.

Another two weeks had passed before Ainsworth ventured into the park. After inspecting the new paths, he turned to the coverts and found that they had become quite neglected. He must speak to Easton about that. Ainsworth's guns had now made a mysterious reappearance in their usual cabinet, all nicely cleaned and oiled for his use, and he was anxious to try his aim. One day he took his shotgun with him and fired at a pigeon and at several rabbits. The pigeon he missed completely, but reasoned that it must have been due to being out of practice. He did bring down one rabbit which he could take to Mrs. Baines for the pot, but he missed several others. He found his eyesight not quite so accurate these days, and when he looked in the mirror, he observed that his eyes were watery and inflamed. That would never have been so in Calcutta, he thought, except perhaps at the height of the rainy season.

There was no horse for Ainsworth to ride now, nor could there be one again without permission and further funds from Sir Charles. So he had Jeb take him out in the pony-trap with James, the skewbald. The pony itself was too light to take the weight of an adult in the saddle. Ainsworth had been angered to discover that Mrs. Jarvis made much use of James to travel to and from her employment, rather than walking as she used to do. He accosted her about it but received a most indignant, and he thought disrespectful reply, that she was entitled to such care at her age and if Mr. Ainsworth wished for anything different he should seek fresh instructions from Sir Charles. As his Guardian, if he had received the Governor-General's letter, was the last person with whom Ainsworth wished to renew direct contact, that was where the matter rested.

The summer had come, Mr. Ainsworth seemed slightly better. By contrast, the condition of Betty's husband, Robert Jarvis, had deteriorated. What had begun as a cold had turned into bronchitis, and Robert spent much of his time in bed at the Bear & Bells. Peter and Margaret Jones were managing the inn very well and made a tidy profit. But Margaret now had a baby to care for, and dividing her time between the infant, the bar, and a bronchitic old man upstairs,was taxing her sense of humour. Betty Jarvis hurried home as early as she could, ignoring any complaints from Mr. Ainsworth since Sir Charles had merely written saying that he 'would be most obliged if Mrs. Jarvis would tolerate Ainsworth's presence for the time being' and sending her an extra allowance for the purpose.

As autumn approached with a wet, chilly September, the condition of both invalids worsened. Mrs. Jarvis wanted to spend time with her ailing husband, but dare not neglect her concern for Jessica. In the end she instructed Jessica that she might sit with Mr. Ainsworth to amuse him, but that if he coughed or wanted for anything she was to leave the room immediately and call for Jeb Hanson who knew what to do. Eventually she was obliged to disclose that Dr. Crowfoot had confirmed his earlier diagnosis, that Mr. Ainsworth had long since contracted consumption.

Meanwhile Robert Jarvis was sinking fast. Jessica had written several letters to Hugo about his uncle's condition and about Mr. Ainsworth's situation too. However none of the family knew the name of Hugo's present ship, save that he had meant to embark on another straight after parting from the *Apollion* now that

England was at war again. Thus she was obliged to send her missives to the Navy Office addressed to "Lieutenant Hugo Jarvis, formerly of H.M.S. *Apollion*" and had no notion whether or not he might receive them. This meant that Hugo was not at home for his favourite uncle's funeral which took place towards the end of October. It was held at St. Michael's Church in Beccles, the one Betty Jarvis and her husband had always attended so assiduously. Robert was buried in the graveyard on the sunny side of the Tower, whose clock and its chimes, he had appreciated from the doorway of the inn for most of his lifetime. A fine gravestone of white marble was added later to the plot. Naturally Carrie Martin had attended the service, together with her husband and her first infant, now more than a year old. Whenever she accompanied Betty to place flowers on the new grave, she thought of asking her about Alicia's tomb which was not so many yards away, but without having Hugo's consent she decided she had better not do so.

When Betty Jarvis lost her husband she also lost her home. Peter and Margaret Jones were anxious to make more of the upstairs bedrooms at the inn available for the use of paying guests and for their own family. For instance, the bedroom that Robert Jarvis and his wife had occupied would make a most delightful nursery. As she still had a financial interest in the inn - her husband's half-share had been passed to her in his Will, Betty decided to compromise. She moved all her most precious treasures and memories into one of the smaller bedrooms, and used another for storage of those items she might yet need if she moved to another property. Now that her husband was no longer there, Betty saw no point in driving back and forth to Beccles each weekday, so she made up a bed in one of the attics at Roos Hall instead. Whilst Mr. Ainsworth was still present she dare not take a room on the first or second floor, but if he were to depart, one way or another, she thought no-one could object if she were to take for herself a modest room nearer to Jessica.

Ainsworth Rich was almost entirely bedridden by now, and these large bedrooms were cold in winter, even with the blessing of a well-stoked fire. When he felt better Ainsworth would sit in his chair beside the window, either reading or writing at his desk, or sometimes watching Jessica playing ball games with Horatio on the lawn below. At other times, when he lacked the strength for any activity, he would sit in bed, well-backed by pillows, and ask that Jessica come to amuse him. In the early days of his illness, quite apart from the matter of preserving Jessica's health, Betty Jarvis had been afraid that they might form an attachment for one another. Jessica was still at an impressionable age and caring for a sick man could evoke the maternal instincts of a woman. Besides, Betty was not entirely sure whether the two were related; half-brother and sister they could be if Sir Charles had fathered both of them. Many a gentleman appointed himself "guardian" to his illegitimate offspring, as Sir Charles had done with Jessica. If Sir Robert Rich had been Ainsworth's father, on the other hand, and he had been the boy's first Guardian, there was no blood relationship as Sir Charles was merely Sir Robert's son-in-law. Nevertheless, Betty did not wish her granddaughter to squander her affections on someone who had been a wastrel for most of his life.

Gradually the two of them had begun to talk to each other. Ainsworth spoke about his life in India, the climate, his house, his servants and their ways; the city, its people, their clothes, food, customs, religions, temples and houses. He spoke about the countryside and the great River Ganges, its floods and its transport systems. He told of his adventures, the journeys up-country to Lucknow and the military campaign against Tipu Sultan. Ainsworth did not enquire about Jessica's life in return, not being curious about the lives of others, though he did eventually tell her about his meeting with Hugo Jarvis aboard ship. Then he made of Jessica rather an odd request. Would she kindly enclose with her next missive to Hugo a letter he had addressed to a Mr. Nicholas Wilmington who, he informed Jessica, was a friend and colleague of Hugo's and likely still to be serving with him on the same ship. There being no obvious objection to this course of action, Jessica complied. Ainsworth's letter read as follows:

Roos Hall, Beccles: 3rd November 1803

Dear Mr. Wilmington,

Please excuse my forwardness in writing to you but I am diagnosed with consumption, have taken to my bed this two months and am not expected to survive the winter. I beg of you that you will most kindly communicate my situation and my whereabouts to your Aunt Marianne and that you will use all persuasions to induce her to call upon me. I believe it is the natural wish of all parents to be reconciled with their offspring at the instant of death, and although I shall be the first to depart this life, she may nevertheless wish to give me her final blessing.

Your humble and grateful servant,

Ainsworth Rich.

The New Year, 1804, found the establishment at Roos Hall sunk in gloom. Mr. Ainsworth's condition appeared to worsen daily. His feverishness had increased and he was now as thin as a skeleton. Jeb Hanson had also taken to his bed, suffering badly with rheumatism in the damp weather, and Mrs. Jarvis felt that she and Mrs. Baines were running a hospital. January and February crawled by with foggy days and frosty nights when Betty scarcely had the courage to drive James as far as the church of a Sunday, or into Beccles town to make any purchases necessary for the running of Roos Hall. For Jessica, having had no news from Hugo for several months, the highlights of her leisure time were the days she occasionally spent at the Ringsfield Farm, joining in their more carefree celebrations, and the equally occasional visits of Mr. Russell who came to report to Mrs. Jarvis on the business matters of the estate and to communicate to Sir Charles the condition of his ward.

It was on one such cheerless day that a plain black carriage drawn by two dark bay horses entered the drive of Roos Hall and drew up in the courtyard. It contained an elegantly but soberly-dressed lady, heavily veiled. She stepped across to the doorway and her coachman pulled the bell. Jeb answered the door. The lady, still veiled, asked if she might call upon Mr. Ainsworth Rich. Jeb, much impressed, invited her to enter, pulled up a chair for the lady to sit upon, and waddled away on his bandy legs in search of Mrs. Jarvis. She, much surprised, dismissed Jeb and sallied into the hall, introducing herself as the Housekeeper. "I understand that you wish to see Mr. Ainsworth, who is unfortunately in his bed very ill indeed and quite unable to receive visitors," Mrs. Jarvis said.

The newcomer threw back her veil, revealing a finely drawn face, still beautiful, though pale and anxious. "I am Lady Wilmington," she said. "If you would be kind enough to ask Mr. Rich, I feel sure he will agree to receive me." Betty Jarvis struggled her way upstairs - her arthritis was not improving with her years - and entered Mr. Ainsworth's room after the briefest of knocks, knowing that Jessica and Horatio were sitting with him.

"There's a visitor for you downstairs, Mr. Ainsworth. She gives her name as Lady Wilmington. Will you receive her?" Ainsworth's response amazed them both; he burst into tears and then into a fit of atrocious coughing.

When he had calmed a little he: replied, "Yes, thank you, in private if you please." Jessica, the dog and Mrs. Jarvis left the room. Jessica had resolved to retreat into her own bedroom whilst the visitor was with Mr. Ainsworth, but could not resist peeping over the balcony at the stranger below. The woman, sensing the movement, looked up, and Jessica immediately thought she perceived a family resemblance. Did this woman have any connection with her too, she asked herself? What Ainsworth and Lady Wilmington said to each other no-one recorded, but when the woman emerged from the bedroom nearly two hours later, her veil had already covered her face, even as she walked slowly down the stairs, and Ainsworth cried himself to sleep that night, just as if he was a child again.

After the carriage had left, Jessica descended to the kitchen with the excuse that it was time for Horatio's supper, but really still savouring the gossip below stairs, as she had often done when Mr. Ainsworth had banished her there as a child. "Who was she, what did she look like.? " Mrs. Baines asked as she poured Jessica a cup of hot chocolate by way of encouragement. "I asked Jeb, but 'tis hopeless asking a man those sort of questions."

"She looked a real lady," Jessica replied, and then, "and a little like Mr. Ainsworth too."

"Is she his mother, do you think, Miss Jessica?" Mrs. Baines asked in a whisper.

"I would not know, Mrs. Baines, but I'll ask Mrs. Jarvis as soon as I can catch her in a good mood."

Betty Jarvis could have overheard the gossip, or more probably she knew that gossip would be taking place, for she entered the kitchen at that moment and called Jessica into her room. "I am sure that you, Miss Jessica, and the servants must all be consumed with curiosity, but I think Mr. Ainsworth would wish us to respect his visitor's confidentiality. However I also need to be sure of her identity. She told me her name was Lady Wilmington. You converse so often with Mr. Ainsworth these days. Does the name mean anything to you?"

"Yes, it does, Mrs. Jarvis. It must be nearly three months ago now that Mr. Ainsworth asked me to enclose a note of his in a letter I was about to write to Hugo. He addressed that letter to a Mr. Nicholas Wilmington. He explained to me that he had met the gentleman during his return voyage from India and that he was an officer and a friend of Hugo, so that they would probably still be serving together on the same ship. I must write to Hugo and let him know that this meeting has taken place.

"By-the-by ," Jessica continued more slowly, "did you not perceive a resemblance between Lady Wilmington's features and Mr. Ainsworth's? Do you suppose she may be his mother?"

"I think it possible," Mrs. Jarvis replied cautiously.

"Then has she any connection with me also?" Jessica enquired softly.

"I think not, my dear," Mrs. Jarvis replied, adding hastily, "Miss Jessica," and went on, "No, I much doubt it."

Ainsworth Ignatius Rich departed this life on 29th February 1804, at the very last moment, that is, before the feast of St. David announced the heralds of Spring. He was aged just thirty-five.

Mr. Russell, to whom Mrs. Jarvis had sent an urgent note, came riding over from Norwich immediately and announced that he had already sought in advance Sir Charles's instructions on the arrangements to be made for the funeral. Apparently Sir Charles required that Mr. Ainsworth be buried "in some quiet rural churchyard where the name 'Rich' would not provoke any interest." Mr. Russell thought the Barsham churchyard would serve well for this purpose and he would himself ride to the Rectory and discuss the matter with Mr. Horace Suckling. As to Mr. Ainsworth's personal effects, his clothes were to be burnt to avoid infection, his books were to be placed in the Roos Hall library, and his papers and personal effects were to be gathered together for Mr. Russell's inspection on the day of the funeral. Mr. Russell stated that he was prepared to stay overnight if Mrs. Jarvis would kindly make up a bed for him. Mr. Russell enquired if it was known whether Mr. Ainsworth had made a Will, but as no-one seemed to know the answer he would look into that matter at the same time.

The congregation at Ainsworth's funeral was a small one, the staff from the Hall, the Jarvis family as Sir Charles's tenants and the neighbouring tenants from Redisham, the Martins from Ilketshall St. Andrew and Mr. Russell himself, but disappointingly not Sir Charles Rich. When they returned to Roos Hall for the funeral supper, Mr. Russell indicated to Mrs, Jarvis that he had instructions to deliver to Sir Charles any possessions and papers belonging to Mr. Ainsworth for which there was no other indication of ownership, or any expression of intent. For instance, the pair of very handsome pistols which Mr. Ainsworth had brought back from India and which had soon come to light in his room, would when sold nicely defray the funeral expenses which Sir Charles had incurred. Mr. Russell spent two days sifting through the piles of miscellaneous scribbles, drafts of letters and copies made during Ainsworth's service with the East India Company. He judged many of these matters to be or have been confidential to the Company and consigned them to the bonfire of Mr. Ainsworth's clothes which Easton was tending in the grounds. Mr. Ainsworth's few remaining pins, studs and rings (for he had been obliged to sell some in London to purchase his ticket for the stage coach), were put aside in a box. As they were trifles, Mr. Russell thought them not worth taking to Sir Charles and suggested they be given to Jeb Hanson who had done more to tend the invalid than anyone else.

As the very last item, Mr. Russell came to a small metal strong box to which no-one had been able to find a key. Easton was called to come with coal chisel and mallet to break the lock, which he did with consummate ease, and returned the box unopened into Mr. Russell's hands. By this time Jessica, Mrs. Jarvis, Mrs. Baines, Easton, Jeb and the maids were all standing behind Mr. Russell as he sat at Mr. Ainsworth's desk, wondering what the box contained. Mr. Russell brought out of it a small coin-purse marked with the Rich coat of arms, and a folded scrap of paper. He opened first the paper and after a moment's hesitation read out:

I, Ainsworth Ignatius Rich, being of sound mind, despite ill health, desire that the contents of this purse be sold and the funds resulting be given as a dowry to Miss Jessica Rich by way of apology for the many sorrows I caused her in her youth.

The note was signed, and dated 1st January 1804. At these words a mutual sigh of satisfaction arose from all the staff present, many of whom had witnessed Jessica's torments at Ainsworth's hands. Mr. Russell turned and said, "Miss Jessica, would you like to open the purse?"

Jessica did so, peeping inside the purse first before carefully tipping it over and scattering its contents on the flat table slide of the desk. "What are they?" Jessica asked.

"They're diamonds," Mr. Russell replied with some amazement, "uncut diamonds, and some other gems in a semi-cut state. They cannot be sold in this country as they are. 'Tis illegal to do so. I expect Mr. Ainsworth discovered that on his return from India, which is why he was so short of funds. Mrs. Jarvis, with yours and Miss Jessica's agreement, I shall take these to Sir Charles who will know how best to handle them. I will give you a receipt, so Miss Jessica, please take a seat and count how many there are. Here is pen and paper, so write them by their colour, and two copies if you please." The excitement over, the rest of the onlookers returned to their duties, although it was a long while before silence reigned in the Roos Hall household.

At the beginning of May Mrs. Jarvis received a summons, not a legal summons indeed, but the kind of summons that causes one to tingle with anticipation. "Sir

Charles Rich requests that Miss Jessica Rich and Mrs. Elisabeth Jarvis would travel by post-chaise to Waverley Abbey House at Farnham, in the County of Surrey, so as to arrive on or just before 15th May 1804. Mr. Anthony Russell has been instructed to accompany the ladies so as to assure them a peaceful and pleasant journey. It is Sir Charles's intention,"(the letter had been written by his Secretary) "to felicitate Miss Jessica Rich personally upon the occasion of her twenty-first Birthday." Mrs. Jarvis immediately penned a note to Mr. Russell reporting receipt of Sir Charles's letter and asking him to confirm what arrangements he had made. The answer arrived by return; they should have Jeb drive them in the pony-trap to Bungay on the tenth of May, to be there by 10.30 a.m. so as to join the post-chaise which he would have taken from Norwich at nine.

One can imagine the excitement of these two ladies, both of whom had spent most of their lives living in or near Beccles, Mrs. Jarvis entirely so, when faced with the task of packing a valise or two to take with them. What to pack? What to wear on arrival? Would their best gowns be spoilt by travelling? Would the weather be chilly or warm? At Roos Hall, Mrs. Jarvis had recently moved into a first floor bedroom next to Jessica's to which, being more spacious, she had been able to bring from the Bear & Bells most of her limited wardrobe. So the doors were set open between the rooms and the two ran back and forth chattering, whilst down below in the kitchen and the grounds there was much speculation as to what changes this event might bring.

The great day came and the weather was kind, so that they did not get wet during their ride to Bungay. Jeb waited with them at the King's Head until the post-chaise arrived and the horses were changed. Then he helped the coachman secure their luggage behind the vehicle, which they were fortunate in having to themselves. Mr. Russell assisted the ladies into the carriage and then climbed in and sat opposite them. Jessica had never seen him smile so broadly, as if many of his cares had suddenly been shed, and she realised that the return of Ainsworth to Roos Hall must have burdened him with anxieties too. "Good morning, ladies," he greeted them again as if he were about to make a speech, which indeed he was. "Today we shall travel as far as Ipswich and shall put up tonight at the Suffolk Hotel where I have reserved rooms already. Then tomorrow we shall drive into London, leave this carriage at Holborn and take a cab to the Kensington Palace Hotel, where I have obtained rooms overlooking Hyde Park. For the following two days Sir Charles has asked me to escort you around some of the famous sights of London, the Parks, the Palaces, the Tower, St. Paul's Cathedral, Westminster Abbey, and an evening at Vauxhall Gardens, should you so wish. At the same time Sir Charles invites you, ladies, to visit some of the new emporia to be found in Oxford Street, Bond Street and thereabouts. I have been granted an allowance for that purpose, and I am sure you will wish to discuss between you what will best suit your needs."

Jessica flushed with excitement and Mrs. Jarvis, having guessed what Sir Charles's intentions might be, found her eyes full of tears. Jessica enjoyed the journey to Ipswich. Having travelled by that route to her last school, she was able to point out the location of Faithful Street and to describe for Mr. Russell's benefit some of the establishment's lesser attractions. "However did Sir Charles come to make such a particular choice?" was Mr. Russell's comment at the end of it. Staying at an hotel was a new experience for Jessica and as the ladies had adjoining rooms they were able to assist each other to dress. Dining in the hotel dining-room, seeing strangers at other tables, having a wide choice of menu, all these were new experiences for Jessica, and Mr. Russell gently guided her among the strange dishes and wines.

Arriving in the Metropolis was even more exciting, although Jessica was horrified to observe so much poor housing, so many filthy streets, and so many beggars and ragamuffins as they made their way through the East End to St. Paul's, where an air of greater respectability seemed to descend. Mr. Russell supervised their transfer to a cab, complete with all luggage, and as the shadows began to lengthen they were driven along the pleasant lanes and between the mansions, gardens and trees that surrounded Hyde Park until they reached their hotel. Entering into their new rooms seemed less strange and novel after their stay at Ipswich, except that the porters and waiters bowed lower but expected much larger tips. However Mr. Russell was on hand to take care of such matters.

Shopping in the Metropolis proved quite different from the experience at rural Beccles. There every shopkeeper was an acquaintance, favours were done in both directions, medicines were made up, boots mended and goods could be ordered overnight. Here the stores were much bigger and one dealt with an army of assistants under the eagle eye of a manager, or sometimes a manageress if ladies' unmentionables were involved. At Beccles and in the countryside, servants and the poor made their own clothes or purchased second-hand, whilst only the wealthy would employ a tailor or tailoress to make up bespoke fitted garments. There must be so many rich people here in London, Mrs. Jarvis surmised, for the poor seemed to have been left behind at St. Paul's and she saw nothing but elegant ladies selecting materials for later confection. This would scarcely serve her purpose of looking smart for her first meeting with Sir Charles, her employer, for more than twenty years.

Strictly speaking, Mrs. Jarvis was still in mourning after her husband's death, but more than six months had passed since she had buried him and she thought she might now indulge in something in a maroon colour, dark and restrained of course, since she was already wearing her best black. Then she found by enquiry that one or two departments did have made-up garments, just a few. Some had been used for advertising in the shop-window, displayed on tailor's dummies, and one or two had been returned by dissatisfied clients. So she was most gratified when one assistant offered her a gown retrieved from the back of the store which might just suit. And it did, and Mrs. Jarvis emerged from the fitting-room looking more radiant than she had done for years. Two smart hats and a silk but oh-so-expensive shawl later, and she felt well-satisfied. Jessica meanwhile had other priorities. The new fashion for pleated muslin dresses, gathered to fit the individual by means of interlaced ribbons, meant that a young woman of average proportions might purchase a ready-made garment with little hesitation, something the manufacturers and store-keepers were just beginning to realise. Thus Jessica bought herself three gowns of different prints, a most becoming bonnet, and some long white lace gloves, since she imagined that Sir Charles would undoubtedly greet her by kissing her hand.

Sight-seeing from the seat of an open carriage seemed an excellent means of viewing the Capital, whilst only Westminster Abbey and St. Paul's required a pilgrimage on foot. They also walked in Hyde Park, visited the Round Pond and the gardens being planted out beside Kensington Palace, and were even able to view the King and Queen as they left Buckingham House one afternoon for their customary weekend retreat at Windsor Castle. By the time they left their hotel again on the fourteenth of the month, in the morning, they felt they had 'done' the Metropolis, and could be quite blasée about its attractions in future. And Mr. Russell had been such a perfect guide, full of lively anecdotes about the places they passed, and sitting quietly reading a small volume that he took from his pocket at those moments when the ladies should be left on their own.

The vehicle that collected Jessica and Mrs. Jarvis from the Kensington Palace Hotel was a large and comfortable carriage whose doors bore the Rich coat of arms. "Oh my goodness me, Sir Charles could not treat us more splendidly than he has," Mrs. Jarvis exclaimed. "You might think we were royalty! " whilst Jessica just stood still in amazement and disbelief that anything so magnificent could have any connection with her, the poor little orphan. Actually it was Mr. Russell who had suggested to Sir Charles the convenience of using a private coach rather than any public conveyance, and knowing full well that there might never be another such occasion for Miss Jessica to receive the full honours of belonging to the Rich blood.

The route to Waverley Abbey led through the village of Farnham with its picturesque cottages, thatched roofs, bow windows, timber-frame and lathe gables with latticed windows, to its southern side. Here a lane led downhill between a high wall that ran in waves to keep its single-thickness bricks upright on the one hand, and a charming wooded dell complete with mill-stream and tumbledown mill on the other. Half-way along the wall stood a pair of castellated towers and a gateway beneath them. Dark windows, uncurtained, peeped out of the dark masonry, as if they would surreptitiously inspect each arrival. In fact the gates were open and the carriage swept through. A long drive led across the scarp of the hill among dark yew trees, only to bring one to a wide gravelled corner where a panoply of a view lay spread out below. A carriage drive and wide lawns swept down to an elegant brick and stone mansion in the Palladian style, three storeys high and with a shallow roof of grey slates rising gently above it. To either hand were two wings of equal height topped by a classical pediment, wings which Betty Jarvis recalled that Sir Robert Rich had added. A large stable block with a substantial clock tower lay to the left hand side, together with a fine walled garden. Beyond the mansion, Jessica remembered that Ainsworth had told her how the lawns stretched down to a lake, with a stone bridge over it leading to the ruins of the old Abbey on the far side.

At the door they were greeted by a Mr. Tupman, Sir Charles's butler, who led them to their rooms on the third floor of the eastern wing where they might overlook the stables and the garden. The ladies had been assigned rooms with a communicating door which Mrs. Jarvis soon knocked upon to make sure that Miss Jessica was dressed to her best advantage. Mr. Tupman called upon them half an hour later and shepherded them downstairs. In this mansion the ballroom and all the grand saloons were situated on the first floor. They were reached by twin staircases under the tall arch over the front of the house, or by a beautiful curving double staircase of white limestone which led up from the lawns on the sunlit side. This meant that the rooms for everyday use were sunk into the lawns in the nature of a basement, whilst all the bedrooms and servants' quarters were two or three floors up, just beneath the roof. They were informed that Sir Charles was expecting them in the Green Drawing-Room. There was no sign of Mr, Russell, so presumably he would not be joining them.

Sir Charles Rich and Mrs. Jarvis, his Housekeeper at Roos Hall, knew one another well, for they had corresponded quite regularly and with much mutual trust, but they had not actually met since Sir Charles had attended Jessica's christening. As a young man, at the age when he had yielded to Alicia's temptations, Sir Charles had had a trim figure and dark curly hair. Now, for this informal occasion, he had put aside his wig and one observed that his body was comfortably corpulent and his hair, though still curly, had grown thin and grey. For his part he found Mrs. Jarvis much stouter than he remembered her, and walking rather stiffly these days. By contrast he thought Miss Jessica an angel descended from heaven, with her white dress bound, coincidentally, with dark green ribbons that matched the drapes around him, with her cascades of pale gold ringlets, and her large dark eyes that watched him with the nervous delicacy of one of the fallow does in his park.

After a moment's hesitation as Mr. Tupman announced them, Sir Charles stood up and strode across the room to take each of them by the hand, with a firm handshake and no bowing and kissing the hand as Jessica had romantically imagined. The ladies were shown to a chintz-covered sofa, whilst Sir Charles resumed his comfortable armchair facing them. Tea was served, and once Mr. Tupman had assured himself that the ladies had everything they needed he respectfully withdrew. Sir Charles turned to Mrs. Jarvis first of all and began to speak whilst the ladies daintily sipped their tea.

"I owe you many apologies, Mrs. Jarvis, and you too Miss Jessica, for having obliged you to care for Ignatius during his last illness." (He persisted in the use of Ainsworth's hated middle name which Sir Robert had selected for him.) "Mr. Russell has kept me fully informed of his condition and of his often uncouth behaviour. I regret also that I was unable to attend his funeral. The reason for that, if I may inform you in the strictest confidence, is that my wife, Mary Frances Rich, is unaware of the financial responsibility for his misdeeds which I assumed on the death of my father-in-law. I wish to maintain that secrecy, for Ignatius has been such a burden to me that sometimes I have not known where to look for relief. Although, before he left for India, Ignatius was well-known in certain raffish gambling circles, I tried to keep his connection with my part of the family known only to a select few, lest it affect my position or that of my wife at Court. If I may request you to have the patience to listen further, I will continue my explanation.

"I should disclose first of all," Sir Charles went on, "that, whatever he may have said to you, Ignatius was not my son, nor that of Sir Robert. He was in fact a child born out of wedlock of Sir Robert's colleague and assistant, a civil servant employed by the Government by the name of Ralph Ainsworth - hence the rather peculiar name given or rather left with Ignatius as a child. There was a movement, hardly a conspiracy, but let us call it so, to have Sir Robert dismissed from his position, which eventually he was in 1775, and that began the decline in his health that you witnessed, Mrs. Jarvis, all those years ago. Ralph Ainsworth had loyally defended my father-in-law and had taken the brunt of the pressure put upon him to resign. Due to that extreme stress, and he was some years older than Sir Robert, he fell sick and died. On his death-bed he confessed to the existence of his love-child and told Sir Robert where to find it. My father-in-law agreed to take on responsibility for the child, and I, as a clerical friend of the family, was sent to retrieve him from the orphanage where he had been lodged. I was to identify him by means of a silver locket which had been deposited with him. I was also forewarned that upon opening it I would recognise the likeness within, that of Ignatius' mother.

"She was a girl of only sixteen," Sir Charles went on, "brought up in a respectable and genteel home in Kensington village where Sir Robert often visited. Upon occasion so did his assistant Ralph Ainsworth, and completely to everyone's amazement one day the girl simply vanished. All inquiries failed to find her and only subsequently did her family learn the truth. Ralph Ainsworth had carried the girl off to Brighthelmstone for a romantic weekend by the sea. He was at least forty years her senior at the time so we would never have suspected it of him, especially as he returned to his employment afterwards as if nothing had happened. The girl decided that she dare not return home for fear of her parents' displeasure and disgrace, so obtained a position in service, which she lost as soon as it became obvious that she was expecting a child. She wrote to Ralph Ainsworth, but that gentleman was too involved in helping my father-in-law to be able to do anything about it. Consequently the girl sought help from the authorities who sent her to a workhouse at Lewes in Sussex, and it was there that Ignatius was born."

A sigh of shock emanated from Mrs. Jarvis and Jessica who were learning these details for the first time. Sir Charles continued, "Eventually his mother obtained another position, in service with a retired Brigadier living in Brighthelmstone. Again he was many years older than she, but as his wife had died some years before he soon married her. They had no children, but the Brigadier already had two sons. The elder one had been bought a commission in the army which had nearly bankrupted his father. He was sent to serve in India and may well be there still. The younger one the Brigadier had had in his retirement, and his wife had died in bearing it. Being unable to cope with a mischievous young boy he had paid for him to be placed in a nearby orphanage. At this point Ignatius' mother revealed the existence of her illegitimate offspring still residing in the Lewes workhouse. Much shocked but, since they were now married,the Brigadier had the child transferred to the same orphanage as his own son, whence I later retrieved him.

"Now the Brigadier died shortly thereafter and Ignatius' mother, as a young and still beautiful widow, was taking the sea air at Brighthelmstone one day when she captured the attention of yet another elderly widower, a gentleman by the name of Sir Everard Wilmington."

"Oh," Betty Jarvis and Jessica exclaimed together.

"They soon married," said Sir Charles, "and Sir Everard, not having had any children of his own, took on responsibility for the Brigadier's two sons. Lady Marianne Wilmington is my younger sister and her husband, Sir Everard, is the villain who obliged my father-in-law to resign his Government position."

"Lady Wilmington called upon Mr. Ainsworth just before he died," Betty Jarvis interposed immediately.

"So she has written to me," Sir Charles responded. "We have been in touch for some years now, ever since her husband Sir Everard discovered the scandal after meeting Ignatius at the gaming table. My sister did not wish me to learn the tale from a stranger. I am glad that a reconciliation occurred. Ignatius returned to her the silver locket with her portrait, to which he had added a curl of his own hair.

"Perhaps you may now appreciate that all along I have been dealing with a most delicate situation, a question of rivalry and dislike between two families highly-placed at Court, so that the less anyone else is aware of the scandal, the better. Even then I will not dare to disclose to you those misdeeds which caused Ignatius to be sent home from India. The Governor-General, the Marquess Wellesley, wrote me a personal letter with the information, so there is yet another highly-placed courtier whom I may not look in the face." Sir Charles paused, took up his cup of tea which must have grown cold long since, but he drank it just the same, replaced cup and saucer on the low table beside him and continued.

"Having finished with that unpleasant business through the unfortunate but fortuitous death of my nephew, Ignatius, let me turn to the much more pleasant business of this day." Sir Charles turned towards Jessica, smiled and spoke more softly as he said, "Mrs. Jarvis has told me that you have often enquired of her whether I, your Guardian, am also your father. I am now able to reveal that it is true. With Ignatius no more I have been able to confess the matter to my wife. She has been gracious enough to forgive me and knows of our meeting here. That will also explain why it was difficult for me to call upon you at Roos Hall."

"Oh, thank you, thank you," Jessica exclaimed, her large eyes alight with joy but also with remembered pain. "I had always hoped you were, indeed I dreamt of it quite frequently."

"I should now wish to give my daughter a fatherly embrace," Sir Charles said, rising from his chair. Jessica rose to her feet and stood pink and trembling whilst Sir Charles held her gently by the arms and planted a paternal kiss on each cheek.

"Thank you, Papa, if I may now call you that," Jessica murmured. "Then who, pray, was my mother? May I know that too?" She did not glance at Mrs. Jarvis, for if she had she would have observed tears streaming down the elderly lady's cheeks.

"Your mother, dear girl," Sir Charles replied, "was a most delightful young lady named Alicia."

"Oh yes, that's my middle name," Jessica interposed, not knowing whether she should expect more.

"Her name," said Sir Charles, enjoying the element of surprise, "was Alicia Jarvis, and she was Mrs. Jarvis's daughter!"

"Mrs. Jarvis? Then she is my grandmother," and Jessica, turning to the lady in question, observed the tears and realised what all the reticence had cost her. She rose and embraced the old lady. "How could you keep it from me all these years?" she demanded. "I thought I had no-one," Jessica protested. "But then, you have always taken such good care of me, taught me to read and write, sent letters to Sir Charles, my Papa, requesting a pony, the pianoforte, and I know not what else. How I shall delight in calling you Grandmama in future, instead of ordering you about imperiously as I have often done. You must forgive me that."

Sir Charles sat chuckling to observe the jollity and pleasure he had created. "Jessica, now that you are officially my daughter," he broke in, "I am able to make you a personal allowance that should permit you to live comfortably, whatever you decide to do with your life," and he mentioned an annual amount which to both of his listeners seemed the height of generosity. "Now I come to matters which may not please you both so easily," Sir Charles continued. "I have reached a decision to dispose of Roos Hall. I have received a good offer for it from a Mr. Thomas Rede of Beccles - you may know of him, Mrs. Jarvis?"

"Indeed I do, Sir Charles, his family has one of the large box pews at the Church."

"I understand from Mr. Rede that his ancestors owned the Hall in centuries past, so perhaps it will signify a homecoming for him. I also understand that at present he is hard put to it to raise the necessary funds, so that your removal thence cannot be expected for some months. However I thought this might be an opportune occasion for me to forewarn you both, and for you, Mrs. Jarvis, to seek an appropriate moment to advise the remainder of the staff. As most of them are elderly, they will receive a good pension, more generous now that there is no Ignatius to provide for. As for you, dear ladies, I am conscious that I must rob you of your home, and as I do not wish my daughter to reside at a public inn, might I suggest that you select a suitable property where you may live together, say within the town of Beccles. Once the sale of Roos Hall is arranged, Thomas Rede is to make me a handsome down-payment. I wish to employ those funds in purchasing for you whatever property you choose."

"Oh, Sir Charles, how generous of you," Mrs. Jarvis exclaimed. "I have been meaning to dispose of my remaining interest in the Bear & Bells now that I am a widow, and with the closure of Roos Hall I would have had nowhere else to go."

"Precisely. Would you be content with such an arrangement, Jessica?"

"Yes, Papa, I would look forward to it and to caring for my Grandmama as she has cared for me."

"I'm glad to hear it, my dear," Sir Charles responded. "Furthermore," he added, "you may remove from Roos Hall such of the furniture and effects as may be useful to you. I am thinking of the pony, the pianoforte, and occasional tables and suchlike. Jessica, if you wish to take any books, please do so, for Mrs. Jarvis has often stressed your devotion to them. For any items you intend to remove I should be glad if you would kindly prepare a list for Mr. Russell's approval. He is to act as my agent in this matter."

"Now, there is one final ceremony I mean to perform today. Jessica, your grandmother once reliably informed me that you were born upon the fifteenth of May, just after midnight. It is the fifteenth tomorrow, but as clocks are notoriously unreliable, we shall say that one was more than a few minutes fast, which allows me to present to you today my gift on your coming of age."

Sir Charles rose from his chair and took from a side-table a modest rectangular package wrapped in silvered paper and tied with a silver ribbon and bow. He placed it gently in Jessica's hands. She murmured her thanks, wonderingly, unused as yet to her new status, and began to undo the wrapping. Inside she found a box some nine inches long by three inches wide and about an inch deep. It was covered with dark blue velvet. Jessica lifted the clasp and opened it. A long gasp came from her lips as she regarded the contents. Carefully spread out within was an exquisitely delicate silver chain made of S-shaped links. Where the curls of the shapes overlapped, a diamond in a claw setting filled each curl. In the centre was a pendant containing a fine sapphire perched upon a sunburst of diamonds. Jessica was completely overwhelmed. "For me, Papa?" she asked eventually.

Mrs. Jarvis, who had risen and stood behind Jessica, gave a long gasp and then asked, "Are these some of Mr. Ainsworth's gems, Sir Charles?"

"They are indeed, Mrs. Jarvis, and only the first few of the stones to be cut and polished. With Jessica's permission I propose to withhold the remainder for the time being and to keep them for my daughter's dowry, just as Ignatius intended. At such time as she is ready to marry, I shall realise their market value and she shall have the benefit of them. If Jessica consents I will have my lawyer draw up an agreement to that effect. There is one further matter which I wish to be understood at this time. As my relationship to Jessica must remain a matter of some discretion, even though it can be openly observed within my family now, I have decided to permit her complete freedom of choice regarding a husband. I lay down no requirements at all, other than that he shall have an income, be it modest or large, and shall not be a gambler! You know of whom I speak."

"I propose to allow you ladies to discuss all these matters between you and to let me have your responses before you leave for home at the end of the week. And do put on your necklace, Jessica."

Mrs. Jarvis obliged, helping to close the clasp beneath Jessica's ringlets. "I have one more question, Sir Charles," she said. "Do you plan to retain the remainder of the Roos Hall estate, the farms and so forth?"

"Yes, indeed I do. I ought to have made that clear. I intend to build a new manor house in due course, but have yet to decide whether it should be on Redisham or Ringsfield land. I shall be sure to compensate Mr. Alfred Jarvis if I choose his acres as my new site. I am aware that he has an agreement with Jake Martin of Ilketshall St. Andrew, and it may be that a just bargain would be to unite the two properties into my ownership. Now, may I leave you two ladies to dress for dinner when we shall be joined by Mr. Russell. He is aware of much of what I have disclosed to you today, except of course for my own family's scandal regarding the parentage of Ignatius."

When Jessica and Mrs. Jarvis returned to their rooms, they spent some long while in an embrace. Neither could believe that their years of restriction had come to an end and in such a beneficial manner. "I shall ask Mrs. Baines to teach me to cook and to lend me the receipts for some of her best dishes," Jessica vowed, "then we may live together very comfortably."

Mrs. Jarvis laughed. "I even believe that Lizzie might be prepared to take us on," she said. "If we choose a property in Beccles town, near to the Church so that I can still walk to service, Lizzie would be able to look after us and her own parents at the same time. They are older than I and there is no sign of Lizzie wishing to be wed. We must tell them all as soon as we return. They will be envying to know what has happened, but we shall need to continue to be discreet about Sir Charles. You see how he defers to his wife who holds the purse strings - thus money may make life miserable for others."

"I should probably need to continue to call you Mrs. Jarvis, perhaps, for the time being," Jessica replied, "except when we are alone. I wonder how much I may tell Hugo, or Carrie for that matter?"

"Oh, I think we shall be able to tell them. Alfred and Martha Jarvis have known all along, of course," Betty said. "Your mother Alicia stayed at their farm while she awaited your arrival. As you know already, she died a few days afterwards. Her grave is in the churchyard at Beccles. We shall go to pay our respects together upon our return."

"Grandmama, I wish you to tell me all about her, every detail."

"Well, I shall do, but perhaps not quite every detail, for I do not wish you, dear granddaughter, to follow her fate. Now, hurry, my dear, or we shall be late for dinner."

In the days that followed Jessica spent many hours of the warm sunny weather walking around the grounds of Waverley Abbey, both the mansion and the old Abbey ruins. There the hay had just been scythed and lay spread out on the ground to dry. Its sweet and dusty perfume filled her nostrils as she walked over it, peeped into the groves of trees and cascades of ivy that concealed the crumbling grey ruins, sketched for her own memories the arches silhouetted against the sky, and noted how the setting sun stole into the undercroft of the old Refectory. Sometimes she paused beneath the great yew tree, and realising its venerable age, wondered at the spirits of those bygone centuries, the monks, the nobles and fair ladies it had sheltered. She remembered that Ainsworth, now curiously proved to be her cousin, had mentioned the tree, and she imagined him as a carefree boy, clambering among its branches. It seemed to her that there was another boy with him, for she could hear distinctly two tones of laughter. "My necklace shall be named 'The Ainsworth Diamonds'," she said with resolution, and walked back towards the house.

CHAPTER XXI

Victory - But At What Cost?

"All the praise and acclamations of joy for our victory
only bring to my mind what it has cost."
Admiral Collingwood to Mrs. Mary Moutray,
mutual friend of Lord Nelson - October 1805

Now we shall have some rare sport, Hughie boy," Captain Devereux turned to his new First Lieutenant Hugo Jarvis as they stood beside the quarterdeck rail and left guidance of *La Belle Helène* out of Portsmouth Harbour to the Pilot, the Master and the leadsman. In the distance H.M.S. *Apollion* already awaited them, together with a fleet of ten military transports for delivery to the West Indies. Events had moved swiftly since these two had last sailed in these waters, when they had been taken before an Admiralty Board hearing to face a possible charge of piracy. The matter had been settled in their favour in May 1802, and a year had passed during which the *Apollion* had again been employed in the convoy escort business, in her former battleground of the West Indies once more. She had completed her latest voyage at Sheerness on 11 May 1803, and a week later war with France had been renewed. The peace terms agreed at Amiens had proved unworkable: Britain wished to retain Malta and the Cape of Good Hope rather than return them to their previous owners. Napoleon Bonaparte had made good use of the truce by strengthening his dictatorship at home and refining his plans for further military conquests in Europe. Nor had he relinquished his intentions to invade England and to rob Britain of her nascent empire in India.

At Sheerness, the Medway pilot cutter had arrived with urgent despatches commanding their sister-ship, the *Aeschylus* to sail to Yarmouth and make her services available to the North Sea Fleet as soon as she had taken on fresh water and supplies. H.M.S. *Apollion* was similarly to re-supply, but to head in the other direction, calling at Portsmouth for her final instructions. Moreover Lieutenant Salmon, also known as "Fish", had received his promotion to captain at last and was appointed to the command of the *Apollion*. Since there cannot be more than one captain aboard a ship, it was a matter of much speculation by Captain Devereux as to what fate awaited him on his return to Portsmouth, the scene of his recent acquittal. Upon entering Portsmouth Harbour ten days later, the matter was easily and happily resolved. There in one of the shipyards the beautiful

La Belle Helène that he had bargained for with the Portuguese a year since was being fitted out by dockyard artificers and she was almost ready to sail.

On taking the ship's gig to Admiralty House together with Captain Salmon and Lieutenant Jarvis, they received more detailed orders. Captain Devereux was indeed appointed to the French warship, together with Lieutenant Jervis (spelt with an 'E') as her First Officer and choice of other Petty Officers from the *Apollion*. A crew had already been recruited for the warship, mostly by the Press-Gang, so Captain Devereux insisted that the *Apollion*'s Master, Mr. Brightman, join him, since he wished to rely on known skills of navigation at least until he had the measure of the refitted vessel. Captain Devereux and Hugo interviewed all the other aspiring officers and petty officers and were satisfied that they had been furnished with a workable team. Moreover the Gunner, Mr. Sanderson, had served aboard one of the French prizes seized at the Battle of the Nile and was familiar with the type of cannon found aboard *La Belle Helène*, though these had now been fitted with British flintlock detonators. Hugo, being much interested in the gunnery side of naval warfare, spent some hours touring the two gun decks with Mr. Sanderson, listening to his exposition of the weapons' refinements and making suggestions about the better positioning of their carriages, the distribution of shot and the more advantageous use of her carronades, points the French tended to neglect in favour of close combat with firearms and steel.

The instructions received from the Admiralty bade the two ships escort ten military troopships full of soldiers destined for combat or garrison duty in various West Indies locations where the peace-time garrisons had been much decimated by disease, especially by typhoid and Yellow Jack. The British islands now faced renewed attacks by French troops despatched from Martinique and Guadeloupe. After delivering the troop transports the two warships were to join one of the British squadrons blockading the large island of Hispaniola* which English settlers and their French Royalist allies had been forced to abandon in the 1790s, due to the combined threats posed by disease and by negro and mulatto rebels led astray by misguided enthusiasm for French 'Jacobin' principles. Late in 1802, whilst the Peace of Amiens was still supposedly in force, Napoleon Bonaparte had sent an army of twenty thousand soldiers to the island, accompanied by his sister Pauline and her husband General Leclerc. These gradually captured the towns and settlements one by one and tricked the black leaders into submission. The renewal of hostilities in Europe made Hispaniola and its huge French garrison an obvious target for British attention and squadrons were despatched to blockade the principal ports and deny the French supplies of food and equipment. The *Apollion* and *La Belle Helène* were to expect fresh orders concerning which squadron most had need of their services.

Having watered at Barbados, which had always remained in British hands, the convoy set out for St. Lucia which had just been recaptured from the French by a force led by Commodore Samuel Hood and Lieutenant-General William Grinfield. The fresh troops were disembarked, the two empty transports took on

Now Haiti and the Dominican Republic

board the disabled and sick and wounded soldiers, and would then sail north to a rendezvous at English Harbour, Antigua, before recrossing the Atlantic under escort. The squadron's next call was at the island of Dominica in its vulnerable location between the French islands of Martinique and Guadeloupe. General George Prevost commanded British forces there from the west-coast town of Roseau. Again two transports were emptied of their Regulars, though the General would have welcomed more. Care was taken not to embark any poor soul already suffering from yellow fever, since it was thought the disease was air-borne, and medical science had not yet reached the conclusion that it derived only from infected mosquitoes.

Proceeding northwards from Roseau into the Dominica Passage, when the convoy reached the vicinity of the French island of Marie Galante the sound of gunfire was heard. Sounds carry a long way at sea, and as it was broad daylight firing flashes were not so noticeable. Marie Galante seemed to be resting peacefully enough upon her azure couch, but Captain Devereux was impatient for some action. The voyage so far had been unexciting and he had resented the regular gunnery practice and small arms exercises which his second in command had instituted with Mr. Sanderson and the detachment of Marines under Lieutenant Hacker. So he ordered the course to be set towards the bay of Pointe à Pître, the capital of Guadeloupe's eastern isle.

A dozen miles further north and it was plain to Captain Devereux that a serious battle was in progress. The whole broad bay was filled with smoke which, when it was blown aside by the easterly breeze, suddenly revealed a British squadron of half a dozen assorted vessels firing upon what appeared to be a French fleet of blockships and gunships in the making. Aboard *La Belle Helène* the decks had already been cleared and her guns run out; she was eager for the fray, pressing forward under all sail. Then one of the nearer of the British ships tacked and fired a shot across the warship's bows. The British were firing on their own! Captain Devereux immediately realised that his ship was so clearly of classic French build as to be mistaken for the Enemy. He ordered the signal officer to run up additional British flags and a message offering assistance. By this time the *Apollion* and the squadron of readily identifiable troopships had hove into view astern and the British ship concerned hoisted a pennant of acknowledgement by way of apology.

It had all made excellent gunnery practice and Hugo was pleased with the performance of cannon and crew. When sufficient of the blockships had been sunk so as to litter the enemy harbour, the British ships withdrew. As the wind had veered to a southerly breeze they presently anchored for the night off the eastern shore of Guadeloupe, though well out of range of any French gunfire. Ships' visits were exchanged, giving Hugo a chance to meet the officers serving on the other ships, some of whom had sailed alongside the *Apollion* back in the 'nineties when Captain Sterne had commanded her and Hugo had been just a humble midshipman. He also learnt at the same time that the French blockships they had sunk had apparently been destined to sail for Antigua where, if they had closed off English Harbour, they would have seriously interrupted British shipping and perhaps have offered French troops an easy conquest of the island.

Their next destination was Antigua itself where they would part company with two more troopships with soldiers assigned to the defence of Falmouth in English Harbour. The four hospitalised transports would stay there whilst the remaining squadron of four would accompany the warships to St. John's on the other side of the island where one more troopship was due to unload. One might have thought the tiny island overmanned, except that experience had taught that half of each shipload of five hundred souls would be dead of some disease or other within the year. That was the reason why many commanders tried to avoid being assigned to the West Indies station. Hugo was not so concerned for his own health, having survived the Yellow Jack already, but though he recognised the hand of his distinguished relative in his Captain's and his own appointments, he would have preferred to have served in one of the many European theatres of war, in the Downs under Lord Keith, in the Channel off Brest with Admiral Cornwallis, off Ferrol with Admiral Calder, or, best of all, back in the Mediterranean with Lord Nelson.

The quay at St. John's harbour was not extensive and Captain Devereux ordered the transport that was to unload to moor alongside, whilst the remaining five vessels anchored offshore. Once they had done so there was a good deal of to and fro-ing in launches and boats as supplies were replenished, particularly casks of water which never kept fresh for long in the Tropics. Captain Devereux went ashore with his colleague Captain Salmon from the *Apollion* and Hugo and his fellow-officers settled into the boring routine of shore watches, when all is "as idle as a painted ship upon a painted ocean". Hugo was therefore leaning nonchalantly over the quarterdeck taffrail when he was hailed from the *Apollion*'s jolly-boat by a rower whom he recognised as Nicholas Wilmington and by a fellow in military uniform whose aspect seemed familiar but whom he could not place. It was only when that person climbed the ladder up the side of the ship, and held on with his left arm without a right arm to keep it company, that Hugo realised with joy that it was his old friend and former shipmate Pip Harris. Tall, brown as a berry and every inch a lieutenant, Pip had come out to the *Apollion* in the hope that Hugo might still be serving aboard her, or that he might obtain news of his whereabouts. Hugo swiftly found a junior officer to take his place on watch whilst he led his friends to the well-furnished and elegant ward-room aboard *La Belle Helène* and ordered a bottle of the best claret from the officers' steward.

Pip related how well he had been cared for by Madame Joly, such that his lost arm now gave him little pain, whilst the burn to the side of his face was scarcely visible, though no beard grew there and he always had a half-shaved appearance if one looked closely. Pip reckoned that Madame Joly had lathered his wounds with so many good herbs and potions that it had left him free of other sickness all these years, and he was not surprised to learn that Hugo had similarly kept his health. Once recovered, Pip had made good his wish to become a soldier, despite his lost arm, and had been moved from one West Indies island to another as British fortunes had fluctuated. He had taken part in several skirmishes, but reckoned disease to be far worse an enemy than the French or the mulattoes.

Pip told them he had sailed as far as Trinidad where he had served in the garrison left there under Colonel Thomas Picton following the recapture of the island from the Spanish in 1797 by Rear-Admiral Harvey and General Abercromby. However the garrison had been reduced to half its strength by sickness and had had to be relieved after only a year. Much more pleasant had been their invasion of the Dutch island of St. Eustatius, where the French garrison had agreed to leave peacefully and the Dutch Governor and the island's administration had been permitted to continue its normal daily existence as if nothing had happened. Pip then related that he had obtained information from the St. John's Harbourmaster that some troops from the present convoy were destined for service in Hispaniola. This had aroused his interest since he had served there briefly under General Maitland before the British and their allies were finally forced to evacuate the island in April 1798, after forty thousand people, settlers and slaves alike, had succumbed to disease in one year. At the same time, a revolt among the slaves led by a mulatto named Toussaint L'Ouverture had captured one town after another till the whole island had been subdued. Pip had learnt of the French invasion under General Leclerc and he felt an urge to take part in the island's recapture. Accordingly he had come to enquire whether he might join this British force, either as a soldier or as a marine, he did not care so long as someone gave him a berth. He was confident that the Commandant of St. John's garrison would give him leave to go now that the fresh recruits had arrived. Would Hugo be so kind as to put the matter before Captain Devereux?

As Pip was speaking the door opened and that gentleman entered. "So this is what happens when I leave my ship in your care, Mr. Jarvis," he said. "And a bottle of my best claret too!" He turned to Hugo with a twinkle in his eyes and said, "Have my steward bring another bottle." Hugo introduced his friend Pip Harris. "Ah, another officer lacking a right arm," Captain Devereux remarked. "Let us hope you achieve as much without yours as our great Admiral has done," he said with a reference to Lord Nelson. Learning of Pip's request to join the convoy, Captain Devereux questioned him about his military service. He concluded, "I can offer you a berth on either of my ships if you'll serve as a member of the crew, or I can recommend you to the captain of one of the troopships if you would feel more at ease among the military." In the end it was decided that Pip would sling his hammock among the Marines in the foc'sle of the *Apollion*, the ship upon which he had first served some ten years since. As the squadron's next port of call would be Basseterre at St. Christopher's, they planned a joint visit to Madame Joly to pay their respects.

On reaching that island, the *Apollion* escorted the one transport whose complement was to be left there to Sandy Point, whence the march to the fortress on Brimstone Hill was but an hour's toil in the hot sun, along with all their equipment and plenty of cannon shot for the fort's guns. Then she rejoined *La Belle Helène* and the remaining two transports in harbour. Their troops were destined for Port au Prince at the western end of Hispaniola to reinforce existing numbers in the event that the present blockade became an assault on the town.

In the meantime, three "young gentlemen" had paid the planned visit to Madame Joly. Alas it was not the aged Melissa who opened the door, but a young slip of a girl with big dark eyes full of giggles. Madame Joly greeted them with great warmth and was pleased to make Nicholas' acquaintance. "Another fine young English gentleman," was her not unexpected comment. "My dear Melissa passed away a year ago," she explained. "She died of old age -I think she was about eighty years old, but which slave, even when freed, remembers a long-ago childhood far away in Africa? I buried her in the blacks' cemetery and gave her as fine a gravestone as any white settler has in the churchyard. You should visit it, Mr. Hughie and Mr. Pip, to pay your respects. My new maid, Maria, she was born here. Her parents were slaves and still are, but I've paid for her freedom. She's merry and laughs a deal, but eventually I'll succeed in her house-training. She probably thought you three were some of my customers!" There was general laughter at that.

"And you, Mr. Hughie, are you still minded to speak out against slavery, as you promised?" Madame Joly reminded him.

"Yes, indeed, Madame," Hugo replied with a flush in his cheeks.

"I see some English newspapers here from time to time," Madame continued. "It seems there is much talk of it in England right now. A gentleman named William Wilberforce is making many speeches in your Parliament. Do you know him, Mr. Hughie?"

"I know of him, Madame Joly," Hugo replied. "My uncle keeps the newspapers for me, such as he thinks may be of interest, so when I have leave to return home I always collect from him those pieces he has retained. I promise you that I shall continue my attachment to the topic, Madame Joly, I surely will."

The orders which the squadron of *La Belle Helène*, the *Apollion* and the two remaining troopships received at St. Christopher were quite specific and unusual. They were to cruise along the southern coast of Hispaniola until they reached the port of Santo Domingo where they could expect to find a large French presence, with British ships from the Leeward Islands Fleet forming an outer ring preventing the passage of any commerce or reinforcements. They were to check that the blockade was in place, report to its flagship, and take on board any seriously wounded who might later be transferred to the military transports once they had landed their complement at Port au Prince. All being well, the convoy should continue westwards, keeping the shoreline under close observation for signs of military activity which were to be logged most thoroughly. They were also to report upon any large movements of mulattoes, and if runaway slaves tried to approach them in boats they were to take them aboard and question them, always being careful to keep them under armed guard and no more than a few aboard any one ship at a time, no matter how friendly they appeared to be. When such information as seemed likely to be forthcoming had been secured, the slaves were to be returned to the shore, either whence they had come or at a place more remote if they feared for their own safety, short rations being supplied to them at the Captain's discretion.

The voyage proved long and tedious, with frequent anchorings to permit parties of marines and soldiers to investigate the shoreline. They had passed the wild features of Punta Salinas and Cabo Beata almost without any sign of life, and it was only as they approached Jacmel that some fugitives claimed their attention. One was a negro who paddled out to the *Apollion* in a small canoe. The first question he asked was whether he was in British hands for he had feared that *La Belle Helène* might be a French ship sailing under false colours. Captain Salmon had the man transferred to *La Belle Helène* where he was questioned by Captain Devereux and Hugo.

The fellow was strongly-built and muscular, but was covered in deep scars.He claimed his name was Samuel and that he had been a slave but had been liberated by a decree from General Leclerc who had sought the slaves' cooperation in driving from the island the remaining British settlers and their French Royalist allies. Then the situation had changed abruptly. Toussaint L'Ouverture had always been suspicious of French intentions and had had a pitched battle with them on the northern coast of the island near Cap François. The French had then opened negotiations with Toussaint and his fellow mulatto leaders Christophe and Dessalines, promising to involve them in the government of the island.One dark night Toussaint had mysteriously disappeared from his home (he died in prison in France a year later), and the rumour reached Hispaniola that Napoleon Bonaparte had ordered the re-establishment of slavery. Generals Christophe and Dessalines had fled into the forests of the island and had renewed their struggle against the French, who had immediately reinvested all the main towns. Thence they had pursued the fleeing slaves through the fields, marshes and forests, even to the seashores, with the aid of bloodhounds. Samuel himself had twice fought off couples of the hounds but now his strength was failing. Food was in short supply, he told them, the harvest having been ruined by this internecine chaos, and he feared that some of the guerrilla bands had resorted to cannibalism. Samuel regretted the enforced departure of the British who on the whole, he averred, had behaved rather better towards their servants, slaves and workers. Samuel was returned to shore at dusk at a location of his choice, together with sufficient provisions to keep him alive for a week.

From Jacmel they were fired upon by the guns of the port. The missiles fell well short of the British ships, but even through a good telescope it was difficult to tell who was firing, Frenchmen or mulattoes. As they neared the western end of the island at Cap Tiburon, signs that the slaves had begun to reverse the tide of war in their own favour became more numerous. Plantations and churches could be seen in flames, and the sight of the Union flag at the masthead of the passing vessels occasionally attracted a wave from an isolated black hand or a shout of excitement from a group of black children seen running along a beach.

In the light of this change of circumstances, and because his ships were now very short of water, not having tried to obtain supplies from the hostile territory they had just passed, Captain Devereux decided to take his vessels on to Port Royal, Jamaica, and to confer with Rear-Admiral Sir J. Thomas Duckworth, now resident commander at the naval headquarters there. Captain Devereux argued that it seemed pointless to proceed further with the troop transports if the slave forces had already driven out the French from Port au Prince. Could the rebel slaves be relied upon to further defeat the enemy, aided by hunger and disease, and without the need for British intervention on land? Admiral Duckworth agreed with this assessment, since his spies before Port au Prince had supplied the same information. To his knowledge the French forces were being driven back towards the north coast of Hispaniola. The Admiral therefore gave instructions that the remaining troopships should be held in reserve at Port Royal and that Captain Devereux should pass by Port au Prince, currently adequately blockaded, and continue along the north coast of the island to Cap François where there was another important British blockade.

Thus it was that on leaving Port Royal, *La Belle Helène* and the *Apollion*, now on their own, proceeded nor'east through the Windward Passage between Cuba and Hispaniola. They counted a dozen British ships grouped between Cap Tiburon and Cap à Foux, and another half dozen before La Môle St. Nicholas, an easy landing-place still heavily invested by the French. Support vessels in the form of snows and cutters sped busily between the various British squadrons, and Captain Devereux did no more than to order the colours dipped as they passed in order to reassure their British colleagues that his warship was a British naval vessel. He had discovered that commanding a ship that so obviously belonged to another nation could have its drawbacks: he was about to discover its advantages.

Off the island of Tortuga, named after its turtles, the officer of the watch reported a large French vessel on the horizon standing in for the mainland. Could they intercept her before she reached shore and take possession of her cargo? "What do you make of her, Mr. Jarvis?" Captain Devereux asked with unaccustomed formality as he handed Hugo the spyglass. "A merchantman, is she?"

"She's certainly long enough and broad in the beam," Hugo replied. "I think she might be a slaver."

"In that case we must intercept her," his Captain responded. "Those poor devils on shore have enough sorrows fighting with the Frenchies without being driven off into slavery elsewhere."

As the Captain was speaking, a strange sound wafted across the water, rising and falling like a siren's call. The crew of *La Belle Hélène* looked at each other and shivered at the unearthly tones. What dreadful tortures were being applied to the slaves that could cause such wailing?

"Quick, Hugo, have French colours run up all our topmasts and signal to the *Apollion* to do the same. 'Fish' will guess my intention," Captain Devereux exclaimed. All hands were summoned, and Hugo supervised the clearing of the decks in record time. He had the foredeck carronades loaded with heavy thirty-two pounder shot so that they might make the maximum impact when landing on the unsuspecting French ship's decks. The guns on the main deck he had loaded with chain shot so that it might achieve the greater damage to the French vessel's rigging. He hoped to immobilise her as quickly as possible and without sending too many heavy missiles into her hull, where in his mind he could picture the rows of slaves shackled hand to hand and ankle to ankle, with only the whites of their fear-frozen eyes visible in the darkness, just as he had found them on the two Portuguese slave ships he had known.

The French slaver continued on her leisurely way, obviously unaware that two enemy vessels had crowded on all sail in order to cross her bows. The *Apollion*, which had been astern of *La Belle Hélène* by several cables' lengths, with her sleeker lines began to overhaul her French-built companion, much to Captain Devereux's chagrin, though Hugo let out a secret chuckle as his old ship showed her paces. The two British ships swept into action simultaneously, the *Apollion* now forward of the French slaver, with *La Belle Hélène* astern. Four thirty-two pound missiles landed simultaneously on the main deck of the vessel, followed by a broadside from each on her starboard quarter, one after another as they passed. Then *La Belle Hélène* delivered another upon the slaver's larboard flank. Mr. Brightman drew his steed neatly alongside. Ropes, ladders and grappling hooks were swung aboard and the Marines swarmed over the enemy decks.

In front of her, the *Apollion* had tacked about and held her guns at the ready in case further punishment was required. There was no resistance aboard the French vessel. She had a crew consisting only of seamen without any military contingent at all, and her decks were as sparsely crewed as any peaceful merchant ship. She had not even thought to run out the light guns she did possess.

The Marines from *La Belle Hélène* had the enemy crew in shackles immediately - there seemed to be plenty of ironware to hand - and herded a number into the French ship's foc'sle. Only then did they have time to turn their attention to the hatches and to examine the contents of the hold, whose inhabitants had grown strangely silent once the gunfire had ceased. The hatches were opened and Captain Devereux and Hugo watching from the quarterdeck of *La Belle Hélène* could not understand why their Marines suddenly started falling about in fits of laughter. Had they been struck by some strange malady? Had they wasted good ammunition on a cargo that was worthless?

Captain Devereux stepped aboard the French vessel, taking Hugo with him.

On the *Apollion*, Captain Salmon ordered his gig lowered. When they peered over the hatch coamings at the cargo below, they were indeed met by the gaze of hundreds of eyes, doleful and red-rimmed as they were - not human slaves but bloodhounds! Scores of 'em!

"Whatever do we do with that lot, Fish?" Captain Devereux stood arms akimbo in puzzlement.

"I would rather feed a regiment than all of those," his colleague replied. "Do you realise they'll eat twice an able seaman's allowance of bully beef every day?"

"I wouldn't feel easy stepping down there to feed them!" Captain Devereux remarked. "Any ideas, Hughie?"

Just at that moment the lookout aboard the taller 'Belle Helène' cried out, "Sail in sight!" After a pause and further consultation of the spyglass, "She's wearing American colours." The strange ship was approaching fast. They had to decide quickly whether she was friend or foe and whether the captains should return to their own ships, cut the cables linking *La Belle Helène* to the slaver and prepare for battle once more. Hugo took a long, hard look at the raking masts of a frigate, then snatched up the French captain's telescope which lay upon the binnacle and ran up the ratlines to the mizzen-top, the only one which their combined gunfire had left standing.

When Hugo descended and rejoined his colleagues his face was wreathed in smiles. "Who is she?" the two captains chorussed together.

"She's the *Beacon* out of Boston, gentlemen, Captain Anderson in command, if indeed he is still as he was in 'ninety-six."

"Friendly?" the two captains demanded.

"He should be, especially if I remind him of our previous hospitality when Captain Sterne commanded the *Apollion*."

"Hugo, have him sent a signal to come alongside," Captain Devereux ordered. "I think we may just have found a solution to our little problem."

The U.S.S. *Beacon*, for indeed it was she, drew up alongside the *Apollion*, that being the vessel that her commander, still Captain Anderson, recognised. Captain Salmon had his gig rowed back to his ship and invited the American to accompany him to meet his colleagues aboard *La Belle Helène*, one of whom he should recognise since they had met previously. Much intrigued, and ordering his own crew to stay alert, Captain Anderson complied and Hugo was soon reminding the American of their previous encounter.

"I scarcely recall meeting you in person," he told Hugo,"but I certainly recall Captain Sterne. Where is he now?"

"He is in retirement, Captain," Hugo replied. "He took a bad wound to his shoulder from a French vessel in these waters."

"I remember well how he robbed me of my prize, that Portuguese slaver, and he only released the *Beacon* after he had recorded it with his Admiralty as a British capture. All that red tape!"

Hugo could see Captain Devereux's moustache beginning to twitch as he listened, for Hugo had hurriedly related the rest of that tale to him whilst Captain Salmon was absent bringing the American aboard. "Well now, I think I may just be able to make amends to you for that little contretemps," Captain Devereux smiled encouragingly. "Come this way, Captain Anderson," and he led him across the netting and fallen rigging to the deck of the French slaver which the Marines and crewmen from *La Belle Helène* were busy swabbing down and clearing.

The hatches were opened once more and the inhabitants, finding themselves again the centre of attention, began to howl piteously. The stench was also overpowering, as Hugo now had time to notice. "Oh, nice!" said Captain Anderson as he peered within. "They use those a lot in Florida, you know, the Spaniards do, and in Cuba too. They're so good at hunting felons through the swamps, slaves and persons lost also. You must have quite a number there. Should fetch a good price in the right market."

"I thought," Captain Devereux said slowly and deliberately, "that as you are already heading northwards, you might be interested in escorting them to a suitable destination?"

"Oh, rather," Captain Anderson seemed quite taken with the idea.

"I should expect something by way of consideration, of course," Captain Devereux hinted.

"I have no doubt of it," the American replied with a grin. "Now, on the previous occasion when this young fellow first met me," he said, jerking his fist towards Hugo, "I had been foolishly deceived by a rascally Spanish pirate who deprived me of my ship and my prize. That too I have but just reversed. Off the coast of Algiers I met up with a Barbary pirate towing a Spanish merchantman from their Plate Fleet with a broken rudder. I took the Corsair, relieved him of the bullion, and set the Spaniard free! Shall we cross to my vessel, Captain Devereux, and discuss the matter further? If you gentlemen," he said, addressing Captain Salmon and Hugo, "would care to take a tour around my ship, she's a particularly fast sailer and I know you'll appreciate her qualities." Hugo thanked him, for he had not had an opportunity of inspecting the *Beacon* on the previous occasion.

When Captain Devereux emerged from Captain Anderson's quarters half an hour later, a large and exceptionally heavy strong-box was transferred to *La Belle Helène*. Captain Anderson confessed that his vessel lacked sufficient supplies to satisfy so many hungry canine appetites. Captain Salmon immediately offered to have his Purser look out some spare barrels of beef and asked Hugo to arrange the same aboard *La Belle Helène*, "those that have passed beyond the point of human consumption," he added in a whispered aside. Some discussion then took place between the three captains as to what should be done with the French crew. The British captains were loath to release them on the island of Hispaniola where they would either fall victim to the mulattoes or cause additional problems for the British forces. In the end Captain Anderson obliged by promising to land them all in Florida, whence it would take them a while to find their way home. Crews from both the British ships assisted the *Beacon*'s crew to jury-rig the French vessel before they parted company with her, and some of the Marines had volunteered to feed the dogs, though they wrapped themselves in spare canvas while they did so and hosed down their boots rather well afterwards!

"Your American acquaintance has done us no little favour," Captain Devereux said to Hugo as *La Belle Helène* and the *Apollion* set sail from the shores of Tortuga Island after filling their water-casks. "What could I have done with all those dogs? There was at least a hundred of them. Could I have let them loose on Hispaniola to maraud whomever they encountered? If I had sunk the ship and the dogs with it, and I confess I had not the heart to do that, I would still have been obliged to return to Jamaica with the prisoners. French prisoners and no ship would have rendered me a laughing stock, and an outcast for killing the dogs. Those might well have been dead by the time we arrived in port, since they'll only stand a short journey aboard ship while confined below decks. I just hope that Captain Anderson makes the Florida coast swiftly and without mishap. You are aware that he will realise for each dog double the sale price for a healthy slave?"

"What shall you write in the log?" Hugo enquired somewhat tentatively, for he felt instinctively that the Royal Navy might not have approved the transaction.

"Oh I shall report that we fired on a French merchant ship off Tortuga Island but that she escaped inshore before we could detain her. 'Fish' knows my mind and will inscribe the same. What do you intend, Hughie, when this war ends and the Navy is stood down again?" he asked in an effort to divert his First Officer's attention.

"My father is a farmer, Captain," Hugo replied, "but my younger brother Peter seems likely to succeed him in that rôle. I would envy to stand for Parliament to speak on the slavery issue, but that requires funds which I presently lack, and support from prominent people."

"What about your famous relative, Lord St. Vincent, will he not assist you?"

"Perhaps he might. When last we spoke at Portsmouth he told me that with his support Commodore Troubridge had just taken his old seat of Great Yarmouth and will speak in the current Parliament on naval affairs. But Troubridge has a public record for gallantry, and is also well-connected."

"At least I can provide the funds you require," Captain Devereux murmured, and as Hugo turned towards him he added, "your share of the contents of that bullion chest I brought from the *Beacon* will furnish you with a down-payment on that Parliament seat."

The next port where Captain Devereux had received instructions to call was Cap François where General Leclerc had landed with twenty thousand French troops less than a year ago. As they approached the bay, a half-circle of British ships anchored offshore was clearly visible. Remembering his previous warm welcome from a British squadron, Captain Devereux made sure that *La Belle Helène* and her sister-ship were fully be-flagged for the occasion. Once they obtained a direct view into the bay Captain Devereux was surprised to see it equally full of French shipping. He counted a dozen troop transports and four ships of the line of various gun-power. In addition there were two fast French corvettes normally used for the carrying of mails and despatches. On the hills above the harbour Captain Devereux caught the glint of steel. As his telescope swept from one wooded summit to another he realised that the hinterland of the port was one vast military encampment. Swiftly he had his gig lowered, collected Captain Salmon from the *Apollion*, and was rowed across to the British flagship where he was briefed on the situation ashore.

It seemed that some months since General Leclerc had himself succumbed to yellow fever and had been succeeded in command by General Rochambeau. He was encamped in the port with eight thousand of his men, nearly all that survived of the original force. They had been driven northwards progressively by the mulatto-led armies, and it was General Dessalines who had invested the surrounding hills with superior numbers of irregulars with their cannon trained upon the French ships in the bay. Spies sent ashore from the British fleet had reported that the French were almost out of rations and that General Dessalines had poisoned their water supply by floating diseased corpses downstream. The General, with British prompting, had sent the French an ultimatum that they should take to their ships and leave his island, never to return, or he would bombard their vessels in port and let the soldiers starve to death. The date now was the 29th November and the ultimatum was due to expire at the end of the month, so the situation was extremely tense. The British fleet waited with its guns run out and its decks cleared for action. The *Apollion* and *La Belle Helène* formed a welcome addition to their strength and were ordered to make the same preparations. Double watches were set in case the French tried to steal provisions from the British ships.

The following morning the port was alive with the sounds of activity, the clink of steel on steel, the march of measured steps, the creaking wheels of a laden cart. From the British fleet every spyglass was trained upon the settlement, but as the surrounding hills threw much of the valley into shadow in the strong tropical sunlight, it was difficult to discern what was happening. Then, to a rat-a-tat-tat of drums, they appeared, the French infantry, each group marching four abreast and twenty-five deep, the muskets over their shoulders gleaming as though they were new, their blue uniforms, white cross-belts and dark tricorne hats all in place. It was an impressive sight. They marched along the mole and sailors appearing from behind each group were observed to assist them into the French fleet's launches, some of which had been moored by the quay. The boats which were full pulled away to the most distant of the French warships and then returned for more. Time and again the boats were filled and departed, until the rowers were too exhausted to continue. As each ship's complement was achieved, a white flag of truce rose somewhat shakily and uncertainly to the main topmast and no other colours were broken out.

It was soon evident that the healthiest of the French soldiers had been the first to embark. As the morning progressed there were many who could scarcely walk, let alone march. Some of the troopships had been warped alongside the mole so that embarkation might be better facilitated. The watchers noted that each shipload had been followed in the column by a single cart carrying what appeared to be water casks and personal effects. The carts were hauled by hand; it seemed that all the cavalry horses had been eaten, and that the heavy guns the French had landed would have to be left ashore. As the military column staggered on, hand-carts made a more frequent appearance, now filled with the sick and injured, all scared stiff, no doubt, at what the victorious mulatto forces might do to anyone left behind. After all it was they, the French, who had encouraged the slaves to rebel in the first place, with their fiery rhetoric of Republican political freedom, they who had prompted the slaves to attack their masters, the settlers, and to slaughter them wholesale, men, women and children. Pip Harris had a wealth of anecdotes upon the subject as he stood beside Hugo on the quarterdeck of *La Belle Helène* and noted down for later reference the numbers of personnel being evacuated.

At that moment Captain Devereux stepped out of his cabin and joined them, asking for a report on the proceedings. When they had obliged, the Captain sent Pip to ask the Purser, Mr. Evans, what supplies he might spare by way of water and provisions, bearing in mind that Jamaica, where the prisoners were to be delivered, was less than a week's sailing distance, fair weather permitting. Pip returned with the Purser's list half an hour later, when Captain Devereux endorsed it and ordered him to take two seamen and the jolly-boat and hand it to the officer of the watch on the British flagship, along with his written message that once the French fleet was safely at sea under escort he was prepared to contribute towards a modest delivery of provisions. Captain Devereux heavily underlined the word 'modest' since he did not trust those treacherous Frenchies not to try to escape.

Meanwhile the marching columns on-shore had come to an end and the French flagship had been towed to the mole. The watchers on the British ships realised that General Rochambeau and his staff were about to make their final retreat from their headquarters, and all the British crews had turned out to witness it. Each vessel's rigging was fully manned, Marines crowded the fore and poop decks, and captains and officers thronged each quarterdeck rail. Out from the shelter of the shoreside cottages came a single figure astride a very thin and shambling horse, the only one that had been kept alive in the French encampment. General Rochambeau rode very upright, his sword unsheathed and held erect in his right hand, his left resting upon his horse's withers as he controlled the stumbling beast with his knees. Behind him came a dozen officers on foot, some of them bandaged or missing a limb, and they staggered their way proudly along the mole. As they reached the ship the officers went aboard, the horse was hoisted in a sling and landed on the main deck, where the poor creature collapsed forthwith, and General Rochambeau had himself rowed out to the British flagship where he surrendered his sword to the accompaniment of a distant patter of drum-beats from his own vessel. He was then rowed back to his warship and his own standard fluttered from its main-truck, beneath the white flag of truce.

By this time the British fleet had been ordered to stations, boats had been lowered and ships not placed to sail in a westerly direction had been warped around till their sails could fill with the breeze that was fortunately favourable. It was a magnificent sight to see the French fleet sail out of harbour in line astern led by their flagship, then followed by the troopships with the two corvettes in the rear. Not long afterwards one of the latter made a dash for freedom, as Captain Devereux had anticipated, and the *Apollion*, being one of the faster ships of the British fleet, was able to chase after her and bring her back into line. Otherwise their voyage was uneventful until they reached the Windward Passage between Hispaniola and Cuba on the third of December, 1803. There they found a battle in progress between the British fleet blockading Môle St. Nicholas and half a dozen French ships trying to slip out of port whilst firing their guns indiscriminately in the hope of keeping their enemy at bay. But the British squadron were having none of it and returned fire with more application and greater interest. As the Cap François fleet approached five of the French vessels struck their colours, but the fastest did make its escape and this time the *Apollion* was not closely positioned to retrieve it.

Thus it was quite a procession of captured craft that made its way into Kingston harbour and delivered its prisoners and their vessels to the docks at Port Royal. A few weeks later, on 1 January 1804, General Dessalines issued a proclamation severing all Hispaniola's links with France and returned to the island its aboriginal name of Haiti.

Although the settlement of Santo Domingo remained in French hands, a similar surrender to the British was anticipated, and ships no longer required for service off Hispaniola were ordered to report to Commodore Samuel Hood, Admiral Duckworth's second-in-command, at his headquarters on St. Christopher, for further instructions regarding naval actions underway in the Leeward Islands. These included the *Apollion* and *La Belle Helène* who were likely to be assigned to further trans-Atlantic escort commissions. Both ships' crews were eager to reach Basseterre, since this would be their first opportunity to receive mail from home since setting out in the previous May. Amongst the incoming correspondence was Jessica's letter to Hugo of 3rd November 1803, which had just arrived with the latest despatches from London. Enclosed within it was the note which Ainsworth Rich had written to Nicholas Wilmington. It happened that Nicholas had brought the package to Hugo, since it had been addressed to him "Care of H.M.S. *Apollion*" and Hugo then realised that neither

JESS OF ROOS HALL

Jessica nor his family had received news of his latest posting. At the same time Nicholas opened the letter from Ainsworth and noting its contents, gave it to Hugo to read. Both young gentlemen agreed to respond at once, Nicholas to apprise his Aunt Marianne of Ainsworth's illness and condition, and Hugo to advise Jessica of his whereabouts. Of the two texts, only the second one remains:

Dear Jessica,   *St. Kitts, 10th January 1804*
This day I received your letter of 3rd November last, addressed to me aboard H.M.S. Apollion *and thus realised that previous letters from Beccles may not have reached me and that mine to my home and to yourself from Funchal and Antigua have also gone astray. Quite a breakdown in service! I am presently engaged as First Officer aboard H.M.S. La Belle Helène, the French ship which we brought home from the Cape Verde Islands nearly two years since. My chief, Captain Devereux, is a fair-minded person and I continue to find my employment with him most agreeable. Fortunately H.M.S.* Apollion *is our sister-ship and keeps us company still. My friend Nicholas Wilmington yet serves aboard her as Second Lieutenant and thus was able to bring me your letter, which I opened in his presence.*

"I was saddened to learn from your letter that Ainsworth Rich is so ill, though truth to tell he was not himself when we encountered him upon the Beaumaris Castle *in which he voyaged home from India. Nicholas informs me that he will act immediately upon the request contained in Ainsworth's note, and I hope that his wish may be fulfilled satisfactorily. For my own part, please inform Mr. Ainsworth that of late I bear him no grudge for his having delivered me into the hands of the Press-men all those years ago. Time heals many scars, and the Royal Navy suits me exceedingly as a profession.*

"I was also most saddened to learn of the loss of my Uncle Robert who had been a great favourite with me, since it was he who had made me aware of the course of publick affairs, and he always had some yarn or other to relate. Please give my most heartfelt condolences to my Aunt Jarvis and my sorrow that I was unable to obtain home leave when we docked last May, as I would most surely have visited Uncle Robert on that occasion.

"I note that you have named your new hound Horatio and am glad that his Lordship's fame continues to be celebrated in his home counties. Here in the West Indies I am sensible of being far from home and quite out of kinship with the Fate of our Navy in Europe. I hear that Lord Nelson stalks his prey in the Mediterranean again and wish that we might be summoned to that service, rather than sawing back and forth across the Atlantic on convoy duty. Yet I suppose it necessary to ensure that you have sugar to spoon into your afternoon tea, milady!

"Of our adventures this last voyage I shall relay more anon, for I wish this letter at least to catch the next mail. One pleasant surprise, however, was to encounter my old friend Pip Harris, he who lost his right arm to a French cannon years ago, but I believe I had told you of that. He is well recovered from his injury

and is serving here as a soldier, having even made lieutenant. He joined us for the present voyage but has decided he enjoys this warm climate too well to wish to return to England.

"I promise to request home leave when next we return to English waters and until then remain,

Your sincere friend,
Hugo Jarvis"

But it was to be a long while before Hugo could return home to Britain. Orders received at St. Christopher sent them across the Atlantic indeed, but only as far as Funchal where the larger escorts guarding incoming and outgoing East Indiamen in wartime would take over. They were often obliged to defend their charges and sustained damage and injuries in the course of such scraps. Once Spain entered the war against Britain in December 1804, they frequently met with hostile and aggressive shipping in the vicinity of the Canary Islands. Moreover, there were ever fewer ports where British vessels could take refuge. Napoleon had persuaded the Portuguese to deny Britain access to the River Tagus, and although this ruling did not yet extend to Funchal, Messrs. Iver and Evans were often denied supplies or obliged to pay a higher price for them. In fact Gibraltar became the only port where British ships could be sure of a warm welcome, and even that port had to be supplied from home, especially with timber for repairs, ship-chandling manufactures and bulk rations.

In truth Britain stood alone against the ambition of Napoleon and the power of France. The Treaty of Amiens had been a lack-lustre armistice, obtained by a lack-lustre administration which then failed to pursue the renewed war with vigour. Henry Addington's government fell from power in May 1804 and William Pitt was recalled from early retirement to head the new administration. Immediately he set about reorganising Britain's armed forces and her systems of defence. Henry Dundas, Lord Melville, Pitt's former Secretary for War and President of the Board of Control for India, replaced Earl St. Vincent as First Lord of the Admiralty. It was found that the rigorous economies which Lord St. Vincent had imposed on the Navy in his quest to extirpate fraud and corruption, had also led to a serious reduction in the availability of trained men and of vessels in a seaworthy condition. In the Mediterranean Lord Nelson complained that he had to do more with less and make them (the ships) last longer. Fortunately British skill at seamanship through being ever at sea on patrol whilst the French spent most of their days in port, in the long run proved the more reliable weapon.

Meanwhile Prime Minister Pitt was trying to build an alliance of nations willing to stand up to the French dictatorship. Russia, under its new Tsar Alexander I, and Austria both joined the Coalition, only for Napoleon to defeat both of them militarily in the following year, the Austrians under General Mack surrendering at Ulm whereby Napoleon could occupy Vienna, and a combined Russian and Austrian army being routed at the Battle of Austerlitz. William Pitt, thrown into depression by the unravelling of his Coalition, died in January 1806 predicting with accuracy, "Roll up that map (of Europe); it will not be wanted these ten years."

Napoleon, who had just had the Pope, no less, crown him Emperor in true Roman Imperial fashion, had continued to develop his strategy for invading and conquering Britain. From the moment that war was renewed in May 1803 he had caused new quays and a huge dock basin to be built at Boulogne where he would gather together the bulk of his 'National Flotilla' of two thousand flat-bottomed barges to carry 160,000 men and ten thousand horses across the Channel. But there the plan came to a halt. How was his army to cross that confounded twenty-mile stretch of choppy water without a French Fleet in command of the Channel to protect it? All the fleets at the Emperor's disposal, in the Texel in Holland, at Brest and Rochefort in Western France, at Ferrol, Cadiz and Cartagena in Spain, and at Toulon and even further east in the Mediterranean, were imprisoned in their ports by Britain's blockades in command of the seas. Napoleon's plan was for all these squadrons to break out suddenly from their ports, evading capture as and when they could, and to rendezvous in the West Indies. There they should gather in force to sweep back across the Atlantic in such numbers as to overwhelm any British Fleet which might be summoned against them. They were then to sail up the Channel and secure the Pas de Calais for the crossing of the Grande Armée.

Admiral Ganteaume, now anchored at Brest, would lead the combined French Fleet, with as his second-in-command Admiral Pierre Villeneuve, he who had escaped from Aboukir Bay in the *Guillaume Tell*, and who was now trapped in Toulon with Lord Nelson sailing up and down nearby, like a cat watching a mousehole. Early in January 1805 Rear-Admiral Missiessy broke out of Rochefort with his squadron and crossed the Atlantic to Martinique, the rendezvous selected by Napoleon. Rather than wait about for his fellow commanders to join him, he invaded the nearby British island of Dominica and obliged General Prevost to evacuate Roseau and march his troops across the island to the relative safety of St. Rupert's Bay. Missiessy then moved from one British island to another, charging each an indemnity levied on every citizen and passing thus through St. Christopher, Nevis and Montserrat. In search of further amusement he proceeded to Hispaniola where the French garrison was still besieged in Santo Domingo by mulatto-led forces. Finding that there was little he could do to assist his compatriots other than to land some supplies, and with no sign of the arrival of Admiral Villeneuve, Missiessy returned to France where he was severely rebuked by Napoleon for not adhering to the master-plan.

In fact Admiral Villeneuve had already left Toulon with his squadron of eleven warships, and Nelson receiving the news at his anchorage in the Maddelena Islands, off Northern Sardinia, had chased all round the Mediterranean looking for the French Fleet before learning that storms had forced Villeneuve to return to base. Villeneuve broke out of Toulon again at the end of March, dodged Nelson's fleet and sailed through the Strait of Gibraltar while Nelson was again checking that the French destination was not within the Mediterranean. Instead Villeneuve had been joined by six Spanish warships from Cadiz under Admiral Gravina and had sailed across the Atlantic, arriving at Martinique on 14th May. Nelson, having got wind at last of a transatlantic rendezvous quite unanticipated by the British Government, set out in pursuit and reached Barbados on 4th June.

But at Martinique Villeneuve, finding none of his fellow-commanders present, and after burying there a thousand of the three thousand French and fifteen hundred Spanish troops he had brought with him and who had succumbed already to disease, amused his fleet by besieging Diamond Rock. This is a pinnacle of rock six hundred feet high which rises abruptly from the sea like the Rock of Gibraltar, near the harbour of Port Royal in the south of Martinique. More than a year previously Commodore Samuel Hood, who had recently returned to England from his post as commander of the Leeward Islands Squadron, had had Lieutenant James Wilkes Morris with one hundred and twenty sailors and some heavy guns winched up that cliff to perch upon its narrow ledges and fire upon passing French shipping supplying Martinique, at which they had achieved considerable success. Villeneuve spent fourteen days blockading attempts to supply those perched on the rock with fresh water and food, and three days bombarding it from his warships, till its defenders were obliged to surrender. The diversion was fatal to his cause since it permitted Nelson time to cross the Atlantic.

On the basis of incorrect information received, Nelson had begun his search of the West Indian islands at Trinidad, but finding all peaceful there he immediately headed north. He soon learnt that Villeneuve, having heard of Nelson's pursuit, had hurriedly passed through the Dominica Passage south of Guadeloupe on 9th June and had headed back across the Atlantic. On 13th June Nelson reached Antigua, left there the troops he had embarked at Barbados which were no longer needed, and made ready to return across the Atlantic. Before setting out, he sent despatches to England via the sloop *Curieux* in order to alert the Admiralty to Napoleon's plan. There the First Lord, now Lord Barham, a former Comptroller of the Navy, ordered Admiral Cornwallis to cruise between Cape Finisterre and Ushant with his Channel Fleet, whilst Rear-Admiral Charles Stirling should lead his squadron from Rochefort to link up with Vice-Admiral Sir Robert Calder and both should patrol the seas west of Finisterre.

Villeneuve's objective was Ferrol where he hoped to release the twelve Spanish warships which had been blockaded in that port. Sir Robert Calder had placed his fleet in their path; his force consisted of fifteen ships of the line, two frigates and two smaller ships, whilst the Franco-Spanish fleet of Admiral Villeneuve contained twenty warships, seven frigates and three other vessels. The action was fierce and continued into the darkness, the British securing a couple of prizes. The following day there was an opportunity to renew the conflict, but neither side took it. Villeneuve's excuse was Napoleon's instruction that he should reach Ferrol without seeking out the enemy, but Sir Robert Calder had none. He was much vilified by the Press in England and was later court-martialled. Lord Nelson, who had returned to Gibraltar from the West Indies, watered there and learnt that Villeneuve had not re-entered the Mediterranean. Off Cadiz he found Rear-Admiral Collingwood on patrol with still no sign of the enemy, so he proceeded further north till he met with Admiral Cornwallis off Brest with whom he left his fleet. As Villeneuve had taken the Franco-Spanish fleet into Ferrol, Nelson had applied for and been granted some home leave. His reception by the public when he landed at Portsmouth was quite rapturous.

Meanwhile the *La Belle Helène* and the *Apollion* had spent much of the Spring of 1805 anchored in English Harbour waiting for their next convoy to foregather. The comings and goings of the Enemy fleets from Europe and the actions of Admiral Missiessy in the Leeward Islands had rendered all the islanders jittery. Harvests were hasty and curtailed, machinery was boarded up or abandoned as settlers made for the forts or the highlands in an endeavour to keep their families safe from French attack. Everyone remembered the events which had occurred in Hispaniola and this was not the time to be making investments in trade. The arrival of Lord Nelson so soon after Villeneuve's departure did restore some kind of confidence. *La Belle Helène* and her sister-ship had lent their launches to assist the disembarkation of the troops which Lord Nelson had brought from Barbados, and instructions were sought from St. Christopher's as to where these regiments should be sent. The two warships then participated in the dispersal of those forces to various British-owned islands, in particular to reinforce General Prevost in Dominica and to add to the garrison of St. Lucia. This was a pleasant way of occupying the balmy summer months, especially as they managed to capture two prizes, one Spanish and one French, which they were delighted to deliver to St. John's, where Hugo and Nicholas spent a few days ashore in the company of Pip Harris and his colleagues.

By the time they returned to English Harbour to pick up their convoy late in July, the hurricane season had commenced and everyone was anxious to see them depart. In the previous year, 1804, there had been an especially vicious hurricane in which seas had swept over parts of some islands and many ships had been lost, thirteen off St. Christopher alone. Having paid the French ransoms, the islanders were short of cash and need to have the benefit of their cotton and sugar crops accredited to their London bank accounts. There were twenty merchantmen in the convoy, a large number for the two warships to keep under constant surveillance in hostile waters.

The weather turned rough and stormy as summer calms gave way to autumn gales. High seas took their toll of spars, sails and rigging, and one of their charges sprang a serious leak. The westerly gales drove them closer to the Canary Islands than they wished, with the result that the Spanish squadron based at Santa Cruz located them and gave chase. The two British warships tacked across the

Spaniards' path and returned their gunfire until darkness fell, when they slipped away and rejoined their convoy, taking them safely into Funchal. Captain Devereux's first concern was to have the leaky merchantman patched up so that she might continue to England where more permanent repairs could be effected. His next concern was to obtain supplies of spars, timber and ropes to repair the damage done to his own two ships. On this the Portuguese authorities proved more adamant. They could agree to repair a merchant vessel, they decreed, but to repair a warship would be to favour one combatant above another. Besides, they needed to retain such supplies of timber as they had for the sake of their own home-coming East Indiamen.

More worrying still was the fact that no Admiralty orders or despatches awaited *La Belle Helène* and the *Apollion* at Funchal. Either the orders had been lost at sea, or else the Navy had forgotten them in its anxiety about more strategic matters. There was a huge East Indiamen convoy already in port together with four British frigates which had escorted them from the island of St. Helena in the Southern Atlantic, and which proposed to take them on to London, together with the newly-arrived trans-Atlantic fleet. The frigates were unfamiliar to Captain Devereux and, suspecting some form of trickery, that their colours were false, that spies or even explosives might be aboard with the intention of causing mayhem among the British fleet or in England's ports, he found an excuse to visit all four of the escort ships and insisted on examining their official documentation before he handed over responsibility for the West Indies convoy. Everything seemed to be in order, but he and Hugo still watched their departure with misgiving. If Captain Devereux had erred in his judgment in wartime, his own life could have been forfeit, as had happened to Admiral Byng when he had failed to relieve Minorca half a century before.

Lacking instructions to come or go, Captain Devereux decided that as they needed certain repairs quite urgently, they should sail to Gibraltar and take the opportunity to have some careening and re-caulking carried out at the same time. Escort vessels were not supposed to occupy valuable dock space at Royal Navy yards except in cases of emergency. Was a deprivation of alternative sources in an hostile ocean a sufficient excuse, he asked himself? The *La Belle Helène* and the *Apollion* berthed against the mole at Gibraltar at the end of August 1805 for what Captain Devereux estimated as a five or six-week period of repairs. Hugo observed that the artificers there worked more willingly these days, for after the mutinous years their pay had been improved, slightly, and, as a result of Lord St. Vincent's reforms, rations were now issued in full measure rather than every middleman taking his cut. He walked around the yards and made notes, thinking that his impressions might one day be useful to him if he ever did manage to obtain that seat in Parliament which he now coveted.

When the repairs to the two ships were almost complete, Rosia Bay at Gibraltar received a distinguished visitor. Rear-Admiral Sir Thomas Louis brought in H.M.S. *Canopus* (80 guns) and half a dozen smaller vessels, apparently needing nothing more simple nor more vital than supplies of fresh water for Nelson's fleet. Now Admiral Louis had served as Nelson's second-in-command during that lightning trans-Atlantic chase after Villeneuve, and Captain Devereux had made his acquaintance during the disembarkation of the troops from Barbados. He therefore sent a note aboard the *Canopus* requesting an interview, thinking first of all that he ought to excuse his own presumption in using prime dockyard services by explaining the lack of assistance to be found at Funchal, as well as his own lack of instructions. However Admiral Louis welcomed his guest, entertained him to dinner and questioned him at length about his experiences in the West Indies, in particular the effect on trade and business there, the settlers and the garrisons, of the depredations by Admirals Missiessy and Villeneuve. This led naturally to the subject of Lord Nelson's trans-Atlantic chase, which led, again naturally, to Admiral Louis disclosing that which he was supposed to keep secret, namely that Lord Nelson, together with several divisions of the British Atlantic-coast blockade fleet, namely twenty-seven ships of the line and sundry support vessels, was at that moment patrolling at sea off Cadiz where the Franco-Spanish fleet had taken refuge. Nelson's strategy was to lure the Enemy out of port by pretending not to be there! Instead he was relying on a number of inshore vessels acting as scouts to keep him informed of the Enemy's movements.

Thanking Admiral Louis for his hospitality, Captain Devereux again mentioned his lack of orders from the Admiralty and his proposal to sail to Spithead to discover what had happened to them. It had occurred to him that en route he might offer his services to Lord Nelson with those of the two ships under his command. Admiral Louis assured him that he would probably be made welcome and as he was leaving Gibraltar on the next tide he would inform his Lordship of the Captain's offer. Unfortunately the Admiral omitted to mention one minor detail, that he had instructions to escort a convoy of troop transports past the Spanish port of Cartagena to the east, before returning westwards through the Strait. Thus it was that *La Belle Helène* and the *Apollion* entered the Atlantic before the Admiral, and Captain Devereux's offer of assistance was never transmitted. Of course the Captain thirsted after an opportunity for taking valuable prizes, not having secured any since he had left the West Indies, whilst off the Canary Islands he had very nearly been captured himself.

La Belle Helène and the *Apollion* left the Gibraltar dockyard on 20th October 1805. The wind was light and blowing from the North-West, so they made slow progress in clearing the Strait and decided to anchor overnight near the African shore of the Gut so as to make a better start in the morning. They set out at dawn but were obliged to tack westwards into the Atlantic before being able to catch the now South-Westerly breeze and head for Cadiz. About noon Hugo alerted Captain Devereux to the sound of distant gunfire, and there were flashes of light along the eastern horizon. As at the Battle of Cape St. Vincent, it seemed to Hugo that the conflict had begun without them. The breeze, or rather the lack of it, had obliged the two ships to tack well to the westward and it was mid-afternoon before they arrived in the battle zone. Captain Devereux had anticipated that this would have been nearer the Bay of Cadiz, another reason for his longer tack, rather than twenty miles offshore of a mean little headland known by the Moors as Taraf El Agar ('Cape of Caverns').

As they approached the battle scene they found it shrouded in smoke and fog, above which a bent topmast or a drooping pennant would occasionally emerge. Obviously intensive action had been in progress for some hours. Immediately to starboard Captain Devereux identified H.M.S. *Prince* (98 guns) and the *Thunderer* (74) which seemed not yet to be participating in the action. Half a mile ahead over the forepeak of *La Belle Helène* he espied H.M.S. *Africa* (64 guns), whose Captain Henry Digby he knew well. Captain Devereux instructed Mr. Brightman to bring the ship alongside the *Africa*, which he obligingly did, with the *Apollion* to starboard and slightly astern. Captain Devereux had his gig lowered from the davits and boarded the *Africa* to learn what instructions Captain Digby had received and how these new arrivals might be able to contribute to the action.

Captain Digby had just started to inform his friend that he was himself awaiting instructions from the flagship, H.M.S. *Victory*, when to engage the van of the Franco-Spanish Fleet yonder, and the Captain waved his telescope in the direction of the sea-mist through which vague shadowy vessels might just be discerned, when there was a thunderous crash as a stray 32-pound shot landed on the *Africa* and buried itself in the cabin section at the stern. At the same instant another hit *La Belle Helène*, smashed through the poop-deck rail and encountered the right leg of Hugo Jarvis who happened to be standing there on duty. Thence the missile fell through the hole it had made, missed the helmsman at the wheel by inches, and rolled into the scuppers with a mighty sizzle as it met with sea-water.

At first Hugo did not realise he had been hit; there is a natural anaesthesia which arises initially from shock. Temporarily blinded by smoke, Hugo reached for the poop-deck rail, found only empty air and fell along the deck with his injured leg poking through the hole. It was the steady stream of blood dripping on to the deck below which drew Mr. Brightman's attention and he sent a seaman to investigate. He ran back with a face as white as a sheet and called for assistance. "'Tis Mr. Jarvis," he shouted, "been hit in the leg and his bones are all over the place!"

They carried Hugo below to the orlop deck where their surgeon took one look at the injury and said, "I cannot deal with that. 'Tis beyond my skills. Send him over to Mr. Dunstan on the *Apollion*." He did, however, fix a tourniquet around the shattered limb above the injury.

At that instant, back on deck, a gust of wind blew aside some of the battle-smoke and the *Victory* drifted clear momentarily. She signalled H.M.S. *Africa* to "engage the Enemy Van closely", and as Captain Digby's crew sprang to action, she hoisted a further signal indicating a shortage of medical supplies. Captain Devereux, observing both signals and aware that *La Belle Helène* had also been hit, but unaware of the damage done, made haste to descend to his gig and return aboard. He arrived just as the two seamen carrying the unconscious form of Hugo Jarvis emerged from the after hatch. They gave him their surgeon's verdict and he replied, "Yes, take him over to the *Apollion*. Use my gig - 'tis already below." Observing the battered hulk of the *Victory* as she continued to drift in the breeze, her helm having been shattered so that she was being steered manually by gangs of seamen heaving at tackles rove to the tiller below decks, with all three mizzen masts shot away, other masts and yards at rakish angles, and such sails as remained aloft hanging in tatters, Captain Devereux understood immediately that she had been given a hard drubbing and could have a hundred men or more awaiting medical attention.

While the inert form of Hugo Jarvis was slid into a sling off the yardarm and lowered into the gig, he sent a middie scampering below to the orlop deck and thence to Mr. Evans for whatever supplies of bandages and ointments might hurriedly be mustered. Then he had them wrapped in oilskin and thrown into the sling with its occupant. When the gig reached the *Apollion* he observed an avid discussion in progress on deck. Presently more packages of medical aid were forthcoming but there was no sign of Hugo being lifted aboard in the sling. Captain Devereux took a megaphone and with irritation demanded, "Fish? What are you about there? Send the boy down to Mr. Dunstan!"

"I cannot, sir," Captain Salmon replied by the same means. "Dunstan's out cold. He's dead drunk!"

"How dare he, on this of all days?" Captain Devereux raged. "I'll flog the blackguard myself if I catch hold of him!" After a moment's thought he said slowly and then with increasing conviction, "Then you'd best send him across to the *Victory* along with the bandages. They have two or three physicians there and one of them will surely know what to do. Send a note with him, Fish, so they'll know who he is, just give his name, no ship."

Captain Salmon thought for a moment as his steward fetched paper and pencil. Then he wrote, "First Lieutenant HUGO JERVIS. Would be gratified if you would kindly treat *all* these provisions with equal care and attention." He had the note tucked into the braided cuff of Hugo's uniform, instructing the sailors to bring it to the notice of whoever hoisted the sling aboard the *Victory*.

As the little boat bobbed its way over the swell till it reached the flagship's side, Captain Devereux watched it for several moments. Then he had all sail set, and staysails and stun'sls billowed as he followed the *Africa* into battle. He could now see quite clearly the Enemy Van of five ships which had been able to tack in the light wind and were bearing down on the *Victory*. The *Apollion*, which carried only fifty guns and was classed as non-combattant, he ordered to remain out of firing-range and to be "ready to pick up any pieces".

The orlop deck and cockpit of H.M.S. *Victory* were no larger, nor any better illuminated than those of other ships of her class. The companion-way was a steep and the injured were carried down manually, adding to their pain and to the gravity of their injuries. Lanterns flickered and dimmed as the ship rolled and the guns reverberated, each with a sickening thud of recoil. The wounded lay in rows, packed in side by side, while the surgeon's mates assessed their injuries, salved and bandaged what they could and took the urgent cases to the head of the queue. Blood ran everywhere, and only the thunder of the guns half-concealed the groans and cries of the men. There was a pause in the gunfire as the *Victory*, having rid herself of the French warship *Redoubtable*, with which she had been locked in fierce hand-to-hand fighting, following timely intervention by the British *Temeraire*, and having done such irreparable damage to the French flagship *Bucentaure* that Admiral Villeneuve presently surrendered her to Captain Pellew of the *Conqueror*, emerged briefly from the battle-smoke and proceeded towards the Franco-Spanish Van, sending a signal to all British ships that were not yet engaged to join the combat.

In that brief pause, Hugo Jarvis was carried below decks on the *Victory* and the seamen drew Surgeon William Beatty's attention to the note tucked into Hugo's cuff. The surgeon removed it, stood beneath a lantern and read it aloud, ending with a "Hrmph!" as he realised the import of the message.

"Who is it?" a voice demanded of him, a voice that Hugo could not see, being blinded by darkness and by the pain that swept over him if he moved.

"Lieutenant Hugo Jervis, my Lord. I suspect a relative of Lord St. Vincent, brought from another ship, confounded impudence!"

"Young Jarvis, Hugo Jarvis? I know him well, Beatty. He has served with me more than once." There was a pause while the voice gathered strength, and then it continued, "You must see to him, Beatty. He has all his life before him. I am done for."

Hugo could not see, but he knew well enough whom it was, that disembodied voice in the darkness. The great Admiral had taken an injury, and this time it was fatal. Hugo felt himself lifted on to the table that served for operations and amputations alike. His own voice croaked as he begged the surgeon's mate to tie the gag in his mouth very tightly and to continue pouring the rum. "I would not wish to disturb the Admiral with my mewings," he gasped finally before lapsing, fortunately, into unconsciousness as the bonesaw began to bite at his shattered leg.

* * *

A great storm marked the passing of England's Hero; it shattered victor and vanquished alike. Seventeen of Admiral Villeneuve's allied fleet of thirty-three vessels had struck their colours, and one more, the *Achille*, had exploded and burnt to the waterline. Four of the Allied Van had escaped under Admiral Dumanoir but were captured a few weeks later by Sir Richard Strachan. Eleven vessels managed to creep back into Cadiz, bearing the Spanish Admiral Gravina seriously wounded. Twenty thousand of Admiral Villeneuve's force had been taken prisoner with him, and six thousand had perished in the battle and its aftermath. Britain had lost 449 men killed and 1,241 wounded, though not a single ship sank or was taken. The violence of the storm made it impossible to retain all the prizes, though the British frigates, the *Apollion* and *La Belle Helène* among them, made strenuous efforts to rescue the drowning and to tow the dismasted hulks to safety. But Cape Trafalgar was a lee shore swept by strong currents and often the cables had to be cut and the enemy vessels foundered in the heavy seas. Others were scuttled subsequently, including the huge *Santissima Trinidad* (130 guns) which was never to serve Britain's enemies again.

News brought out of Cadiz indicated that the city's hospitals had generously opened their doors to British and Allied wounded alike, so Captain Devereux had his two ships deliver there all the personnel they had rescued who did not belong to their own crews. When the storm had subsided after three days and visibility in the Bay of Cadiz improved, Captain Devereux noted that there was no sign of the *Victory*. He soon learnt that she, along with others of the British warships, had been last seen under tow heading for Gibraltar. Was Hugo Jarvis still aboard the flagship, he wondered? He called Captain Salmon aboard and ordered him to send Nicholas Wilmington and any of his crew who spoke Spanish to tour the city hospitals and enquire whether anyone had landed wounded sailors from the *Victory*. *La Belle Helène* would proceed straight to Gibraltar in search of the British flagship, and the *Apollion* should follow immediately her enquiries were complete.

Indeed the *Victory* had reached Gibraltar safely, towed first by the *Polyphemus* and then by the *Neptune*, but it had taken a week to make the journey. Only a few of the prizes captured were still afloat, such that quite exceptionally the Admiralty made a special grant to compensate all Trafalgar veterans. But nothing would compensate the Navy for the Hero who had died as the battle came to an end. The schooner H.M.S.*Pickle* under Lieutenant Lapenotiere bore to England the formal despatches written by Admiral Collingwood, now left in command of the Fleet. He landed at Falmouth and took a post-chaise to Whitehall without pause. At the Admiralty he awoke Lord Barham in the early hours of 6th November, who dressed and sent the news to the Prime Minister, William Pitt, in Downing Street. He then despatched a messenger to the King at Windsor Castle.

King George, on learning of the death of Admiral Nelson, could not speak for a full five minutes, and his subjects were in much the same state, not knowing whether to cheer for a tremendous victory or to wail for the loss of a beloved leader. In the end they did both: bells were rung, bonfires lit, guns saluted, and after Lord Nelson's body had been brought home in a temporarily-rigged *Victory* in December, it was laid in state in the Painted Chamber at Greenwich and was given the finest state funeral England had seen early in the New Year.

Meanwhile Captain Devereux had awaited the arrival of H.M.S.*Victory* at Gibraltar, not wishing to trouble a ship under tow with his minor enquiry when every vessel he passed en route was dressed overall in mourning for the commander they had lost. Indeed his own mood was just as sombre, for the injury to Hugo had reminded him all too painfully of his own personal tragedy. Back in the early 'nineties' he had taken his fifteen-year old son to sea with him and the boy had been wounded in one of many naval actions in the West Indies in which the Captain had taken part. The son had been transferred to hospital in Jamaica while his father continued with his naval duties. He had never seen his son alive again. To some extent Hugo Jarvis had taken the place of his lost son, and Captain Devereux felt a great affection for him. In addition, Hugo was well-liked by the crew and was a good navigator. Captain Devereux ordered his gig lowered and rowed across to the *Victory* almost as soon as she anchored in Rosia Bay, since he observed that many of her seriously-wounded crew were being sent ashore to the local hospital.

The first person he met aboard the *Victory* was her captain, Nelson's flag-captain Thomas Masterman Hardy, with whom he was but vaguely acquainted. Captain Devereux explained his mission, to which his interlocutor responded, "Oh that was you who sent over Lieutenant Jervis for treatment, was it? And I suppose that your surgeon was too drunk to amputate?" Captain Devereux did not reply as Captain Hardy continued, "By-the-by, which ship was he from?" Captain Devereux pointed out *La Belle Hélène* and the *Apollion* which had just arrived in port. "But you're only support vessels," Captain Hardy almost protested. "I mistook your sixty-four for a Frenchman having taken an English prize, till I observed the Union flags you had pinned to every yardarm!" Captain Devereux then explained that at Funchal they had found no instructions from the Admiralty and had proceeded to Gibraltar for repair. There they had encountered Admiral Louis and had offered their services. "Admiral Louis has not yet returned from his mission in the Mediterranean," Captain Hardy said drily. "Your lieutenant has gone ashore to the hospital along with the rest of our wounded, those that still survive." He sighed as he accepted Captain Devereux's somewhat belated condolences for the loss of his commander. "If you are still minded to assist," Captain Hardy concluded, "I suggest you seek instructions aboard the *Euryalus* over there. That is where Admiral Collingwood has shifted his flag whilst he awaits the arrival here and repair of his *Royal Sovereign*."

Captain Devereux personally toured the Gibraltar hospital till he located Hugo Jarvis. Conditions there were not as bad as he had feared, but he sensed that any reduction in numbers to be cared for would be welcomed. A stretcher was sent and seamen carried the still unconscious Hugo to the gig. They rowed him out to the *Apollion* where Mr. Dunstan, long since cold sober and extremely contrite, promised to take the greatest care of him. Returning aboard his own ship, Captain Devereux had Hugo's sea-chest brought up from the hold where it had been packed and sent down when clearing for battle. He found the key to its lock attached to its handle and opened it. Right on top lay Hugo's little tin box which had fallen open due to the motion of the ship. Curiosity about his young protegé overcame him as he remembered his lost son. He examined the book of poems and dipped into the letters, noticing that the very latest one written in April 1805 had been signed simply "Jess". He closed the little box and turned its key. Then he took a larger box of fine ivory inlay which had always graced his desk and ordered his steward to have his *Beacon* chest brought up from the hold.

Half an hour later he was back aboard the *Apollion* with Hugo's sea-chest whose key he handed into the personal care of Nicholas Wilmington, instructing him to put the lanyard around his neck and if Hugo should die before they reached England he should ensure that the sea-chest safely reached Hugo's family. That said, he gave orders to Captain Salmon to sail for Portsmouth as soon as he had taken on fresh water, and to deliver Hugo to the naval hospital there. Then he might call at the Admiralty Office and enquire after the missing orders. On his return to these waters, Captain Devereux continued, he might expect to find his chief either on watch with the British ships that still lingered off Cadiz or else here at Gibraltar. Then Captain Devereux returned to his gig and directed his men to row him across to the *Euryalus* where he offered his services to the acting Commander-in-Chief of the Mediterranean Fleet.

* * *

When Hugo eventually regained consciousness it was to find himself in familiar surroundings, namely the sick-berth of H.M.S. *Apollion*. A seaman watching over him immediately called Mr. Dunstan who examined his wound with care, sent one of his assistants to apply more ointment, and enquired if Nicholas Wilmington might be spared from his duties in order to cheer his friend. Nicholas told Hugo about the key to the sea-chest which he kept about his person and the two of them speculated as to what Captain Devereux might have enclosed within it that required such care. The *Apollion* made good time to Portsmouth and Hugo was soon installed in the naval hospital with his sea-chest beneath his bed. A few days later Nicholas Wilmington handed over the key, saying that the *Apollion* had orders to escort a convoy to the West Indies again, picking up *La Belle Helène* off Cadiz or at Gibraltar on her way. Nicholas ascertained that Hugo had received funds from the Navy Office, had written to his family explaining his whereabouts, and he gave his friend carte blanche to call upon his own family at Norwich whenever he fancied after his return home to Beccles.

Staff at the hospital had spoken to Hugo about being fitted with a wooden leg. With a rueful smile Hugo thought of Stan Stevenson and imagined himself stumping about Beccles, and feeling rather inadequate whilst his healthy younger brother Peter ran the farm. He began to wish that the cannon-shot had killed him outright. One day he awoke from a doze to the sound of sea-boots on the flagstones beside his bed and sat up to find himself staring into the frame and features of Big John! "They told me you was here," he said, "I knew they couldn't mistake the name." Much rejoicing and exchanging of news followed till Big John explained the purpose of his visit. "I've come to fit you for a leg," he said, took off his sea-boot with his other toe and displayed his own apparatus. Beneath a standard upper fitting that cradled the fleshy stump, the wooden shaft was holed at the ankle and fitted with a movable wooden flange by means of a metal loop. "I was watching the cavalry pass by one day and noticed the movement of their feet in the stirrup," Big John said, "so I bethought me of this. 'Tis like a stirrup, just a bar under the foot covered in leather and a metal loop joining it to the leg. Had a blacksmith make up some for me in iron, though they can snap and would be better made of steel, as a stirrup is. As for the 'foot' here, well that's my whittlin' for you. Can be designed to fit a shoe or a boot. You can even put a stocking over it, if you wish. I've started a little warehouse now with half a dozen old salts giving me a hand, making crutches, hooks, hands and stumps we are, all customised to fit the person concerned."

Big John then unwrapped a spare stump he carried under his arm and explained further. "The first step we take as soon as your wound has healed proper, is to make a plaster cast of it. Then we can carve the socket to exactly the right fit, making it much more comfortable. Then we line it with woollen cloth to keep it warm, and a layer of velvet to make it soft. Then we fit the top just so. Next we cut the stump to the right length with you standing on your good leg, and I carve a foot similar to your own and depending upon what boot or shoe you fancy wearing with it. Some of our customers have had two or three made, one with a shoe and another with a riding boot. I'm even having my device patented," Big John continued. "You remember that naval architect we sent aboard that American ship, the *Beacon* she was called, a Mr. Mackenzie? Well, he's here in Portsmouth with his son looking at the designing of the new dockyards ."

"Mr. Mackenzie!" Hugo shouted joyously. "Daniel Mackenzie is my brother-in-law, he's married to my sister Lucy. Are they here in Portsmouth?"

"If she's the little lass with the fair hair, blue eyes and a very pert nose," Big John replied, "that's the one. And she's expecting a child from the last I saw of her."

"Will you bring them to visit me, John?" Hugo asked eagerly.

"Well, surely I will. Anyways, 'tis Mr. Mackenzie senior that's done the drawings of my patent foot, just as if they were the lines of a ship's hull, and he says he will have my device registered or some such, so that I have the rights to it."

A nurse came by at that moment, unwrapped Hugo's bandages and showed his patched stump to Big John. "The inflammation has nearly gone," she said. "You'll soon have need of one of those, and then you must find yourself a place elsewhere."

Daniel and Lucy Mackenzie called upon Hugo the following day. They came with the offer of a room at their lodgings till Hugo could be fitted with his new leg and could travel home to Beccles. They had only just learnt from Carrie of his whereabouts or would have sought him out before. Hugo emphasised that he had only told his family of an injury and pleaded with Lucy that they should not mention details of his disability to Jessica. "Oho, so that's how it is," his sister said. "You know that she is one of our family now? Roos Hall has been sold and she lives in a pretty place in Northgate, along with our Aunt Jarvis who turns out to be her grandmother. Jessica isn't related to us by blood, though, which means you can marry her without any dispensation."

"Thank you, Lucy," Hugo said with a laugh once he could get a word in. "I did know, for she wrote and told me of it."

"Did she now, then you must have a fair chance with her, dear brother."

One other step which Hugo took before he left Portsmouth was to write to Lord St. Vincent detailing his injury and inquiring after firstly an administrative position in the Admiralty, or alternatively the possibility of a seat in Parliament on a similar basis to that Commodore Troubridge had occupied. He received a reply from the Earl's Secretary, Benjamin Tucker, to the effect that Commodore Troubridge 'intended to relinquish his seat at the next election and that his Lordship, having now left the Admiralty, he did not propose to lend his name to any future Parliamentary aspirant. Moreover, since his Lordship's retirement, he had little influence over the daily organisation of naval affairs, and with the unfortunate and lamented passing of Mr. William Pitt, his Lordship's influence at Whitehall had much diminished. As for Mr. H. Jervis's disability, his Lordship was of the opinion that it should not prevent him from taking his place upon the quarterdeck again, whenever the National need should arise.' As if to emphasize the implication contained in the final sentence, that very month, March 1806, Hugo read in the newspapers that the Earl of St. Vincent had been called to sea again, hauled out of retirement and put in charge of the Channel Fleet.

As soon as he felt well enough to travel, Hugo bade farewell to his sister and his in-laws, obtained from Mr. Mackenzie senior a recommendation to a reliable London banker and set off for the City in a post-chaise. He had also taken with him a fine pair of pistols which he had acquired at Portsmouth at the sale of a dead naval officer's effects. The reason for this precaution was that, upon opening his sea-chest in the privacy of his sister's lodgings and unlocking the ivory box which Captain Devereux had slipped into it, he discovered that the contents consisted entirely of some very solid gold! As he carried a letter of recommendation from Mr. Mackenzie, the Banker accepted the deposit with few questions asked, especially when Hugo disclosed that he had been First Officer aboard one of the ships present at the Battle of Trafalgar and that his injury had been caused by a shot from the Enemy. (Captain Devereux had at last been granted his coveted gold medal for his services in support of H.M.S. *Africa*, but Hugo had no such expectations.) Hugo arranged for the interest from his bank deposit to be paid six monthly to a bank in Norwich where he intended to set up an account; it was the firm used by Mr. Russell for the Rich family estates.

Hugo spent a few days in the Capital which yet mourned the death of Lord

Nelson, as well as his famous victory. There were still illuminations to be seen at some of the fashionable mansions, and regular theatrical performances took place of the "Battle" which Hugo considered tawdry and inaccurate. His own recollection was far too sacrosanct a memory; of the voice that had come out of the darkness and had urged Surgeon Beatty to save his life.

Hugo had decided to travel home by sea. There was a naval packet that left Deptford dockyard of a Friday to deliver despatches and supplies the day following to the North Sea Fleet's headquarters at Great Yarmouth. He secured a ticket and some prize-money owing to him in respect of his services aboard *La Belle Helène* in his last trip to the West Indies. He had already written to his family of his plans and trusted that they would send the haywain to meet him to save him the stage service with his injured leg. Besides, this might turn out to be his last sea voyage, should the Navy not recall him to duty. The month was April and the weather fair though breezy as the packet scudded along in a brisk south-easterly under a generous press of canvas. Hugo felt a tingle of pleasure and excitement as the little ship reefed most of her sails off the Roads and waited for the pilot to come aboard. Then she eased her way along the river mouth to the quays he knew so well.

Hugo could already see his family waiting for him, seated in the haywain with the two Fen Blacks, Major and the new recruit Brigadier, standing at ease in the shafts on three feet apiece with their noses deep in their hay-bags. There was his father, looking stocky and brown as ever, his mother looking slighter and more frail beside him, and in the back of the waggon, Carrie and her two young children, a girl and a boy so far -no sign of her husband Benjamin, but he was no doubt at business - and Peter with his fiancée Susan whom Hugo had yet to meet. Then Hugo's glance strayed to another waiting vehicle, and suddenly he saw Jessica and his Aunt Jarvis sitting in the pony-trap drawn by the skewbald James. As he looked, Jessica's glance met his and for a moment her hand fluttered in her lap. They too had come to greet him.

Hugo was not to know that Benedict Mather, having witnessed the disposal of Roos Hall - indeed his father had handled the conveyance - and observing the removal of Jessica into a pleasant but modest dwelling in Northgate, along with Mrs. Betty Jarvis whom he now understood to be her grandmother, and with her father's identity still discreetly concealed, so that none knew yet of the Ainsworth Diamonds, he relinquished his partiality for her and had become betrothed to a commercial heiress living in Norwich instead.

Hugo had paid a sailor to follow him with his sea-chest now that it contained nothing more valuable than a pair of serviceable pistols. Thus he paused unfettered at the head of the gangway that had been set up against the side of the vessel. There was something about his pose, the way he stood with one leg not quite at the same angle as the other, that attracted Betty Jarvis's attention. Then suddenly she realised the reason. "Oh, my poor Jessica," she exclaimed. "He has a wooden leg!"

Hugo descended carefully to the quay and walked, a little stiffly but with a measured stride, across to the haywain. He shook his father's hand -the words would come later - then Peter's, whose grasp was strong and vigorous, and was introduced to Susan who blushed easily but looked plump and capable. Then he walked round to the far side of the waggon and received a chalorous hug from Carrie, whilst her two youngsters peeped over the side of the haywain believing that the possession of a wooden leg only made their visitor all the more interesting. Hugo came to his mother, a little tearful with relief to greet him and at the injury to her poor boy. He took her in his arms with the most gentle of embraces.

Hugo saw his sea-chest stowed in the waggon and paid off the sailor. Then, fighting for control of his own emotions after his mother's embrace, he strolled across to the pony-trap, gave James a distracted pat and said, "Afternoon, Aunt Jarvis, Miss Jessica."

"Welcome home, Hugo," Aunt Jarvis said stoutly, blinking a tear from her own eye. "We thought you should be met by *all* the family, did we not Jessica?"

"Oh, Hughie, so good to see you home at last," Jessica uttered with a slight flush stealing into her cheeks. "Would you care to call upon us tomorrow afternoon?" There, he had it, the invitation he wanted from her, and she had called him by the old childhood diminutive, Hughie. Perhaps a future as a quiet country gentleman of modest, but not too modest means, might not prove too tedious after all.